The Devil's Cathedral

The Devil's CATHEDRAL

A Mystery of Queen Anne's London

David Fairer

Matador
9 Priory Business Park,
Wistow Road, Kibworth Beauchamp,
Leicestershire. LE8 0RX
Tel: 0116 279 2299
Email: books@troubador.co.uk
Web: www.troubador.co.uk/matador
Twitter: @matadorbooks

ISBN 978 1800464 452

British Library Cataloguing in Publication Data.
A catalogue record for this book is available from the British Library.

Printed and bound by CPI Group (UK) Ltd, Croydon, CR0 4YY
Typeset in 11pt Adobe Jenson Pro by Troubador Publishing Ltd, Leicester, UK

Matador is an imprint of Troubador Publishing Ltd

For Adam Bray

. . . Not only the *Play-House* which is called the *Theatre-Royal,* and is as it were the *Cathedral Church* of the *Devil* in this Kingdom, but the other inferiour *Temples,* which are but as *Chappels of Ease* to the former, ought to be remov'd, as *Obstacles* and *Hindrances* to *Vertue,* and the *Reformation of Manners.* The *Drolls* and *Interludes,* at *Smith Field* and *Southwark Fairs,* at *May-Fair* under the very Nose of the Court . . . *Play-Booths* and *Musick-Booths* are directly contrary to the Nature of a *Fair,* which is Established for the benefit of Trade and Commerce; yet are our *Fairs* turn'd into *Buffoonry,* set off with *Booths* instead of *Shops,* and Peopled with *Merry Andrews* and *Jack Puddings* instead of *Trades-Men* . . .

The *Societies* for *Reformation of Manners* ought principally to be taken Care of; they have entred themselves Voluntiers in the Service of Heaven, and have hitherto subsisted themselves in their Spiritual Warfare . . . it is high time they should be brought on a National Establishment . . . They want nothing but a National Authority to carry on a National *Reformation.*

John Tutchin, *England's Happiness Consider'd, in Some Expedients . . . Humbly Offer'd to the Consideration of both Houses of Parliament* (London, 1705), p. 20

Characters

Historical figures marked with *

STATE POLITICS

*Queen Anne, *the last Stuart monarch, niece of Charles the Second*
*Prince George of Denmark, *Anne's ailing husband*
*Robert Harley (later Earl of Oxford), *wily politician with Tory sympathies, Anne's confidant*
*Abigail Masham, *Harley's cousin, now Lady of the Bedchamber*
*John Churchill, Duke of Marlborough, *the great general, victor of Blenheim (1704) and Ramillies (1706)*
*Sarah Churchill, Duchess of Marlborough, *Queen Anne's friend and adviser, now out of favour, supporter of the Whigs*
*Wriothesley Russell, *2nd Duke of Bedford, a Whiggish young man who owns most of Covent Garden*

THE BAY-TREE

Mary Trotter, *the widow who now rules in the Bay-Tree*
Henry Trotter, *memorably deceased*
Tom Bristowe, *budding poet born under Saturn; a Juvenal with ambitions to be a Virgil*

Will Lundy, *Tom's best friend, mercurial law student of the Middle Temple, future Westminster Hall orator*
Mrs Dawes, *creative in the kitchen*
Jenny Trip, *barista princess with a sharp eye*
Peter Simco, *skilful coffee-boy with a bright future*
Jeremy Jopp (Jem), *does errands and hard lifting, but learning to be elegant*
Old Ralph, *sweeps and cleans*
Jack Tapsell, *Whig wine merchant*
Barnabas Smith, *Whig cloth merchant*
Samuel Cust, *Whig with a Caribbean sugar plantation*
Laurence Bagnall, *poet and critic with laureate ambitions, author of 'The Shoe-Buckle'*
Captain Roebuck, *old soldier of Marlborough's Flanders campaign*
Gavin Leslie, *down from the glens of Scotland*
David Macrae, *his friend and compatriot*

ST JAMES'S

John Popham, Second Viscount Melksham (Tom's Uncle Jack), *Deputy Keeper of the Privy Purse, an unwilling courtier*
Sophia Popham (*née Doggett*), Viscountess Melksham, *a young step-mother, enjoys London's social whirl*
The Hon. Frank Popham, *Tom's cousin, politically ambitious young man returned from the Grand Tour*
The Hon. Lavinia Popham, *Tom's other cousin, lively and advanced for eighteen*
The Countess of Welwyn, *of St James's Square, friend of the Pophams*
Lord Tring, *her Italophile son, fresh from the Grand Tour, Lavinia's admirer*
Arthur, *the Pophams' footman*
Julia, Lady Norreys, *friend of Lady Melksham, helps weave Arachne's Web*

*Delarivier Manley, *controversial journalist and fiction-writer, chief weaver of the web*

THE THEATRE ROYAL

*Christopher Rich, *hard-pressed manager of the Drury Lane Theatre*

The Sixth Baron Tunbridge, *theatre patron – of actresses especially*

*Colley Cibber, *popular comic playwright and actor, later Poet Laureate*

*William Pinkerman, *chief comedian of the Drury Lane company and fair-ground impresario*

*William Bullock, *Pinkerman's partner in comedy, second witch in* Macbeth

*Christopher Bullock, *William's son, young actor and future playwright*

*Anne Oldfield, *young actress becoming the star of the company*

*Thomas Betterton, *the renowned Shakespearean actor-manager, now 72*

*Elizabeth Barry, *a celebrated Lady Macbeth*

*Will Keene, *plays Duncan in* Macbeth

*Robert Wilks, *plays Mosca to Powell's Volpone, and a seductive Dorimant in* The Man of Mode

*George Powell, *plays Macduff in* Macbeth, *and Volpone to Wilks's Mosca*

*Anne Bracegirdle, *celebrated actress of star quality, just retired, now looking down on the Bay-Tree*

*Lucretia Bradshaw, *actress having her benefit night*

Sally Twiss, *young actress attracting admirers*

Gilbert Angell, *ambitious young actor, an admirer of Sally, third witch in* Macbeth

Mr Bolt, *intrepid lightning-man at the Theatre Royal*

Mr Grant, *exasperated prompter*

Mr Bridge, *under-prompter*

Mr Bannister, *housekeeper*
Mr Howell, *chief carpenter*
Amos Jackson, *burly scene-man and carpenter*
Mrs Moody, *theatre-sweeper, handy with broom and bucket*
Betty, *the new assistant sweeper*
George Bellamy, *script-man, arrested at the molly house*
*Owen Swiney, *theatre impresario and shareholder in the Theatre Royal company*
*Richard Estcourt, *actor and shareholder*
Mr O'Malley, *a disappointed playwright*
*Sir Richard Steele, *author of* The Tender Husband (1705)
*Joseph Addison, *poet, critic and cultural authority, partner with Steele on* The Spectator (1711-14)

THE CHURCH

*Arthur Bedford, *Bristol minister, Chaplain to the Duke of Bedford. Moral reformer and enemy of all things theatrical, author of* The Evil and Danger of Stage Plays (1706)
The Revd. Mr Ebenezer Tysoe, *reformist preacher and saver of souls*
*The Revd. Robert Billio, *popular dissenting minister at Hackney*
*Henry Compton, *Bishop of London, 73, hates Papists*
*Thomas Tenison, *Archbishop of Canterbury, 71, hates Papists even more. Ardent campaigner for moral reform. Advocates government surveillance of the theatre and censorship of blasphemous publications*
Abraham Gell, *Nonconformist minister of Shoreditch, big in the Society for the Reformation of Manners*

THE LAW

*Sir James Montagu, *Her Majesty's Solicitor-General*
Benjamin Hector, *conscientious new-broom magistrate*

George Grimston, *aggressive magistrate humiliated at the Fair*
Richard Sumner, *respectable Middle Temple barrister and Will's pupil-master. Lady Norreys's brother*
Elias Cobb, *Covent Garden's chivalrous Constable, with semi-official interests, long-time friend of Mary Trotter*
Tobias Mudge, *Elias's bold apprentice who's shaping up*
Bob Turley, *Toby's fellow-watchman*

THE FAIR

*Edward Shepherd, *May Fair landowner*
Dick Middlemiss, *landlord of the Dog and Duck*
Charles, *pot-boy of the Dog and Duck*
*Isaac Fawkes, *man of tricks renowned for his sleight of hand*
*Mr Finley, *entrepreneur and Pinkerman's rival, owns a popular booth at May Fair*
*Mr Miller, *another rival May Fair showman*
Edwin Price, *runs his waxworks at the Fair*
Francis Flinn, *his talented apprentice, a budding artist*
Sophie, *the amazing rope-dancer*
*Hannibal, *Pinkerman's African elephant, star of the May Fair*
Tiny François, *big in tumbling. Has appeared by Royal command at Versailles*
Bob Stanley, *playing the apothecary in* The Tender Courtesan
Lizzy Wright, *playing Agnes, the novitiate nun*
Joe Byrne, *playing the hot-headed Don Felipe*
Peggy Evans, *playing the Abbess of St Clare*
Jake Sawyer, *scene-shifter at Pinkerman's booth*

HACKNEY

Mr Justice Oliver Lundy ('Hemp'), *Will's father, Old Bailey judge, strict upholder of the Law and guardian of morality*

Aunt Dinah, *his sister, a spiritual judge*
Aunt Rebecca, *her equally upright sister*
Mr Hodge, *the Lundys' gardener*
Mrs Pearson, *their skilful cook*

ELSEWHERE

Adèle Ménage, *of Katherine Street, retired from the bagnio business, Widow Trotter's friend*
Charles Denniston, *runs a toyshop in Katherine Street, Mrs Ménage's landlord*
John Pomfrey, *his friend, private secretary to the Duke of Bedford*
Humfrey Proby, *surgeon of long experience, with clean hands*
*John Radcliffe, *extremely eminent hands-off physician*
'Booming Billy', *vocal hawker of pamphlets in the Covent Garden piazza*
Jessamy Smith, *dancing milkmaid who helps run the family milk business*

Saturday

29 April 1708

Chapter One

'WHAT! *NO ERECTIONS?*'

'That's what it says, Pinkey – None are to be allowed! – 'tis a *pro-hibition!* And in the black-letter too.'

'The devil it is! Hand it here!'

The gentlemanly hand reached across the table, and with a neat turn of the wrist the broadside was seized upon. The paper was thick and its ancient Gothick script looked incongruous against the man's elegant lace cuff and the dish of dark coffee. He drew it nearer his face and studied the printing. In character it was like an old Tudor manuscript and had the smell of a summons to the scaffold – a proclamation not to be resisted! With furrowed brow he began to read the thing aloud, and at once the Bay-Tree Chocolate House began ringing to the tones of the Drury Lane stage – a voice that in a few hours' time would be that of the chief witch in *Macbeth*. It lent the document a weird solemnity:

'"*An order ... To prevent the great profaneness, vice, and debauchery so frequently used and practised in the Fair, by strictly charging and commanding ...* (a man of few words is our proclaimer!) *all persons concerned in the said Fair, and in the sheds and booths to be erected and built therein or places adjacent, that they do not let, set, or hire, or use any booth, stall, or other erection whatsoever ...*" No erections at the Fair? You may as well prohibit breathing! ...'

A flush rose on his cheek, and the eyes widened further as he read on.

"*... or other erection whatsoever to be used or employed for interludes, stage-plays, comedies, gaming-places, lotteries, or music meetings*" – But it will be no Fair at all! A mere market! ...'

His hand came down hard on the table.

"*... We earnestly desire that the said orders may be vigorously prosecuted, and that the said Fair may be employed to those good ends and purposes for which it was at first designed.*"

'*Good ends?* Well, there we have it! Trinkets and fancies! – Mere skittles and a hog roast! Is this what the May Fair will come to? *Over my steaming corpse!*'

William Pinkerman, player and chief comedian of the Theatre Royal, now had the attention of the whole coffee-room, and there was a ripple of applause from his audience. Over by the fireplace a familiar figure was eyeing him with a fixed look – not ungenial, but one that placed him under scrutiny. The actor returned the look and held up the broadside as if he were holding a rat by the tail. His voice boomed across the room:

'Elias, my friend! Dost know aught of this mouldy article? Where has the thing crawled from, and what's its authority? I don't like the smell of it!'

Constable Cobb rose to his feet and came over. A private word, he had decided, was preferable. He took his seat by Pinkerman's side and set down his pipe carefully, giving a nod over the table to his friend Bullock (another of that evening's witches) who was training an indulgent smile on his fellow actor.

'The thing is not what it seems, Mr Pinkerman,' said the constable.

There was a stirring, and the wig twitched slightly.

'Seems?... *I know not seems ...*'

Elias Cobb noticed that the actorly cheek was lifting the corner of the mouth just enough to signal wit, and he felt emboldened to continue:

'It purports to be from the magistrates, and it's dressed up like a Royal decree. But in truth it's a mongrel, Mr Pinkerman – a new reprint of an old proclamation against Bartholomew Fair.'

'Aha! 'Tis a nice *satirical* thrust, then? ... Well! I admire the impudence of it! ...'

Pinkerman laughed. He liked a text that played clever games, and he respected it as he would any fellow-actor.

'... But seriously, Mr Cobb, you know how we of the profession are being threatened. Do you think this has been cooked up by the *ranting brethren? ...*'

He rolled his r's aggressively. With contracted brow he leaned confidingly toward the constable.

'... What does it *presage?* The May Fair will soon be upon us, and you know how much I am invested in it. Pinkerman's booth is building as we speak, and I assure you, that particular erection will exceed any of former years! A most brilliant cast is in prospect – one that will draw the public forth like nails to a magnet. The Theatre Royal will decamp to Brook Field and create a brave new world of good humour and adventure! There will be a sparkling satiric comedy and a dramatick romance that has the finest sentiments imaginable ... and this year I have secured a troop of tumblers who defy all physical laws—'

He broke off and left his words hanging in the air as in an empty theatre. Seconds later the eyebrows swept together and the face assumed a more melancholy cast. With a scarcely suppressed sigh he reached for his dish of coffee.

'... I tell you, Mr Cobb, there's trouble brewing. And if the Fair is suppressed then I shall be a foul way out. Are you certain this piece of Gothick flummery is a fiction? Or does it *portend?*

You recall the disaster a few years since. Something tells me it is ready to flare up again.'

Elias shook his head:

'None of us shall forget it, Mr Pinkerman! Justice was done and the butcher hanged for it – but the others ...'

'I allow Constable Cooper thought he was doing his duty, but the man was a fanatic – hot for the reformers!'

'Yes, he was always boasting how he and his officers would sweep away the ungodly and abolish the Fair entirely.'

'Well, they met their match, did they not? Waving their warrants in the air was no defence against drunken soldiers with swords in their hands ... But tell me, Mr Cobb, do you have wind of anything from the Association? Rumour has it they are determined to try the same again, only this time with a gang of their own. They say the magistrates want to bring matters to a crisis. If so, I swear it will be more than a skirmish – it will be *warfare*, pure and simple! That's what I truly fear – nothing less than a *riot*.'

Elias Cobb removed his pipe from his mouth and contemplated it. His hands were large, but they held it lightly as if conscious of their strength:

'You know what I think of the Association of Constables. It's all hugger-mugger. Untrustworthy men like me are kept well away! And their informers are everywhere – perhaps even here. Who can say what they're planning? ... But if it will set your mind at rest, I'll make what discreet inquiries I can. Another death at the Fair would be the final curtain.'

'But there are always miscreants, Mr Cobb. Villainous gangs can form and melt away in an instant – a blow or a blade – in the wink of an eye! A scuffle. A corpse ... Constable Cooper tangled with the wrong people. And yet ...'

Pinkerman's colour began to rise and his eye sparkled.

'... *Licence* is the very life-blood of the Fair, is it not? ...'

He leaned forward and shifted his haunches on the bench.

'... 'Tis a strange thing, but my pulse always beats quicker on that little boarded stage. In the booth the scenes are even more magical, and the gasping and roaring can't be matched. You can feel the breath of the audience – they seem to be at your fingers' ends! ... I tell you, two weeks at the Fair lifts our spirits and gives us the heart to endure the dog days ... But I'm very fearful, Elias. Our enemies are circling and there's a new confidence about them. *Reformation of Manners* indeed! What a mealy-mouthed title! The *Society* has such powerful friends – even the ear of the Queen. Can our old liberties be coming to an end? It is unthinkable ...'

The player broke off and looked at the constable almost pleadingly. Elias Cobb took his cue and nodded in sympathy:

'You've hit the nail there, Mr Pinkerman – Liberty and Licence! In truth, the world is growing polite, and the Fair has always thumbed its nose at correctness. The danger is indeed from that quarter – the *puritanical saints!* A terrible preaching crew! And what fear they can strike!'

At that moment, charged with a sudden spiritual electricity, Pinkerman leapt to his feet. He turned to face the room, eyes ablaze, and hoisted his right hand in the air, the palm thrust outwards and his whole body tensed as if struggling to hold back the Devil. In response, across the table William Bullock cowered in his seat, somehow managing to erect the hairs on his head as he sank under the shadow of the curse. In the twinkling of an eye the coffee-room had become Shakespeare's blasted heath. There was a moment of suspended, silent terror ...

Bullock pulled himself up again and broke the spell:

'Well, they certainly frighten me, Pinkey! But it's not just their waving arms. In the words of our immortal Mrs Behn ... *''Tis their damn'd puritanical, schismatical, fanatical, small-beer faces!*'

The three of them burst into laughter, and the constable pounded the table joyously. But the release of humour was only momentary. Pinkerman was soon sober again and spoke quietly, in a tone he had never employed on the stage:

'But I begin to fear for the Theatre, Elias. We have no protection. The pamphlets fly off the presses, and the sermons pour from the pulpits. They are calling us *the Cathedral Church of the Devil!* We are Her Majesty's company of players under the Royal Seal – and yet the Queen shuns us. She deplores our stage and everything it represents. Worst of all, she bends an ear to the reformers and their precious new *Manners!* We are all to become virtuous and right-thinking – or at least profess it. We are at the mercy of a universal *Reformation!*'

The chill sound of that word troubled the air inside the coffee-room. It was as if the street door had swung open and a freezing blast was lifting the newspapers from the table-tops and making the dust whirl about their feet.

Elias Cobb, the Covent Garden constable, clapped the actor on the back. It was not a consoling gesture:

'And if Reformation comes, Pinkey, must a *Civil War* follow?'

Truth to tell, at its inauguration a few months earlier the Bay-Tree Chocolate House had itself undergone a *Reformation* – and so far, civil strife had been avoided. The regulars of the old Good Fellowship Coffee House still regarded the spruced-up place as their parlour and eyed the politer crowd with suspicion. But generally, the grumblers and the wits managed to rub along together – indeed the eccentricities of each fed the amusements of the other.

Of course, Covent Garden itself was a jumble of high and low. From the elegant squares out west, it drew gentlemen seeking their pleasures in the neighbourhood of Drury Lane. And from the east, the merchants and men of business with offices in the City were happy to relax from their labours in a bagnio, a tavern, or a coffee house. And for both of these the celebrated Theatre Royal was there for entertainment. Within the playhouse all sorts of folk, the polite and the vulgar, were crammed in together. Orange peel flew down from the gallery, silk fans shivered in the boxes, and down in the pit, citizens' wives and elegant whores rubbed shoulders with critics of taste and gay young bucks of the Town, all vying with each other to pass judgment on the show.

In its new character, the Bay-Tree had begun to attract the theatrical crowd. The chocolate house was two minutes' walk from the playhouse, tucked around the corner in Red Lion Court, which provided a passageway from Drury Lane into Bow Street and the Covent Garden piazza. In its genial surroundings, and with an image of the great Mrs Bracegirdle in her famous role as the Indian Queen gazing down on him, an actor could take refreshment before the ten o'clock rehearsal or settle in for a sociable hour after dinner. He might warm himself with a spiced chocolate in advance of the evening's performance at five-thirty. And later that night, if the omens seemed favourable, he would make an anxious return for the inquest. The Bay-Tree was one of the places where reputations were decided and the Town sat in judgment on a new prologue or a promising début.

The chocolate house was a place of many moods, and on this Saturday morning, the 24th of April 1708, the atmosphere was animated and bustling. The proprietorial Mary Trotter stood in her place behind the bar, beaming at the scene before her. She made a queenly figure herself, with her ample red hair swept up under a tall tiara of lace and her arms spread wide on the counter as if to embrace the room. In the few months since her husband's memorable demise Widow Trotter had taken the place in hand and stamped it with her own character, which was generous and accommodating, ready to welcome all conditions of men. It warmed her heart to see those two great comedians, Pinkerman and Bullock, settled in together and enjoying what was obviously a lively conversation with her old friend Elias Cobb. There even appeared to be some stage business going on.

It was a special delight today, because in the evening, as a favour to herself, she would be taking leave to watch a performance of *Macbeth*, with the great Mr Betterton in the leading role. The anticipation was itself a pleasure, and she looked forward to seeing her two new customers in action. The antics of the witches would introduce some welcome moments of hilarity into the dark play – Pinkerman especially could be relied on to enliven things with a little seasoning of his own. If Mr Betterton and Mrs Barry brought Evil itself into the theatre and made the audience shiver with horror, Pinkerman and Bullock would add a pinch of grotesque humour. The thought reminded her to bring a handkerchief, since the Macduffs would infallibly draw quiet sobs from the more sentimentally inclined. Altogether, the play would be a feast for the emotions!

After a few minutes of contemplation Mrs Trotter was brought out of her reverie by a familiar figure emerging from the door next to the bar. Her poetical young lodger, Tom Bristowe, looking all spruced up in a new coat with his dark curls brightly polished, saw her watching the two actors and caught her eye. He beamed in his turn, and there was a chuckle in his voice as he greeted her:

'Well well, Mrs T! I see the famous pair are here again. The Bay-Tree is becoming a home-from-home for the players ...'

He glanced at the table where Pinkerman was now making some odd gestures with his arm while Bullock mirrored him. Elias Cobb was peering through his pipe-smoke and giving them his concentrated attention.

'... I see they are rehearsing even as we speak. What a treat we have in store tonight!

Double, double, toil and trouble!
Fire burn, and Cauldron bubble!'

'A rare one for me, Mr Bristowe – I haven't set foot in the playhouse since December. And that was Mr Shakespeare too – *Timon the Man-Hater*.'

'Ah yes, I recall it vividly. Our Mr Pinkerman was at his most inventive – though I fancy it was more Shadwell than Shakespeare.'

'Well it certainly was very comical. And Mr Pinkerman was remarkably convincing as a second-rate poet.'

She gave Tom a knowing look. The young man winced and bowed his head as the embarrassment of the occasion washed over him a second time:

'It was a disgusting travesty, Mrs T – an outrageous slur on a noble profession!'

'Yes, I think he was a little hard on your poem ... but you must allow the parody was an ingenious one.'

'It was too close to home. On that evening my poor "Myrtle Garland" received its death blow – though I have to admit he set the gallery on a roar.'

'I thought he caught the boyish innocence of your verses well – and in his singing he was romantic devotion to the letter ...'

Widow Trotter knew she had carried the teasing far enough, and deftly shifted her ground:

'... But it was Timon's pastoral masque that really delighted me – the dancing and the music.'

'Now there I can agree with you. Mr Purcell's music was very fine – and the new costumes also. The whole thing was lavishly done. And we shall be having more music tonight, shall we not? And a good deal of *flying about*. I trust our witches have been rehearsing it?'

They both looked over at Bullock, who was now on his feet, crouching slightly and whirling his right arm like a windmill.

'I must say, Mr Bristowe, it is a privilege to watch these fine actors close at hand. We are having our own request performance – *At the desire of the patrons of the Bay-Tree Chocolate House!*'

Tom laughed and reached for a sweetmeat, leaning a little across the counter towards her as he did so. He felt now was the appropriate moment to convey his message:

'Well, Mrs T, I have some news for you about tonight's performance – or rather, a proposal to put to you concerning it … I hope you will feel able to agree.'

'What is this?'

Something was afoot. She looked directly at him with narrowed eyes and bent her head. The lace tiara above her coiffure tilted dramatically as if posing its own question. Tom felt a little intimidated, but pressed on:

'You know that tonight my uncle has taken a box …'

'A box? Yes, but …'

She halted, and shook her head decisively.

'… O no, Mr Bristowe. I must stop you at once! You must go no further.'

The lappets were swinging violently across her cheeks.

'Please hear me out, Mrs T … an opportunity has arisen …'

'Lord Melksham's box? No, I couldn't possibly.'

'But Mrs T, please listen! You know that you and I were to sit together in the pit? … Well, Lady Welwyn is indisposed, and so the box will have only four. My uncle insists that you should be invited to take the fifth place. I know he'll be disappointed if you do not.'

'But that would leave you by yourself. And the box is not my place at all. I would feel horribly exposed. You know the propriety of these things.'

'Propriety be damned, Mrs T! You have the style and wit to carry it off perfectly. And I know you can out-stare anyone. But I do understand your uneasiness ... Of course, if you shrink from it you can always hide behind your fan.'

'But I can hardly put myself on display like that, Mr Bristowe. For a woman of my rank in society it will be viewed as brazenness – and you know how that can be misinterpreted. Someone in my position has to be careful.'

'But you may quite happily – and appropriately – take an *inner* seat. Leave the lolling and ogling to the superficial beauties – the gaudy tulips! You can plant yourself in the shade and quietly observe all.'

'But I'm no shrinking violet, Mr Bristowe – as you well know.'

Her jaw lifted slightly. Tom gave a triumphant smile:

'Excellent! That's just what I wanted to hear. The Mary Trotter I know would never *cringe*.'

'But you will be alone in the pit.'

'No-one is ever alone in the pit, Mrs T – it is convivial to excess. And in any case, my friend Will has expressed a wish to come along ... So you see, you would really be *de trop*, as Sir Fopling would say ... Are you ready for it? Will and I can pay our respects to you from below.'

And so, Widow Trotter was prevailed upon. The proprietor of the Bay-Tree would be gracing a box at the Theatre Royal. Tom's uncle, Viscount Melksham, was a good-natured gentleman, and she had heard enough from Tom about his cousin Lavinia to arouse her curiosity – she sounded an independent young lady, witty above her years, and Mrs Trotter suspected they would have some sharp observations to exchange ... Lavinia's admirer, Lord Tring, had been known to pop into the Bay-Tree on occasion to sample one of Mrs Dawes's delicacies, and he seemed to her an agreeable young man ... It was just Tom's aunt who made her feel apprehensive. By report, Sophia Popham would not take kindly to sitting in the same box as a Covent Garden landlady.

Mary Trotter thought about it for a moment, but then drew herself up to her full height and lifted her tiara proudly. What nonsense! That night she would be the match of any Duchess!

Chapter Two

THE THEATRE ROYAL looked at its best in candlelight. It was no morning beauty; but as darkness settled and the sconces and chandeliers flickered, the amphitheatre began to glow, and its complexion took on a velvety bloom. The touches of gold along the side-boxes glittered like jewels, and what seemed small quivering butterflies were in fact coloured fans catching the light. It also possessed a richly mingled perfume, which the fans helped waft around: rose and lavender from the middle gallery, peeled oranges from the crowd in the upper one, and French fragrances and bergamot snuff emanating from the boxes. But the strongest odour came from the pit, where tobacco-tainted coats were rubbing against the bawds' taffetas enhanced with Arabian scents of myrrh, cinnamon, saffron and cassia. Whatever presented itself from the stage had to compete with the exotic atmosphere being generated around the body of the theatre.

In good time Tom Bristowe and Will Lundy had settled themselves on one of the green-baize benches in the pit. The two young friends had found a place behind a diminutive couple who were talking quietly with each other. But within a few minutes all forethought was in vain. Larger bodies, swaying bulky coats, feathered hats, and wigs like knotted carpets began hovering over them and squeezing round them, and they found themselves shunted along the row. And the ambient conversation was also growing in volume, turning into shouts as patrons hailed their friends, and young men bawled compliments to their *toasts* and defiance to each other. The theatre musicians played louder in response, and so the shouting became even stronger. Two rows in front of them, a tall stripling beau was on his feet displaying his angular features to the audience, a silk handkerchief waving in one hand and a silver cat-call grasped tightly in the other.

'That spark has come prepared!' said Will.

'Yes,' said Tom. 'His kind are the loudest critics of all – and certainly the *shrillest*.'

'Which is it to be, do you think? Weeping or whistling? Let's hope the instrument stays in his pocket!'

Seated in the pit, Will Lundy was conscious of his height, and his neck was tingling with embarrassment. He was new to the delights of the playhouse and was trying not to let his shoulders stoop in anxiety. Now a student at the Middle Temple, he had attended enough court cases to know that a show of confidence could bring advantages. He had learned to be bolder and valued being able to see over all but the loftiest of lofty wigs – a fashionable extravagance that ought to be discouraged in the playhouse! Will cultivated longer hair as his own little protest against the excessive wiggery of others; but a career in the law (if he rose that high) would inevitably compromise his principles as much as it would test his patience. The legal profession was not the natural home for a mercurial temperament.

Beside him, a modestly bewigged Tom Bristowe cut a more saturnine figure; but the character of a determined satirical poet was not yet imprinted on his face, and its melancholy could be easily dispelled with a disarming grin. While Will looked around at the crush of bodies moving in on them, Tom was peering up at the side-boxes to his left. For many in the audience these boxes were as much part of the performance as those wooden boards trod by the players, and their little dramas were sometimes more entertaining. On this occasion Tom was anticipating with no small anxiety the moment when Widow Trotter would make her entrance on the social stage. For the hostess of the Bay-Tree Chocolate House, a place in Lord Melksham's box represented an unlikely – and potentially embarrassing – elevation.

At last there was a stirring, and Tom glimpsed the box-keeper ushering in Lord Melksham's party. He nudged Will in the ribs, and his friend looked up with a smile.

'Ah yes! The big moment. What a stately minuet they're giving us!'

The figures were doing an elegant little dance around the chairs, with silks and fans swaying, arms guiding, and hands gesturing. Finally matters seemed to be settled, and Tom saw to his delight – and apprehension – that the group was displaying its three beauties in the front row, with his cousin Lavinia placed in the middle, a rapidly-fanning Lady Melksham to the left with her face turned to the stage, and on the right, angled more toward the auditorium, Mary Trotter was returning the curious gazes of the audience.

It was a look that was striking in its simplicity: she was dressed in a gown of darkish blue muslin bordered with black, her auburn locks folded under a small silk cap, and a gauze scarf playing more freely round her shoulders. A string of jet clung closely to her neck, and a single white silk rose nestled against her bosom. Yes, it was a simple but distinctive look – that of a recent widow who was just beginning to reconcile herself once more to life's pleasures.

Will Lundy was open-mouthed for a moment, then whispered loudly in Tom's ear:

'I don't know how you managed it, but manoeuvring Mrs T into an aristocratical box is a feather in your cap. And I thought *I* was the schemer!'

Tom responded in kind:

'Well, it needed some quick-footed negotiation. There was a bit of practical sense, a sprinkling of flattery – and then a direct challenge. I think it was the last that won the day. I suggested it might be more decorous for her to hide in the rear of the box and cover her face with a fan.'

'Genius, Tom! And now look at her! I don't think she's hiding, do you?'

Mrs Trotter, who had been scanning the pit, finally located her two young friends, and her eyes lit up. As one, both Tom and Will got to their feet and made her an elegant little bow (anything more might embarrass her), which was acknowledged with a nod and a slight smile. It was all very polite. But they knew that behind the smile was a gleeful laugh holding itself in.

The theatre was still in commotion. Underneath the shouts from the audience and the last-minute cries of the orange women, there was a murmur of expectation which got louder by the minute. For decades, Mr Betterton's Macbeth had been one of the highlights of the stage, and the grizzled and slightly stooping thane could still draw them in. Now well into his seventies, the great actor must surely be bowing out very soon, and every performance might – who knows? – be his last.

The pit began to seethe and was becoming noticeably warmer as people fought for space and recognised more of their friends. Then suddenly everyone realised that the overture had come to an end. A scattering of applause was followed by shufflings, fidgetings and doffings, all carried out to cries of 'Down! Down!' 'Hats off!' 'Quiet!' 'Down!'

And then there was silence. On this occasion there was no prologue to ease the audience's mood and allow them to settle. Instead, an eery hush descended, and everyone fixed their eyes on the curtain, which twitched expectantly.

At once, a single indeterminate note broke *fortissimo* from the band, then another, then another, followed by a harsh, quivering chord that refused to become a melody. Again there was a second of empty silence, before a tremendous crash made everyone jump in their seats, and the roar of thunder made the whole place vibrate. A storm was in the theatre. It was as if a cascade of rocks were tumbling down on them. The curtain swept up to reveal a dark and dreary heath. The stage looked empty of humanity, but in the wings everyone was busy. Off to the right, the lightning-man threw his rosin-powder up at a line of candles hidden behind a wooden cloud, and there was a sudden brilliant flash, accompanied by another apocalyptic rumble of thunder from the heavens. In the wings, at either side, two stout stage-hands pulled alternately at ropes, causing a long wooden box suspended above the proscenium to swing violently up and down like a see-saw. Inside it, three large cannonballs rolled at speed and crashed before being swung back again.

And then the witches appeared! A single dark figure slid diagonally down from the flies; and then another, at an angle, swept down beside him. To more crashes, a dazzling white flame lit up the scene, and a third figure swung out from the wings, a large branch waving in his hand, and landed a little unsteadily on the stage. All three of them were uttering unearthly cries. And then a wild incantation began as they danced to and fro with stamping feet, while squibs exploded around them and smoke began to rise:

'—*When shall we three meet again,*
In Thunder, Lightning, and in Rain?
—*When the Hurly-burly's done,*
When the Battle's lost and won.
—*And that will be e'er set of Sun.*
—*Where's the place?*
—*Upon the Heath!*'

They chanted in turn, like demented priests of a dark religion. And then—

'There we resolve to meet MACBETH!!'

The talismanic name was shouted in unison, at full volume, answered by a hollow shriek like the cry of an owl. An evil spirit was calling back its own:

> *'Paddock calls!*
> *To us fair Weather's foul, and foul is fair!*
> *Come hover through the foggy, filthy Air—'*

With those words, the three grotesque creatures danced on their heels, until with a sudden twitching of their garments they lifted off into the air, which was now thick with smoke. As they soared back up through the clouds, a voice – which Tom and Will instantly recognised – was heard to cry: '*We'll be back!*'

There was a burst of relieved laughter, but tinged with apprehension. The stink of gunpowder slowly drifted out into the audience, so that the opening battlefield scene took on a distinctly nitrous flavour. Fans began to wave in earnest and handkerchiefs were pressed to noses. A few old faces in the audience were silent and grim as they re-lived the smell of Civil War.

The auditorium may have been gleaming with candlelight, but the darkened stage seemed to be drawing everyone in. Nevertheless a few conversations had already begun, with elegant figures in the boxes leaning out to acknowledge friends and offer greetings. On stage, while King Duncan listened attentively to the wounded captain giving his report of the victorious battle, a cork popped in one of the boxes. His character's severe injury didn't prevent the actor from employing the appropriate dramatic emphases with one arm, and as he was carried off the stage to receive the ministrations of a surgeon he gave a grateful bow to the audience.

Another ripple of applause greeted the entrance of Macduff – or rather George Powell, a tall, convivial gentleman whose martial steps on this occasion appeared to be reasonably steady and his voice unslurred. Indeed, he delivered his message from the battlefield with a becoming nobility of phrasing. Young Mr Keene as King Duncan looked distinctly relieved, and with the audience now quietened, he brought the scene to a dignified close, the actor's eye projecting the command of Majesty itself:

'No more the Thane of Cawdor shall deceive
Our Confidence! PRONOUNCE HIS PRESENT DEATH!
And with his former Title greet Macbeth.
He has deserv'd it! …
What HE has lost, Noble MACBETH has won!'

The royal procession formed, and departed the stage to warm applause.

Seated in the front of Lord Melksham's box, Mary Trotter had begun to feel uncomfortable. Not that she hadn't been made welcome, but she was acutely aware of heads turning and eyes stealing glances at her. It was a little like sitting in a shop-window, but without the glass. And to her right she could feel the indignant breeze of Lady Melksham's fan wafting her shoulder. This annoyed Lavinia, who was sitting between them:

'Mamma, don't you think your fan deserves a rest? I'm quite chilled enough!'

Her step-mother could not conceal a scowl, but remained silent, inspecting Widow Trotter with mixed feelings. Sophia Popham, née Doggett, was distinctly uneasy at sharing the attentions with a Chocolate House hostess, especially one who was not attempting to outshine her – indeed tonight the Popham jewels had an undiminished lustre. But Mary Trotter's widowed simplicity was drawing notice. Among the female figures gracing the boxes she was distinctive in restraint. Set against all the glitter around her she gained dignity by default. Her very lack of show drew interested eyes toward her.

But looking down on the stage from a side-box was very awkward. She longed to turn her chair round and lean out to see the full stage to her left, but it was clear that a woman in her position was intended to divide her attention equally between the play and the public, and be herself part of the show. She longed to huddle in the pit and gaze up at the stage as if she were viewing the work of her own imagination. From the box there was simply too much brilliant distraction, and all the time she was conscious of holding her face under control. Down in the pit her two friends sensed her isolation, and Tom began to wonder if he had done right in encouraging his uncle's offer.

But all thoughts, whether in pit or box, came to an abrupt end. Another shuddering bang rang out from the heavens, and the lightning-man in the wings threw his handful of rosin (he had very big hands) up at the candles. This would be a flash to end all flashes!

It nearly proved so. There was an almighty explosion, and this time the brilliant incandescence was sustained. One of the painted wooden clouds had felt the full force of the sublime electricity. The thing began to burn with increasing ferocity and fell to the stage in flames. The skies were seriously troubled. But this time it was not only the witches who danced wildly: alongside them a pair of scene-men were stamping the protesting cloud into submission. Oblivious of this, the band played with even more intensity, delighted at the encouragement the audience was giving them. Rhythmic applause was now filling the theatre, and the onstage jig seemed more diabolic than ever. From the side-scenes the prompter was waving his hands and shouting: '*The play must go on! Go on, witches! Thunder – do your worst!*'

The two stage-hands needed no further encouragement and responded with superhuman energy. The thunder-trunk received a truly Herculean tug and swung wildly, the cannonballs flinging themselves along the box. Down below, Pinkerman, the leading witch, was undeterred and strained to make himself heard above the din:

'Aroint thee, Witch! The rump-fed Ronyon cry'd.
Her Husband's to the Baltic gone, Master o'th' Tyger.
But in a sieve I'll thither sail,
And like a Rat without a Tail
I'll do, I'll do. AND I WILL DO!'

Pinkerman clinched the effect with a remarkable scurrying motion, sliding his leg across the boards like a rat's tail, and spinning while the others stamped in unison. The audience, who had given up listening to the words, were in ecstasy. Never before had Shakespeare's witches released such elemental power! And as if in confirmation the thunder rolled for a final time, louder and more urgently than ever. The gods were angry!

And then suddenly Jove's thunderbolt itself seemed to strike the stage. But this was no illusion. It was all too real. One of the timbers of the thunder-trunk had sprung loose, and instead of Scottish hail, three elemental cannonballs descended. A loud cracking sound was followed by another – but the third crash was a muffled thud.

As one, the audience gasped. Their simultaneous intake of breath almost sucked the scenery into the pit. People were leaping to their feet, and Will was on tip-toe:

'It's one of the witches, Tom! It's Pinkerman I think ...'

He craned his neck over a particularly lofty peruque while Tom tried to mount the bench beside him.

'... No! It's the *third* witch ... It's poor Mr Angell! The ball has struck him!'

Above the scene a few clouds still lowered menacingly, and stage left, the cauldron continued to breathe smoke, but alongside it a pair of figures in witches' garb were crouched over a prostrate body. The potions they held in their hands gave the arrangement an extra gruesomeness. But young Gilbert Angell appeared to be beyond the aid of any potions, however magical.

The audience in the Theatre Royal began to realise they were witnessing a truly elemental performance of the Scottish play. Dancing round their cauldron, the witches had summoned up fire and hail, and the heavens had duly obliged. But one of their number was now writhing on his back and shouting harsh imprecations on the company. This energetic response was taken as a reassuring vital sign, and the prompter strode to the front of the stage with arms outstretched and tried to reassure the spectators: the curtain would be lowered to allow Mr Angell to be attended to, but they hoped after an intermission to continue with the evening's entertainment. Meanwhile the band would divert the audience with a concerto by Signor Corelli ...

At this there were some encouraging cheers, and a couple of cat-calls began screeching from the pit, where many of the younger folk were standing on the benches. By now, to add to the precipitation, a light shower of orange-peel was descending from the upper gallery, with a few interspersed walnut-shells pattering on the boards. It was altogether a lively scene.

In Lord Melksham's box, Sophia Popham was fanning the air vigorously:

'This place becomes more and more like a fair-ground booth! What do you say, Lavinia? Are they not turning poor Shakespeare into a farce!'

'I think Shakespeare is beyond caring, mamma … I just hope the same isn't true of the witch. He seemed such a sprightly dancer!'

Young Lord Tring, who during the performance had been experimenting with a miniature telescope brought back from Venice, was able to be more precise. He leaned forward to Lavinia's ear:

'The ball missed his head – I think it took him on the shoulder.'

'Well, his vocal chords appear undamaged,' said a less than sympathetic Lavinia. 'Some of his expressions are very unShakespearean.'

The curtain began closing with a funereal slowness. Lord Melksham was looking concerned:

'What do you think, Mrs Trotter? I'm afraid this has turned into a horrible travesty. I cannot believe they are set on continuing.'

'The machinery does seem to have a life of its own …'

'Well, I for one could manage with less flashing and banging,' interrupted Lady Melksham – 'and less of the flying too. I was feeling quite giddy!'

'But don't you see, mamma, they're all rehearsing for the *May Fair* – and it's gone to their heads. They'll be off on holiday soon!'

Widow Trotter was looking down into the pit, where Tom's eyes met hers. There was an anxious expression on his face and he was shaking his head slowly. At that moment she longed to join him, and given a convenient ladder she would have scaled down it eagerly.

But this was not only for her friends' company. While the unlooked-for stage business had been going on she had noticed something puzzling. Her angle of vantage gave her a direct view into one of the opposing boxes, where she had seen a tall figure in the shadows calmly observing the stage antics. Everywhere in the theatre people were engaged and restless, peering, gesticulating and chattering; but this man stood stock still, his attention glued to the stage and a cold half-smile on his classical face, like a Roman emperor incised on an old coin. The figure moved not a muscle – even the eyes were motionless. It was as if something rich and satisfying were playing out before him, just as planned.

But her attention was distracted by words from the other side of the box:

'I understand the witches are customers of yours, Mrs Trotter? I trust they behave with a little more decorum in the chocolate house?'

Lady Melksham's wrist fluttered as she spoke, wafting an air of amusement towards Widow Trotter, who turned and met it with a gracious smile:

'Ah, my Lady, at the Bay-Tree we discourage the dark arts. Good conversation is always preferred!'

'And very good conversation I find there, Mrs Trotter!' said Lord Tring, his silver snuff-box held open in one hand, '… and ambrosial delicacies for the palate too! I'm glad you encourage Mrs Dawes's culinary invention. She is a miniature artist in that line.'

'I like to cater for all my guests, my Lord. Pies and pasties for some – and daintier fare for others. I encourage variety!'

'You run a most civilised house, Mrs Trotter,' said Lord Melksham. 'And beside your actors you have a sprinkling of poets too … our dear nephew is still soliciting the Muse, is he not?'

'Mr Bristowe does seem to be attracting notice – and of the right kind. He has just been invited to write a prologue for this very theatre.'

'A *prologue?*'

Lady Melksham expelled the word with distaste, and her fan became busier than ever.

'Calm yourself my dear,' said her husband. 'The art of the prologue is not to be despised. The late Mr Dryden was a specialist in that line – and Joseph Addison is too.'

Widow Trotter seized the moment:

'Yes, I recall Mr Addison's visit to the Bay-Tree when he spoke very highly of Mr Bristowe's verses.'

The fan snapped shut.

'What of that? To think that Tom is turning his back on a career in the Church. And for satire too! Such an unedifying trade – playing with the worst in life!' She turned to Lord Melksham. 'Can you not drum some sense into him, my dear? With the Monkton living he could be so happily settled. It would be such an eligible appointment.'

'I have pressed him as much as I can, my love, and I would like nothing better. But he does at last seem to be making his way.'

'His way to *what?* A life of anger and mockery! How edifying can that be?'

Widow Trotter was hesitant about intervening – these were difficult family matters. But she knew how much Tom dreaded the thought of becoming a country clergyman, and how ambitious he was for poetic fame. She longed to speak, but fortunately Lavinia Popham pre-empted her:

'I can assure you, Tom is now set on higher things. He told me he has put Juvenal aside and is imitating Virgil.'

Her step-mother looked quizzical rather than impressed:

'Virgil? You don't mean he's attempting epic? Heroes and gods?'

'No, mamma. Vegetables. And flowers too – he's writing something about Covent Garden.'

Lady Melksham shivered:

'You mean … the *market?*' She could hardly bring herself to use the word. 'But you said Virgil …'

'Yes mamma, The Georgics – the poem about country life – vines, and olives, and things. Tom has become very interested in vegetation – the fruits of the earth.'

'Both entertaining and useful!' declared Lord Tring chirpily. 'What a splendid idea. The garden in the city. *Rus in urbe!* What do you think, Mrs Trotter? Might there even be a place for the *Bay-Tree?* Long may that piece of vegetation flourish!'

There was a ripple of laughter from all but Lady Melksham, who peered down at the closed curtain. Signor Corelli's *allegro* was coming to an end. The whole occasion was becoming painful to her. Suddenly she saw the curtain twitch.

'I think something is stirring!' she declared. 'Perhaps the pantomime will soon be starting up again.'

And indeed, with a slight creak the curtain was tentatively lifted, and Christopher Rich, the theatre manager, bent forward under it. More cat-calls sounded, mixed with some scattered applause. A whole orange hurtled past Rich's head, threatening to repeat the earlier accident. His hands stretched out in supplication and he begged for silence. There was a momentary lull during which he was heard to declare that Mr Angell had badly dislocated his shoulder but was on the way to recovery. Nevertheless, given the uncertain state of the clouds and the difficulties with the machinery – especially the thunder-box which was dangling precariously above the stage – it had been thought wise to terminate the performance … unforeseen events … profound apologies … the safety of the actors …

His words were overwhelmed by an immediate roar, and something distinctly unpoetical from the market thudded onto the stage beside him; and so, after a couple of rapid bows to the auditorium, he retreated behind the curtain, which shivered to the floor. The place was suddenly loud with cries of disappointment, shouts of complaint, and several more projectiles. The band, with thoughts for their own safety, seized their instruments and made off as best they could.

Widow Trotter turned and looked over into the facing box, but the figure in the shadows had disappeared. Had she really seen it? There had been such drama in every direction that she began to lose certainty. The ghost-like apparition had added an extra strangeness to the occasion; and while the hooting and shouting continued she began wondering if more had been going on than they had realised. Or was she being fanciful? One thing was certain: she had hoped for a memorable evening in the playhouse, and very memorable it had proved to be! The theatre was a world of conflicting moods and turbulent passions, but it had its dangers too. Her mind raced, and a succession of images struck her: Pinkerman and Bullock playing in the Bay-Tree coffee-room – the wild dance of the witches – the explosion – the flaming cloud – the huge hailstones – the moment of terror – the furious oaths of Gilbert Angell writhing in agony ... It was a weird pageant altogether. While the others talked, she was pensive and a little uneasy. *When shall we three meet again ... ?* That April night, for a few terrible minutes, the Theatre Royal had cast a spell and dark forces seemed to have been released. *Paddock calls* indeed! ... But who was the familiar? And what did all this bode?

Down in the pit, Tom and Will had a more constricted perspective. The two young friends were hemmed in by a protesting jumble of bodies, some of them anxious to leave, others spoiling for a fight. Nearby, a bench had overturned, and to cries of '*heave!*' the ample frame of a citizen's wife was being hauled up from the floor, where her bottle of *sal volatile* continued to roll around and spread its choking fumes along the rows. This did little to calm the mood. The noise was undiminished, and the stripling beau, who had been deafening everyone with his cat-call, was now improvising a duet with another critic seated on the edge of the stage. As this cauldron of unsettled humanity bubbled away, Tom and Will held their places in the belief that staying put was the better option.

But Tom was restive and couldn't suppress his annoyance:

'Damn the theatre! All that machinery! Why can't we trust the *words?* Spectacle is all very fine, but the poetry … the poetry …'

'Ah, Tom, don't lament its passing just yet. Tonight the words were hardly given a chance, were they? Poor Mr Betterton – and poor Mrs Barry – waiting in the side-scene! They would surely have won the day and *soothed the savage breast* – the magic wand of the poet, and all that! In the end we would have wept for the Macduffs and their *poor babes* …'

Tom sighed:

'All machinery!'

'But better weeping than raging, surely? Tears are more civilised than blows.'

'Yes, I'll allow you that … though too much of either can be dangerous. Even Mrs Trotter had her handkerchief ready!'

'Yes indeed – and she's not of the blubbering persuasion.'

Tom looked around at the unruly audience who seemed unwilling to leave the theatre, as if the unfinished business had cheated them:

'But I'm fearful, Will.'

'What about?'

'The whistling and the orange peel – all that anger! Did you hear what they were shouting? In an instant the theatre can become a bear-garden.'

'But where's the fear?'

Tom's head lowered:

'My prologue ...'

'Ah ... !'

Will swallowed as he remembered. There was a moment's pause while he shared his friend's uneasiness:

'... Yes of course, your stage début! But that will surely be different? Prologues are indulgently treated – the audience are ready to be charmed and amused. Now, if you were writing an *epilogue* ... well ... A prologue is altogether safer! You won't have to retrieve anything. It's in your own hands.'

'In the playhouse, yes. But in the coffee-houses afterwards? That's where the critical axe can fall.'

Tom knew that a prologue was a tempting morsel for the town critics to chew on – and perhaps spit out. In the Bay-Tree he had heard some cruel verdicts that would have blasted an oak ...

Suddenly there was a tinkle of glass as one of the wall-sconces in the auditorium received a direct hit. Tom looked over and saw that the Pophams' box was empty – the party had clearly left for somewhere more salubrious. At that instant a fidgeting neighbour sneezed violently and deposited a trail of oily snuff across Tom's sleeve. He began scrubbing at his coat, while Will reached into the pocket of his own for a small orange. This was not turning out to be an elegant evening.

'About your prologue ... Have you read the play yet?'

'No, but I'm to attend a rehearsal on Monday morning. It should be little more than a reading. The play lacks a title as yet, but Pinkerman is toying with *The Tender Courtesan*.'

'I'm sure he is!' said Will with a chuckle. 'Who would not?'

'Well, we've already had *The Tender Husband*. I take it this is going to be rather more daring.'

'*Daring* is the word, Tom. I suspect the thing will be a severe provocation to our reforming friends. I can see it now: a charming rogue and a soft-hearted whore! A courtesan is combustible material – your only hope is that the action ends in Bridewell or at Tyburn!'

Tom and Will looked at each other in silence for a moment. Suddenly they both wanted to be elsewhere.

'The Bay-Tree!'

It was said almost in unison, and the two of them rose laughing. But as they struggled to make their way out of the pit, their minds turned to Widow Trotter and what her thoughts on the events had been. They hoped soon to find out. In the playhouse that evening all of them had become unwitting performers in a dark comedy that stirred the passions. Whatever you might say about the theatre world, it was always ready to spring surprises – delightful ones and dangerous ones.

Chapter Three

CHRISTOPHER RICH JUMPED back under the curtain as it lowered to the floor. It was a fragile barrier but a welcome one, and he winced when he saw the cloth ripple violently as another message was delivered from the auditorium. He knew the theatre's greencoats were even now encouraging the audience to calm themselves and depart in an orderly manner. The place was simmering, but it hadn't yet boiled over, and as he stood by the curtain he cocked his ears and tried to fancy that the noise was dying a little and he could detect the shuffling of feet. The prompter, Mr Grant, was off in search of the chief carpenter, but his damned house manager was nowhere to be seen. The man was probably even now settled in the green room with his feet on a table chatting hugger-mugger with George Powell and saluting the contents of a claret-bottle.

Rich knew things had been too good to last. It was late in the season, but business had held up well, and the past few days had seen warm houses and vigorous applause. Mr Betterton's Macbeth was always a good draw. In advance of the May Fair recess he liked to slip the audience one or two popular pieces – a few jewels to glow in their minds during the quiet months ahead. Now, in the final days before the release of the Fair, his surest hope rested on Tuesday's performance of *The Fox*. Jonson's comedy never failed, and in Powell's Volpone and Wilks's Mosca he had a pair who always struck sparks off each other ... *Sparks?* It was an unsettling image. He checked himself and glanced down at the cumulus of charred wood. He sniffed the stink of burnt paint that was rising from it and shuddered.

His anger was mounting:

'Lug that blasted cloud off the stage!' he shouted. The scene-men continued to hover.

'... and someone fetch a broom!'

The men looked at each other.

'... Damn the weather! Why do plays need *weather?* From now on we shall perform nothing but pastorals!'

The three scene-men approached the overcast fragments, and a quick-thinking fourth ran on with one of the witches' broomsticks which had been abandoned in the wings.

Mr Rich looked around him in disbelief: language was beginning to fail him:

'And where the devil is the lightning? I want him here! – *now!*'

He looked down at his feet where the iron cannonballs rested, two of them nestling in splintered hollows in the boards. There was the sound of a voice behind him.

'And to think that could have been my head!'

The reflection came from Will Pinkerman who was approaching with an almost cheerful sparkle in his eye.

'Ah! Here has been some mischief, Mr Pinkerman! I warrant there's malice behind this – I would swear to it!'

'Well, I've never seen a flash like it. I know the three of us were raising the very devil tonight – whirling the elements as never before! – But that explosion ... well, it was surely beyond our capacities – even Bullock's ...'

Pinkerman's eyes widened and his voice began to tremble, spectre-like.

'... Unless, of course, this is the Lord's judgment on our stage? ... *the hand of Heaven!*'

'The only hand I'm concerned with is Mr Bolt's! Where *is* the man?'

The name was not coincidental but a piece of company humour which recognised the lightning-man's elemental powers. As he spoke, the manager looked in the wings to his left and espied a figure half-crouching behind a section of Birnam Wood which on this occasion had signally failed to make its way to Dunsinane.

A short while later a house inquiry was in progress. Mr Bolt, along with Mr Howell the chief carpenter, Mr Grant the prompter, a couple of the more senior stage-hands, and the two surviving witches, were convened on the forestage, perched on stools that awaited the banquet scene. Beyond the curtain the auditorium seemed to have gone quiet, but no-one dared investigate. A little way behind them a pair of smart fellows who claimed their liberty of the scenes were lounging against the royal throne and chatting nonchalantly. One of them was trying on a painted wooden crown.

In face of Rich's questions the lightning-man was adamant. When he flashed his rosin for the final time he knew something was wrong. It felt different – he was sure somebody had been tampering with it.

'You mean ... *gunpowder?*'

Pinkerman was no longer grinning.

'Well, I delved deep,' said Mr Bolt almost proudly. 'It felt different in the hand – and just look at this!'

He held out his bowl of rosin, and there amongst it were unmistakable black grains. He stirred it with a large finger, and the powder grew darker still, a change not discernible in the night-scene of the performance. Under the direct light of a candle there could be no doubt: tonight the witches' spells had been augmented by hellish alchemy. The playhouse itself had very nearly taken fire.

The manager twitched his nostrils, and his eyes narrowed. This was something deep and dangerous, he hardly knew what. A stunned silence had descended.

'And what about the thunder, Mr Howell?'

He could see from the chief carpenter's face that nothing reassuring was to be expected. The normally taciturn fellow was murmuring to himself, his white knuckles gripping a hammer that hung from his apron:

'There's been some dirty work, Mr Rich! And if I find out who … his nose will be as bent as those nails!'

'What nails?'

'In the thunder-trunk. I swear a body's been tampering with it – and loosened one of the planks.'

One of the burly stage-hands agreed.

'Three of the nails have been bent round, Mr Rich – and that was surely done before the accident. You can just make them out from here.'

Rich craned his head upwards where the loose plank was hanging down.

'But how is that possible, Jackson? It hangs so high. Out of reach … except by the gods.'

At the word *gods* the intrepid Mr Bolt gave a shiver and voiced an uncomfortable thought:

'Well, Mr Rich … perhaps there's been an intervention *from above?*'

'Stuff and nonsense! The thing must have been in bad repair. After all, it's had all hell knocked out of it! May is approaching and we've had a tempestuous season. Every new author seems to require a storm or a crash of thunder …'

As if to emphasise his point he jumped to his feet.

'… Look what we've had! There's been oracles prophesying,

gods endlessly descending, banditti lurking round their caves, terrible shipwrecks, hurricanes, portents and tumults – and romantic lovers who can only meet in a dark forest with lightning flashing over them. No wonder the poor trunk was close to bursting!'

'But Mr Rich ...'

The manager swung round:

'Silence! I'll have none of this superstitious nonsense! And you, Mr Bolt, must *look to your powder!* From now on you'll find another source for your rosin, do you hear? ...'

He lifted his eyes in pious frustration, driving home his words with a waving hand.

'... Thank Heaven the house is returning to comedy! Good old Ben Jonson didn't need such stuff. *He* had no recourse to tempests! We'll have beds and bolsters, simple desks, tables and cupboards. No divine anger! With nothing more combustible than Spanish snuff – and no wind stronger than the breeze of a fan!'

On those words, Christopher Rich seized his hat, and with a final ferocious glance over his shoulder, made an exit worthy of Betterton himself.

A few minutes later he was stalking around behind the scenes. It was hardly possible to do anything else, given it was such a warren of little rooms and twisted passageways, improvised stairs and subdivided closets. Since he became the theatre manager, Rich had delighted in internal architecture – *nook-building* as he called it – ingeniously finding places where yet another body could be accommodated. There were dressing-rooms and costume-rooms, offices and store-rooms, a script-room, a copying-room, a room to house the account-books and musical scores, and some rooms that didn't deserve the name. But one of them was larger and more amply furnished than any other, and was the place where the company could come together to relax. Here they could converse, laugh, drink, seduce, gossip, grumble, accuse, squabble, threaten, fight ...

When he pushed open the door of the green room, Rich could not be certain which of these would be playing out. But after that evening's fiasco he rather hoped to find some of the players to commiserate and reassure – anything to escape from the cursed auditorium, where carpenters, cleaners and scene-shifters were now busying themselves. He was weary of the whole complicated business.

The hinge creaked, and he knew that all had fled: the place was dimly lit and unexpectedly quiet. But he could detect a low murmur and some stentorian breathing from the direction of the couch at the far corner of the room. His own candle gave a little more illumination. After a couple of steps he stopped in his tracks.

'My Lord! This is unexpected. I did not know you were in the theatre.'

'I didn't announce myself, Mr Rich – just thought to slip in after the third act and catch a few friends ... I understand that tonight the elements conspired against us! Devilish bad!'

'A disaster, my Lord – nothing less. I take it you have had the particulars?'

'I have! I hear the pit was boisterous – and with good reason! Flames and thunderbolts beyond control – I've never known such a thing! You must sharpen your axe. We need a head!'

'But I suspect ...'

'A *head*, Mr Rich. 'Ods life! The stage-manager must go. The place is becoming lax. No discipline! Our reputation is at stake. At times like these we must be beyond reproach ... like Caesar's wife – eh my dear?'

Lord Tunbridge, ageing and infirm, yet still elegant in his movements, bestowed a smile on the young actress who was squeezed up beside him on the couch, and began withdrawing his hand from beneath her petticoat. His free hand set down a glass of port. His face was carved from alabaster.

Sally Twiss was blushing pinkly, yet somehow managed an unruffled smile. But as she rose to her feet, Rich caught a look of disgust and relief.

'Good evening, gentlemen. I'll leave you to your theatre-talk. You'll not be wanting distraction.'

She adjusted her dress with dignity and turned to give her admirer a peck on the cheek, to which his arm responded with more than a gentle reminder:

'My coach is waiting in Bridges Street. I shall join you shortly.'

The sixth Baron Tunbridge held a substantial share in the theatre and was someone who had to be listened to. And so Rich responded to his inviting gesture and helped himself to wine. He avoided the couch and sank into an armchair close by. The Baron raised himself to a more upright position and placed one buckled shoe above the other. Both men lifted their glasses in silence.

Lord Tunbridge had always interested himself in the fortunes of the company's younger females, and Sally Twiss, he had decided, was a talent to be nurtured. Unlike some others of the nobility who graced the stage-boxes, Tunbridge was happy to encourage a girl's ambitions – after all, he hardly looked for a wife, but rather for a grateful protegée who could be coached into spirited performances and learn those little tricks of casting a spell over the pit. The Baron maintained that it was in the slighter movements – an eager glance, a thoughtful half-closed eye, a modest drooping of the head, a hesitant turn of the wrist – that the secret lay. 'The eloquence of the body', he would say, 'is a tender thing: the body breathes and sighs. But through it you must find the *soul* and animate that too. Let your soul breathe – *and let it fly!*' Christopher Rich could almost hear the words now as he hesitated to speak, wondering what more should be said about the evening's accidents. But Lord Tunbridge's thoughts were elsewhere. He began smiling and half-whispering to himself.

'Ah ... Miss Twiss! ... Miss Twiss! ... She is indeed the sweetest thing. What an air she has. I *lisp* it aloud ... Misstwiss! Mistwiss! ...'

Rich was taken aback.

'... . She will have to change her name. We cannot have the pit getting hold of that. The poor girl! I'm surprised she has not already done so.'

'There's a euphony to it, my Lord, but I agree it has an unfortunate ambiguity,'

'Ah, but what *capabilities* she has. A little charmer! A creature so pretty, and yet so civil; so innocently wanton, and so good-natured. You must treasure her, Mr Rich – and *forward* her. We must make plans!'

As a patron of the theatre, Lord Tunbridge was someone who could make life difficult for an uncooperative manager, especially one whose position was becoming precarious. But on this matter Rich tended to agree: young Sally had talent and in time might rise to be a star in the theatrical firmament. But it must be managed with delicacy. There were sensitivities that had to be negotiated, company rivalries to be carefully handled ...

'I have been thinking,' the Baron continued, fixing Rich with a direct stare. 'This new play of yours ... *The Willing Mistress* ...'

'*The Tender Courtesan*, my Lord.'

'Indeed, yes! The *Courtesan*. It is to be the centre-piece at the Fair, is it not?'

'That is the plan – with a view to bringing it to the main house if it should *take*.'

'Well, we must make sure it does take! Have you cast the thing yet?'

'We begin rehearsals on Monday, my Lord. A reading only.'

'And does young Sally have a part?'

'A considerable one, my Lord – Agnes, the novitiate nun. It is a considerable step for her, and a role that helps drive the plot: the girl *conspires* and shows some spirit. I thought ...'

'Some spirit? Yes, an *ingénue* I suppose? But *I* see Miss Twiss as possessing more *extensive* talents ...'

Lord Tunbridge tasted the word as he spoke it, and lifted his goblet close to his face.

'... I was hoping ...'

He swirled its contents slowly, watching the deep red liquid coat the inside of the glass as it rose and fell in a smooth rhythm.

'... I was hoping, Mr Rich, that you would consider her for the main part – the tender mistress. Tenderness is well within her range.'

'I'm sure it is, my Lord, but Mrs Oldfield ...'

'*Mrs Oldfield?* She will be in your *booth?* How did you persuade her?'

'Mr Cibber and I ...'

'Ah, Cibber! I might have known! But are you certain of her?'

'It was arranged with the promise of securing her the part for the main house.'

'As if Anne Oldfield didn't have parts enough! Beware of monopoly, Mr Rich! Poor Mrs Bracegirdle has already felt it – driven from the stage! Mrs Oldfield must allow others room.'

'But these things have to be decided carefully, my Lord. There are contractual matters ...'

'But playing at the fair surely cannot be in Oldfield's contract?'

'No, of course ... but we have agreed matters verbally.'

'What is arranged verbally can be *re*-arranged verbally! If this is a *tender* part, Mr Rich, then it is not much in Oldfield's line. You need someone with the most delicate and *wooing* ways. I have been coaching young Sally, and I know she can set the heart-strings in motion like no other. I assure you she will repay your confidence.'

'But the role is so much more than that, my Lord. Mr Cibber and Mr Pinkerman have given Tamara a heroic – even noble – aspect.'

'*Tamara?* An exotic? Even better! This is the chance for young Sally to show her mettle. The company needs a new face – one to stir the pit to ecstasies! I tell you, Miss Twiss will not fail you. And it will extend her range.'

The manager was more than uneasy. In these early months of her career Sally Twiss had no *range* at all.

'I do not doubt it, my Lord, but this is all very difficult, and at this point in the arrangements … I would have to consult Colley.'

'Mr Cibber will do as I tell him!'

By now Lord Tunbridge's complexion had assumed something of the hue of the port, which at that emphatic moment was disappearing down his throat. His Lordship set down the glass with considerable force on a small lacquered table, and rose to his feet.

'I cannot stay to argue this out, Rich. But I know you won't disappoint me. I have the good of the theatre at heart, and in this I suspect you share my opinion – if not my eagerness. You're a shrewd man, and I'm confident you can manoeuvre things satisfactorily …'

The Baron was about to open the green-room door but stopped in his tracks and turned round. There was a slight curl of the lip – was it contempt? – and he was suddenly more formal and assured:

'… I was going to raise this with you at an opportune moment, Mr Rich, but given the circumstances I ought to tell you now … It may help your deliberations to know that I have today negotiated a transfer of *shares* …'

Christopher Rich heard the word and was at once uneasy. It was a term that was never spoken lightly in the theatre – if spoken at all. A share was more than a token of power – it was power itself. And the word *transfer* …

'… Mr Swiney and Mr Estcourt are willing to make over their shares in the theatre to me. The financial settlement needs to be completed, but I can confidently say that by next week I hope to be the leading sharer in the company.'

Rich went cold. At that instant he almost heard the rumble of distant thunder as an unwelcome picture flashed before him:

'My Lord, I …'

'I have already spoken with Mr Cibber, and although he seemed not to rejoice at the news, he came to see how the new arrangement might bring *opportunities* … I am anxious to take a more active role in the company. You know my devotion to its best interests.'

Rich had to speak:

'But Mrs Oldfield is formidable …'

'Indeed she is – but actresses, however froward, can be made to see sense. I'm sure you can compensate Oldfield in some other way … or you can take refuge in confusion …'

He opened the door slowly.

'… I leave it to your well-known *ingenuity*, Mr Rich. I sometimes think you employ an art of muddle in order to keep everyone on their toes. It is your own mischievous scheme of order. Well, we shall see! This challenge will try what stuff you are made of.'

With that, Lord Tunbridge left the room in determined fashion. As the door closed, the manager felt he was re-living the earlier stage disaster. He raised his eyes in disbelief. But this was no empty bluster. It sounded like a direct threat, and how the company would react he really didn't know. The room was suddenly less familiar, and less comfortable.

'Death, Hell, and Furies!' he shouted to the ceiling, and as he did so he half expected it to collapse on his head.

Chapter Four

REPORTS OF THE apocalyptic events in Drury Lane didn't take long to reach the Bay-Tree, where the evening's disaster became the chief topic of conversation. The goings-on at the theatre were often a cause for mirth among the older regulars, and any over-excited playgoer was considered fair game. For the 'men of business', who tended to huddle together in spite of Widow Trotter's best efforts, the very idea of watching a set of extravagantly-costumed performers declaring love or war to each other across a wooden stage appeared a ludicrous waste of time. As for the new 'opera' – as it was called – well, they considered it a cultural assault little short of a Catholic invasion.

These Whiggish gentlemen, gathered at the table nearest the fire, seized on the latest news with relish and began offering their observations freely. The hilarity was rising. But on the wall above their heads, and somehow remaining superior to it all, was Anne Bracegirdle, the former toast of the Theatre Royal pictured in one of her more exotic roles. The Indian Queen looked down from her frame in all her feathered finery and brought a touch of theatrical *panache* to the room. Needless to say, Widow Trotter's introduction of this image of female self-assurance wasn't popular with those gentlemen, who had draped a black scarf over it when it first appeared.

So, it was not a propitious moment for their two wayward friends, Gavin Leslie and David Macrae, to come in through the door. The young Scotsmen had been deeply disappointed at the curtailed performance, but they were given no time to settle themselves before the ribbing began.

Jack Tapsell, a wine merchant of harsh nose and vinegary aftertaste, waved his hat in the air and saluted them as intrepid travellers:

'*All hail* gentlemen! You have returned safe! We hear your sojourn in Scotland has been full of incident. 'Tis a wild place at the best of times, and you've certainly had *heavy weather* of it tonight!'

'All *hail* indeed – more than enough!' said Sam Cust, importer of sugar, as he stirred some of the stuff into his coffee.

'And yet *not a cloud in the sky!*' added a grinning Barnabas Smith, cloth trader, not wishing to be left out of the repartee.

'Scotland is a bonny country ...' began David Macrae unadvisedly; but the young man was cut short by Jack Tapsell, who was determined to keep the hare running:

'Your *Scotia* is a romantick promontory, Sir. It clings to the edge of the civilised world – a realm of witches' spells and second sight, of boggarts and bogles! You must both be mightily glad to be back in Red Lion Court. Our Mrs Trotter may be terrifying but at least she doesn't suspend the Laws of Nature!'

'You're free of wizardry in the Bay-Tree,' echoed Sam Cust rather lamely, and beckoned them to sit down.

But Jack Tapsell was warming to his favourite topic:

''Tis surely Heaven's judgment on *the Union*, is it not? ...'

His eyes took on a mischievous glint.

'... Such happenings are a terrible warning. We should have left *North Britain* where it was and not allowed those dangerous Scots to meddle in our affairs. Had we only had second sight ourselves! But thanks to Mr Harley and his Tory crew, all's gone arse over head.'

'Yes, *the time is out of joint!*' commented Barnabas Smith with a hopeful grin.

'I think you have mistaken your play, sir!'

Gavin Leslie offered all three of them a genial smile and seated himself in an easy manner. He and his friend were familiar with such banter and had come to enjoy the sparring:

'What we witnessed in the theatre tonight, Mr Tapsell, was English anarchy. On stage the Scots gave us courage and noble sentiments, while in the pit the polite English became a howling mob. The storm was nothing in comparison!'

David Macrae picked up the idea:

'The Union, Sir, will surely work to your advantage? If you English will let us teach you how to be civilised, then we can all boast of being *British*.'

At this Jack Tapsell spluttered into his coffee and managed to spill most of it; but the two Scotsmen, with the instinctive generosity of their race, called upon Peter the coffee-boy to replenish his dish and supply their own, and within a few minutes they were telling their tale to a contented company. All the talk was of explosions, blazing clouds, and deadly thunderbolts.

When eventually Tom Bristowe and Will Lundy came through the door it was clear the drama would continue. Tom was pale and wigless and a little unsteady on his feet, and he was pressing a handkerchief to his temple. His other hand clutched the bundle of brown curls but for which his injury would have been considerably greater. Jack Tapsell, emboldened by Widow Trotter's absence, was once again playing the usher:

"Ods-life! A pair of English refugees! Is the battle still raging, gentlemen? Have you fled the field?'

'The trouble is over now,' said Will. 'The Watch have a couple of 'prentices by the ear and they'll be soundly whipped. Half a dozen of them were stoning the theatre windows – but some widened their aim to the retreating audience. The handsome wigs were just too tempting!'

'We heard the shouts,' said Gavin Leslie.

'Yes,' said Tom. 'There were some choice insults being hurled – the language of the pamphleteers!'

'You mean they were cursing the stage? Are even the apprentices at it now?'

'Those who've been slipped a coin, certainly. They must have been organised in the matter. We heard the words *synagogue of Satan!*'

'Well, if that's not from the pulpit …'

'And *spawn of the Devil!* too.'

'Aha! Have the Reformers been at work, then?'

'More than likely,' said Will. 'The 'prentices pick up slogans easily enough. Give them another penny and they're as like to pelt the men who hired them.'

Tom patted his sore head and frowned. He drew Will aside:

'After tonight's disaster it only adds insult to injuries. I dread Monday's rehearsal – there's bound to be an inquest. It's not the best introduction to *The Tender Courtesan*, is it?'

'Look at it this way,' said Will brightly. 'It makes an excellent subject for your *Prologue*: the theatre under attack, and the company threatened by dark forces. Don't you think you could paint a lively picture? Curses and thunderbolts! – Insults and cobblestones! With the heroic actors triumphing over adversity. You can work it up to something entertaining … and of course, speaking in his own booth Pinkerman will have the audience in the palm of his hand.'

'Yes, I suppose I could risk something in the defiant line.'

'At the fair you'll have licence to be satirical. You can paint the reformers as empty trunks and damp rosin!'

'But there's a serious point too. I want to say that the stage itself has power to attack vice and ridicule folly. And above all to expose hypocrisy – that's why the reformers are so fearful of it.'

'That would hit the mark, Tom! I know you can make something fine out of this. You'll be saying what needs to be said at this moment.'

Tom glanced at the wig which hung disconsolately from his clenched fist:

'At this *very* moment, Will, I want to climb out of my theatre clothes and wash my face. I've had enough of the playhouse for one evening. But I have to be here when Mrs Trotter returns – she's bound to have a tale to tell! I hope my aunt and uncle have been taking good care of her.'

'The Pophams must have carried her off to St James's and an early supper? What a taste of high life she'll be having! How are you going to keep her feet on the ground?'

'Easily, Will. I warrant she's feeling quite at home around the Pophams' table – there'll be enough chatter to keep her entertained, and I'm sure she'll be contributing her share ...'

He suddenly looked apprehensive.

'... I only hope Uncle Jack and Lavinia will be discreet. I dread to think what stories they're telling about my mis-spent youth.'

'Mrs Trotter will be delighted at that. You know how she draws people out.'

'Especially when madeira is to hand.'

'Do you think your Cousin Frank will be there?'

'Oh, that would make it worse! He'll surely be at his club with his political confederates? At least I hope so. Frank would never miss a chance to have fun at my expense.'

'In that case I'm certainly staying here until the Queen of Sheba arrives. It's been an eventful evening, but it may not have reached its climax yet.'

Tom scowled. He was full of anticipation himself.

The pair settled themselves at a table and beckoned the

coffee-boy over. Peter Simco was light on his feet and gave them a cheery look as he set two china dishes before them with a half-pirouette and a practised sweep of the arm:

'Mr Bristowe! Mr Lundy!'

His eyes were bright under the little bob-wig, and his green livery looked almost regimental paired with an apron that was reassuringly clean. Peter's movements were precise and delicate, and the hot liquid poured in a thin cascade from the raised coffee-pot. It was a delightful performance that turned routine into ceremony and gave the drink more savour.

Will reached out and cradled the blue and white porcelain between his fingers. He was thoughtful, and his face wore an unaccustomed solemnity:

'Well, Tom. What are we to make of tonight's drama? Mr Pinkerman will surely be sobered by it. The whole thing sank into cheap farce.'

'And quickly too. The house wasn't happy, was it? How soon the gallery lost its enthusiasm! At one moment they were whipping things up to a frenzy, and the next ...'

'Yes, it was more Hockley Hole than Drury Lane.'

'People love spectacle, Will – and how eagerly plays pander to them! How they stir up the passions!'

'Take care now, or you'll be a hypocrite yourself. What about the poets? Surely you excite the passions too?'

'Yes of course ...'

Tom checked himself, but only for a moment.

'... But poetry is different – its passions are private ones. We make readers weep and laugh, and we rouse them to indignation – but they don't jump on the furniture. If I make my reader angry I want him to *think*, not throw stones. In a theatre the passions are contagious ...'

He looked at Will with narrowing eyes, and a mischievous smile began to invade his cheeks.

'... I suspect there's a particular theatrical passion that *you* want to keep private, Will? But you must allow others to share it ... Perhaps some already do?'

'I can't think what you mean.'

'*The Rover?* Was there not a certain young actress on Thursday night who set your heart all a-flutter? You were in raptures about her.'

'Ah! You mean Lucetta?'

'Yes, Will, Lucetta – or rather young Sally Twiss.'

'She's a fine prospect.'

'Yes, you said that many times, and your eyes lit up each time you used the word *prospect* ... I only hope you don't think you have *prospects* in that direction yourself?'

'I was evaluating her performance.'

'I know. You said she acted the *jilting wench* to perfection. Perhaps she was only playing in character?'

'She was very spirited ...'

Tom began laughing, but Will was undaunted.

'... She tricked poor Blunt unmercifully. It was so clever. She has a charming way with her.'

'Yes, Will. So be warned. Remember what happened to that young fellow. He lost his breeches and ended up in the sewers.'

Now Will was laughing too:

'A palpable hit, Tom, I confess. But she's a rosebud of a creature.'

'But one with thorns coming, I warrant.'

'Well, tonight she was to have played Lady Macbeth's waiting-woman – if only the performance hadn't broken off as it did.'

'Now I know why you were eager to join me. I hope you've not had two nights without sleep?'

'No, Tom, I've slept very soundly ... but Sally Twiss has all the winning graces. A young Bracegirdle in prospect.'

'*Prospect* again! ... In that case you'll be pleased to know that when we are sitting in Pinkerman's booth to hear my prologue, you'll have a further sighting of her.'

'Ah! So she has a part in *The Tender Courtesan?*'

'Indeed she does. But be warned – she is to play a novitiate nun. An innocent role, but no doubt one in which her *prospects* will once again be in full view ... Mrs Oldfield will have to look to her laurels!'

The mood had lightened, and both of them were now chuckling. Will seized the opportunity to turn the conversation:

'To think that Oldfield will be gracing the Fair with her presence – that will be an attraction in itself.'

'Yes, Pinkerman is determined this year's offerings will be more ambitious than ever. Let us hope everything goes smoothly.'

'Are you anxious about the *Courtesan?*'

'A little, I confess. But perhaps the other production will be more troublesome? *The Devil on Two Sticks* promises to be satirical! I know Pinkerman plans to introduce some remarkable stage business.'

'More machinery, eh? Oh dear, that's just what you were dreading! Let's hope it doesn't require *thunder and lightning*.'

The talismanic words were overheard in the room, and at once Tom and Will found themselves drawn into the general conversation. The offer of a slice of toasted cheese was happily accepted, and the next minute the two of them were making their own contribution to the playhouse incident, which by now had become embroidered with the rich trappings of mock-heroic.

The Queen of Sheba's arrival proved to be a discreet one. There was no very great train or abundance of spices, and certainly no camels. Lord Melksham's coronet coach delivered Widow

Trotter to the end of the court in Bow Street, and she walked from there up to the Bay-Tree, slipping in through her private door round the back. When *Macbeth* broke up so memorably the Pophams had whisked her off to Pall Mall, and after a convivial hour of cold meats, gossip and speculation, she was now well set. Rather than being a disappointment, the whole evening had unfolded very satisfactorily. She had said nothing to the Pophams about the mysterious figure, but her mind was running back over the on-stage antics and the extraordinary *diabolus ex machina*. She hoped to hear what the upshot had been. Lady Melksham had fled the theatre in alarm, so they weren't able to linger and observe the outcome.

Twenty minutes later, now comfortably settled in the Bay-Tree's parlour, Widow Trotter was pleased to have her two young friends to herself at last and to find their sense of anticipation quite the equal of hers. The madeira was poured, and alongside the glasses were three elegant china cups waiting to receive the chocolate.

'Well, that was an evening to remember! ...' she said, hesitating for a moment with the jug poised in her hand. 'I seem to have lived in several worlds today – and none of them quite real.'

'From the look of you, Mrs T, you've enjoyed mingling with the *beau monde*?'

'Yes, Mr Bristowe, and I've survived remarkably well. Your Pophams are a spirited bunch – nothing too stiff or solemn with them – though Lady Melksham was uncomfortable. She's a woman who's learned the *forms*, and having a Covent Garden landlady at her table was something of a challenge.'

'You say *learned*,' said Tom. 'That's true. Poor Aunt Sophia hasn't quite settled into the gracious arts. She embraces the world of fashion but tends to forget the easy and natural. She doesn't see that Nature has its own winning charms.'

'Ah, but Lavinia is a delight! She and I had an amusing *tête à tête*. What a sparkling young miss she is! – a lively fancy, and full of stories too. She had a few to relate about her Cousin Thomas – a young man who it seems hasn't always been so serious and well behaved.'

Tom swallowed hard and felt a blush beginning:

'We can never escape our youth, Mrs T – I'm sure you don't wish to! – but I doubt you discovered anything unforgivable.'

'That depends – at least nothing to put your soul in mortal danger. However, what if I were to mention … *raspberries?*'

The accusing stare on Widow Trotter's face called to mind his old schoolteacher, and he instinctively glanced at the wall to see if there was a birch-rod hanging there.

'Ah … !' he said, in response to Will's inquiring gaze. 'My old theatrical days!'

Will's eyes widened further:

'*Theatre? Raspberries?*'

'I promise to tell you later, Will. It was not an uplifting occasion.'

'Well, in one way it was,' quipped Mrs Trotter.

'More enigmatic yet!' said Will. 'You must unveil the terrible truth when we have beers in our hands. I suspect it's a story that gains in the telling.'

'I'm sure it does,' said Mrs Trotter. 'Lavinia certainly relished it!'

'But what about the events in the playhouse, Mrs T?' said Tom, attempting to guide the conversation. 'What a production that turned out to be. A *Macbeth* like no other.'

'It was very alarming, wasn't it! One of the witches could have been killed. Poor Mr Angell – I hope it hasn't crippled him. He has such expressive hands.'

'Mr Pinkerman has cast him in *The Tender Courtesan*,' said Tom. 'He is to play Ernesto, the young lover – or rather he *was*.'

'*Ernesto?* That's a romantic name. So the play is not set in Piccadilly?'

'No, in Seville. This wasn't the author's idea, but Pinkerman and Cibber thought the love-plot warranted it.'

'And this is the play you are to write the prologue for?'

'Yes, it begins rehearsal on Monday.'

Widow Trotter's hand touched her jet necklace:

'Well, I hope the climate will be favourable – and I don't mean the Spanish one. Might it stir up trouble, do you think? *Courtesans?*'

'Tamara was to have been Moll, a kind-hearted Covent Garden harlot, but that was thought too incendiary – and Mrs Oldfield does like to dress in fashion. So Mr O'Malley, the author, was invited to rearrange it a little … well, to tell the truth, Mr Cibber arranged it for him.'

'And will Mr O'Malley be there to witness the staging of his masterpiece?'

'I fear he shipped himself back to Dublin last week – wishing Mr Pinkerman joy of his *amputated carcase*, as he called it!'

'Oh dear, this doesn't sound propitious.'

'No, but Mr Cibber now thinks he has transformed the thing into a popular piece; and Pinkerman intends it for the theatre – once it has been fully tried at the Fair. Mrs Oldfield has seized on the part of Tamara. She swears the play will be a sensation – a six-nighter at least!'

'Anne Oldfield appearing at the Fair? Well, in that case I predict great things for your prologue.'

During these exchanges Will had been looking pensive, but at this he leaned forward in anticipation:

'But what about tonight, Mrs Trotter? What did you think of the explosions and thunderbolts? We witnessed a remarkable set of accidents.'

It was now her turn to look thoughtful:

'Yes, Mr Lundy, remarkable indeed. But, *accidents?* ... I just wonder.'

Her friends looked at each other.

'What do you mean?' said Tom. 'Do you suspect some mischief?'

'I've been thinking about what I saw – or fancied I saw – while all this was going on ... From the side-boxes you have a commanding view across the amphitheatre, and in the foremost seat you're uncomfortably exposed – it's a little like being a figurehead at the prow of a ship! ... Well, over in one of the facing boxes I could swear I saw a man staring at the stage in a peculiar way.'

'What was he doing?'

'Well that's it – he was *doing* absolutely nothing. As you recall, when the cloud burst into flame and the thunderbox broke open, the whole place was in uproar – people straining to see what was going on, clambering onto benches, exclaiming to each other. And yet this gentleman was standing a little to the back of the box, motionless. There wasn't a flicker on his face – he just stared calmly at the stage. And I swear he was almost smiling – in a cold way – as still as any ghost! He reminded me of a Roman Emperor watching the lions in the Colosseum. But I was distracted by conversation, and the next time I looked the figure had disappeared. It was as if he'd been spirited away.'

'Perhaps it *was* a ghost, Mrs T? That Scottish play conjures up dark forces.'

'Especially when Pinkerman and Bullock are in full flow – then anything can happen.' added Will.

'No, but there was something else about the look on his face ... It made me shiver and my stomach tighten. It was a look of satisfaction, as if a prophecy was being fulfilled ... as if he could see the actors *burning in hell*.'

There was a sharp clatter as Tom brought his glass down directly onto his cup of chocolate. But nothing could distract them now. Will gave a low whistle:

'So, you think this man was watching something unfold which he was expecting?'

'Which he might even have helped to bring about?' added Tom.

'Well, there seemed to be no trace of surprise or curiosity, which was very strange ... but perhaps I'm reading this too closely?'

'Perhaps not, Mrs T. This evening we heard that the theatre has been receiving threats.'

'Of what sort? Are they anything more than pulpit stuff?'

'It's more particular than that. It seems Mr Rich has received some anonymous notes but has kept quiet about them. They have threatened the theatre with the fate of Sodom!'

'But that's just preachers' language – fire and brimstone!'

'Yes, but these were handwritten notes sent to him personally ... and one of them was simply a quotation from *Macbeth* – in capital letters – just two words only.'

'What words, Mr Bristowe?' said Mrs Trotter apprehensively.

'FIRE, BURN!'

Monday

26 April 1708

Chapter Five

It was Monday morning at the Theatre Royal, and Tom could hear the commotion as he walked along the pit-passage. It was a few minutes before ten. Surely the rehearsal hadn't already begun? These things usually started late anyway. He opened the door tentatively and caught sight of the stage, where a lively performance was in full cry. A female hand was raised, a fist being shaken, a foot stamped hard, all accompanying the delivery of an eloquent denunciation. It was only after several seconds that he realised this was not *The Tender Courtesan* – tenderness being in short supply – but some climax to a scene worthy of heroic tragedy. He half expected a dagger to be produced and a cry of triumphal vengeance to echo from the walls. Tom stood transfixed, not daring to move.

He could hardly believe what he saw. It was Anne Oldfield – the normally patient, good-humoured, shrewd Mrs Oldfield – who was caught up in another drama; and it was a role she seemed to be playing with relish. Facing her was Christopher Rich, pressing his hands to his ears as if waiting for the storm to subside – on this occasion stage effects were unnecessary. Was this an angry wife or a jilted mistress? It was hard to decide. The lady had beauty and style all right, but here raised to magnificent indignation. This was a Junoesque heroine. Faced with a character like that, even Jove would quiver.

Tom took a step forwards and began to note what was being said. He heard the words *usurper* and *minx*, quickly followed by *malicious busybody* and *interfering old fool*. More predictably, there was *trust* and *honour* shortly followed by *betrayal* … It was clear that the exit-line was approaching. And then, exactly on cue, it came: *four guineas! Nothing less than four guineas!* And with that precise declaration (hardly the language of the gods) a sheaf of papers was flung to the ground; the jilted beauty turned on her heels and strode off into the wings. Tom imagined wild applause ringing round the auditorium, but the silence that followed was even more effective. He could hear his own eardrums beating.

After a few seconds a single pair of hands began to clap, and a smartly-dressed figure stepped forward, his face enraptured and just a little red. Then, in an elegant gesture, one of the hands reached out toward the vanished actress as if it sought to recall a departing genius:

'Well, Mr Rich! What think you of that? Would she not make a fine *Mrs Loveit?*' If Mrs Barry were to relinquish the role …'

'Indeed, you are right, Mr Cibber. When we play *The Man of Mode* on Thursday, Barry will have to be on her mettle. I think, when she retires, we have a Loveit ready-made!'

The Manager of the Theatre Royal raised a smile at the thought and made his way to a chair toward the back of the stage. Meanwhile the sibylline leaves scattered on the floor were gathered up and Oldfield's part reassembled. Christopher Rich was a practical man and appeared remarkably unruffled by the encounter, although he was seething inside and needed a moment to think. The green-room scene on Saturday still rankled; but after some hard-headed thought he had concluded that Lord Tunbridge must be placated. Unreasonable and impractical as his demand was, young Sally Twiss would have to be given her chance with Tamara.

Rich had hoped to mollify Mrs Oldfield with the considerably less flamboyant role of Agnes, Ernesto's hoped-for bride. It wasn't the title-role, and virtuous nuns were always a challenge dramatically … but with a few added touches here and there perhaps Agnes's devotion might be given more of a *punch?* He and Cibber had promised Mrs Oldfield they would set about it immediately. But whatever might be done, the character was milk-and-water in comparison with Tamara, the outrageously bold courtesan – a woman prepared to seduce the father to aid the son, and who would renounce her young lover so he might win his charming heiress. It was a part to kill for …

Rich suppressed the thought at once and turned his mind to more solid matters. Oldfield's indignation had been wonderful to watch, and frankly unanswerable. Given the Baron's insistence on the last-minute change of roles there was clearly no compromise available – except perhaps financial? Since her re-establishment at Drury Lane Oldfield had been holding out for four guineas a week – an unheard-of sum for an actress of twenty-five. Only Mr Betterton could command as much! … and the agreement would give her a prime benefit each year, with a minimum house-charge … it was hardly thinkable! He hated being tied down by written contracts, but it seemed he would have to concede. It was the only way to placate her, and that night's orphan's benefit would be in peril if she walked out … Yes, a lot was going on in Christopher Rich's mind, and after an inner struggle worthy of Monsieur Racine he reached a determination. With a sigh he stood up and quietly left the stage, hoping to find his injured heroine waiting in the green room for his answer.

But there was one thing for which he could be grateful: the replacement tender courtesan was late for rehearsal! Such tardiness was usually the prerogative of the leading actress who would make her dramatic entrance *in medias res*. He could only hope that Sally Twiss was not going to become a *grande dame* in her teens …

By now the cast was gathering and began to form itself into a semicircle. Pinkerman arrived a little out of breath, and Tom watched him settle his face into the mould of a stern patriarch, the cold-hearted Don Leone. The comic features were being hardened and the brow compressed into an expression of dark disapproval. Tom tried to catch his eye, but he seemed preoccupied. There was still no sign of Sally Twiss, nor of the love-struck Ernesto, who was evidently being expected despite his accident. Would he have his arm in a sling? Colley Cibber was to take the rehearsal, and Tom thought the actor appeared remarkably at ease as he distributed their recently-copied parts to the performers, humming quietly to himself in between saying a few words to each of them. No doubt this distribution of roles was a formal ritual.

In preparation, Tom placed his own chair toward the rear of the stage so that he could watch and listen inconspicuously. It would only be a read-through, but he detected an anxiety among the actors, and his own slightly wobbly legs left him in no doubt that he was on the famous Drury Lane boards.

He had time to look about him and take in the perspective. The theatre was a surprisingly intimate space with the galleries and boxes curving round into an attempted embrace. He was struck by how close they felt, and how natural it would be to play directly to them rather than to the pit, which lurked at a menacingly lower level where judging eyes could scrutinise you. It was down there that the actors' reputations would be made or lost. He looked around and was struck by how handsome the place appeared, with tall pilasters linking the tiered boxes, and gilded carvings interspersed with polished sconces. The building was beginning to show its age and some of the paint was peeling, but the large candelabra gave an air of refined elegance – an actor on this stage would certainly have something to aspire to … And yet on Saturday evening the room had become a noisy bear garden! Tom felt almost ashamed as the phrase 'vulgar herd' came into his head only to be instantly suppressed.

The parts finally distributed, Colley Cibber swung round, and Tom was able to take in his full figure. He was a shortish man, but elegantly dressed and bewigged – a vision in purple and chestnut – with an ebony cane instead of a sword dangling from a tassel at his waist. He had the manner of a brisk gentleman who valued regularity. Everyone had a job to do, and here on the stage of the Theatre Royal there was to be no lapse into informality. As an actor, Cibber may have been celebrated for his outrageous fops – Sir Courtly Nice and Sir Fopling Flutter – but in his hands they never became merely caricatures. They were certainly extravagant, but he gave them a fastidious delicacy too. Their style was ridiculed but its effects precisely observed, and the audience's laughter was always seasoned with delight.

But this morning things were clearly not as they should be, and Tom realised to his discomfort that he himself was becoming the centre of attention. Cibber was walking towards him. The actor's face was lit by a warm smile, and the click of his buckled shoes emphasised the slightly mincing steps. Some dusty sheets of paper were in his hand:

'Mr Bristowe, welcome! You are our *two-guinea man*, are you not? Pinkey tells me we are to expect a fine prologue from you.'

'I have that honour, Sir.'

'Good, good! However, I must warn you that our friend has the highest expectation of your talents. He tells me it will be a composition of wit *and* feeling, of satire *and* good taste – no mean hope! … If you can harness those four headstrong steeds together without upsetting the coach, then you'll be a poet of rare genius! …'

Tom swallowed awkwardly. Cibber stepped closer, and his voice became more relaxed and confiding.

'… But above all, Mr Bristowe, I hope you'll make us *laugh*. Please lift our spirits a little! – I suspect we shall need it …'

Cibber glanced down at the paper and continued before Tom could make a reply.

'... But this morning I have a further favour to ask. As you may have seen, we have encountered a difficulty with our *dramatis personae*. The role will be new-cast shortly, but as things stand we find ourselves without an *Agnes* ... Might I prevail on you to read the role for us? It means you can take part in our rehearsal as well as listen. The part is that of a novitiate nun who moves from the love of God to the love of man – a sensitive role, but I assure you that on this occasion it requires no *actions*. I do not ask you to kneel in tearful prayer; you are not required to speak in soft tones to the listening night; and there is no pressing need to smother Mr Angell with kisses – if our invalid manages to turn up ... But our read-through will be greatly facilitated if you would help us.'

By this point Tom had stopped breathing. There was an endearing fussiness in Cibber's manner. He looked into the man's bright eyes and found himself whispering that he would be happy to do so. What in God's name was he saying? He already felt trapped in a stage comedy. Common sense told him to answer with a firm no, but he was caught up in the moment and, after all, this was an experience never to be repeated ...

Before anything more could be said, or minds changed, there was a disturbance in the wings, and the two missing performers entered. The first glimpse of Sally Twiss and Gilbert Angell brought relief, but then a sudden disquiet. They were putting on a show of normality, but both appeared flushed and their movements were in tension with each other. Their eyes didn't meet. Sally was pressing down her gown a little crossly; Gilbert was wincing in annoyance. Tom saw that the young man's arm was indeed in a sling – a rather elegant creation of pale blue silk – and he noticed the hand was clenched into a fist – with pain or anger? Cibber immediately beckoned the pair over to the side of the stage and began talking with them quietly. Was this the aftermath of a quarrel, he wondered? Or had something else unsettled them?

Tom also felt uncomfortable about the role he was to play. How innocent was this Agnes? A novitiate nun *and* an heiress *and* a lover – *and*, eventually, a wife – that much he knew from Pinkerman. She was sure to be entangled in plots and machinations, and he wondered what passions he would be drawn into, not least his own. The more he thought about it, the more the phrase 'read through' was deceptive. He would have to act on the stage of the Theatre Royal – not with his body admittedly, but with his voice and his thoughts. He glanced across at Sally and Gilbert (Tamara and Ernesto) who were caught up in a whispered little drama of their own. Cibber was shaking his head and appeared concerned.

Tom gave an involuntary shiver and began looking through his part. His speeches were carefully written out and individual cue-lines given, but nothing more – only the prompter saw the whole play. He knew he would have to be alert and listen closely as the plot unfolded. The drama would surely draw him in, and its emotions would become his. He was no doubt destined to weep (not too much, he hoped), but might he have to kill? Would he lie, deceive and betray? He thought about Agnes and about his own innocence, and how he was in many ways a novitiate too. But he mustn't allow his life to become entangled with the play. It was, after all, only a fiction cobbled together by several hands. He smiled ruefully to himself: might that be said of his life too?

The Tender Courtesan turned out to be a mixed affair. There were certainly tears – lots of them – and the scene in which Agnes forswore the veil gave Tom plenty of histrionic opportunities. Her pleas to Don Leone (her cold-hearted guardian and Ernesto's father) were eloquent enough, as was the old man's determination to shut her away and claim her inheritance for himself. Pinkerman gave the role of Don Leone a strong hint of Polonius, which made Tom feel at times like an imitation Ophelia bereft of her tragic power. As a character Agnes did little else than plead – except when she was lamenting. There was a great deal of lamenting. In the end she became Ernesto's wife, but in the most unsatisfactory way possible – through the noble self-sacrifice of his mistress, the tender-hearted courtesan. Tamara's finer feelings turned the fortunes of the play and gave it what little soul it had. The scene where she renounced her young lover would surely flood Pinkerman's booth with tears! Tom could see that the role was a powerful one, and she carried the drama almost singlehandedly. It was Tamara's idea to trap Don Leone in a love plot of her own, when Ernesto would find her *in flagrante* with his father and would promptly take 'poison'; and it was her idea to suborn a doctor to pronounce that Ernesto's life hung by a thread; and it was she who tricked Don Leone into making his crucial vow: that if his son were to live he would withdraw his objections, so that Ernesto and Agnes would be free to marry ....

The plot creaked like an old haycart, and Tom couldn't help wondering whether a real-life Ernesto wouldn't use Agnes's inheritance to find himself an even tenderer courtesan ... but he was ashamed at the thought.

But there was one thought he couldn't suppress, and it made him glow with anticipation: what would Will say when he told him he had acted on the same stage as Sally Twiss? – that they had even played a scene together? Tom could hardly believe it had happened. The dialogue had taken fire a little, especially at her line '*You must learn / That innocence is not the path to love!*', when she had shot him such a look as might char wood. But

Sally Twiss was no Bracegirdle – at least not yet – and Tom saw that pushing her into this role at such a young age would do her no favours. She had a delightfully coquettish manner, and a natural ability to coax and charm – but renunciation and a forceful will were beyond her.

During the reading young Gilbert Angell was uneasy, and at several moments, particularly when he spoke of Don Leone, there was a discomfort and hesitation in his manner. The encounters between father and son had a dark menace: Gilbert's throat tightened and a grudging bitterness distorted his voice. It certainly made for an emotional performance; but in the process style and intonation were forgotten and the speeches broke their natural line. It seemed to Tom that Gilbert was *feeling* more than he was acting. As for their own scenes together, they had a naturalness and ease that surprised him, and he began to think that the play's quieter moments worked better. But the language remained earthbound. Ernesto and Agnes may have been young lovers, but they were no Romeo and Juliet!

No ripple of happy applause broke out at the end of the reading, but there was a murmur of satisfaction – or perhaps it was something closer to quiet relief. The play *would do*. It didn't aspire to tragic poetry, and sparkling wit was in short supply, but there was passion a-plenty, and as a piece for the May Fair … well, it might succeed. Some of the actors were wondering aloud whether this sentimental vein would weigh too heavily on the audience. Such gushes of emotion might be indulged in a lady's closet, but in the tougher world of the public theatre, who could say? And as for the play's language, Tom smiled as he overheard Cibber's definitive pronouncement on the matter: 'In drama, Sir, poetry can be an unnecessary burden!'

He felt a slap on his back and turned to see William Pinkerman's face. There was still a Leonine scowl occupying his features, but his words were cheering:

'You gave us a remarkable performance, Mr Bristowe! Were we but living seventy years back, you would be a sought-after Juliet or Desdemona!'

Tom winced with uncomfortable pleasure:

'That, Sir, is an incontrovertible argument for the superiority of our modern stage!'

At this, Pinkerman's frown intensified, and a sudden anger flashed in his eyes:

'But for how much longer shall we have *our stage?* ...'

He paused, and his gaze swept the gilded amphitheatre as if taking a last look at an old friend.

'... The way events are moving, we shall soon have it snatched from us! We shall become strolling players once more – driven out of town and taking refuge in barns and inn-yards ... We are becoming reprobates, Mr Bristowe! They are wanting to take us away from the people – *our* people. And 'tis because they fear us! ...'

Tom did not have to ask who 'they' were. But he was wondering what had occasioned this heartfelt cry. The anger flashed again.

'... But we shall NOT let it happen!'

Others were glancing over toward them, so Tom drew him apart and they walked to the furthest forestage, looking down upon the empty pit. It was as if both of them felt drawn to the theatre's beating heart.

'What has brought on this dismay, Mr Pinkerman? Our reading went well, and you're likely to have a success. The passions are powerfully drawn, and your actors will give everything.'

'I do not doubt it, but ...'

'And you needn't fear for the Prologue – I promise you the finest of fanfares!'

Pinkerman was touched and seized Tom by the elbow:

'But Mr Bristowe, 'tis not the actors I fear – and certainly not the Prologue –but our stage itself – what it is like to become.'

This was enigmatic. Tom asked him what he could mean, and in response Pinkerman dropped his voice. His whispered words made their way out into the silent amphitheatre. Suddenly Tom was sharing a secret.

'There are changes afoot, Mr Bristowe. You know how the company is threatened and what forces muster against us – well, the picture is darkening … It would seem we are under threat from *within*.'

Tom was about to reply, but Pinkerman hushed him with his finger, and with a hissed 'follow me' he led Tom into the wings and out through a doorway into the backstage area where it would be possible to speak more privately. In one of the labyrinthine passageways he halted beside some stairs that twisted up to a small anonymous closet:

'Here we can speak. Forgive me, but I know not whom to trust.'

'I'm all ears Sir. You can tell me anything you wish. I'm sorry to see you so disquieted.'

Pinkerman gave a slight nod and leaned in an actorly way against the hand-rail as if drawing relief from its support:

'Early this morning I was summoned – graciously *summoned!* – by a man who thinks to take our theatre's destiny into his hands … Lord Tunbridge is someone with whom I have always had uneasy relations. He is uncommonly sure of himself, but the pretence is lost whenever he is crossed. On occasion he has intervened in money matters – which as a sharer he has every right to do. But now he is busying himself with more *political* concerns … He wasted no time in advising me of the great role he is to have in the theatre's affairs …'

The expression on Tom face was question enough.

'… He is to assume the shares of both Mr Estcourt and Mr Swiney, and this will give him a commanding interest in the company. And he intends to exercise this power to the full.'

Tom whistled under his breath:

'Do you have wind of what it will mean?'

'*Wind* of it? He left me in no doubt of it, Mr Bristowe. He spelt it out to me in the most direct way. He is intent on *reformation!*'

'You mean, to close the theatre's doors?'

'No, but he intends to reform *us* and all we represent – root and branch. Henceforward, all *low comedies,* as he calls them, will be a thing of the past. He is utterly set against Mr Congreve and Mr Vanbrugh – the darlings of our stage! Their whole tribe will be proscribed – the Farquhars, Wycherleys, Centlivres – even our complaisant Colley too, I warrant! The company will be about a loftier business – the improvement of the nation's morals! The man was full of pompous phrases – you know the lingo ... *Nothing is more liable to debase and corrupt the minds of the people than a licentious theatre ...*'

Pinkerman was now holding himself erect and composing his face to piety.

'... *The stage undermines the faith and morals of the nation* ... The Baron says that under his *guidance* – as he calls it – the Theatre Royal will be *the very school of manners and virtue* ... In other words, we shall become like the French! He is setting out to be a one-man *Académie!* ...'

The comedian in Pinkerman gave his words a pompous resonance. Tom smiled painfully at the parody, but his heart was sinking.

'... And, would you believe it? He deplored what he called my *divided loyalties* – as if my loyalty to this place has ever been in doubt! When I protested, he said that all links between the playhouse and the May Fair must be broken off. Indeed he's determined the Fair itself will be closed down.'

'But what of *The Tender Courtesan?*'

'Lord Tunbridge is looking to the future. He intends that

the play will stir the finer feelings of the audience. 'Twill be a pious thing and celebrate the rewards of virtue. Its errant hero will finally be redeemed! And young Sally Twiss's Tamara will set the noblest example. At the end of the play, while Agnes and Ernesto enter into the joys of sacred marriage, the tender courtesan will herself *take the veil!*'

'What? You mean Tamara becomes a nun? But that's not how the play ends, is it?'

'No, Mr Bristowe, not yet. But the Baron is set on the re-writing. He insists that Tamara must *rise above* (those were his very words!) the sordid life she has lived. He will demand that the play conclude with the courtesan renouncing her former life!'

Tom whistled in astonishment:

'So, we shall end with a sermon! Can he really do that, Mr Pinkerman? This is your play – yours and Mr Cibber's. Surely he cannot change it in such an important particular – and at the last moment too?'

'According to *my Lord,* once he has the company in his power he will be able to insist that all new scripts meet with his approval.'

'What will the actors say to this? Do they know of it yet?'

'Not generally – and Mr Rich is very anxious on this score, as you might imagine. Even Cibber is concerned this will be a step too far – and you know how timorous he can be about offending the ladies ... It would seem, however, that Sally Twiss is pliable in the matter. But Oldfield is sure to be outraged.'

'Ah yes, we have already witnessed it. Shortly before you arrived she stormed off the stage, breathing fire!'

'That's because of the change of roles. It is the first move in the Baron's *reformation*. He must know that Oldfield would have no truck with her part being re-written! ... My Lord has far-reaching plans. He is determined that the magnificent Tamara will push aside the Biddy Tipkins and Mrs Sullens – the roles that Mrs Oldfield is making her own. Yes, Sally Twiss will become the patroness of Reformation! ...'

Tom gave a low whistle.

'... It will make our theatre an extension of the pulpit, and he will have us all preaching. We are to become *virtuous* – at least in show. Our very thoughts will be policed, and our language chosen for us.'

'But don't you exaggerate, Sir? This surely isn't something he can achieve by himself?'

'No, but with the political weather as it is, and the May Fair approaching, the company is in a delicate position. We may not be able to control events. I've talked with Mr Rich, and he understands the gravity of our predicament.'

'So, Lord Tunbridge has a mission to save the theatre – as he thinks. But what will it become in his hands?'

'We can only imagine, Mr Bristowe. I fear these moves are but the beginning, and the prohibition of the Fair will be the next step. Lord Tunbridge sees a continuing role for our theatre, but there are those who see no future at all – and they won't rest until the final curtain falls. Such men won't hesitate to push the Baron aside. By then the place will have lost its heart and will fall an easy prey. There are too many who believe the reformation of the nation's morals can only come with our extinction!'

Wednesday

28 April 1708

Chapter Six

WIDOW TROTTER ENTERED the Bay-Tree with more circumspection than usual. Instead of a confident push at the door there was a tentative nudge, and she hesitated in the entrance. Her brow was furrowed. Instinctively she scanned the coffee-room, not with the customary alertness of a ship's captain surveying the lower deck, but as someone who badly needed a friendly face. In her left hand was a bundle of lemons tied in an old newspaper and in her right a folded broadside almost warm from the printing, its ink scarce dry – last week's news and this minute's sensation! Her fingers tingled and she felt slightly sick.

Her foray into the piazza had been unremarkable until she passed the old ballad-seller who was unbundling his sheets in the colonnade. The familiar figure of Booming Billy wore his wide-brimmed hat at a jaunty angle, and his jaw jutted out in a toothless grin. The hawker hoisted the papers above his head as if in triumph, and Mrs Trotter gave him a smile as she strode by, only to be pulled up short by the sudden cry behind her: '*The Devil in Drury Lane! … God's Judgment on the Playhouse!*' The stentorian voice echoed through the arches, and she swung round.

A minute later she was leaning against one of the pillars as she pored over the document with mounting alarm. This wasn't the usual street ballad. It was a piece of oratorical prose and read like the climax to an angry sermon. The thickly-printed broadside was surmounted by a woodcut in which a devil sat astride a burning cloud and looked down on a scene of theatrical chaos. The horned figure was pointing to a long wooden coffin which was split open and hanging at a precarious angle. Directly below, three antic figures in witches' hats cowered in terror, arms akimbo, as a pair of cannonballs rained down on them.

The writing oozed with self-righteous confidence, and by the end the preacher's bony finger seemed to be pointing directly at herself. She needed to be back home in the chocolate house before the broadside reached there – she didn't want to leave it on the tables for her customers to read ... But how could that be avoided? Like so much circulating street-paper the thing would be passed around and discussed, read aloud in taverns, quoted with glee or thrown aside in disgust; it would do its work, and finally reach yet more readers in the servants' kitchens wrapped around pies and fruit. The chill of the idea came home to her and her steps quickened ... But was she being a hypocrite? The Bay-Tree was a library of ephemeral scribble and she was no censor – anything could come in, and all opinions were welcomed. Why should this be different?

Now inside her own front door, she clutched the document tightly and looked around the coffee-room hoping to find one face in particular. With relief she saw the wigless figure of Tom at the corner table, a dish of chocolate gripped precariously in one hand. He appeared to be in earnest conversation with Laurence Bagnall, author of *The Shoe-Buckle*, a man of distinctive poetic industry who had contributed not a little to the paper surplus of the age. Bagnall was erect and toying with a spoon, while the younger man lounged slightly and gesticulated as he spoke. Two poets in dialogue! The thought amused her, and she felt a sudden urge to sit with them and hear their talk. But other business was pressing. She approached directly:

'Mr Bagnall, Mr Bristowe! I'm loath to interrupt your conversation …'

'You do no such thing, Mrs Trotter!' said Bagnall graciously, turning his bewigged face in her direction. 'We find ourselves at a stand. I have been advising your young lodger on the art of the *prologue*. He tells me he has a commission for Pinkerman's booth, and I have been recalling my own experience – not a happy one – of prologuizing …'

'Mr Bagnall is fearful, Mrs T, and he urges me to avoid anything that *provokes*. He says I must keep it light and witty.'

The large wig shuddered slightly:

'A prologue is a difficult challenge, Mr Bristowe. You are not yet sure of your audience and what its character is. I merely advise caution! It is like a gentleman arriving at a party – it is always best to open things quietly. A prologue is an *hors d'oeuvre*: it whets the appetite and should not be too *robust*.'

Widow Trotter appreciated that robustness was not Mr Bagnall's forte:

'An apology is needed, Sir. I wish to talk urgently with Mr Bristowe here – not about prologues, but on another matter – if you will excuse us, I shall carry him off to the parlour.'

'I'm sure neither of us will protest, Mrs Trotter, and certainly not Mr Bristowe. I suspect he will be happy to forego any further advice from me.'

With a few nods and bowings the social niceties were negotiated, and Mrs Trotter soon had Tom to herself. Inside the parlour there was no pause for refreshment – business called immediately:

'What can I say, Tom? You must wonder at my behaviour – and Mr Bagnall too … But I need to show you something.'

'I'm in your hands entirely, Mrs T. You look as if you've seen a ghost. What is that you're holding?'

Widow Trotter was clutching the broadside so tightly that it seemed attached to her fist. She held it out to him, and with an effort of will she managed to loosen her grip sufficiently to allow him to take the paper:

'I purchased it not five minutes ago. At this very moment it is being cried in the colonnade.'

Tom waited, but she said nothing more. There was a tautness in her features that he hadn't seen before. He cast his eye down onto the paper and at once took in the significance of its title: *The Devil in Drury Lane*. The crude woodcut was the stuff of a child's story-book, but the text was far from innocent. He read a few lines and saw that the piece took its cue from the disaster of Saturday night. In particular, the writer considered Shakespeare's Scottish play – especially the witches' antics – to be the work of the Devil ('*a noxious brew of regicide, profanity and slaughter'd innocence*') and rejoiced that on this occasion God's anger had clearly manifested itself.

Tom looked up at her, but her attention remained fixed on the paper. Increasingly apprehensive, he read further. There was more on the witches:

> *... These diabolical beings invoke Satan himself and bid defiance to the laws of God. They presume to imitate the Almighty in his wonderful acts and ascribe the Lightnings, Thunder, Storm and Tempest not to Divine Judgment but to their own unholy Spells! They mock the Great Governor of the World who alone commands the winds and seas: they cast God's Providence from the throne and set up the Devil instead. But on this day, when the Demons shriek'd their blasphemies to the Heavens, THEY WERE ANSWER'D. Satan himself smil'd as he conducted his shocking spectacle. But GOD IS NOT MOCK'D, and now He cried "ENOUGH!' In a play of portents, this divine intervention was the greatest portent of all!*

Tom read the last sentence aloud.

'O my Goodness! This is a sanctimonious harangue, is it not?'

'But there's more, Tom. Read on … The writer has a political message too.'

From this point he continued to declaim the thing aloud. The voice was becoming indignant about the theatre itself:

> *'This outrage must be brought to an end. The Play-house is the nursery of that* Profaneness *and* Immorality *against which Her Majesty has issu'd so many proclamations. In vain do we attack Vice in the open field, if it has its* Fortress *– its very* Sanctuary *– in the* Play-house …'

Tom took a breath. His throat was tightening, and the words tasted bitter on his tongue. But it was when he came to the fourth paragraph that he understood why Widow Trotter appeared so disturbed – almost distracted. The writer had turned his attention to the theatre's audience, and he clearly found its diverse nature distasteful:

> *'The Play-house as it now stands is fill'd with a strange mixture of auditors, all cheek by jowl. It is a promiscuous assembly, a confus'd jumble of high and low, Quality and Mobility. Gentlemen and porters gaze at the same spectacle; fine ladies breathe one air with kitchen wenches; and it seems a side-box may now be graced by a* Mistress Quickly!'

Tom gasped.

There was a stunned silence while he registered the implication of those words and the contempt that lay behind them. He and his uncle had urged Widow Trotter, against her better judgment, to defy social forms and expose herself to censure. How easy it had been for them, secure in their own position in society, to imagine she could share their confidence. Well, her fears had been justified. Tom saw with sudden clarity that behind the reformers' zeal was not a love of virtue but a fear of change. For them, the theatre was a threat to the established order. *Mobility!* – that hateful newly-coined word which linked social mixture to the unruly mob. What apprehensions prompted it! What terrible anxiety was hidden there!

'Mrs T ... I'm so sorry. This is shocking ...'

'It is *Satire*, Mr Bristowe, and therefore has a licence to ridicule. I know enough to understand that. I suppose I must bear its scorn bravely and take my place as one of Satire's victims. Perhaps I should be proud and wear this as a badge of honour?'

'I don't know what to say. It's a pernicious piece of work, little more than sneering insults. It doesn't deserve the name of satire.'

'But it tells us one thing, Mr Bristowe, and I'm uneasy at the thought of it.'

'What is that, Mrs T?'

'Whoever wrote those words was in the theatre that evening. He saw me in the box and recognised my face; and while I was surveying the scene, he was looking at me with derision. I wonder ...'

She paused, and there was a distant look in her eyes. Tom could read her face, and perhaps her mind too:

'Ah! Your mysterious figure? I see what you're thinking.'

'Yes, how stupid of me! Fear does strange things, and I'm sure that's all it is ... But I can still picture that sneering face. Such a man could have written this ... I really must stop dreaming! Nevertheless, it troubles me ...'

She took the broadside from Tom's hand. He wondered if she would rip it apart, but instead she folded it neatly in two and smoothed it out with her fingers.

'... I feel as if I've been sent a message – that I'm being invited to play a part in something. Do you understand me?'

Tom thought he did. He looked intently at her and found himself scrutinising her features. For all her forty years, Mary Trotter possessed a youngish face, but one that had evidently smiled a lot. Now he saw that the hatchings about the eyes were also lines of wisdom and determination:

'I think I do, Mrs T ... The *theatre?*'

'Yes, the theatre. The events on Saturday evening were no accident. From what you told me, there's some mischief brewing. Perhaps I should have a word with our constable? Elias will know if anything is afoot. This is becoming an assault on the Drury Lane company, is it not? Do you think it might go further?'

'Pinkerman fears it will. He is concerned about the May Fair and suspects the occasion will bring matters to a crisis. The Fair and the playhouse are always being yoked together by the reformers.'

'And now you've become a part of this, Tom,' she said quietly. 'Your involvement in *The Tender Courtesan* ...'

'Alas, yes, my Prologue! To think I took the commission so gladly – I thought it would be a simple task. But now it has become less innocent, has it not? But I shall steel myself and carry it through. I owe it to Mr Pinkerman and the company.'

'Have the theatre's affairs settled themselves since your rehearsal? Or have there been more disturbances?'

'Nothing significant, Mrs T. My spies tell me that at *The Fox* last night the theatre was packed and generally orderly – until the last act. Volpone and Mosca were applauded in their trickery, and at the end of the trial scene some of the audience were determined to silence their judges with cat-calls and have the rogues set free. Wilks was cheered when he stepped in front of the curtain, and there were cries of 'Release him!' echoing round the theatre. I don't think Ben Jonson would have approved at all!'

'Well he wasn't there to object, was he? It seems the Playhouse is becoming feverish now the recess is approaching.'

'The break cannot come soon enough for Mr Rich. He's longing to leave town and let the Fair take people's attention ... But of course we still have *The Man of Mode* to negotiate tomorrow.'

Widow Trotter beamed:

'Ah, Sir Fopling! What a delight! I take it Cibber will be in his pomp?'

'Yes indeed, and what's more, a certain Miss Sally Twiss and Mr Gilbert Angell will be attempting respectively the roles of a waiting-woman and a valet.'

'Will that be enough to tempt Will to attend, do you think?'

'It has already done so! It is Mrs Bradshaw's benefit night, and he and I have procured tickets for the Pit. It should be a great occasion. The two of us have suddenly become theatre-enthusiasts.'

'Well, I wish you both joy of it. Speaking for myself, I shall be content to stay within these four walls. However lively the Bay-Tree becomes, I suspect things will be quieter here!'

Widow Trotter had no need to send a message for the Covent Garden constable, because less than half an hour later her old friend put his head round the parlour door. Elias Cobb kept his stout body on the other side of the threshold until he had ascertained if an interruption would be welcome. This elegant room, tucked behind the Bay-Tree's busy kitchen, was Mary Trotter's sanctuary, and Elias by long tradition observed the polite forms with her: it was a game they both played, and like any game it had a serious intent behind it.

'Am I intruding, my Lady?'

She looked up at him, and the moment he saw the document in her hand he knew *The Devil in Drury Lane* had reached her. Her arms rested on several sheets of accounts, but it was clear this routine task had not managed to distract her. She had taken up the broadside again, and the look on her face was eloquent enough.

'Oh Molly! – So you have seen the thing already?'

'Yes, Elias, I've read and digested it – every poisonous drop. It's a fine piece of writing. As for my own role in it, I can't think why Mrs Quickly should be a figure of shame. After all, her establishment gave home to a prince – and of course she had her devoted *Sir John* …'

The constable eased himself into the room, boots and all, and lit up the place with a beaming smile:

'Aha, yes! But let's not press the resemblance too far. I'm glad you can make light of it so.'

'No, Elias, I don't do that. It's a pernicious penny-rant; but is it not a part of something more *dangerous*? From what Tom has told me, I wonder if there was some intent behind the havoc at the playhouse on Saturday. I have reason to think so … But first you must let me play the hostess of Eastcheap!'

With that, Widow Trotter pulled out a second chair, and Elias seated himself at the oak table while she reached for the already-opened bottle of claret. She set a second glass down and poured his wine carefully:

'You will think me fantastical, Elias, but there's an image from that evening that won't leave my mind.'

'That's no surprise – it appears to have been a memorable pantomime altogether!'

'But this was not happening on stage. It was what I saw – or thought I saw – in the audience …'

The constable was intrigued, and his face composed itself while she told him of her suspicions. She described the ghostlike figure in the facing box, who in her imagination had become the master-mind of the violence. The constable would normally dismiss such conjectures, but Mary Trotter was not a fanciful creature – far from it. He listened to her attentively, knowing from long experience that, with her, gossip was always filtered through a shrewd understanding.

'… And that's not all, Elias. You must surely know that Mr Rich has been receiving menacing letters – letters threatening the company. And I know Mr Pinkerman suspects something is being planned to disrupt the Fair … Now, do you not think all this activity fits together? …'

She held up the broadside to him as if it were evidence in court.

'… This reads to me like a commentary on events that have yet to run their course – as if some scheme of retribution is working itself out.'

Elias Cobb leaned back in his chair and raised his glass:

'As I've had cause to say many times, you are a remarkable woman, Mrs Trotter! You give voice to my own fears. And I don't think your ghostly figure is to be dismissed – not at all. The *Reformation of Manners* may be a public campaign, but it is also a secret war, and it is drawing many to the cause. We hear much from the public voices – the preachers and magistrates – but in truth it's being driven by nameless tradesmen and citizens, with their paid informers and petty spies.'

'Nameless?'

'Exactly that, Molly. The Societies are tightly knit. They have no lists of membership, and no records are taken of their meetings – and no-one is admitted who has not been twice proposed and fully inquired into. Investigation is made into their lives and conversations … In truth, nobody knows how widespread the system is. Your suspicions could be well founded.'

'But what about the constables, Elias? Don't you play a part?'

'Many of them do – but the Reformers have met with some resistance there! And there are magistrates who will have nothing to do with them. As for the constables – well, the *Association* is hot in the business. I've been approached more than once and had blank warrants pushed into my hand – as if I should spend my time arresting profane swearers and Sabbath-breakers, Sunday tipplers, idle walkers, and street-sellers ...'

'It all seems so petty, Elias!'

'But this is merely the chaff and bran. There is a solid core to it. These people want to build a godly society – to return us to the rule of the Saints. They will not be satisfied until the theatres and fairs are closed, and we are all *righteous*.'

By this time Constable Cobb was looking distinctly grim, but Widow Trotter managed a wise smile:

'Surely that cannot happen, Elias! Centuries have passed since *Convent* Garden was a place of spiritual devotion. These streets are never going to become the paths of righteousness!'

'You may laugh, Molly – but I see things you don't. And I know what these people are capable of. They view themselves as a new national army ... Just listen to this ...'

He reached down into one of his capacious pockets and retrieved a sheaf of papers. One of them was a small closely-printed pamphlet. He turned a couple of pages and bent them back to read ...

> '... *The* Societies for the Reformation of Manners *are volunteers in the service of* Heaven: *theirs is a Spiritual Warfare, and it is high time they should be placed on a proper footing. In war, we rejoice when our prisoners are delivered from the bondage of Tyrants; shall we not much more rejoice, when the souls of our people are redeemed from the bondage of* Satan?

'You see – a call to arms! What could be plainer than that?'

'There's so much violent talk, Elias! … So, you agree the playhouse is under threat? That my suspicions could be justified?'

'Most certainly. For them, the playhouse is the source of the nation's disease and the actors little better than blasphemers and debauchees. There's a strong taste of it here – indeed it's a passage very apt to your purposes. Just listen! I don't think you'll be smiling when you've heard it.'

He turned a couple more pages:

> '*Can anyone believe that* Playwrights *or* Actors *ever give thought to those places in Scripture which speak against* Adultery, Fornication, *and* Whoredom? *If such men thought thereon, they would not venture to debauch our Youth, and turn our Cities into so many Places like SODOM and GOMORRAH, lest when others may be destroyed with Fire and Brimstone, they also should* perish in the Flames.'

Mrs Trotter shuddered:

'God's Judgment! They are forever invoking that aren't they? There's little mention of God's *love*.'

'I don't think the idea appeals to them, Molly. No, this is all *Old Testament* stuff.'

'But how eagerly their thoughts turn to *flames* – the fires of destruction. They seem to speak of it with relish … I always thought the days were gone when we burned heretics to save their souls.'

The two of them looked at each other and lapsed into an uneasy quietness. The soft ticking of the parlour clock seemed less to calm their minds than to move their thoughts further on, second by second, as they wondered about what was approaching. Their mood was solemn, but not peaceful. The constable was picturing the silent figure in the theatre box and found it an unsettling image; while Widow Trotter's mind had turned back to the broadside. She unfolded it and caught sight of the chilling words again. In spite of herself – and for ill rather than good – this man had drawn her into his troubled vision.

Thursday

29 April 1708

Chapter Seven

WAVES OF DELIGHTED laughter filled the playhouse. Act Three of *The Man of Mode* was roaring along nicely, and the old favourite was showing that the brilliant wit of King Charles's day could be as fresh as ever. The sexual intrigues gave the play an undertow of passion that strained its brittle elegance to the limit. Every look was a potential seduction – or a potential exposure. There was little sentiment here and uttered only in epigram. In the world of George Etherege your love boiled and cooled in an instant, your emotions betrayed you, and your character was a fashion to be worn like a new dress or an elegant sword-knot – and dispensed with as easily.

On this special evening the side-boxes were decorated with swags of flowers, and from them the *beau monde* of St James's looked at the stage as into a looking-glass. They saw themselves caught in a mirror which reflected their familiar world but returned it more sharply defined with its tricks and pretences exposed. This was the kind of satire that lured and flattered, but embarrassed too. Here in the theatre you were on display to your own kind, but also to the crowd in the galleries who overlooked both the stage and the boxes – and saw little difference.

In the pit, the benches were closely packed so that shoulders were squeezed and knees jabbed into backs. And the stage itself was crowded. The cream of this benefit-night audience were watching the comedy at close quarters, their chairs almost intermingled with the players. On the left side of the stage, several gentlemen were poised behind a pair of aristocratic ladies who lolled on their red plush cushions and vied with the actresses for attention. The fictional and real were colliding; and faced with this intimate competition, Lady Townley and Emilia were responding with movements of excessive grace, handling their fans knowingly and swishing their dresses with conscious pride. On the right side of the stage were the distinguished patrons seated behind a couple of velvet-covered tables as at a banquet, with wine and sweetmeats before them.

One of their number was of particular interest to two members of the audience seated in the pit. Lord Tunbridge cannot have been aware that he was under such scrutiny, but Tom Bristowe and Will Lundy had special reasons for observing him. Tom was thinking back to what Pinkerman had told him about the Baron's designs on the company; and Will had been eyeing the man suspiciously since the beginning of the Act when young Busy, the lady's maid, had made her entrance.

This was Sally Twiss's big moment, and Will's sudden attentiveness had been more than matched by the Baron, who was in a distinctly favourable position. Not only was he much closer physically to Sally, but he had a glass to raise to her – which he duly did – and elicited a little blushing nod in return.

'I see you have competition, Will!' whispered Tom. 'Lord Tunbridge seems to be enjoying his place of vantage!'

Will reached into Tom's bag of hazelnuts and whispered back:

'What a leering look he has. The man knows he has power, and he's determined to use it.'

Both of them became silent and alert. As the scene progressed, Sally Twiss lent Busy's words a notable sharpness. The maidservant began eyeing her mistress mockingly, much to Mrs Bradshaw's discomfort, and each remark seemed more taunting than the last. Sally gave her a sly, knowing look, and it was clear that Mrs Bradshaw (whose benefit night this was) was taken aback by the young actress. Yes, her maid was meant to be a shrewd character, but never so insinuating as this!

When the moment came for her to request her maid to sing ('some foolish song or other!') it was clear that on this occasion the invitation was issued with considerable reluctance. Mrs Bradshaw had already been obliged to watch the girl being toasted by a Lord, and now the young actress was about to become even more the centre of attention. What she hadn't bargained for was that Sally would accept the request with a graceful turn of the hand, move to the very front of the stage, and face directly into the pit. As the opening chords of 'When first Amyntas charm'd my heart' began to sound, Sally's voice took up the melody, and the whole house went silent – except for a single whisper in the fourth row:

'I didn't know she could sing ...'

Tom dug his friend sharply in the ribs, and the two of them became part of the rapt audience. On stage, Lord Tunbridge was frowning as he gazed at Sally's back; but Will – whose mouth was gaping like a baby robin in its nest – was enchanted, particularly when the final lines of the song arrived. At this climactic moment Sally's roaming eyes settled on the fourth row of the pit, and she sang with true feeling:

'The dangerous passion you must shun,
Or else like me be quite undone.'

Warm applause greeted the end of the song, and an impatient Mrs Bradshaw had to wait a full minute before she was able to continue the scene. Tom glanced at his friend, and Will glanced at him.

'She looked at me!' said Will, as if recalling an angelic visitation.

Tom nodded amicably, although he knew – much to his discomfort – that Sally Twiss's eyes had focused their beam exactly on his own.

The audience, as always, had to wait patiently for the Man of Mode himself to make his entrance. The play had run almost half its course when the moment arrived, and the other actors all took a step back, allowing Sir Fopling Flutter to stride into their midst. Colley Cibber was wearing a luxurious blond periwig which hugged his shoulders, and a stunning long-waisted suit of blue satin. As if to emphasise the radiant effect, he was followed in perspective by a little page-boy clothed as a miniature copy of himself. In the French manner of the previous age, Sir Fopling sported tasselled pantaloons and a pair of fringed gloves that reached almost to his elbows. To complete the effect he carried his head slightly on one side, creating a languishing look that appeared to mimic the ladies in the boxes. The other characters began to move round him, sighing and exclaiming as if viewing an exquisite piece of sculpture. Cibber flirted with his audience, and uttering a tiny exclamation he sauntered over to Lord Tunbridge's table and with a graceful turn of his arm took one of the sweetmeats. To spontaneous applause he placed it delicately between his lips and gave a beatific smile.

'A master at work, Tom!' said Will, chewing very inelegantly on a filbert.

'What a *bel air* he has – outrageous style!'

The scene was played almost as a ballet until, to further applause and cheering, Sir Fopling made his exit with an *à revoir*. 'All the world will be in the Park tonight!' he announced, anticipating the following outdoor scene when the play's sexual manoeuvring would be at its height.

An interval was called. The hallowed boards were now occupied by the stage-audience, who performed their own equally intricate manoeuvres. They had to negotiate their polite chit-chat while being careful to make room for the stage-hands who began shifting tables and chairs so that the flats for the evening Mall scene could be slid into place. A bowl of fruit was being handed round, and in the theatre-boxes bottles were uncorked and packs of cards shuffled. Tom and Will stood up and stretched their legs. They noticed Lord Tunbridge, still frowning to himself, make his way out through the back of the stage.

'Tripping off to the green room, I warrant! – To give the actors a little encouragement perhaps?'

'Or a certain actress some urgent *discouragement?*' said Will, with what he intended to be a knowing smile.

'Or perhaps it's simply the universal Call of Nature? The man is human, I take it?'

'Did you not see how she looked at me?'

'She certainly has a lively way with her.'

'She smiled at me when she sang of the dangers of passion. It was only for an instant, but there could be no mistake.'

'She has a sweet voice.'

'Did you not see it?'

'But how could she single you out, Will? I grant you are a tall fellow – but she surely doesn't know your face?'

'She must have marked it when I threw her the flower.'

'A flower? Did you throw a flower at her?'

'Last Thursday at *The Rover* – it was a pink carnation.'

'Did you hit her?'

'You sound a little peevish, Tom. I can understand it ...'

Will looked into the air and smiled. He was putting on a good performance, and Tom enjoyed encouraging it:

'And when are you to elope? Did you have time to arrange that too?'

'I've ordered a chariot for ten o'clock. She promised not to be late ...'

'This is a dangerous passion indeed – I hope you're not *both* undone by it! She was clearly attempting to warn you, Will. Perhaps Lord Tunbridge has slipped away to find his pistol ...'

'I expect to receive a challenge directly. St James's Park at dawn!'

They both laughed for a moment, but uneasily. The thought – and memory – had become a little too real for comfort.

The interval stretched out for a while. The auditorium was humming, and everyone seemed to be in a relaxed mood, happy to greet friends and exchange pleasantries. A comic spirit was presiding. At one point Tom and Will were hailed from further back in the pit by David Macrae and Gavin Leslie, the two Scotsmen, who had put Saturday's disappointment behind them and were giving the theatre a second chance. It seemed they were relishing Wilks's Dorimant and taking note of the stylish bearing and gentlemanly manners of which he was master. His handling of the snuff-box was a model, and no-one tied a cravat with such consummate skill.

The evening scene in the Mall eventually got under way. Substantial wooden flats of oak trees and elms – as well as something that looked as if it had migrated from the set of *Oroonoko* – were giving a good impression of the park, and the characters strolled up and down the alley with as much easy elegance as they could manage given the restricted dimensions of the stage. The repartee was lively, and the nicely-crafted plot swung gracefully to and fro as the characters encountered one another on their promenade. It was all very mannered, yet the artfulness was so precise that it seemed to move along naturally.

There was only one jarring element to the performance, and Tom and Will found it unsettling enough to take the edge off their pleasure. As they looked at the stage their eyes were repeatedly drawn to the table at which Lord Tunbridge had been sitting. It had been repositioned slightly during the interval, but they were conscious that his glass remained half-full; the dish of sweetmeats was untouched; and the chair on which he had been sitting was empty – and remained so until the final curtain.

Chapter Eight

THE *MAN OF Mode* ended with applause and cheers. Even the curtain seemed to be joining in the celebrations, descending with the flourish of a magician's hand. The theatre had worked its spell, and a relieved Christopher Rich smiled to himself – not because he felt the enchantment, but at the thought of the packed house and the smooth organisation of the evening. Lord Tunbridge's empty chair, however, was a little worrying, as had been the scowl on his face when he strode off at the interval. Rich had looked into the green room to see if his Lordship was solacing himself with company, but there was no trace of him, and he reached the conclusion that the old play's sexual freedoms had simply proved too much. Rich was enough a man of the world to allow that a gentleman's opinions and his actions might operate independently, especially in the sphere of desire. With this thought the smile on his face took on a more philosophical character.

As the applause finally died away, Tom and Will got to their feet in buoyant mood, especially Will, who continued to insist that Sally Twiss had conveyed a message to him during her song. They were perplexed by Baron Tunbridge's absence, but had different explanations: Will, not surprisingly, detected the pique of a jealous lover, while Tom guessed it was official backstage business of a more mundane kind.

'But didn't you notice the angry look on his face?' said Will. 'He resented the way she turned her back on him and gave all her attention to the *audience* ...'

He lingered expressively on the word.

'To a particular seat in the fourth row, do you mean?'

There was a moment's silence as they waited for the crush to clear.

'Well, what are we going to do ... The dressing-rooms?'

Tom knew his friend was serious:

'Now look, Will ...'

'You have freedoms here, do you not? You're practically part of the company now. We can find young Gilbert Angell and see if he'll introduce us. You can congratulate your friend on the elegant way he carried off the role of a one-handed valet.'

Tom grinned:

'Yes, remarkably so, given his name – *Handy!*'

'It was a heroic performance. I was glad he received his own cheer ... Well? Are you going to lead the way? You're an official prologue-writer – all doors will be open!'

'Let's see if we can at least find Gilbert, then. There could be a crush behind the scenes tonight.'

They were right. It was an evening of celebration and all doors had clearly been opened. Etherege's play may have finished and the actors departed the stage, but other performers had taken their place. A fresh set of Dorimants, Belindas and Old Bellairs were gathered in knots around the stage and were conversing animatedly. No doubt other plots were being hatched and reputations roughly handled.

Tom and Will didn't linger for too long but slipped out through one of the rear doors towards the backstage offices and miscellaneous rooms. They could hear animated laughter coming from the green room, and further along the passage a group of figures were lounging and talking more quietly and confidentially. It was only a corridor, but some attempt had been made to give the space a degree of elegance with mirrors and wall-sconces.

'The dressing-room is along this way, up the stairs I think,' said Tom. 'The leading actors have closets of their own on this floor, but Sally and Gilbert will be sharing with others.'

They walked along the passage, which was just wide enough for two petticoated heroines to squeeze past one another. Small carpets of various colours and shapes covered the floorboards and helped muffle the sounds of activity. Further along, a flight of stairs took them up to the next level where the passage was more confined and the floor less even. The air was clammy here, and a slightly sweet, dusty smell hung about the place.

They found the doorless dressing-room along the corridor to the left. It was blessed with a sash window, but the furnishing was sparse. A couple of tables had small hand-mirrors on them, and a long sideboard was piled high with odd accessory items – gloves, perukes, fans, and small knick-knacks.

And Gilbert Angell was there, all by himself, perched on a stool with his bob-wig set on the table beside him. He was bent over and rubbing his face with a towel.

He heard the two of them come in, and spoke without looking round:

'If you're here to admire Miss Twiss, I have to disappoint you. She's left the place in a hurry – for God knows where!'

There was a slightly petulant edge to his voice.

Tom and Will exchanged glances, and there was a moment of awkward silence before Tom spoke:

'We hoped to see *both* of you, Mr Angell.'

'In that case … I'm happy to receive you!'

The young man flicked the towel to one side and swung round. It was an expressive face with delicate, porcelain-like features, and traces of powder still clung to it. His eyes brightened as he saw the two men, one of whom he recognised:

'Ah! – do I see my darling spouse beneath that wig? … Agnes has returned to her Ernesto! *I trust you've been faithful?*'

The tone was endearing. Tom felt a slight blush rising – it was hard to know how to reply. But Will was ready:

'My friend still has a hankering after the chaste life, Mr Angell – unlike myself.'

Tom at once had the presence of mind to introduce his friend, Mr Lundy of the Middle Temple. Will gave the young man a slight nod of the head. The actor returned it:

'Ha ha! *Lundy* eh? Well, sit down gentlemen – Draw up chairs. I trust you'll take some port-wine? Could I ask you to help yourselves? …'

He looked eloquently at his disabled arm.

'… We gave a sterling performance tonight, did we not? What a treat! Wilks was in fine seductive form – and I thought Cibber was sublime!'

'He's a man who knows how to command the stage,' said Will.

'Yes, and in this play we allow him full scope. We are all content to dance in his shadow!'

Tom was struck by the confidence of the actor's 'we.' Gilbert Angell was no neophyte:

'The audience were especially admiring of your *handiwork*, Mr Angell. You performed the valet's duties with exceptional skill.'

'Yes, Mr Bristowe, I'm almost accustomed to this thing now,' he said, looking at his sling. 'It's become my *signature* – I'm loath to discard it …'

And with that, in a single movement, he swung his arm free.

'… I think I shall allow it one further performance, however … but certainly not for *The Tender Courtesan*. As Ernesto, I intend to make full use of *both* arms! …'

Tom and Will were silent, wide-eyed.

'... You look shocked, gentlemen! I'm afraid we actors are never quite what we seem ... I'm happy to say my shoulder is back in place – only very sore. It was decided that *Handy* was an opportunity to show off my juggling skills. It was such a comic opportunity, was it not?'

The friends saw that this young man knew how to command the stage too, and both wondered what acting they were witnessing. It was impressive in its way: Gilbert Angell made the room seem larger than it was.

Will in particular was beginning to feel uneasy, thinking how to raise the subject of Sally Twiss. For once, his tactfulness deserted him, and he broke in a little too early:

'You said Sally Twiss has left suddenly. I was hoping to be able to congratulate her on her singing.'

There was a pause while Gilbert Angell assessed the tenor of the remark. He took up the towel again and began wiping his neck:

'She has a fine light voice, I confess, and a good natural manner. She will have a brilliant future ... if only she will be patient and careful.'

His countenance became more sombre. Will persisted:

'Mr Bristowe tells me she is to play the lead in *The Tender Courtesan*?'

'*Aye, there's the rub,*' said Gilbert with a shake of the head. 'She is full of eager confidence about it – but she is heedless of the danger this puts her in.'

'Danger?'

'Mrs Oldfield has been deplorably treated in the business and will not easily forget the slight. Mr Rich is resentful and takes it as an attack on his position – and the whole company are unsettled by the sudden promotion ... But Sally is blithely unaware ... And in truth, Tamara is a role she is unsuited for. I foresee trouble. The May Fair booth is an unforgiving place, and an audience who thought to see Oldfield … Well, it will be a difficult test – a fearful test of her …'

Tom and Will knew that the conversation had taken a darker turn – and it at once grew darker still.

'… And all this because of that devil Tunbridge! …'

Gilbert stopped unbuttoning his shirt and frowned as he took a drink.

'… The old raven flattered her and coaxed her, and showered her with gifts. He told her the theatre is at her feet … And poor Sally is only eighteen! … I apologise gentlemen – you find me in an unsettled state tonight. Things have been happening here – I should not talk of them.'

Gilbert Angell had emptied his glass of port and now poured himself another. They realised that the bottle was almost empty. Tom leaned forward:

'But Mr Angell … !'

The actor raised his hand. He was flushed and anxious. There was a loud sigh:

'*Angell!* What a name I am burdened with! … In truth, it is she who is the angel, not I … *I*, gentlemen – as you have seen – am something of a magnificent sham. But Sally Twiss is *Nature itself* …'

He set his glass down carefully. Tom and Will were beginning to feel uncomfortable and were not sure where the conversation was heading.

'… But she is so *vulnerable*, gentlemen … God knows what she has done – and what she *may* do.'

It was a maudlin performance, but underneath was something painfully genuine. The lawyer-like Will was determined the remark shouldn't slip by:

'Mr Angell, forgive me – but has something happened tonight? Something to alarm Sally – Miss Twiss? You speak of *what she has done*.'

'I know not ... she would say nothing to me. But after the curtain fell, I could see she was agitated. I think he had made another attempt on her.'

'An *attempt* ... you mean Lord Tunbridge ... ?'

Will realised he didn't want to complete the sentence.

'Young Sally was flattered by his attentions, Mr Lundy, and the gifts he lavished on her. She thought of him as a kindly grandfather coaxing and instructing her. She was not a little ambitious too, and saw how she might use him. A man of his influence could be a powerful patron! But the old carrion fixed his claws in her deeper and deeper. On Monday morning ...'

He paused, and a distant look came into his eyes.

'Before the rehearsal?' prompted Tom. 'When you and she arrived late?'

'Yes ... We had been arguing, Mr Bristowe. She had boasted to me of the re-casting, and what his Lordship had promised her ... but she said he was now becoming violent. Before that, it was mere innocent play – petting and dandling ...'

He drank some more.

'... But now he told her he felt he had *rights* over her. And he wanted to be paid ... She doesn't know where to turn. Her openness has led her along the path step by step, and now she sees no way back – no way but humiliation and the loss of her hopes – all the plans she was making for herself!

'I told her I would confront him and demand to know his intentions. I said I would tell Mr Rich of this ... but she said the theatre was in Lord Tunbridge's hands – that his designs are not to be thwarted. His *designs!* How could the man have gathered such power to himself? She begged me to do nothing ... and that is how we left it.'

'But tonight you believe he took matters further – or attempted to?'

'I cannot say, Mr Lundy – but Sally brushed me away and looked black. She ran off after the performance, and I don't know where she is now … I can't say … I don't know what to do …'

Gilbert suddenly appeared young and lost. His confidence had ebbed as if he was shocked at how much he had said. All passion was spent, and he cradled his face in his hands, his fingers pressed into his eyes.

Tom took the bottle and glass and set them aside:

'You should do nothing more tonight, Mr Angell. But in the morning you should perhaps call on Mr Rich. Tell him what you know of Sally – she may have broached the matter with him already. Do nothing precipitate. It's something that must be resolved carefully.'

Gilbert drew himself up:

'I apologise, gentlemen. You've caught me in an unsettled state of mind. I've given quite a performance, haven't I … ? You've drawn too much out of me. You will make a fine prosecutor, Mr Lundy …'

He attempted a polite smile and looked around as if suddenly noticing an audience.

'… You know, this is an unusual building … It heats the blood and fans the passions into flame – and it also encourages language to take wing … There's something about the air in this place. Behind the scenes all is close and suffocating – it is only when the curtain rises that we actors feel able to breathe freely!'

Will looked at him between the eyes:

'You can count on us, Mr Angell. If Miss Twiss is in danger you must promise to let us know at once. Mr Bristowe lodges at the Bay-Tree Chocolate House, off Drury Lane, and a note will find me there too.'

'It's been a frantic evening, Mr Angell,' said Tom with as much calmness as he could command. 'Things should feel cooler tomorrow.'

With that, they slipped out and left the young actor bending down to remove his buckled shoes. He was still in his valet costume.

Tom and Will walked away from the theatre briskly, as if they too had begun to feel the closeness of those dusty theatrical corridors. They were cheered by the knowledge that the Bay-Tree was only a few minutes away. Both of them had been discomforted by their meeting with Gilbert Angell. Tom had seen a young man who was an actor through-and-through – not false or insincere, but confused, as if on this evening of joyous comedy he felt trapped in a larger plot, and didn't know his part.

During the twists and turns of the conversation Will's anger had been mounting. The picture Gilbert had painted was as shocking as it was predictable – the old story of a young actress and her 'patron.' He choked as he contemplated the cautionary tale. There was so much he wanted to say, but he could manage only a single phrase:

'That devil Tunbridge!'

The two sweepers leaned gratefully on their brooms as they took a few minutes' rest. The theatre was taking its breath too after the evening's performance. The place was empty and quiet now, but the debris of the brilliant occasion was scattered all around. After a good hour in the upper gallery the women's buckets were brimming over with apple cores, orange peel, and nutshells.

The younger of the two looked exhausted:

'There's more trash here than in the market, Mrs M! It must have been a good show tonight.'

'Certainly a comedy,' said Mrs Moody, taking out her wooden snuff box. 'You can always tell. With tragedy it's all handkerchiefs and lavender-water – but a good comedy will have 'em nibbling away like rats in a granary. Anyway, my pig's in for a treat tomorrow ...'

She lifted up one of the buckets.

'Does the Housekeeper allow you?' said the girl a little anxiously.

'Ah, Betty! What Mr Bannister don't know won't hurt 'im ... Here, take a pinch and cheer yourself – you'll soon get used to the job. The worst's over, and Mrs Carter and her boy should be done in the pit by now.'

The two women were lingering in the passageway outside the green room, and Mrs Moody turned an ear to the closed door:

'We always leave the green room till last – there's usually one or two actors still wetting their whistles, and they like to be left alone. I can hear talking in there now. We could make an attempt on the costume room, though the place is such an unholy jumble there's little enough floor to see ... But let's take breath first. With luck we can manage a tot in the green room later – there's often a glass or two to be emptied ... Sit here for a minute – it's my favourite seat in the theatre!'

She indicated a long-backed bench finely carved in black oak, and the girl squatted nervously on it. Mrs Moody lowered herself down beside her and took her snuff in turn. For a moment they felt like two fine ladies in a box. But just as they were settling themselves for a pleasant chat, the green-room door opened.

'What's this with the pair of you? Lounging and gossiping like alehouse whores! If your brooms were as busy as your tongues! ...'

'Mr Bannister! We were just readying ourselves for the green room ...'

'The room is occupied, Moody, and will be for some time. Get to work somewhere else! You're not paid to pass the time of day.'

'We'll do the main costume-room then ...'

The pair were now on their feet.

'No, no – there's little good you can do in there. I've another job for you – you must begin clearing out the closet along the corridor here, where we keep the helmets, shields, swords and suchlike. It seems it's to be fitted out as a dressing-room for Miss Twiss, and we need to move the clutter. It will all have to go into the smaller costume-room – not that we have any space for it ...'

The housekeeper's eyes were beginning to have a desperate look.

'... This place is like a huge attic. Our Mr Rich must needs build another floor! ... I'll get Carter and her lad to help you ... You see how thoughtful I am? And you'll need candles.'

The sweepers were smiling.

'What are you grinning at? Go on! Busy yourselves!'

And so they did.

The closet in question was windowless – it was one of those 'nooks' that Christopher Rich had carved out of several larger rooms in the place and had no furnishings except for a cupboard and a few shelves. Mrs Moody led the way with her candle and lifted it up toward the ceiling. On the walls were hooks from which hung a veritable armoury of breastplates, swords and helmets. Here was all the assorted weaponry of Shakespeare's Tewkesbury, Bosworth and Philippi; they could see an extravagantly plumed helmet that had graced the heads of both Prince Hal and Alexander, and a heraldic banner that had waved behind Caesar and Othello; a couple of muskets which had featured somewhat incongruously in a recent *King Lear*, and English longbows wielded on the plain of Troy.

The candle glimmered, and Mrs Moody and Betty held their breath. It was like being on the stage of the theatre itself, encircled by a troop of fearsome warriors about to give battle. They had never confronted anything quite like it. They imagined the scene coming to life before them.

But after a few seconds they found themselves plunged into a drama of their own. The candle spluttered, and as the door opened further their eyes instinctively lowered to the floor. There, as if on stage at the end of a tragedy, was a man's body. It was stretched out face-down, the hands gnarled in agony. What made the effect even more theatrical was the elaborate dagger that jutted out between the shoulder-blades. For a brief moment they thought this might be a stage prop thrown in here for storage; but the sticky deep-red blood that oozed toward their feet was the real thing. Both of them gave an involuntary scream. The lace cuffs and undrawn sword showed that this was a gentleman …

The housekeeper and prompter heard the cry in the green room and hurried to the scene. As soon as they came through the door and saw the body, they knew why there had been an empty seat on the stage that evening.

Chapter Nine

MEANWHILE, TOM AND Will were reporting their news in the coffee-room at the Bay-Tree.

'Poor Mr Angell – and that was how you left him?'

'Yes, Mr Pinkerman,' said Will. 'He was solacing himself with port and looked sad and lost. But there was anger and frustration too. I'm not sure we've seen the full picture.'

'I think he's genuinely concerned about Sally,' said Tom, 'but perhaps the two of them had quarrelled over Lord Tunbridge. How much of it was jealousy, I wonder? Do you think he's imagining the worst?'

'Tunbridge is a vile creature, and from what you've been saying, Mr Pinkerman, the man sees no check on his power. He wants to rule the playhouse and everyone in it.'

Widow Trotter sighed:

'Mr Angell sounds like a perplexed young man. It seems to me he was wanting to play the hero, but Sally Twiss wouldn't let him.'

'An *avenging* hero? Let us hope not, Mr Lundy!' said Pinkerman, who was becoming concerned for the fate of his Tamara. If Sally Twiss had quarrelled with the Baron and run off in a pet, then he was in danger of losing two courtesans within a week.

'Surely,' said Tom, 'young actresses have often negotiated happy terms with their admirers – look at Mistress Gwyn.'

'But Nell Gwyn left the theatre,' said Pinkerman, 'as she had to. The King wouldn't allow it.'

Widow Trotter gave a knowing smile:

'Yes, the old hypocrisy. Charles wanted an actress in his bed, but not his mistress on the stage.'

The three men were sitting in the Bay-Tree taking stock of the evening's events. A glowing fire and cups of spiced chocolate were helping to ease what had turned out to be a chilly evening. Widow Trotter was standing over them with a linen cloth in her hand, curious to hear how matters had unfolded in the playhouse. As she suspected, the occasion had been eventful:

'You say Lord Tunbridge never returned to his seat. But can it really have been disgust at the play? How could anyone take offence at such a laughing comedy?'

'All too easily!' said Pinkerman. 'Dorimant the rake behaves outrageously: he dangles his lovers by his fingers' ends as if they were puppets, and boasts of his succession of mistresses; he scorns fidelity and constancy … and yet he departs the play unpunished, triumphant in his reputation!'

'Yes, but as I recall, he meets his match in Harriet.'

'His match, yes – but that makes things worse: Harriet has all the makings of a female rake herself.'

Widow Trotter looked at Tom and grinned:

'Well, she's certainly no Agnes!'

There was a sudden earnest look on Pinkerman's face:

'People demand *Poetic Justice,* Mrs Trotter. 'Tis a rule! The virtuous must end happily, and all vice be punished.'

'Well, they didn't demand that on Tuesday night at *The Fox,*' said Tom. 'The audience were cheering Jonson's villains!'

'Yes, Mr Bristowe … and there is now talk of action being taken. The Lord Chamberlain has been complained to! It seems that on Tuesday the performance gave offence to some important people.'

'So, even our Ben Jonson is under threat?'

'Not for the first time. Some years ago, we actors were put on trial for performing in that very play! Mrs Trotter here will remember it – Mrs Bradshaw, Mr Cibber and myself were tried in Westminster Hall – before the Lord Chief Justice himself.'

'Yes, and you were found guilty, Mr Pinkerman,' said Widow Trotter. 'You personally!'

Will shook his head in disbelief:

'In the Court of Queen's Bench? I can't believe it.'

'*King's* Bench, it was then – Yes, Mr Lundy, it was only a handful of offensive lines – and a full century old they were too! – but we actors were brought to trial for them. You lawyers saw to that! And we were in court again for the witty sentiments of Vanbrugh and Congreve. Censors are everywhere, and 'tis the players who take the blame. There are men in the audience taking note of any oaths. A single *'ods life* can damn you – and a *Devil take it!* brings you before a magistrate.'

A momentary silence descended.

'But you'll surely be secure at the Fair,' said Tom. 'There anything goes!'

'Will it? I think a stand could be made this time – that old proclamation was a warning shot. Since the turn of the year we've been half-expecting another royal pronouncement *against profaneness and vice*.'

'But they are still declaiming the old one from the pulpits,' said Will. 'My maiden aunts love to be reminded of it regularly. At the Hackney meeting-house they take a special pleasure in denouncing the nation's sins.'

'Yes,' said Widow Trotter, 'it means they can be virtuous by doing nothing.'

'You hit the nail there, Mrs T – but I would never dare say as much to my father – I know his opinions too well! He's particularly hot against comedies. For him, all laughter is irreverent, and even a smile borders on the immodest … And a *guffaw* damns you to the mines of sulphur.'

'Is Judge Lundy involved with the Society?' asked Pinkerman hesitantly.

'I fear he is. At least he approves of its work. Frankly, the Reformation of Manners is a subject I tend to steer away from. I believe father has attended some of their meetings. It appeals to his Puritan heritage – after all, he's a bit of an old Roundhead. The playhouse is well out of bounds!'

Widow Trotter tried to picture 'Hemp' Lundy in a theatre-box, and smiled. A glare from those hawk-like eyes would make any sensitive actor forget their lines. She turned to Will:

'Have you encountered the reformers at any of your trials?'

'Not directly – it's usually a matter for the magistrates. But as it happens, this morning I was taking notes in Westminster Hall, and one of the cases was a private prosecution for *blasphemous utterances*.'

'Not the theatre this time, I trust?' said Widow Trotter.

'No, it was a trivial thing that had blown up stupidly. It should have been a simple case of alehouse "tippling," but the poor man wasn't quite drunk enough to collapse – far better for him if he had, then he would have slept it off in the round-house. But he had a robust constitution and resilient vocal chords. The gentleman remained conscious long enough to do his very worst with the whole world. It seems he began letting out a string of lively curses, invoking *Christ* and the *Saints*, and damning his dear wife to kingdom come! He drew down the *Devil* on the landlord, *Beëlzebub* on the Ministry, and – unfortunately for him – consigned to *Hell-fire* the local Magistrate, whose nephew happened to be sitting at the next table. He only wanted a bell, book and candle to complete the full Satanic performance!'

'That must have made for a lively case. I hope you made full notes?'

'My usual shorthand, Mrs T – Although some of the more ingenious expressions had to be written out in full.'

'Was it the pillory, then?' asked Tom.

'The sentencing was postponed, but the pillory will be the least of it. It was the man's second offence, believe it or not – and if the full rigour of the law is observed, it could be a forty-pound fine – a year's wage! But his curses were so shocking that there's talk of his being made an example of.'

'That sounds ominous, Mr Lundy.'

'Yes it is, Mrs T. It would involve the boring-through of his tongue – and imprisonment too. The 1694 Blasphemy Act is equivocal on the matter, and there is considerable laxness and uncertainty in its implementation – but by the provisions of the old 1649 Act of Toleration ...'

'Thank you, Mr Lundy! I think that is enough ...'

Tom's tones were uncannily those of Will's father, whom he had witnessed on the bench.

'... The Court is grateful for this illumination of statute law. I'm sure Mr Sumner will be impressed with the progress of your studies.'

'*Mea culpa*, Your Honour!' said Will in response. 'The case indeed remains *sub judice* ...'

There was laughter, but only for a moment. Will was serious:

'... It sounds trivial, Tom, but in these things the *niceties* of the Law can be crucial. The poor gentleman is sweating in gaol at this very moment, wondering if he'll be made the victim of finer detail.'

Widow Trotter knew she had to set about her work, but she lingered by the table, delighting in the talk. Half her mind was over in the playhouse. Her curiosity about Lord Tunbridge's absence was still bothering her: a patron of the company didn't simply disappear from view like that and leave his empty chair to be viewed by everyone in the benefit-night audience. She thought it strange. Sally Twiss's flight must surely be connected in some way? Had the Baron confronted her? Attacked her? ... Heaven only knew – it was an episode from a sordid French romance! She had to be careful about such flights of imagination. But it was strange nonetheless ...

With a slight shock she recalled herself to the here-and-now: 'Well gentlemen, I must leave you to chew on the matter!'

And they did. And they also chewed on slices of toast, and talked; and Tom and Will listened while William Pinkerman recalled some of his theatrical adventures over the years. It was an inexhaustible topic, and he told his tales so genially that his hearers were held in thrall. One cup of chocolate followed another as Pinkerman spoke about the progress on his booth, about rehearsals for *The Tender Courtesan*, and eventually, as the fire grew low, about old Mr Betterton and the fund of stories the venerable gentleman, when in the mood, could be prompted to recall about the antics of Mr Shakespeare of Stratford-on-Avon and his fellow actors.

It was near midnight when the party broke up. The room had for a while been empty except for themselves, and Widow Trotter had re-joined them. Looking at the clock, she decided it had been one of the best nights she could recall since the inauguration of the Bay-Tree. At moments like this the place transformed itself from a public chocolate house to her *home* – a second home too, perhaps, for these good friends of hers.

As the group was stirring, the coffee-room door opened and there on the threshold stood the watchman equipped with his lamp and staff, doing his midnight round. It was Tobias Mudge, Elias's apprentice, and Widow Trotter smiled a greeting at him only to find it freeze on her lips. The young man was not wearing his usual cheery face but was looking grim and apprehensive:

'I have news from the playhouse, Mrs Trotter. Constable Cobb is busy there right now, but he wants me to tell you … a dead body has been found. He says you will be concerned to know of it – a Lord *Tunbridge*. He has been stabbed in the back.'

Pinkerman was the first to react:

'What! Lord Tunbridge dead? … *Murdered?* …'

It was said in wonder as much as horror. The watchman nodded unnecessarily.

'… Did this happen in the theatre? Where was he found?'

'In one of the store-rooms, Sir. Where they keep the armaments. The corpse was discovered by the sweepers about an hour ago.'

Pinkerman forgot to breathe. He was thinking about what this meant – what would change – what it would mean for the company …

'Killed in the theatre?' said Tom. 'It must surely have been during the play, then?'

'Yes, perhaps during the interval?' added Will. 'Can you believe it?'

Widow Trotter was pensive:

'Well, well, well … One mystery is solved, gentlemen – only for another to take its place. A much bigger one!'

A certain look was coming over her – one that Tom and Will recognised. And she lingered on the word *mystery* with the kind of shiver that told them her curiosity had been excited. She was becoming *interested*.

But it was Will who was thinking more immediately:

'Sally …' he said. 'What of Sally? You don't think? …'

Tom looked at his friend:

'It's difficult *not* to think … if what Gilbert Angell told us is true.'

'God save us! I can't believe ...'

Suddenly the horror could not be kept at bay. The watchman hesitated before speaking, wondering if it would be revealing too much:

'Sally Twiss, Sir, the young actress ... She is being sought.'

'*Sought?* Oh God, this is terrible! You mean she is suspected?'

'I can't say more, Mr Lundy. I don't *know* more than that. Mention was made of a quarrel. They are looking for her. You say you've talked with Mr Angell about her. When was that?'

'Earlier tonight, in his dressing-room.'

The watchman's face made a note:

'Mr Cobb will have to know of this. You must tell him about it. The theatre has been in uproar, as you can imagine.'

'O heavens! I must go to there,' said Pinkerman. 'This is certain to have consequences. Mr Rich will still be in the place – I have to talk with him.'

'He was there when I left, Sir. There's an urgent confab going on. Mr Cibber is with him. Everybody is shocked. I caught Mr Rich smiling – but then he put his head in his hands. There seems to be a lot of confusion.'

'I'll say there is,' said Pinkerman in a tone of bewilderment.

'But I have to continue my round, Mrs Trotter – Sirs – I've been delayed tonight ...'

The watchman paused at the door.

'... Mr Cobb says he will call here in the morning. If Mr Lundy could also be here it would save the constable a lot of trouble – he will wish to know of your interview with Mr Angell.'

Thank you, Toby,' said Mrs Trotter. 'I must apologise for not offering you a drink.'

'I'm sorry if my ill news has startled you. Good night all!'

The watchman left them standing in a half-circle as if forming for a country dance. But each was rooted to the spot. Minds were racing as they pondered what this could mean for the future of the theatre. It was far from clear whether the sudden crisis would bring good or ill – the threads were so tangled.

It was Tom who broke the silence:

'Where does this leave His Lordship's plans for the company, Mr Pinkerman? Is this a fifth-act reprieve?'

'It has the look of it, Mr Bristowe. The threat of tyranny is lifted for the moment. But I ask you to remember *Julius Caesar*. You might kill the body, but only to release the spirit – and the *spirit* of a tyrant is a terrible adversary. This murder will be a scandal and be used against us. Our enemies will draw strength from it. We must not run through the streets crying 'Liberty! Freedom! Tyranny is dead!''

'Wise old Shakespeare,' said Tom quietly.

'But Sally Twiss ...' said Widow Trotter, glancing at Will alongside her, 'Toby said she is being *sought* – does that mean she has fled? It would amount to a confession of the crime.'

'That's something I have to find out at once,' said Pinkerman. 'Forgive me, but I must hurry away – things may be changing by the minute. *The Tender Courtesan* is to open in a week's time. If the pair of them are arrested, then our new play is doomed ...'

He was understandably flustered. He stopped at the door and swung round.

'... *'Tis a catastrophe!*'

It was a dramatic exit line, and the door banged decisively behind him. It lacked only a peal of thunder to achieve the full effect.

As if in response Widow Trotter turned smartly:

'Well gentlemen, we find ourselves in a swiftly-moving plot. I wonder what tomorrow has in store? ... You can stay here tonight, Mr Lundy – I'll not have you walking alone to the Temple after midnight. And it means you'll both be on hand in the morning to talk with Elias.'

'Thank you, Mrs T. I'll take up your offer gladly. It's been a crowded day.'

Will looked relieved, but his eyes told her he was occupied in thought. However, by some kind of mental magic the idea of a comfortable bed immediately brought a stifled yawn.

Widow Trotter began securing the coffee-room for the night, and as she drew the bolts she was in a reflective mood:

'But this is a serious matter, gentlemen, is it not? Our friends in the playhouse must feel themselves under siege. Accusations will surely be made against them. The Baron's killing will cast a stain on the place. Whatever the circumstances, it has the smell of scandal. And if young Sally Twiss is under suspicion … No, I can see nothing good coming of this!'

Her face was solemn. The final bolt struck home, and three tired and thoughtful people went to their beds.

Friday

30 April 1708

Chapter Ten

'IT WAS TOWARDS ten o'clock, and on this bright spring morning the Bay-Tree was humming as the day's news began to accumulate. Early soundings had been taken – in the market, on street-corners, in dawn messages or midnight conversations – and now gentlemen were arriving from all directions ready to take stock of what the world was doing – the 'world' being defined by the range of an hour's brisk walk. Behind the bar of the coffee-room, Jenny Trip viewed the scene with amused curiosity, wondering at the masculine character – how men liked to believe that their gossip was really 'news' and their scandal 'business.'

Jenny had worked at the Bay-Tree for six months and had developed a good understanding of how the system regulated itself. The morning scene held a particular fascination. At this time of day the coffee-room functioned like an office of intelligence, and she noticed how it was organised and which roles men played. She could differentiate between the 'repositories of wisdom' (those who stationed themselves to consult and assess the news); the 'post-boys' (who gathered information as they plied between a succession of coffee-houses); and the 'scavengers' (who hung around hoping to collect whatever scraps they could). There were the judges, the wits, the eager novices, the cynics, and the politicians. It was altogether a bustling medley.

The Bay-Tree had its share of these, and Elias Cobb's entrance was often a moment when sensational news might be expected. The constable had to be careful, and sometimes his secrecy was a cause of frustration to the other customers. This was one of those mornings. Rumours of dramatic events at the playhouse had quickly spread beyond Covent Garden, which was a market for news as well as fruit and vegetables. Shoppers took home more than apples and cauliflowers: in St James's the return of a servant from the piazza could set up drawing-room chat for the whole day.

When Elias arrived in the coffee-room he saw Tom and Will sitting quietly while a conversation was conducted round them. On Widow Trotter's advice the pair had agreed to listen and take note rather than reveal what they knew. Nothing was to be gained by talk of Sally Twiss's flight and the suspicion that hung over her, and the two of them understood that Elias would soon be their reliable informant. Fictions took wing: an outrageous rumour that Mrs Oldfield had been arrested for stabbing Christopher Rich persisted for at least five minutes. Confirmation that the deceased was Lord Tunbridge turned speculation in a wholly new direction, and the lack of more certain news proved no obstacle to conjecture.

As he strode to the bar, Elias Cobb had to fend off questions from the tables, meeting them with a patient smile and a shake of the head. He was noticeably unshaven and a little red-eyed, which told its own story. Jenny leaned forward and spoke softly to him, the ribbon of her bonnet dangling in front of his nose:

'Mrs Trotter is in the parlour, Mr Cobb, doing the accounts. She is expecting you, along with Mr Lundy and Mr Bristowe – if you'll go through.'

No well-schooled valet could have performed better.

Elias turned his head to see Tom and Will looking over, and he knew they would shortly follow. It was like a scene in an illicit gaming-house, and he rather enjoyed the hint of mystery.

Five minutes later the constable was seated at the parlour table with a bowl of hot mutton broth in front of him, which Tom and Will eyed enviously. His heavy coat hung on the back of the chair, and as he leaned forward his stubbly chin jutted under the spoon.

'This is very welcome, Molly,' he said, before taking a mouthful of crusty bread.

'Take your time, Elias. You've had a busy night.'

'I've known nothing like it. Things are moving swiftly. A scandal is already bubbling up! I've been trying to contain it – but things are taken out of my hands.'

'What do you mean?' said Will, curious to know what the procedure was.

'Exactly that, Mr Lundy. The killing of Lord Tunbridge – a peer of the realm – is deemed well beyond my competence. I have no official role in the Law, remember, and in something as momentous as this it has to be others who hold the reins.'

'Could I ask who these *others* are, Mr Cobb?'

The constable set down his spoon, as if a mark of respect were required:

'I'm told it's to be the Queen's Solicitor-General, no less! – Sir James Montagu, Lord Halifax's brother. His office will take things into their hands. Her Majesty is being informed at this very moment ...'

There was a tense silence as the three of them took the fact in. This was to be a national investigation.

'... It seems they wish the business to be overseen by someone who will oblige the Court.'

'But what has the Court to do with it?'

Tom's intervention sounded naïve, but the question had to be asked. Will gave his friend a considered answer:

'The killing of a Lord is a State matter, Tom. And on top of that, the Theatre Royal company is under the patronage of the

Queen – constituted by Letters Patent under the Great Seal. So they are effectually *her* players. The royal patent is double-edged: it bestows a privilege, but also imposes a responsibility.'

Elias looked impressed at Will's summing-up:

'Mr Lundy is right. And it appears Her Majesty is giving thought to the affairs of her company. But Anne is no Charles! She dislikes the stage and listens to her friends in the Church who want the playhouse suppressed. The reformers have the Queen's ear and hope one final push will bring her over. But I suspect something is holding her back ...'

Elias took a mouthful of the hot soup and twisted off a piece of bread with his fingers.

'... She is suspicious of the dissenters!'

'But the reformers are both High and Low, are they not?' said Tom.

'Yes, among the clergy perhaps. But it's the low-church sort who are the engine of the Reformation of Manners. The shopkeepers and tradesmen – the kind of busy people who hate plays and fictions, and think a pantomime is a papist conspiracy.'

'They are the ones behind the Blacklist?'

'They are, Mr Lundy. Those men are only happy when they are keeping accounts. The blacklist is their brainchild. It's how they think about spiritual matters – counting lost souls and reckoning the tally of converted sinners. Profit and loss is what drives them!'

At this point Widow Trotter made a sound something between a groan and a sigh:

'Yes. Poor Mr Trotter featured in its pages – but he looked upon it as a roll of honour!'

'What was his offence, Mrs T?'

'Exactly what you would expect, Tom – the heinous crime of serving a few dishes of "coffee" to his friends on the Sabbath ... The difficulty was, *all* the customers of the old Good Fellowship were my husband's friends!'

Elias grinned widely:

'Yes, Molly, we had a few convivial parties on Sunday afternoons, did we not? … But an informer did for us – and the magistrate needed no encouragement!'

'What a mixture this is,' said Will with a half-smile. 'The serious and the trivial all jumbled together.'

Tom met Will's smile with a frown:

'Perhaps trivial to us, Will – oaths and curses, and observing the Lord's Day – but such things are life and death for these congregation-people. Their hope of salvation depends on it.'

There was an awkward moment of silence. Tom's words recalled them to the serious business of the murder, and the possible fate of the young actress. Widow Trotter watched Elias mop up the last of the soup with his bread and concluded that he was now fortified enough to take things further:

'Do you have news of Sally Twiss, Elias? Toby told us she was being *sought*. Has she fled her lodgings?'

'It would appear so. She has not yet been found, and they are looking for Mr Angell who seems to have disappeared also! When Mudge sent word of the killing, I hurried to the theatre and was able to see the body and ask a few questions. The housekeeper and prompter were still in the building, and Mr Rich had been summoned. Young Bullock was in the green room sleeping off his claret!'

'What about the corpse, Mr Cobb? It was found in a store-room, was it not?'

'Yes, two sweepers discovered it. The Baron was lying face-down with a dagger stuck into his back. I had a look at it, and it was no crude stage-prop but a fine ornamental poniard. It was kept in the room with the shields and armour – a clutter of pageant-stuff. Mr Rich confessed it was theirs – a dangerous thing to have around! It was used for special scenes – Italian murderers, or troubled young princes – that sort of thing.'

'What was Lord Tunbridge doing in there?' said Tom.

The innocent question hung in the air, and the silence seemed answer enough.

'Whatever took him into the store-room, it was there that he was killed – the blood showed that. There was none in the passage.'

The picture beginning to form was not reassuring, and Will looked gloomy. He wondered if Sally had been in there with the Baron. No-one spoke, but it was what they were all thinking.

Elias, however, wanted to avoid conjecture, so he moved briskly on:

'When I questioned him, Mr Rich told me somebody had heard raised voices during the interval – angry accusations – supposedly between Sally Twiss and Lord Tunbridge. The theatre passages are such a warren, and he wasn't able to confirm this himself – but he said Miss Twiss was distinctly red-faced and flustered during the Mall scene. He himself saw nothing of Lord Tunbridge, and he told me he was shocked when he noticed the Baron's empty chair.

'Mr Bannister the housekeeper said he had glimpsed Sally and Mr Angell quarrelling outside the green room while the Mall scene was playing (her character doesn't enter for several minutes) and had taken it to be a lover's tiff! This was the sum of what I was able to find out. It was all fragmented and unsatisfactory. Everyone was confused by the events, and no-one that I spoke to had *seen* Lord Tunbridge behind the scenes at all.'

'That's curious. Was it you, then, who sent after Sally?'

'No, Mr Lundy. I had but a quarter-hour to ask my questions before the magistrate arrived on the scene.'

'So, had Toby sent for him?' asked Mrs Trotter.

'I don't know how word reached him. But Mr Hector turned up ready to take charge of matters. It put me in a difficult position. I passed on the few facts I'd been able to gather, but he was more concerned to find Sally Twiss. He and his officer made it clear my services were no longer needed and a higher authority was involved. And this was confirmed when I called back this morning.'

'Are you being shut out, Elias? Is the company closing ranks?'

'I don't think so, Molly – Mr Rich and the others talked openly enough. But the magistrate's arrival changed the mood. It seems the investigation is to be carried on in a more official way. Mr Rich looked unhappy, as if he was being pushed aside himself.'

His friends' faces fell, and Elias saw three disappointed people who had glimpsed an inviting path only to find it closed. Will in particular looked tense and uncomfortable. He was pushing himself forward in his chair as if he longed for action:

'But is there nothing we can do, Mr Cobb? Tom and I are involved in this, and especially in the fate of Sally and Gilbert. And now you tell us he is missing too! As you know, we went to Mr Angell's dressing-room after the play and talked with him ...'

Elias caught the mood and knew it chimed with his own. He decided he was not going to let this affair go. Besides, he had enough experience to sense something did not ring true. The feeling was so strong he could almost smell it:

'Rest assured,' he said, looking at his three friends, 'I am not intending to walk away. And as a first step, I want you and Mr Bristowe to give me a full account of your interview with Gilbert Angell. There may be things we can glean from it.'

The atmosphere became purposeful, and Tom and Will began telling their story. As Elias listened, he knew it boded ill for Sally. There had been a confrontation with Lord Tunbridge, but of what nature? The evidence was painting a vivid picture, but so much was dependent on what others may have glimpsed, or heard, or surmised. It was as if, while the stage comedy was playing, the old Baron and the two young actors had been caught up in a behind-the-scenes drama of their own.

By the end of their tale Elias understood why Tom and Will were disturbed by the killing. He wished he could be confident that Truth would out, but with the Queen's Solicitor-General directing things he felt himself becoming suspicious. He looked at Widow Trotter. One thing was clear: all four of them were now pulling at the leash. They just needed a direction.

Their deliberations were coming to an end when there was a polite knock on the parlour door, and Jenny Trip showed her face. Her mistress was urgently needed in the coffee-room – and a letter had been brought in for Mr Bristowe:

'The thing is sealed, Mr Bristowe, and the boy says it's to be put into your hands only. He's sworn to it and won't even let me bring it you.'

Jenny opened the door wider to reveal a youth of about nine with tousled sandy-coloured hair and an earnest expression. They immediately looked at his feet and were glad to see there were shoes beneath his worn linen trousers. The letter appeared big in his small fist as he stepped through the threshold, and it was handed over with some formality.

After the boy's departure the door closed again and the four of them were left contemplating the marvellous object. No-one spoke, but in each mind there was a barely-suppressed hope ...

Tom broke the seal and opened the document. His eyes quickly scanned the contents. The letter was hastily written and sprinkled with urgent underlinings. After a few seconds he began reading it aloud.

Mr Bristowe –

I write in great haste – *News has no doubt reached you of the killing in the playhouse* – Lord Tunbridge! Stabbed! – *I can scarce believe I write those words! From our talk yesterday you will guess how greatly I am shocked by this. My worst fears have been realised – and more violently than I could have imagined.*

Last night you and Mr Lundy appeared as welcome visitors – you were kind and showed yourselves interested in my fate – and in Miss Twiss's also. You urged me to seek your help if I needed it – and I do now – most urgently. *Last night I took you into my confidence – you are the only people to whom I have spoken, or to whom I dare now speak.*

Sally has fled – and she has fled to me!

Lord Tunbridge raped *her during the play – it was a* manner *of rape – and after the performance she rushed away in confusion and distress. She returned home only to find she could not stay there lest the Baron follow her. And so she came to my door! She is* innocent, *Mr Bristowe – but now knows she is suspected of the crime. She does not dare to return home.*

And so I have taken her away – I knew they would call at my lodgings at any moment.

I write with Sally's agreement. *We seek your help and advice – Mr Lundy's particularly. He has experience in the Law, and perhaps can advise us what to do. We are today with my cousin and her family in Holborn* – Snow Hill – *the address is Green Arbour Court – Mr Rudd's house. We dare not venture out, and beg you both to call on us. We put our* entire trust *in your* secrecy.

I will say no more till we meet. God grant you will help us.

Gilbert Angell

While Tom read the letter Elias Cobb was scowling and tutting his tongue. At the close he could hold out no longer:

'Mr Angell has done her no favour by fleeing. And he has served only to implicate himself in this affair!'

'It's certainly a frantic letter,' said Will. 'Sally must be very frightened.'

'And her state is worse than ever,' said Mrs Trotter. 'If she is indeed innocent, she would have done better to face it out.'

There was a pause before Tom looked at his friend:

'I think we must go, Will. Do you agree?'

'Yes. We cannot do nothing. We have to go to Holborn – if only to talk some sense into the pair of them ...'

Will saw that the Covent Garden Constable was frowning in silence beside them.

'... Mr Cobb ... Do you think we are being foolish? Should we perhaps inform the authorities?'

Elias gave them a guileless look:

'Hmmm ... *Authorities?* And what might those be in this business, do you think? ...'

Will responded with a collusive smile.

'... Yes, Mr Lundy, talk to the young runaways, both of you – we need to hear Miss Twiss's account. If *she* is not Lord Tunbridge's killer, then we are involved in something much more dangerous ... I think you should venture into Holborn, gentlemen – but be *vigilant!* ...'

Imperceptibly the constable found himself slipping into the familiar role of instructing the Watch.

'... Given that others will be pursuing the suspects, some care must be taken. Make your way separately, while keeping one another in sight at all times. Meanwhile I shall see if I can sniff out what is being organised between Mr Hector and Sir James Montagu. Our *authorities* no doubt believe they have everything in hand. But we shall see ...'

Widow Trotter escorted her friends out of the parlour with mixed emotions. She was disgusted by the story that was emerging – of rape and murder, power and ambition, of a simplicity that might prove to be deception, and innocence that might truly be guilt. But another part of her was relishing the thought of investigating this dark world. She wondered whether the forces ranged against the playhouse had been active during Thursday night's performance – and were they working now? Whatever was about to unfold, Lord Tunbridge's murder could give the theatre's enemies new heart.

Chapter Eleven

After receiving their charge from Constable Cobb, Tom and Will were aware of being on a mission. Making their way eastward towards Holborn they tried to follow his advice – to remain separate while keeping each other in view. But after crossing over the Fleet River they decided to take their chance. And so they walked up Snow Hill ridge together, negotiating the notorious Breakneck Steps side-by-side, and emerged through a passage into Green Arbour Court, a bit breathless but pleased to have found the place so easily. Its name had been generously bestowed: this was no pastoral retreat but a closely-built cobbled yard, and the Rudds had given the two runaways sanctuary in the garret above their lodgings.

Tom and Will knew theirs was a double commission – as sympathetic listeners but also unwelcome messengers. They would have to encourage Sally and Gilbert to give a full account of the goings-on at the theatre, but also make it clear that their immediate return was required, and any delay would be disastrous. It had been decided that any mention of the Solicitor-General or even Constable Cobb should be saved till the end. Sally would surely talk more freely without the threat of the Law looming over her.

After a further climb to the third floor of the building, they paused, and Tom knocked on the door with some apprehension. There were a few seconds of silence before it was opened tentatively and Gilbert Angell's face appeared. When he saw the familiar figures the relief in his eyes was unfeigned and they were welcomed in like friends.

It was a cramped room with a small lacquered table at its centre, at which Sally was seated as if ready to welcome guests for tea. Her light brown hair was neatly pinned, and a dress of yellow muslin completed the impression of polite comfort – she didn't look like a fugitive who had fled her home only hours before. Around the table the four of them formed an oddly domestic scene, but with the conversation conducted over bottled ale rather than cups of tea. Tom and Will noticed their parts from *The Tender Courtesan* lying on a stool by the door. An easy tone was established, and for a few minutes, with talk of the spring weather and the route they had taken, they were able to avoid mentioning the circumstances that pressed on them all. Until silence fell.

It was Gilbert who spoke first. He stuttered slightly, with impetuosity rather than hesitation:

'I – I had not hoped to see you both so soon! … Young Joseph told me the letter came to hand immediately. He said he thought you might not be far behind him.'

'We were both in the Bay-Tree when it arrived,' said Tom. 'I have to say your messenger delivered it very smartly.'

'Yes – my cousin's son. He swore he would put it into your hand and nobody else's. I was loath to send him – but his father takes pride in the lad's boldness and honesty, and Joe was happy to be a volunteer in our service.'

'As are we!' said Will impetuously, offering Sally a reassuring smile. 'Mr Bristowe and I are here to help … but you need to help us too. We have to know about the events in the playhouse, and what led up to them – and anything else that might be material, however trivial.'

'We need to know what happened,' added Tom. 'And especially from you, Miss Twiss. We learned a little from Gilbert yesterday evening, but to have the full circumstantial story about Lord Tunbridge ...'

Sally was giving him a concentrated and expectant look. He consciously lowered his voice:

'... Please don't feel embarrassed ...'

'Have no fear, Mr Bristowe. I've no time for embarrassment ...'

She gave a full-lipped smile which lit up her face.

'... All I can do is tell you the truth. It is not *I* who should be embarrassed by it.'

It was a forthright remark, and it made Tom think that innocence and boldness could go together. This was indeed no Agnes.

In the end, Sally needed little encouragement in telling her story, and she began recalling her first encounter with Lord Tunbridge – how he had come into her mother's millinery shop and chanced to overhear her in the next room reading a play aloud. She was giving a spirited performance of the different parts, catching their individual humours and manners of speech, and he had asked to see her ... Such a fine old gentleman! ... invited her to read more ... persuaded her mother that she would have a future as an actress ...

It was a story out of romance – but whether wholly true or not, it had led to her introduction to Sir John Vanbrugh and acceptance into the company at a salary of fifteen shillings per week! ... She talked with remarkable confidence, as if destiny were guiding her.

It was the eyes that struck Will most forcibly: they were the colour of violets, he decided – not quite sapphires – and as he looked into them he was half-expecting to see them bedewed with tears while she told her tale. But the young actress talked frankly and gave no thought to the poetic impression she was making. She wasn't projecting her charms from the Drury Lane stage but was in a garret room in an insalubrious suburb, hiding from the Law. The charmless setting, Will thought, seemed only to emphasise her naturalness.

Next to him, Tom was listening closely and trying to judge how sincere her story was. He was struck by the way she spoke to them directly, without uncertain glances toward Gilbert Angell who sat beside her on the couch. Tom had expected some collusion, but he was reassured that Sally seemed to be speaking for herself. His was a shrewder and less coloured assessment than Will's, but their conclusion was the same: Sally appeared to be a guileless creature, not yet caught up in what they both thought of as theatrical playfulness.

Sally told how the Baron had advised her on ways of presenting herself from the stage – how to convey the passions by facial expression and establish character through bodily gesture. But as the days passed the attentiveness had become closer, the advice more pressing, the little gifts more extravagant, the expectations more demanding. Lord Tunbridge's ambitions for her grew in proportion to his infatuation, until her self-belief knew no bounds. The path seemed smooth and open ...

'I had never met discouragement, gentlemen, and everything seemed possible. The Baron had infused his confidence into me, and so when he determined I should take the role of Tamara, I saw no difficulty. When warnings were given and unwelcome advice offered, I took it badly. I felt no inhibition or constraint. A brilliant career stretched out before me ...'

Tom continued to listen intently. Sally's words grew into a fine speech, although the sentiments were natural enough. It was oratory – but was it false? Tom was unsure. Did Truth only come through hesitant confession and whispered doubts? Or could it also be bold and rhetorical? He really didn't know.

Will was becoming increasingly impressed by her composure and found it disconcerting. He had expected a more ingenuous – frankly a more girlish – performance. But he checked himself. Sally was beginning to fascinate him, and the lawyer in him could sense the danger. But did enchantment disallow Truth? Could it not enforce it?

Sally Twiss's story was approaching the Monday rehearsal when she and Gilbert made their flustered entrance. She told how Lord Tunbridge had secured Rich's agreement to the change of role – and that the manager had been persuaded to launch her as a leading actress. Tamara would be a triumph!

'The Baron broke the news to me on Sunday night and came to my lodgings. When he told me, I floated on air. I could think only of myself and what a fine prospect was opening up for me ... but within minutes I was grovelling on the earth! Hitherto Lord Tunbridge had made no *demands* – nothing beyond little pettings in the green room and some fumblings in his coach ... Such intimacies were distasteful to me; but a real affection for him made it easier – and something of gratitude too. There was little other way I could show my thanks – and they were genuine!

'But on Sunday night, as he watched me, I saw a different look in his eyes ... I was catching my breath and almost spinning round, when he seized me of a sudden and pulled me to him. He pressed his face to mine and could not contain his passion. I pushed him off, but this only heated him more, and he became violent ...'

Will's face was expressing horror; Tom glanced at Gilbert, who was looking distinctly uncomfortable himself.

'... I found I could not scream – the moment appeared unreal, and the cries were stifled in my throat ... It was a strange fancy, but at that instant I thought myself in a novel and heard myself cry out to him like a heroine of romance: "*For the love of God, spare me! Spare me!*" ...'

She paused and took a breath:

'... The words worked like a spell – and instantly he drew back. Somehow, without knowing it, I had given him his role ... And so, like a lover whose ardour is finally conquered by his virtue, he fell onto his knees and sobbed ... . Yes, gentlemen, we acted out a powerful scene together!'

There was a stunned silence in the attic room. Tom and Will were holding their breath, and Gilbert was looking at Sally with wonder. No-one was ready to speak.

At that moment they heard a sudden scraping sound along the roof-tiles and a scuffling outside the open attic window. Sally gave a shiver of alarm, and Gilbert sprang to his feet. Had he worn a sword he would have unsheathed it ...

Unaware of the consternation it had caused, a pigeon peered into the room and jerked its head from side to side as it scrutinised their little *cabal*. Its feathers were sleek and its eyes had a questioning expression. The creature had heard the commotion and come to take a look.

Sally's body relaxed again, and an amused relief passed across her face:

'I have an audience, gentlemen!'

Tom had noted Gilbert's volatile response to the bird – which was now being shooed back onto the roof – and it prompted him to speak:

'I recall that at Monday's rehearsal, when you and Miss Twiss – Sally – came onto the stage, there was a coldness between you – you were both discomposed and appeared to have been quarrelling. Am I right?'

Gilbert turned from the window:

'There was an awkwardness, yes. Sally had just told me of

Lord Tunbridge's assault … To be brief, I urged her to break with him and inform Mr Rich of it. I told her to decline the role of Tamara and not let herself be the cause of ill-feeling within the company. I was distressed to hear how the Baron had been harassing her.'

'Distressed, or *angry?*' Will interjected.

Gilbert lowered himself back onto the couch beside Sally and gave her a kind look:

'Yes, angry of course – who would not be? I was furious at the old *lecher!* I fear I gave vent to it during our play-reading and somewhat startled poor Pinkerman with my vehemence. In old Don Leone I saw the Baron standing before me!'

'It certainly added spice to your performance,' said Tom.

'It was a memorable reading,' said Sally with a look of disarming innocence. 'The play unlocked our hearts, I think. The words were simple enough, but there was much feeling in them.'

Tom found that both Sally and Gilbert were looking at him. He ran a hand through his dark curls and immediately moved the conversation on. He addressed himself to Sally, clearing his throat nervously, conscious of stepping onto uncertain ground:

'Will and I need to ask you about what happened yesterday at the theatre while *The Man of Mode* was playing – particularly what occurred during the interval … It seems you were overheard quarrelling with Lord Tunbridge … and Gilbert told us you were *disordered* …'

At this point Sally began to look a little uneasy and blushed slightly, but she did not attempt to interrupt him.

'… Is that so? …'

There was silence.

'… What happened, Sally?'

Tom spoke quietly, almost in a whisper. By his side, Will was holding himself back, though he itched to speak. It had been agreed his time would come shortly – this must not become a courtroom.

Sally crossed her hands on her lap as if to compose herself, and responded calmly enough:

'That evening Lord Tunbridge was in a strange mood. During the play he was flirting with me from his seat on the stage, He had a complaisant smile on his face as if I were performing for him alone, and I was being distracted … So, when I began my Act Three song I resolved to put him behind me – literally so. I turned my back and addressed myself to a friendly face in the pit …'

Sally looked down into her lap, and now it was Tom's turn to blush. Next to him, Will was gazing intently at a pinned-up ringlet of her hair. She hesitated, but then moved matters on, still looking downward – in embarrassment? Modesty? Shame?

'… The Baron took that as a public slight, and during the interval when I returned from my dressing-room I encountered him in the passage. He had his back to me, so I turned tail and waited. I knew I had angered him … When I returned, the coast seemed clear, but as I skirted the passage that leads down to the back door I saw him walking towards me …'

She suddenly paused and looked straight at Tom and Will.

'… I'm sorry – you did wish to know the circumstances …'

'Of course, please continue!' said Will, unable to disguise his eagerness.

'The Baron was looking thunderous, and I stopped in my tracks. There was a brisk exchange – but then his eyes seemed to shine, and he put out a hand. He glanced around and whispered a grovelling *apology* to me. "I have something urgent to say to you," he said, "– something of great import. We must not be overheard!" It was dramatic, and he was so eager he half-pulled me into the store-room. There was a lit candle in there, which I thought odd …'

Will looked at Tom, but said nothing.

'… To be brief, gentlemen … He took my hands in his, and held them … and promised to make me his *wife!*'

Tom could not help himself:

'A marriage proposal? But that's absurd! – In the store-room?'

'It was a scene from burlesque, Mr Bristowe. He had been drinking heavily. His eyes were bright, yes – but they sparkled with brandy ... He swore he would *arrange it all* – if only I would surrender to him. He said he could *hold out no longer* ... I tried to pull myself away and told him it was ridiculous – *absurd* – yes, I used your very word! But this suddenly turned him – it was too much for his pride. He became angry and was shaking with indignation. He told me I mocked him and must be taught a lesson ...'

Sally had now lost her composure and was visibly trembling.

'... He forced me down on my knees and pulled me close to him ... and he ... he attempted to humiliate me ... but then suddenly his hand fell to his side and he drew back. His mouth was open and a strange sound was coming from him – a moan. He rocked backwards and had to steady himself on one of the shelves. He was looking at me helplessly ...'

She paused and took breath.

'... The bell rang, and I knew the Mall Scene was beginning – and though my entrance is some way into the scene I needed to watch from the side. He had gone silent, and just stood there ... so I slipped out of the door and left him ... I did no murder, gentlemen – I swear to you. *I did not stab him!*'

Will had been keeping a disciplined silence, but could hold back no longer.

'So, when did your exchange of words with Mr Angell take place? We understand that the two of you were seen quarrelling – when the Mall Scene had already begun.'

Gilbert glanced anxiously at Sally. The young man was suddenly looking uncomfortable and knew the beam had shifted to himself. Tom and Will were watching him, expecting a response. He had been taking a mouthful of beer, and set the glass down on the table as nonchalantly as he could, wiping his small mouth with a cuff. Sally was looking apprehensive, but Gilbert calmed her with a gesture of his hand:

'Yes, Mr Lundy, we were not wishing to keep this from you. But it was no quarrel – just a sharp exchange of words. I had been in the green room during the interval, and when the bell rang I opened the door just as Sally was approaching ...'

He looked reassuringly at her and waited in case she wished to speak. She remained silent, and so he continued:

'... Sally appeared flushed, and I knew something had occurred. I had seen the Baron's behaviour during the play and suspected another confrontation ... I challenged her, but she said she was troubled by a different matter. We were both anxious and irritable, and exchanged words. The play had re-started, and Sally was eager to be off. It was only later that she told me the truth of what had occurred – how that foul ravisher ... !'

He checked himself, realising that a show of anger would be unwise, and reached out to take her hand.

'... I now understand why you were so agitated.'

Sally and Gilbert composed themselves into the picture of a loving couple, and at that instant, as if to seal the bond, a beam of sunlight lit up the chamber, exposing the bareness of its walls and the dust on the floor. Tom noticed mouse-droppings along the skirting-board.

Will watched and was becoming even more restless. He pushed back his hair which had worked loose from its tie, and shifted on his haunches. He decided that now was the moment to confront the pair of them with reality. But he trod carefully, glancing at Tom as he spoke:

'You've both been open with us – indeed you could not have been more so – and we're determined to help if we can ... But first we must impress on you the extreme danger you are in – especially you, Sally. You must know this yourself – you would not have fled otherwise.'

'I fled in fear of the Baron, Mr Lundy – not from guilt.'

Will was cheered to hear this:

'Exactly so! That is how it must be … And that is why you must both return immediately – this very instant …'

Sally looked at Gilbert. The urgency had clearly unsettled them both.

Will didn't pause and began setting out the matter plainly. When they were tracked down, he said – as they undoubtedly would be – they would be renegades from justice. They could not argue their innocence if they were hiding from the Law. And the longer they hid, the worse their position would be.

'… whereas to return now – *voluntarily* – will work in your favour. Sally can argue that she fled Lord Tunbridge's violence and did not know of his death until Gilbert brought the news …'

He turned directly to Sally:

'… That revelation has cleared the way for you, do you see? Your return will be understood – even commended! And it will throw all the emphasis on the Baron's *assault*. You will be regarded as the victim.'

The logic of this was clear to Will and Tom, and so they were surprised to see that Sally was still frowning. Gilbert also looked fearful:

'You say we are suspected already? Both of us?'

'The wheels have been turning quickly, Mr Angell. You are being sought. Your flight *together* – and that is how it is seen – makes you appear as outlaws. If you are discovered here, it will be the end of you – the Law will treat you as accomplices and look no further for Lord Tunbridge's killers. Guilt will be stamped on you!'

'What you are really saying, Mr Lundy, is that we already bear the mark on us. You are asking us to surrender to people who believe we are guilty. What Justice can we expect from that?'

It was an awkward point, but Will remained insistent:

'Believe me! You must submit yourselves to the Law – there is no other way. Your flight was most unwise.'

A now white-faced Gilbert unclasped Sally's hand and looked directly into Will's eyes:

'You speak of *the Law* as an impersonal thing – but I wonder? Could there be some vindictive spirit driving this? Is someone hunting us?'

Will knew they had reached the nub of the matter:

'The murder of a member of the House of Lords is something in which the State has an interest. It is *aberrant*. This is no everyday Covent-Garden killing. It is best that you know … the Solicitor-General himself is involved, and his office is now pursuing the case. It is out of the constable's hands, and the local magistrate is superseded.'

'So, you advise us to return at once and face this "Justice" of yours, Mr Lundy?'

Will nodded in silence – he had said quite enough. Gilbert and Sally were looking at each other, and still hesitating. A further moment of awkward silence passed.

'*This is not a play!! …*'

Tom was becoming angry:

'… You must take Sally back at once! – Not within the hour, but this *minute!* You must face what you have to face as responsible people who trust to Justice. *Not as fugitives!*'

Tom was suddenly conscious of the open window and imagined his shouts echoing across the rooftops.

The runaways were clearly shaken. Full realisation seemed finally to have struck them. Seizing the dramatic moment, Tom and Will stood up. Gilbert sat looking stunned, but Sally got to her feet:

'We are grateful to you both – truly we are – and we shall do as you say. But … you must allow us to tell our own story, as we think best … Will you agree to one thing? What happened to me in that store-room has to remain a secret – for now. It must not become matter for coffee-house gossip …'

She looked down fondly at Gilbert.

'… The truth has to come from *us*, Mr Bristowe. I have opened my heart to you both – please do not betray my confidence!'

The speech was made with no little assurance. She looked intently and pleaded eloquently. It was Will who spoke:

'We shall keep your secret, Sally. I give you my word.'

'But you must tell the truth,' added Tom.

'I have just done so, Mr Bristowe – and very uncomfortable it has been. But I feel I owe you no less.'

'You must allow us to tell Mrs Trotter and Constable Cobb. We keep no secrets from either of them. They are our friends and close collaborators in this business and already know of our visit here. The four of us are your greatest allies, believe me!'

She cast her eyes down, drew her hands together as if to reassure herself, and nodded assent:

'I do, Mr Bristowe … For our part, we must now try and repair the damage our flight has caused. You speak to us like naughty children – not without reason. It will take us but ten minutes to pack and take our leave. Will you wait for us?'

'No, no, Sally,' said Will, who was feeling immensely relieved. 'We must depart separately. No-one must see us escorting you. You must make your own way back. Tom and I will leave immediately and find a tavern.'

Gilbert was stirring and pushed himself off the couch, at last coming to terms with the situation:

'We shall go to the playhouse at once. That will be the best course, do you agree?'

'Yes,' said Will. 'It will be the natural thing. We shall tell no-one of our visit here. As we said, the Covent Garden constable knows – but Mr Cobb will keep our secret, I assure you.'

The leave-taking was extremely brief, and a minute later

Tom and Will were walking out of Green Arbour Court – not down the Breakneck Steps this time but eastward towards the Old Bailey with the intention of turning south to Fleet Street and the Temple. They said nothing for a moment or two, both feeling as if they had been acting in a court-room drama. They longed to sit down together and compare notes, and so, when Tom pointed out that if they took a small diversion they would be at the Saracen's Head in two minutes, their own direction was decided.

Chapter Twelve

Tom and Will may have been heading for a tavern, but as they walked away from Green Arbour Court some distinctly sobering thoughts began to close in. It didn't help that their route had less than cheerful associations. A few strides brought them in sight of Newgate, a place whose nauseous stench still lodged in their memories. They glanced across at the old barbican with its turrets and barred windows sharply defined by the noonday sun. But however brightly lit, the building still managed to be a brooding presence over the scene.

Maintaining an uneasy silence, they turned left into Snow Hill, putting the infamous gaol behind them. They were now on the Tyburn road, the processional route to the gallows. Neither spoke of it, but they knew that only two days earlier it had been thronged with a crowd in holiday mood, hanging out of windows and perched on walls to watch the condemned in their open carts being carried to the place of execution. The young traitor William Greg, Robert Harley's clerk, had been among them. 'Tyburn Fair,' as it was affectionately called, was the one fair of which the authorities approved – the only one that did some moral good.

The melancholy picture was confirmed as they walked past St Sepulchre's church whose tolling bell always accompanied the Tyburn procession and ensured the occasion didn't lack solemnity. On the night before the 'Fair' it was the custom for the church clerk to carry a hand-bell over to the gaol and ring it outside the condemned cells, calling the prisoners to repentance: '*All you that in the condemned hold do lie, / Prepare you, for to-morrow you shall die* ...' How eagerly, thought Tom, religion sanctions the ritual of death – embraces it even!

And here finally, on their right, was the church porch where the line of Tyburn carts halted briefly while each criminal was given a nosegay to hold. It was the most delicate part of the ceremony. Did the gesture cheer them, he wondered? Or did it remind them of the fragile world of beauty they were about to leave?

Tom shivered and looked down, where his eye caught something colourful on the ground by the iron palings. Two or three scattered flowers were trodden into the pavement. Perhaps they were a pathetic remnant of that ritual moment, flung away by a prisoner? Or had they simply dropped unnoticed? All this time Tom had been thinking of the fate of Sally and Gilbert, and this image concentrated his mind. He stopped in his tracks and turned to Will, finally giving voice to the thought that was troubling both of them:

'Do you think we've saved their lives, Will? ... Or have we condemned them to death?'

It was an uncomfortable question, and Will had no decisive answer. Instead, quite out of character, he found himself reaching for a platitude:

'Who can say, Tom? Only Time will tell ...'

As if to echo the sentiment and lend it a deeper note, the hour of noon began to strike from the tower, scattering the birds that had been huddling quietly there. There was no doubt about it: the two of them were moping like a couple of melancholy lovers. It was fruitless. They needed to unbend their minds and lift their spirits. Perhaps with tankards in their hands they might think more practically. How easy it had been to lecture Sally and Gilbert about *facing Justice* – but what was the Justice that awaited them? And what must the pair be feeling, having to retrace their steps to a place that held such a dark secret? They were the ones with some reason to mope.

The Saracen's Head was a venerable hostelry tucked in behind the church tower. The Great Fire of 1666 had stopped right here, as if the wall of flame had finally relented and decided to slake its thirst. Tom and Will strode through the entrance-gate under scrutiny from a couple of larger-than-life Saracens who guarded their posts with glaring eyes, their mouths shaped into a battle-cry. These wooden warriors had seen off the Fire and were now offering patrons a threatening look that had somehow slipped into grotesque humour. Tom gave them an appeasing nod as he passed, wondering if Shakespeare or Ben Jonson had once done the same.

The cobbled courtyard was relatively quiet – the morning coaches had left hours earlier and the evening arrivals were to come. But there was a bustle about the place, and up in the galleries the servants were airing the bed linen, draping sheets over the balconies and gossiping loudly to each other. In recognition of the fine spring weather a few tables had been moved outside, and Tom and Will took occupation of one of them. A jug of ale was promptly ordered, along with a barrel of Whitstable oysters. They sat back on their stools and looked up at the patch of blue sky where a buzzard was circling elegantly. On the far balcony a carpet was being beaten. The cheerfulness of life began to seep back into their veins.

But it would take a while. Will knew that Tom was holding gloomy thoughts at bay. The sight of Newgate's walls had been a reminder of its horrors – how close at hand they were.

The wall at their backs was beginning to heat up in the sun. Will laid his hat on the table and loosened his cravat:

'They *had* to return, Tom – it was the only way. Any other course would mark them as guilty. You do see that?'

'Yes of course. Our mission has been a complete success: we have heard their stories and have persuaded them to return. I think Elias will be pleased.'

This sounded resigned rather than hopeful. Will looked askance at him:

'You say *their stories*. Were you not convinced? You sound uncertain.'

'You're the lawyer, Will – but don't you think it's a complicated business? I do believe them … at least, I don't like to *dis*believe them.'

'Ah! A nice distinction.'

'I was moved – and yes, convinced … but both of them are players …'

Tom checked himself, aware of where his logic might lead him.

'… It's the old problem, isn't it – the theatre? Actors imitate human nature and convey the passions truthfully, and yet it's always a performance. It must be hard to set that aside – to forget your audience.'

'Do you not think they are being honest with us?'

'I suppose I do – but more troublingly, I wonder if they are being entirely honest with each other? There was a show of affection and trust, but something has been bubbling up between them – what Gilbert called *exchanges of words*. Neither of them took that further.'

Will caught the drift:

'Yes, we learned a lot about the Baron's passions, didn't we? All that lust and anger! But what about Gilbert's? I detected a note of jealousy – a hint that Sally was a little too independent. I think Mrs Trotter caught that.'

'And what about Sally?' said Tom. 'She must know her power over men, and what they might be prepared to do for her …'

He looked at Will invitingly and received an uncomfortable look in return.

'Take care, Tom. You seem to be turning them into the Macbeths.'

It was a shocking thought, and not one that either of them wanted to pursue.

'But we must keep Sally's secret, Will – now that you have given your word.'

'Should I not have done so?'

'A moment ago I wasn't sure, but now I see we had to agree. It was the most private of confidences. The scene in the store-room was shocking and she was brave to tell us. And, who knows? Should the turn of events warrant, we may finally speak about it?'

'Yes, Sally and Gilbert must be allowed to tell their own story. I only hope they will see that truth is the best ally of innocence.'

The beer and oysters arrived opportunely, and they were glad of the interruption. Smiles and raised tankards lifted the mood, and they plunged their hands into the icy cask. The knife was wielded, and by tradition, after pausing face to face, they interlocked arms, and after a spirited *hurrah!* the little bluish molluscs slid simultaneously down their throats, the brine dribbling from their chins.

'The thirtieth of April,' said Will. 'We've timed it well!'

'Yes, these delicious creatures are the unlucky ones. Another day and they would have been safe.'

Their talk began to relax a little; but before conviviality took over entirely, they knew they had to return to the difficult topic of the murder. The threat of scandal hung over the Drury Lane company, and the Baron's death would do them damage whatever the outcome. But if Sally and Gilbert were innocent, then a dirty political motive began to loom. Widow Trotter's suspicions about a conspiracy were becoming persuasive. Pinkerman seemed to be taking the same view, and if they were right, then the plot would surely reach its climax at the Fair. Any later, and all would unwind and disperse with the summer.

Tom was puzzled:

'But if the reformers *are* conspiring against the company, what would they gain from the Baron's death? Yes, it embarrasses the playhouse, but that can be achieved in less terrible ways. And why murder the man who was planning a reformation himself?'

'Yes, that's a problem – unless we imagine a *counter-*conspiracy in the theatre ...'

Will broke off. His phrase brought a wry smile to his lips – it sounded far-fetched. But Tom didn't smile:

'It alarms me, Will. Lord Tunbridge's plans for the theatre must have stirred up a lot of fear and anger. Seen in that light, his death is an easy solution. Might it have tempted someone?'

Will was astonished at the thought:

'Christopher Rich, do you mean? ... Surely not? – No, no, this is turning Drury Lane into the Turkish court.'

'Well, such a scene has been played out on that very stage, has it not?'

'More than once, yes. But ...'

'But what?' asked Tom pointedly. 'The whole thing has a dramatic character to it. The murder took place during a performance, in a costume store, and with an Italian poniard. If someone was wanting to make a theatrical gesture, then they succeeded!'

'Yes, it's theatrical – but what kind of drama is it? The murder is real enough, but everything else is conjecture. Is it a love plot? A political conspiracy against the theatre? A struggle for power in the company? If this was a court of law we would have something solid to work with – a charge brought, arguments to construct, and evidences to challenge.'

'That's your world, Will – not that a law court doesn't have its own dramas.'

'True, but we need some facts to build on – and we have to decide what we can best do. We can't simply let events take their course.'

'No, we're already involved. And in any case, Elias and Mrs Trotter wouldn't allow it! … But where shall we start?'

A pensive silence, and more oysters. Tom was the first to speak:

'I think we should begin with the reformers. If something is being planned for the May Fair, then we have little time left – only a few days.'

'Yes, that makes sense … So, if they are hatching a plot, how can we find out what it is – and who *they* are?'

The discussion came to a pause again. They raised their mugs of beer (that age-old stimulus to ingenuity) and pondered the question to the accompaniment of oyster-shells popping and creaking. Tom was thinking about the anonymous letters, and whether they might ask Christopher Rich for more details about them … Will was thinking about his father …

'I have an idea, Tom – a practical suggestion. It may give us a slim chance of knowing what faces us.'

'I'm all ears!'

'I wonder if *His Honour Judge Lundy* might yield something? My father has knowledge of the Society, and Reformation of Manners has been his favourite theme for years – he has delivered many a lecture from the bench on the subject.'

'It would certainly be worth trying. But they are such a secretive cabal – *clandestine* is the word – how could you entice information from him?'

'Well, that would be the challenge … What would you say if I walked over to Hackney on Sunday for the Lundy ritual? A heavy sermon in the meeting-house, a delicate negotiation of my spiritual state with my aunts, a hearty Sabbath roast, a furtive game of chess – if my aunts allowed it? There would be no drink to loosen father's tongue, but I might draw something out of him. It would allow him to preach to me, which he always enjoys. And if I show myself curious about the *excellent work* of the Society …'

'That's devilishly clever, Will. But would you get away with it? Of course, you could link it to the Law – perhaps that blasphemy case of yours?'

'Yes – he might not be able to resist talking about that. And I could raise the topic of the theatre … He doesn't know about my recent conversion to the delights of the Drury Lane stage, so perhaps if I were to *waver* and manifest some dangerous curiosity in that direction, it might bring out the minister in him? … But I would have to be very careful.'

'And Lord Tunbridge? Would that be pushing things too far?'

'It might be. But we shall see … So you think it would be a good plan?'

'An excellent one. I only wish I could be a tiny mouse in the corner of the room, so I could overhear your talk.'

'I would not advise it. Aunt Rebecca would squash you with her broom. She's ruthless – and very agile for one of the Elect.'

A second jug of ale was ordered, and gradually the two of them brought their discussion back to the Drury Lane company and the forthcoming adventures of the May Fair. This would begin on Monday with three days of trading in cattle and hides until the traders emptied their pens and left Brook Field to the vagabonds and sharpers, acrobats and players. Then would come thirteen days of carnival, when the boundaries of Nature and Decorum would be tested to breaking-point.

It was several minutes before the conversation progressed to *The Tender Courtesan* and Will was able to pose the crucial question:

'How is your prologue progressing? Is anything down on paper yet?'

In his reply Tom attempted nonchalance – it was a mere thirty lines after all, not an epic:

'I have a few ideas. Pinkerman told me he needed it for the first booth rehearsal on Monday. The opening performance is to be Thursday – but now I don't know what will happen. If Ernesto and Tamara are taken into custody, then he's facing disaster.'

'I suppose he must be arranging deputies?'

'Surely, yes – but at this stage it would be a patched-up job – it throws everything out. He could postpone it, and open with *The Devil on Two Sticks*.'

'Ah, the satirical piece! Have you got wind of what he's doing with that?'

'Something highly irresponsible, I assume – the show is being written as we speak! By all accounts Pinkerman is in such a bustle over the set, which is to be something new. Of course, as usual he has to compete with Miller's booth, which promises a monstrous mish-mash of *The Tempest* and *Macbeth!* He says Miller is to give us singing mermaids, Neptune's chariot drawn by sea-horses, and lots of other stuff – and three comedy witches to provide the humour ...'

'That sounds like a crowd-pleaser!'

'Pinkerman isn't impressed – he's intending *The Tender Courtesan* as a more classic drama – much against advice – but he says he's already giving the rabble plenty to hoot at with *The Devil!* ... Oh yes – this will please you – we're to have the Dutch dancing dogs again.'

'Hurrah!'

'And of course there will be the elephant ...'

'Ah – the elephant! No other booth can compete with that! ... Oh dear, Tom, I've just had a thought ... your prologue ... you don't think ... do you?'

Will broke off, and received the kind of eloquent look that said 'yes, I *have* thought of that, and it makes my blood run cold.'

'... like Ned Ward's epilogue last year?'

In one of the more memorable performances at the previous fair, Pinkerman had delivered an epilogue while seated on the back of a nine-foot elephant. The animal took the whole thing in its stride, but the audience's response was ecstatic. Needless to say, the epilogue itself slipped into immediate obscurity while the elephant triumphed – it was the sensation of the Fair. The splendid beast had been one of Pinkerman's more speculative investments, brought over from Guinea with its boy handlers – and by popular acclaim it was due to reappear at this year's fair – though in what role was yet to be determined.

Will downed his beer and watched Tom do the same. He hesitated.

'... I suppose your prologue could work the beast in somehow? Remember, in the Garden of Eden Milton has an elephant entertaining Adam and Eve ... it's the first laughter in Paradise! ... You could talk about the creature as a comic *original* – the innocence of a sportive humour ...'

Tom's hand began making its way surreptitiously towards the oyster barrel.

'... or perhaps it's the figure of the *satirist?* ... I can see the bulky form making a point about the robustness of the satiric poet ... you could stress the creature's memory of past grievances which it stores under its hide – with large ears to hear what is said ... and the trunk to feel its way around and sniff the air ... and those formidable tusks to tear its enemies when roused ... No enemy can touch it! The thing is immune from mockery, being itself the mockery of Nature ... it is itself a *satire* ...'

Tom's hand came closer to the barrel, the fingers flexing.

'... And of course, the elephant has a remarkably thick skin – the barbs of critics are mere pinpricks to it. The creature stands its ground. It may not be beautiful, but it's a four-square animal – admittedly a bit stubborn … but devilish difficult when roused …'

Will's meditation was cut short by a generous cascade of icy water, a satisfying amount of which – with immediate satiric effect – crept down his neck and along his backbone.

At the sudden shock, Tom's victim gave a shrill whoop that was something between outrage and exhilaration:

'*Pax!*' he cried, '*Pax* of your prologue! …'

Tom was grinning widely.

'… I plead the licence of satire!'

Will's own hand spontaneously went to the jug, but it was now empty, so that only drips emerged when it was inverted over Tom's head.

'I see we need more supplies. Shall we call a truce?'

The negotiation was brief, and when the next jug of beer arrived Will's retribution was suspended – in exchange for the full story of *the raspberries*.

'You said it belonged to your *theatrical days*. When were they? I didn't know you'd had any!'

'Childhood innocence, Will! In the summer holidays I was the Betterton of the Monkton Court theatricals!'

'An excuse for dressing up, eh?'

'Yes, and for exercising my talents with the pen. I wrote a few little plays – on big subjects, and always with a heroic part for myself.'

'Didn't the Pophams find this a bit wearing?'

'On the contrary – I had the resources of the estate carpenter and a local seamstress at my disposal. Uncle Jack was very encouraging.'

'But where do the raspberries come in?'

'Ah – that was Julius Caesar!'

'You performed Shakespeare?'

'Oh no – it was Bristowe's *Death of Caesar* – a playlet that achieved a single momentous performance. Unlike Shakespeare's version, it has not entered the repertory ... For the assassination I hit on the idea of using bags of blood – not real blood of course, but raspberries from the kitchen garden (when crushed they make a wonderfully rich colour). For the murder scene I hid a bag of juice beneath my toga – without telling the conspirators. I also couldn't resist consuming a great deal of the delicious fruit myself – rather too much as it turned out ... Well, the audience in the great hall were treated to a vivid representation, and some rousing poetry – it was Bristowe at his finest.'

'You wrote in verse?'

'Of course – I didn't wish to be outdone by the bard of Stratford! ... Well, after a deal of ranting and buffeting, the moment of my death was quite a spectacle. The bag of crushed fruit burst to great effect under my white toga – but I hadn't allowed for the sensitivities of my young murderers (Frank and Lavinia included) – wooden daggers in hand, they were horror-struck by the blood that seeped everywhere – through the toga, down my legs, and onto the stage in liberal quantities. By this time my stomach was queasy, and so a further surge of raspberry fluid was projected from my mouth ... I'm afraid the audience were not immune from the *coup de théâtre* ... and at the end of the drama the stage was like a butchers' shambles.'

Will was dumbfounded by the picture – the world of aristocratic theatricals! He thought of his own childhood when the mere presence of a playbook in the house would have brought a lightning bolt from heaven.

'What would the old Puritans have said to that, Tom? Their worst nightmare come to life!'

'There were never many Puritans in the vicinity of Monkton, I can tell you! The house was a royalist stronghold. Lots of fancy dress, and music and masquing in the old days. But then the Civil War ...'

'The estate was sequestered, was it not?'

'Yes, for a time – and the living too. The Pophams were outlawed by Cromwell's generals.'

'Just as my grandfather lost his living when the Restoration came.'

'What a chequered history, Will! – Cromwell and Charles – Parliament and the Court – Lundys and Pophams! It's all of half a century ago, yet the old divide is still with us, isn't it? The *Saints* and the *Sinners!*'

By this point, both young men were gazing philosophically into their foaming ale.

'Not here though, Tom – *not now!* Let us heal the wounds – we two!'

Their slouching bodies were brought to attention, and their tankards charged and formally raised.

'To *Great Britain!* The new nation!'

'The new nation!'

Will was eager and animated, but Tom's face betrayed a lingering uneasiness.

'But we're a frivolous people today, are we not? We love *shows* of all kinds – it's everywhere you look.'

Will laughed:

'How solemn you are! Do you see what's happening to us? – I'm about to become a frivolous theatrical Lundy – while you are showing every sign of an emerging Puritanism. Shall we blame the exchange on the oysters?'

Tom saw the irony and joined in the laughter:

'Happily! And tomorrow is a holiday, remember – the First of May ... So, if we're looking for frivolity, it will be easy to find. The Strand will be thronged around the great maypole.'

'Good King Charles's glorious legacy! There's sure to be

enough dancing and prancing to make Cromwell turn in his grave.'

'Yes, we'll all become pagans for the day. I understand Mrs Trotter is to swathe the Bay-Tree in greenery.'

'It will not be a comfortable day for the reformers, Tom. I hope they don't show themselves.'

'They would be wise not to. There's little to match a crowd of May-Day revellers when the drink is flowing!'

'I take it the serious-minded Bristowe will be shut away in his study penning his Prologue?'

'I think not. A prologue mustn't be studious and over-worked – it should have an air of spontaneity and liveliness. A touch of the festive!'

'I'm relieved to hear it ... So, if we were to join the crowds at the maypole, you might find some holiday inspiration?'

'Undoubtedly. I need to put myself into the mood of *The Tender Courtesan*.'

'I'm not sure tenderness is quite in your line, Tom? ... But tomorrow on May Day, love will be in the air! Perhaps that will spark off something?'

'Let us hope so ... But just now, can I play the Puritan once again? ...'

He looked at Will, who was having tender thoughts of his own and was attempting to build a tower out of the empty oyster shells.

'... We need to report back to Elias and Mrs Trotter. Today we're still on duty, remember!'

'Ah, the stern goddess Duty! She's a formidable lady! ...'

Will swung round and his elbow caught the shell-tower, which collapsed in a heap.

'... Let us go, then – while we still can ... but perhaps some dinner first?'

Saturday

1 May 1708

Chapter Thirteen

May Morning, and the day had dawned bright and cloudless. For a few precious hours it seemed as if a purer world were being unveiled and London was a virgin bride decking herself in pastoral garments – bright greens, pinks, and yellows. By eight o'clock the countryside appeared to be invading the city, with little groups of holidaymakers strolling in from Islington, Clerkenwell and Moorfields, their faces lit by the early sun. The hopeful Damons and Sylvias had gathered plunder from the hedgerows and were holding switches of hazel and laurel, sprigs of sweet-briar still with the dew on them, and knots of apple and cherry. And of course there was white hawthorn in profusion, the May-blossom itself. Lots of it. The girls were freshly beribboned, and the boys wore daisies in their hats. The less optimistic expressed a love-melancholy by girding their heads with garlands of willow. It was a centuries-old springtime scene, and it had the innocence of all beginnings – the thought of what the day would bring, and what might unfold for each of them with the arrival of the new season.

In Red Lion Court, Covent Garden (a distinctly unpastoral corner of the metropolis), the decking of the Bay-Tree Chocolate House with greenery was a communal enterprise. A start had been made with Widow Trotter's new prize: a little bay-tree, which now graced the front door and offered both an invitation and an aspiration to the patrons. Jenny Trip had lived up to her name, bouncing in early with an armful of spiky beech-twigs gathered on her morning walk, and Tom had been busy in the market, happy to have secured a few chestnut branches, their buds sticky and just about to burst. With the help of a ladder, the energetic Jeremy was nailing the spoils along the bar canopy and over the doors, while Peter arranged small pots of spring flowers on the tables. By the time Old Ralph began sweeping the floor, the place was on its way to becoming a leafy bower, although its peace was broken periodically by tumultuous sneezes.

As usual, the news of the day began to flow in with the early customers, and with each arrival Widow Trotter was increasingly apprehensive. She expected the door to burst open at any moment announcing the sensational arrest of the young actress and her jealous lover, with appropriate embellishments of intrigue and passion. But the minutes passed routinely, and nothing arrived to disturb the calm of the place. Even the goddess Rumour seemed to have gone quiet, or was still a-bed.

Mrs Trotter had received a full report the previous evening when Tom and Will returned from their adventures in Holborn, and a message had been conveyed to Constable Cobb who had promised to call at the Bay-Tree once he had a spare moment. But it seemed this would now be delayed, given what had happened during the night.

In the early hours, down in Henrietta Street a gaming-house had been 'visited,' and in the upstairs room a convivial extended family had been discovered celebrating May Morning in the modern way with the domestic pleasures of drinking, dining, coupling, and relaxing. The happy band consisted of mothers and fathers, brothers and sisters, aunts and uncles, all joining in the venereal ritual – and all found upon investigation to be men. The new Covent Garden magistrate was eager to root out the 'mollies,' and Elias had found himself having to take details from a group of weeping and pleading gentlemen in various kinds of costumed embarrassment.

But there was still no news of Sally and Gilbert. Tom had gleaned little from his early visit to the market which was buzzing with the 'molly-house' business, and he had headed down Drury Lane to see what was stirring at the theatre. As she stood behind the bar twirling a hawthorn-twig round her fingers, Widow Trotter ran over the situation in her mind.

From what Tom and Will had told her, the two young fugitives had a convincing story. The Baron's assaults on Sally were only too plausible, and Gilbert had evidently been angered by them. She sensed that during the interview it was Gilbert who had appeared the more uneasy – or was it simply that Sally had been the more brazen?

She wondered about everyone's movements during the interval of *The Man of Mode*. One or two things niggled her. Was Gilbert in the green room throughout? – there must have been witnesses – and was his hurried exchange with Sally quite as he had reported it? Why did she not tell him of the attack? And if the Baron had left the stage in order to confront Sally, why did he not look into the green room for her, where Gilbert would have seen him? And why was there a lit candle in the store-room? …

Mary Trotter ran these questions through her mind. Each one hinted at a slightly different story, but could they be made to fit together? With a slight shiver she realised that one scene was taking hold of her imagination, and it was not a comfortable one. She fancied that Sally, as she hurried back to the stage, had told Gilbert of the attempted rape and that the Baron was in the store-room gripped by some kind of momentary seizure – that Gilbert had rushed to confront him, and there had been an angry altercation … and Gilbert's hand had driven the dagger home …

The scene was worthy of a stage tragedy, and this gave her pause. It was easy to picture a love-plot. But she knew that another plot was possible – one that made the killing part of a larger story of political and religious intrigue. She couldn't erase from her mind the fact that Lord Tunbridge was a man with *reforming* ambitions. What precisely were his relations with the Society? This was something they needed to look into. There were other passions beside lust and jealousy which could lead to murder – a dagger through the heart could also be cold and calculating.

The coffee-room was filling up, and Mrs Trotter's attention was claimed by routine matters. Her thoughts on the murder had begun tumbling over each other, turning everything into a question, and churning it like butter. So it was a relief to be faced with immediate problems that needed practical solutions: a dropped snuff-box; a sudden shortage of lemons; a dispute over the rules of backgammon; the ripping of the curtain that screened the commode.

And all around her was the familiar background music of the chocolate house itself – the hum of well-modulated conversation enlivened by notes of genial laughter and accompanied by the regular percussive clink of pennies on the bar. Whatever enormities were happening in the world outside, she liked to think the Bay-Tree offered some relief – a refreshment for body and spirit. It was a place of sociable relaxation where thoughts could expand and ideas engage. The world was surely a better place for these busy harbours of the mind?

The world eventually found its way in again when the front door opened to admit Tom and Elias in conversation. The two of them approached the bar purposefully. Their eyes were bright and their brows unfurrowed, so at least the news would not be chilling. With a lightened heart she gave them the nod and silently led the way to the back parlour. If they had a story to tell, it was not for sharing with the rest of the room.

While they were settling themselves in her domain, Mrs Trotter began pouring the coffee. She arranged three slices of cheese tart on a plate – one for Tom, and two for Elias who had not breakfasted.

'You know the way to a man's heart, Molly,' he said approvingly.

'I know the short cut to yours, Elias! ...'

She put the plate down between them.

'... Has Tom been telling you his story?'

'He has – at least a sketch of it. My two young deputies did an excellent job yesterday ...'

He smiled approvingly at Tom.

'... You may have saved two lives. I hear the runaways took your advice and strolled into the playhouse as natural as you please, full of eagerness to help and expressing sincere concern for what had happened. They couldn't have performed better!'

Widow Trotter hesitated, uneasy at the idea:

'But did Sally give her account of the Baron's assault? I'm concerned you talk of them acting their parts – I hope she told the *truth,* however embarrassing?'

'Who is to say, Molly? ... But I can tell you the matter is still unresolved. Both Sally and young Gilbert were taken before the Magistrate to give their statements – that much I've learned.'

'Ah yes, was this your Mr Hector? You said he had shut you out of the investigation.'

'Yes – but I have friends who are happy to keep me informed. Our Mr Hector is new to the business. They say *a new broom sweepeth clean,* but in my experience it can be a bit stiff and miss the corners.'

He bit into his tart with a wicked glint in his eye.

Tom intervened:

'Mr Cobb says that neither Gilbert nor Sally has been taken into custody – at least not yet.'

'Is that true, Elias? I had expected the Magistrate would pounce on them.'

'I think he would gladly have charged them – but remember, the "new broom" is in the grip of the Solicitor-General. Our Mr Hector has to tread carefully and not alarm his political masters.'

'So, you think this investigation is being politically directed?'

'I'm sure of it, Molly. The thought troubles me – but it also gives us cause for hope.'

'What makes you say that?'

'Well, from what my friends tell me, there's a good deal of consternation in high places. Lord Tunbridge's murder has been a terrible shock to some important people. The Baron was well connected, and I'm beginning to think his ambitions for the theatre were more than personal – that he was the public face of a larger policy.'

'A *conspiracy*, you mean?'

Widow Trotter relished the word:

'The one often shades into the other.'

He took another bite of the tart and began to chew enigmatically.

'Mr Cobb thinks that Sally's claims of rape would threaten the enterprise of reform ...'

Tom paused. He was impatient, but knew the constable had to be allowed to tell things in his own time.

Mrs Trotter's curiosity was now wide awake:

'So, you think Sally's accusation has upset their plans?'

'I don't know how much Sally has told them; but if I'm right, then Lord Tunbridge's killing becomes a problem for them. It may be they are trying to decide how the affair should be managed.'

'*Managed?* This is a conspiracy indeed!'

Now Tom was lifting his brow:

'I wonder, Mr Cobb, might it suit the reformers' cause for the

Baron to become a martyr to reform – the victim of a company plot? It would be the final nail in the theatre's coffin? Would they steer matters that far?'

'The thought had occurred to me, Mr Bristowe. The more zealous of the reformers might.'

Widow Trotter was beginning to feel anxious:

'Do you mean they will try to present the killing as a company dispute? … but how would that work?'

'It would mean letting Sally and Gilbert fade into the background as an inconvenient complication.'

It was an extraordinary suggestion, and the three of them sat in silence for a moment. Tom was looking puzzled. He wondered if they were allowing their imaginations to run too far:

'Wait a moment, Mr Cobb – are you saying that the Solicitor-General is pressing the Magistrate to direct his fire towards Mr Rich and the company?'

'It sounds fantastic, but I hear that some persuasion is being applied, and Sally is being encouraged to forget that Lord Tunbridge was anything other than a generous patron.'

'And what does Gilbert say to that?' said Mrs Trotter sharply.

'Now, that I don't know. It's certainly a curious state of affairs.'

'Neither of them has been seen at the Playhouse since yesterday,' said Tom. 'Indeed, the people there know less than we do. I had to pretend ignorance … but what I did learn is that tonight's performance of *The Unhappy Favourite* has been cancelled.'

'But it's being advertised …'

'Yes, and the loss of it will be felt. It's a popular play, and with it being the last performance before the Fair – and a public holiday to boot! – Mr Rich was expecting an extremely profitable evening. He's understandably irate.'

'But perhaps a part of him is relieved the theatre is closing for a spell.'

'Yes, that's some compensation – though you know how attached he is to his accounts!'

The conversation had reached a pause, and the three of them sat back in their chairs pondering. Elias was enjoying the last of his second cheese tart, while Tom and Mrs Trotter were more quietly contemplative.

'So, what are we to *do*, gentlemen?' said their Field-General, pushing her cup to one side and leaning forward in purposeful fashion. 'I know Tom and Will have a plan for tomorrow – at least Will does.'

Tom accepted the hint and turned to Elias:

'Will is to have one of his Hackney Sabbaths, Mr Cobb. The plan is to draw out his father on the subject of the Reformation of Manners. Judge Lundy is a bit of a reformer himself, and Will is sure he has links to the societies.'

'That's an excellent move, Mr Bristowe. Something is afoot, and the reformers are organising themselves. During the past week they have been more active. Last night's raid on the molly-house is sure to provoke a pamphlet or two.'

'Yes, we heard about that,' said Mrs Trotter. 'The coffee-room was abuzz with it earlier.'

'The market too,' said Tom.'

'Well, it was a sad affair altogether. The gentlemen were pathetic creatures, I fear. Some were defiant, but there was a deal of shaking and sobbing … I give little hope for the chances of two of them.'

'What do you mean, Elias?'

'I mean that they were caught in the heat of their performance. The act was witnessed and cannot be denied … You know what will happen, especially now the societies are feeling so confident.'

'Death?'

'Yes. No quarter will be given … There's a chance one of the pair could be reprieved, depending on how they sort out the pleas between them – but certainly not both. It's another case of making an example.'

'Oh dear, Elias. This is more ammunition against the playhouse, is it not? You know the charges that are always being made against the actors.'

'Yes, it plays right into their hands. "*It is an abomination!*" as the Bible proclaims. I'm sure we'll be hearing more in that vein ... As I say, I fear for them.'

Tom was looking darkly thoughtful:

'And the holiday celebrations today – they will surely raise the heat even more ... and when the Fair begins next week ...'

'Yes, early May is a difficult time, Mr Bristowe – the burst of springtime energies – the blood rising with the sap!'

'That's a distinctly pagan idea, Mr Cobb.'

'It's a very ancient one.'

'Do you think the *old gods* are stirring?'

Elias said nothing, but his raised eyebrows gave a kind of answer.

'Well, something is,' said Widow Trotter. 'Today the Strand will be a Fair in itself. And folk will be dizzying themselves around the maypole. Last year with the celebration of the Union the crowds were larger than ever, and today's fine weather is bound to draw people in. It's always a happy occasion, but things grow a little wild as the day wears on. This year I'm being prudent – the Bay-Tree closes its doors at *twelve*. I'm happy to forego the pennies and let the *merry mayers* have the streets to themselves.'

'Will you be joining them, Mrs T?'

'I'll certainly walk down to the Strand. I love to see the milkmaids parading, and the chimneysweepers too – those poor children rarely have the chance to dance! I'll be taking a bag of copper with me. I love these old customs ...'

She lifted her head, and a distant look came into her eyes – it was one Tom hadn't seen before. She was almost smiling.

'... When I was a little girl my mother used to take me to watch the May Day dancing there – we would get up at dawn and walk down the hill from Highgate. She used to tell me how much the great maypole meant to her. Of course, when she was a child there was none of this *celebration* – there was no holidaying, no dancing, no parading, no costumes – and (heaven forbid!) no maypole! Cromwell's generals didn't allow it. She used to tell the story about seeing the great pole being first set up after the Restoration – just where it stands now. In those days it was an even mightier thing – *one hundred and thirty-four feet,* would you believe? It was a great occasion. King Charles and his brother were there supervising its erection. There was a gigantic pulley, and a whole troop of sailors hauled on the ropes. She told me they were powerful men with massive brawny arms! It must have been an unforgettable day ... Of course, there was such happiness in the air – they all thought the dark days were over ...'

She looked at Elias.

'... Ah well – I'm beginning to sound like a sad spinster, aren't I!'

'No, Molly. I remember the old May Days clearly. Your Henry and I were always given an afternoon's holiday – but you know what apprentices are like! We were expected to misbehave, and we did. But somehow the Watch never caught us – we kept dodging into the crowd.'

Tom smiled at Elias. The Covent Garden constable clearly knew the law from both sides.

The three of them continued happily chatting and reminiscing. It was as if time stood still, and they were beginning to feel a holiday mood growing in them ... But it didn't last long. They had begun talking about the Bay-Tree's own apprentice, Peter Simco, and how the coffee-boy was fast becoming the spirit of the chocolate house – such a smart, skilful young fellow, always good-humoured and patient with the customers … when there was a sharp noise in the distance, and a sudden cry. Widow Trotter swung round. A door banged, and a shout came from the neighbouring kitchen. A second later the parlour door burst open to reveal an alarmed Jeremy, his eyes wide, and his mop of hair shaking like straw in the wind.

'You'd better come quick, Mrs Trotter!'

He turned tail and ran back towards the coffee-room, closely followed by the three of them. There they found Jenny Trip standing in front of the bar, holding something in her hand. Broken glass littered the floor. A group of bewigged gentlemen were looking shocked, some peering out of the front window, which had a gaping hole in it. What had happened was all too clear. Elias ran out of the door, but knew there would be nothing to see, and he stood there, his face burning with anger. The small bay tree by the entrance had been kicked over, and was lying on its side, half-uprooted.

'Who has done this?' said Mrs Trotter. 'Did anyone catch them?'

'They were too quick, Mrs T,' said Jenny. 'By the time someone ran outside they'd disappeared – we don't know in which direction.'

Widow Trotter's heart sank. Jenny handed the stone to her – it was quite small, about four inches across. But it wasn't just a stone. Tied tightly around it was a scrap of paper.

'I think it's carrying a message,' said Tom grimly as she tried to pull off the thick thread that encircled it. She unfolded the paper.

'Yes. Let's see … it's not a message, Tom – just a reference – to the Bible.'

She handed it to him, and his brow furrowed as he read:

'*Deut. 12:3* … Deuteronomy! – No doubt some reminder of the *Old Law*, wouldn't you think? How predictable is this! … I'll fetch my bible …'

He hurried off and was back downstairs within the minute, clutching the sacred text. He gave it to Widow Trotter, who turned the leaves clumsily – she was annoyed to see her hands were shaking. When she came to the passage, she spoke the words clearly and loudly – loud enough, in fact, for the whole room to hear them:

'Deuteronomy, Chapter Twelve, Verse Three …

"And ye shall overthrow their altars, and break their pillars, and burn their groves with fire; and ye shall hew down the graven images of their gods, and destroy the names of them out of that place."'

There was silence.

'Idolatry! So that's what we're being accused of, are we? Setting up images and worshipping in our sacred groves … So much for the May!'

Elias was now standing beside her. He looked up at the green boughs hanging from the bar-canopy, at the bright flowers on the tables, and Tom's sticky chestnut buds now drooping above the window – and at young Peter in his green livery holding a jug of chocolate, his face wide-eyed and frightened.

Elias nodded:

'The struggle is beginning, Molly … and now I think we know what we're fighting for.'

Chapter Fourteen

AFTER THE SHOCK of the morning's events, Widow Trotter was determined to enjoy the release of May Day even more. With the Bay-Tree secured, she walked along Drury Lane with a spring in her step, ready to mingle with the holiday throng. At the point where it met Little Drury Lane, the Strand swelled to create a natural oval – almost an amphitheatre – and there at its centre was the maypole, which seemed to preside over the large crowd and could be seen along the length of the street, from its western end curving down toward Whitehall and St James's, to the east sweeping up to Temple Bar and Fleet Street. The Strand was the main thoroughfare linking Westminster and the City, and on this special day people had poured there from all directions. One or two aristocratic coaches huddled in the distance – unlike the Lord Mayor's Day this was not their occasion. The silken fashions of St James's were best kept hidden. This was a defiantly homespun assembly.

Not that there weren't costumes a-plenty – but these were holiday clothes decorated with ribbons, with dresses sporting wilder frills and flounces according to fancy. The style was certainly not strait-laced – gowns were loose and flo[illegible]air was unbound, and everywhere there were sashes an[illegible]s, which also hung in mimicry from the street lamps. A slight breeze kept everything on the move. Widow Trotter had caught the spirit of the occasion with a dress of pale green cotton topped by a bodice embroidered with roses, and a silk gauze scarf hung past her waist. The châtelaine of the Bay-Tree was not by nature ethereal, but there was more than a hint of Titania in the coronet of May-blossom that girded her loose auburn hair.

There was music all around, and as Mary Trotter moved along, sounds from different directions caught her ear. Somewhere a band was marching to the accompaniment of fife and drum, while behind her a softer tabor and pipe with jingling bells suggested that morris-men were prancing. In the far distance a ballad was being rather beautifully sung in a clear soprano, its strains intermittently snatched away by the breeze. Accompanying it all, and bringing the open-air concert to life, were the cries of the hawkers and street-vendors, hallooing their wares: 'Dainty Sweet Nosegays!' 'Fair Lemons and Oranges!' 'Holland Socks – Four Pair for a Shilling!' 'Four for Six pence – Mackrell!' The chants echoed one another across the street, the sounds curving through the air in lengthened notes as if mimicking the antiphonal singing in one of the new City churches whose spires were rising to the east. But today it was the people's music, and the whole thing made an extraordinary symphony.

She made her way through the press of bodies, checking that the bag of coins was still secure in her pocket. She had a handful of farthings ready. This was a day when begging was licensed and purses were opened generously, but also 'twitched' along with watches and snuff boxes. The young pick-pockets worked in pairs, one causing a distraction while the other fingered away the booty with a delicate twitch of the hand. The coming May Fair would be the chief theatre for this distinctive skill, but the May-day gathering was a useful rehearsal.

There was also a sombre element to this miscellany. Every few minutes she passed a soldier returned from the European war with a leg or arm shot away, cap in hand, leaning on a crudely-fashioned wooden crutch. She caught sight of a legless young man squat on a low trolley who was pushing himself along with a pair of hand-crutches. She winced at the pain of it, but not in disgust. These raw, discomforting figures were not alien, she thought – on the contrary, they were at home in this London scene, and on a day like this they were as much on parade as any gentleman with wig and cane.

And there, in a holiday dress of its own, was the towering maypole. Above the heads of the onlookers she could see the long ribbons entwining themselves as the dancers wove around each other, in and out, up and down. The distinct colours formed a braided diamond pattern that worked its way gradually down the pole, before being unwound as the dancers reversed and untwisted the fabric. She had watched the effect so many times over the years, but the blending of music, dance and weaving colours never ceased to fascinate her.

She scanned the crowd, and across to the right, individual faces came into profile. People were smiling and gazing in wonder; some pointed gleefully, others nodded their heads to the beat as if longing to join the dance; here and there, infants were perched on the shoulders of their parents, silent and transfixed.

And then, amidst all the delight, she saw a face that wasn't smiling. The figure was standing on the far pavement, a little detached from the main body of the crowd. He was dressed in a grey woollen suit which looked funereal amid the holiday colours. Widow Trotter could hardly believe it, and stared. She felt a sudden chill at her neck and knew her mouth was open … It was the man in the theatre-box – she was sure of it. Her angle of vision was the same, and so was the unforgettable look on that face caught in imperious profile. It was a cold half-smile, like an absolute monarch conscious of his power.

In her imagination the crowd seemed to melt away and leave just the two of them sharing that vast space. It was a strange sensation. She could feel his presence so strongly that he must surely sense hers too? Instinctively she moved slightly to the left behind a tall neighbour and began thinking quickly. This time she wouldn't let him out of her sight! She had arranged to meet Tom and Will in an hour's time and wished they were here now so they could work as a team. But she was on her own. It was an uncomfortable situation. She stood stock still and waited.

Suddenly the man swung his face in her direction, and their eyes seemed to meet. It was as if he sensed her watching him. She pulled back, heart pounding, feeling she must have been noticed. Anxious seconds ticked by before she attempted another look. He was now in close conversation with another man, their heads almost touching. Through the milling crowd she saw his head nodding gravely. Someone moved in front of her and she was forced to stand on tiptoe in order to hold the picture ... Was something being handed over? She couldn't quite tell. There was more intense talk, and then the man's hand rested itself on the visitor's shoulder. It was a formal gesture – almost a comradely blessing. Something was going on.

But there was no time to consider further. The visitor bowed his head slightly and turned away – in her direction but thankfully not exactly towards her. He had a distinctive grey beard trimmed short in continental fashion, and the eyes had a furtive look. Widow Trotter quickly decided she must follow him. It was a difficult choice, but something important – a message perhaps – had passed between them and it could be crucial to know where the man was heading. She sensed that he held a secret.

What came next was an awkward version of the maypole dance as the two of them wove in and out among the holiday throng. The figure was strolling easily through the crowd, and

Widow Trotter was able to do the same. She adopted a slightly distracted air, trying to avoid faces as much as possible, and glanced at her prey through the corner of her eye.

Beyond Somerset House the crowd began thinning out, although there was still a good number of Saturday strollers and shoppers. She found herself walking about fifty yards back along the pavement – any nearer and it might look suspicious. Thankfully her quarry appeared to have little thought of being tracked – least of all by a respectable widow of forty dressed as a Covent Garden Pastorella. She fixed her eyes on the leather satchel he was clutching to his shoulder. What wouldn't she give to know its contents! She began to wonder what Elias would do. Had she been right to leave her post and trail him? Step followed step, and still the man didn't turn round.

Approaching to her left was the arcade of the New Exchange where groups of elegant people were conversing on the pavement and under the arches. This was no longer the holiday crowd but a sample of the *bon ton* of St James's. She had left *the City* behind, and here was the beginning of *the Town*, where the money made in the City was spent. Widow Trotter wondered if the man was heading towards an aristocratic address near the palace – or was governmental Whitehall his destination? Well, she would soon know.

She was readying herself for the busy junction of Charing Cross, when the man was suddenly nowhere to be seen. He must have turned into the open arcade of the Exchange. She put on a spurt and made her way inside. The vaulted space echoed to the hum of conversation and the clicking of shoes on its marble floor. The shops were upstairs, but some very fine things were on display here at ground level – not least the latest styles in ladies and gentlemen, who were promenading along the concourse. There was also a good selection of men of affairs holidaying from their offices. On this day even more than usual, the arcade was the site for romantic assignations, both polite and mercenary. Some of the finest-dressed women were strolling alone, trailing exotic perfumes. Widow Trotter stood in the middle of the throng and turned her head to left and right, not knowing which direction to take and unnervingly aware that she might be mistaken for a woman of 'business' herself.

At last she saw him at the far end of the arcade. Amidst the colour and movement, his very inconspicuousness singled him out. At once she surged forward in pursuit. It was a tricky manoeuvre – in this place the women's dresses took up a lot of room and gentlemen's canes swung out from their hips. Couples glided swan-like in a leisurely style she couldn't attempt to emulate. She squeezed past them like an over-eager spaniel.

Ahead of her, the man began mounting the grand staircase that led up to the shopping galleries, and his head disappeared behind the balustrade. She strode on, but happened to catch the dress of a young belle who was flouncing before her beau. The genteel Belinda swung her ringlets in annoyance and her eyes narrowed satirically. Whispering to her friend, she pointed her fan at the May-day coronet that still decorated Mrs Trotter's unruly locks – clearly a rustic creature from the wrong end of the Strand! It was a timely hint, and so, as she mounted the broad staircase, she discarded the garland and began setting her mind to the serious business of shopping.

Now there was a dilemma. There were parallel galleries. The right-hand gallery, or the left? She chose the right – no point in hesitating – and hoped for the best. The long walkway stretched ahead of her, a row of upper windows giving the whole space a bright aspect. On either side of this indoor street were dozens of tiny shops, each one partitioned off from its neighbour, with a little opening alongside the counter so the purchaser could examine the wares. Shelves of goods were displayed, and dangling from the ceilings were stockings, scarves and handkerchiefs. The whole place was a polite bazaar, but instead of Arab traders there were frock-coated gentlemen, and ladies with servants and lapdogs in attendance. Behind the counters were shop-girls chosen for their delicate hands, and sparkish boy-apprentices in white linen cravats trying to catch the eyes of potential customers.

Widow Trotter made her way slowly down the avenue, glancing to either side. To her right was a handkerchief shop with samples hanging from a cord stretched above the counter. She moved towards it, taking the opportunity to glance round – and there was the man – behind her! She paused to cast her eye over the handkerchiefs, then moved on at a natural pace, keeping a couple of yards behind him. Smoothly done!

She wondered what had brought him to this place of fashionable indulgence, the preserve of haberdashers, perfumers and milliners. But he wasn't looking at any of the wares on display. He was a man with a mission.

At last the moment arrived. He suddenly checked himself, and his face inclined slightly to the left. He appeared to be eyeing the Haberdasher's shop three stalls along, in front of which an elderly gentleman was trying on a hat while the shopkeeper held a mirror before him. Widow Trotter sensed this was his destination – but he would have to wait till the customer had been served. And so, while he hesitated, she eased past him and allowed her interest to be caught by the shop that was next along. Fortunately it was free and was selling gloves. Like a boat steering gracefully into harbour, she drew nonchalantly to the side and dropped anchor.

The young shop-girl was attentive, and they discussed material, size, colour ... For once Mrs Trotter became the fussy shopper, wondering aloud if the grey kidskin might look a little too formal – perhaps something more colourful and embroidered? The girl kept returning to sort through her stock.

After several minutes of to-ing and fro-ing she told the girl she would like to try them on again quietly, one by one, so as to make up her mind.

At last, before the scene descended even further into social comedy, the old gentleman at the haberdashers moved off, and the hair on the back of Widow Trotter's neck prickled as she heard another shopper take his place. Her shoulder was touching the wooden partition, and she could hear some breathy muttering and the creak of leather. She didn't need to turn round to know that it was the man with his satchel. While her gloved hands followed a practised routine, all her attention was being given to the conversation that was beginning a yard behind her back.

She didn't hear every word – far from it – but she caught some phrases, and they chilled her, all the more so for the terseness of the exchanges. The two men were being deliberately enigmatic, though they were evidently paying no heed to the mature, auburn-haired lady next to them, who was now removing a blue velvet glove from her hand with some difficulty.

The connections between the fragments of speech were not always clear, but there was enough to work on.

It is arranged, she heard her man say. *His Lordship has given approval ... it will be in exactly half an hour ... the man is supplied and ready ... a huge crowd ...*

This seemed terrifyingly suggestive. Then, a moment later:

... We have recovered the papers – in here ... This was followed by a creak.

And then the haberdasher spoke:

Is Monday's meeting to proceed, then?

Yes – Middlemiss has everything set up – though it has to be noon – no earlier.

There was more hugger-mugger talk; then she distinctly caught the phrase *adventure at the Fair ...* She strained to catch the precise words that followed, displaying an elegantly gloved hand in the air and leaning back to admire it properly.

Behind her there was a muffled laugh.

Their sins will find them out, eh? ...

This time it will be decisive ...

The tone was gloating – some action was being anticipated. Their voices had lowered further. What were they saying?

She realised they were talking about *the players*. Then she distinctly heard *The Tender Courtesan,* and Pinkerman's name mentioned with derision.

She knew she was on the brink of a crucial discovery.

'I think the *kidskin,* madam, don't you? – they sit so beautifully on your hands ...'

The shop-girl was close to her again and smiled winningly. *Damn!* she thought, and tried to listen, but could make out nothing more – the girl insisted on attending to her discerning customer.

The men's talk was now ended. She caught the words *Till Monday* ... and with that, things went quiet. There was another creak, but no further talk. The man had moved off, back down the gallery.

It wasn't much – sparse pickings – but they were vital ones, and they had imprinted themselves on her memory. It was beyond question a plot – and a carefully planned one. But along with the teasing snippets of information came questions, not least who was *His Lordship?* What *papers* had been recovered? And what was to happen in half an hour's time?

And, worryingly, there was more. What retribution was being planned for the May Fair? Why did the men seem interested in Pinkerman and *The Tender Courtesan?* Tom would have to know about this at once!

Widow Trotter peered at the clock in the distance and saw that she was due to meet with her friends in exactly half an hour!

The coincidence made her shiver. What was going to happen at two o'clock? ... She dared not think of it. But she knew she must return to the maypole without delay. There was important news to share with Tom and Will, and it would be a relief to be in their company. What she had overheard at the Exchange was remarkable, but it brought yet more questions. She needed her friends' wise heads to help make something out of it.

Mary Trotter was not a vain woman. As she made her way back down the sweeping staircase of the Exchange, she never thought to congratulate herself on having played the part of informer so expertly. Instead, she was anxious and thoughtful. She couldn't help feeling that, as well as the kidskin gloves (which she had indeed coveted), she was carrying back something explosive.

Chapter Fifteen

AT THE FAR end of the Strand the maypole-dancing had come to a pause, but a little distance away a solitary fiddler kept people's feet tapping with a country dance-tune. The man's elbow was busy while his coat-tails swung from side to side and his festive cockade nodded along to the melody. The pulse of the festivities was quickening. The crowd was milling around, and everywhere the pie-sellers were doing a brisk trade. Savoury smells wafted on the air with hints of rosemary and mint as country garlands rubbed against each other. With so much living flesh, the tang of sweat was in evidence too, but it floated by on the breeze. Even the scent of Virginia seemed sweeter out here as it mingled with the aromas of cinnamon-cake and gingerbread.

The hawkers were in fine voice, but their cries now had competition from the street children playing hide-and-seek in the throng. The ragamuffins hooted and screamed as they tried to tag each other, slippery as eels, weaving in and out, crouching low, diving under the food-stalls. Their electric energy was beginning to animate the scene. A wheelbarrow of apples was overturned, and a wicker cage full of chickens flew off one of the tables, with the birds beating their wings and screaming in protest.

The Maytime spirit was spreading fast. Revellers emerged from the alehouses light of heart and head. Bosom-brothers embraced one another, and holiday friendships were inaugurated in a mood of patriotic euphoria. Glasses were lifted to the confusion of the French and the hated Louis – toasts drunk not in *Nantes* or *Cognac* but in good honest beer and English gin. Madame Geneva was the lady in fashion, and at a long table the liquor was being dispensed from jugs; fruits were squeezed into it, cordials added to it, dry biscuits dunked in it. The drink brought a glow to the cheeks and seemed to lend a rhythm to every step.

But Mary Trotter was unable to attune herself to the heartbeat of the occasion. Back amidst all this jollity, she felt uncomfortable. She was longing to catch sight of Tom and Will, but every glance threatened to reveal the face of the stranger once again. She wondered if he had fled from the Satanic spectacle, or was he still surveying it with contempt, and perhaps watching her?

'Hey-ho! Mrs T!'

The cry startled her. She turned and noticed a hand raised, and saw to her relief that it was connected to the tall figure of Will Lundy, who had Tom in tow behind him. The pair were grinning broadly, and both were suitably decorated. Will sported a flamboyant blue ribbon tied in a knot above his elbow, while hanging precariously from the side of Tom's head was a garland of bay-leaves, held there by the curls alone. This uneasy laurel-crown did him no favours: the look had slipped from poetic *gravitas* to rakish impudence – a votary of Dionysus rather than Apollo.

'Well met, Mrs Trotter! We've been lucky to find you in the crush ...'

Tom was attempting to adjust his laureate headgear, which had been irreverently tweaked by a hand in the crowd.

'... There's no respect for poetry here! This thing was meant to give me some dignity.'

Will gave him an indulgent look:

'I think people are leaving their dignity at home, Tom. I've tried to encourage him, Mrs T – we saw a fool's cap on one of the stalls which fitted him very nicely. It was scarlet and had a silver bell on top – but he declined it.'

'Not without reason! I was concerned the crowd would take me for a Merry Andrew and expect me to perform.'

'I think he's saving that for the Fair, where there'll be even less dignity on show!'

They were both looking at Widow Trotter, who was smiling at them but had not yet spoken. Something wasn't right, they could see. The expression was fixed, and her eyes were not smiling. There was a moment's silence before Tom spoke:

'You look anxious, Mrs T. You must try to banish what happened this morning – we're here to lift your spirits!'

'Thank you, Tom – I'm relieved to see you both. I've just had an adventure and have been wishing you with me. I have some urgent news. Things are as we feared – we've little time left. Minutes in fact.'

'*Minutes?*' said Will. 'Do you mean it? ...'

Widow Trotter nodded silently, her eyes restless.

'... We need to talk urgently, then. Can we escape the crowd?'

'I don't want us to move far – something may be about to happen ... If only Elias was here, or someone from the watch! We may need them ...'

'Let's move over that way,' said Tom, 'beyond those stalls, by the barrels. We should be able to talk there.'

They had begun making a path through the throng when they heard a sudden bang, and a shriek – and then another bang, and more screaming. It was several seconds before they realised a prankster had detonated some squibs which were creating a merry dance among a knot of girls.

'I thought it had started!' said Mrs Trotter enigmatically.

When they reached the corner by the barrels they saw it was something of a miniature farmyard. A goat was tethered alongside a pile of chicken-coops full of birds clucking away, unaware of the fate that awaited them. With luck the three of them would not be overheard. The minutes were ticking by, so she gave a brisk account of the fragments she had overheard at the Exchange. They could discuss it fully later.

'*In exactly half an hour*, did he say?'

'Yes, Tom, he was very precise. He spoke of a man being *ready*, and being *supplied* ...'

'Supplied with what, I wonder,' said Will. 'A bundle of pamphlets perhaps? ... Or a pistol?'

'And you're sure it had reference to this place?'

'Well, he spoke of the *huge crowd*. And there's nowhere at this moment with such a press of people. He must surely mean something is to happen here? It could be an attack, or a protest ... But *supplied?* Yes, I suppose it might be a bundle of handbills against the May-day celebrations.'

'Let's hope that's all it is,' said Will. 'But you said a *Lord* had given *approval?* And in *exactly* half an hour. Why be so precise? It must be something sudden – some action.'

'It's five minutes before two,' said Tom, consulting his watch. We mustn't take a chance. We do need to find someone. There's such a mass of people here – a sudden panic would be very dangerous.'

They felt helpless.

But before they could think, they were jolted by a high-pitched wheezing that might have come from an old gentleman clearing his throat. This was the unmistakeable sound of bagpipes settling into their drone. And sure enough, the air became disturbed, and there emerged from behind the barrels a little squat fellow with a bloated sack tucked under his arm pumping away merrily. His cheeks swelled as he blew into the pipe while his fingers danced over the stops. The man began walking forward into the smiling crowd, who cleared a way for him – and there, in his wake, appeared one of the most popular May-day sights: a young milkmaid dancing.

On this one day of the year, an exhausted girl stooping under a heavy yoke was transformed into a creature of grace and dignity. She was clothed in a fine linen chemise beneath a pink bodice tagged with ribbons. With her back straight and shoulders set, she was miraculously balancing a decorated milk-pail on her head, wearing it proudly as if it were a queenly crown. Silk ribbons fluttered round it, and the structure was hung with well-polished silver tankards, plates and bowls, the whole creation surmounted by a silver-gilt teapot. The glittering pyramid bobbed up and down as the girl's feet tapped and swung to the music. One of her bare arms supported the majestic structure while the other held her apron out so that it formed a wide pouch for farthings and pennies.

Just for a moment Widow Trotter and her friends stood transfixed at the sheer joy of her dance. The merry milkmaid was a figure plucked out of an innocent pastoral, but there was an urgency too in the way she gripped her apron and darted her eyes around. Her smile was a proud one, but it was still the smile of a beggar making the best of a day when generosity was in the air.

'What strength the poor girl has!' said Tom. 'Even on a holiday she has a weight to carry!'

'That's Jessamy Smith,' said Mrs Trotter. 'She's following her mother in the business – her father keeps a few cows out toward Marybone. We used to take our milk from them.'

'Jessamy! – that's a beautiful name,' said Will. 'Sweet-sounding and sweet-smelling!'

'I wish their milk was the same! When I saw the nasty hovel and the poor beasts kept over their hooves in excrement, I quite lost a taste for it ... We use Chelsea milk now – real country milk – but the Smiths seem to make a decent living nonetheless ...'

Her eyes were still anxiously scanning the scene. All three of them were looking to see if there was any sign of disturbance or if they could glimpse someone in a uniform.

'... But what are we to do, gentlemen? We can't stay here. Something tells me we ought to work our way to the maypole – after all, the pole is the centre of things.'

'Yes, that's a thought,' said Tom. 'We should move there now.'

And so they began walking in the direction of the maypole, whose ribbons were hanging loose while the dancers and musicians sought refreshment. They found their steps synchronising with the bagpipe-tune, which was holding its own amidst all the cries and chatter. Over to their right Jessamy Smith's pyramid of silver was still jogging to the rhythm above the heads of the crowd, like a stately galleon breasting a turbulent sea.

In these circumstances Will had the advantage of height, and so it was he who caught sight of a familiar face treading the pavement at the corner of Little Drury Lane.

'I see *Mudge!* He's over the road. Quick now!'

Without a word more, Will darted off, leaving Tom and Mrs Trotter standing. He navigated the crowd with the skill of an eager law student in the throng of Westminster Hall, and within half a minute he was standing in the young watchman's path. It was a daytime patrol, so Tobias was equipped only with his staff, and in place of the thick watchcoat he was wearing a suit of brown serge. Nonetheless he cut a robust figure amidst all the gay streamers and holiday flounces.

Will hailed him, and Tobias's face lit up. His small turned-up nose was contradicted by everything else about him, which was solid and powerful. If something was to happen, then Mudge was your man.

'Mr Lundy – you look alarmed, Sir!'

The watchman was removing his hat just as Widow Trotter and Tom were approaching.

'We're glad to have found you, Mr Mudge. Glad indeed! We can't explain all here, but will you accompany us to the maypole immediately? We have wind of something that might require the use of your staff!'

All three of them were standing before him, and the watchman's eyes glittered as if he'd been invited to mount guard at the palace:

'Say no more, Mr Lundy – you can explain as we walk. Follow me!'

And so the troop set off, and Widow Trotter began giving him an inkling of what she had overheard, and the threat that might be about to be realised.

Everything now happened at once. Out of their sight, and exactly on cue, a figure with his back to the maypole was bending over a wheelbarrow full of onions – or so it seemed. He flung up the layer of sacking on which they rested, and as the onions scattered he seized a large, brightly-polished axe. Within the blink of an eye he made three rapid strides up to the pole, and with a mighty heave struck the cedar trunk with full force and incised a deep gash in the wood. Another blow followed, heavier than the last, and before anyone could register the outrage, he had fallen into a rhythm, one stroke following another.

Suddenly there were terrified screams. Some in the holiday crowd saw what was happening, but held back helplessly – the man was swinging his weapon like an avenging angel, and it swept furiously through the air. Another blow – and another. It seemed the gigantic maypole was to end its days in ignominy.

But how many people would die when that great trunk fell? As panic began to take hold, one man threw himself forward and tried to grapple, and another followed him – but they were flung back onto the cobbles, and another blow was struck. Some demon was giving this figure a superhuman strength.

The man was lifting his axe yet again, when suddenly a stout oaken staff caught him on the back of his skull. He tottered as if drunk, and the axe swung wide, missing the pole entirely. A second later he felt the full weight of the staff strike him across the back of his knees, and he sank down as if in prayer, his kneecaps dashed against the stone. Mudge stood over him, staff in hand, and reached for his handcuffs. The other men rushed forward and seized the axe, which was now hanging limply. The man's eyes were closed and his hands raised, and as the weapon was taken from him he gave a great cry.

'Ye shall make no idols! These abominations have the men of the land done – and the land is defiled!'

A cobble from the crowd struck the man on the ear, and he swayed with the blow. People were standing back in awe.

The man was still crying out:

'I will destroy your high places, and cut down your images! My soul shall abhor you!'

Another cobble hit him on the shoulder.

'Judge them O Lord! For their shows are evil. Their monuments are the Devil's! Bring thy Judgment down on them! Reclaim the Land! Bring us back into thy holy ways! For such things are abomination in thy sight!'

The crowd had heard enough and surged forward. Before Mudge could attach the handcuffs the man was grabbed by his arms and legs. Fists pummelled him, boots struck home; his hair was being pulled out in handfuls, his face scratched and bleeding as nails gouged him. Mudge tried to interpose his own body and struggled to save him.

'Hold off! Let the man alone! Let him face justice!'

But no-one heard, and the young watchman began receiving blows in his turn. The crowd's fury was unstoppable. Mudge staggered back, one hand steadying his forehead, and he watched in horror as the kicking continued. Suddenly a soldier burst through the press of people, musket in hand, followed by another, and then a third. The crowd drew away as if in shock at what they had done. Mudge was left standing, and with blood beginning to trickle from his temple he looked at the surrounding faces in disbelief. It had been the work of a moment, an explosion of terror and anger – and how quickly, he thought, the one became the other, like the flipping of a playing-card. He swallowed drily and his ever-practical eyes turned toward the maypole. Although a deep slice had been taken out of it, the mighty trunk would hold. Thank God, he muttered to himself, thank God.

Widow Trotter and Tom were held in the crush and were struggling to see what was going on. Ahead of them the shouts and cheers of the mob had offered a commentary on the scene as if it were a Hockley-Hole boxing match. Will was a little nearer and had glimpsed the violent action as it played out. He turned round, grim-faced, and shouted back to them:

'The pole is safe! But the man is in a bad way … Mudge is hurt – not seriously I think!'

And as Will spoke the words, there was a sudden lull, and the noise of the crowd fell to a whisper as if a sea-wave had broken into a quiet hiss. The ribbons of the maypole continued to flap gently in the play of the breeze, and from the far distance they could make out the tones of a bagpipe continuing to play its sprightly melody.

Chapter Sixteen

THE TRESTLE-TABLE IN Elias Cobb's office was untidy at the best of times, but on this May-Day afternoon it was encumbered by more than papers and watch-house paraphernalia. Occupying one end was a surgeon's bag and a scattering of bandages and bottles (one containing cheap brandy), a pair of scissors, brown paper, and a couple of ointment-jars. The surgeon was drawing his work to a close and winding up the relentless commentary that had accompanied it. Mudge, the beneficiary of his skill, was returning a wan smile, detectable beneath the dressings that swathed his cheek and forehead. Humfrey Proby charged a substantial fee, but his smart clothes and clean hands somehow inspired confidence. Tom, Will, and Widow Trotter, who formed the audience seated around the table, had been admiring his deftness – a painter's fingers adapted to the surgical art – but they were impatient to begin their conference and for the moment had little to say.

Over in the Strand, the mysterious axe-man had received no such tender care: his still-living body had been unceremoniously carted off by the soldiers. The man's identity was a mystery, and whether he would survive to be questioned was in doubt. Tom had tried to stress that his identification was of great importance; but for the soldiers this seemed less a priority than removing him from the scene before he could prompt more violence. The crowd were pressing round, and above their dark murmurings, the occasional shouts of *Fanatic! Ranter! Damn'd Puritan!* and *Papist!* suggested the mob's impatience with particularity. It was best to take the man away at once. The maypole-dancing, needless to say, would not be continuing.

Constable Cobb had been full of praise for the boldness of his young watchman, and yet again had cause to wonder at the resourcefulness of the 'Bay-Tree militia' – as he was beginning to think of them. Elias had promised them news, and while they awaited the arrival of the surgeon, Widow Trotter gave him an account of her exploits at the Exchange. Everyone was stunned by the drama of the past hour, and apprehension was mounting. The attack on the maypole was a spectacular outrage, but they were wondering if more was to come. The fact that Constable Cobb had let slip that he 'had something to show them' aroused curiosity even more.

In the end, their patience was rewarded, and Mr Proby was ushered out of the room with as much grateful attention as they could spare. As for the drowsy patient, he was happy to sit by the window nursing his wounds and a pot of ale, encouraging the contents of his head to settle themselves back into their old order.

'You promised us news, Elias!' said Mary Trotter as the door finally closed. 'Is it from the playhouse?'

'Have things been taken further with Gilbert and Sally?' asked Tom.

'Have any charges been laid?' added Will.

While the questions tumbled out, Elias returned to the end of the table, reached for his pipe and tobacco-pouch, pulled back his comfortable elbow chair, and sat down ceremoniously, as if he were about to chair a committee:

'It's hard to know where to begin ... One thing I do know

is that you ought to be sitting here, Molly. Your mission to the Exchange was a triumph. No informer by profession could have done better ...'

He beamed at her, and there was a ripple of approval around the table. Widow Trotter half expected a formal vote of thanks.

'... and what's more, you were on the scent from the beginning! This is indeed a dangerous *plot*, and it is shaping up to be a State matter. Your strange figure in the side-box – whoever he is – gives us a link from the playhouse to the maypole. And what is now a terrible possibility is that the Baron's murder may be a part of it ...'

The constable picked up a candle and ignited the combustible material in the bowl of his pipe. Smoke began billowing round his face.

'... Rich's threatening letter – the *Macbeth* business – the apprentices' shouts outside the theatre – that *Drury Lane* pamphlet – the stone through your window, Molly, complete with its bible verse – all is ...'

He paused, and the cloud began to lift itself above his head.

'... thoughtful activity!'

Tom and Will looked at each other.

'What is your drift, Mr Cobb?' said Tom. '*Thoughtful?*'

'I mean these are not random bolts – mere bursts of anger. They are conveying messages.'

'Yes,' said Will, 'it's as if a consistent thought is behind all this – a wish to bring fear to people and put them in mind of their sins.'

Widow Trotter jumped slightly in her seat:

'*Their sins will find them out!*' – Of course! That's what I heard the man say. He was talking about the Fair, and about *The Tender Courtesan*. I heard him mention the play ...'

She looked at Tom apologetically.

'... I'm sorry, Tom – the phrase has just come back to me. I can hear him saying it now. It was in connection with your play … *Their sins will find them out!* … and they *laughed*.'

'That's the key, Molly,' said Elias. 'And, what is more, the raid on the gaming-house may be part of the picture. One of the sodomites who are facing death is a gentleman from the Drury Lane company – not an actor, but a script-man – George Bellamy. He supervises the copying and revising of the parts.'

Tom gave an audible sigh, and Will's head sank down. All four of them were beginning to feel uncomfortable.

'But there was something more, Elias. We need your help to explain it – it could be important.'

'What is that, Molly?'

'They spoke of holding a meeting on *Monday* – that it was to take place at *noon*. And that *Middlemiss* had set it up. I think that was the name of the man. It was distinctive – *Middlemiss*.'

Elias's eyes widened:

'Well, well, Molly, I think you must have heard right! Dick Middlemiss is the landlord of the Dog and Duck.'

'Lord bless us! The tavern at Brook Field? – The one next door to the May Fair?'

'The very same.'

'That's it!' interjected Will. 'If they are to attack the Fair, then we know where they will gather.'

'But the place is a busy hive, especially during Fair-days,' said Mrs Trotter. 'All sorts gather there – they will be meeting in a private room.'

'Likely so,' said Elias. 'But if people are assembling on Monday at noon, it should be possible to keep watch and see *who* is gathering. I warrant the plotters will be sitting round a table much as we are now – hatching their evil designs!'

'All the more reason to be vigilant. Do you think we should tell Mr Pinkerman about this meeting?'

'That may be a risk – until we know more. Once the picture is clearer he must be told, of course.'

'Poor Pinkerman,' said Tom. 'This is just what he's feared. I wonder what these *evil designs* are ...'

He broke off and noticeably blanched. Widow Trotter was the one to ask the inevitable question:

'Could you have one or two of your men there on Monday, Elias? We must do something, surely?'

The constable hesitated:

'It's difficult. These people will be meeting in private, so there will be little to overhear – but it would be good to observe who is involved. Your haberdasher will be there with his mysterious colleague. But there's a good chance my men would be recognised. These plotters mustn't suspect they have been sniffed out ...'

There was a pause.

'... No, we need somebody who would be there quite naturally, and whose business takes them to the Fair. It's the first day, so the place will be crammed with livestock-traders and hide-dealers – one of those would be ideal!'

The fanciful thought was followed by a spirited tug on his pipe. In response, Tom stirred himself, and spoke quietly:

'Or perhaps, Mr Cobb, somebody connected with one of the booths – perhaps a person who is rehearsing there – or even someone *handing over a prologue* ...'

'But he mustn't be alone,' said Will. 'A solitary drinker would arouse suspicion. He would have to be taking his ease with a friend. What's more, a couple sitting opposite each other can see in front and behind. And they would need to compare notes.'

Widow Trotter brightened:

'Ah! The team harnessed up again! Are you sure you can do this, both of you?'

'Well, for me it's either that or Westminster Hall,' said Will.

'A painful choice. A long day listening to the drone of lawyers – or the two of us cracking a pint together at the Dog and Duck.'

'I was planning to walk over to Brook Field on Monday in any case. I have to deliver my prologue to Pinkerman – and I want to see how the booth is taking shape. I hope to encounter Gilbert and Sally at rehearsal too.'

'And while we're there, we can scout round the site and look out for anything suspicious.'

'And if there's any tracking to do …'

Tom grinned.

'… we have the *widow-spy* to emulate. You've fired us, Mrs T!'

They were expecting a smile from her but met a frown instead.

'This is no holiday jaunt, Mr Bristowe. You must both take extreme care. This morning at the Exchange I was practically invisible – just a woman trying on some gloves – and those men were not on their guard. But your plotters will be watchful and suspicious. You'll be in a place where a sudden fight would cause hardly a stir – and a knife could flash in an instant.'

'And remember, gentlemen,' added Elias, 'the tracker can become the tracked. These gentlemen-conspirators may be practised *hole-and-corner* men.'

Tom and Will felt chastened, although there was something in the warnings that added to the excitement.

'But that is for Monday,' said Widow Trotter. 'By then we may know a little more about the reformers …'

She turned to Will.

'… If your father is in an easy mood tomorrow, you may glean something useful.'

'Much depends on the sermon, Mrs T – a good long Hackney rant may fire him up and make him unguarded. Indeed, I'm wondering if I might try and rouse him to indiscretion.'

The constable smiled:

'That's a lawyer's skill, Mr Lundy. But be careful not to make him angry. It might be better if he would confide in you?'

'I think that's unlikely, Mr Cobb. We usually find ourselves playing adverse roles. As a child I had to argue points with him and give good reasons for everything I wanted. Over the years there's been very little *confiding*, believe me!'

'Ah well, I wish you a fair wind with that – it bids to be Westminster Hall in Hackney ...'

Elias laid down his pipe and looked at the others.

'... But I promised I had something to show you all ...'

The look on his face was enigmatic. It suggested he was about to give them a present they might not like. His chair scraped on the floor as he reached forward to a pile of papers, and his hand closed round a small pamphlet. He was conscious of having a rapt audience.

'... This unsavoury item was brought in not an hour ago from Fleet Street – it was being cried over there. I don't think it will surprise you, sad to say. The thing is anonymous of course, and it's wretchedly printed – schoolboy-work! The pamphlet is meant to make trouble and has been rushed off as news – though it's more of a crude sermon, as so many of these things are.'

He handed it to Tom.

'You're right, Mr Cobb – this is crude – but what a title!'

He held it out. The title-page was displayed, and as he declaimed it to the company, the words read like a menu of poisonous dishes.

> *'An Account of the Frightful MURDER IN THE PLAYHOUSE, that Notorious SANCTUARY OF SATAN; together with the terrible BLASPHEMIES lately utter'd in that Place; the DEVILISH PLOT hatch'd against the Reformers of Manners; and the MANIFOLD OUTRAGES against public Order and Decency committed in that SCHOOL OF VICE*

AND DEPRAVITY. With a Prayer for the Soul of the Late Baron Tunbridge, Reformer and Martyr.'

There was a moment of stunned silence.

'My God!' said Mrs Trotter with a look of wide-eyed horror. 'What a charge-sheet! It's precisely what we feared. Has everything led up to this?'

'It reads that way,' said Elias. 'The thing may have a sneaking, hang-dog look, but it's a clever piece of story-telling, and its climax is the Baron's murder. There's no mention made of Sally or Gilbert, or of any motive outside the theatre. Indeed it's exactly as you predicted, Mr Bristowe: the man who was planning to bring the company to order becomes a hero, and his death is a *martyrdom* – it even ends with a prayer for his soul – an oddly Popish touch! The Societies now have a banner to proclaim their cause, which is nothing less than to hasten the final battle between God and Satan!'

It was a chilling thought.

Tom cast his eye over the title and began leafing through the pamphlet. The constable continued:

'... Yes, everything is there: the incidents at the playhouse; the old charges of blasphemy and idolatry; the unruliness of the theatre audience; the promiscuity of the actors; the vicious tendency of the plays; the public display of vanity and frivolity. It all builds into a conspiracy within the company to resist reform. The theatre, it says, is out of step with *the new manners of the age*, and is in defiance of the Queen's proclamations against profaneness and vice.'

Will had been listening intently, and by this time his usually bright countenance had assumed the look of an attorney who sees his client's case is hopeless.

'So, Mr Cobb, what about Rich, Pinkerman, and Cibber? Are they named – or is the accusation a general one?'

'They are not named, Mr Lundy. But the argument leaves little doubt that a company plot has been laid against the Baron – and an *execution* carried out.'

Tom gave a whistle of amazement. Widow Trotter was making hesitant sounds that were not quite speech:

'But ... but that's a monstrous accusation. Is it not libellous?'

'No-one is named, Mrs T, so the writer *keeps the windy side of the Law* – but only narrowly.'

There followed a moment of shocked silence, and then the others heard Tom reading aloud:

> *'The Playhouse is a vile Sink of Iniquity, a common Sewer for Vices not to be spoken of. From its stage, the most shocking Oaths and Blasphemies are put forth; vicious characters are indulged with Laughter; the solemn Bonds of Duty and Matrimony made mock of; Virtue is scandalised and Vice rewarded. At this time of national danger the Theatre and the Fair serve only to bring comfort to our Enemies, to corrupt the natural Vigour and Manliness of our Kingdom, and sap the Prowess and Valour of its People.'*

'National danger *my arse! ...'*

The voice came from the far side of the room, by the window, where Mudge was now turning round to face them.

'... Excuse me, gentlemen – and Mrs Trotter – forgive me, but that's preachers' language, not soldiers'! They don't know what true *Valour* is – and they've never faced an *enemy* in their lives. Not like those poor wretches begging in the Strand – shot to pieces, eh Mr Cobb?'

'Tobias, young fellow! I sense you are well on the way to recovery!'

'No apology needed, Mr Mudge!' said Widow Trotter. 'None at all!'

The watchman hesitated: it was not for him to join their conversation. But he was bold for a moment longer:

'All I can say is, I for one will be off to the Fair next week – and I don't take kindly to busy-bodies telling me what's good for me!'

Tom was looking down at the pamphlet:

'Well, you won't like this sermon, Toby! … I see our preacher has something to say about the Fair.'

'The May Fair?' asked Will.

'Yes, he rails against the iniquity of the theatrical booths – it's the usual stuff about rope-dancers, mountebanks, and raree shows. Even Pinkerman's elephant finds a place, would you believe? … And alas, Will, I see he disapproves of the dancing dogs! They are evidently things of the Devil … and …'

He broke off suddenly, and his jaw sank. His eyes continued to run over the paper.

'What is it Tom?' said Will.

'There's more …'

His lips were forming a lively oath, but he held it back just in time.

'It's *The Tender Courtesan* …'

'You mean, the play is mentioned?'

'It is indeed … listen … "*The Tender Courtesan – a piece that promises to celebrate Whoredom and reward Depravity – which makes Nobility contemptible, and Marriage a Smithfield-bargain.*"'

'Is that what it says? That's not a bad summary, Tom!'

'I wouldn't laugh it off. This is no frolic … And there's more: "*Let the performers know what dangers they run themselves into in enacting a piece of such lewdness … May they be hiss'd from the stage as they deserve!*"'

'*Dangers?* That sounds like a warning to the actors,' said Mrs Trotter. 'It's coming very close to home, is it not?'

'As close as can be, Mrs T,' said Tom quietly. 'There's a threat behind it.'

Elias Cobb was now looking solemn. He set his hands on the table in front of him, as if to add substance to his words:

'I think we all need to be alert during the next few days – you in particular, Mr Bristowe. I wonder if that Prologue of yours …'

He left the sentence hanging, not quite sure what he was in fact wondering. This had a menacing effect.

'Yes, Tom – you must be careful,' said Widow Trotter.

Tom surveyed their anxious faces. This wouldn't do, he thought – they mustn't allow themselves to be cowed by a bit of hectoring rhetoric, however grand a flourish it made … No. It was a warning, but one they must use to their advantage. If there was an enemy, that person was now stepping into the open. He looked over at Mudge, from whose heavily-bandaged face a defiant smile was struggling to emerge, and the sight gave him courage and confidence:

'I swear I'll be careful. But my prologue will proceed. I had set aside tomorrow to write it, and that's what I'll do … and after the events of today, I think I can see my way.'

Sunday

2 May 1708

Chapter Seventeen

FROM HIS LOFTY pulpit, the Reverend Mr Tysoe looked out at his congregation as if he might shake every person's hand. In the cramped space of the Mare Street Meeting-House the preacher was not only on display himself, but could scrutinise each individual at close quarters, particularly those in the balconies which projected on three sides and seemed almost to touch the pulpit itself. This was a much smaller theatre than Drury Lane, and its whitewashed walls and plain wooden roof were a long way from the velvet, gold and filigree-work of the playhouse; but the principle was much the same, and this actor was holding his audience in thrall as powerfully as Betterton or Barry ever did. Dressed in plain black gown and clerical bands, the gentleman was well launched into his soliloquy, and a further hour would pass before his disquisition would begin drawing to a close.

Will's Hackney Sabbath was under way, and like many in the dissenting congregation he felt as if the preacher's eyes were peering into his soul. At these services the brethren were indeed brothers and sisters concerned with each other's spiritual wellbeing and on the watch for any lapse into sin. It didn't help Will's peace of mind that he was seated up close to his father, who as usual was occupying the front row of the centre balcony and was conducting his own intimate scrutiny of the minister. The same piercing Lundy eyes that glared down from the judge's bench managed to turn the pulpit into a witness-box. But on this occasion the testimony was being well received. 'Hemp' Lundy's look was an approving one, and from the deep purrings in his father's throat Will guessed he was finding the sentiments in tune with his own.

Will had anticipated something rousing from this invited preacher. The resident minister, Mr Billio, knew how to stir his hearers when need be, but he tended to remain in encouraging negotiation with his flock. If the people wanted their vitals pierced, then they had to look elsewhere – and the Reverend Tysoe was the man to do it. From the moment he announced his text, Will could sniff the nitre in the air:

'The First Epistle of John, Chapter Three, Verse Eight: *He that committeth Sin is of the Devil; for the Devil sinneth from the Beginning.*'

To his right, Aunt Dinah gave a delighted chirrup, and her elbow caught him in the ribs. Will tried to settle himself on the bench but couldn't find a comfortable position. In every way the next hour would be a restless one, a contest between the forces of light and darkness – God pitted against the Devil – '*the Two Powers contending for Dominion over Mankind!*' The preacher's drama of spiritual combat was, he declared, '*a Holy War for the Recovery of the World from under the Tyranny of Satan.*'

Such notions were common enough, and Will found himself only half-listening as the usual phrases came forth. From his lawyer's training he had come to prefer argument to assertion; but he knew that in the world of religion the language of precedent, authority, sanction, judgment and punishment was equally operative. The Old Testament had its legal codes too – and what great piles they both made! He could see them in his mind's eye: a hide-bound mountain of case and statute law on the one side, and the hallowed scrolls of Deuteronomy and Leviticus on the other. Why should he see any difference between them?

But after a while, as the Reverend Tysoe set out his battle-plan, the tone became more urgent and the preacher's gaze more penetrating. His audience were drawn even closer as he began invoking another theatre – the one where the Devil himself presided.

Will was now giving the words his full attention:

> *'I look upon this task as merely taking the outworks of Satan's fortified place among us. I trust that the* Citadel *itself, the PLAY-HOUSE, in which the Devil's militia have their retreat, will soon fall into your hands! O ye faithful Servants of God! In this* Great War *between Christ and Satan, there is no standing neuter – you are for* God, *or for* Baal! *For the* Lord's *altars or for* Satan's!*'*

Will glanced about him. What he saw reassured him that the good folk of Hackney appeared quite happy with the altars they already had. But he shivered at the man's vision of the Theatre Royal and the confident expectation of its overthrow. Will sensed the congregation was warming to the speech – although it may have been the increasing heat in the room: the people were swathed in sober woollens and muslins, and the place was packed.

The minister was now pointing toward them all, like a recruiting officer seeking for volunteers:

> *'But how shall you act your own part in this enterprise? Why! if you have a noble and heroic spirit – if you thirst for* Glory *– then TURN INFORMER! These people bravely scale the walls of Sin; these carry the Devil's vassals captive! In primitive times the* Martyrs *bore the brunt of Satan's fury – faithful Soldiers of*

> *Christ who gave their lives in defence of his Truth against the Antichrist. And now, the most noble and heroic of our band are our* Informers.
>
> *'In this task you exert your zeal for your Saviour's Glory … and shall not* The Society for Reformation of Manners, *and their noble band of informers, be honoured? The war they are engaged in is a* war against the Kingdom of Darkness!'

Will could hardly believe what he was hearing. It was as if the preacher were speaking out of the experience of the past few days. At any moment he expected the man to wave the latest pamphlet in the air. But thankfully he was caught up in painting his own vivid scene of the LAST BATTLE.

By the time the Reverend Tysoe came to his peroration, Will was gloomy and tense, and his stomach was clenched so tight it was beginning to ache. The sermon's concluding words were intended to be hopeful ones, but even here the preacher couldn't dispel the nightmare from his imagination. Will watched the man closely as the words came in a last desperate plea:

> *'Thanks to this great work of the* Reformation of Manners, *the streets of our Metropolis are being cleansed of the rotten and filthy carcasses strolling and crawling there. The air is being purged of the infectious breath that steams forth from those contagious persons and places – air more infectious than that from a Pest-House.* The Play-House *is the one nursery of impiety and abomination yet remaining among us. Let us carry on the War! Let us give the enemy a decisive blow! Prostitutes are now less seen in our streets, oaths are less heard in conversations, and profanations of the Lord's Day are not so public as before … Yet alas! we hear of a much more fearful, and a far more abominable Host approaching: the SODOMITES are invading our Land! Here we must maintain our ground against Satan's efforts and repel*

> *this enemy the* Sodomite, *to the driving him out of the Land – cost what it will… . You are engaged in a necessary war against the* Powers of Darkness, *and you must be actively engaged in it. Nothing of a neutrality will be permitted! The matter is brought to one single issue, and that is this: ARE YOU FOR GOD, OR FOR SATAN? … For God's Sake, let us not be for the Devil! Oh, let none of us be on the Devil's side – whatever may befall us!'*

With those words the Reverend Tysoe ended. He was practically in tears as he looked out at the endangered souls before him. His eyes were glistening as if he could see them all, every one of them, slipping inexorably downwards beyond reach of salvation. Alas, thought Will, the poor man will never be at rest! His life is a warfare upon earth, and his Christian vision will forever be darkened by fear of the world around him – haunted by the thought of a plague-ridden Apocalypse.

The preacher made his way down from the pulpit, and at once from every part of the meeting-house there rose a swelling hum like the sound of bees seething in a hive. To his right, Will felt Aunt Dinah give a slight shiver, as if an electric current had passed through her; and to his left his father drew himself away from the balcony's edge with the slow satisfaction of a man sitting back after a fine meal.

'So … There's a good warfaring Christian, is he not, William? Food for thought, eh?'

'He's a powerful speaker, father, I admit. But you would need to be careful using such words in Westminster Hall. In that place argument is conducted with more nicety – you and I both know that.'

'But the Law is adversarial, William. There is *Guilty* or *Not Guilty* – and I hope you agree there is *Right* and *Wrong!*'

'Yes father, and there is *Black* and *White* too … but are there not many other delightful colours in the world which bring every scene to life? Very few *living* things are black and white.'

'Now you speak as a poet, not as a lawyer. You must not indulge in such fancies – certainly not as a ground for argument. *Clarity,* William! *Clarity!* How often have I stressed that to you?'

'Well, let us hope the Reverend Tysoe is as strict with himself as he is severe on others! I wonder if he ever looks around him and loves what he sees?'

'In our different ways, he and I are both *judges,* William. And so may you be some day, I trust – one who values the Law and respects its statutes ...'

He paused, and Will saw the corner of his father's eye tighten into an ironic glance – it was as near as he could come to playfulness.

'... So, you consider Mr Tysoe a bit of a dry stick, do you? Well, we shall both see shortly.'

'What do you mean, Sir?'

'I mean – that the good gentleman is invited to take dinner with us this afternoon. You'll have the chance to study the phenomenon at close quarters.'

Will was not expecting that. He was briefly lost for words. How would it affect his plans?

'In that case, father, I trust his voice will be less resounding over the dinner-table. I don't want to be frightened out of my appetite.'

The talk over dinner wasn't as loud and uncomfortable as Will had feared. Old Mr Hodge's efforts in the kitchen-garden and Mrs Pearson's culinary skills had combined to good effect. The new season's lamb and the home-grown asparagus were both sweet enough to draw Will's attention whenever the talk became oppressive; and by the time the first tiny strawberries of the year were put on the table, to the delight of Aunt Dinah and Aunt Rebecca, the mood had become almost genial.

At the sisters' prompting, Mr Tysoe was more than happy as the meal progressed to talk about his commanding mission – the rooting out of Satan. Will found himself listening to an embattled man who, when he wasn't fighting the Devil directly, was carrying the struggle onto other fronts in disputes with committees, Boards of Governors, landowners – anyone who didn't share his conviction that if Good was to be done then it must be done at once. The man's zeal would let no-one rest.

Even his kindness and warmth of heart had to be channelled into the fight, his benevolence be made forceful, and his pity uncompromising. The education of the poor, his current concern, was for him a campaign as significant – and as frustrating – as Marlborough's soldiering on the Rhine.

'Charity schools, Mr Lundy, are the greatest force for Good in our time. They are the readiest way to root out Satan from the minds of the young and instil in them Godly piety and discipline! But we are being constantly frustrated. *The Society for Promoting Christian Knowledge* has shown the path, but it is an Anglican stronghold, and we dissenters are shunned and despised. We are forced to go our own way and make our own provisions. In this worthy cause I meet nothing but opposition – and, what is worse, downright laziness – at every turn!'

Yes, a good warfaring Christian, thought Will. But the more he heard of Mr Tysoe's charitable zeal, the more uneasy he became. The sheer uncompromising energy of the man's convictions made every question a challenge, every choice an ultimatum, and every disagreement a betrayal. In an unsettling way, the Reverend Tysoe's *Good* seemed to override humanity and make humanity itself shameful and unworthy.

It was Aunt Rebecca who moved the conversation in the direction Will had been both wanting and fearing. After a discreet pause she gave a quiet little cough that commanded attention like a Town-crier's bell. As she spoke, she remained straight-backed and turned only her head:

'If I may speak for myself, Mr Tysoe, I rejoiced especially to hear you celebrate the reform societies. God is surely working through them, is he not? In the present activity of *Reformation of Manners* we feel his guiding hand directing the nation's affairs.'

'Indeed we do, Miss Lundy. The Society as a body is a beacon of hope. At this time especially, when the forces for Good are beginning to advance, we rely ever more on their vigilance – their readiness for the fray.'

Opposite him, Aunt Dinah's eyes sparkled with a vitality that defied her age:

'Your vision was truly an inspiration, Mr Tysoe, and your tribute to the informers was a noble call to arms. Were it within my sphere ... I would even enlist myself!'

'We need informers amongst all ranks of people, Miss Dinah, and especially in the suburbs of our metropolis. I regret to say that even Hackney has its blasphemers, and there are some profane wretches who break the Sabbath – one fears that deep in their hearts they break even more of the Lord's commands.'

'We need windows into men's hearts,' said Aunt Rebecca, narrowing her eyes as if peering into a darkened room. 'Vice may do its work in quiet corners – and a retired indifference is a soil ready for the Devil to sow.'

At this, the minister turned, strawberry in hand, and gave her the full weight of his attention:

'You put it most eloquently, Miss Lundy ... "*Because thou art lukewarm, and neither cold nor hot – I will spew thee out of my mouth!*"'

It was spoken with passion, face to face. Will noticed his aunt's complexion flush slightly and fought to suppress a smile.

All this time, with the exception of a few polite remarks, he had been keeping his counsel; but now he sensed that his silence was becoming audible amidst all this eagerness of declaration. He had been hoping their mood would mellow and the easy sociability of the dining-table allow wit and fancy to find their way in. But he should have known better. This stiff and polished table had seen little of those over the years!

'Of course, in your present studies for the Law, Mr. Lundy, you must meet some of the very worst of humanity – and some of the blackest crimes ...'

The man was speaking directly to him.

'... For any young man, that must prove a challenge to your Christian scruples, I've no doubt.'

Will felt the eyes of his father on him. The place was suddenly like a court-room:

'My studies have been mainly in the civil law, Sir, and in the area of litigation. I must confess that in that particular branch of the Law the worst motives and meanest passions seem to emerge. There is so much dispute and mutual accusation – it is hard sometimes to steer a path to the Truth ... But of course one constantly tries.'

The minister warmed:

'Nicely said, young man. I sense your delicacy about the matter. As your father's son, I know you will have imbibed the best of principles – as you have had the finest model.'

The Reverend Tysoe nodded to Will's father, who responded with a look that managed to conceal his uneasiness. The reply came at once:

'William pursues his studies conscientiously, Mr Tysoe – and I interest myself in them, as you would expect. The two of us enjoy some spirited engagements on the workings of the Law – its rule and conduct. And on matters of principle too. We have been known to thrash things out vigorously.'

'That is as it should be ... As the great Milton says, "*I cannot praise a fugitive and cloistered virtue!*" I am glad you engage yourselves like this ...'

He paused, allowing Will to take a breath and feel the precariousness of the moment.

'... Mr Billio speaks well of you, William (I hope I may call you that at this table?), and wishes you might make your way to Hackney more often. He told me he has heard that one of the benchers at Middle Temple, Richard Sumner, sings your praises. You assist him, I gather?'

'Yes, Sir, Mr Sumner allows me to help him with some of his cases – mainly civil and chancery proceedings. The experience is invaluable.'

'I shall not ask you about any case in particular – but I'm glad if you are able to steer clear of the sordid criminal matters which come your father's way. Civil law is the way to go – and the route to success. You will mix with better people and avoid the less edifying elements of humanity ... "*He that toucheth pitch shall be defiled!*"'

Will was now finding the man's talk unpleasant. How much more of this would he have to take? He knew the Hackney congregation was a close-knit family, but was nonetheless shocked that his activities had been inquired into and his character canvassed.

He found himself responding more sharply than he intended:

'But surely, Sir, the Law must reach into every part of life? We must bring its weight to bear on any criminal – whether felon, defrauder, or murderer. If anything can shine a light into the darkness it is the Law. Dirty hands or not, the Law must grapple with wrongdoing of every kind. We should not step aside.'

The minister was taken aback – but although he flinched for a second, his face assumed a radiant expression: this was a language he understood. He recognised in this young man all the ardent idealism of youth.

'You speak well, William, and I like your fervour – you will go far in the profession ...'

Will was being scrutinised.

'... For one thing, you have eyes that a man might trust – open and honest. I am rarely deceived in such matters! They are the beacon of the soul, and yours is *good*. I pray to God you will guard yourself through life. These are terrible times, and there is temptation and viciousness at every turn.'

'The haunts of Satan are everywhere in the city,' said Aunt Rebecca. "*Our adversary the Devil, as a roaring lion, walketh about, seeking whom he may devour!*"'

The minister beamed:

'Indeed he does, Miss Lundy – and nowhere does he walk more openly and boldly than in the *Playhouse*. That is his sanctuary! Elsewhere in the city his power is being challenged and his stratagems frustrated. Only in the Playhouse can he lift his head high and gather his friends about him. There he swaggers in full confidence!'

'The theatre is a place of deception,' said Aunt Dinah, who had never been in one in her life.

'You say true! All is false. On the stage the meanest actor can wear a royal crown, and the foulest whore deck herself out as a blushing virgin. A coward may impersonate a general, and a reprobate atheist a man of the cloth. Every costume, every machine, every trick of the face, every sentiment spoken – is a show. Nothing is as it seems.'

The voice of the preacher was reasserting itself. By now Will was attempting to keep his mind on the glass of elderflower lemonade that he held up to his chin; he was examining its fragile tracings and wondering about the skill of its making. But as a means of distraction it proved unsuccessful – he was really thinking about what he would say if his opinion was sought. Whatever happened, he had to rein himself in and be nonchalant.

Seated at the head of the table, his father was solemn-faced: 'The theatre, Mr Tysoe, is also a place of *murder*.'

Coming from Judge Lundy the word was especially chilling.

'Ah yes – Lord Tunbridge!' said the minister, shaking his head in the manner of a headmaster recalling a troublesome student. 'What a scandal! I spoke of touching pitch ... What greater instance could you have? His Lordship was a shareholder in the playhouse – and seems to have made the place his second home. There is a terrible *consummation* to his fate. A stage dagger! I understand the manager, Rich, is suspected – if not himself then some hired assassin. The playhouse is a common shore – the very worst types have entrance there.'

Will decided he must end his embarrassed silence and say something. He set his glass down and turned to the minister, who was now slightly red-faced and drinking from his own glass of the cooling liquor.

'I heard, Sir, that the Baron was intending to reform the theatre's company. Can that be true?'

'Indeed, yes – that is how he was dirtying his hands. The place can never be *reformed!* – it is too deep-dyed in sin and blasphemy. The man would not be told! He thought to work with the Society – and as a peer he was well placed to do us good. But such a person could never be a reformer. He should have begun by reforming himself!'

The Reverend Tysoe's anger was beginning to show.

'So, you do not see him as a martyr in the cause of Reformation?'

'*Martyr?* No, William – indeed I do not! It is a ludicrous idea ... but there are some in the Society, I admit, who are all for making him such. But for me, only the pure and virtuous can win a heavenly crown. The thing is too solemn to be made light of – the very thought is a blasphemy!'

Will's heart began pounding. He knew something important was stirring:

'Are you suggesting, Sir, that there are disagreements about how reform should proceed? One could hope the Society would be of one mind on the matter. This is no time for divisions, surely!'

'Young man, you speak very judiciously. How right you are! If only we could persuade all our members to pull together. There is, sadly, a *faction* who will stop at nothing ...'

Will's father intervened:

'I think, William, such a contentious topic ought to be left alone. These affairs are highly sensitive and not for discussion over the dinner table – and certainly not in the presence of *ladies*.'

The sentiment was unexceptionable, but at that moment Will detected in both of his aunts a flicker of disappointment. Judge Lundy gave the two women a brotherly look as he spoke, and the silent message was received. After an awkward pause, they rose simultaneously from their chairs. They would, said Aunt Rebecca, go into the garden and breathe its pure air ... if Baines could send out some coffee and sweetmeats ...

In the absence of the ladies the three gentlemen refilled their glasses and settled themselves in their chairs. The minister continued to give the junior Lundy an approving look:

'Your son has a wise head on his young shoulders, Mr Lundy ...'

The Reverend Tysoe was smiling upon Will, who responded with a modest lowering of his head. His hair fell across his face.

'... I only wish we could recruit him to our ranks ... I wonder – might we consider it, do you think?'

Will's father was looking distinctly uneasy. There was much in his offspring that he admired – but the boy was a renegade in religious matters, and Judge Lundy knew he ought to intervene before the taint of atheism could show itself and his dinner-guest flee from the house as from a leper hospital.

Although unbending in the cause of moral reform, Will's father was no zealot on the doctrinal side of things, and he hesitated to embarrass his son. He remained silent, comforted by the assurance that Will would recoil from the man's suggestion and step aside gracefully.

Will's response was therefore a little disconcerting:

'Coming from you, Mr Tysoe, I take that as a compliment to myself and a tribute to my father. But I'm sure he'll agree that I am simply not equipped to join your ranks – at least not yet. I fear I lack your zeal for the cause. And I could never go beyond ideas and argument into the sphere of action. In anything that required an act of a direct nature I would be a poor infantryman, believe me!'

Will was not a little pleased with himself. It was a sinuous speech – one might almost say serpentine – and the Reverend Mr Tysoe, as Will thought he might, warmed to the challenge:

'You are becomingly modest, William! But I have to say, were you – as I might hope – to give allegiance to our cause, you would not be required to *perform*. Certainly you would not. We already have in our ranks several men who are only too eager to involve themselves in action – men, it might be said, of a *violent* tendency. Indeed, it concerns me that they are following their own lights in this. It remains hard to keep discipline ...'

Will's father jumped in:

'I think, Mr Tysoe, that William will need to turn things over in his mind. Neither of us would want to push him further than he wishes to go.'

'Indeed not, Mr Lundy. I apologise if you think I have urged matters too far. It is an early stage ... but if your son would wish to explore the possibility, then it might do no harm if he came as an observer to our next meeting – I stress as an observer only ...'

He turned to Will and softened his voice.

'... is this something you would consider, William? Of course, you must say no at once if you have any doubts on the matter.'

'I believe I should follow my father's feelings in this, Sir ...' said Will, cringing in embarrassment at the words he was using. He wondered what his father was thinking.

'... Nor would I wish to be an intruder. You may have sensitive business to consider. I know your meetings are properly secret ones, and I deeply appreciate your trust in me – but I would not want to betray it by making your friends uneasy.'

The gestures of delicacy continued. The three of them were becoming distinctly polite, each stepping carefully, like courtiers dancing a minuet. As the moments passed and matters began to resolve themselves, Will could hardly believe what was happening. In the end, after a little more graceful to-ing and fro-ing, Will allowed himself to be persuaded that at the next meeting of the Society his attendance as an observer would be welcome.

Monday

3 May 1708

Chapter Eighteen

'ATTEND A MEETING! Can you be serious? You are to attend a *meeting?*'

'Yes, Tom, tomorrow evening. What do you say to that?'

'Wonder of wonders, I say! I know how persuasive you can be, but this is beyond expectation … We must tell Mrs T – she's longing to hear your news. She said she would come up here when things are quieter downstairs – I can't wait to see her face!'

Will had delivered the revelation in a nonchalant way while the friends settled themselves early on Monday morning in Tom's chamber at the Bay-Tree. Tom had also promised to show Will the draft of his prologue, the manuscript of which lay on his desk alongside a number of crumpled-up pieces of paper. While the two young men talked, a restless Widow Trotter remained down below, trapped behind the coffee-room bar like a human soul that longed to make its upward journey – in her case up two flights of stairs.

'So, your preacher was a Reformation man? – And dinner too! That was a stroke of good fortune … Did he *unwind?* Perhaps Mrs Pearson's cooking helped a little?'

'I was simply being the charming youth, Tom. It was fortunate that the Reverend Mr Tysoe possesses a feeling heart underneath his Christian armour – one that warmed to a potential disciple with eloquent eyes. I think he longs to initiate me into the reformers' cause. He had evidently been inquiring of my character, and Judge Lundy didn't wish to reveal my apostasy. My father had a most uncomfortable hour, although in the end I believe he thinks my attendance at the meeting could do me some spiritual good. He's not lost faith in me yet!'

'Be careful – you've only just discovered the pleasures of the theatre. I'd hate you to revert to your old indifference.'

'No, Tom, indifference never! – But who knows? I may see the light and convert to the cause.'

'Don't jest about it. Some of these people are fanatical, and they may not take kindly to having a stranger in their midst. They are dangerous adversaries.'

'From what Mr Tysoe said, they have adversaries enough in their own ranks. There are certainly factions among the reformers.'

'That comes as no surprise. It's a coalition of high church and low, and I imagine the Dissenters are *tolerated* so long as they don't press their religious views. But it must make for some ticklish discussions. It will be interesting to see if anything flares up at your meeting tomorrow.'

'Mr Tysoe said he was concerned about *men of violence* taking matters into their own hands. He said it was becoming hard to keep discipline.'

'Ah, plotters! That's exactly as we thought. Did he offer any detail?'

'No, I was wanting him to say more, but finally his discretion took over – helped by my father, who seemed unhappy with the topic. I suspect there's a group within the Society who yearn to be *soldiers of the Lord* more literally.'

'I'm sure there must be. The Church Militant isn't metaphysical. It needs real enemies.'

'Well, if there is one thing that unites the reformers – high and low – it's hatred of the Catholics! That's something we can be sure about – their fear of Popery.'

'And that, Will, I can truly say, you have no taint of.'

'But it's strange, isn't it, how people are drawn into alliance by hatred and fear.'

'No, not strange at all. The bond of hate is much easier to manage than the bond of love. It has fewer doubts, and the more it spreads, the more certain it becomes. It gains strength from numbers.'

'You're being philosophical again, Tom.'

'No, just thoughtful. Perhaps I'm anxious about what we shall encounter at the Dog and Duck this morning. A cabal of hate, I warrant … We ought to be in place by eleven, don't you think? We can settle in and take the lie of the land. We must try not to draw attention to ourselves.'

'We'll only be distant observers at best. I doubt we shall learn much, unless we can smuggle ourselves into a cupboard.'

'That's more Mrs T's kind of thing. The most we can hope for is to gain some sense of who these people are – and how many.'

'It will be good to have two pairs of eyes, and compare notes …'

Will noticed Tom's furrowed brow, and paused.

'… You really do look uneasy. What's troubling you?'

'It occurs to me … thinking about your reformers' meeting tomorrow … Some of the plotters may well be attending it.'

'And?'

'And … you could be recognised. These will be suspicious men …'

'You mustn't be concerned about me, Tom. I'll try and slip into the background. Or perhaps you want me to go in disguise? … If it will make you happy I can call in at the playhouse – a large pair of Mahometan whiskers, perhaps?'

'Then you certainly will be noticed.'

'With a fine turban and jewelled scimitar to complete the effect? What do you think?'

'Excellent. And to match, I shall go along as the Indian Queen – exotic feathers and all.'

'And so, Tom, together we shall bring the theatre to *them!* – it will frighten the reformers out of their wits!'

'It will be their Apocalypse!'

Widow Trotter could hear laughter as she mounted the staircase and quickened her steps in response. She only hoped the news she was carrying wouldn't dampen their spirits too much.

A moment later Tom opened the door to a deep-breathing Mrs Trotter who was wearing a look of such eagerness that she could have been Curiosity personified. Tom spontaneously stepped aside, allowing her to stride over to the armchair he had just vacated. She flung herself into it:

'I mustn't be very long, gentlemen – I promised Jenny I would return once I'd heard your news ...'

She swept her hair back and gave Will an encouraging look.

'... What tidings from Hackney? Did you manage to wheedle something from your father? I'm thinking more and more that his dissenting friends could hold the key.'

Will grinned at her as she took a breath:

'Not only do they hold the key, Mrs Trotter, they appear to have unlocked the door and are inviting me to enter ...'

She grappled for a moment with the allegory.

Tom helped her out:

'You'll not believe this, Mrs T ... but Will has been invited to attend one of their meetings – tomorrow!'

Widow Trotter's eyes and mouth widened simultaneously. Suddenly the emblem of Curiosity had turned into Astonishment:

'But I thought they were held in the utmost secrecy? Elias says you have to be proposed and investigated – this is extraordinary ... You'll be entering the *lion's den*.'

But the figure in the chair next to her had a more confident demeanour as he recounted his Hackney adventure and what an indiscreet Mr Tysoe had revealed about the Reformers' agenda. Mary Trotter began to have a fuller picture of what they faced – though not necessarily a clearer one.

'Hypocrisy!' she declared, with an outraged flourish of her hand. 'It's scarcely believable! So, Lord Tunbridge did have links to the Society! The lecherous gentleman was happily seducing actresses and hanging about the green room – and all the time he was pushing for *Reformation of Manners*. The old rogue!'

'I doubt there was any formal connection,' said Will. 'The Society presents itself to the world as a single body, but in truth it's formed of local groupings. They have a mission, and it's certainly secretive – but I don't think it's closely organised.'

'Perhaps it tries to be,' said Tom, 'but from what you say, its policy is in dispute.'

'Yes, the end may be agreed, but the means ...'

Widow Trotter had been listening carefully and thinking about the Baron's plans for the playhouse:

'Perhaps, gentlemen, Lord Tunbridge had *agenda* of his own? Could he have been using the Society to forward his own ambitions?'

'For the theatre? I suspect he was. And now it seems that certain members of the Society are using *him*.'

'Yes, Will – as your reverend gentleman said, he makes an odd kind of a martyr. That's the biggest hypocrisy of all.'

Widow Trotter shook her head:

'I wonder what Mr Pinkerman is thinking of all this – and especially of the new pamphlet?'

'Well, I'll find out this afternoon when I take him my prologue ... He must feel like a prophet – everything is working itself out as he feared. When we talked in the playhouse, he said Lord Tunbridge was set on the moral reformation of the company – to make it virtually a state theatre.'

'I certainly smell ambition there,' said Widow Trotter.

'That would please the Church,' said Tom. 'Our old Archbishop would be delighted if he could bring the stage to heel, and we all know the Bishop of London's views – he is forever announcing them! They think the theatre is a running sore. Every sin and moral outrage is tracked to *Drury Lane* – it's becoming a byword for depravity ...'

Mrs Trotter felt a slight chill. It was true. In the language of sermon and pamphlet – and in satires too – 'Drury Lane' was a badge of dishonour.

Tom noticed her slightly downcast look and changed tack:

'... I'm longing to talk with Pinkerman again and find out how the rehearsals have been progressing.'

'And you'll have news for him too,' she replied. 'And after your visit to the Dog and Duck, you may have even more ... but I hope you'll both come round here later. I may be stuck in the coffee-room, but I want you to think of this place as your centre of operations.'

Tom and Will swore their fealty, touching their hearts like a pair of medieval knights.

'It is indeed our office, Mrs T. And while we're over at Brook Field we'll expect you to gather any Bay-Tree gossip. There may be a few scraps worth picking over?'

'I'll be all ears, Tom. I'm expecting a visit from Elias too ...'

She leaned forward conspiratorially, and her voice took on a confiding tone.

'... But I already have a tit-bit that could be important ... it concerns Sally Twiss ...'

Her two friends glanced at each other apprehensively.

'This is dramatic, Mrs T!' said Tom.

'Sally? Is she ... ?'

Will didn't complete the sentence.

'I thought I should tell you – even though it may not be anything more than hearsay – you know how these reports flit around ...'

She paused shamelessly.

'... Sally has given up the role of Tamara.'

'What!' cried a horrified Tom. 'When did you hear this? That will surely wreck *The Tender Courtesan*? ...'

He glanced over at his desk.

'... And poor Pinkerman – what is he going to do? The play has its opening on Thursday – and it has been advertised.'

Widow Trotter had been expecting this:

'Mr Bagnall heard it this morning from a gentleman who had come from the playhouse – he stayed hardly longer than to deliver his news. It's evidently the talk there.'

Will was uneasy:

'A *gentleman*? ... Could this be a deliberate rumour? We've had so many attempts to damage the theatre. Is this the latest?'

'Well, Mr Bagnall didn't recognise the man. Are you suspicious, Mr Lundy?'

'Yes, a little. False rumours can cause great embarrassment.'

'It all adds to the confusion,' said Tom.

Will's suspicions were mounting:

'You said "poor Pinkerman" ... but I wonder? Might this be our friend's latest manoeuvre? – something he and Rich have been cooking up?'

'Do you mean ... keeping Mrs Oldfield *waiting in the wings*, so to speak?'

'Plots upon plots!' said Widow Trotter. 'I hadn't considered that. Really, you two gentlemen are talking quite like politicians!'

'Well, we shall soon know,' said Will.'Whatever the outcome, I sincerely hope your *prologue* will have its airing, Tom – I'm expecting it to be more memorable than the play.'

He looked over at the desk.

'I hope you're not keeping it a secret until the performance?' said Widow Trotter.'I'm on tenterhooks!'

She also looked over at the desk.

The manuscript remained in full sight – Tom had made no attempt to hide it. That was partly because Will had knocked on his door just as he was honing the final couplet. He had not read the thing aloud to himself yet – let alone to an audience.

There was stillness in the room. Seconds passed. His two friends were determined to say nothing, knowing it was their best hope of having a foretaste of Tom's latest inspiration.

'The ink is scarce dry on it,' he said.'I'm not sure it's achieved its final form ...'

His friends remained silent, continuing to look at the desk.

'... . I suppose there is distinguished precedent for prologues being hastily written – even on the very day of the performance ...'

Will started laughing, and Widow Trotter began to smile expectantly:

'We are a friendly audience, Mr Bristowe. If you were to honour us with a reading, there would be no cat-calls, I promise you.'

Tom's stomach tightened at the thought. Yes, this was a small, indulgent audience. And he might have Pinkerman declaiming his verses that very afternoon, and so it would be good to hear how the thing sounded ...

'Perhaps if I were to read a few lines from it – would that content you?'

'We would be honoured to have just a single couplet, Mr Bristowe.'

'A *phrase* only!' added Will, who was now holding his laughter in.

It struck Tom that he must stop playing the sensitive poet and behave more like an author. He walked resolutely over to his desk, picked up the single sheet of paper, and swung round to face his friends, who folded their hands and sat back in their chairs, imagining themselves in Pinkerman's booth.

Tom cleared his throat:

'"Prologue to *The Tender Courtesan,* spoken at the May Fair, the Sixth of May 1708 ..."

You dread REFORMERS *of our sinful age!*
You awful cat o'nine-tails to the Stage!
To gain your favour we'd your rules obey
And offer you a MORAL *piece today,*
Design our play to give you satisfaction:
We would be PURE *in Language, Thought, and Action.*
To do you right and in your Cause enlist
No rogue would thrive, no virgin e'er be kist;
No Man of God hypocrisy display,
No Lord from paths of virtue ever stray;
No paid Informer ever take a bribe,
No Tradesman curse, no Magistrate imbibe ...

The couplets unwound elegantly as Tom's face radiated innocence. His audience were smiling to themselves, waiting for the 'but' to arrive, and when it did, the poet's brow knitted itself into a frown, and the tone hardened to defiance. A satiric picture began to form of a set of modern Pharisees who had won their virtue cheaply by sounding their trumpets against others' vices. There was genuine indignation in Tom's voice as the prologue came to its end:

... Such Men attack the Sins that they're inclin'd to,
And damn the very Vices they've a Mind to.
Thus REFORMATION *doth discharge its Rage*
And claims the Virtue of a spotless Page,
Sees Crimes in others roundly sent to Hell
While they indulge and think themselves quite well.
OUR *Stage presents a true Democracy,*
Whose greatest enemy's – – – HYPOCRISY.'"

The upper room of the Bay-tree ignited into spontaneous applause; but it took only a few seconds for a more guarded response to follow.

'Tom!' cried Will. 'What bold words! Fearsome words ... You don't hold back.'

'My neck is tingling!' said Widow Trotter. 'I salute your bravery – you turn the reformers' own language against them.'

'Is it *too* strong, do you think? ...'

Will and Mrs Trotter looked at each other.

'... Hearing myself deliver those words, I began to feel like a ranting preacher myself. Is the tone too bold? The lines looked strong enough on the page, but spoken out loud ...'

'That's the mark of a fine prologue,' said Will. 'It comes alive when it's delivered ...'

He paused.

'... I'm proud of you Tom! Those are such powerful verses – and they're bound to cause a stir. And as a rallying-cry for the stage, they more than serve the turn.'

Tom could sense a slight uneasiness:

'But you think them dangerous, Will – I know you do. You think they may run me into trouble ...'

Will was about to reply but Tom stopped him.

'... I acknowledge it ... but with all the hatred and contempt now in the air, the accusing spirit everywhere, the lack of toleration … I want to speak out. I don't want to produce a milk-and-water prologue about young love and the virtues of renunciation!'

'You must do what you think is right, Mr Bristowe,' said Widow Trotter quietly. 'I think your lines are wonderful. And in Pinkerman's booth, before a fair-ground audience, every heart will echo your sentiments. I predict the lines will be resoundingly cheered.'

That thought didn't make Tom feel any easier. But he knew his resolve was firm, and that this was something he had to see through, however uncomfortable the result.

As the three friends sat together, they could still half-hear the words of Tom's prologue ringing out. In truth, all three of them were apprehensive, but they somehow felt there was no turning back – not now. The path was set for the adventures of the Fair, and all it would bring.

Chapter Nineteen

WALKING WESTWARDS ALONG Piccadilly, Tom and Will made a less than elegant sight. As they strolled past a succession of aristocratic mansions guarded by lofty railings and stone pillars their practical coats identified them as gentlemen heading out to the market at Brook Field. The decorum of that place was felt hats rather than dress-wigs, and with the ground softening under foot solid boots and canvas leggings were going to be of more use than buckled shoes and ebony canes. The Fair proper (or improper) wouldn't begin until Thursday. Until then the site would be given over to butchers, livestock-dealers, and hide-merchants drawn to the market from London's outlying villages. From as far as Edgware and Enfield in the north, from Lambeth and Camberwell in the south, and out west from Brentford and Hounslow, the traders converged. On this sunny morning it was proving to be thirsty work negotiating for the early bargains and renewing old acquaintances; and by eleven o'clock the nearby Dog and Duck was beginning to hum with business.

The alehouse was an old timber structure that had done duty in earlier times as a hunting-lodge, and its rickety balcony still commanded a view. But what had once been the haunt of deer and game was now a patchwork of fenced-off scrubland, small ponds, cattle-pens, and stabling for horses. The brook that ran through it was already changing from an Arcadian stream to a convenient drain, and the fact that it flowed from nearby Tyburn hardly enhanced its character. A few open fields bordered by solitary trees were interrupted by a line of huts and a couple of large barns that already sported banners for the Fair; and further along by a forlorn-looking hedge a blacksmith's forge was busy, cheek by jowl with a neat row of houses in shiny brick which sat beside the muddy roadway and announced that the city was encroaching fast. Brook Field would soon lose its name and its character, and the May Fair be an embarrassing memory lost under elegant streets.

'Whoah! What a fug!' muttered Tom as Will half-pushed him across the tavern threshold. 'The true cattle smell, eh?'

Will stepped in after him, his hat striking the lintel where the words 'Richard Middlemiss, Proprietor' were boldly carved.

'Close your eyes, Tom, and you'll guess where you are – I'm scenting blood, are you?'

'Yes, raw meat – and cooked meat too – I'm not sure which is worse!'

'Damp sheep's wool ... And a vinegary smell ...'

'That will be the tanned hides.'

'Ah yes of course! And unmistakeable *pig!* The genuine scent of sty ...'

'Nicely mixed in with fried bacon, though – it's quite a stew in here!'

And indeed, somewhere out of their sight a big stew-pot was on the go, in which various meats bubbled away, intensified by the living odours that exuded from bloodied aprons, shit-caked boots, and coats reeking of horseflesh. To complete the effect, this banquet of the senses was smothered in a rich gravy of tobacco smoke.

'We shan't need any food, Will. Just breathe in and swallow!'

'No, but a drink, certainly.'

The beer, they discovered, was good. It was being delivered on tap from four large barrels at the far end of the room. There were smiling faces all around, and animated talk. It was a big merry meeting of market-folk, and the atmosphere seemed to wrap around everyone like a welcoming cloak.

Will's eyes scanned the scene:

'It's a strange place for a reformers' meeting – a drinking den!'

'I'm beginning to wonder about this Middlemiss fellow. To be a Reformation man and a tavern landlord … How does he square his conscience by it?'

'Does the author of *Prologue to The Tender Courtesan* need to ask?'

'Ah, our old friend Hypocrisy?'

'The very same. The brethren clearly have no qualms about gathering in Satan's parlour.'

'It's not the Sabbath of course. Perhaps they'll redeem their weekday indulgence by their Sunday piety?'

'That's true of many, Tom!'

'And look behind us – surely these are *pews*, are they not?'

'I do believe they are – well, well! Were you to put this in a satire, you'd be thought a fanciful creature.'

It was hardly to be credited, but along the wall were three partitioned box-pews in dark oak, which must have been removed from a local church. They were high-backed, but had their doors removed and their facing panels lowered. Tom marvelled at them:

'Snug little alcoves, aren't they! – and they look old. Imagine the thousands of sermons their occupants have slept through …'

He noticed a pair of bewigged gentlemen huddled together in one of them.

'… It's what you call *superior* accommodation!'

As they laughed, a pair of livestock-men dressed in belted

smocks emerged from the nearest one. They were carrying notebooks and had whips slung at their waists. Their determined faces suggested they were ready to drive some hard bargains.

'Perhaps not so superior after all! But quick, let's have a seat – they're certainly good enough for us.'

They stepped into the pew and settled down side-by-side, their heads leaning against the wooden panel. It was quite a comfortable billet – too comfortable perhaps, and Will stretched himself to full length:

'I'm feeling drowsy already – and there's not even a sermon.'

Tom grinned. His mind was working:

'Will,' he said quietly – almost in a whisper. 'Those two gentlemen in the next pew – they looked *incongruous*, did they not?'

Will's eyes suddenly brightened with his mind:

'My God, you're right – sorry Tom! It's fortunate one of us is alert. You don't think … ?'

'Beginning to assemble for the noon meeting? Why not? That's exactly what we're doing, after all.'

They were now whispering, knowing that the two bewigged figures were in the neighbouring pew. By this time Will was smiling beatifically at how events seemed to be unfolding:

'I think you may be right … If only Mrs Trotter could see us! I'm beginning to know how she felt at the Exchange – we're officially spies, are we not?'

'The game's afoot, Will. Hush!'

The two of them sat back and raised their tankards to their lips. The room was noisy, but there was definite talking in the pew behind them. Their hearts started beating faster.

Tom scrutinised the oak panel against which their backs rested, and made a discovery.

He beckoned to Will, who leaned over:

'There beyond you, Will … is that a *hole?*'

Will looked, and indeed high up in the pew, about a foot away, a knot in the oak had been pushed through and a chink, hardly more than an inch across, was visible. Will said nothing, but slowly edged himself along the seat and drew himself up to his full height. The tiny gap in the panel was now just by his right temple, and as he cocked his ear he detected conversation.

He turned back to Tom and spoke in a low voice:

'I think we're about to learn if these are just a couple of market-managers – or if someone is blessing our enterprise …'

He gave a conspiratorial look.

'… Shall we sit and have a quiet drink? See if sleep overtakes us?'

Will settled back in the pew, and for the next five minutes they sat in silence. Will had removed his hat so that his ear rested close to the hole, eyes half-shut, and Tom watched the responses play across his friend's face. He found himself reading its contours like a child intent on a dumb-show at the Fair. The idea amused him, but his impatience was mounting. He made as if to speak, but Will raised an admonitory finger. Will's eyes were now trained on the blackened beams of the ceiling, and Tom watched as a look of puzzlement touched his face before a slight smile took over. The suspense was building, and Tom tried to calm himself by taking another gulp of the deliciously hoppy ale. He knew he would simply have to be patient and wait.

A further minute passed before Will finally relented and relaxed himself:

'You're not going to believe this …' he said, shifting his position and taking a sip of his beer.

'Well there's a way of finding out,' said Tom, filling the pause a little peevishly. 'I'm waiting.'

'Land!'

'Land?'

'Speculation – the price of land!'

Tom was at once downcast. His hopes had been building. These were evidently two City men – nothing of moral reformation there! … But Will was looking pleased with himself.

'Why are you smiling?'

'Because … there's clearly another aspect to this affair which we've been ignoring.'

'To do with land?'

'Yes – it's obvious when you think of it. The *value* of Brook Field … Perhaps there are others – besides the Reformation of Manners people – who would be happy to see the end of the Fair?'

Tom saw the light:

'Of course, that makes sense … But are they here for the meeting?'

'They most certainly are – I heard them talk of it. But it's not the gathering we have been expecting. These are men of business.'

'So, what did you learn?'

'They spoke of a *Mr Shepherd,* who appears to be a young friend of theirs. And I think he is expected at the meeting. This Mr Shepherd *owns* a large part of Brook Field – he collects good rents from the Fair, and he's begun erecting one or two houses at the edge of the site. It seems these men are hoping to persuade him to relinquish the rest of the land to them – for a price, of course.'

Tom began to give a loud whistle, but checked himself:

'I think I see … If the Fair was to be banned as a nuisance, then the young man might be encouraged to sell.'

'Yes, I think men are eyeing these acres hungrily. But the grant of the Fair is an obstacle. It was a royal warrant under the Great Seal – the late King James of blessed memory!'

'Ah, so his daughter …'

'Yes, Tom, it is within Her Majesty's prerogative to proscribe the Fair and cancel the grant …'

'And so, a great obstacle to building would be removed. This complicates matters, does it not? You're the legal man.'

'It adds to the picture certainly. I wonder how much the religious brethren know of this plotting.'

'Well, it wouldn't be the first time God and Mammon have made common cause.'

'And once again everything seems to hang on the Queen's *proclamation*. With a wave of her hand she could shut down the May Fair and discontinue the theatre's patent.'

'Such is the breath of Queens!' said Tom. 'Are we really still in that world?'

'In matters of prerogative, yes ... and that is what gives the Society for the Reformation of Manners its power. They may find it hard to carry all the magistrates and constables with them – but if they win round the Queen ...'

'So, the killing of Lord Tunbridge in the Playhouse really does make things precarious.'

'It links all together, Tom – theatre and fair. The Queen may consider it the final provocation.'

'And so, it bodes ill that her Solicitor-General is building a case against the company – and Rich in particular.'

'It looks very bad. The ground is being prepared – and if they can prove the company conspired to murder the man who was setting out to reform them ...'

This time Tom's whistle ran its course:

'But what about these business people and the Fair?'

'I don't know. They may be working for the Grosvenors or the Berkeleys, who own the adjacent land. Or there could be a royal connection – after all, St James's Park is nearby, over the road. These are influential men. To find common purpose with them would strengthen the reformers even more. Each has an interest in seeing the end of the Fair.'

Powerful forces were at work; and as the two of them chatted, the holiday world of May Fair began to appear innocent in comparison. What price Joy? they asked themselves, somewhat sentimentally. But a chilling echo came back: What price Debauchery? Vice? Crime? Perhaps there was no genuine innocence in any of this, only different kinds of power?

A glumness was settling over them, so Will beckoned to the pot-boy and ordered another drink. Small beer this time, they agreed, for lubrication only – they needed to keep their heads clear.

'You have a meeting-room here?' Tom asked the lad as he was turning to go.

He didn't reply immediately but gave them both a sly look. They suddenly felt uncomfortable. Perhaps the question had not been a wise one.

'You 'ere for the meetin' then? …' he asked.

Tom shifted in his seat.

'… Mister Dick says it's a secret *do*, and we're to keep quiet about it. Do yer want me to tell 'im you're 'ere?'

His free hand twitched spontaneously.

'No, no, we're with the Fair,' said Will awkwardly. 'Just thinking of a private room for dinner.'

'Yer don't sound like Fair folk to me,' said the lad. 'Tables for food are out back …' He dropped his voice. 'The *meetin*'s in Mister Dick's chamber, upstairs – *if yer need to know*.'

His grin was now cheeky, and his palm brazenly extended.

Will gave him tuppence:

'Just bring us the beer, eh?'

As the boy moved off Will was shaking his head.

'Oh Tom, Tom! …'

'I'm sorry, Will. That was unwise – no, it was downright stupid! I was thinking …'

'I know what you were thinking. But what did we say? We mustn't draw attention to ourselves? The lad's a bright spark – he's clearly the *Peter* of the Dog and Duck.'

'I just hope he's as honest. He looked a mischief-maker to me.'

Both of them began to sense each other's anxiety, and their glances around the place became more guarded. They were trying to be aware of customers' faces without letting their curiosity show. Widow Trotter was right: this wasn't the genteel New Exchange where everyone had their own space. This alehouse was taking on the character of a private drinking-club.

It was thoroughly packed by this time, and the smoky air was even more suffocating. There were no seats to be had, and men were standing together in close-knit groups. They themselves were now sharing their pew with a couple of carters, who thankfully were morose and distinctly unsociable. One had eased his boots off and was rubbing his feet, encouraging a smell of ripe cheese to rise from his socks. Outside their pew the noise was increasing. Bursts of laughter drew everyone into the joke, and raucous shouts flew across the room; taunts were being delivered, backs slapped, friendly insults offered, doubts raised about parentage or mental competence.

After a few hours of trading, some of the market-men had good coin in their pockets and were determined to lay it out in pleasure. The mood had progressed from cheerfulness to ebullience. Female company was available, and women's voices were joining in the banter. Here and there a daggled calico skirt or muslin dress tripped from group to group; thick arms slid around delicate waists or squeezed bolstered hips; male fingers explored ribbons and flounces. From time to time a couple would separate out and swagger to the rear door.

It was still an overwhelmingly male huddle, and now its warm closeness was more evident than ever. The butchers' blue aprons were rubbing up against the worn leather breeches of the horse-coursers, and the floor was wet with spit and spilt beer. A couple of bedraggled lurchers were licking the boards and nuzzling among the stools for scraps of food.

'Am I wrong, or does everyone here seem to know each other?'

Tom's question hardly needed an answer. Will took out his watch discreetly and consulted it:

'Ten minutes!' he whispered.

They had begun watching the staircase furtively, but as the place filled up it wasn't easy to have a clear view. The money-men in the adjacent pew still had to make a move. Any plans for keeping a lookout were proving easier in theory than in practice. Everything was so close, and they felt hemmed in. Will had his hat on again and found himself inching it forward over his face.

Suddenly they were aware of a figure standing by them. He had emerged out of the huddle, smiling at the customers and returning their greetings. He briefly caught their eyes, and then stretched out an arm.

'Gentlemen, come this way!'

For a moment Tom and Will were terrified, until they saw it was their neighbours who were being beckoned. This character, they guessed, was *mine host* himself, Dick Middlemiss. Now their hearts were truly thumping. Both of them sank into their seats and waited for the moment to pass. It was with relief that they saw the host and his bewigged guests make their way over to the staircase. The two gentlemen, satchels clutched to their stomachs, processed through the huddle to the accompaniment of mock bows and hoots of admiration.

Tom and Will were unsettled but remained vigilant, and five minutes later they were rewarded with the sight of the landlord on the stairs again. He descended quickly and made his way to the door, where two wary-looking gentlemen clothed in black were standing, their faces set in cold disapproval, lips pursed against the unholy air. Middlemiss ushered them inside, and like a pair of excisemen in a smugglers' den, they half-crept, silent and purposeful, along the far wall.

Will looked at Tom:

'What eloquent faces! I think we know who they must be. That grey beard – it's just as Mrs Trotter described. And the squat red-faced fellow ...'

'The messenger and the haberdasher, yes! ... But look, Will. Who is that, do you think?'

Will glanced back to see a third man following them up the stairs. This individual was more of a Dog and Duck character. He was short, dressed in shirt-sleeves and breeches, a coat under his arm, and carried himself confidently, almost like a wrestler. Tom had noticed an angry scar curving under his left ear:

'Now that gentleman looks like trouble.'

Will nodded:

'A motley company altogether. What a party they must be having – landlord, city-men, the brethren – and ...'

'... and one who knows how to wield a knife, I expect.'

'If those gentlemen *are* plotting something, then it's not just money-matters. These mean business of another sort.'

The words brought a shiver. Sitting in their little box-pew, the two friends were beginning to attract a few glances. The place was seething, and they could see almost nothing of the room. And so, after another five minutes they decided their seats were no longer comfortable.

But just as they stepped out of the pew, a sudden gunshot rang out. It came from outside the alehouse and was a little distant, but unmistakeable and startling. An immediate hush descended on the company, followed by an excited gabble. Several men began leaving by the garden-door, and they heard the word 'ducks!' being uttered.

'It seems the place is living up to its name, Will!' said Tom, mightily relieved at the distraction. 'Let's slip out while we can ...'

Will looked puzzled.

'... The *dog and duck!* ... I think we are about to witness the unholy sport itself.'

'Of course! This looks like a popular show. Better than the playhouse!'

They began moving nonchalantly towards the rear door. The aim was to appear as inconspicuous as possible, and so they avoided any appearance of hurry as they wove between bodies. Their eyes were fixed on the door, and they reached it without interruption, emerging into the brightness of the garden with some relief, not a little pleased with the nice manoeuvre and altogether happy with the results of their tavern eavesdropping – it had proved a profitable hour. They were unaware that a little way behind, another figure slipped out quietly after them, and with thoughts that were very similar: yes, the pot-boy's report had been right – here were a pair of smooth playhouse-men interesting themselves in their meeting. A dangerous curiosity, the man thought as he pulled up his coat collar.

Tom and Will found an eager crowd assembled to the rear of the building. Sure enough, there was a large duck-pond shaded by willow-trees, with a scattering of men and women gathered along the gravel walk that skirted it. The participants were readying themselves. Dogs had been tethered to a line of posts and were pulling angrily at their chains while their owners tantalised them with scraps of raw meat held over their heads.

'And there are the victims, Will!' said Tom, pointing to a large coop where the unfortunate birds were huddled together in conditions not dissimilar from those they had just left.

'... Rural sports, eh?'

They were about to turn away when Will snatched Tom by the sleeve:

'Look there – on the balcony!'

Tom glanced upwards to see a group of familiar faces gazing out at the scene.

'Well I never! Middlemiss's private party – and with a commanding view! Whatever they're discussing is going to have to wait, it seems.'

'And look, there's someone behind them – a tall young man. I think he must be Mr Shepherd?'

'The monarch of the market! – but not for long perhaps?'

The sport was beginning. Three of the ducks were tossed into the pond, and a moment later two huge mastiffs and a sleek pointer were released after them. At once the ducks began flapping frantically with pinioned wings that refused to lift them into the air, while the dogs leapt and barked, splashing water everywhere. The chase looked one-sided, but the ducks had the advantage in diving, and the leading mastiff suddenly found its prey had disappeared. Another dog dived after them, but almost immediately emerged coughing and shaking itself in annoyance.

There was cheering from the crowd, and the odds were being shouted by men taking bets. People were crowding to the water's edge, their boots touching the boards that formed the pond's protective fence. There was mayhem in the water, with the creatures flapping and splashing while cries of encouragement rang out all around. A couple of boys were throwing stones at rival dogs, while another took aim at the ducks. One of the birds was struck and began flapping helplessly as the pointer swam towards it and closed its jaws around the creature's neck. Suddenly the shouting was wilder than ever. Tom and Will looked up and saw great excitement in the balcony where the two gentlemen in black were smiling broadly and shaking hands.

'I see they have no objection to this kind of theatre!' said Tom bitterly.

'No qualms at all, evidently.'

'Come on, let's leave them to their entertainment. It's time I thought about other matters. We need to find Pinkerman's booth.'

Will nodded in assent:

'I don't know about you, Tom, but I have a desperate need to *smile* ... After what we've seen and heard this past hour, *The Tender Courtesan* has such a delightful ring to it, don't you think?'

Tom felt into his coat pocket, where his prologue nestled:

'A smile, *yes* … laughter, *no!*'

The two of them walked off, able at last to chat freely and relax into the holiday mood. They were anticipating a more congenial interlude and felt hugely relieved to have put the Dog and Duck behind them.

Chapter Twenty

WHILE TOM AND Will were on their mission to Brook Field, in the Bay-Tree's coffee-room Widow Trotter and Elias Cobb were leaning head-to-head across the bar like a pair of alehouse conspirators. Jenny Trip was eyeing them with an amused look on her face. Heavy matters! she thought. And her guess was not wide of the mark.

The normally easy-going constable was giving vent to his frustrations:

'... But I'm hamstrung, Molly! Things are moving on apace and I'm left to catch what hints I can. The Justices are closing ranks and Mr Hector is happy to see the business carried on by Montagu's people. It's all backstairs-work!'

'This new magistrate – has he no authority?'

'He would have more if he chose to exert himself. But there's always an easy path when the politicians decide to meddle – you simply stand back and reap a reward for your silence.'

'But does he not have a responsibility?'

'That's the thing, Molly – he can hide behind the scenes while the performance goes on, knowing it's been taken out of his hands.'

Widow Trotter looked at her old friend with a mixture of admiration and concern, shaking her head:

'And that's something you've never been able to do, is it Elias?'

'No, and I'll not begin now! …'

He seized his dish of coffee with a gesture of determination.

'… Old Mr Dignum did things by the book. He was exceedingly testy at times, but you had to respect him. This fellow Hector is a sharp City man with the manners of a court flunky – it's a dispiriting combination! He's not prepared to ask awkward questions. There's no *grit* in him!'

Mrs Trotter smiled to herself. She suspected it was a clash of personalities as much as principles:

'Did Mr Hector have the door shut on you?'

'Not physically, but I was told the Baron's death was not a matter for inquiry. The words "Her Majesty's Solicitor-General" were spoken in hushed tones and I was briskly ushered out.'

'And you say things are also quiet at the theatre?'

'Hardly quiet – there's a deal of sawing and hammering going on. The boatyard at Chatham isn't busier! But there's no sign of Rich or Cibber, and none of the other actors are there because it's the recess.'

'So, the crisis-meeting …'

'Never happened! It seems Mr Swiney and Mr Estcourt turned up, but there was no-one to meet them.'

She tried to be encouraging:

'Perhaps they are at the Fair. The place must be busy now – and our two young scouts will surely glean something over there … You've heard nothing more about Sally Twiss?'

'No, not since the news of her leaving the play – if that's what she's done.'

Widow Trotter sighed:

'If only I could be at the Dog and Duck with Tom and Will! I'm being eaten up with curiosity.'

'We'll both have to be patient, Molly.'

'But I wonder ....'

'Do you think .... '

'Perhaps ... ...'

And so, as often happens, a dearth of news generated its own sense of urgency. With nothing firm to build on, imagination was left to paint the scenes, and their talk continued to feed on the very absence of information.

When the news finally came into the coffee-room, it arrived with a refreshing waft of air from the door. Christopher Bullock was standing in the entrance, surveying the scene. His eyes lit up, and the young actor gave the kind of cry that would pacify a Roman mob:

'Ah, Constable! There you are!'

He swept off his hat and with a few easy strides joined them at the bar.

'Mr Bullock! You enter like a messenger – not with ill news I hope?'

The room had instantly gone quiet. Around the tables, half a dozen conversations had broken off and wigs swung round in anticipation.

'The worst, Mr Cobb! The very worst! ...'

News from the battlefield of Shrewsbury could not have been delivered more solemnly.

'... *Mr Rich is in custody!* – And poor Mr Cibber has been carted off as well.'

'Arrested?'

'Yes – and had the charge read to them. They've been taken out west for questioning.'

'Out *west?* This is not the Magistrate then. What sort of a procedure is this?'

Elias knew only too well – *politicians* were taking a hand. No doubt of it.

'Tipstaffs came to call at Mr Rich's lodging – and a couple of burly gentlemen they were too! I was there with my father and Mr Cibber. There was little consideration shown, and no-one was allowed to accompany them. It was a formal arrest – *on the orders of the Solicitor-General*, they said.'

Widow Trotter was listening closely. She had half-expected this, but the shock wasn't lessened. She was trying to think clearly:

'What *charge* was it?' she asked, afraid of hearing the answer.

'It cannot have been a formal one,' said Elias. 'Not without a magistrate.'

'They were charged with conspiring.'

'*Conspiring?* – conspiring *what?* ...'

Elias was looking at Widow Trotter as he asked the next question.

'... *Murder?*'

There was an audible gasp from the coffee-room.

'No, Mr Cobb, it was not murder directly, though Lord Tunbridge's killing was mentioned. They were accused of bringing about his death.'

'Well!' said Elias, 'this is a strange notion. It sounds an awkward procedure to me, intended to frighten them and embarrass the company.'

'But a formal charge could be made at any point?' said Mrs Trotter.

'Certainly, but at this stage they need do nothing more – it serves their purposes very well.'

'What it suggests to me, Elias, is that they lack the evidence for a murder charge, at least for now.'

'Well, they have wedged the door open, Molly. The playhouse is more vulnerable than ever. If only we knew what evidence they have been collecting – who they have questioned, what clue they may be following ...'

By this time the constable had drawn himself up to his full height and was looking into the distance as if trying to make out something on the horizon.

'... I wonder ...'

It was a private thought, and Elias was suddenly aware of the room's silence. He turned and spoke softly to his hostess:

'... Might we move to somewhere *quieter?*'

Widow Trotter didn't need to be asked – their audience would simply have to be disappointed. She turned to her listening customers:

'I'm sorry, my friends ...'

And the contrition was genuine: she was aware that hot news was the Bay-Tree's stock-in-trade as much as hot coffee and hot chocolate.

'... You've all heard the report. It seems there's nothing more to add at this moment. Make of it what you will, gentlemen!'

Two of the wigs were already tripping smartly towards the door with that very intention.

'Come, Mr Cobb,' she whispered, '– and you too, Mr Bullock – the *parlour* is calling.'

The eighteen-year-old was a little shocked at the privilege being accorded him. Mrs Trotter patted him on the arm for reassurance:

'I want to hear more from you, Mr Bullock. I'm sure things have been happening in the playhouse that will be of interest to us.'

Over in Brook Field, Tom and Will had reached the busy market area where trade was bustling. It was a distinctly fleshy experience. Along the cinder-strewn promenade was a line of stalls piled high with tanned hides and untreated skins, while others displayed heaps of offal in various shades of cream and pink, decorated with bright green cresses. Less picturesque was a row of bloody carcases that swung from metal hooks, some of them opened up for inspection and attended by men in blue aprons, knives at the ready.

Just beyond this scene of carnage were some sheep-pens where an auction was in progress. Tom recognised one of the burly stock-men from the Dog and Duck, here in his element shouting the prices and shaking his whip as if taming a lion.

But Will's eye had caught something else. He nudged Tom's elbow and pointed to a large timber noticeboard, in the centre of which a boldly printed broadside was nailed:

TO BE PERFORMED AT MR PINKERMAN'S DROLL BOOTH FOR THE ENTERTAINMENT OF THE QUALITY, GENTRY, AND OTHERS

THE TENDER COURTESAN

A DRAMATIC PIECE NEWLY WRITTEN FOR THE FAIR

EXHIBITING

THE SOFT PASSIONS OF A FEELING HEART
SENTIMENTS OF AMATORY AFFECTION
A NOBLE SACRIFICE TO LOVE
– & –
THE TRIUMPH OF MARITAL DEVOTION

ALSO WILL BE PERFORMED A SATYRICAL TABLEAU

THE DEVIL ON TWO STICKS

A SPECTACLE NEVER BEFORE SEEN AT THE FAIR!!!

WITH A CONCLUDING PAGEANT OF

the Seven Deadlie Sins

MR PINKERMAN IS ALSO PROUD TO PRESENT
A COMPANY OF ROPE DANCERS, VAULTERS AND TUMBLERS
THE FINEST IN ALL EUROPE
WHO ARE EXCELLENT IN THEIR SEVERAL PERFORMANCES
AND DO SUCH WONDERFUL AND SURPRISING THINGS AS THE
WHOLE WORLD CANNOT PARALLEL

AND TO DELIGHT HIS DISCERNING PATRONS
MR PINKERMAN IS PLEASED TO ANNOUNCE
THE RETURN OF

THE DUTCH DANCING DOGS

WHO WILL PERFORM AT THE SMALL PAVILION EXHIBITING
SEVERAL NEW TRICKS

Whenever theatre and fairground meet, there is bound to be a touch of the burlesque, and Tom couldn't help smiling at the bill of fare – *soft passions* and *dancing dogs!* But his heart sank when he thought what the play's reception might be. *The Tender Courtesan* was a domestic romance of the social affections, with none of the spectacle a May Fair audience might expect – no heroic adventuring or epic machinery, and there was a marked absence of battle and shipwreck. Beyond that, it had little of the verbal wit that might keep people entertained. It was a play of feeling, and everything depended on the actors' gripping them with the emotions of the piece. It suddenly seemed like an experiment in a new style of drama, and one that might go terribly wrong.

Will, however, was untroubled by such niceties and was grinning broadly at the unfolding scene. To their left, cries of "forty shillings!" and "two guineas!" arose from the nearest of the sheep-pens where some brisk bidding was going on. The centre of all this attention was an ugly ram who was strutting before his admirers like a victorious general. Ahead of them a team of oxen was being harnessed, ready to show their paces in tugging a tree-trunk across the field. And a little further on, over to the right, somewhat incongruous amid the scenes of the cattle market, stood William Pinkerman's booth, or rather the larger part of it.

The miniature theatre was still under construction. Its entrance was shrouded in wooden scaffolding on which builders were erecting a balustraded platform – an important feature of the booth. Along this raised walkway the performers would soon be parading in costume by way of advertisement, trying to entice customers with bits of stage business and snippets from the play. The poorer folk in the crowd would be content simply to gaze up in wonder, before moving on to a puppet-show nearby. The May Fair booths, it had to be admitted, were hardly Temples sacred to Thespis – they were more akin to a street bazaar where the ancient dignities of the theatrical art were happily sacrificed.

Immediately before them, the concourse of the fair was largely empty and gave a dreary impression; but it was easy enough to picture the scene in three days' time when the place would explode into life. There was some activity around Pinkerman's booth, and Tom recognised one of the stage-hands from the Theatre Royal, who seemed to be giving directions. The canvas covering was being pulled back to reveal the timbers. The two of them strode over to him.

'That's an elegant piece of work, Mr Jackson!' said Tom, looking up at the balustrade. 'Rather more solid than the rest of the booth, I have to say!'

'It's the old story, Sir – spend big on the shop window and you can stint on the rest – once folk are inside it will be too late to complain! The tent is a draughty place, but when the crowd are all packed together it will be cosy enough.'

Tom and Will shared the laugh.

'That's what makes the Fair so special,' said Will. 'I'm sure we can dispense with boxes and chandeliers!'

'I don't hear any activity inside,' said Tom. 'Is Mr Pinkerman here?'

'They're rehearsing in the old tithe-barn, Mr Bristowe. You'll find him over there ...'

He indicated a large structure at the edge of the field.

'... Excuse me, but they tell me you're penning the Prologue?'

'I see word travels fast, Mr Jackson. Yes, I'm about to hand it over now.'

'Well, I wish you luck with it! The play's an odd piece of work.'

Tom hesitated, trying to keep the anxiety out of his voice:

'Is Sally Twiss at the barn also? I did hear ...'

'Ah! Word's been travelling ... None of them are speaking of that! Young Miss Twiss has been – shall we say – *reluctant*. There's nothing to match an actress for airs and flights and rolling of eyes! They've had as much drama offstage as on. But as things stand they're hoping she'll be made to stay. Meanwhile the rehearsal goes on – they've been three hours in there. I wish you joy of the business!'

The stage-hand's words unsettled Tom even more – this particular burly gentleman had clearly not been won over by the sentiments of *The Tender Courtesan*. But it was some relief to know that Sally was still on board, however much the vessel might be listing. He only hoped they wouldn't soon be clinging to the wreckage.

As they walked on in silence, Will was trying to feel relieved but with less success. It had struck him that Sally and Gilbert might not welcome their arrival. They would hardly enjoy being reminded of their earlier flight – especially by two young men who knew certain things best kept secret. Why did it all have to be so involved? He wished he could simply take enjoyment from seeing her …

As the path neared the barn, they began to hear animated sounds coming from within. Their steps became slower, and a moment later Will stopped in his tracks. It was a hesitancy much unlike him, and Tom turned round.

'This won't be easy, Will – for either of us.'

'You've read my thoughts.'

'Are you sure you want to come in with me? I have to report to Pinkerman, but you're a free agent. You could go and watch the oxen – or buy a sheep?'

There was a half-smile on his face. Will responded by throwing back his head and taking a deep breath:

'No no – we go in together. I'm wondering whether more persuasion is going to be needed. It's unfinished business, isn't it?'

'Yes, things are far from settled. Sally is sure to be in a quandary – I'm not surprised she wants to flee again. Amos Jackson is right: there are *two* dramas playing themselves out here.'

The door swung free with a creak as they stepped into the barn, and the scene revealed itself. As well as being a space for rehearsal, the cavernous building was in part a working barn, part property-store – and evidently not just for Pinkerman's troop. They could see it was offering temporary home to a jumble of props and costumes, all of them displayed in the bays amongst odd pieces of farm machinery and bales of dirty straw. *The Tender Courtesan* was being rehearsed at the far end; but first they had to negotiate their way round an unusual vehicle stationed by the door. It was constructed from pieces of board nailed together, all brightly painted in yellow and green, with naked figures blowing curled horns and a child sitting astride a dolphin. There were reins hanging down from the thing, and cart-wheels were bolted onto its side. For a moment Tom and Will were distracted by the exotic object, and Will was frowning in puzzlement.

'Neptune's chariot!' declared Tom helpfully. 'It's for Miller's booth. The thing will soon come into all its glory – though what use wheels will be in the ocean I cannot think!'

He reached out a hand and grasped an iron trident that was leaning against the side. As he shook it heroically, Will looked upward and pointed to the mighty timbers that soared from floor to ceiling:

'We are in the abode of the gods, Tom.'

'If only we were! … I think some distinctly earthbound things are happening over there.'

And indeed, as they approached, they could see that an altercation was in progress. Gilbert Angell was crouching in front of a distinctly unhappy Pinkerman, who had stepped out of character as the cold-hearted Don Leone and was pointing to his script.

'No, no!' he was shouting. 'You must stay on your knees until I make my exit. Only then do you turn round. Your speech will come much better from a recumbent position. It shows your character. Remember, at this point Ernesto is *in despair*.'

'But am I not also *defiant*, Mr Pinkerman? And if I'm on my knees I shan't be able to do the gestures properly. Am I not defying you?'

'Yes, Mr Angell …' said a red-faced Pinkerman, who was trying to remain calm in the face of annoyingly reasoned argument.

'… But you defy me once I've left the stage – not before! …'

He sighed.

'… But if you insist, then you can rise to your feet on the words *honour's call*. I suppose that would fit the sentiment well enough.'

Gilbert Angell sank once more to his knees and composed his features to despair; the cold-hearted Don Leone was back in character, and the scene played itself out satisfactorily enough, though there was little animation about it. The hours of rehearsal were beginning to take their toll.

It was with obvious relief that Pinkerman saw Tom hovering in the distance, and his eyes lit up when he glimpsed the sheet of paper clutched in his hand.

'Mr Bristowe! Step forward, Sir! You come most carefully upon your hour!'

Tom shuffled forwards, suddenly caught up in the performance. Don Leone's fearsome stare was still operating, and a few yards to his left the young Ernesto was viewing him with something between despair and defiance. It was altogether unsettling.

'I don't wish to interrupt your rehearsal, Mr Pinkerman, but indeed I bring the Prologue with me, such as it is.'

'*Such as it is?*' said an indignant Don Leone. '*Such as it is?* I don't want apologies, Sir! The words of your Prologue must lift us up! Fire us with a zeal for our play. I expect *Genius* to take wing – nothing less!'

At that moment Tom would have turned and fled from the barn had not the face suddenly broken into a wicked grin and the genial Pinkerman been restored. Tom wasn't sure how to respond, and it didn't help that his attention was distracted by a large pair of angel's wings propped up on the far wall, their buckles hanging loose. Could it be an ominous prophecy?

Behind him to one side, Will had settled himself on a straw-bale, his eyes trained on Sally Twiss, who was similarly seated at the back of the acting area, her elbow leaning against a military drum and her sleeve pulled back to reveal a white forearm under the froth of lace. She looked strikingly innocent and vulnerable in these chaotic surroundings, and he needed to remind himself that this was no novice, but the resourceful – and scheming – Tamara. He flinched slightly at the thought.

Pinkerman beckoned Tom nearer:

'Come, Mr Bristowe, shall we hear your prologue? We are full of anticipation. Will you do the honours yourself – or do you wish for Pinkerman's rich tones to bring the script to life?'

Tom hesitated for an instant, then held out the paper. But Pinkerman demurred and spoke more softly:

'No, no! 'Tis your piece, young man – your workmanship. I think we should hear you deliver it, if you would like to? ...'

He smiled at the assembled troop.

'... You can rehearse me later!'

And so, Tom was brought centre-stage, and as he looked around him, the ancient barn took on the character of an auditorium, its cruck timbers bending over them in place of chandeliers, and with side-lofts instead of boxes. Around him the players were all seated, only too glad of the chance to hear a fresh voice. Even a pair of wood pigeons up in the rafters ceased cooing and were giving him their attention. He saw Will wink at him encouragingly.

Tom cleared his throat and imagined himself in Will's meeting-house, with the Reverend Mr Tysoe in his pomp addressing the ranks of Hackney believers, all of them comfortably seated, stern of soul and unforgiving of countenance. He took a couple of deep breaths, and began ...

'You dread REFORMERS *of our sinful age!*
You awful cat o'nine-tails to the Stage! ...'

He saw smiles beginning to light up the faces around him.

'To gain your favour we'd your rules obey
And offer you a MORAL *piece today ...'*

There was a sprinkling of laughter, but he kept his own face composed, lifting his eyebrows into a supercilious expression.

> *'Design our play to give you satisfaction:*
> *We would be* PURE *in Language, Thought, and Action ...'*

Pinkerman was already beaming with pleasure, and Tom began to relax into the part, drawing confidence from his audience, who were hanging on every word. The rhymes seemed to chime nicely, and with each of them the irony mounted. By the time the Prologue was reaching its end he knew he had them. He could see his favourite couplet approaching and gave the lines a wicked lightness of tone:

> *'Such Men attack the Sins that they're inclin'd to,*
> *And damn the very Vices they've a Mind to ...'*

There was an immediate burst of laughter, and some anticipatory clapping rang out, so that he had to pause before continuing. A murmur of approval was already beginning, and the poem's final words had a satisfying sense of climax:

> 'OUR *Stage presents a true Democracy,*
> *Whose greatest enemy's – – –* HYPOCRISY.'

The last word released everybody like a cork coming from a bottle, and there was a burst of spontaneous applause. Amidst the rapturous clapping he could not avoid noticing Sally Twiss. She was staring at him intently, motionless and thoughtful. Well ... it was done!

Tom was uneasy. He was thinking of Shakespeare's Mark Antony in the forum winning the crowd to his cause – a crowd that would a few minutes later become a murderous mob.

But Pinkerman was on him, seizing him warmly in his arms as if greeting a returning hero. Tom was blushing and flustered, embarrassed by the sudden electric fervour in the air around him. His eyes searched for Will, and he saw him transfixed – not smiling, but with what could almost be a look of concern.

Yes, Will knew.

Pinkerman held Tom by the shoulders and turned toward his troop of actors:

'That will indeed do, Mr Bristowe! 'Twill do mightily well! … You have not only given us heart – you have given us a cause!'

Tom knew he had. And on that thought his face presented a look that might easily have been mistaken for modesty and shyness but was something much more disquieting.

Chapter Twenty-One

'I TRUST YOU will join me in a bottle of claret, Mr Bristowe? …'

Pinkerman's arm guided Tom towards the side of the barn, where an upturned barrel and some stools gave the appearance of an improvised tavern-corner. He was rather red-faced and breathing awkwardly.

'… You have heard the desperate news from the playhouse? Things look black indeed …'

Tom gave a silent nod. He glanced round for Will and caught sight of him slipping out after the actors, who were happily trooping from the barn in the direction of the market and its refreshments. Sally Twiss was with them.

Pinkerman was obviously restless, and with a fussy shake of the hand he beckoned Tom to sit down.

'… We are under attack – a direct attack that seeks to bring us down. 'Tis a mockery of Justice!'

He reached into a deal box by his feet and retrieved a bottle and two glasses. It was evidently his private bar.

'Yes indeed, Mr Pinkerman. Elias showed us the pamphlet on Saturday. It's a poisonous thing – nothing short of a libel on the company.'

'Ah, the pamphlet, yes. What a rant! It seems we are *Satan's sanctuary*, a very *school of depravity* – a sodomitical conspiracy prepared to kill anyone who opposes us. 'Tis a mad piece of work.'

'Is there any action you can take?'

'None directly, Mr Bristowe. We can only hope it will be seen for what it is – yet another pulpit fulmination. But 'tis a crushing piece – the killing of Lord Tunbridge is made to bear down on us ... and now it has led to *this!*'

He sank lower on his stool. The words sounded ominous.

Tom checked himself. *This?*

'You say *led to this* ... Has something occurred?'

'Ah! You do not know! ... Yes, something most certainly has. I allude to the arrest of Mr Rich and Mr Cibber.'

Tom felt the blow. So, their suspicions were all too true.

'This is what we feared, Mr Pinkerman – a concerted attack, is it not?'

'Yes, our enemies clearly have a battle-plan. And I suspect it has not yet reached its culmination ...'

He shuddered and grasped the wine-bottle tightly, hovering over Tom's glass.

'... but things have moved on this afternoon. We have heard that Colley has been released. But, can you imagine the shock to the poor fellow? The indignity! ... Mr Rich, however, is still being held – and with bail fixed at an almighty *five hundred pounds.* Would you believe? 'Tis a huge ransom. He would have to pawn the theatre!'

'Bail? But has he been charged?'

'Word is, he is *awaiting a charge* of murder – whatever that means. They are trying to build a case against him. Rumour has it they have found someone prepared to swear they heard him plotting the death of Baron Tunbridge – or at least wishing it. The whole thing's uncertain – but no less dangerous for that.'

'But this is flimsy, Mr Pinkerman – does it have any basis

in law? We must ask Will. It sounds very improvised. There's so much rumour swirling about.'

Pinkerman shook his head:

'*Our Reputation,* Mr Bristowe! *Our Reputation!* We theatre people have plotted to kill Lord Tunbridge! – that is what everyone will now believe … and it is what Her Majesty will be *made* to believe …'

He began filling his own glass, shaking his head.

'… This whole affair is being planned simply to defame the company. We shall be anathema! Although I suspect any charge will be dropped in a day or two once the damage has been done.'

Tom was thoughtful – behind Pinkerman's theatrical bluster was an astute mind:

'I think you may be right, Mr Pinkerman. Why should they risk a trial? Particularly if young Sally Twiss is waiting to step forward and accuse the Baron. A public trial would be dangerous for them. The Baron would no longer be their martyr, but a villainous predator.'

Pinkerman gave Tom a piercing look:

'An *accusation,* Mr Bristowe? I see you know of the liaison – the actress and her patron! But *predator?* You arouse my curiosity. Might she be willing to accuse the dead man publicly? That would be dangerous for her too, would it not?'

Tom was suddenly circumspect and paused to sip his claret. Pinkerman was speaking of a *liaison,* nothing more … Had Sally not spoken about Lord Tunbridge's attacks? Or could it be that their relationship was more *regular?* The thought unsettled him. He didn't want to believe it.

'To tell truth, Mr Pinkerman, I was not expecting to find Sally here. This morning's chocolate-house gossip was that she had given up Tamara – it was intimated that you and Mr Rich were contriving to bring back Mrs Oldfield.'

'Oldfield? Confounded gossip!'

'Will and I met Amos Jackson just now, and he spoke of Sally's *reluctance* – he said you've had some dramatic scenes.'

'Jackson should keep his mind on his work and not pry into what doesn't concern him! … But I owe you the truth, Mr Bristowe – now that you are associated with the company …'

He set down his glass and looked around him.

'… Sally Twiss is afraid. She has been receiving notes – threats to herself.'

'Threatening notes? Have you seen them?'

'No, but they have evidently scared her. I think it must be somebody jealous of her sudden success.'

'Someone within the company?'

'I take it so – though I don't like to think of it. I told her it must be a childish prank, but she seems truly frightened. She wouldn't say more.'

'Then why has she stayed?'

There was a sudden flicker of the cold-hearted Don Leone:

'Because I gave her no alternative, Mr Bristowe. I told her she would be betraying the company and would find it hard to work again. The tantrums of a great actress can be borne – they are almost contracted for – but a mere novice? To flounce out of a role at the last minute? *No!*'

Tom was becoming alarmed. He thought about what he and Will knew of Sally's final confrontation with the Baron:

'But if you've not seen the letters, how can you know? – they may carry a serious threat.'

'We are *all* under threat, Mr Bristowe. The whole company. Now is the time to find common cause.'

Tom was wondering how much he ought to reveal about the plot they were uncovering, and how far it reached. He felt he owed it to Pinkerman – and to Sally – to say more. But he would have to be careful:

'Not just the theatre, Mr Pinkerman. I take it you've heard about that terrible business of the maypole?'

'Indeed we have. I understand Toby Mudge was the hero of the hour! What a brave fellow! Such a desperate attempt, was it not? I hear the man was spouting prophecies as he wielded his axe – a lunatic!'

'Mad perhaps, but clear-headed. The outrage was minutely planned. The axe was well hidden and the man chose his moment. He came prepared to be a suicide.'

'And he nearly was, by all accounts. Has he succumbed, do we know?'

'I don't, but Mudge said he was in a parlous state. The crowd exploded into anger and tried to tear him apart.'

Pinkerman's eyes were taking on a haunted look:

'There is such violence in the air, Mr Bristowe …'

He gave a great sigh.

'… 'Twill take very little to ignite it … Just think of our *Macbeth!* What a disaster, and at the worst time. The air ignited indeed! – I thought my last hour had come … But believe me, Mr Bristowe, the violence in the audience frightened me more. A mob – a crowd – an audience – I sometimes wonder if there's much difference … And did you know there was another outburst at *The Fox* last week? Mosca and Volpone were loudly cheered, and the gallery were throwing oranges at the judges. We very nearly had to alter Jonson's ending!'

'Has the Lord Chamberlain been placated?'

'Hardly. We've done what we can, but our credit is exceeding low. We have yet to hear. And now the Fair is upon us …'

A swig of claret helped suppress another sigh that was escaping from him.

'… But your *Prologue* is a fine thing, Mr Bristowe – very fine indeed. Something of a call to arms!'

'If that disturbs you, then perhaps I could …'

'No! You must not think of softening it in any way. I shall perform it as it stands – but not, I think, astride Hannibal.'

'Hannibal?'

'Our elephant – a noble beast deserving of his heroic name ... No, I shall do you the credit of delivering it on my own stout legs – solemnly too. It deserves an appropriate dignity of utterance. I shall put on a holy face.'

Tom smiled:

'Thank you. I was beginning to have doubts about the directness of the verses.'

'There are times when we have to be direct, Mr Bristowe. And this is one of them. I shall not rouse the rabble but speak to the hearts and minds of our audience – I shall give them the credit of understanding. It will be no rant, I assure you, but a piece of holy rhetoric. Only with the final word – *hypocrisy* – will it strike home.'

Tom felt reassured – and also infinitely relieved that it wasn't he who would be standing in front of the curtain:

'But you must be concerned about the Fair itself, Mr Pinkerman? It would be well if some peace-makers could be organised – people who would be vigilant and prepared for trouble.'

'I'm sure we shall have our share – there will be a phalanx of constables patrolling the Brook Field. The Justices have sent out a proclamation, and if the call is answered then we'll have a great press of them. They are to *preserve Her Majesty's Peace* – but I fear they will antagonise rather than pacify. And we are sure to have informers mingling with the rascality, holding their noses and taking notes. All of them determined to *suppress vice*. What an easy phrase that is! ...'

Pinkerman was now well into his stride.

'... What are we to expect, I wonder? – Is there to be no whoring and drunkenness? No gaming, and no lotteries? No cursing and swearing? – ha! – And what about *idle walking*? – they are sure to find plenty of that at the Fair – not to mention those delights of *congress* that a sunny field in Maytime always offers.'

'It does sound a vain hope,' said Tom.

'They'll be poking their noses into the droll booths too – strutting about the place like Zeal-of-the-Land Busies sniffing roast pork. You recall the last time the constables and their troops tried to *suppress* the Fair. The crowd didn't stand for it.'

'But with *The Tender Courtesan* ... Can we not hope ...'

'Ha! I fear our *Courtesan* is very much in their thoughts. This new pamphlet has ill intent. 'Tis a deliberate provocation. I am concerned that the play will be vulnerable.'

'Vulnerable?'

'To mockery and malice. We all know how ridicule can damn a play in seconds ...'

He leaned forwards and his voice softened.

'... Our *Courtesan* is a delicate thing, Mr Bristowe. It must work *in sympathy* with the audience, and draw out their sympathies in turn.'

'I understand ... You think it might meet resistance?'

'Some hearts are hardened to the social affections. But at this perilous time Colley and I are determined to appeal to the *finer* feelings ... 'Tis a risk – a *great* risk – but one we have to take. I am determined our play will touch the heart ... and on Thursday – let me assure you – Tamara will NOT take the veil!'

Pinkerman ended with a rhetorical flourish, and Tom felt like applauding. He began to see that *The Tender Courtesan* was intended to offer a message about our human passions: how they could be channelled towards good and find a path from selfishness and cruelty to benevolence and love ... Perhaps he had been too cynical about the piece?

'But I have to ask about your satire, Mr Pinkerman – *The Devil on Two Sticks*. How is that progressing? I've read Monsieur Le Sage's novel ...'

'Ah, Mr Bristowe, yes. Then you will know a little of what to expect, and what malicious fun we are like to have. There will be an opening panorama, and lots of amusing business – tricks and transformations – capering and tumbling – and flying too. Plenty to delight the groundlings! And I predict that our miniature devil will be a triumph. He is a fellow who can jump and tumble with the best of them – Tiny François has performed in front of King Louis! He must be seen to be believed!'

'And will he be on crutches?'

'Of course! And he has cloven feet to wear too. The boy is the finest little sprite you can imagine, and he prances about on his sticks faster than any athlete. This young *diable boiteux* is our guide and master of the ceremonies.'

'And I trust the satire won't be forgotten?'

Pinkerman took the cue. He settled himself on his stool, and with a gesture of supreme elegance lifted his glass, radiating a look of benign innocence:

'Ah, the *satire?* ... Yes, Mr Bristowe – you are right to remind me. We hope to find *a little something* – after all, our materials are everywhere, are they not? And one or two things do offer themselves. Perhaps we may touch on the way we live now – on those who rule over us, and those who would *wish* to rule over us ...'

Tom was smiling.

'... There are a few comfortable *hypocrisies* that wait to be exposed ... Yes, Mr Bristowe, I think there will be something for you to relish. And we plan a grand conclusion that will draw our satiric scheme together – a pageant to lodge itself in the mind. 'Twill not be soon forgotten, I assure you.'

This is enigmatic – are you keeping the thing a secret?'

'As much as we can. We are rehearsing it elsewhere, and the set is in pieces ready to be assembled. You smile, Mr Bristowe! But remember, the effect of these more *extravagant* performances is much the greater if the audience are *in the dark*. Never underestimate the power of the unexpected.'

'Well, my expectations are considerable!'

Pinkerman looked up and saw Amos Jackson hovering nearby, hesitating to interrupt. He was awaiting his instructions:

'Mr Jackson – yes, of course! I'll come with you immediately. Is it completed?'

'That's for you to say, Sir. But it looks pretty well to me.'

Pinkerman reached into a leather purse that hung from his waist:

'Good, good! Forgive me, Mr Bristowe, but I have to inspect the new balcony. What would a booth be without its promenade, eh? ...'

He drew out a fine two-guinea coin and held it out to Tom.

'... This has been well earned, Mr Bristowe! I shall always be grateful to you. If our *reformers* will permit us to survive, then I hope your association with our playhouse will continue ... Lead the way, Jackson!'

William Pinkerman marched off, buoyant and eager in an almost childlike way. The man, Tom thought, was fashioning his own magical world here at the Fair, and offering that magic to others. 'Pinkerman's booth' would soon be on everyone's lips. He deserves well, Tom thought.

The bright gold coin nestled in his palm, and for a brief moment he held it there, unwilling to pocket it. Here was his fee – and for the first time he felt every inch an author by profession. He looked at King Charles's head in profile. It was crowned with a garland – was that an omen? He smiled at his own presumption. But just as his fingers were about to close around it, he saw something he had never noticed before ... There at the coin's edge, nestling beneath the Monarch's head, was unmistakeably – and inexplicably – a tiny elephant.

Chapter Twenty-Two

THE ACTORS WERE dispersing, and Will followed them out of the barn across to where food and drink were on offer. He thought it best to leave Tom to his discussion with Pinkerman and venture on his own. Beyond the fence that skirted the field an improvised stall was dispensing hot food, and a few trestle tables were scattered about, at which homely appetites were being satisfied. Some of the market traders had retired here from their haggling over cows and sheep, and the trenchermen among them were feasting on veal pies and mutton stew – clearly devotees of meat, alive or dead. Will saw that Gilbert and Sally were talking together a little behind the others, and when the main group began settling themselves at one of the tables the pair continued strolling on towards the cattle-pens and hide-stalls, caught up in each other's company.

Will was hesitant, wondering whether to follow them or join the rest of the troop who were talking animatedly and laughing aloud, clearly in a holiday mood. (Three hours of *The Tender Courtesan* might do that to anybody, he thought, ungenerously.) It was his own hunger that tipped the balance, and so he ambled up to the party and introduced himself.

Five minutes later he was being refreshed with a pint of ale and a beef pasty, enjoying the actors' lively conversation; and when they discovered he was a particular friend of 'Mr Bristowe' he found himself raising his glass in a toast to Tom and the *Prologue*.

'Here's to Hypocrisy!' was the first cry.

'And here's to *what I've a mind to!*' was the second.

'Aye, I'll always drink to that!' cried a third.

'Your friend has certainly done us proud, Mr Lundy – he launches us into the play with spirit – if the Prologue doesn't raise a cheer, then I'm a Puritan!'

'It begins the play vigorously enough,' remarked Bob Stanley, to whom had been entrusted the rather routine part of the apothecary. 'I only hope we can keep the piece jogging on with as much spirit!'

Given the change of roles, Will was curious to know who was now playing Agnes the novitiate nun – the part that Sally Twiss was originally destined for. He asked the question directly and was met with spontaneous smiles.

'Take a bow, Lizzy!' said a voice.

A round-cheeked and round-faced girl jumped to her feet laughing, and bobbed a girlish and far from nun-like curtsey that showed she was well rounded in other ways too. Although not the most obvious candidate for the veil, she would no doubt settle into the role and make Ernesto a good-humoured and devoted wife by the end of the play ...

Will smiled in turn:

'I'm glad you'll win a good husband, Lizzy! It's a happy ending, I gather!'

'Yes, a happy one in her case, Mr Lundy,' said Joe Byrne, who was taking the role of Don Felipe, Ernesto's devil-may-care friend. 'But speaking for myself, I'd prefer to come to a violent end. If you can't get the girl, then you can at least die like a man! A bloody battle or a good sword-fight is just the thing.'

'And are you favoured with either in this play?' asked Will.

'Happily yes. Being a rake, you see, I have to end with a rapier through my guts!'

'Ah, Poetic Justice!' said Will. 'Where would we be without it? But I thought this play was less correct in that way?'

'Not really,' said Lizzy Wright. 'But this being the May Fair I hope we can ruffle a few feathers. My Agnes will be no simpering little novice. I'm determined to give her some mettle – after all, I have to win *dear* Mr Angell away from his devoted *Misstwiss*, don't I?'

There was a burst of laughter. It was clear that young Sally Twiss was not the darling of the company, and Gilbert no popular favourite either. The fact that they had wandered off together only confirmed it.

'What does Mr Pinkerman say to that?' said Will, amused at the thought of how these real-life antagonisms might play out in performance.

'My Agnes has been well behaved so far, Mr Lundy – but on the stage, who knows? Our exotic Tamara might find her renunciation very easy. Noble sacrifice indeed!'

'And as for young Ernesto,' added Joe Byrne with a curl of the lip, 'he's all curds and whey – a moping lover with nothing solid about him. Whereas the bold Felipe ...' He sighed. 'Of course that's why I'm fated to die ...'

So much for the nicely-judged relations of the drama, thought Will.

'... Did you see the pair of them just now? Strolling off like royalty – beef pasties not good enough for 'em.'

'They'll have a long walk to a pastry-cook's!'

More laughter. Will felt a chill in the sunny air – this was something more than good-humoured baiting. He wondered whether to probe further. It might not be a comfortable conversation, but it would be useful to find out what these people knew, or at least suspected, about the goings-on at the playhouse.

It soon became clear that Sally Twiss was resented, and the reason was not far to seek: the young lady was a cuckoo in the nest. It was Peggy Evans who was most forthright, expressing herself in terms hardly befitting the genteel Abbess of St Clare:

'Hang her! She's a dimple-faced girl! – And to be favoured over Ann Oldfield! Hardly two months in the company and the chit is insinuating herself with her ladylike notions. Poor Mrs Bradshaw was very *put out* at her benefit when the young minx started giving herself airs – a maidservant toasted by a Lord!'

'Come now, Peggy, beware of jealousy! I'm sure you'd be expensively *patronised* yourself if you could. We all know where she got her graces from, don't we?'

'Indeed we do, Mr Stanley. But *I* wouldn't want to buy 'em at such a rate, however fine the coach and six! I would never venture into it – not with all that bouncing and tossing. 'Tis beneath even an actress's dignity.'

'Perhaps the role of courtesan will become her?' said Lizzy. 'Who knows but she may *grow into* the part.'

'Let's hope so! A shilling whore isn't going to do the business.'

'Well, she'll have to set about it soon,' said Joe. 'But our young Gilbert is no Lord Tunbridge. Perhaps that's why she finds it so difficult? He doesn't have the badger-smell of the nobility in heat.'

At this, Lizzy rocked back on the bench and nearly over-set it. Bob Stanley remained more serious:

'Who knows, Joe – perhaps by Thursday she'll have found something? Frankly, I think Tamara is a part that needs more poetry – a touch of the *memorable*. If only Shakespeare could have written her a soliloquy!'

'Ah yes! – do you mean something like this …'

Joe Byrne put on a tragic face.

"… Tamara, and Tamara, and Tamara … . ."

A wave of hilarity swept over them, and for several moments speech was impossible.

'Poor Sally!' said Bob Stanley. 'She's very unsettled. We are being cruel about her. The Baron's death has been such a shock.'

'His *murder*, you mean,' said Lizzy. 'Let's call things by their right name. *Murder most foul* …'

She turned to Will.

'… You'll know by now, Mr Lundy, that Sally's patron, Lord Tunbridge, was found behind the scenes at the theatre with a dagger in his back. It was horrible.'

Suddenly the bright mood passed into shadow. The four of them looked at each other awkwardly, and Will was confronted by a dramatic silence. He felt he had to speak, and did so hesitantly:

'It must be a terrible thing for the whole company. Am I allowed to ask … are they near to finding the killer? …'

The word sent a shiver through the air. Will sensed it.

'… Is the death being investigated?'

They looked at one another.

'On that, we're in the dark, Mr Lundy,' said Bob Stanley. 'We are no better informed than anyone else. The playhouse is closed to us during the recess, and all we have is gossip and speculation.'

'Word has it the Queen interests herself in the killing,' said Lizzy.

'I'm not surprised,' said Will. 'It is the *Theatre Royal* after all – *her* company.'

'That's true indeed … and Mr Rich is being questioned. They are making a star-chamber matter of it …'

Will looked curious, but said nothing, so Joe continued.

'… Do you not know the news about Mr Rich and Mr Cibber?'

This sounded alarming:

'What news?'

'The pair were arrested last night, Mr Lundy. We now hear that Mr Cibber has been released, but Mr Rich has been charged, and is on bail for a vast sum.'

'Five hundred, they say,' added Lizzy.

'*Bail??*'

Will held his peace. There was little more they could tell him, but from the scraps of rumour he began to pick up, the arrest seemed a vexatious procedure. He was anxious to hear more but would have to be patient.

He raised the tankard to his lips and looked about him. The buoyant mood had gone, and everyone was turning to their pasties and pies. Over by the pens the cattle were becoming restless, and the sing-song cries of the auction were being wafted over on a rising breeze that was animating a line of flags and slapping their ropes against the wooden poles. With a natural sense of decorum, the sun disappeared behind a cloud. The hot food suddenly seemed a good idea ... So, was Sally Twiss suspected? She was certainly resented, but there was nothing certain, no direct accusation. But he was beginning to sense what their unspoken thoughts were.

He was half-expecting to see Tom at any moment and knew he needed to push the actors further while he could:

'A cold-blooded murder in the playhouse! – That must be unprecedented, surely? There have been theatrical fights before now, but nothing like this.'

'No, this wasn't a man-to-man fight, Mr Lundy,' said Joe glumly. 'It was a crime of passion. A sneaking knife in the back – and in one of the costume-rooms too. It smacks of some backstairs work. What was the Baron doing in there, I ask?'

He looked at the others, whose expressions gave silent assent. It was Peggy Evans who spoke:

'What could draw him into such a place? What had *charms* enough to lure him into a property-store during the interval ... ?'

Expressed in those terms the question was itself dagger-like, and the thrust went home. But no-one was ready to continue. Will pressed on:

'Mr Bristowe and I went behind the scenes ourselves. The place is such a warren of passages, is it not? It would be easy for someone to hide.'

'The rear door is a problem, Mr Lundy – it opens into Vinegar Yard. The thing is seldom used by anyone but us – it gives a short cut to the green room and the dressing-rooms. But people have been known to sneak in there – particularly the behind-the-scenes gentlemen.'

Will gave him a questioning look. Bob Stanley explained:

'We think of them as the playhouse butterflies. They like to flutter around the theatre and never settle anywhere. They're in and out of the boxes to meet their friends, sniffing around the dressing-rooms and slipping into the green room. They think a handsome suit and a fancy sword-knot are their passport to all.'

'And of course,' said Joe, '*The Man of Mode* was Mrs Bradshaw's benefit, so on that evening we had a generous share of 'em. Flounces and fine waistcoats by the score, with more Sir Foplings than you could shake a silk handkerchief at!'

'So you think it might have been an intruder? Or perhaps a quarrel during the interval?'

'What *we* think, Mr Lundy, is not to be spoken of ... But Peggy's question needs to be answered. *What took His Lordship into the property-room?*'

Will knew he must be careful with his questions. He was having to curb his lawyer's instinct to prod, provoke, and burrow. He was only their acquaintance, and they would resent an inquisition. But perhaps one nudge more might be risked – with a little reminder that he was a close friend of the 'Prologue.'

'Were people in the company alarmed about Lord Tunbridge's plans for the theatre? My friend Tom tells me His Lordship's ambitions were far-reaching – distinctly *reforming* ones.'

Bob Stanley spoke:

'We are supposed not to know of those, Mr Lundy! But rumours abound, as you might guess. Mr Pinkerman and Mr Rich have been outraged, but Mr Cibber appears more sanguine about it. In any case, nobody consults us. If it's to be all preaching and moralising from now on, then we'll be the last to know.'

Joe picked up the theme:

''Tis said the Baron was pressing for a licensing of the stage – with all scripts submitted to a censor – namely himself. That would be death to the theatre. There's more than enough policing as it is … Tunbridge's demise has been nothing short of a blessing.'

The others murmured approvingly.

'Yes, we've been given a reprieve, thank God,' said Lizzy, 'and we're mighty thankful for it.'

'The sooner the Baron is buried – and his plans with him – the better!' added Peggy decisively.

'But we're still at war, Mr Lundy,' said Joe Byrne. 'We may have seen off one enemy, but there's others circling. The pamphlets are branding us as Satan's crew, and they're intent on destroying us. We all know what we're facing, do we not? …'

He looked around him.

'… The reformers would burn us at the stake if they could!'

For an instant, everyone knew this was no figure of speech. The shock was palpable, and it ran through Will's bones too. But the uncomfortable thought served to jolt them out of the hellish vision. It was Lizzy who drew them all back to life and laughter:

'But, take heart my friends! We're forgetting this will soon be the Fair – the glorious *May Fair!* Remember, this is our world – not theirs! We're bringing ourselves to the people and giving them wonder and laughter. There'll be plain folks and fine folks, and pompous folks and delicate folks …'

'… – and drunken folks!' added Joe.

'... Let's hope so! But there will be no preachers! And if anyone tries to preach to *me*, they'll get a blood pudding in their face!'

A cheer of relief went up.

The mood became convivial again, and talk returned to the play and its prospects – but only briefly. Without warning, there was a sudden flurry of wind, and heavy drops of rain began swirling in on them. Glancing to the sky, they saw a black cloud rising above the scene like a giant anvil. With cries of surprise, the actors leapt to their feet and instantly began scampering back in the direction of the barn. Their whoops of wild delight were those of liberated children racing out of school. Will smiled at the irony and finished off his beer with a single gulp as the rain beat down on the table with a clattering sound. Rather than run after them, he turned toward the stalls and saw a canvas awning that would give him some shelter.

He ran for it and swept a lock of wet hair away from his eyes. As he did so, he noticed another figure with similar intention running light-footedly in his direction.

It was Gilbert Angell.

But there was no sign of Sally Twiss.

Chapter Twenty-Three

WILL PEEPED OUT from under the awning and shouted to Gilbert Angell, who was running through the rain. The young actor looked up, glimpsed shelter and a friendly face, and lengthened his stride. A few seconds later he was by Will's side, huddling in the tight space along with three or four of the market-traders whose business had been dramatically curtailed.

Will's immediate question was half-shouted above the noise of the rain buffeting the canvas:

'Where's Sally, for heaven's sake?'

This was not an occasion for polite niceties, and Will had only one thing on his mind.

Gilbert wiped the rain from his face. There was a smear across the left cheek, which emphasised the startled look in his eyes, and he took a moment to respond while he reached into his pocket for a handkerchief:

'We've had a quarrel.'

'What!'

'A disagreement …'

He blew his nose like a schoolboy.

'… She's still refusing to speak about the Baron and what he did to her! …'

This wasn't the place for a private talk, but Gilbert was obviously wrought up to a pitch of annoyance and frustration.

'... She says she wants to forget that anything happened ... But I keep pressing her to be honest and open ... I'm concerned the facts will be discovered, and then she'll be plunged in deeper.'

'But you must let her choose for herself. She's sure to be afraid, Mr Angell, don't you see that?'

Will spoke the words softly between his teeth in hopes of calming him.

'Of course I do!' said Gilbert petulantly. 'She has told me about the notes!'

'Notes?'

'The threatening notes – but I suppose you don't know about those?'

Will looked out at the lowering sky which gave no sign of clearing. What else didn't he know? If only he could lead the young man off somewhere. This was becoming desperate and he needed to settle him down.

'We mustn't talk here, Mr Angell. We must wait till the storm is over.'

'Yes, but you agree, don't you? I know your friend Mr Bristowe was adamant that she has to tell the whole truth. The Baron may be dead but the business is far from done – and now Mr Rich is being accused. The whole company is under suspicion! Where will it end?'

Will suddenly saw what was driving the young man. It was the only explanation. He looked Gilbert in the eyes:

'You think she did it, don't you? ... From the very beginning you've suspected her.'

There was no immediate denial. Perhaps this was something Gilbert hadn't wholly admitted to himself?

'She was his kept mistress, Mr Lundy. There's no other way

of seeing it. I don't know what to think ... How else could it have happened? ...'

Suddenly Gilbert's voice went quiet and he looked down at the muddy grass. The whole place would soon be churned into a morass.

'... I'm in love with her, Mr Lundy ... but ... but I cannot trust her!'

'You mean you don't *believe* her – that's different. You should not confuse the two. Are you not asking too much of her?'

'I only ask her to be honest with me.'

'Perhaps she *is* being honest but doesn't want to bare her soul. You mustn't think you can claim that of her. Perhaps Sally wishes to be private. Concealment isn't deception.'

This wasn't a comfortable thought for the ardent young lover, and Gilbert appeared not to welcome it. Will wondered how much of Ernesto was ingrained in him, and at once his mind turned to Tamara and Agnes – the courtesan and the nun. Such a neat opposition, and a theatrical one. If only life didn't so often confuse the two!

'But where is Sally? Have you left her? ...'

Gilbert seemed in a trance, and at that moment Will wanted to shake him. The young man's mind was half-elsewhere.

'... Has she run off?'

'She does not wish to return, Mr Lundy. You see, one of the notes threatens her with death if she persists – if she continues in the part.'

'Ah! I understand ... So, you are urging her to ignore the note and risk her life for the role? And you also want her to tell everything about the Baron's violence? Do you wish to kill her yourself?'

Put like that, the idea was outrageous. Gilbert was stunned:

'Why, no. Of course not! But ... Mr Pinkerman is insistent – and the company ... What would happen to our play? ...'

Gilbert was trying to bring his mind to order:

'... I don't know what to think – or to do for the best ... Do you want them to win, Mr Lundy?'

The questioning had suddenly swung round:

'*Them?* Who do you take them to be, Mr Angell?'

'Why, those who would abolish the May Fair and close our theatre – the ones who believe plays to be the work of the Devil. Who else could it be? They want to destroy Mr Pinkerman and suppress the Fair for good.'

Will hesitated. Young Gilbert sounded so certain. And perhaps he was right? Perhaps the jealousies within the company were only petty resentments and the serious threat to their theatre would unite them in a common cause? Now it was Will who was thinking hard ... But whatever was happening, he needed to find Sally at once.

'Where did you leave her, Mr Angell? Tell me!'

'In the garden of the Dog and Duck. We wished to talk quietly, but there's a baiting going on, and the place is wild and noisy – we were having to speak loudly. And then we began shouting in annoyance ... I wanted her to tell the truth and confess all to Mr Pinkerman ... I'm convinced she is safer with the company around her. We are her friends, Mr Lundy, and at a time like this we are all surely stronger together ... But she refused to return with me. She said she wanted time to gather her thoughts ...'

Gilbert paused and began fumbling for his handkerchief again.

'... What will Sally do if she has no future with the Playhouse? ... I dread to think ... I really don't ...'

His throat dried, and his voice trailed off into a cough.

'You'd better make for the Barn, Mr Angell. The rain appears to have relented a little.'

'And you?'

'I'll wait for Mr Bristowe ... Go now!'

Will had thought it best to end their conversation at once. The worst of the storm seemed to be over and he was conscious of being within earshot of others. It had been an uncomfortable meeting for both of them, and the news about Sally was the last thing he wanted to hear.

He stepped out from under the awning and looked over to the distant field. There was no sign of Tom – perhaps he should make his way back to the barn? But in his heart he knew what he had to do. He pictured Sally sheltering at the Dog and Duck – if indeed she was still there and hadn't left the market entirely. It was no place for a woman on her own, at least not a respectable one, and she might be lost and afraid. The rain was still pattering quite heavily – but he had to find her. He pulled up his collar and glanced behind him as he launched himself into his run. In doing so, he momentarily met the eyes of his neighbour, a roughly-clad market type huddled in his coat, who shot him a knowing look. Was it a glance of sympathy? – or perhaps something less friendly?

As he approached the alehouse Will could see that the duck-baiting was over. With the violent ritual at an end, two men were wading through the pond with a large cloth strung between them, gathering up the floating feathers. It was a good haul; there was perhaps enough to stuff a small pillow, and tomorrow the bill of fare at the Dog and Duck would feature the house speciality. The wind had thankfully died down, but the rain was still falling lightly. The noisy crowd had dispersed and only a few mournful figures remained sheltering under the trees as they contemplated the deserted battlefield. Alongside the empty coop a young man was tending his dog as it lay on its side – one of the pointers had been savaged by the mastiffs when they grew tired of the skittish birds.

Will noticed that the balcony was empty. The meeting would surely be under way by now; but he paused outside the building, wondering if he should enter, and what he might find.

And then he saw her. It was certainly Sally – he could tell from her dress gathered a little loosely round her shoulders, and the way the lace fell as her arm moved. She was a good distance away, and her face was concealed by an oiled umbrella which allowed a glimpse of the side of her neck where a light brown curl hung down. Will stopped in his tracks. She was in animated conversation, and there was a male hand holding the umbrella, a sword visible at the side of his coat. This was not what he had expected. The gentleman was bewigged and well dressed, but not in a showy way, and when the umbrella lifted for an instant he caught an interested look lighting up Sally's face. It was an easy meeting: this wasn't a lost girl bedraggled by the rain and not knowing where to turn, but a confident young woman, entertaining and being entertained. At that moment the man appeared to be her protector.

Will hesitated, and watched them. He felt bedraggled and distinctly shabby in his market-coat. His hair hung down limply and the damp was spreading under his collar. He wondered why the two of them were standing together like that, and what they were conversing about. Neither seemed anxious to move on – in either direction. Well, there was one way to find out. And so he strode towards the pair, a little apprehensively, consciously adopting a casual manner.

'Mr Lundy!'

She greeted him in a surprised but not unfriendly voice. The gentleman beside her swung round, and Will at once recognised the face. Sally introduced him:

'Mr Cibber – this is Tom Bristowe's friend, Mr Lundy of the Middle Temple.'

Polite nods and pleasantries were exchanged, and after a few moments a relieved Will was able to commiserate with the actor on his recent arrest and inquire about the fate of Christopher Rich. Given Sally's presence, the conversation could have taken a difficult turn, but Colley Cibber was master of the moment and somehow made them both feel at ease. Beneath the elegantly-cuffed arm holding the silk umbrella it wasn't Sir Fopling Flutter standing there but his downright, affable, and very English cousin.

'How kind of you to concern yourself, Mr Lundy. It is a desperate time for all of us, and we at the playhouse need friends! I was telling Miss Twiss about my ridiculous adventure this morning and reassuring her that our friend Rich will survive the ordeal. When last I saw him he was firing off his indignation from both barrels! I was saying she must not let the matter trouble her.'

'That's good to hear, Sir,' said Will. 'The procedure appears to be vexatious – designed to create anxiety and uncertainty. I suspect the politicians feel they have to be a-doing. There's a deal of bluster about the whole Reformation business.'

'You are right, Sir! And I sincerely hope common sense will prevail on all sides – Miss Twiss and I have been talking on the subject. I feel the company can only be strengthened by this organised attack. We must help each other and leave suspicion and accusation to others – it is *fear* that will damage us most. No, Mr Lundy, we must hold to our ideals and carry on defiantly. And poor Pinkerman needs our support. The man is carrying a lot on his shoulders – enough to break anyone less tenacious. I am making my way to the booth right now to talk with him and see how our *Tender Courtesan* is faring. Miss Twiss has been telling me we have a defiant Prologue at least. I gather Mr Bristowe has done us proud!'

The actor was voluble, and Will sensed that his own presence was allowing Cibber to speak indirectly to Sally:

'They are stirring verses, Sir, and hit the mark. The barn rang with applause. I am heading in that direction myself to meet Mr Bristowe ...'

He half-turned toward Sally.

'... I know Tom is eager to talk with Miss Twiss about the play, and to hear her thoughts on the Prologue. He thinks that Tamara is a majestic part, and that she will do great things with it.'

He gave Sally a warm smile and saw that his slightly fictional truth had registered with her. Cibber beamed in his turn:

'Then we shall all walk up together ... Miss Twiss will make a third, I trust? ...'

He gestured to her with his arm.

'... There is so much I want to ask you about, my dear – so many possibilities for the future ...'

At that instant a transient spark of amity flickered in Cibber's eyes. He pulled back his umbrella and glanced at the sky.

'... I do believe the rain has stopped and the welkin promises to smile on us again ... I hope Pinkey has his *box* with him – a bottle of claret is in order, do you not think, my friends?'

Cibber, with an entirely natural turn of his body and a gracious sweep of his hand, began leading the two of them smoothly in the direction of the barn. A shepherd and his dog could have learned much from the accomplished actor.

And so, Will and a silent but now bravely smiling Sally, her arm locked into Cibber's, found themselves walking along together. Complaisance had triumphed, and the three performers made a handsome group as they made their way past the cattle-pens, which were stirring into life again.

Chapter Twenty-Four

'I SIMPLY HAD to escape, Mr Lundy. Forgive me!'

'You managed it most adroitly, Miss Twiss. I think Mr Cibber was half-admiring beneath his obvious disappointment. He is himself a *connoisseur* of such niceties.'

Sally raised an eyebrow:

'And so are you, it seems ...'

She picked up the gingerbread man by head and shoulders and delicately bit its foot off.

'... I was beginning to feel the pressure of his hand too much. Suddenly I felt dizzy and simply had to sit down and take some nourishment – sweet food especially ... The gingerbread is restorative! It was good of you to insist on accompanying me ...'

The bench moved as she settled herself and turned toward him.

'... I'm glad to have the chance to talk.'

'I was hoping in any case to talk with you privately, Miss Twiss ...'

She smiled at the awkward formality:

'You must call me *Sally* – and I shall call you *Will* ... Otherwise I shall think you are instructing me!'

'Heaven forbid! ... But I confess I came to find you – I encountered young Gilbert, who said he had just left you at the Dog and Duck – and naturally I ...'

'... And naturally you pictured me in an alehouse all alone and without a protector. I may be the tender courtesan, Will, but I know when to leave a role behind ... But it was very thoughtful – although I suspect it wasn't only my safety that concerned you. As you say, we have matters to talk over ...'

She glanced down, as if touching on a difficult subject.

'... I haven't thanked you and Tom for your intrepid expedition to Holborn. It was foolish of me to run away like that, and the two of you saved me from much more than embarrassment. Had I not returned when I did ...'

She paused. Will swallowed hard and stopped toying with his coffee-spoon:

'We're both glad you took our advice. It was the only wise thing to do ...'

Will was longing to ask her directly about the Magistrate's questioning, but he held back. He knew his own zeal for interrogation and felt this wasn't the moment to press her. There were other things to discuss, and perhaps he ought to let the story emerge when she was ready to tell it. He set down his dish of coffee.

'... It is being said you wish to resign the part of Tamara – is that true? I do understand, believe me – Gilbert let slip about the letters.'

'Ah, the notes! Yes, I've had two of them. Foul little things scratched out in hate, threatening me with a horrible death unless I give up the part ... One tells me we are about the Devil's work and are sure to burn in hell! ... .'

It was just as he'd thought: the language of the pulpit. Sally was giving him a searching look.

'... Did Gilbert tell you he's received one also? ...'

Will looked surprised.

'... No, I thought not. I do believe his alarm for me is the greater because of it.'

She paused, and Will found himself thinking aloud:

'But Gilbert wants you to stay. He's fearful the company will break apart and the theatre's enemies triumph – I don't say I agree with him, but I think he's genuinely anxious on your behalf.'

'I know all about Gilbert's anxieties – I was regaled with them not twenty minutes ago. And I share them, I assure you. I have fears on every side! If I remain, I put my life in danger – If I leave, I destroy my career before it's begun ... but my biggest fear is Tamara herself ...'

Will was nonplussed.

'... I did not choose the part – it was forced on me. You know how it was done: I was Lord Tunbridge's protégée, and he fancied me as *the whore*. But Tamara is a big heroic role, and I have no right to play it. This morning I saw the looks of the company and could feel their contempt. I've become an interloper, don't you see? A novice raised above herself – an *ingénue* playing a heroine. And it disturbs me. I look at Agnes and know that it is *as Agnes* that I feel, not as Tamara.'

Will's imagination was becoming delightfully confused, but he thought he could comprehend the idea. It must be an actor's dilemma:

'The role is a challenge, Sally, I see that – but perhaps *your* Tamara can be the stronger for it? Tom has given me an account of the plot – of her renunciation of Ernesto – and it seems to me that she understands too well what she has lost. She has gained her experience, but at what cost? Yes, she feels *just as Agnes feels*, but that role can no longer be hers. And with that knowledge, her sacrifice is all the more tragic. Tamara sees how in the end it is youth and innocence that will reap the rewards of love.'

Will surprised himself with his eloquence – but an image of Lizzy Wright's buoyant Agnes instantly flashed on his mind, and he felt the improbability.

Sally's eyes widened. This was a presumptuous young man, but well intentioned:

'So, you think I could naturally play a fallen woman, do you? That this is a role I should be able to understand? ... You think I have *gained my experience?*'

He was tongue-tied. That was not what he meant at all ... Or was it?

'No, no. I speak of the *role*. I just think that you could understand Tamara through Agnes – Oh dear. You must think me confused.'

Will suddenly found himself blushing crimson.

'I was not the Baron's mistress, Will ...'

The statement was shockingly direct, and it reverberated in embarrassing silence.

'... I told you the truth. Had I surrendered to him, he would not have attacked me as he did. Do you not see that? ...'

Yes, he did see that, but perhaps he had not trusted her enough – had not believed her ... He hardly knew what he thought any more.

'... I know what people are thinking. They believe I really did stab Lord Tunbridge ... that we had an assignation ...'

The thought struck home. Will's mind was racing, but he still said nothing, and this made the seconds of silence even more electric.

'... Suspicion is a terrible thing, Will ... I know this myself. You see, I cannot drive from my mind the thought that it was Gilbert who dispatched the Baron to his Maker – that he slipped into the store-room and vented his anger in violence. He was certainly angry enough when I left him ...'

Sally's eyes were bright, as if she was seeing something clearly for the first time.

Will suddenly flung his head skyward:

'Yes – a paradox! A wonderful paradox – do you not see it, Sally? ...'

Now it was her turn to be thoughtfully silent.

'... The two of you have let your suspicions rankle – and look what has happened! You are stalking each other like hunters in the night. I believe you when you say you think Gilbert did the deed – but I can assure you, he in his turn suspects you equally. He told me so himself, and it pains him deeply. He thinks you killed the Baron. Do you see? Each of you thinks the other may be guilty – but of course you are both innocent. Your festering doubts of each other are the clearest proof.'

The irony seemed too simple, but like a touch of warmth on rounding a sunlit street-corner, the atmosphere changed.

'Yes, Will, you are right – of course! It was something we could never prove to each other, wasn't it? However strong our protestations, there would always be a nagging doubt. We are both actors, after all.'

She broke off the little gingerbread man's head and handed it to him. Will took it with a slight hesitation, and scrutinised her. The insouciant expression on her face reassured him that the gesture was innocent of symbolic significance. He smiled to himself, and ate. The role of a sybil was not yet within her reach – but in the future, who was to know?

'I must go to him, Will,' she said. 'The two of us need to have our first truly honest conversation. I think Gilbert and I have been too delicate with each other!'

'But this is only the beginning, Sally – the first step. Now you and Gilbert must help *us*. You see what we must all do – we have to discover who it was murdered the Baron. The politicians and the Reformation Society are pursuing Mr Rich – and they are organising evidence against him. The Queen and her Solicitor-General are directing affairs, and at any moment a trial may be brought on. And that could mean doom for the playhouse – and certainly for the Fair. We have so little time!'

Sally half stood up, as if eager to set matters in motion:

'Gilbert and I will put our heads together. And when we have set things right between us, I know I can assure you of him.'

'So, you and he will play your parts? – Both in our investigation, and in *The Tender Courtesan?*'

'Yes, Will. Now is not the time to divide the company against itself – you've made me see that. If only I could speak to the other players ...'

'You mustn't reveal too much – not yet. Be friendly and natural with them – I mean, be your true self. You must be open, both of you, and not hold yourselves aloof. But you should talk with Mr Pinkerman if possible – I think you might confide in him. Assure him you are with us! And let *him* speak to the company. It is in his hands to unite you all ...'

Will paused, almost breathless at the sense of release his words were giving him.

'... And perhaps even *The Tender Courtesan* will work what magic it can – who knows?'

'Yes, I suppose it may. Once Thursday comes, its spirit could bind us together. I may even give everyone a Tamara they can believe in!'

There was a fresh determination on her face, and Will found himself mirroring it:

'I can say nothing of this now, Sally ... but I assure you, we already have several irons in the fire. Mrs Trotter and Constable Cobb are with us, and Tom and I are returning to the Bay-Tree for one of her *conferences*. And Widow Trotter's conferences are always fruitful! Between us, we shall certainly have some news for you by Wednesday ...'

Amidst all this enthusiasm, a flicker of uncertainty showed in her face, and he noticed it.

'... But don't be alarmed. We shall keep your secret between us – the secret of the store-room. It will have to be revealed eventually, but at the proper time … When we have identified Lord Tunbridge's killer.'

'*When?* You are remarkably confident!'

'We *must* be confident. The truth is becoming clearer with each discovery we make – and I know there are more to come …'

Now Sally was looking at him, intrigued by his assurance.

'… And once things fall into place, then you can reveal the disgusting truth about Tunbridge, the *Blessed Martyr* of the Reformation Society – exactly what that man was, and what he did. You must expose the Baron's hypocrisy to the world.'

'I shall try to fulfil your expectation – try to live up to that duty.'

Noble phrases, both – the words of a true heroine!

'You and Gilbert can give each other strength. You must work together from now on – and keep hope alive.'

Sally Twiss laid her hand on his, and spoke to him slowly and quietly:

'You are a good man, Will … I take to heart what you have told me of Gilbert. Thank you. I shall go to him …'

She stood up and gave him a killing half-smile.

'… I think you know what you have done – it is not lost on me … *Tamara!*'

Will remained seated on the bench for a few minutes more, letting the talismanic word echo in his mind, and pondered on the enigma of Sally Twiss. He watched her as she walked back at an even pace in the direction of the tithe-barn, a slight spring in her step kept gracefully under control, and he thought about the strange interwoven plots they were involved in. Gilbert and Sally were both difficult to read – and as a pair impossible! He was familiar with legal entanglements, but in cases of law it was argument, probability – and thankfully, on occasion fact – that could decide the matter. But within the environs of theatre? ... This was a new world to him, and like that other New World across the sea, it existed as much in imagination as reality.

He suddenly knew that he needed Tom badly. During the past hour his mind had been wrenched this way and that. He wanted above all else to be back in a world where he could talk freely and hear the comfortable voice of a friend, with no need to check himself before every sentence. With a sudden lightness of heart he got up and followed Sally's route towards the tithe-barn.

The rehearsal had resumed, and cold-hearted Don Leone was again in action at the far end of the barn, only this time he was being defied by his ward, Agnes. Will smiled to see Lizzy Wright acquitting herself nicely as a rather cherubic novitiate nun; but the presence of Peggy Evans as an over-demonstrative Abbess of St Clare seemed to be complicating matters unnecessarily. Emotions were rising into rhetoric, and Will found his attention easily distracted. He walked further in and looked around for Tom. He cast his eyes into all corners of the place, right and left, but there was no sign. He should have known. They ought to have arranged a meeting-place, but both of them had let events take their course.

He slipped out of the barn by the rear door and gazed forlornly across the field in case Tom had wandered off in that direction, but there was nothing. Had he come along by the market he would certainly have seen him. Will was about to be annoyed with himself when he caught sight of Joe Byrne, who had just been pissing behind a nearby hedge. From this disrespectful source he learned that a while ago Tom had wandered off to investigate 'Pinkey's booth.'

'The front of the thing is looking pretty smart – but *we'll* be crammed in at the back like fish in a basket. Pinkey makes a comfortable roost for our *worthy Patrons*, but leaves his poor players falling over each other behind the scenes.'

'I expect there's never enough room, Mr Byrne.'

'Not if you need a modicum of dignity! You scrabble around like a beggar, and a second later you're thrust on stage to strut it like a king.'

'That's the illusion of the stage, Mr Byrne. But I'm sure Don Felipe will be every inch the Spanish nobleman!'

In response, Joe performed a stately and excessively hispanic bow.

And so, Will strolled over to the booth, his curiosity mounting. He was expecting the place to be a busy hive, but by now the workmen had melted away, their job done – or at least suspended. The place was not secured, and he was free to walk in through the main door beneath the newly-completed balcony. The interior was still and quiet, except for a solitary house sparrow which was chirping tunelessly from somewhere in the canvas roof. At the far end, the stage was still not fully erected and some of the supports were exposed. The backstage area was curtained off, and at the side a stack of timber planks indicated this was a job in progress. There was a workbench covered in folded canvas sheets, and a selection of buckets, brackets, and a few chairs, with other assorted items that must have some use or other. After the elegant joinery at the front of the building, this business end remained a mess – though by Thursday everything would no doubt be ready.

But as yet nothing was stirring. Will turned back and was about to make his way out again when something made him pause and call out *'Tom?'* It was for form's sake as much as anything: he had no expectation of a reply, and there was none. He was surprised by the intimate sound of his voice, which was muffled by the grass – the floor was as yet uncovered. He looked over his shoulder to the stage and called again, this time louder.

Again there was nothing, and so he began walking back towards the door. But as he did so he detected the faintest sound at the far end of the stage. One of the planks had shifted slightly as if a ghost had touched it. He shivered at the thought and realised he had halted in mid-stride. It was stupid – was it a cat or a bird?

Will knew he had to investigate. He turned, and slowly began approaching the place from where the sound had come. After only a few steps he felt a cold hand touch his heart. He stopped in his tracks, surprised by his own fear. This would never do! He was about to shout 'Tom?' into the silence for a third time, but checked himself. His legs were protesting. A few more deliberate steps brought him to the edge of the stage. Beyond the neatly-piled planks, others were strewn about, as if a stack of them had fallen over – and there on the ground, partly hidden by the rear curtain, was the sight he had been dreading.

His sudden cry of 'Tom!' now had a horrified ring to it as he half-leapt across the strewn timber. His friend's body was stretched on the grass, partially covered by a tangle of curtain, with the head bent over to one side and a plank against the neck. Another lay across the chest and another had fallen on the legs. Now treading carefully, Will crouched down beside him; he slowly lifted the curtain away from the forehead, and swung the plank off him. His face wasn't stiff and white, and there was no blood that he could see. He put a shaking hand to the neck and, thank God, felt a pulse.

Absurdly, he began whispering his friend's name as if he didn't want to wake him, searching the face for a tiny movement that would bring Tom back. The forehead was warm to his touch, and the hair slightly damp. He knew he mustn't move the head, but began rubbing it gently with his hand, repeating the name.

Only then did he think of shifting the other timbers, which lifted off easily enough. His judgment was beginning to function.

He noted that the planks looked almost arranged, as if someone had laid them on top of the body while it was lying there, the head against the curtain. He knew he should run for assistance, but he remained still, transfixed.

And then he thought of shouting.

He bent over and shouted out the name, as if calling to him across a river.

'Tom!'

The effect was electric. There was a responsive movement of the cheeks, the eyelids twitched, and then a low moan came from the chest. He was moving.

Tuesday

4 May 1708

Chapter Twenty-Five

HIS PINIONED ARMS wouldn't move. The heavy garment clung to him, pulling him down further into the viscous liquid. His fingers tore at the suffocating, feathery softness. His loins swung this way and that, but with every thrust his body only sank in deeper – the alien fleshy clothing was mastering him. Above his throat, a partly-human face began to dilate, its features twisted into a smile that began breaking apart, punctured by a disconnected bony finger which turned and pushed towards his eyes. Dark laughter bubbled up from below as the element into which he was merging came alive, mocking him while it congealed. Encroaching over his forehead, a dark Medusa-wig was writhing, and at once the feathers that coated his neck began to respond: they grew erect and reached out, clasping the serpentine curls in a devil's embrace, each entwined with the other. Now hellish voices were everywhere, a sinister choir of barking, quacking, human laughter. Around the edge of the cauldron toothless smiles muttered an incantation, and three distorted half-faces, partly Pinkerman, Angell, and Cibber – pink, angelic, cibberian – gave their last benediction. He was exhausted. He ceased to struggle, and submitted. And then the curtain came down – and with it, the dark.

Tom's eyes opened to see Widow Trotter easing the sheet that had wound itself round his body. She felt him shudder.

'You have come back to us!'

She was smiling joyfully.

Tom's forehead creased as he adjusted to the evening sunlight that was streaming through the window:

'Mrs T! … Thank God!'

His voice was hoarse, and he was breathing quickly, as if he'd been suffocating.

'Don't talk, Tom – lie still and take a breath. You've been having a bad dream.'

He lifted his head slightly, and his eyes surveyed the room with all its familiar furniture reassuringly in place. Every inanimate thing seemed to be quiet. Nothing was shouting or gesturing, and there was no activity save for Widow Trotter who was sitting on the edge of his bed pouring a glass of water.

He was dizzy for a moment and his head dropped back onto the pillow:

'Home!' he said. 'How did I get here … ?'

His voice was now a whisper.

'Don't think of it. You'll hear the story later. Take some water.'

The drink was refreshing, and he swallowed thirstily:

'Will … Where's Will? Is he here?'

'No, Tom, he's out – but he'll be back presently. He promised to call in on his way to the meeting. He's been sitting with you half the day.'

'*Meeting?* … But we've been at the May Fair market … I was at Pinkerman's booth … There's so much to tell you … I was … *someone hit me!* …'

'Yes, Tom – and you've been sleeping like a baby ever since. Keep quiet now – we've brought you home.'

Tom was unsettled, and baffled by the sudden clarity of everything – except his own mind:

'But ... what meeting?'

Mrs Trotter was concerned not to let things crowd in on him too soon, but she had to answer:

'The meeting of the Society – the Reformation of Manners – He is to be there at seven, with his father and the Reverend Tysoe. But rest easy. He should be here very soon.'

Tom's mind was clearing, and he was beginning to understand. He was in his own bed, and it was evening, but ...

'But ... Is it *Tuesday*?'

Widow Trotter smiled:

'Yes, Tom. Tuesday evening. You've had a long sleep – and a healing one, I hope. Mr Proby gave you a heavy opiate. You've been very calm most of the time. How is your head?'

'Have I lost a day? No wonder I'm feeling hungry ...'

He lifted himself off the pillow, but winced and fell back.

'... I was hit on the head, wasn't I?'

'Yes, and you've an almighty bump to show for it ...'

He lifted his arm and felt a bandage wrapped round his skull.

'... But nothing is shattered, thank the Lord! Are you able to see clearly?'

'Everything is sharp. Mrs T – like a Dutch painting. The light is beautiful ... those flowers! ... But they move around a little ...'

He shut his eyes again.

'... I've had a terrible vision – I've been in *Hell*, Mrs T.... I've seen devils ...'

He started catching his breath again.

'Don't talk of it, Tom! Try to forget. Keep your eyes open. Just lie still and it will slip away. Dreams always do.'

'I was in a theatre, Mrs T ... a duck-baiting. I was being hunted ... feathers ... the witches ...'

He shuddered.

'Hush, Tom!'

'No, you must let me talk – I have to talk ...'

And he did, eagerly. And Widow Trotter listened as he told her about the frightening images of his dream, which were already beginning to run into each other like watercolours. It was as if his mind were staging the events of recent days as a wild pageant, badly rehearsed and relapsing into chaos. But as the minutes ticked by he grew calmer and began to understand more clearly. *Aegri somnia!* he thought to himself, and smiled:

'I'm not making much sense, am I, Mrs T?'

'It all sounds very theatrical to me. But you've been living so much in the theatre these past days. We all have! ...'

She handed him more water.

'... Will has told me about your visit to the Dog and Duck yesterday – and while you were at the rehearsal in the barn he was able to talk with Gilbert and Sally ... But I'll let him tell you about that himself. I think you should stay quiet while I arrange for some food. Are you sure you're hungry? – you said you were feeling dizzy.'

'I'm ravenous, Mrs T. I could eat a *whole* pasty!'

'Well, I'll see what we can do.'

Without any fuss Widow Trotter slipped out of the door. She was feeling hugely thankful and made her way down the stairs with care, checking each step to stop herself from running down. Tom had come back to them! She knew that Will would be inexpressibly relieved. It had been a difficult day for everyone.

Left to himself, Tom tried to keep a hold on the agitated thoughts that threatened to burst out of him. During the dream a curtain had been lifted, and he shuddered to think what lay beyond it – things terrible and arousing by turns. Thankfully their vividness was fading, and he had no wish to raise the curtain again.

Suddenly he heard a tread on the stairs. To judge from the creaks they were being mounted two at a time, but carefully ... It must be Will, he thought – and he must be carrying a tray.

The deduction was faultless. A few seconds later a beaming Will Lundy pushed open the door, a japanned tray grasped between his hands. On it was arranged a venison pasty sliced in half, a piece of buttered toast, a small bowl of ragout, and an orange. Alongside them, a jug of chocolate and two delicate china cups completed the picture. Will placed the tray carefully on the bedside table. Tom contemplated the still life, admiring the way it refused to keep still.

'The toast is for me!' said Will in admonitory tones, before cracking the broadest smile possible.

A few minutes later Tom was devouring the pasty while Will told him some of his news. The words began tumbling out on both sides, all the more because Will needed to leave shortly for the rendezvous with his father and the Reverend Mr Tysoe in St Martin's church hall.

Will had been hesitating to ask about the attack, but Tom soon turned to the subject himself. He looked at his friend knowingly:

'You've not asked me what happened in the booth ... I know you don't want to distress me, but I need to describe it while the picture's still vivid. Images are swirling in my head, but I think I have the memory clear enough ...'

Will interrupted him:

'No, Tom, I've been hesitating because I don't want to distress *myself!* This would not have happened had I acted right – if I'd returned to the barn to collect you. I went in pursuit of Sally Twiss instead. Gilbert had left her at the Dog and Duck, and I thought ...'

'You thought right, Will! You had to try and talk with her, and you say you learned a lot ... I would have done exactly as you did ... No, it is *I* who should have gone to find *you*.'

This contest of penitents was soon resolved, leaving Tom to try piecing his recollections together. His head was aching, and he held his hand against the back of his skull, eyes half-closed.

'I can recall Pinkerman going to view the new balustrade – it was after our talk – he'd been telling me about Sally's threatening letters – and he spoke of her *liaison* with the Baron. Yes, I remember he used that French word with a curl of the lip – he seemed not to have heard of any *attack* on her – I don't believe she's told them everything ... He went off, but I thought I would wait so you and I could view the inside of the theatre together. He'd left behind the script of *The Tender Courtesan* – the full thing – and I was leafing through it – so many crossings-out and alterations! I'm surprised the actors know their parts at all ... And then the storm came – I remember it clearly. The players burst in screaming like children! And then Pinkerman returned – and he said the rain was easing. They were setting up the rehearsal again – so I thought I would go over to the booth and take a look ...'

'Slow down a little Tom. We have enough time – it's all making sense so far ...'

He handed his friend a cup of chocolate.

'... You must take the next part carefully. Close your eyes if it will help.'

Tom sipped at his chocolate and tentatively closed his eyes, seer-like:

'It was still raining slightly – I remember that – and there was no-one in the booth – the door was open – I was trying to imagine the place thronged with people – it's a larger theatre than last year – and the stage – it was still being erected – there were tools about – and a workbench – as if the men had just walked out and left everything – perhaps they had broken off suddenly – I remember there was water coming through the roof over by the edge of the stage – and the canvas was sagging

– I hoped it would be watertight during the performance! ...'

Tom opened his eyes a little and took another sip of the chocolate.

'... I can see things clearly, Will – the scene is coming back to me.'

'I'm there in my mind's eye, Tom. Carry on!'

'It was strange, but there was something in the air of the place – I had the feeling of being watched – I told myself it was because I was concerned about the play and was imagining an audience – but I *knew* someone's eyes were on me.'

'That's not like you, Tom.'

'I felt uncomfortable – and it was then I saw the curtain – out of the corner of my eye – I was convinced it had moved – twitched slightly – and then suddenly a bird started chirruping! – a sparrow somewhere – and I almost jumped out of my skin – it sounded like a warning ... All the time I was thinking how stupid it was! ...'

Tom shook his head and opened his eyes. Every detail was clear.

'... Yes! It was the curtain to the right of the stage – it was hanging over the edge and down to the grass – a kind of partition – ill-fitted – folds of the stuff – and somehow I knew it couldn't be the wind ... And so I walked up to it boldly – mocking myself for being such a fool! – I reached out ...'

Tom swallowed the remains of the chocolate in a single gulp. Will saw that he was shivering and almost called a halt. But he knew he must let him be. It was a kind of ritual, like watching the Delphic priestess with the rapture on her.

Tom's voice was suddenly harsh and loud:

'... It came alive, Will! The *curtain* reached out and twisted round my face! It was dusty and smelly – pah! – and I felt a blow – a hammer-blow at the back of my head – and a second one I think. Everything was whirling round and I was choking – I felt a splitting pain – yes, and I heard a *grunt* – distinctly! – not a word or cry but an animal grunt – I remember my legs gave way … and then nothing at all … nothing … and since then, oblivion – except for the visions – the nightmares! … . Oh God!'

Will saw that Tom was suddenly pale, and reached over just in time to prevent his cup from falling:

'It's the opiate, Tom. You mustn't distress yourself. Mrs Trotter says it's only to be expected that your brain is confused, and things will soon settle themselves.'

'Yes, you're right … but the images are so vivid. What tricks our minds can play!'

'Well, you've given an exact account. There's nothing wrong with your mind, believe me. With a little more rest …'

'But I've had too much rest. It will be good to exercise my God-given Reason. I've been in the grip of Imagination – and you know what a wild enchantress she is …'

Tom's face was beginning to relax.

'… It will help to have something for my mind to work on. I've been asleep for a whole day! You must tell me everything … I need to know what I've missed.'

'*Everything?* That's a hard task! I have to walk over to St Martin's for the reformers' meeting at seven. I only hope Mr Tysoe hasn't discovered the shocking truth about me. If I can just get into the meeting, I'm sure there will be a lot to learn – the Society is usually so secretive …'

In truth, Will was more than a little fearful about what might be facing him. But he thought it best to leave his own worries aside and bring the talk back to Tom's concerns.

'… But before I go, I need to tell you about Gilbert and Sally.'

'Ah yes, Mrs T says you had conversation with them.'

'Yes – not both together. There had been a disagreement. I talked with Gilbert during the rainstorm, and then with Sally, once she had extracted herself from Colley Cibber's attentions …'

Will's account was brief and to the point, and Tom listened closely. He spoke of the suspicions Gilbert and Sally harboured of each other, and what that must mean.

'... So you see, Tom, each has had misgivings. That's been the cause of the distrust. Gilbert thinks Sally must have stabbed the Baron – and Sally can't rid herself of the thought that it was Gilbert who slipped back into the property-store and did the deed ... They are both innocent, Tom, I'm sure of it.'

'Yes, I see ... but Pinkerman talked of Sally's *liaison* with the Baron. Do you think she has been less than open with us?'

'But that doesn't make her a killer, does it?'

'No, but it questions her candour ...'

Tom could see Will was becoming unsettled by the drift of their talk.

'... I'm sorry – I don't accuse her – far from it. But I wish I could share your faith in her ... You may well be right.'

Will was struggling to set aside his trust in Sally's innocence, and engage his lawyer's brain:

'Gilbert told me she was Tunbridge's *kept mistress* – but that could just be his suspiciousness ...'

He sighed uneasily as he recalled his talk with the players.

'... The other actors suspect her too – but that's all mixed up with jealousy and gossip. Some of them were envious of her having a "protector" – and they all resent her dazzling rise in the company. But the hold she had over the Baron was surely her resistance to him, *not* her submission? She swore she had not been his mistress – and I believe her, Tom! It was the manner in which she said it – the pride – the indignation – I think I know when people are lying – I've watched it in court so often.'

'Yes, but your witnesses have not been actors.'

'Ah, that again! We keep meeting that, don't we! Oh dear ... so you think I'm being blinded by my feelings?'

'No, Will, not at all. And I don't ask you to distrust her. I think it's good for one of us to take a different view. An image can be clearer for being seen from two angles. So ... you must go on trusting Sally – and I must be allowed to be just a little sceptical. Are we agreed?'

'Agreed!' said Will.

At that moment he was reminded how good it was to have Tom back. Strange, he thought, how the two of them acted as an encouragement, but also a check on each other:

'I must be leaving, Tom – but before I go, I have to tell you about the players. I sat with them and had an entertaining conversation – they are a witty and outrageous bunch, and some of their talk was for effect – but I sensed a tremendous resentment against Tunbridge and his plans for the theatre. They knew he was setting himself up to be the company's dictator – that's how they see it ... And all of them expressed relief – no, more than that, *delight* – at his death.'

'The feeling was that strong?'

'They all spoke of it.'

Tom was thoughtful:

'That's something we must keep in mind. Perhaps we shouldn't discount the idea of a conspiracy – a company plot?'

'Or the action of a determined *member* of the company?'

'It's a troubling thought, Will. These people are becoming our friends ...'

He took a deep breath and posed the inevitable question:

'... Then who was it attacked me? Who was behind the curtain? ...'

It was a rhetorical question and reverberated in the silence.

Will was suddenly uneasy, as if he knew of something else that Tom was yet to hear about. Tom sensed his friend's hesitation:

'Will? ... What's on your mind? Who would do that to me?'

'I think there's something you need to know. You'll find out soon enough ... I have it here.'

He reached down into his pocket and drew out a scrap of paper.

'What's that? Oh no! ... *Not me too?*'

'Yes ... It was found thrust into your pocket.'

Will held the thing out. Tom raised himself a little in the bed and took it from him gently. It was a torn-off piece of paper, folded over – a veritable 'scrap'. For several seconds he held it between his fingers, unopened.

'I'm feeling dizzy again. Read it to me, Will ... What does it say?'

Will took it from him:

'It's a pencilled message. Short and simple. It reads: "Hell awaits you Bristow!"'

Will spoke it in a voice that was soft – even kind – but that gave the words an even more sinister edge.

'Is that all?'

'Yes. It's a brisk thing – direct! It looks hurriedly written, as if scribbled over your body when the deed was done.'

Tom tried to sound unperturbed:

'What does Mrs T say to it? At least this one doesn't quote scripture!'

'She didn't want you to see it – but I thought you should know you're now one of the proscribed. It's an honourable club, Tom ... It's your *prologue* that's done it. You've been meddling with the theatre and are destined for eternal torment!'

'That person could have killed me, but they didn't. Perhaps they really do believe what they say and are leaving me to damnation? The note surely can't have come from any of the players – none of them believes Hell is awaiting us.'

'Who knows? Such things can be done in mimicry ... but I think you're right. It's the language of the ranting preacher again ...'

Will consulted his watch and stood up.

'… And I am about to hear more of it – much more I suspect! I wonder what form of damnation is awaiting *me?* Do you think these people will drive me out of the place?'

'Being "Hemp" Lundy's son will be your passport, surely?'

'Yes, but that has its own embarrassments – he doesn't approve of my going.'

'Mr Tysoe will shield you.'

'Ah yes, my *protector!* It's always good to have one of those …'

Will allowed himself a wry smile.

'… My protector – or my *guard?* Whatever happens, I promise to be on my best behaviour.'

'I wish you luck, Will. It won't be easy – but this meeting could unlock so much for us.'

'I know, and I'm extremely curious. I only hope the things I'll hear won't frighten me too much …'

Tom was about to speak, but Will cut him short.

'… Rest easy – I shall come back and give you a full report, I swear. Mrs Trotter has already insisted!'

'It's supper for three in here, then?'

'Something like that …'

Will paused at the door, and hesitated.

'… It's so good to have you back, Tom. I can't say how good. This has frightened me. I don't want to go through anything like it again.'

Chapter Twenty-Six

As he stepped in through the tall double-doors, Will was struck by the elegance of the room. He had been expecting plain walls and solid benches – something not unlike the Hackney meeting-house. But this upper room was of a different order. There were chairs with gracefully curved backs, Turkey carpets, wall-sconces, and – the biggest surprise of all – a splendid chandelier almost the match of those in the Theatre Royal. Adorning the walls were gilt-framed portraits of men with clerical bands and puffed-out sleeves in postures of worthiness and dignified command.

His second impression was of unrelieved maleness. Before him were rank upon rank of solid backs, some of them surmounted by wigs that draped over shoulders; others were supporting squat shaved necks or straggling locks that lacked the tender touch; and here and there a neat periwig was tied with a ribbon. At the far end of the room, a row of substantial bewigged characters occupied comfortable armchairs. All hats had been removed and there was no common style – quite the contrary: here were *all sorts and conditions of men*. Will was taken aback. This was less a congregation than a crowd: churchmen, City men, shopkeepers, gentlemen of the professions, some labouring men too, and three or four younger people who were hardly out of their apprenticeships. All were gathered in this place to profess a common cause. It was impressive, but also unsettling.

Will had paused to take in the prospect when he felt the Reverend Tysoe's hand on his arm. His father had walked ahead towards the front of the room, but his protector was guiding his elbow.

'You sit by me, William, and If need be, I shall introduce you to the meeting – though I doubt it will come to that, so you must not be anxious. I have informed the committee that your father and I are bringing you here, and we have vouched for you ... If you listen and observe, then you will appreciate what we are about and imbibe the *spirit* of the meeting ...'

There was a gleam in Mr Tysoe's eyes at the thought.

'... The spirit does not come as a rushing wind – but its work is strong, and I know the Lord will be guiding us in our deliberations.'

It was seven o'clock, and the two of them took seats in the penultimate row, much to Will's relief, although as he reached his place he noticed a pair of eyes fixed on him. Stationed at the side of the hall was a stern-looking figure whose job it seemed was to scrutinise each person as he entered.

A dark murmur filled the room. Some sixty or seventy men, Will calculated, were conversing in low tones, with no lighter grace-notes or tinklings of laughter. All were about the Lord's business.

There was a sudden announcement:

'Brothers in Christ!'

It was delivered in reverberant tones by a distinguished-looking gentleman who had risen to his feet on the dais – not a clergyman, so far as Will could see. The man surveyed the room with evident satisfaction; then, after a short pause:

'May the Lord guide our councils this day ... *Trust in*

the LORD with all thine heart; and lean not unto thine own understanding. In all thy ways acknowledge him, and he shall direct thy paths.'

There was a general 'Amen,' some muttering it quietly, others making a louder declamation.

'That's Mr Hector, the Magistrate,' whispered the Reverend Tysoe. 'He is to give the Justices' report.'

Will caught his breath. So! Mr Hector, the man directing the investigation into the Baron's death, was active in the Society for the Reformation of Manners! Will couldn't help glimpsing the whole thing as a conspiracy – from the Queen's Solicitor-General downwards. He noted the courtly bearing of the man, his head bowed just a little in humility before God, and tried picturing Elias Cobb in conversation with him. They would not see eye to eye in any sense.

There was no immediate drama. The routine business opened with a report from the London parishes on a remarkable number of convictions – the largest ever recorded in the metropolis in a single week. Will listened carefully as the figures were given: a haul of more than two hundred prosecutions for lewd and disorderly behaviour, with a similar number for the sin of Sabbath-breaking on the previous Sunday alone. In their own parish of St Martin's, Mr Hector announced, no fewer than forty warrants had been issued on the Lord's Day past, with fines totalling sixty-eight pounds.

The Magistrate lowered his paper and lifted his face slightly toward the ceiling as if to acknowledge their benign sponsor.

'This account,' he declared, 'added to those of recent months, indicates that this Year of Our Lord, Seventeen Hundred and Eight, will see by far the largest step towards the moral reclamation of our city ...'

There was a loud hum of approval from all corners of the hall.

'... It is gratifying,' he continued, 'that the *blank warrants* are proving a most effective means of ensuring the Fourth Commandment is respected. *Remember the Sabbath Day, to keep it holy!* continues to be our watchword, and I am pleased to say that this Sunday past, in our parish alone, no fewer than two tailors and three shoemakers were apprehended pursuing their work; seven shops were discovered to have their windows open; and the traffic on the streets of Covent Garden included two carts conveying vegetables, a baker bearing his baskets without explanation, a shoe-boy with his tripod and bag, and a hatter with a periwig-box containing a dress-wig, which was being openly carried down Drury Lane ...'

He surveyed the room again, remaining solemn of countenance.

'... These are no petty misdemeanours, brothers. They are symptoms of the malignant traffic in sin that disfigures our city, and which puts us all in danger. Debauchery was fatal to the Roman state, and ours is under notice, is it not? ... But as we continue to advance, the day is near when whoring and drunkenness, swearing and cursing, and profanation of the Lord's Day will no longer plague our streets. Only then will our country be saved from the retribution that hangs over it!'

He sat down to a ripple of applause, and the audience settled themselves in their chairs. At Will's side, the Reverend Tysoe beamed:

'Amen!' he said in a quivering voice. 'We look to that day, William. Let us hope it is not far off!'

Will was hesitating over his reply when another figure rose to his feet, this time a member of the dissenting clergy whose untidy hair added to his generally dishevelled appearance. His linen bands were a little creased, and the folds of his chin made his head appear to be bouncing with enthusiasm as he spoke. This gentleman responded with formal thanks to the magistrates and constables; but then he determinedly moved matters on, taking the tide that had begun to swell through the hall.

'Mr Abraham Gell, Minister of Shoreditch,' whispered Mr Tysoe, helpfully.

But in comparison with Mr Hector, this man's words were less easy to catch, and there was some jowly mumbling that reminded Will of a turkey cock.

'... In this *Crusade*,' he was declaring, 'I have to say, our growing band of *informers* ...'

He paused, and an approving murmur surged again. This was a subject of intense interest, and Will gave it his full attention.

'... these men continue to pursue God's work fearlessly! These brave soldiers in Christ, I tell you, are bringing us *informations* of a most dangerous tendency – I can say no more. They do their work in secret – but assuredly their names are known unto God, and we can be certain they will be recorded on heavenly scrolls ...'

'Amen to that!' echoed in Will's ear, and he felt Mr Tysoe shift in his chair. The speaker swallowed hard and shuddered slightly.

'... My friends – we know the day of trial is coming! We are being tested as never before. What can I say? My tongue dries as I approach the subject ...'

He gave a hollow cough.

'... I need not tell you that we continue to harbour in our midst ... Satan's very own temple – a shrine to *Baal!* – an establishment which infects the body of our Nation. The place corrupts our youth, and our women above all – the Fair Sex! – In every way it defies God himself... I allude, gentlemen, to ...'

He paused, as if it needed all his will power to force the words from his lips:

'... . to the Playhouse ...'

More murmurs, this time growling and threatening, rose from the body of the hall.

'... This is a school where the Devil teaches his own. I tell you! Each day we see it grow more defiant, more shameless in its outrages! ... but, my friends. I lack the words – and the capacity – to speak on this subject with true authority.'

A cry of 'Speak, Abe!' came from his audience.

'Yes, speak!' shouted another.

His hearers wanted more. The man's oddly stumbling rhetoric was having an effect: his very hesitations seemed to be prompting them.

'But fortunately, friends, we have with us today a man who *can* speak with authority. He is an honoured guest, and I am happy to invite him to address us. I wish to introduce the Reverend Mr Arthur Bedford – a gentleman whose writings will be known to many of you ...'

There was a stir in the body of the hall, which seemed to confirm it.

'... Mr Bedford, an inhabitant of Bristol and Vicar of Temple Church in that city, has had signal success in promoting the work of the Society there – so that the theatres in both Bristol and Bath are now established on a new footing of morality and decency. He assures us his work is but half done, and that the utter abolition of those playhouses is his ultimate aim.

'Mr Bedford has recently come among us with the laudable aim of continuing the fight here in the metropolis. We can take heart from what he has achieved in the nation's second city, and his example should inspire us. He is convinced that success is within reach, and he is helping organise our efforts to bring down our own temple of iniquity ...'

A comment of 'Yes indeed!' was heard. 'He has showed the way!' called another.

'Mr Bedford's writings have found their way to us in London – and I can say with confidence that his book ... I have a copy here! – is admired by all who have read it ...'

He held the volume aloft and displayed it to the room as if it were the sacred Host.

'... *The Evil and Danger of Stage Plays* is its title – and in it, the reverend gentleman offers an account of some two thousand instances of immorality and profanity taken from the stage-plays of the two last years alone ... *Two thousand!* And what a shameful catalogue it is! ... He tells me that in the few weeks he has been in London he has added greatly to that list.

'The Reverend Bedford has the honour to be Chaplain to His Grace the Duke of Bedford (his namesake, though not – he feels bound to point out – a blood relation). And that noble young gentleman is happy to have it known that he regards his chaplain as the champion of a noble cause!'

Some cheers rang out. Will was clenching his teeth, trying not to let his amusement show: the Theatre Royal was part of the Duke's estate, and His Lordship was happy enough to lease out the land on which it stood. Yet again, the whiff of hypocrisy! What would Tom make of that?

The speaker offered more in this vein of oily compliment until the audience became restive. For a man lacking words, he seemed to have an excessive supply of them. In the end, the gentleman whose praises were being sung got to his feet and silenced the speaker with a gracious sweep of the hand. There was relieved applause, and the Reverend Arthur Bedford swung round to take in the warm reception.

A gratified smile played about the man's lips as he turned – and Will's mouth opened involuntarily. The profile was an imperious one – eyebrows arched, chin firm – with a distinctly handsome Roman nose completing the picture. What had Widow Trotter said? A face like an emperor's coin ... Yes, it was surely her gentleman in the theatre box – the man who had watched the maypole-dancing, no doubt with that same self-pleased smile! Things were beginning to make sense. This was someone not afraid to enter the halls of the damned and contemplate their future torments. But today, here, he was amongst his own.

The man was a practised pamphleteer, and he spoke like one. He began by paying tribute to the work of the London parishes, of which St Martin's was a beacon, and he noted how greatly the Lord's work was flourishing there:

'I heartily concur with Mr Gell in his praise of our informers. Without their strength, gentlemen, we should be so much the weaker; without their dauntless courage we should be timorous and ineffective ...'

Then his voice became solemn and his face thunderous.

'... Alas, friends, I have to tell you – and I drop a tear pronouncing it! ... we have today lost one such – one of our very finest ... the bold spirit who, armed with his weapon of righteousness, sought to bring down that pagan idol which lords it over the Strand – the May-*pole* – that foul Popish erection which offends us every day by its very existence ... He set his axe to its root! – But alas, before he could succeed, the frenzied worshippers of Baal struck him down and tore him to pieces. His death, I fear, was but two hours ago ...'

There was a shocked silence, and a tense whisper began. Then the Reverend Bedford, his eyes now closed, launched into something close to a prayer. His voice almost chanted the words, as if he were speaking to the dead man himself:

'... To lose your life in the war against Satan is to dispose it to the very ends for which it was given you. In dying, you glorify the Lord. It earns you the reward of MARTYRDOM! ... for is it not written: *Be thou faithful unto Death, and I will give thee a Crown of Life?* A Martyr is one who, at the expense of his blood, attests the TRUTH. He suffers for righteousness sake, and GREAT is his joy in Heaven. God removes him from his earthly Work to a Heavenly Reward. Can this be counted an Injury? No, I say, – it is a blessed ETERNITY!'

His words rode above the dark muttering of his audience like a golden chariot soaring over a thunder-cloud. It seemed to Will an ambiguous sound, part wonder, part consternation. But this was only the beginning. Arthur Bedford now turned to the Nation's sins, especially as evidenced in the theatre.

The sentences unrolled at an even pace, moving in and out of scripture with a preacher's confidence. All the old accusations against the stage appeared; but from his lips they assumed a special dignity – as if human waywardness was also a lapse of taste. Will listened carefully as the Reverend Bedford's voice became more impassioned:

'The fault lies also in those persons who *attend* plays! They openly delight in swearing and cursing, in blasphemy and profaneness. They fear not God, and regard not Man! The theatre audience are men of corrupt minds and debauched practices – reprobates who are resolved to go the furthest in sin – until *Vengeance* comes upon them at last – and it shall! – It shall come upon them *to the uttermost!* ...'

These last words were delivered with a coldness that froze Will's spine but seemed to kindle warm enthusiasm in his audience – at least in some of them. Arthur Bedford surveyed the room with his imperious gaze:

'... My friends! – We are all of us joined together in the cause of *Reformation*. A noble ideal! But what are the means we espouse? Do we wish to *improve* manners and *encourage* virtue? We do indeed! But is that enough? Do we wish to *advise*, to *admonish*, to *guide?* We do indeed! But, I say again, *is that enough?* Surely the Nation's sins are too ingrained to be washed away with pious exhortations. Men of the stage – aye, and women too (let us remember that in the playhouse whoredom and debauchery are universal!) – these are persons *openly in the service of the Devil* ... Nothing less than their TOTAL SUPPRESSING can work Reformation! We must wield the sword of Righteousness!'

The murmurs grew; but now Will began to sense some questioning amongst the general affirmation. To his left, Mr Tysoe was growing restless. He wondered if he might be imagining this; but then it occurred to him that the Reverend Bedford's rhetoric was beginning to sound like a rant, and their meeting was becoming a conventicle, an assembly of the disaffected.

The speaker was now gleefully prophesying a time of *weeping, wailing, and gnashing of teeth,* and as the words rolled on, Will sensed uneasy shufflings in the seats around him. The Reverend Bedford needed to remember he was addressing a mixed company. Many of the Dissenters would be aroused, but Will knew that the solid Anglican gentlemen in the room might detect something more suited to plain oak benches and whitewashed walls.

But now a sharpness entered the Reverend Bedford's voice as he turned to the 'pressing case' of the Theatre Royal. The playhouse, he said, was not merely a symptom of the Nation's ills, but the very disease itself. Will's heart was beating fast as he waited for the picture to form.

With undisguised glee, the preacher instanced the disasters of *Macbeth* ten days earlier. He painted a lurid scene. The life-threatening thunderbolts and lightning were a direct sign of Our Lord's anger, 'a warning of that *ultimate retribution* when the Revelation will be fulfilled – "*And there were voices, and thunders, and lightnings; and there was a great earthquake, such as was not since men were upon the earth, so mighty an earthquake, and so great.*"'

The Apocalypse could always be a crowd-pleaser; but as he listened Will suspected that the more comfortable gentlemen in the audience were not eager for the Last Day – whatever benefits it might bring in the way of judging the Nations and separating sheep from goats.

The end of the world, however, was not to be the climax of the oration. That honour was reserved for Baron Tunbridge. Will had sensed the approach of the topic and was now literally on the edge of his seat – partly to evade the excited motions of the Reverend Tysoe, but also to gain a fuller view of the responses across the room.

If anyone was expecting a tribute, then they were to be severely disappointed. From the outset, Arthur Bedford's eloquence clothed the Baron not in the pure garments of martyrdom, but in the costume of a stage seducer. Will was astonished. Whatever might be thought of the reverend gentleman, he was clearly not someone to run from a fight. Indeed, seeing a skirmish in progress he would rush in and make it a battle.

'Lord Tunbridge's end,' he declared, 'was as sordid as his ambitions! Dead on the dirty floor of a costume-room, his place of assignation with one of the actresses! The blood of the playhouse ran in the Baron's veins, and it was this same blood that spilled out of him, overlooked by all the false trappings of stage nobility – pompous helmets worn by vagabonds, noble swords wielded by cowards, the robes of false monarchs – all the mimic regalia of stage performance ...'

There had already been a few quiet voices of dissent, mixed with half-stifled cries of 'No!' and 'Disgraceful!' – and these began to mount as the rhetorical charge-sheet grew.

'... It was a fitting end to a debauched life! The Baron haunted the theatre and took its pickings of easy virtue – and indeed he was about to build a glorious future for the place. I know he has been hailed by some of you as a Martyr to our cause ...'

'Cries of 'Yes!' and 'He is so!' were heard, but Mr Bedford strode on:

'... No! – he was no martyr! He was a *confederate* rather, who sought to establish the company on a new footing and secure the patronage of the Great. Yes, the theatre was to offer plays commending virtue and Providence – but I tell you, there can be no accommodation with that place. Our *Reformation* cannot reach a compromise with those that sup with the Devil!'

Whether or not the Reverend Bedford had intended to end his speech there, it could go no further. The noise in the room was simply too great. The audience were now actively in debate themselves. Discordant voices predominated, and opposing views were being made known. To call the response 'mixed' would give a false impression: this was faction. Suddenly Whigs and Tories felt at variance; Dissenters and Anglicans were pulled in different directions; Puritans and Royalists donned their old divisive colours. And the Reverend Tysoe was joining in. With a cry of 'He is no Martyr!' Will's protector was exchanging warm sentiments with a gentleman further along the row.

At the front of the room, Mr Hector was on his feet trying to make himself heard. The Magistrate was looking like thunder and had already been in argument with the Whiggish Mr Gell on the front row. Everywhere in the room other conversations were turning into disputes.

Finally, Mr Hector was able – partly by his commanding presence, but also by dint of shouting loudly above the noise – to bring some calm to the meeting:

'Gentlemen! – *Brothers!*' he cried – 'May I remind you, that is what we are! I beg you! Calm yourselves! ...'

The hubbub lessened.

'... The murder of Lord Tunbridge has been a great shock to us all – and I know that many of us were looking to him to reform the Stage. Feelings run high, but I must warn you that his death is currently being investigated by the Solicitor-General himself – with, I have to say, the interest and full support of *Her Majesty the Queen* ...'

At those magical words the silence was sudden – as if Anne herself had entered the room.

'... Let me remind you that the Theatre Royal is Her Majesty's own company. She is greatly concerned at its debaucheries – but I must declare to you, most solemnly, that she has intimated to Sir James Montagu – and through Sir James to myself as the examining Magistrate – that she wishes all sordid speculation about Baron Tunbridge to end – *forthwith!*'

Mr Hector's angry brow and commanding eyes brooked no dissent. It amounted to a Royal Proclamation. He paused but for an instant:

'... We shall accordingly move on to other matters!'

Will relapsed back into his chair, but his mind was racing. He had suspected the Society would be at variance with itself but had not appreciated how the killing of Lord Tunbridge had exposed its deep divisions. The Society for the Reformation of Manners, he decided, was in crisis.

'I'm sorry you had to witness such a scene, William ...'

Mr Tysoe was speaking softly in his ear.

'... Such outbursts are most regrettable. I trust the remainder of the meeting will be conducted in a more peaceable spirit.'

And indeed it was, given that discussion now moved to the forthcoming May Fair. No topic was more likely to unite the Society in a common cause. To warm approval, Mr Hector confirmed that the Middlesex Justices had issued a strict charge to the magistrates, ordering them to be vigilant during the time of the Fair and bring in their judgments briskly and rigorously. They were to ensure that *Her Majesty's Peace* was preserved, and have a special eye to drinking, gaming, raffling, and lotteries.

'Our dear Queen's Proclamations leave no room for doubt. She is troubled and questions why her wishes are constantly frustrated ... At the Fair, abominable acts of lewdness are openly committed in the surrounding fields, and a disorderly mob runs into every excess and riot. And this *Sodom* is permitted to encroach almost into the very precincts of Royalty itself. How rapidly an unruly mob could threaten Her Majesty's person, I need not ask you to imagine! ...'

Mr Hector allowed his audience several seconds to do just that.

'... The May Fair harbours thieves and pickpockets, vagabonds and tricksters, whores and sodomites – but let us not forget that other nefarious troop, the *players!* In their persons we find the diseased blood of the Fair. These are called *Her Majesty's Servants* – and the fact that their nasty booths stand so near Her Majesty's person is a shameful affront. How glorious will that ROYAL HAND appear, that shall pull down this HIGH PLACE of Iniquity!'

The Magistrate's language was florid, and it buffeted the mind like a swirling wind, but its message was simple. Will shivered, and for the first time felt he wanted to be elsewhere. He was trying to shut out this cant, but it went on, and others had their say – with less of the rhetoric but much the same vehemence.

Time, as it often does, came to Will's rescue, and eventually the meeting was drawn to a close. But by now he had ceased to listen. As the general conversation resumed, he looked around at the elegant furnishings of their upper room and could not avoid casting his mind to that other room of Scripture. Here under the great chandelier there had been no speaking in tongues, and thankfully no actual rushing of a mighty wind – but the spirit of Reformation had been released, and it was not to be taken lightly. In spite of the divisions, it was clear there was a burning resolve not only to suppress the stage but to bring about a moral revolution in the Nation, whatever the cost might be.

Chapter Twenty-Seven

'AND JUST WHEN I thought the ordeal was over! ... it was then that things began to happen ...'

Back in the Bay-Tree, Will was holding his audience of three in rapt attention with his account of the Reformers' meeting. Widow Trotter had agreed that an immediate conference over supper might be allowed and had organised a light repast and a bottle of choice burgundy, which were brought up to the invalid's room. Mr Proby had been told that a further opiate was out of the question, and so it was an eager but aching and slightly dizzy Tom who sat up in bed to welcome his visitors.

'So, yet more things happened, Mr Lundy?' said Mrs Trotter. 'Surely your meeting had been eventful enough!'

'Ah! But you often learn more in casual talk, Mrs T. That's when unguarded words are spoken. The mind relaxes and things are allowed to *slip* – aren't they, Tom?'

This bit of private banter was lost on the others, and Tom let it go with only a flicker of recognition:

'So, what did happen, Will?' he asked. 'Or rather, what was *let slip?*'

'After the formal part of the meeting, people went into huddles: the big wigs clustered together, and the shaven-headed brethren were muttering solemnly, while the thin, watchful ones tended to hover … I, of course, had my two sponsors at either shoulder: Mr Tysoe was anxious to have my ear, and my father decided he should pin down my other flank in case I roamed unguardedly.'

'You were their prisoner,' said Elias with a laugh. 'That's exactly how it's done!'

'Yes, I think Mr Justice Lundy would have happily escorted me off the premises; but he hadn't allowed for the Reverend Tysoe's zeal – for my education in the divine mission of Reform …

'My father gave me one of his "I can see you – no point in running for it" looks and asked what I thought of the proceedings. Of course, with Mr Tysoe on my other side I was politeness itself. I remarked on the quality of the speeches and said I hadn't expected to hear such oratory. My father confessed he'd found some of it excessively florid – "I have too much of that in Court," he said – rather gruffly I thought – "But we must surely approve the sentiments."'

'I suspect you wanted to escape yourself by this time!' said Elias. 'Were they holding you fast?'

'Mr Tysoe was gripping my arm, and I could tell he was aching to talk. But what he said surprised me. He told me he deplored the "maypole business," and I began nodding in agreement … until he added that he'd been for chopping the thing down during the night!'

Tom was wide-eyed:

'What! Do you mean to say they had debated it?'

'Evidently, yes. He must be one of the Society's inner council. My protector wasn't being discreet, was he?'

'Far from it! This is extraordinary. Your new friend reposes such trust in you … if only he knew!'

'Well, it seems there was a big dispute about the pole, and it was Mr Bedford's urgings that won the day. They decided a public act at the height of the celebrations would be immensely more powerful ...'

'And put innocent lives in danger!' said Tom.

Will looked surprised:

'Yes, that's exactly what I said ... I could feel my father stiffen; but the Reverend Tysoe was sympathetic and said he couldn't approve the excessive violence – that he abhorred it. "But as for their *innocence*," he said, "alas, those poor creatures knew not they were worshipping the Devil. They are sure to dance eternally," he said, "– but not to May-day music!"'

Widow Trotter shuddered:

'He's thinking of the Dance of Death, isn't he?'

'Yes, something like an old woodcut – perhaps one with horned devils pricking sinners with their forks and roasting human arses like chestnuts.'

'And all this under that fine chandelier!' she added. 'These men have such dismal fancies.'

'Every drawing-room conceals a sulphurous pit, Mrs T ... and as for the playhouse – the very mouth of Hell is gaping. I heard the word *Hell* more than once.'

'But did you manage to overhear anything of the conversation?' asked Tom.

'I certainly did – and I heard it from the man himself.'

'Arthur Bedford? – No!'

Will nodded:

'The same. He glided over in order to converse with Mr Tysoe and my father, and the poor man found me stuck between the ornamental pair – like a mantelpiece clock ... so they had to introduce me.'

Widow Trotter blanched and set down her wine carefully:

'You came that close?'

'Yes, I met that face directly. He's a tall gentleman and we saw eye-to-eye, which made the moment even more perturbing.

There were a few polite questions, but fortunately he didn't interrogate me – I think my father's presence dissuaded him. But I'm sure he was curious.

'Well, as Bedford turned his attention to Mr Tysoe, my father tried to draw me off, but I stood my ground and held him with questions, so that while he answered I could set my ear to my two neighbours. There was some tension growing between them, and it was then that I heard it ...'

Will shamelessly paused – his hours of attendance in Westminster Hall had not been in vain.

'... Arthur Bedford was speaking. I think the unwary Mr Tysoe had raised a question about the society's *agents* – I heard the word distinctly – and I knew they were touching on preparations for the Fair. They did not appear to be in agreement – and their voices were raised well above a whisper!'

'You're becoming a practised sneak,' said Tom admiringly.

'Well, Mr Tysoe mentioned two agents by name. And ...'

'Not by name, surely?' an astonished Elias interrupted.

'Yes, but not their own ... he referred to them as "Brother Merlin" and "Brother Redcrosse." Would you believe it, Tom? It's the world of romance – your beloved Spenser!'

Tom could indeed scarcely believe it, but he saw the meaning. Widow Trotter was looking at him questioningly.

'It's *The Faerie Queene*, Mrs T. – *Merlin* is the old magician who holds the future of the Nation in his magic mirror – and *Redcrosse* is the knight of the True Faith, who rescues the Church from Popish error.'

Elias was smiling at his young friend:

'Well well! Who would have thought these reformers could be so witty? It's good we have a poet with us.'

'But that's remarkable!' said Tom. 'It really is a secret society – with cyphers and watchwords too, I don't doubt. And they will be sniffing about the Fair, don't you think?'

'I'm sure that's their plan,' said Will. 'I strained to hear what I could, but all I caught was something about the fair-ground booths. And the *Devil* was mentioned. I think it was *The Devil on Two Sticks* they were talking about – they were arguing upon it. I'm convinced something is being organised. It was frustrating that I caught so little.'

'But this is valuable,' said Elias. 'It means we can be confident there will be spies at the Fair, and someone will be interesting himself in Pinkerman's booth. We have cause to be vigilant.'

'But that's not all, Mr Cobb. I wasn't going to slink away from the meeting as a mere eavesdropper, was I?'

Widow Trotter's wine-glass remained poised at her lips: 'No?'

'*No*. I had the imperious Arthur Bedford within reach, and the temptation was too great.'

'What did you do?'

'I can hardly credit what I did … I intervened, and asked him a direct question about Lord Tunbridge …'

Three people took a breath simultaneously.

'… I inquired if Mr Christopher Rich had been charged with his murder.'

'Will!'

'It was an entirely innocent question, Tom. And I asked it in a genial, inquiring spirit. I was simply an angler casting my fly into a quiet pool.'

'And did the trout bite?'

'He circled around – definitely curious. He said the Solicitor-General was being over-scrupulous – that time was being wasted – that there was difficulty with any *conspiracy*. We discussed the matter, and I was trying to be helpful to him. I even suggested that a witness of some kind would be necessary …'

'I don't believe this!'

'… and that was when his jaws closed on the fly. He told me

a witness had come forward who was prepared to swear that Mr Rich had called for the Baron's death, and in the clearest terms. He had been overheard in a tavern expressing a wish that the killing could be *arranged*.'

'So – they have someone ready and waiting – bribed, I take it?'

'I don't know, Tom. Such a scene *is* possible, isn't it? … and if Rich was in his cups …'

Widow Trotter crossed her arms decisively and glanced at her friends:

'But he wasn't the only member of the company who must have wished the Baron dead – they all knew the threat. But would one of them dare to do it?'

Will's brow furrowed as he recollected his earlier conversation with the players:

'Just so, Mrs Trotter. I heard the actors talking, and they all bade him good riddance. They were delighted he and his reforms were no more – happy to see them both buried! It was his plans for the company that concerned them – after all, their livelihoods are in question.'

Widow Trotter nodded:

'And they all know every inch of that theatre …'

'The actors killing him? That would be a formidable conspiracy!' said Elias. 'From the things you've said, it's more likely to be a political plot, perhaps with this Mr Bedford as the master-mind? It's clear Lord Tunbridge was stirring up violent disagreements among the reformers. He was caught either way – both sides might have an interest, and …'

His voice tailed off as his thoughts brought another scene to mind:

'… You didn't mention Sally Twiss to him, did you?'

'No, Mr Cobb, I thought that would be dangerous. My father was listening, remember, and I was giving a good show of commenting on the legal question. I gave Mr Bedford to understand that no such charge as *conspiracy to murder* exists – it's not a statutory offence. Though I suspect he had been hoping something of that kind could be fixed up by the lawyers.'

Tom was beaming at him:

'I can hardly credit this, Will! You find your way into a secret meeting of the Society for the Reformation of Manners. You hear all their latest news. You learn about their spies. You discover the man who may be the ring-leader of a plot against the theatre … and you end with offering him legal advice … I don't know what to say!'

'So, you think my mission was successful?'

'Conspicuously so, Mr Lundy!' said Elias. 'And what is more, I think you may have gained us more *time*. If these people are hesitating about bringing charges against Mr Rich, then we can exploit the delay. The more uncertainty there is, the more opportunity we have of finding out who did kill the Baron.'

'You really think it possible, then?' asked Widow Trotter.

'We have a fair chance, Molly. It's intricate, but the truth is in there somewhere. After all, I would rather have three possibilities than only one.'

'Three possibilities?'

'At least three, are there not? … the first, a plot within the company – perhaps an actor taking his chance? … second, killed by one of the Reformers' agents … or the third, a crime of passion – Sally – or Gilbert.'

Will winced as the constable named the young actors. He was convinced of the pair's innocence, and the imputation was hard to take. But the lawyer in him knew the idea shouldn't be closed off. He glanced at Tom:

'I know we have to keep that path open; but when I talked with Sally and Gilbert yesterday, I didn't get any sense of their guilt. Each feared the other might be the killer … Tom and I have agreed to differ on that.'

Widow Trotter was thoughtful:

'What I've been asking myself is, if Lord Tunbridge was murdered by our Reformers, why not kill him in a street brawl or a robbery? His death in that property-store seems so random. The "crime of passion" looks most likely to me … and what I heard from young Mr Bullock didn't dissuade me.'

'Of course,' said Tom. 'You and Elias talked with him yesterday?'

'Yes, he brought us the news about the arrest of Rich and Cibber. I have to say he made a fine performance of it in front of the whole coffee-room, waving his hat and declaiming. The young fellow is shameless – he's shaping up after his father!'

'What did you learn, Mrs T?' asked Tom.

'Only a little. He was surprised to be ushered into my Holy of Holies. An offer of madeira helped.'

'Young Kit Bullock wouldn't say "no" to that. He's something of a tippler – although the evening is his time, especially in the green room.'

'Yes, so I hear – and he was certainly there – and far from sober – on that fatal evening. Yet Elias tells me he was never questioned.'

'Nor was he, gentlemen! By ten o'clock the fellow was sleeping off his indulgence, utterly dead to the world. He had no part in *The Man of Mode*; but he sometimes uses the green room as a club, and on that night he was already half-seas-over by the interval. He thought he recalled some of the comings and goings – but only confusedly.'

'Not your ideal witness, Mr Cobb!' said Will.

'No – but a few random things imprinted themselves on his *cerebellum*. He does remember Gilbert arriving in the green room at the interval and immediately throwing back a whisky – he recalls it because he was offered a glass himself! He said Mr Angell seemed unsettled.'

'Ha! No wonder!' said Tom. 'But did the two of them exchange words? Does Kit remember?'

'It seems they drank a toast to their mistresses – although it could have been to *Miss Twiss* – he's not sure. He remembers drinking, though.'

Will groaned. By this time he was despairing of anything coherent emerging:

'Is that all?'

'He heard voices raised outside the room – the door was a little ajar.'

'Ah! Dare we ask if he recognised them?'

'One was Mr Grant the Prompter exclaiming against the scene-shifters. The scene hadn't been set to his satisfaction – I suppose the benefit-night clutter wasn't helping!'

'But this sounds like the usual interval panic – nothing more.'

'Yes – but then, he insists he heard Sally's voice – as if she was angry at someone.'

Will turned to Mrs Trotter:

'I don't suppose our witness recalls exactly when this occurred?'

'He's uncertain about the order of events ... But he does remember the end-of-interval bell – which finally sounded after some delay.'

'Well, that's a miracle in itself,' said Tom. 'It's a blurred sketch, is it not?'

'Better than nothing,' said Will. 'If only he could place things in order, we might be able to make more sense of it.'

Elias gave a rueful nod. Their conversation had reached a pause. The four of them looked at each other as if waiting for a spark from Heaven. Widow Trotter's burgundy, though excellent, was no substitute – and little inspiration was to be had from a tray of cold meats, however spicy the pickle.

Their hostess was fighting off discouragement:

'I don't think we *can* make sense of the murder, Mr Lundy –

not yet at least. Not out of the pieces we have. We need a fresh approach ...'

And with these words she suddenly jumped to her feet and threw her hands in the air. The others were startled. It was the energy of frustration – as if she wanted to grasp something elusive that was almost within reach. The others watched, fascinated, not knowing what to say.

'... I've changed my mind – I think our learned friend Mr Lundy is right. We *have to* trust Sally and Gilbert – there's no other way forward – otherwise we'll be endlessly questioning and suspecting when we should be acting decisively ... You're a chess-player, Mr Lundy, are you not? ...'

Will looked intrigued, and nodded.

'... Am I right in thinking that sometimes, when you have a difficult position on part of the board, you let it alone, and it clears as the game goes on?'

Will's eyes shone brightly. She was an amazing woman!

'Yes, Mrs T – that can happen. It's easy to become distracted by sorting out your own position, when your opponent's moves may do it for you ...'

'Exactly! ...'

Widow Trotter was now beaming – this was talk she wanted to hear.

'... The attack on Mr Bristowe was a hasty move, and it has alerted us. Our attacker has gained a brief satisfaction – but it is we who can learn from it. And it's telling us we must shift our attention to Brook Field. That is where the battle is to be fought. Things have moved from the playhouse to the Fair!'

There was a pause for thought.

'Yes,' said Tom'... that note my attacker left ... it was improvised – but it was someone carrying a pencil. The attack wasn't planned.'

'And your attacker was already in the booth, was he not?' said Mrs Trotter. 'He cannot have followed you in ...'

'Ah no, Mrs T. You see, there was a flap open at the rear, behind the stage – access for the workmen I assume. I'd noticed it when I walked up, but I went round to the front entrance to take a look at the balcony. Anyone could have slipped inside the booth during that time.'

'In that case,' said Elias, 'someone was keeping watch on your movements. Are you sure the two of you weren't followed from the Dog and Duck? Did you arouse suspicion? I thought my new apprentices would know to be careful.'

The two friends looked at each other. It was Will who spoke:

'We entirely forgot your rules, Mr Cobb! We left the tavern feeling pleased with ourselves and never thought to keep an alert eye. We were taken up with the duck-baiting, then we strolled off. I fear we never gave a thought …'

'It was worse than that,' interrupted Tom. 'I'm afraid I had been very stupid …'

He described asking the pot-boy about the meeting-room – an inquiry that now appeared supremely foolish. The constable gave him a sympathetic look, but his slow shake of the head was eloquent:

'Both of you still have much to learn! I think you may have been more conspicuous than you suspected.'

Widow Trotter leaned forward in her chair:

'You must take care. When the Fair begins on Thursday there will be such a crush of bodies – and we know the Fair's enemies will be there. It's going to be a dangerous time.'

'It will be confounded hard to police the place,' said Elias. 'And from what Will has told us, Pinkerman's company are likely to be in the line of fire.'

Tom was looking thoughtful:

'I can't help thinking … The naming of those agents – *Merlin* and *Redcrosse* – There's a witty mind behind all of this – one that thinks in symbols. Every act of violence seems to come with a message. Could it be Arthur Bedford's imagination?'

'I do believe he's smiling at us,' said Mrs Trotter, her eyes half-closed. 'I keep seeing that cold imperious smile.'

'Yes,' said Will, 'I see him too – observing everything from a distance.'

'As if he's in a theatre of his own creation,' said Tom, 'and watching his cleverly-scripted drama playing out – *untouchable!* ... Do you think he really is behind this? It would be the biggest hypocrisy of all.'

Widow Trotter's face took on a sudden determination:

'Well, gentlemen, we shall have to find some way of *touching* him ... I must think carefully how it may be done. We need some inspiration!'

There was a sudden electricity in the air – a sensation heightened at that moment by the sound of footsteps on the stairs, coming ever closer. They were slow and heavy (this was evidently no wingèd messenger), and it took several seconds for the door to open, revealing a beaming Jeremy, who was holding out a letter:

'A liveried gentleman has just brought this into the coffee-room, Mrs Trotter. It's an aristocratical letter for Mr Bristol ...'

He walked over to the bed and placed it in Tom's outstretched hand.

'... The gentleman is waiting for a reply – just a word, he says.'

Curiosity was intense, and no-one spoke while Tom broke the elaborate wax seal and unfolded the sheet. His eyes fell at once on the signature, and a reassuring smile lit up his face.

'It's from cousin Lavinia!' he said, and began reading it in silence.

The missive was certainly enthusiastic in its underlinings:

Tom!

Everyone here is agog for your Tender Courtesan *– we were in* *the Park this afternoon and saw it advertised in fine* Gothick *lettering – on more than one post! One of the bills was defaced by a shocking drawing (some lewd apprentice I think) – but the others were all perfectly legible. The dancing dogs intrigue me! – Anyway, we shall be coming on Thursday to see it – the play, that is – though it would be good to stay for the dogs, especially if they are going to be satirical. When I said* everyone, *I did not of course mean your aunt – who regards the Fair with* absolute horror *and rushed off to her room at the very mention of it – and your serious cousin Frank, who – need I say? – is presently in Wiltshire cultivating his precious* electors *… But your uncle and I shall certainly* both *be coming. We hope the thing won't be a disappointment after your* Prologue *– which we are sure will be a wonder of its kind.*

But first things first, Tom – you are to come to dinner on Thursday. *Then we can all take the coach to the Fair. My father says you must come! I know that is reason enough – but just hear what I've arranged to tempt you – I have prevailed on mamma to invite two special people who are now great friends of mine … What say you to dining with* Lady Norreys *(your* admirer*) and (**sound the trumpets!**) the distinguished Mrs Manley!*

I know that will surprise you – but I shall explain all on Thursday. Suffice to say that Arachne is still weaving her web *(you understand the meaning!), and the two ladies have a* joint interest *in the Fair – that is all I can possibly say. It is an* inviolable secret *– which means I can speak nothing here but will reveal every delicious particular when you come.*

You now know why you cannot decline this invitation. Just tell Arthur 'yes,' and our arrangements will proceed.

Your enigmatic cousin (from whom much more later) –

Lavinia

Tom folded the letter and looked at his friends, who were sitting in expectant silence as if their fates depended on its contents.

'Well?' asked Widow Trotter, '– is it something we can share?'

'I'll explain all in a moment – but first, Jem, will you tell Arthur the answer is *Yes* – and you must say nothing to him about my accident, do you hear?'

The stout Jeremy gave a silent salute and pulled the door closed with a thud. Tom knew he had some explaining to do.

Widow Trotter was uneasy about his venturing to dine in Pall Mall before heading for the Fair, concerned that the exertion might overtax him. But the arguments in favour, added to her own curiosity, won the day. She herself would be escorted to the Fair by Will, while Tom formed a party with the Pophams and the two literary ladies. It was agreed that Tom's visit would allow him to have a private talk with his uncle. Her Majesty's Deputy Treasurer knew all the news of the Court, and the Theatre Royal affair was sure to be absolutely sterling gossip around St James's. Widow Trotter also knew that in the battle to come – and that was how she saw it – Lord Melksham could be a valuable ally.

'Well then, gentlemen!' she announced with a flourish, 'Our next move is decided. We must turn our attention to Thursday and the Fair!'

'And until then, Mrs T,' said Tom, 'I promise to behave myself. Tomorrow I shall be the perfect patient.'

'I shall hold you to that, Mr Bristowe. We must build up your strength for the challenges to come – Mrs Dawes will see to it!'

Will, who was beginning to feel left out of this enthusiastic muster, gave a little cough and raised a hand like a shy schoolboy:

'I know that after this evening I ought to be resting on my laurels ... but I may sniff out something in Westminster Hall tomorrow. My studies are calling, and there's no better place for legal gossip – I'll see what I can gather.'

'Excellent!' said Mrs Trotter. 'As for me, it's high time I consulted my Friends in the Garden ... On the matter of the Reverend Arthur Bedford there must be more to uncover. The gentleman has been in town for over a month now, and I can't believe he hasn't left some traces of himself. Something tells me the trail may be a sticky one – a man with such a fine profile must have something to hide?'

Thursday

6 May 1708

Chapter Twenty-Eight

THE MONKEY GAVE a wild squeal and sent a handful of nuts cascading over the heads of the crowd beneath. From its vantage-point at the top of the flag-pole the animal commanded a sweeping view of the May Fair, which stretched from the clustered streets in the east, over nearby fields toward Tyburn in the north and Hyde Park in the west. It was the opening day of the Fair proper, and the tide of humanity was in holiday mood. Hats, scarves and colourful bonnets wove a restless pattern below, churning to the beat of a military drum, with penny trumpets and cat-calls supplying the chorus. Competing cries of the stallholders and hawkers came from all directions. The monkey's nose twitched as the smell of seared crackling ascended from the roasting-spits upwind. Swirls of tobacco-smoke and cheap perfume eddied around.

It was a bright and lively scene this Thursday morning in early May. Flags fluttered in the sun from the nearby roofs, and banners hung out of windows. On the gable-end of a nearby house a large painted cloth advertised the extravaganza in Miller's booth: a bejewelled Venus was pictured alongside a singing mermaid and three witches in pointed hats, and beneath them a trident-waving Neptune rode in his chariot drawn by a pair of sea-horses. As with any fairground droll, this romantic tale was exploiting whatever props and costumes were obtainable. The adjacent banner proclaimed: 'An excellent new Droll, call'd THE TEMPEST, or *the Distressed Lovers*. With the *English Hero* and the *Island Princess*, and the comical humours of the *Inchanted Scotchman*; or *Jockey* and the *Three Witches*.'

Far above it all, the monkey curled its tail around a hempen rope that stretched from the top of the pole through the air to a nearby roof, and began watching the performance. The rope shuddered as the woman swung herself down on it and lay full length, stretching her arms behind her neck and lolling one leg as if enjoying the most comfortable of hammocks. The crowd's gasps turned to smiles when the monkey, not wanting to be left out, lowered itself in turn and clung to the rope by its toes, swinging gently to and fro. Was this a satiric parody, or did it catch the wonder of the performance? Everything about the May Fair seemed to be a mixture of the two.

At ground level, one individual was moving through the crowd with watchful eyes, glancing down at people's belts and pockets, and alert to what their hands were doing. This kind of patrolling came as second nature to Constable Cobb – the Fair was a place where nimble fingers earned a good living. But today Elias was also scrutinising faces, searching for any look that had some malicious intent.

It wasn't pickpockets or sharpers who were on his mind today, but a threat that was less definable: he felt he would know it when he saw it. This was not a very professional approach, but it had stood him in good stead over the years. It had also made him naturally suspicious – a tendency that was thankfully countered by an innate good humour and a propensity to enjoy his friends.

At that moment there was another gasp from the crowd, louder than before, and Elias swung round in alarm. He glanced at the rooftops where the intrepid dancer was now clinging onto the rope by nothing but her own toes – she in turn was mimicking the monkey! Many spectators had ceased to breathe; but a minute later the fair-ground rang with cheers of delight as she curled round and swung herself up again, using the rope's momentum to right herself. Strength and grace combined! There was spontaneous applause, and the dancer's harlequin-clad assistant chose that moment to hold out his velvet hat and begin collecting some appreciative halfpennies.

William Pinkerman looked up from the entrance to his booth and smiled. The crowds were vast – more than he ever remembered before – and he couldn't help picturing the hundreds of purses and pockets, knotted around waists and buttoned beneath skirts, all impatient to open as the exuberance of the Fair took hold. That rope-dancer Sophie was good – very good! – and he was anticipating some pretty fair takings when she performed with the rest of her troop in his booth that afternoon. Connoisseurs of the rope-dancing art would be eager to view her at close quarters, balanced on one hand with her trunk-hose and stockinged legs pointing to the heavens. He mentally made a note to ready the wheelbarrow with its grooved wheels ...

The final rehearsal of *The Tender Courtesan* had been unremarkable – not the disaster he had feared. The cast weren't word-perfect yet, but a little improvising had got them through it. The company had assembled at an unearthly hour shortly after dawn; but once sleep had been rubbed from their eyes and the jugs of strong coffee emptied, they made a good run at the thing – and who knows? In front of an audience the piece might catch fire? The words on the page desperately needed the burnish of stage performance to bring them alive – but the magic would surely come?

Pinkerman's mind took refuge in practicalities: a small adjustment to the stage was needed; they were a couple of cushions short for the 'box' seats; the rugs by the door needed securing; oh ... and the elephant boys would be arriving with Hannibal at five o'clock, in time for him to do his little performance – at which point (he liked to think) the May Fair could officially begin.

A ripple of delighted laughter and a surge of applause came from the booth behind him: the dancing dogs were enchanting their audience as always. What admirable creatures, he thought. They were remarkably well disciplined, always eager to entertain, reliable, and tirelessly skilful! There was a lot to be said for canine performers: they didn't arrive the worse for drink, didn't need their vanities soothing – and they never haggled over their contracts.

He broke off his whimsical meditation when he saw the familiar figure of Elias Cobb making its way towards him. The two men hailed each other:

'What a press of people, Mr Pinkerman! So many sixpences!'

'And some florins too, Mr Cobb! Things are humming nicely. I've spotted a few polished buckles and not a little braid and velvet – and with very *giving* faces – it bodes well! I hope the day will pass without incident.'

'For all their noise, they're a good-humoured crowd this morning – but Sir John Barleycorn is yet to make his entrance!'

'The rogue will have his way no doubt, give him an hour or two. But at the moment I have a smile on my face ... You will have heard about Mr Rich?'

'Yes – that must have cheered the company!'

'To a degree – but they have succeeded in tainting us all. Suspicion will always leave a mark.'

'But there's no charge they can bring – or so I hear.'

'They will be in no hurry, Elias. It suits them to keep the pot bubbling. And he's not been exonerated, just released on bail. The gossips and scribblers will enjoy themselves. *Speculation* is the Muse of Fiction! ...'

It was a neat quip, and both men smiled.

'... But I'll tell you what has unsettled me ...'

There was another burst of applause from within the booth, and a melodious howl was followed by spirited laughter.

'... This morning we were granted a *magisterial* visit – one of the local Justices with a constable at his shoulder and a couple of bruisers hovering behind – and not a smile between 'em.'

'Oh, and what did they want?'

'It was no courtesy visit. I was offered – *gratis* – a little lecture on order and decency – or rather *dis*order and *in*decency. He gave me to understand that we are here *upon suffrance* until the Queen sees fit to close us down, *which she will certainly do!* That was when I caught a hint of pleasure in their faces. The message was solemnly delivered. You'd have thought Her Majesty was about to materialise in her coronation coach and command us all to disperse.'

'Arriving in your booth, I trust ... That would be a crushing blow to Miller – he'd never withstand it!'

Pinkerman grinned:

"Twould be the death-blow to Neptune and his appalling chariot. Have you seen the thing? It was patched up and creaking at the last Fair – and this year it looks even more like a painted haycart.'

'Cart-wheels across the ocean!'

'But 'tis what people love, Elias. There's nothing like an Olympian God to make mouths open – look at Finley's booth! And a Triton blowing his horn is the *very thing,* wheels or no wheels ... Alas, in *The Courtesan* there are only human beings – but real ones I like to think. I'm saving the magic spells for *The Devil on Two Sticks*.'

'And Rumour has it you have a remarkable Devil,' said Elias appreciatively. 'A devil on the stage! That should tweak the noses of the Magistrates!'

'I fervently hope so. The four noses that were sniffing at me this morning needed pulling, I tell you … They inspected my booth as if it was a public privy, and were on their way before you could say *Abracadabra*.'

'If they turn up for your satire, you must set the Devil onto them!'

'I'm sure Tiny François would lead them a merry dance! But seriously, Elias, I suspect the reforming guardians will have a presence here tomorrow night – and at our *Courtesan* this evening. It seems I've become a person of interest.'

'You are never less than that, Pinkey! But we shall keep an eye on your booth. Are you taking precautions?'

'As best I can. I'm hiring a pair of helpers, and I'll have the burly Amos at the door tonight – he's reliably testy and won't stand for any nonsense. But if you could spare one of your watch …'

'I've already spoken to Mudge, who considers it his duty to enjoy everything the Fair has to offer. And I'll be there myself of course, if only to hear Mr Bristowe's Prologue.'

'I've no concerns on that score. I'm going to make it something our reforming friends won't forget – if any pays his sixpence to hazard his immortal soul …'

He noticed the constable raise an eyebrow.

'… Why do they damn us, Elias? Are we truly consigned to Hell? In the great Scheme of Things we players are surely harmless – simply the comedy and tragedy of life – and the make-believe of it, nothing more. And yet we arouse such hate, such terrible anger.'

'The *make-believe* is what they fear, Pinkey. Don't you see? They fear the imagination: it's something they can't control.'

The two friends shared their philosophical grumblings for several more minutes before Elias made off. And all the while the innocent dancing dogs in the booth behind them continued to prance and strut and leap and twirl as if there was nothing more natural in the world.

Eleven o'clock, and the Fair was taking on a rhythm of its own and releasing every kind of human inventiveness. Distraction was the rule where all was higgledy-piggledy and nothing permanent or ordered. On this patch of ground things were piled up, cast off, disarranged, distorted, exaggerated. Flimsy timbers projected as temporary balconies; bare wooden planks were nailed into structures of every shape and size, from which miscellaneous stuff hung down, or across which curiosities were spread. A 'shop' could be little more than a table shoved against a wall, and a 'booth' a dirty piece of canvas stretched out on poles. Banners and painted show-cloths waved everywhere. Anyone might set themselves up on a patch of ground by a fence and make a stand. Others were continually on the move: card-sharpers crept around looking for a place to unfold their tables; fruits, biscuits and bags of nuts circulated on wooden trays strapped around shoulders. Through the press, a variety of performers from the drolls intermingled with the fair-goers, and your elbow might be caught by a wooden sword or a raised drumstick. A Persian satrap or Plantagenet queen brushed by you; a Mahometan turban or feathered helmet loomed at you; a ragamuffin filching from the stalls dived past your legs.

As for the terrain, it was already becoming sticky as the sprinkled cinders mixed with the underlying mud. Little patches of grass and clumps of weeds were a sad reminder that these were fields as well as streets. May Fair was an incongruous thing – an urban desecration of the sweetness of the fields, and a dirty rural invasion of the town.

Tom smiled to himself as he and Will began to catch the holiday sounds that grew ever louder. The Fair was a challenge to any writer; but a georgic poet could perhaps make something out of it, and Thomas Bristowe was determined to try. His ambitious poem had been set aside while thoughts turned to *The Tender Courtesan;* but now his imagination was working, and it occurred to him that a May Fair episode might have a place in his poetic scheme. After all, this was an occasion when human ingenuity took many forms, and if Virgil could celebrate the restless sociability of the honey-bees, then the Fair also offered a busy nation in miniature. If Rome needed reminding of its old republican virtues, then a May Fair digression might do the same for Anne's 'Great Britain' – perhaps with a slight satiric edge to give it a modern touch?

Tom was pondering these poetical questions while he and Will strolled into Brook Field, now transformed from the working cattle market of three days earlier. They were determined to enjoy the Fair's simpler pleasures before Tom had to leave for Pall Mall – only a short walk away in St James's, but a different universe.

'Cheer up, friend Tom!' said Will after their few minutes' silence. 'Pinkerman and his troop will rise to the occasion tonight, I'm sure – and your Prologue will have a fine effect.'

'Not *too much* of an effect, I hope. You know my fears over it.'

'I do – but you'll not start a riot, if that's what you mean. Your words will draw the audience together and sharpen their expectations ... If anything, it's Sally we should be fearful about. I hope she won't have apprehensions. Tamara is a big step for her.'

'Well at least she and Gilbert won't be flinging plates at each other. What you said to them was remarkable – I do believe you brought them into harmony.'

Will nodded agreement, but then gave an audible sigh:

'But that rumour I picked up in Westminster Hall yesterday ... if word should reach Sally before tonight ...'

'We must hope it doesn't. You're right not to speak of it – the news would only discompose her.'

'It would disable her, Tom! How could she give herself to the play with such a threat hanging over her? ...'

Will had slowed down almost to a stand as the troubling thought returned.

'... I feel so helpless, Tom. But it was told me with serious intent – it wasn't frivolous gossip. Mr Sumner said there was a sure basis for it.'

'Well, if they *are* going to arrest her, it confirms what we've suspected – that there's a battle in high places, and the Baron's murder is being used by both sides.'

'Yet another struggle of Whigs and Tories! Can you credit it? Everything seems to sink into faction.'

'All too easily. I must ask Uncle Jack this afternoon. He's thoroughly sick of the party bickering – he meets it every day.'

Both of them hesitated. This gloom would never do, and there was little flesh left on that particular bone. It was time to let the May Fair work its magic. As they looked around, everything was conspiring to do just that. It was a sunny, fresh morning, and they were now on the avenue leading up to the main concourse. *Have at the Fair!*

At once, to their left at the corner of a yard they caught sight of a young fellow in a tattered greatcoat much too big for him. He was hugging some bagpipes to his chest and drawing a lively jig out of them. As his foot tapped away, an ingenious mechanism of wires, scarcely visible under his shoe, was working a pair of wooden dancers ten inches high, who spun round in a circle to his tune. Alongside, his pet dog balanced on its hind legs, a little cocked hat on its head and a walking-cane dangling from its paw, just like a miniature beau jaunting down Piccadilly.

'A smart little chap!' said Tom with a smile, throwing a halfpenny into a handkerchief spread on the ground.

'A pert *St James's* puppy, you might say – in comparison the lad looks like his scullion.'

'But it's a flourishing trade the boy has – I wonder who owns him?'

It was a pertinent question: it was likely someone was exploiting the lad's talents and he was being run by an enterprising gang-master who would be calling by to collect the takings.

'I hope he gets a fair cut. He'll have sore knees by the end of the day – if his breath holds out.'

They turned, and the piper disappeared in the crush of bodies that enveloped them. They checked their tightly-buttoned pockets and gave themselves to the flow, swimming with the tide of the crowd, shoulder to shoulder past a row of stalls where hawkers were crying their wares.

'Look over there, Tom! Can you see what I see ...?'

Tom craned his neck as Will pointed to a table beneath a canvas awning, where a bewigged conjurer was juggling eggs in the air. With a flourish of lace cuffs, he caught and swung them round until there were three of them in the air at once. A huddle of people clustered round him, one of whom was an intent-looking Gilbert Angell. He was gazing at the hands as the man set down the eggs, one by one, on the green baize – four of them – and then slipped them into an embroidered bag.

'... Fancy a bit of conjuring?' said Will.

Tom nodded happily, and the two of them succeeded in peeling off from the crowd. A moment later they tapped a startled Gilbert on the shoulder just as the spectators gave a little gasp: the man was turning the bag inside out and shaking it – it was completely empty.

'Mr Lundy and Mr Bristowe! You must keep quiet and watch this – it's what *theatre* ought to be. So simple – but a perfect illusion!'

They watched together as the man reached into the empty

bag and took out the eggs again – not four, not five, but one after another, and another, until there were a dozen of them lined up before him.

A smattering of applause greeted this, and smiles of puzzlement, followed by a sudden intake of breath as his hand dipped into the bag once more to emerge with a handsome white bird, which hopped onto his arm and looked quizzically at the spectators. With yet another swirl of the cuffs a long paper scroll appeared out of nowhere, and he announced in ringing tones that his complete show – "a spectacle like no other!" – would commence in exactly five minutes. He promised to introduce them to a world of the supernatural and cause them to scratch their heads and "*doubt reality itself* ..."

'I suspect our play is going to have much the same effect!' said Gilbert.

Tom and Will laughed a little uneasily, but he swung round and beamed at them:

'Rest assured, gentlemen! We shall give you a memorable performance this evening. Fear not!'

'Are you for the full show here, Mr Angell, or have you seen enough?'

'I know Mr Fawkes's tricks, Mr Bristowe – he is a young genius! But just now I have another idea ... If the two of you would care to join me, we can refresh ourselves and have a little excitement at the same time.'

'That sounds intriguing,' said Will. 'What do you have in mind?'

'I need, gentlemen, to visit a raffling shop. I'm determined to raffle for a fan – and I'm sure there may be a trinket or two that you might want to venture for yourselves?'

This seemed a suitably festal thing to do, and so the three of them made their way across the field to a row of old cottages which had been converted into temporary shops. Some canvas roofing projected on poles, and strips of rush matting were laid out along the front. The Fair was a boon to these householders, who could earn a fortnight's good rent, and the 'raffling shop' was in the largest cottage at the end of the terrace. Above it, the painted banner had sagged a little and was now giving notice of a 'Grand Raff ottery.' But the message had come through and the threshold was tight with spectators. Under the awning were three or four wooden tables where refreshments were being offered for sale 'to patrons of the raffle' – a touching bid for politeness. These particular 'patrons' decided to wait for the next session when the crush would have cleared; and so, after a few minutes they were sitting at a rickety table with cider, bottle-ale, and a bag of nuts, while Tom gave Gilbert an account of his painful adventure in Pinkerman's booth.

Not surprisingly, the attack had caused alarm among the actors, and Gilbert visibly shivered as he commiserated. Company talk had been of a 'fairground ruffian' who must have sneaked into the booth to steal any tools left lying around – a plausible fiction, but one that had called forth no evidence except for the hammer that had been found on the floor.

Tom hesitated; but he caught Will's eye and remembered Mrs Trotter's resolution that Gilbert and Sally should be trusted. And so, he told Gilbert about the note:

'I too was given a threatening note, Mr Angell. It was left in my pocket ...'

The young actor blanched.

'... Sally told me you've also received one?'

Gilbert looked even more uneasy and acknowledged with a slight nod. He spoke quietly and hesitantly:

'So – this is our threatened *nemesis* again, is it? ... I'm sorry you've been caught up in all this, Mr Bristowe. No doubt it was your Prologue which prompted it.'

'I hope that's all it is. As you know, Will and I have been interesting ourselves in the threats to the theatre ...'

'Yes, Sally told me you wanted our help.'

This was terse, but appeared well meant.

'It is to be hoped we can assist each other, Mr Angell. We know Mr Pinkerman is feeling beleaguered, and with just cause. We're sure the *Reformation of Manners* people are organising against the Fair, and we have evidence of it. With the theatre in recess they'll be bringing their forces to bear on the Brook Field – Pinkerman's booth in particular.'

'Yes, poor Pinkey told us he was fearful. This morning he warned us to be vigilant, but insisted our shows must go on. He's doing his best to bear up, though he feels it as a personal threat. At the rehearsal he held the very latest pamphlet in his hand and declaimed some of it to us. Flatulent stuff! The thing is fresh from the press today and was personally delivered to him – anonymously of course. Such a terrible vision! We are all to be *eternally damned*.'

'I hate these anonymous attacks,' said Tom. 'If they believe God directs them, why do they conceal themselves?'

'But this one did not, Mr Bristowe. The author goes by the redolent name of *The Reverend Ebenezer Tysoe*. It's on the title-page as bold as anything. A Hackney sermon preached this very week! I'm happy to say that Pinkey tore the paper in half and said he would *put it behind him*. Indeed he's made a fine joke of it, and has had the thing hung in one of the privies!'

'What?'

So, Tysoe's sermon was in print! It was now Will's turn to go pale, though the picture was an amusing one. How did Pinkerman manage to keep the comic spirit alive? It was genuinely heroic. Stoical heroism!

Will seized the opportunity and told Gilbert of his visit to the Mare Street Meeting-House and his direct encounter with Mr Tysoe over the family dinner-table. Gilbert was curious about what opinion he had formed of the preacher, and as Will was speaking a look of recognition came into his eyes. The reason was soon revealed:

'Well well, Mr Lundy! Indeed you have him to a T! And you judge him shrewdly ...'

Tom and Will exchanged glances.

'... It will interest you to know that I have encountered Mr Tysoe myself.'

'Not in the playhouse, surely?' said Tom. 'That would be a revelation!'

'No – it was a social occasion of a different kind ... How can I express it without seeming to accuse him? – or without tarnishing myself? ... but I owe you the truth, and it may help you ...'

Tom and Will lived through the pauses.

'... We theatre-folk, you know, are sociable fellows and mix in many a circle – some of them genteel, others distinctly impolite. This was an elegant gathering in a private house in St James's, an informal club where gentlemen are able to find companionship and easy talk. It is a place where young gallants, literary men, men of affairs – clergy also – can escape from the formalities of life and be *themselves*, in whatever way they choose. It is a place to which I and a friend might retire after a performance, and unwind congenially ...'

The euphemisms were accumulating. Tom swallowed hard, not quite knowing where this preamble would lead.

'... The Reverend Mr Tysoe was brought there by a fellow clergyman; but from the outset he was uneasy, especially when he learned it was a place where *actors* occasionally resorted. I think he had expected a scholarly and Platonic gathering – certainly not one with closets and alcoves for more specialised communings. And yet the place seemed to fascinate him equally. His host introduced him, and from the first I knew he was *interested* – in me and my precarious profession – repelled and aroused in equal measure. But I ask you to believe he had no base motive – quite the opposite. There was a delicacy that made him a fish out of water. He was anxious, and panted slightly as he spoke. Little did I know he was a reformer who railed against plays and players!

'The man may roar from the pulpit, but I have to say that in that place he was a softly-spoken confessor. And would you believe it, gentlemen? – he made a valiant attempt to *save my soul!* His hand seized mine, and I felt the dampness of his palm – which may have been balm but was possibly a more feverish extrusion. It was hard to tell. There was something carnal in his spiritual fervour. He said he longed to take me away from that place – and from my *sordid life*, as he called it. It was strange, but the more he insisted he wanted to remove me, the firmer his grip became. He was pressing me … "You are an angel indeed!" he whispered … "You do not belong here!"…'

For an instant Gilbert's features took on a choirboy naivety, eyes raised to a world beyond.

'… I was thoroughly embarrassed at the intimacy and wanted to flee, but he held me there like a fly in his silken web. And then he turned to matters of the flesh, and I caught the full force of his pulpit oratory. But it was delivered in a tone of hushed disgust. The man *hates the body*, gentlemen! He spoke of "the Deed of Darkness" as if it could not be named, and his hold on me tightened even more … And finally came the dreadful word "Sodomy" … it was uttered like poison expelled from the lips …'

Gilbert paused, almost in wonder.

'… The Reverend Tysoe is inflamed by purity – thrilled by innocence! Trapped in his own mortal flesh, he is stung with an intense desire for release! I have not met such a thing before.'

The picture was a highly-coloured one. There was silence, and for a few seconds the three of them were no longer sitting outside a raffling-shop: they resembled a little group of startled onlookers in an Italian fresco who had stumbled on a scene of religious ecstasy. Tom and Will stared at each other, hardly knowing what to say. Gilbert Angell reached for his pot of cider, letting his eyebrows speak for him.

It was Will who broke the silence, and with words that were no less unsettling:

'So ... I now see what I must do.'

This was enigmatic.

'*Do?* ...' said Tom at once. He caught a look of determination on his friend's face.

'... What do you mean? What are you resolved on, Will?'

'There's some unfinished business between myself and the Reverend Ebenezer Tysoe, which I now see has to be settled. I think I glimpse an opportunity ...'

There was a flash of wit in his eyes that reassured Tom.

'... I think I need to twitch the silken web myself!'

Tom at once saw the import of Will's remark, but he was still curious:

'Where did things stand between you? He was very indiscreet at your Reformers' meeting – are you hoping to push him further?'

'Yes, Tom – though *pull* might be the more exact term.'

The others were taken aback, but it was Gilbert who spoke, giving a little laugh as he did so:

'That sounds like a seduction, Mr Lundy. Is that what you are plotting?'

'You put it crudely, Mr Angell. Let us say that I can see a way to draw further indiscretions from him. The man indeed has a web – you are right about that – but it is a considerable network. Along with Mr Arthur Bedford, he is close to the heart of the Reformation society, but also at odds with its more violent members. I sense a growing disaffection – an unease over the direction events have taken. And we can exploit this. We know his misgivings about the maypole – perhaps murder doesn't sit well on his stomach either?'

'But how can you arrange another meeting?' said Tom.

'I think it could be managed. I know he considers me a potential disciple, a young man ready to commit to the Society – perhaps even with thoughts of becoming an *informer*? ... After what Mr Angell has told us, our Mr Tysoe – *my* Mr Tysoe – may not be averse to drinking tea with me tomorrow – perhaps in *St James's*?'

There was a palpable shock around their table.

'A nice thought, Mr Lundy,' said Gilbert, astonished. 'But he will not have access to James Street – unless by invitation.'

'Ah! James Street! That's what I need to know. You must give me more exact directions ...'

'Will!'

'Don't be concerned, Tom. My plan is a very simple one. There will be no return visit, I assure you! But I suspect the mere mention of that place may encourage an indiscretion ... and given that my father is "Hemp" Lundy, the Reverend gentleman could soon find himself in some embarrassment.'

'Now who is the spider, Will? This is a hazardous manoeuvre – and a shameless one.'

'Yes, shameless perhaps – I'll concede that. But not excessively hazardous. I believe Mr Tysoe is something of an innocent. I don't see him as a dangerous plotter – he is too unguarded for that. The man puts his name to things. He preaches what he feels, and publishes what he preaches. I may be able to draw more out of him if we can talk on an intimate footing.'

'What we need is more about Baron Tunbridge and the Theatre Royal. That's the gold dust! If you could find out what he knows ...'

'So, you think I should do this? ...'

Tom hesitated and said nothing, torn between discretion and opportunity, but his look was encouraging.

'... Then I shall write a note accordingly. Who knows what will come of it? I think this is called *laying a fleece before the Lord?*'

'No, it's called *taking a chance,*' said Tom. 'I wouldn't claim more than that.'

Gilbert brightened:

'Perhaps that's our cue, gentlemen? The raffle awaits. Shall we see if the dice run in our favour?'

Chapter Twenty-Nine

As the three of them gathered round the raffling board, Gilbert Angell's face took on a look of willed concentration, as if seriousness of intent would somehow win the fickle goddess to his side. The raffle was of course mere play – a game of luck for which no skill or concentration was required, and Tom and Will had purchased their tickets in a spirit of happy chance; but alongside them the young actor had the demeanour of Prince Hamlet pondering the mysteries of Providence:

'You know what they say, gentlemen – "There are but few casts at dice between a rich man and a beggar" – well, I hope to reverse the dictum!'

It was certainly a very splendid fan: pleated silk in a floral design of lemon and pink, with fine ivory sticks – a good three guineas worth, Gilbert insisted.

'And yet only twenty tickets – and I have a double chance!'

This was presumptuous. His two friends had come in for a half-crown ticket each, which, added to Gilbert's two, brought the odds down to five, a number that seemed to fill him with entire confidence. Given merely a half-smile from Fortune, Sally would have her beautiful fan in time for that evening's performance.

Gathered around them were the other ticket-holders, a distinctly more fashionable group than the ones who had raffled for the previous item. The Duke of Marlborough on horseback had commanded thirty tickets at sixpence, and the young apprentice who won the prize had presented it ceremoniously to his mistress, who tried to look as if a pottery Churchill was her very heart's desire.

It was a small, tight room which was growing smaller and tighter by the minute as people squeezed themselves in. The raffle was a popular show, and the press of spectators was turning the place into a cock-pit. Every shoulder seemed to have a face peering over it, and there was enough sweat and stinking breath to curl the wallpaper, had there been any. Jostled wigs were billowing hair-powder, and scented handkerchiefs wafted an uneasy sweetness into the mix. By the far door a couple of the house ladies were befriending young men, hoping to become mistress of their winnings – a proven way for the proprietor to tilt the odds even more in his favour.

The raffle got under way as the deal box was offered to the first player. After a needlessly thorough shake and a muttered incantation, the dice eventually tumbled out only to form themselves into a miserable trio: *deuce-trey-cinque* – a mere *ten* with no doublet. The gentleman looked up at the ceiling accusingly and passed the box on. The second ticket was handed in, and a sparkish young fellow touched his heart and his forehead in turn before sliding the dice gently onto the green baize … *Sice* and a *cinque* doublet. He brightened hopefully, but 'false throw!' was immediately declared by several of the players, and the bank gave him a disapproving look: 'The gentleman will throw again! You must *shake*, Sir – as well you know. We'll have no slurring here!'

The shake did little for his cause, and he slunk humiliatingly from the race with a *trey-quatre-sice*. The look on his lady-friend's face hinted that such disappointment was only to be expected.

Four more throws followed, and four more downcast faces – a *trey doublet* was there to be beaten. Now Tom handed in his ticket and clasped the box. He smiled to himself at the little drama that was gripping the audience and decided to woo the gallery. With a stylish flick of the wrist he made a neat performance of it. But there was substance as well as style, and a spontaneous murmur ran round the room: *quatre* and a *sice* doublet! Only a *cinque* with the same, or a triplet *raffle* could beat it! Eyes glanced at the young hero who had the prize in his sights – but there was no doxy at his side. One of the house ladies standing by the door made a move in his direction.

When his turn came, Will's throw was good, but not good enough: a *cinque* doublet; and Gilbert's first throw, after so much expectation, was a miserable one, with nothing above a *quatre*. As the purchaser of a second ticket he could claim the right of last throw and so he silently passed the box on. And so it continued around the room as each hopeful player in turn handed over their ticket and took their chance, only to fail. Tom was nearing the prize, and – in spite of Gilbert's plans – began picturing himself bending the knee as he presented the fan to Mrs Trotter. More sighs and curses followed – and at last the box came into the delicate hands of the sole lady who was bidding for the prize, a young woman who had been still and quiet during the proceedings but was now seen to blush elegantly, her eyelids set in delicate motion. The hands were shaking and she was ill at ease. The spectators leaned forward, interested in her fate and wondering about her character: this maiden evidently lacked a gallant who would venture for her. Or less romantically, perhaps she was a whore with pretensions?

The woman was flustered, and as the spectators crowded in, a gentleman behind her caught her elbow and one of the dice fell to the floor. There was an embarrassed cry and the man knelt down to retrieve it from beneath the table, making profuse apologies. The box reappeared, and the woman's gloved hand took it gratefully. There was a pause of a second or two as she collected herself, and then the dice were cast … The drama was intense, and the sensational moment duly delivered itself: *cinque* and a *sice* doublet – Tom's throw was beaten!

Exclamations and cheers rang out, and the woman made to rise from her seat – only to see Gilbert's hand outstretched. His second ticket was being offered for another cast of the dice. The woman looked disconcerted, and her mouth opened – but nothing could be said. The young actor must have the last throw. The banker took the ticket from him, and the final moments of this ingenious little scene played themselves out.

Of course, Gilbert's second cast was also an excellent one – indeed it was an impeccable one. The little platoon of three dice lined up along the green baize as if pleased with themselves: a six, a second six, and a third six – an unbeatable *sice raffle!*

It took the three of them several minutes to extricate themselves from the shop. There were congratulations and back-slappings, and Gilbert became the centre of attention among the house ladies, one of whom interlocked her arm with his and gave him the sweetest smile imaginable. The young actor, while admiring her performance, knew the plot, and returned a polite dismissal:

'Alas, I fear this fan is promised to another!' he said, and began making his way carefully through the entrance door.

Will was warm in his praise and expressed wonder at Gilbert's brilliant success:

'What a climax! Deliver a performance like that tonight, Mr Angell, and you will be the sensation of the Fair.'

'Alas, I'm no hero, Mr Lundy – merely the cleverer trickster! That little playlet was intended to end with the heroine's triumph – and what a neat exchange the two of them made! He jogging her elbow, then substituting the dice. The lady supposed she would be the last to play – but of course she was unaware of my second throw. A set of dice weighted to show only *cinque* and *sice* greatly lessened the odds! I do feel a little sorry for the two of them. Their talents are wasted here – but perhaps they'll be more successful tomorrow?'

'But the proprietor will surely exclude the pair of them?' said Tom.

'On the contrary, I suspect they are part of the business,' said Gilbert. 'Dame Fortune isn't a guileless lady – and she sometimes has to be bribed!'

It was a worldly sentiment uttered with a knowing smile, and the mood of the party at once lightened – although Tom couldn't help regretting that his own luck hadn't held. At least Sally Twiss would now have an elegant fan to wave in the booth that evening. It was undoubtedly a *Tamara* fan!

Tom offered that observation to Gilbert, and the three of them began laughing. But in an instant the mood changed. There was a noise, and the smiles froze on their lips. Several burly men were pushing past them, shouldering fair-goers aside as they directed their strides towards the scene of Gilbert's triumph. The cohort began pushing their way into the raffling-shop, followed by a pair of gentlemen in Justices' garb who were attempting to strike a note of civil authority in a scene that was about to descend into riot.

It took only moments for the screams to begin. The fox was in the hen-coop, and human fur and feathers were flying. To the accompaniment of a loud crashing and shouts of indignation, a mixed crowd began spilling through the doorway, baffled to be thrust out from their entertainment. Hands were desperately clutching velvet bags and pigskin purses, and a couple of ladies limped onto the grass, shoes in hand, torn scarves dangling from their shoulders. All dignity was lost. Figures emerged with disordered coiffeurs, hats hanging askew or being kicked along the dirt; pockets were ripped, and cuffs torn. Inside the door a violent skirmish was in progress, with fists flying to the accompaniment of wild halloos. The cottage itself seemed boiling with energy and about to explode.

And sure enough, a few moments later one of the upstairs windows burst open, and a roly-poly wheel flew out, metal tokens cascading round it like sparks from a bonfire. For a brief moment the object resembled an eccentric planet thrust from its orbit. In defiance of Newton, it crashed down into the garden, narrowly missing a stout gentleman who began attacking the thing with his cane as if fending off an intruder. Above his head, playing-cards spiralled downwards like snowflakes.

'So,' said Will, 'it seems the *deep play* was upstairs! Have you ever played the wheel, Mr Angell?'

'Only once, Mr Lundy. I prefer to be a spectator! Believe me, Roly-poly is a game best played *sober*. The spinning wheel draws you in like an enchantress, and it can lure you to destruction. I have seen tragic scenes played out around the table that might challenge Othello crying for his handkerchief.'

There was no reply. The three of them were stunned and stood for a moment watching the chaos. It hardly seemed real.

'Well, we seem to have escaped just in time!' said Tom. 'We can do no good here, gentlemen – shall we seek out more innocent pleasures?'

'I'm not sure how innocent they may be,' said Gilbert, 'but my pleasures await in the tithe-barn, and I must return there. That amorous fellow *Ernesto* has an assignation with a certain tender courtesan – purely for matters of rehearsal, you understand! We are to run through our scenes together. We aim to make each other perfect for this evening.'

'I trust the fan will work its magic,' said Will.

'Let us hope the audience will be generous,' said Gilbert. 'We shall be relying on our friends. Thank you gentlemen!'

Thrusting the precious fan deep in his pocket he gave them a brisk bow, and they watched him stride off into a gathering crowd whose attention was turned in their direction. The disturbance in the raffling-shop was audible for some distance, and this free show was attracting more and more onlookers curious to see what was playing out.

There was a sudden cry of 'the Justices!' But this only acted as a rallying cry, and around them several men in the crowd, not content to be spectators, began running to the cottage where the fight had spilled out into the garden. Others joined in until the odds were distinctly unfavourable to the Law. One of the magistrates was having a hard time fending off blows and was soon joined by his fellow Justice, who was half thrown across the lawn by a pair of bruisers. Thankfully, mocking laughter had taken over, and the hail of blows was now a shower of fruit. It was a signal that the two law-men would escape with their lives, while leaving their pride and self-respect hostage. And so they ran – or rather scampered, tails in the air – accompanied by laughing fair-goers determined to escort them from the site. It was not a dignified departure.

'Whoah!' said Tom. 'This isn't good, Will! What are we to make of it?'

His friend was frowning:

'A provocation, I'd say! Something so bold on the first morning of the Fair? It was calculated to stir up trouble. If a summons was to be presented, it needed to be done quietly and formally, not by bursting into a house like a pair of bum-bailiffs with their gang.'

'Hardly the dignity of the Law, was it? ... Do you think they had come over from the Dog and Duck?'

'By the smell of them they were primed and loaded – but fortunately only with drink. I wonder what Mr Cobb will say to this? I was half expecting to see him.'

They surveyed the restless scene and, as if the thought had beckoned him, caught sight of Elias approaching from the far side of the raffle-shop. Toby Mudge and several other watchmen were with him. The group were walking in close order, their faces set and quarter-staffs gripped in their hands. It was an opportune moment to arrive; and as they came nearer, the remaining fighters drew back, recognising that their sport had come to an end.

'That's *authority* for you,' said Will quietly. 'Hold your peace, choose your moment, and keep your weapon close, like you mean to use it.'

The procession of watchmen closed in and had an immediate effect. With remarkably little fuss the eager scrappers were separated and some semblance of calm re-established. Everyone had had their fun, and within moments the holiday mood returned.

Elias was wiping his brow and saw Tom and Will approaching:

'Well, what think you of that, gentlemen? A nasty little scuffle – and one that should have been avoided. Our Justices will never learn. A time and a place!'

It was a terse phrase but summed up their thoughts well enough.

Tom and Will told him of their sojourn in the raffling-shop and what they had seen of the sudden invasion by the magistrates.

Elias nodded:

'It was a calculated incitement, gentlemen. We saw it coming ...'

He gave a knowing wink.

'... thanks to the report of my *two spies*. I had the Dog and Duck watched this morning, and my informant saw the trouble-makers gathering there, fuelling themselves with courage. We followed them and waited behind the cottage till the worst had played itself out. Had we poured in earlier the violence might have been hard to contain and could have spread to the whole Fair – an equal fight is usually a more protracted one. And it wasn't for us to shield those Justices from the consequences of their folly! ... It has the smell of a plot, don't you think? ...'

That was exactly what Tom and Will were thinking.

'... It was to spread alarm and confirm the fears of the authorities. The Queen's Justices chased out of the Fair! You can be certain Her Majesty will hear about it within the hour. Yes, gentlemen, it was a tactical foray to strengthen the hand of the magistrates and give fuel to the reformers. We must hope it's not a rehearsal for the show to come.'

This was a grim prognostication, and Elias's last phrase struck home. Instinctively their thoughts turned to Pinkerman's booth and that evening's performance of *The Tender Courtesan*.

'Mr Angell seems cheerful about the play's prospects,' said Tom.

'And so is Pinkerman,' added Elias. 'I left him reckoning up shillings and sixpences in his head. I suspect the booth will be crammed for the inaugural show. People are intrigued – it's not the usual fare for a droll-booth!'

'Our friend is risking a lot; but he trusts his actors, and although Rich has washed his hands of it, Cibber has been encouraging from the start.'

'Well, we shall see ... I know a certain landlady who is humming with anticipation ... and I gather the *nobility* will be gracing the tent with their presence?'

He gave Tom an impish grin.

'Uncle Jack and cousin Lavinia insisted on being there, Mr Cobb – and not just for the Prologue: they at least pretend to an interest in the play. Mr Steele's *Tender Husband* is a favourite with them, and they think this piece may be out of the same drawer.'

Elias shook his head:

'From a husband to a courtesan, eh? Well, it's a step many take ...'

'But it's an improving play, Mr Cobb,' added Will. 'In the end, the joys of marriage triumph.'

'The joys of marriage? Hmmm – so, this is a comedy rather than a tragedy?'

'A little of both,' said Tom encouragingly. 'You could call it a tragi-comedy – a bit like life.'

'*Life,* Mr Bristowe? I don't know about that – but I hope the audience will know where they are with it. The ladies won't know whether to laugh or cry.'

'Well they can always *smile*. That's a pretty safe response to most things!'

And that was their own response at this moment. The men's critical dialogue may not have been worthy of Dryden or Dennis, but it set the affair in a just perspective, and to face the coming events with a smile seemed the right course. In a few hours' time the various players would be assembling – those on stage and those in front of it – and the result of that mixture was impossible to predict.

Chapter Thirty

THE RITUAL OF the tea-table was not something Mary Trotter had studied or much practised, and she was thankful that her particular friends were not ones to expect straight backs and fine silks, with talk confined to routine pleasantries. Tea with Adèle Ménage was certainly very pleasant, but the drops of Nantes brandy with which she enlivened the Chinese leaf ensured conversation wasn't inhibited by the demands of formality. Thoughts could be aired freely, rumours tested, stories told, informations circulated. Anything indiscreet was prized above all. In this regard, Widow Trotter's 'Friends in the Garden' rarely disappointed.

On this Thursday afternoon the talk was flowing along nicely, and with just the three of them it was more intimate and unconstrained than usual. The third figure around the japanned table was Mr Denniston, a man of business whose toy-shop occupied the ground floor of the building. Far from being one of those categorical men who dismissed the tea-table as a feminine indulgence, Charles Denniston was only too happy to indulge himself – not merely in the tea and cake but in everything that went with it.

One of his favourite subjects – the cog-wheel that always set him in motion – was the shop itself, its contents and its clientèle. Any awkward lull in the conversation could be overcome by a simple enquiry as to *how trade was*. This opened up most topics, and on this occasion the question led directly to the May Fair and the very *un*fair competition from the Brook Field traders with their so-called 'shops.'

'Mere tinkers and gipsies!' Mr Denniston declared, setting down his china cup and reaching for a slice of cheesecake. 'Give these people a plank and a couple of barrels, and they'll set up for a toy-shop. The Fair overflows with fiddle-faddle stuff – nothing but cheap imitations! And the raffling-shops? I never cease to wonder how some folk are happy to throw away a guinea or two rather than pay a fair price across the counter ... I would even consider becoming a raffling-shop myself if it wasn't for those cursed magistrates. As we know, ladies, there is one law for the Fair people and another for the rest of us. The end of it can't come soon enough for me!'

With a precise turn of the fingers he placed a remarkable amount of cheesecake across his tongue and bit into it gratifyingly. Mrs Ménage gave her guest an approving nod and turned to Widow Trotter:

'Do you picture the delightful scene, Marie? Our friend Charles in his polite little raffle-shop? What a decorous establishment it will be! Only the beau monde will have the *entrée* – and he will bar the door to riff-raff ... Katherine Street will once again be fashionable!'

'Do you see the May Fair coming to an end, Mr Denniston?'

Mrs Trotter's question could not avoid striking a serious note; and after a moment's pause while he savoured the creamy filling, he leant over to her with a confiding gesture:

'It is doomed, Mrs Trotter! I have it on good authority that after this year the Fair will no longer outrage the good folk of St James's. As our pulpiteers insist on telling us, "the end of all things is at hand!" – and the May Fair will undoubtedly be the first to sink into the pit!'

'You mention the magistrates, Mr Denniston. Is this where you have your information?'

He gave a sniff:

'Ah no! The magistrates merely do others' bidding … no, no, I have a *higher* authority – no less than our mighty landlord himself.'

He said nothing more and reached for his tea-cup, allowing the *frisson* to register. There was a pause. Mrs Ménage's hooded eyes began to glitter eagerly:

'*Mon Dieu!* Can you mean His Grace? …'

The question was met with a knowing smile.

'… Is this from your friend Mr Pomery? The Private Secretary to the Duke is a valuable gentleman to have as your acquaintance, especially in our Covent Garden …'

Wriothesley Russell, Second Duke of Bedford, was a name more often whispered than shouted in this part of the capital, and Mr Denniston chose not to sully it with his breath, which was now inhaling more of the cheesecake:

'… Of course, Marie, you are fortunate. As mistress of the Bay-Tree you possess your Freehold. But we others pay our rent. We are tenants – and subtenants – and *sub*-subtenants, are we not? But there is no escaping the great Duke: it is he who rules over the Garden. He might demolish this building tomorrow if he wished – as he did his own house – to squeeze in more properties for rent.'

While her friend Adèle was feeling the chill of the idea, Widow Trotter was warming to the conversation. She could see possibilities if it could be steered in the right direction. She turned on the shopkeeper her best playful manner:

'Have the magistrates been giving you trouble, Mr Denniston? I hope you've not been opening your doors on the Sabbath? I would hate to see you on the blacklist!'

He shivered dramatically, as if a cold draught had invaded the room:

'Ugh! I wouldn't dare, Mrs Trotter – not now! For these people, even washing your doorstep on a Sunday is an invitation to the Devil. They are a noxious crew altogether. They talk of *reforming manners*, but they really want to drain the joy from our lives. You are not going to believe this ...'

He gave a nod to his hostess, who had stood up and was holding the teapot poised above his cup.

'... I had a gentleman in here yesterday who informed me in no uncertain terms that selling silk ribbons and snuff-boxes was an encouragement to debauchery. He sniffed at my perfume jars as if they were brimstone! And as he fingered the bodkins and brooches, I could hear him muttering to himself about *female fripperies*. It was all I could do to stop myself throwing him into the street.'

'O my goodness!' said Mrs Trotter sympathetically. 'What was the man looking to buy, then?'

'A mere pair of scissors, Mrs Trotter. He gave me a little lecture on how scissors should be large and practical – not small and discreet. *Little mincing things* he called them and looked at me as if I were a toy myself. He leered at me and left the shop with a disapproving grunt.'

'Did he not buy the scissors?'

'No – he seemed embarrassed even to hold them. He had such big gnarly hands! He had been examining a paper-knife, and when it was held in that fist, believe me, it looked like a murder weapon. I was glad to see the back of him. I confess I had to sit down and collect myself ...'

He sipped at the tea and his face took on a thoughtful cast.

'... Perhaps I'm being fanciful, but two of my windows were broken during the night, and I cannot but think the man's visit had something to do with it. Silly of me, I know – but I can see those hands holding the stone. How our fears paint pictures in the mind!'

'Mr Denniston,' said Widow Trotter, placing a sisterly hand on his shivering knee, 'you must not think like that. These men are street-ruffians, nothing more, whatever title they give themselves, or whatever banner they march under. At the Bay-Tree on Saturday morning, *our* stone had a threatening message attached …'

The revelation was greeted with exclamations of sympathy; but the mood began to lighten a little as she told them about the passage from scripture with its accusation of idolatry.

'… So much for the deadly sin of decorating our coffee-room with May-Day greenery! The cobble was probably thrown by some poor urchin who had been slipped a penny to deliver it. And at worst, yours would be the same, Mr Denniston – although I wager it was some drunken sot dragging himself home.'

At this thought the shopkeeper looked somewhat easier in his mind, and when he shook his head it was at the violence of the times generally.

Widow Trotter persisted:

'Your friend Mr Pomery – may I ask what more he had to say about the Fair? I'm curious to know because I shall be there myself this evening.'

Mrs Ménage burst in unhelpfully:

'Marie is to venture into the Fair tonight, Charles – she is to see a play in one of the booths.'

Mr Denniston looked a little startled, as if some secret liaison were being uncovered; but then he recollected himself:

'Ah! Could this be *The Tender Courtesan*? I have seen it advertised. It sounds something more than a droll.'

Widow Trotter seized the opportunity to tell him about the play, and about the Prologue, and about her lodger, and about her lodger's distinguished uncle, Viscount Melksham, and how she herself would be a member of the Pophams' party …

This was perfect tea-table, and Mr Denniston drank it in. Within moments he had revised his assessment of her evening's entertainment; nevertheless, the idea gave him little pleasure. He knew that the nobility frequented the May Fair (it was, after all, only a short walk from St James's) but the thought unsettled him. He was, however, eager to hear about the Pophams' arrangements. This took several more minutes, and it was some while before Mrs Trotter – her credit now extremely high in the gossip account – was able to turn the talk back to the Fair and the dire prognostications of John Pomery – Mr Denniston's special friend, and His Grace's indiscreet Secretary:

'You say the Duke is somehow concerned in this threat, Mr Denniston? I would love to know more of what your friend had to say – the Brook Field is not part of the Russell estate, is it?'

'No indeed not … at least, *not yet* …'

The words had been spoken. He paused, and as if sensing the hiatus, Mrs Ménage's bullfinch decided to join in the conversation. From his cage by the window the bird offered a disconcerting whistle and a snatch of broken melody. Mr Denniston glanced over at his little accompanist, suddenly feeling part of a performance. This prompted him to continue:

'… This is not generally known, but the Brook Field land is possibly to be sold, and His Grace has expressed an interest in it. He is not the only party – the names of Berkeley, Cavendish and Grosvenor are also being whispered …'

Widow Trotter kept still: Tom and Will's report from the Dog and Duck was not to be mentioned, but this tallied with their story. She was longing to know more. It was clear to both ladies that Mr Denniston's enthusiasm was struggling with his discretion, and so the two seasoned newsmongers simply waited. Bully had gone quiet again, and the silence was inviting – or perhaps it was the brandy which tipped the balance? Anyway,

Mr Denniston could resist no longer. He leaned forward in his chair, as if wanting to draw them close:

'There is such a tale to tell – about the Fair – and it goes back several weeks. I hardly know where to begin … And not just the Fair – the playhouse also – especially the playhouse! Believe me, ladies, there has been such plotting and conspiring – John has been quite shocked at the business. I have had him here in tears more than once. And all because of that interloper!'

Widow Trotter instinctively moved further along her seat:

'Interloper?'

'John thinks of him as such – Mr Arthur Bedford, His Grace's Chaplain. Have you heard of him? He is piping hot for reform!'

'Yes, I know the name. Has he not written against the theatre?'

'Indeed he has, Mrs Trotter, at inordinate length and most violently! He is an implacable enemy of the stage – a very *Seraph* among the Saints! The man has wound himself entirely into the young Duke's confidence, but we are convinced his first loyalty is not to His Grace but to the Society.'

'The Reformation of Manners?'

'The *Holy Army*, John calls them … Well, the man has now rooted himself in the household. Until six weeks ago he was ensconced in his Bristol living, but the Society have beckoned him here to London, and the Duke has been favouring him more and more. The man has taken so much power to himself – in all matters – and poor John has been increasingly snubbed. It is Mr Bedford who is listened to, and John has become a mere scribe – literally so! With His Grace presently in the country the Reverend Mr Bedford expects John to be his amanuensis!'

Widow Trotter liked to think of herself as well-temper'd, but this was a challenge to her composure. It was pure gold! She did her best to remain calm and attentive and allow the story to unfold. Mr Denniston, however, needed no prompting. He was astride his horse and loosening the reins:

'The Brook Field business is a hare-brained scheme, and the Duke is in danger of over-extending himself. Mr Arthur Bedford thinks he is playing a clever game and has convinced His Lordship that it offers an *opportunity*. But Mr Shepherd is unwilling to give up his investment, and the price goes ever higher. At the same time Bedford pretends the abolition of the Fair will forward the Duke's plans, but it's clear he is using him for the Society's ends.

'The man is a *conspirator*, John says, always hurrying to meetings, holding consultations, and receiving visitors – late at night sometimes – and there's a secrecy about it all. On Monday, would you believe? John saw him with some odd-looking characters by one of the outbuildings in the garden! What in Heaven's name can the man have been doing? I'm sure he wasn't supervising the topiary!'

'Perhaps your Reverend Bedford is a *Guy Fawkes* in secret,' said Mrs Ménage, mysteriously glancing toward the door. 'An agent of the despicable *Louis?*'

The words were almost hissed. Since her escape from the notorious *dragonnades* of '85, this was the kind of conjecture that thrilled through Mrs Ménage's soul – and not without a degree of relish.

Mr Denniston would have none of this:

'Far from it, Adèle! The man is a hardened Whig. And quite a tub-thumper when he's in the pulpit. That's why the Duke favours him. You know His Grace will never trust a Tory, not even to wait at table – not after what they did to his poor father! No, the Duke sees eye-to-eye with Mr Bedford on many things. The man would not be so active if he wasn't favoured ... But he is certainly hatching some plot.'

He broke off to take another sip of invigorating tea. Widow Trotter was anxious to keep the talk moving and felt that a nudge toward the theatre was in order:

'From what you say, Mr Denniston, this Mr Bedford is attacking the Fair and the playhouse together. I understand that Mr Pinkerman is anxious on that score?'

'Exactly so, Mrs Trotter. You snatch the words from my lips. I'm sure the Reverend Bedford's intention is to close the playhouse – no doubt of it! *The Devil's Cathedral* they call it, and that's no figure of speech for them. The May Fair is somewhat of a holiday indulgence, but the *Theatre Royal* is the heartbeat of our nation. I hold no brief for those droll-booths! But I have to say I would greatly mourn the loss of our Drury Lane theatre. John and I have taken so much pleasure in it over the years, especially from the divine Shakespeare – that is how we think of him ...'

There was a moment of distraction before he recollected himself:

'... Yes, Mrs Trotter, you can be certain Mr Bedford has the players in his sights – especially Pinkerman. Our Pinkey is something of a Merry-Andrew, is he not? He laughs at himself and loves to mock the dignity of the profession, and that gaiety has been his strength. But the times are grown dark – do you not sense it? The world is losing its playfulness. No longer can we laugh at our own reflection. Even Comedy is under threat. And as for Satire – it has sunk to bitter accusation. All its delightful inventiveness has gone!'

Mr Denniston was becoming slightly flushed. Widow Trotter gave him a moment to collect himself. She looked concerned:

'You say Mr Bedford has been plotting against the playhouse? Can you truly mean that? Are you suggesting ... not that terrible murder?'

Mr Denniston burst into new life:

'Ah! Lord Tunbridge! A shocking business! ...'

He flinched at his own words and almost dropped his china cup onto the table.

'... We are being kept in the dark, you know. This is where John thinks Bedford is most active ... but ...'

He suddenly stopped in his tracks.

'... No – John and I have agreed to secrecy ... I really cannot say more.'

Widow Trotter was startled, and she hesitated about whether to speak. But Adèle Ménage, who had been listening intently with a look of increasing fascination, stirred herself. She reached across and touched him gently on the arm:

'My old friend Charles! – over the years we have revealed to each other so many secrets, have we not? We have shared such confidences. Mrs Trotter and I understand the *réticence* you have. You must not tell us anything that will endanger dear Mr Pomery, for that is what holds you back, is it not? – thoughts of your friend? We both of us know ... But do you not think it would assist John if the machinations of Mr Bedford were exposed? Only you can say ... but we are here to listen – and to help, if we can.'

Mary Trotter never ceased to wonder at Mrs Ménage's wisdom and shrewdness, and at this moment she felt like hugging her old friend. There was a difficult silence before Mr Denniston spoke again:

'You are right, Adèle. But it is fear for myself as much as for John. We are both threatened, you see ...'

His chin was shaking slightly as he spoke.

'... I suppose it would do me good to speak of it – and to such *sympathetic* friends ...'

They were now forming a *tête-à-tête*, and his voice was hushed.

'... As I told you, John handles the Duke's correspondence, which has included some communications from Mr Bedford.

The busybody thinks he can express a view on anything! … Well, he has been pressing hard on the playhouse, retailing to His Grace the worst of the gossip – about Lord Tunbridge and the actress, about the scandalous behaviour of the audience, the incompetence of Rich, and the farcical happenings of recent days – the accidents and indignities – anything he can turn to the disadvantage of the company.

'The Duke may be the owner of the theatre, but of course the Queen's power over the company is supreme, and Bedford has been urging the Duke to add his weight to those who are demanding she revoke the company's Patent entirely – and His Grace commands some authority.

'Well, the Duke returned one of Bedford's private missives annotated with some scribbled notes, and – surely by accident – the thing was enclosed in John's bundle. Clearly the original letter had been a secret, intended for His Grace's eyes only, and what it revealed was extraordinary … *There is a spy in the playhouse!* – would you believe? Not only that, but it seems this informer has been causing trouble there. He has been unsettling its affairs, and a certain "accident" was attributed to his "ingenuity." This spy has been taking his orders from Arthur Bedford … What do you think of that? Not only is our chaplain attacking the reputation of the Theatre Royal – he would appear to be arranging the mischief himself!'

He paused for breath while his two friends took in the uncomfortable idea.

'Did the letter give any particulars, Mr Denniston?'

'Not precisely, but the drift was unmistakable. The expression was couched in hugger-mugger terms. But with some teasing out, its meaning became clear. The three witches were mentioned, which made me think the *Macbeth* disaster was the accident it spoke of.'

'Can this spy be identified?'

'Alas no, but it is a member of the company – and I assume a man. He was referred to, with satisfaction, as "*our Red Cross Knight*." What a strange idea! That is *St George* is it not? Saint George of England! It was the only interpretation John could put on it …'

Widow Trotter's mind was working furiously as another piece of the puzzle slipped into place. Her thoughts turned to 'Merlin,' but she decided to say nothing. It seemed their conjectures about Arthur Bedford were more than justified – and here was the evidence.

'… But there is more – and his plotting runs deeper. He spoke of plans being put in place for the Fair – there was nothing more particular than that. But it appears that the work of Mr Bedford and his spy may not be finished.'

'What did Mr Pomery do with the letter?' said Widow Trotter, maintaining a calmness she did not feel.

Mr Denniston's face froze. He hesitated, and gave a slight groan:

'John did, alas, what a good and honest man would do: he took it to Mr Bedford himself. If only he had thrown the document on the fire and disclaimed all knowledge of it! But he didn't. No, John handed the letter over to Mr Bedford personally and asked him what it meant – what on earth he had been doing.'

The two women said nothing. They understood the import of this and hoped they were wrong.

'Bedford was furious, and – would you believe? – accused John of spying on him! It was all bluster of course, and both of them knew it – and after a few moments Bedford saw simple outrage would not do – that a sharper weapon was needed. It was then that he made his threat …'

Mr Denniston looked at his two friends. His voice was shaking slightly.

'… The man knows John has power over him, and he thinks

to meet it with a greater power of his own … This, ladies, is where *I* enter the picture! …'

He spoke the words like a miniature fanfare, which somehow caught the absurdity. Within moments Widow Trotter began to see that a touch of humour could be a strength, a means of resistance.

'… As you know, nothing terrifies these reformers more than *sodomy*, the Great Evil that will bring God's wrath down on our whole nation. And Mr Bedford, it seems, is no exception. He has been urging the Duke to press for the rounding up of the "mollies" throughout his estate, and for the closure of their *places of resort*, as the phrase is. The Magistrates are being readied, and there is a feverish mood stirring. The raid last week in Henrietta Street is a sign of things to come … And this, ladies, was the threat he decided to turn against *us!*

'Believe me, John was struck with horror – at the man's ignorance and absurdity! "You and your friend Mr Denniston are suspected to be a pair of *hermaphrodites*," he declared. "Indeed, I have more than a suspicion – and would feel duty bound to inform His Grace."'

'*C'est un scélérat!*' shouted Mrs Ménage at once, with some vehemence. 'He is a hypocrite scoundrel! He thinks to try a *blackmail* on you both, does he not?'

'Yes, it is a kind of a blackmail – a threat to humiliate us – or perhaps something much worse. It is hard to say what he might be capable of. John and I are apprehensive – but we trust he will hold off so long as John knows what he knows. It is a frightening state of affairs.'

Widow Trotter spoke at once, and with surprising urgency:

'You must tell Mr Pomery to do nothing hasty! This Mr Bedford is extending himself recklessly, and I can only believe he is heading for a fall. I can't say more; but both of you must remain quiet and alert, and wait on what the next few days will bring. You must *not* force a crisis – that's very important! … Do you understand? He is a dangerous man.'

Mr Denniston was taken aback for a moment, registering that this was more than casual advice. It was certainly presumptuous; but the determined look on Widow Trotter's face told him she must know more about Mr Bedford and his affairs than he had thought. Her look was at the same time warm and sympathetic, and he soon found himself assuring her that John and he would do nothing precipitate – and that if any further news came their way he would be sure to send a message to her.

Chapter Thirty-One

'YOU WERE *ATTACKED?*'

There was sudden drama around the Popham dinner table. Tom Bristowe flinched at his uncle's question, which put the matter directly. He himself still wanted to think of it as an accident – being in an awkward place at an unfortunate time – but he knew that was ridiculous: the scribbled note had been eloquent enough.

He was gathering a reassuring answer together when Aunt Sophia intervened:

'That determines it, Lavinia! You shall *not* go to the Fair! The very idea is preposterous. The place is full of low-life ruffians. No decent person will be safe.'

'But mamma, we shall be a party. None of us will be wandering off beyond the concourse. We shall not be peering behind curtains I assure you.'

'I should hope not! Curtains are there for a reason … It is a wild scheme altogether. No respectable young lady would dream of it …'

She turned to her nephew.

'… Why have you become embroiled in this Fair nonsense, Tom? If you *are* to be a poet, can you not be a polite one? …'

Lady Melksham shuddered as she spoke. Further along the table, two distinctly impolite poetical ladies looked at each other and suppressed a smile.

'... Must you hire yourself out like a hack? A prologue in a droll-booth!'

'My dear,' said her husband in softened tones, 'this is an important occasion for Tom. We shall be there to give him support ... And *The Tender Courtesan* is no raree-show. It is a serious play and may feature at the Theatre Royal next season.'

'Hah!' exploded Lady Melksham. 'As if that were a commendation! Can you be sure the lover won't be pursuing his *tender courtesan* through the clouds and throwing firecrackers at her? That is what the audience will be expecting – and Mr Pinkerman is never one to disappoint a crowd.'

There was a grain of truth in the remark, enough to bring a few seconds of uneasy silence. Knives and forks had been laid down in acknowledgement of the difficult moment.

'I'm sorry aunt. Please be lenient with me. All I have to offer is a *prologue*, I admit; but it is my own voice, and one I'm not ashamed of – on the contrary! And this is a time when it is important to speak out. There are voices that need to be heard, and things that must be said.'

Tom was looking at his aunt with intense eyes, and for an instant she saw the young priest she fondly hoped he would become. The expression disconcerted her:

'Well – you will all have to go without *me!* It is a foolhardy adventure, and I'm shocked your father thinks to take you there.'

At this point Lavinia decided a degree of reassurance was necessary:

'Do not fret yourself, mamma – I shall hold a tight rein on father's every step! You will be pleased to know that I've already dissuaded him from taking his chance in the supreme raffle ...'

'*Supreme raffle??*'

She turned an alarmed gaze on her husband.

'Yes, mamma – though the prize is certainly a tempting one ... I told father we should need a bigger garden.'

'*Garden?* What on earth is to be raffled?'

'Mr Pinkerman's elephant.'

For a moment Lady Melksham's sublime imagination swept all before it:

'John! What were you thinking of? An elephant!'

The immediate laughter round the table told her all, and a blush rose up her face.

'Ah my dear!' said Lord Melksham fondly. 'Lavinia is being satirical. You must not let your fancy run away. The elephant is quite safe, I assure you! And as for the play, we shall be a distinctly literary party. You must not think we are venturing to Hockley Hole!'

At the other end of the table Lady Melksham pushed back her chair:

'Well, I am going to leave the five of you to your arrangements – I'm sure you have much to discuss, and many delights to anticipate.'

'Nay, Sophy! You must not take it ill ...'

The plea came from the figure seated beyond Tom, a homely-looking woman of ample proportions whose genial face beamed out from under billowing ash-coloured hair.

'... We're cruel to bait you like this – and at your own table! But you can be assured we shall be a most respectable set this evening, and you must surely want Mr Bristowe to have his supporters. We intend to lead the cheers.'

'Ah, Dela! You know I wish Tom well ... But the Fair is a violent place. And the crowds press in so. You must be sure to keep together at all times and not lose one another. I dread what may happen ... and in a booth! The thing is nothing more than a draughty tent!'

'We shall have some superior seats my dear,' said her placating husband – 'We are in a box – and have been promised cushions.'

'A box? You'll be wobbling on a bit of rough carpentry. Let us hope it will be the *only* box you'll be in tonight ... And I wish you joy of your *cushions* – I'm sure they will add to the elegance of the occasion!'

The conversation continued in this spirited vein for a few moments more, with Lady Melksham showering friends and family with fresh sallies of indignation. It was taken in good grace; but Tom knew enough of the mounting threats to the Fair, and Pinkerman's booth in particular, to find his laughter uneasy. If his aunt only knew! ...

The cut-and-thrust came to an end with her standing by the open door, commanding the scene with her gaze and uttering a gnomical warning:

'... And I'm sure you recall what happened to *Arachne!*'

With a swish of dress-silks, Lady Melksham left the room, and a bemused Arthur the footman closed the door on her as quietly and politely as he could.

At the head of the table, her husband's good-humoured features crumpled into a frown. He looked over at Tom:

'Arachne ... She was transformed to a spider, was she not?'

'Yes, uncle. The girl was punished for weaving too beautifully. She challenged Minerva with her skill, and the goddess couldn't endure defeat!'

'Then what on earth can Sophia mean? ... *Spiders?* I think your aunt has left us with a puzzle! What do you make of it, Lady Norreys?'

At his right elbow, Julia Norreys was patting her lips with a napkin, her dark eyes glistening with amusement. Before replying, she glanced at her friend Mrs Manley across the table who was suppressing a smile:

'Mr Bristowe is entirely right, Lord Melksham. Poor Arachne was, you will understand, a *poet* – but being a woman, her voice was silenced and she could speak only through the eloquence of her loom. Her skill with the shuttle has never been matched. But the images she wove spoke the truth about the cruelty and deception of the gods – and so she had to be punished.'

'Arachne is one of art's great truth-tellers, my Lord,' said Mrs Manley, 'and she continues to weave. Minerva finally relented and gave her immortality.'

'Yes – but as a spider! Trapping innocent flies in her sticky web! … I'm still puzzled by Sophia's allusion. My wife's weaving has never got beyond the sampler stage … I'm beginning to think there is a joke here that I may have missed …'

He was scanning the table from left to right.

'… Lavinia, can you enlighten me? Am I being more than usually stupid?'

'No father, you're not … I mean – not stupid at all. I think what mamma meant to say was …'

She made a fatal pause. On this occasion youthful ingenuity failed her. It was Lady Norreys who came to the rescue:

'Let me answer for your daughter, Lord Melksham. There is a story behind this which you need to know. Your wife has kept our secret from you …'

'Your secret?'

'"Arachne's Web" was your wife's coinage – an ingenious name we have now adopted.'

'A name for what, Lady Norreys?'

'For our band of female politicians, my Lord …'

She paused, expecting a look of amusement – but there was something closer to an interested curiosity:

'Ah! I see! Your little circle! … Yes, I had come to suspect that your tea-table was more than a set of female tattlers. Am I right?'

Mrs Manley interposed:

'A female *tattler*, my Lord, can be a politician too – just as gentlemen politicians can certainly be tattlers.'

'Now there you hit the mark, Mrs Manley. I have had my fill of those, I tell you. A gaggle of "men of affairs" can put cackling geese to shame!'

'Your Lordship is enlightened enough not to begrudge us taking a view on matters of State?'

'I would encourage it, Mrs Manley! I encounter more good sense in the fair sex than in many a self-important man of affairs – and I meet an unconscionable number of those ...'

He glanced at Tom and Lavinia, who seemed to be communicating with silent looks across the table.

'... I know that my daughter has *views* – and is not backward in expressing them.'

'Your daughter has recently become one of our number.'

This was an awkward moment. Delarivier Manley was not one for letting secrets lie hid. Lavinia herself looked startled, but her father's smile reassured her:

'Well well! – You are eighteen my dear, and more than capable of rational thought. But why the *secrecy*? ... What do you know of this, Tom?'

His nephew had been maintaining a judicious silence, but he now felt the urge to speak:

'I have to say, uncle ... I'm not the only person whose words will be heard in Pinkerman's booth. Arachne has also been at work ...'

'We were intending to tell you, papa. But we wished to keep it close until all was settled. It has been a profound secret – even from Tom here.'

'Not even the players know of it!' added Lady Norreys.

Lord Melksham was beginning to feel like a cat with its claws stuck in a ball of wool:

'Do you mean *The Tender Courtesan*? Have you all been writing something?'

'Yes, my Lord,' said Mrs Manley firmly. 'We have indeed. But no soft-hearted romance – that's not in our line … No, we have been assisting Mr Pinkerman with *The Devil on Two Sticks*.'

Lord Melksham found himself swallowing hard:

'The satire? I know Pinkerman has been furtive about the piece, but I confess I'm surprised. It's not something Lady Melksham would countenance, is it?'

'Indeed not – and you have seen how strongly she disapproves! Your wife was formerly of our number, but she now finds us an embarrassment.'

'But, you say that Lavinia …'

He was momentarily lost for words.

'It has been a cause of dissension, father. Poor mamma originally introduced me to her circle, but now she heartily regrets it.'

By this time, all four of them, Tom included, were looking unblinkingly at him; and the expansive Mrs Manley was giving him a radiant, knowing smile, the heat of which was almost palpable:

'In expressing our opinions, my Lord, we have had recourse to the *scourge* as well as the pen.'

'Lashing the corruptions of the Age, eh? Well, there's much in need of correction, Mrs Manley. And of course, young Tom here – with some help from Mr Juvenal – has spoken out, has he not? And fine verses they are too!'

He looked proudly at his nephew. And the look on Lady Norreys's face was not dissimilar:

'His *Crime and Punishment* is an admirable poem, my Lord, and it has given us a motto for our times:

"… *The virtues are in exile: nothing's left*
But murder, treason, perjury and theft …"

Although he cannot be one of our number, we regard Mr Bristowe as something of a shining knight – a champion in our cause.'

Her eyes encountered Tom's in a brief silent dialogue. The young knight in armour knew he should speak but could find nothing to say.

Lord Melksham's mind was trying to absorb these revelations. He knew that across history, many a crime had been committed for a *cause* ...

'You speak of a *cause*, Lady Norreys. Forgive me, but I take it this is something beyond everyday party differences?'

'Oh yes. It is the antithesis. The cause is the joy of life itself ...'

This was unexpected. Lord Melksham did not respond in words, but offered her an open expression, a willingness to be convinced.

'... There are those, my Lord, who would think *for* us – who would make us all virtuous by law. But ... people must be free to be good, and there is no freedom without choice – and no *virtue* without either. Otherwise, all is cant and hypocrisy – being good by form – being virtuous by prescription.'

It was a striking speech. The table itself seemed to be listening.

'Ah, I see! Or I think I do ... and I think I see why you want to deliver this message at the Brook Field. The Fair is under threat, is it not? – and from forces you consider malign and oppressive?'

'And *violent*,' added Mrs Manley. 'And the threat is not only to the Fair, but more gravely to the Theatre Royal and everything it represents.'

'Ah yes. I shall never forget that terrifying *Macbeth*. It is seared into my memory. The repercussions of that evening are continuing, and I know the Bay-Tree has felt them particularly ...'

He caught a look on Tom's face that told him he had found the mark.

'... The *threat* you have in mind is the Society for the Reformation of Manners, is it not? I have been hearing a lot of those people in recent days – and I confess to finding them distressingly sanctimonious. They would wish us all to become saints.'

'They would return us to the rule of Cromwell's generals,' said Mrs Manley.

'Just so. There is little compromise with them. They are *root and branch* men!'

Lady Norreys managed a rueful smile:

'Entirely, yes. *Men*, one and all.'

Tom was listening with some encouragement. As the conversation continued, he was impatient to talk about what he and his friends had discovered – but this had to wait until he could have a private word with his uncle.

The opportunity wasn't long in coming. The three women were increasingly conscious of their hostess's absence, and Lord Melksham detected an uneasiness when his wife's name was mentioned. And so, when there was a break in the talk, he dispatched Arthur with a small tray up to Sophia's room, and intimated that they might wish to accompany it:

'I do think Sophia would welcome your company, ladies. Would that be agreeable? I'm sure Tom and I have things to chatter about.'

During the past week, Tom had longed for the opportunity to consult with his uncle. Residing in distant Winchester, Canon Bristowe was a benign but demanding father, and over the years it was to his Uncle Jack that Tom had gone for wise advice free of the sanctions of Holy Writ. At Monkton Court he had spent the long summer days with his cousins Frank and Lavinia in a setting less stifling than a cathedral close. Above all, he had been glad to escape the proximity of the school, where his father and the headmaster between them had kept a sharp eye on all his doings.

Once the women had departed, Lord Melksham beckoned Tom to the vacant chair beside him and pushed the decanter of brandy in his direction. At moments like these Tom always hesitated between formality and ease. Uncle Jack said nothing, but simply raised a glass, and at once his nephew sensed a reassuring presence. His uncle's dress-wig draped its arms round the lordly shoulders and lent his figure a calm confidence; but the gravitas was lightened by a pair of eyes that were looking to be informed and amused:

'Well, young fellow, I think you owe me a fuller story than the one I've heard so far! Throughout dinner I felt you had a great deal to say but were unable to say it – am I right? Are we back in the world of secrets and suspicions?'

It was said with a twinkle of curiosity.

'Both, uncle! I can keep nothing from you – nor would wish to … Much has been happening, and the attack on me was part of it. We need your advice – and help too.'

'*We?* I thought so! Are our good friends Will and Mrs Trotter caught up in this? I heard about the May-Day events – all very troubling – and Lord Tunbridge's murder … I don't dare ask if the Bay-Tree militia are somehow involved. I don't think I want to hear your answer – I know what it will be.'

A moment of silence followed, which confirmed Lord Melksham's apprehensions.

'We think we have uncovered a plot against the playhouse, uncle – and we suspect that Baron Tunbridge was more than knee-deep in it.'

'And the Society for the Reformation of Manners …'

He looked at Tom, hesitantly.

'… Do they have a hand in this?

'Several pairs of hands, uncle – including those that struck at the royal maypole with an axe. The outrage was planned in detail ... Will attended a meeting of theirs on Tuesday.'

'What? – A *meeting?* I don't believe this. I know his father is strong for reform, but Will? ...'

He checked himself.

'... You are going to tell me he was there as a spy, are you not? ...'

Tom nodded his head. In response, his uncle shook his own – violently.

'... But that is so dangerous! Foolhardy in the extreme. Do you know how zealously they guard their secrets? You must tell me all you can, and what you know about Tunbridge – everything! Then I shall tell you what *I* know. Let us see if we cannot build a clearer picture of this "plot" of yours.'

Half an hour later, with his uncle's wig now forming a graceful pile on the table between the fruit bowl and the brandy decanter, Tom was drawing the threads of his news together. Lord Melksham was listening intently, leaning across the arm of his chair as if wanting to absorb his nephew's words directly.

Tom told him about events in the playhouse on the night of the killing; about the interview he and Will had conducted with Gilbert Angell, and their strange mission to Holborn. He tried to be discreet about Sally's story and hoped this guardedness didn't show. He narrated Widow Trotter's adventure at the New Exchange and described Mudge's heroism at the maypole in the Strand. He spoke particularly about Arthur Bedford and the directing role the man appeared to be taking. And then there was the visit to the Dog and Duck, the rehearsal in the barn, and the relief of the actors at the Baron's death ... He made himself re-live the attack in Pinkerman's booth and gave what details he could of all that Will had learned at the reformers' meeting. Finally, he brought the story up to that morning's violence in the Raffling-Shop.

It was a jumble of events and discoveries worthy of Miller's booth, and the tale poured out of him with relief. It was useful to set out the whole story, and he began to glimpse how some parts might fit together. Perhaps his uncle could help fill the gaps.

He seized his glass and sat back in the chair:

'Well, there you have it, uncle – the bare bones at least. I've spared you our many conjectures! I wonder what you make of it all?'

'I'm awe-struck, Tom. What adventures you've been having – and what dangers you've run yourselves into! Had I but known … Give me a moment.'

Lord Melksham popped a sweetmeat in his mouth and ruminated with it while the clock ticked quietly. His fingers beat time on the walnut table. Then he stirred himself, his right hand now clenched into a fist:

'Politics, Tom!'

'*Politics*, uncle?'

'Yes. It should not surprise you to learn that our political friends are at their tricks again! This is my province, and what you've told me makes sense. The picture is a curious one. You're right – the key is Tunbridge – and of course the Queen. None of this is accidental.'

'We suspected not – but we didn't want to imagine too much.'

'Matters of state, Tom! These things always work their way down from Ministers, Bishops and Dukes, to players, shopkeepers and shoe-boys. It's the old story. Our masters are like drawing-room generals – they strut around caballing and working their interests, while all the dirty business is conducted as far from them as possible. I meet it all the time around the Court.'

'Conspiracy?'

'No, Tom, that's too grand a name. But political machinations? Yes. Everyone is using somebody. There are principles lurking somewhere, but too often they disappear in the sheer bustle of plotting.'

'How far does this reach, uncle?'

'Oh, the Queen, of course – the fount of all preferment and influence. *Turning the Queen* has become the grand sport of politics.'

'Turning? Are we back with the Duchess and Abigail Masham?'

'No, not on this occasion. Now it's the *Church*. The battalions are much the same, but this time you can detect the swish of lawn sleeves and the smell of well-scrubbed benches. Cathedral chapters and meeting-house conventicles!'

'But no-one could ever turn the Queen from Church to Chapel.'

'Hah – no, indeed. Sooner make grass grow red! But in the matter of the *Theatre Royal* Her Majesty is distinctly suspicious and fearful. Add *national morality* to the mixture, stir in concerns about *public order,* hint at *disaffection,* and then pour in the murder of a peer of the realm ... and you have a potent dose of poison. They concoct nicely. Think of the witches!'

'But is the Church not being lost in all of this?'

'By no means – quite the contrary. The Church is never lost. Religion is political, Tom – you know that well enough – and has been so for nigh on two hundred years. It will always be the field of party strife.'

'So, what is the picture, uncle? You say it's not a conspiracy – but it's certainly conspiracy-*hunting*.'

'Exactly so. The cleverest plotters are those who expose another's plots. I'm proud of you, Tom – you are learning policy. You'll have to teach Frank some of it! The lad still has such trust in human nature. If he's elected this summer, I fear for him.'

'You believe the Queen is being persuaded a conspiracy threatens her authority?'

'Yes, that is the tendency of all this activity, Tom. Everyone knows she is being pressed hard; but now I see the mechanism of it – the workings from below. The Drury Lane playhouse is the battleground. The culture of the nation is at issue, and with it the Queen's authority. The two are bound together ... I happen to know that the Patent of the Theatre Royal is about to be revoked.'

'The Patent? The company's warrant to perform?'

'Yes, the Letters Patent under the great Seal of her uncle Charles. During these recent weeks the warrant has been reconsidered.'

'So, it's true! This is what we've been fearing. But do you mean *re-drawn*, or *withdrawn*?'

'Ah Tom! There you touch on the very nub of the matter. This has been a closely guarded secret ... Lord Tunbridge was to have become the Patentee under a new dispensation. The *Patentee!* No longer a mere shareholder, but a man with dictatorial powers. Clauses have been inserted about actively encouraging virtue and morality, with all scripts to be submitted to a censor, and only plays of "serious import" being admitted. Anything of a "vicious tendency" to be banned, every oath expunged! It has all been negotiated, Tom – every stipulation in place ... Great Britain's new *national* theatre ...'

'But this is everything Mr Pinkerman fears – his nightmare come true! We had wind of the Baron's share-holding – but not of the Patent.'

'... But then came his killing. As you can imagine, it has thrown all into confusion. The man who was to have been the Queen's champion in this affair, murdered! You can surmise what the Queen's advisers – especially Sir James Montagu – are now urging on her – what picture presents itself as to how the Baron met his death.'

'Yes ... someone in the company? We thought as much. And that's why Cibber and Rich were arrested, is it not?'

'Indeed, Tom. It is held as certain that the assassin is somebody within the theatre, or a man hired to do the deed. Her Majesty is being persuaded that her own company will do anything it can to challenge her authority … and so the jaws have closed on poor Rich – a man who has all to lose by the reforms, and who has hitherto run the theatre like his own fiefdom – and whimsically too …'

Lord Melksham's hand reached out to the abandoned wig, as if he needed to grasp at something tangible. His fingers began threading the curls.

'… What your story is revealing, Tom, is something else. We are presented with a scene in which the Society for the Reformation of Manners is taking the leading role. Far from being outraged by events, the Society appears to be initiating them. This is extremely serious! If these occurrences are connected, and if Arthur Bedford is the instigator, then it makes the killing of Lord Tunbridge assume a very different character. It does indeed.'

'But you say the Queen is about to act – and that it will mean not reform, but the closure of the theatre?'

'Yes, that is about to happen. The determination is now for abolition. Her *heart* is still for thorough reform, but everything is now pulling her towards revoking the Patent. But at this moment, she is waiting on events.'

'The outcome of the investigation?'

'Yes. If the company are shown to be involved in the Baron's death, then the way will be clear. It will be impossible to gainsay the matter.'

'But to close the theatre Royal … it's unthinkable!'

'No, Tom. At this moment it is all too thinkable. Things are brought to a crisis.'

'But – about the murder – what of the third possibility, uncle?'

Lord Melksham gave a little harrumph, and hesitated:

'Do you mean Gilbert Angell and Sally Twiss? Did that amount to much? You said they had been made to see sense, and you seemed to make light of Mr Angell's jealousy of the Baron's attentions.'

Tom was caught in a trap of his own making. He and Will had sworn secrecy, but ... what would serve Sally's interest best at this moment? She was facing arrest, and it was important that his uncle saw the full picture. Tom's conscience was pulling contrary ways, but in the end he could see no alternative.

In strictest confidence, he gave Lord Melksham an account of what had occurred in the property-store – Sally's account, at least – and told him of the rumour of her imminent arrest. His uncle pushed the wig away and shook his head:

'I see ... Oh Tom! Things are making more sense. This would explain Montagu's hesitation. What you say about factions among the reformers is common knowledge, but from Will's meeting it seems the anger in the Society is boiling over. There is an almighty struggle going on, and again Tunbridge is the key. Was the man a martyr or a ravisher? That is the decisive question now ... Is Sally prepared to make a public denunciation?'

Tom was uncomfortable:

'I honestly don't know, uncle. Will and I urged it but left the occasion to her. The more I think of it, the more unlikely it becomes. However, if she is arrested ...'

'Yes, Tom. If Sally were to make a public denunciation of Tunbridge, and a crime of passion proved, it would lift the threat from Rich – and probably from the company too. Do you see? An accusation of rape ... well, that would be a huge embarrassment to the Queen. Her *reformer* a *ravisher!* There would be the stink of hypocrisy about it, and it would paint the company as a victim, and reform as a kind of violation ... I think she would draw back ...'

Tom was thinking of his prologue and smiled to himself. His uncle continued:

'... A mere *liaison* between Sally and Lord Tunbridge can be managed – it is a two-hour scandal at best. But rape ...'

There was a sudden silence. Tom reached for his glass, slightly shaken by the vehemence of his uncle's responses. The things he and the others had discovered were clearly important. Even more hung on them than he had imagined. But Tom was still puzzled:

'But where does the Church come in? I assume the Society for the Reformation of Manners is increasing its pressure on the Queen. Is that so?'

'Yes indeed. Her Majesty favours them. After all, the Society are putting their weight behind her Proclamation (*their* proclamation, in effect). She is speaking through them, and they through her. They are ensuring that her words are heard from every pulpit in the land. Vice and immorality are being universally castigated! Yes, the Queen is well disposed to the Society – at least to its reforming aims.'

'I can hear a *but* approaching.'

Lord Melksham smiled:

'But ... she flinches at the low-church people. The Society is a coalition, and you know how she detests the language of the ranting preachers. The attack on the maypole has horrified her! After all, the thing is the very symbol of the monarchy.'

'Of course!' said Tom. 'Her Uncle Charles's gift to the citizens of London – a pledge that the new King was to bring everyone joy and hope.'

'You put it perfectly. No, our reforming friends overstepped the mark there! Violent acts are abhorrent to the Queen ... And you are now saying the Society was behind the maypole business?'

'Yes. The Reverend Tysoe let slip as much to Will. It wasn't the act of one fanatic.'

'This is shocking. What would our Bishop say to that, I wonder?'

'Bishop? … So this is where the Church enters the scene?'

'It has always been there, Tom. Whenever the nation's morals are in question, the Church is ready with its advice. That is its own *patent*, and it guards it jealously … I hardly need ask you who are the two most important churchmen in London?'

Tom looked into his uncle's eyes. This wasn't merely rhetorical:

'Well, Compton … and Tenison, I suppose – though they are out of the Queen's favour, and have been so for years. Their power ebbed long ago.'

'Exactly, Tom! Two elderly gentlemen in their seventies, still lodged immovably at the top of the Church – *London* and *Canterbury!* Her Majesty has tried to ignore them, but they are both commanding figures still, are they not?'

'Yes uncle, indeed. But not of the Queen's persuasion.'

'Certainly not – a pair of thoroughly Whiggish clerics, disgruntled at being ignored by Her Majesty, who is simply waiting for them to die so she can install men more to her taste. Their views are routinely dismissed, and their advice shunned … Well, the two of them have taken up the theatre as their cause. They are good friends to the Society and have been active in its campaign – not just from the pulpit, but by actions behind the scenes – Compton especially. They have been pressing for a full revocation of the Patent – the closure of the Playhouse. And they have been gathering support from some important men. The Duke of Bedford, for one – the owner of the theatre! That young man is a bit hot on reform himself and easily swayed by these avuncular gentlemen … and your Arthur Bedford is the Duke's chaplain. Can you see the picture?'

Tom certainly could. He was coming to understand the larger scale of their local events. Pinkerman's booth was more than a draughty tent, and what was to be played out on its stage was part of a bigger drama. But there was something he felt he had to ask:

'Uncle … I'm thinking of the play this evening – and my Prologue. From what you say, I suspect my voice will be heard well beyond the Fair …'

At that thought his tone was suddenly quieter.

'… Are you certain that you and Lavinia should be at the performance? I shall not take it ill if you think it wiser to stay at home. I'm a little afraid my aunt's concerns may be justified.'

'Thank you, Tom. You are right to ask. But I've discussed this with your cousin … I use the word *discussed* loosely – you know how determined she can be! … No, Tom. All four of us will be gracing Pinkerman's booth this evening, ready to cheer – and we shall also be ready to outface any critics.'

'But it's not the critics who concern me, uncle …'

'I understand, Tom. But I'm more concerned about you – are you ready to venture into that tent again, after what happened?'

'I'm sure I'll shiver a bit when I walk into the place – but only for a moment. After that cowardly attack I'll relish hearing my words spoken out. They're defiant ones, and Mr Pinkerman will do them proud. It will help diffuse my anger! …'

Lord Melksham looked alarmed and was about to speak; but Tom cut him short:

'… Have no fear, uncle. We shall not use violence – we sink to their level if we become angry ourselves … But we have to fight these people, and not just with words. We must turn their own weapons against them – it is their own violence that will defeat them. The more they preach, the more their fear and hate show themselves. In the end, surely, hate will always be seen for what it is … *bad faith*.'

'That's well enough for a rousing speech, Tom. But these people are dangerous. They have established power on their side – and they don't lack self-belief.'

'But perhaps they are becoming too confident? The balance may be about to turn.'

'Well, we must wait on events – and no doubt the Brook Field will have its surprises ... Who knows? Perhaps tonight Tom Bristowe will be the talk of the Fair?'

Chapter Thirty-Two

THE MAN WORKED deftly. He held the final quill between his fingers and began tamping down the black powder as tight as it would go inside the tube, right up to the wax seal. The nail's head was perfect for the task, and the effect was neat, close-packed. Firmly but delicately he wedged the last twist of paper into the end, and there they all were – four of them, tied loosely together with string, splayed like a small skeletal hand. He wondered if he should add a fifth as a kind of joke. But no – four of the lively little things would be enough! He rolled them in a page of newspaper and slid the bundle into his pocket, quietly satisfied. Instinctively he picked up his pipe, only to lay it down again with a smile – best not take any chances. Instead he reached over for a rag and rubbed hard at his own fingers. There was a taste of nitre in his mouth, and he spat generously before finishing his mug of ale. With a casual air the man got to his feet, set his hat at a jaunty angle, and by force of habit adjusted the cotton kerchief round his neck, pulling it up slightly under the left ear so as to hide the livid curving scar.

'It's tradition!' declared Widow Trotter with some authority as the four of them paused, hemmed in by the throng. 'At the Fair, you have to eat *pork* – pork, cider, and gingerbread. They're the flavours of May Fair! The roasting-shops are just over here.'

'Aye – a' can tell.'

David Macrae was hesitant and sniffed the air like a heifer sensing an approaching storm. He looked at his friend for support, but his fellow-Scot's eyes were already half-closed in ecstatic anticipation. Gavin Leslie was impatient for the feast:

'Come, Davie,' he said encouragingly, 'you must gie yoursel' tae the Fair! And that means pork – can ye no smell that *cracklin?*'

'All a' can smell is burnt flesh! A' hardly need tae eat it.'

'But we are men of taste, remember – and *taste* we shall! Ye'll not refuse Mrs Trotter's generous invitation? It's nae time for delicate appetites.'

As the shops came closer, the smoke was billowing in their direction.

'You'll find the taste is less overpowering than the smell,' said Will. 'No-one needs snuff in here!'

He grinned at the two young Scotsmen, who were beginning to come to terms with the Fair's impolite festivity. David in particular thought he must be trapped in a Brueghel painting. As a panorama it was delightful, but down on the ground there was some discomfort and embarrassment. The pair hadn't heeded Widow Trotter's advice about leaving their wigs behind; and after only ten minutes swimming along the tide of the main concourse, the Macrae peruke had suddenly flown from his head like a leaping squirrel, and within seconds the thing had hopped from hand to hand and been bagged tidily somewhere far off in the crowd. There was nothing to be done except wonder at the dexterity and sheer cheek of it.

It struck them both that for all its coarseness, the May

Fair wasn't the random experience they had anticipated, but a scene where things were skilfully choreographed. Roughness and danger were delivered with style. They had shivered in admiration as the fire-eater swallowed his coals with nicely judged care; the card-sharpers were brilliantly practised at their manipulations; and they saw the tumblers twisting themselves into exquisite knots as if their limbs were made of dough. They had watched a young girl dance with a pair of swords whistling round her face; and they held their breath while the high-rope flier swept down from the church tower, finely balanced on his grooved breastplate, hands and feet akimbo. Somewhere deep down they could even find a grudging admiration for the wig-snatchers and their confederates, the nimble-fingered gentlemen of what was endearingly called the 'diving mystery.'

After this, appetites had been sharpened, and a haunch of pork was declared to be necessary, if only to confirm that they had thoroughly immersed themselves in the experience of the Fair. The two young Scotsmen knew they must leave metropolitan politeness behind, but neither was quite prepared for the Fair's intoxicating rhythms and its overloading of the senses.

Davie's fears seemed realised when he saw the roasting spits – three of them set up in front of the booths, each turning round merrily to the accompaniment of boastful cries about the choiceness of the pig and the juiciness of its flesh. The flanks of the animals were blistering, and the dripping-pans filled rapidly while the competing cooks basted and sweated in turn, with their greasy shirts flapping round their own haunches. One of them paused from his labours and began rubbing his neck and armpits with the same cloth he applied to his pig.

'Tradition!' shouted Widow Trotter again, encouragingly. 'Avert your eyes, gentlemen, close your mouths – mind the flies! – and in we go!'

Twenty minutes later they were lolling with their elbows on the table, the four plates empty save for the last scrapings of pig sauce. Scattered around them, customers of all kinds were consuming the pork of the Fair, chewing and crunching with a will, and easing their throats with cider. A doting couple with moistened lips gazed into each other's eyes while slivers of meat dangled from their fingers; to their side a small child was occupied in throwing bits of greasy bread at the wall, fascinated by the way the canvas shivered when it was struck. Over in the far corner, a pair of lavishly dressed ladies, masks still pinned over their painted faces, were eyeing a couple of gentlemen in homespun suits who showed country complexions under their woollen caps. The flavours of the Fair were sinking in. Gavin Leslie's wig was by now well marinated, and he knew he would be taking a little reminder of Brook Field away with him. At his side, Will ran his fingers through his hair and voiced what they all were thinking:

'Well, His Greasiness does serve a sweet bit of meat, I'll allow him that. The May Fair pork has taken possession!'

'Och, Mr Lundy!' said David Macrae, 'we are now truly *one flesh*. A' sincerely hope me and ma' stomach will remain on amicable terms.'

'Then it's not going to be the whirligig for you, Davie?'

'No, but if a' dinna move mysel' right now, a' never shall.'

The party got to their feet, and Widow Trotter smiled to herself as she led them out into the open air. The polite young Scotsmen were beginning to fall into a holiday mood, and she noted how their chocolate-house accents were slipping back into something broader and easier.

Out in the field again, they re-joined the swirling throng and steered their way towards the main concourse and the theatre booths. The ground was becoming sticky, and some of their steps took them into inch-deep mud. Mary Trotter knew it was time for her pattens, and so they paused while she fitted the irons under her shoes and tied the straps. This was deftly done. Thinking practically, she turned to Gavin and held her bag open:

'Don't you think we should conceal your crowning glory, Mr Leslie? It should fit in here at a pinch?'

A pinch it was; but together they managed to squeeze the protesting curls into their hiding-place, and Gavin was glad to be rid of the anxiety: now he could enjoy the distractions of the Fair without fear of the wig-snatchers. In this place it was best not to look conspicuous.

Gavin's loss of height was Mrs Trotter's gain, and she led the way in the direction of the droll-booths, guiding her friends past a puppet-show, where a screaming Mr Punch was cudgelling his wife without mercy. A row of children's faces gazed up at the miniature stage, watching open-mouthed as Joan fought back with her wooden fists and the pair of them boxed it out. Will thought of Tom, and winced at the sound of the cracking skulls.

The cacophony was making their ears hum. The air was full of 'Knives to grind!', 'Pickled cowcumbers!', 'Fine Holland socks!', 'Pears and pippins!' Each call seemed to provoke another. As if in protest, a tired infant was determined to assert his claims to attention against anything the Fair could muster. People were shouting to make themselves heard.

And suddenly, wafting through the confused noise, a single word began to make its way towards them. Widow Trotter heard it first, and her ears pricked. A nearer voice picked it up, and others in the crowd began murmuring as if they were a single excited consciousness.

'*Elephant!*' declared Mrs Trotter. 'I think it must be Mr Pinkerman's elephant. Can you see anything, Will?'

Gavin and David looked at each other in disbelief. Now they knew for certain this was a place of conjurers!

Something appeared to be stirring in the distance, Will said, but there was no sign of the giant creature just yet. As so often, Rumour was flying ahead of events. And so, the four of them pressed on in the direction of Pinkerman's, where the phenomenon would be making its appearance. It turned out that the imperturbable Hannibal was pursuing its leisurely progress through the further reaches of Brook Field, surrounded by cheering children and waving handkerchiefs – a guard of honour that seemed to delight the beast rather than disturb him.

When Widow Trotter and her young friends reached the vicinity of Pinkerman's, they saw that across the concourse Miller's booth was already putting on an impressive show. Parading along its balcony, the various characters of THE TEMPEST, or *the Distressed Lovers* were exhibiting themselves in full costume. An impressive gentleman with a crown and long white beard was waving a trident in the air; and next to him a hero of romance was offering what looked like a dead rabbit to a bejewelled Island Princess; further along the timber promenade, two of the three witches waved their broomsticks at a figure in a ginger wig and feathered cap, who was easily identified as Jockey, the soon-to-be-enchanted Scotchman. The crowd was delighted, and all was going well. But within moments the actors began losing their audience. They gazed down in consternation as backs began to turn and all the crowd's attention was given over to Hannibal, who was now approaching Pinkerman's in full majesty. Miller's droll simply couldn't compete. It was clear that the spectacular TEMPEST would be opening to a thin audience.

Meagre compensation though it was, the players' vantage-point on the raised walkway gave them an excellent view of the elephant, on the back of which William Pinkerman was seated in state, dressed in a silk robe and an incongruous Maharajah's turban. His legs were astride an improvised wooden saddle and his hands gripped the pommel. The man was looking remarkably at ease, no doubt reassured by the presence, on either side, of the animal's young guides who had accompanied him from the Guinea coast a year earlier. Hannibal's ears flapped contentedly as the boys offered words of encouragement in a language the creature obviously understood. To them, he was *ngajba* – the great tusked one.

Widow Trotter and Will found themselves smiling at the extraordinary scene; and beside them Gavin and David were silent and open-mouthed as Pinkerman somewhat gingerly raised himself in his seat and reached out a hand to the crowd.

'Welcome to the Fair!' he cried presumptuously – a greeting that brought wild cheers across the concourse.

Pinkerman unrolled a vellum scroll in true herald's style and was about to make his proclamation, when a sharp crack rang out somewhere to the rear of the animal. A second louder crack came, and a sudden silence in the crowd was followed by alarm as the creature lifted its head and waved its trunk in the air. The third crack resounded like gunfire, accompanied by a great cry from the creature who was outraged and baffled. A fourth crack like an angry whip drove him into motion, his huge feet lifted high and his haunches swaying menacingly. The animal swung round, not knowing where to turn, and Pinkerman was now half hanging off his chair. With each swish of the giant ears he slipped further down. Screams were echoing around as the alarmed animal began to stride forwards, his trusted young companions desperately calling out his name and trying to pat his head. The elephant appeared to be dancing, swinging to left and right as the crowd drew back on all sides. People crashed into each other and began falling over in the mud; shouts of alarm rang out as the creature gathered momentum and trotted on, slowly as yet, but with a terrifying weight and impetus. It seemed nothing could stop him. The brave Pinkerman gripped the seat with whitened knuckles, fearful of falling under the massive legs. From the balcony of Miller's booth came sounds of jeering and laughter. On this occasion their rival, like Milton's Lucifer, had aspired too high – and here was his fall. Literally so! Before their eyes Pinkerman was sinking from glory into ridicule. That would show him!

But a moment later the mood changed, and the dire situation became clear, not least because the animal – all five tons of him – was heading directly across the concourse towards Miller's booth, ignoring the urgent shouts of 'Wart-u! Wart-u!' from the two boys running beside him.

Neptune was the first to show alarm – command of the sea was one thing, but an elephant quite another. Alongside him, Jocky the Scotchman froze in terror, and the witches' cries stuck in their throats. The bejewelled princess lost interest in her kneeling hero and looked for an escape route.

But it was too late. Hannibal had them in his sights and was by now writhing his trunk up at them, much taken by these exotic specimens who were all shouting and waving their arms. Almost affectionately, the creature snuggled up to the wooden balcony and gave an almighty heave with his tusks. One of the struts gave way, and the promenade tilted at a crazy angle. The crowd watched in horror as the players slithered down it like children on one of the Fairground slides – trident, broomsticks, and stuffed rabbit along with them. They all dropped to earth like discarded toys, and sat there for a moment, baffled in the mud.

With quiet skill Hannibal's two protectors had managed to steady him. 'Waal-u', 'waal-u,' the boys were whispering into his ears; and astonishingly, after only a few seconds the giant beast spread out its legs and sank, with no little elegance, to the ground – with Pinkerman still aboard.

At once the recriminations began. An outraged Miller flew out of his booth with fists in the air, shouting dire imprecations against his rival, who it seemed had declared open war with a fiendish new weapon. Around him, the actors were picking themselves up and feeling their limbs to check for broken bones, thankful for the softened ground but all too aware of their bedraggled costumes. In the process of the fall, Neptune's trident had somehow managed to skewer the rabbit, and the play's hero had ended up clutching a broomstick in place of his sword. Around them, the stunned crowd were gathering again, but not to jeer: they were thoroughly delighted at the performance. It had been a show to remember; and as the players staggered and recovered themselves, the informal audience began applauding a truly memorable climax. Mr Miller had arranged an ingenious burlesque, and at that moment many of them resolved to come and see the show once performances resumed.

Sensing the shift of mood, the ever-resourceful Pinkerman dismounted the elephant with as much composure as he could muster and approached a transfixed Miller with arm outstretched. The pair shook hands; and to roars of appreciation the two impresarios stood side by side, arms raised aloft to receive the applause.

From their vantage-point at the far side of the booth, Will and Mrs Trotter had watched the whole adventure with alarm. The firework was yet another malicious attempt to cause mayhem; but by some miracle a disaster had been averted and the comic spirit of the Fair reasserted itself. As for the two young Scotsmen – they decided on reflection that the May Fair itself was one vast playhouse in which actors and audience performed together – a carnival world that offered humanity a stage for ever more spectacular effects.

Chapter Thirty-Three

After their elegant dinner in Pall Mall, the Popham party arrived at the Fair in style; but their coach was able to proceed only a short way before the press of the crowd became too great. The Popham crest on the coach door had attracted attention, even more when it opened to reveal a pair of vizarded ladies among the occupants. The celebrated Mrs Manley favoured anonymity, and Lady Norreys was happy to wear a mask too. Both knew the disguise suggested brazenness rather than discretion; but this was May Fair, and such titillating ambiguity was very much in character.

Tom Bristowe was himself in two minds about being in a formal party, and part of him longed to mingle with the Fair more freely. The five of them were attracting the notice of hawkers and pedlars, who could picture full purses beneath the fine clothes; and one figure in particular was giving them undue attention, hovering around with a dancing gait, twisting his body into grotesque shapes and beckoning them to follow. His face was comic, but in a way that played for nervous laughter rather than a smile of pleasure. Others in the crowd were calling out his name. 'Lead on, Andrew!' they shouted happily – but Tom had always found clowns unsettling – more facetious than funny, with their smiles fixed in a menacing way.

This Merry-Andrew was drawing them towards a booth that they saw was exhibiting 'Curiosities of Nature.' The board in front of it boasted a roll-call of capricious forms: a cat with three legs, a woman carpeted with hair, a child with a bear-cub supposedly growing out of its back – and others. Such a freak-show was not for them; but as they turned away the clown took out a reeded pipe and began playing a strange tune, as if it would magically draw them back to the booth. The figure blocked their path and rolled his eyes beseechingly.

A small audience had now formed around them, and they were feeling uncomfortable. It was Lady Norreys who took the initiative and reached into her glove for a handful of pennies. She gave the man a bright *thankyou* for his entertainment and tossed them down, much to his delight. At this, there was relief and smiles all round, and the party walked on. But Tom was unsettled. He knew his mood was at odds with the spirit of the Fair. He comforted himself with the thought that it was a forgivable anxiety about the events to come: *The Tender Courtesan* and his defiant Prologue.

Something more to their taste offered itself a little further on. Waxworks were always amusing, and sometimes the more ridiculous and unconvincing the better. In this case there was a mismatch between the solemnity of the subjects and the crudeness of their execution. Tom conjectured that the Olympian gods had rarely been exhibited to such disadvantage, even in satire. These were no pure marble forms: the painted wax seemed to give them a fleshiness that was all-too mortal. The figure of Venus sported breasts of unclassical awkwardness, and the look on her face resembled a Fleet Street oyster-seller in mid-cry. Next to her, Diana had all the accoutrements of her character, but her quiver hung down heavily over her brawny arms, and she was wearing a tired scowl.

A smile lit up Tom's face, and beside him Lavinia's expression was one that he knew well – an eyebrow raised in ironic amusement.

'Love and chastity, Tom – a hard choice for you! Do you go for the fishwife or the scold?'

'I would hate to tangle with either of them. The gods have little to recommend them!'

They took a few steps further, and another female figure confronted them, this time to very different effect. Here the wax was shaped into pleasing curves with everything in proportion. The eyes gazed ahead in a visionary way, and the helmeted countenance was radiating a mood of calm authority.

'Well, Tom,' said Lavinia, 'what do you make of her? Not the same artist, surely? A favourable omen?'

Lady Norreys was now standing beside them, and her eyes lit up:

'Excellently done! This is no woman to meddle with!'

Tom looked down at the label propped up against the statue's feet.

'Ah of course!' he said, castigating himself for his slowness. 'Minerva! No indeed, I would never dream of challenging *her!* – or any of her votaries.'

'This one knows her own mind, Mr Bristowe,' said Lady Norreys. 'Surely there's no choice? If only Paris had been confronted with these three figures a lot of trouble would have been avoided.'

Tom caught her eye:

'No doubt she would have caused trouble of a different kind – Wisdom can be dearly bought.'

'Well, he was a silly boy altogether,' said Lavinia conclusively.

Along from the distinctly human gods, the exhibition next presented a line of godlike humans, commanders of earth and sea: a stiff Marlborough was the first (without his horse and simply carrying a baton), then Admiral Rooke, the craggy hero of Gibraltar, a telescope in one hand and a brass sextant dangling from the other. These were followed by a bemused King Charles the First whose wax head was unconvincingly attached to the torso; and finally a motherly Queen Anne who was clutching orb and sceptre to her bosom with a tired expression, as if she were nursing the nation itself.

But it was the next group of figures that brought them up short. Things came to life again. There were three of them, caught as if acting a scene on stage. The hands of the two men were in gestures of accusation and denial, and the woman's were clutched together in a plea. The faces were eloquent and words almost redundant.

'Well, well!' said Lord Melksham as he approached them. 'Very *expressive!* Mrs Barry and Mr Betterton – to the life – and Mr Cibber too. I wonder what they are playing? … Well I'll be damned!'

He stopped in his tracks, and the others likewise. They were suddenly looking at a face that belonged to a pageant in Hell. It was Cibber. The figure had the actor's lively eye and witty mouth. But his head was turned slightly, and when the full face came into view the left side of it was distorted into a terrible grimace. The wax had melted, and the features hung down like a bloodhound's jowl, the colours smudged into a stain.

Clearly an accident had happened; but the thing was uncomfortably real, and they could almost hear Cibber's groan of pain.

None of them spoke, but their thoughts were racing; and as they left the booth they couldn't help but question the proprietor who was sitting in a wicker chair by the door.

'We did notice, Mr Price …' began Lord Melksham hesitantly – but there was no need to say more.

'Alas, yes!' the man replied at once. 'Mr Cibber! …'

There was a nod.

'... Shocking! It happened yesterday. Sheer destruction!'

'Did you see who it was?' said Tom, not holding out much hope.

'Alas, sir, no – I can't explain it. We've had only respectable folk in here – none as would do such a thing. I did leave the place for a minute or two sometimes – for a pee – so I reckon it must have happened then. I reckon as someone slipped in from that raree-show next door. Wanted to make my beautiful figures as horrible as theirs! We are uncomfortable neighbours, sir, and don't see eye-to-eye ... Anyway, Francis was mightily upset.'

'Francis?' asked Tom.

'My apprentice, Francis Flinn. He's a bit of a genius with wax and paint – especially the painting. The young man has real skill in it.'

'So, is he responsible for the figures?' said Mrs Manley, suddenly interested.

'Only the theatrical group, ma'am – though I let him try his hand at Minerva too. Not a bad job he's made of her. The previous figure was a sad frump – looked like a governess who had a fondness for the bottle.'

'He's a true artist,' said Lady Norreys. 'A fine touch, especially with the actors – he's caught them in the act of speaking – and thinking. It's terrible to see his work defaced.'

'It's cruel, ma'am. I have high hopes for Francis – if I don't lose him to the stage first!'

Tom's ears pricked up:

'He's keen on the theatre, is he?'

'He haunts it, sir! The group of players was his idea. He's a lover of the playhouse, when he can sneak in there. He likes to hang about the place sometimes – has a sketching-book with him. Well, he swore he could "do" Mr Betterton to a T, and so I gave him a free hand. Then the others followed ...'

The proprietor rejoiced to have some people interested in his figures.

'... Indeed, we've had the idea – for next year – of setting up a whole scene of Shakespeare. *The Merchant of Venice*, we thought – the trial scene.'

'That would make a good show,' said Lord Melksham. 'Very dramatic!'

Tom was thinking fast:

'Mr Price ... when Francis arrives, could you invite him to come over to Pinkerman's booth? There's a performance there tonight that he might enjoy – I'll leave word at the door for him to be admitted.'

'Well sir, I reckon I could spare him. *The Tender Courtesan*, eh? He'd like that – and he might manage to have a proper seat for once!'

'But I don't want him to be too comfortable. From what you say, he has a sharp pair of eyes. Can you ask him to use them, and take note of all that's going on? – particularly in the audience ... And tell him to bring his sketching-book!'

The two groups joined forces outside Pinkerman's booth, hailing one another and eager to tell their stories. Widow Trotter, Will, and the two Scotsmen were still talking about the adventure of the elephant, while the Pophams' party couldn't expel Cibber's melted face from their minds. The Pophams had arrived too late to witness Hannibal's caperings, and they were aghast to hear the account, especially when the firecrackers were mentioned. They knew how close things had come to disaster.

'You say people applauded and cheered?' said Lord Melksham in disbelief.

'They thought it just another show, my Lord,' said Widow Trotter. 'A Pinkerman spectacle to surpass all the others.'

He shook his head:

'There's always danger lurking about the Fair – some violence waiting to happen. People crave it!'

'Risk is part of the entertainment,' said Will. 'We saw some heart-stopping work on the high rope.'

'Aye – and the fire-eater!' said Gavin, rolling his eyes. 'The laddie was chewing hot coals! – and a' have to blow hard to cool ma' porridge!'

Talk of the coals brought Mr Price's waxworks into the conversation, and there was more shaking of heads.

'It was an act of deliberate cruelty,' said Lady Norreys. 'Mr Cibber mustn't see it.'

'I think we should say nothing to him,' said Lord Melksham.

'Yes, I hope they'll remove the thing,' said Lavinia.' It was a face from nightmare. Nothing of the comic spirit about it!'

The exchanges continued in this vein; and amidst all the concern and conjecture, the forthcoming play and its prologue were forgotten. But not by Tom, who stood by quietly and attempted to listen to their talk. Widow Trotter noticed his silence.

'I think Mr Bristowe here needs some time to himself. Perhaps you should go and seek out Mr Pinkerman, Tom, and see that everything is settled? You must be wondering about the arrangements.'

'Thank you – yes,' he said quietly. 'And I can have a word with the players – if only for my own peace of mind.'

'Well,' said Mrs Manley, 'perhaps we others could seek out a little refreshment? – or at least sit down?'

The suggestion was welcomed. Tom's mind was on other things. He turned to his uncle:

'I hope you don't mind if I watch the play with Will and Mrs Trotter? You and the ladies can have the cushions to yourselves.'

'Of course, Tom! We can't have you bowing to the audience from a box, can we? It would be too grand. You must receive the cheers from the body of the audience. A man of the people!'

There was a twinkle in his uncle's eye which transformed sarcasm into gentle ribbing. Lavinia intervened:

'*Grand?* I hope you're not expecting more than a few little chairs, father?'

'No, Lavinia. But my posterior has to be pampered. I wouldn't want to contemplate a tender courtesan from a bench. In a fairground booth, a chair counts as *luxury*.'

Tom made his way round to the back of the booth to see if anything was stirring. There was some shouting and hammering going on behind the stage area, where a few rather crude props were stacked. Part of a street in Seville was receiving urgent attention, and one of the workmen was attaching a bit of greenery to a wooden flat representing the exterior of Don Leone's mansion. The slit-deal was painted in yellow so as to capture the magic of sunny Spain, and alongside it an ironwork balcony was bedecked with paper roses. The shouting was directed at a stage-hand who was unrolling a backdrop too eagerly and some of the paint was flaking off. If the street was to have a convincing fountain, then he would have to take more care.

Tom suddenly heard his own name called, and turned to see Gilbert Angel in the doorway. The actor was not yet in costume and had something of a strained look, as if a thought was troubling him. He hesitated a moment, then took a step forward.

'Mr Angel! How goes it?'

Tom spoke with a jaunty air, but Gilbert's face was flushed and tense:

'We're determined and in good heart, Mr Bristowe – in spite of events.'

'Yes. I've just been hearing about the elephant. How is Mr Pinkerman? That escapade must have shaken him. Is he all right to continue?'

'Our Pinkey is a resilient creature, and he seems to have turned the whole thing into a triumph … But it was a miracle no-one was killed. If it hadn't been for those two boys … This has got to stop!'

'A firecracker, was it not?'

'From the crowd, yes. The young lad ran off – people thought it a joke! The elephant was dancing, and they were cheering him the more. There were screams, but mainly at the thrill of it. I think if a tiger had been prowling around, they would have cheered that.'

Tom shook his head, but then brightened:

'Well, let's hope the festive mood will continue tonight. What did Sally say to her exquisite fan? She must have been delighted?'

'She was. Now she'll *flaunt* more than ever – quite the enchantress … but I'm afraid my sweet Agnes isn't at all happy. That was something I'd not considered – female jealousy!'

'But it's in the play, Mr Angell.'

'You're right of course – but if fiction comes *too* close to life …'

'It will add some spice to their performance!'

Gilbert was grim-faced:

'We can do without that. Matters are tense enough already. Events have gone too far …'

Tom noticed the furrowed brow and felt things weren't at all right. A blushing Gilbert reached into his pocket. He was angry.

'… I think you should see this. We found it pinned up in the shed where we dress. It's clearly directed at the actors … I've not told Pinkey about it.'

Tom looked at the paper and his eyes nearly burst from their sockets:

'Have they all seen this?'

'Enough of them – word has already got round.'

It was a picture drawn in ink with the vividness of caricature. It showed a stage on which stood a row of actors – men and women – identifiable by the names written above each of them. It was the players in *The Tender Courtesan*. They were all presented totally naked – the women leering and displaying their breasts, and the men with their tools in their hands. Along the bottom was inscribed three words in stark capitals: SODOM WILL FALL!

Tom was aghast:

'This is sick!'

'Yes, it is disgusting. Our enemies are sinking into the gutter, are they not? …'

Both of them stood in silence, taking in the implications of the paper and its being displayed in the actors' shed.

'… Well, I've come to a resolution, Mr Bristowe. This whole affair of Tunbridge and his friends has got to stop. I'm done with all this secrecy – this covering up of the truth. Things must be brought to their crisis!'

'What do you mean?'

'I've told Sally I'm going to expose Lord Tunbridge.'

'Against her wishes?'

'She doesn't know her own mind! Matters have to be resolved, and I'm going to resolve them for her …'

Gilbert took the paper and folded it roughly, with a determined look on his face.

'… Tomorrow I have a part in *The Devil on Two Sticks* – did you know that? – Well, I intend to take some liberties with it … Names will be named, Mr Bristowe! My contribution will be greater than anyone has bargained for. The true Devil will be exposed. That ravisher will be shamed in front of all! Thinking of your prologue has resolved me. I have to speak out!'

Tom swallowed hard:

'You say "ravisher" – but ...'

'That's the *truth*, Mr Bristowe. I know it for a fact. Sally confided in me; but then she thought better of it, and she tried to suggest it was somehow less than that ... No, Mr Bristowe, that fiend *raped her*. It was Zeus making one of his violent conquests. He left his mark on her. I only hope to god he hasn't impregnated her.'

'I had no idea – from what she said, I wondered ...'

'What Sally *said* was out of delicacy. She wished to wipe the idea from her mind. I can understand it ... but things have gone too far. This business has to be resolved!'

'But what of the Baron's proposal – his offer of marriage?'

'A sham. Like everything else about him. The man thought he could unlock the door with a single word, and that Sally would fall at his feet ... No, there would have been no marriage – the very idea is preposterous! ...'

Gilbert was becoming agitated, his eyes wild. The nearby hammering wasn't helping to calm him.

'... Nothing could be allowed to stand in his way. The man was a Machiavel, Mr Bristowe!'

Tom looked at the young actor and suddenly saw more than anger and anxiety. The Baron was becoming an obsession with him. Gilbert Angell was possessed with an idea he couldn't let go, and it was bubbling up inside. How closely it corresponded with reality was hard to say. Tom wondered if there might be a further indiscretion ready to rise to the surface ... It would be good to find out:

'Are you not being over-dramatic, Mr Angell? This is real life, not a play.'

'Ah, Mr Bristowe! It is you who are being naïve ... I happen to know ...'

He paused.

'... Sally has forbidden me to speak of it – but I'm sick of concealment ... The Baron wanted to draw the two of us into his plot, would you believe? To make us his confederates – report to him on doings in the playhouse.'

'What? – do you mean as spies?'

'That's what it would have been. It was Sally who disillusioned him – told him exactly what she thought – what *we* thought!'

Tom allowed himself to look a little sceptical:

'Did the Baron confide in you also? Or was this revealed only to Sally?'

Gilbert flinched slightly: it was not a question he appreciated. There was a moment's pause:

'He hardly needed to! You see, I knew what he was up to. I could see what was happening in the theatre. Milord Tunbridge *already had his informer*.'

'What?'

'I had my suspicions, and things confirmed them. You see, I'm observant. I watch and listen! You can learn a lot from glances and silences – from a person being where he shouldn't be – and lingering when he should be leaving – and asking what he shouldn't ask ... I watched the watcher, Mr Bristowe! ...'

A complaisant, knowing look possessed his face.

'... Do you think all these accidents over recent days have been a matter of chance? No, of course not! ...'

He suddenly checked himself, as if realising he was being drawn into the open himself.

'... But I can say no more.'

'But Gilbert – if you know anything ...'

'No! – You must wait for tomorrow. *The Devil on Two Sticks* will be my moment. This has to be spoken before an audience ... It will come!'

And with that he suddenly seized Tom's shoulders in both his hands, flushed, eyes glistening:

'Together we are going to defeat these people, Tom! Your prologue too – You and I! – what an adventure!'

And with a shiver of resolve, the troubled young actor turned on his heels and walked off, almost skipping. Tom watched him go, and trembled slightly. There was something in Gilbert Angell that electrified the space around him, a kind of nervous agitation that was forever creating a scene and drawing others into it. After the whirl of their conversation, Tom knew that a rather different picture was forming of Gilbert and Sally. Perhaps the two of them had been closer to Lord Tunbridge than they admitted, and confederate in other ways? Gilbert and Sally's isolation within the company was becoming explicable. Above all, he couldn't help reviewing the events on the evening of the Baron's killing. He didn't like to think of it, but he wondered if Gilbert and Sally had been concocting a story between them ... Were they playing a scene together? That was not something Will would like to hear.

Chapter Thirty-Four

THE MOMENT HAD come at last. After so much anticipation they were all finally seated in Pinkerman's droll-booth, crammed in tightly like apples in a barrel, waiting for the curtain to part and the Prologue to show himself. On this opening day of the Fair the place was full, and one or two people were standing at the back. In this makeshift theatre the benches were, if anything, more closely packed than in the pit of the playhouse – but that was where any resemblance ended. In Pinkerman's booth everything was practical, with nothing there for show, the message being that all the wonder and delight was to come from the little stage which jutted out almost to the knees of the patrons in the front row, as if beckoning to them.

The room was well enough lit but lacked the dazzle of the Theatre Royal. This was not a place for diamonds to shine and silks to shimmer. Instead of chandeliers, a couple of solid wooden stands held the candles. The room itself was largely a tent, with large canvas panels stretched over a slight framework. Here the 'boxes' were a line of small cushioned chairs arranged along a dais to the right – easier on the backside, certainly, though reminiscent, Tom thought, of a jury-box at the Old Bailey. In this place, however, the verdict of life or death would be decided by the audience, whose eager conversations had now settled into an expectant hum.

All around him, eyes were checking the curtain, and little adjustments were being made to clothing. There was some shuffling and wriggling, and as Tom surveyed the room, he caught a restless mood. Never had he scrutinised an audience so closely. One or two faces made him uneasy: he noticed a disapproving scowl here, a supercilious brow there, and in the second row a dark-suited gentleman had a self-righteous look; a red-faced character in a patched coat was consulting his watch. There were a few respectable couples scattered about – mainly dull husbands dwarfed by wives swathed in layers of muslin.

And the sounds were disturbing too. A burst of silly giggles came from a group behind him, and a harsh cough (of impatience?) from somewhere else. And then suddenly – horror of horrors! – as if to offer a comment on the whole enterprise, a prolonged and mellow fart rang out, much like a bassoon tuning itself for the overture. At once, a wave of laughter swept through the booth. The cold hand gripping Tom's stomach tightened even further. The evening was going to be a disaster of the first magnitude.

'Stop fidgeting! …' said Will to his right. He was grinning widely, as if this was just another theatrical entertainment.

'… It looks a pretty friendly audience to me – and quite a respectable one.'

To Tom's left, Widow Trotter was radiating reassurance:

'I know you're imagining the worst, Tom – but whatever happens, we're all going to survive the performance, You'll have to trust Pinkerman! … Look, your uncle is smiling at you.'

Tom glanced over to the right and saw his Uncle Jack beaming happily from his cushioned seat. It was an encouraging gesture, but offset a little by Lavinia, who was sitting by his side holding her nose.

The irreverence cheered him, and his spirits lightened. This was a fairground booth for Heaven's sake, not a command performance! Shouts, whistles, cat-calls – yes, and farts – were only to be expected. It was the music of the Fair.

Tom's eyes shifted to the 'box' next to the Pophams, where Lady Norreys and Mrs Manley were seated. The vizarded ladies had been generating a ripple of curiosity through the crowded tent. Now they were in whispered conversation with Colley Cibber, who was half-leaning on them in rapt attention. Tom smiled to himself when it struck him how much the exotic pair resembled courtesans themselves. Instantly, as if they had heard his thought, the two black masks swung toward him, and he gulped. It felt like an accusation, and the nods and smiles that followed seemed a polite afterthought. The seconds ticked by. He felt more and more exposed – but this was nothing to the exposure that would come in a few seconds' time! What was being expected of him? Why couldn't he simply hide away and write delightfully inoffensive verses ... odes, and elegies, and sonnets? A *Prologue!* What had he done? ...

But there was no time to call back events and reorganise his life. After a dozen rapid heartbeats, Tom saw a human hand part the curtains, and William Pinkerman stepped out to the front of the stage.

Applause burst forth, and a cry of 'Pinkeeeey!' came from several members of the audience. They were welcoming an old friend and acknowledging a figure who, more than anyone, personified the May Fair itself. So far – Tom thought – so good ...

But this time Pinkerman was not his genial self. The expression on his face was solemn, and his costume as the cold-hearted Don Leone was made even more brooding by a long black scarf that hung down from his shoulders like a churchman's stole. With a slight shock, Tom noticed a small volume clasped in his left hand – could it be a prayerbook? An old-fashioned velvet cap was settled on his head, and Tom felt he was looking at the Newgate chaplain about to take a last confession.

There was an uneasy murmur in the room as Pinkerman reached out a hand apologetically. The man looked humble, even cowed, before an audience he would normally have commanded. A mystified hush fell, and then some words began to come from a pair of lips that had shaped themselves into a complacent half-smile:

You dread REFORMERS *of our sinful age!*
You awful cat o'nine-tails to the stage!
To gain your favour we'd your rules obey
And offer you a MORAL *piece today,*
Design our play to give you satisfaction:
We would be PURE *in language, thought, and action …*

He paused. There was no doubting the speaker's sincerity. Members of the audience began to glance at their neighbours. None of them had been expecting this, and the prospect of settling their haunches onto a hard bench for an hour's moral lecture was beginning to frighten not a few.

Pinkerman continued his propitiatory speech; but gradually, as the neat couplets fell into place, a glint in his eyes began to tell a different story. Smiles of recognition were now lighting up some of the faces in the audience as, line by line, a majestic mountain of irony rose up before them:

… To do you right and in your cause enlist
No rogue would thrive, no virgin e'er be kist;
No man of God hypocrisy display,
No Lord from paths of virtue ever stray;
No paid informer ever take a bribe,
No tradesman curse, no Magistrate imbibe …

There was a deep intake of breath, and then Pinkerman's voice boomed out in full Puritanical confidence:

'Tis MANNERS *rule! – And* Manners *you shall see!*
Nothing but Virtue, Faith, Propriety –
A righteous and REFORMED SOCIETY!

His hands were now working hard to drive the point home. The man's whole body was tense, and the eyes began to blaze. There before them the audience recognised a familiar figure – the hectoring preacher! But this one was taking his hearers into his confidence, stripping away pretence and laying his intentions out for all to see:

Now you must listen while we rant and preach
And curse – we know no other way to teach! –
The PULPIT*'s voice is all we have to give,*
And by its strictures we would have you live …

Pinkerman paused again. There was a palpable tension throughout the booth, as if a spring had been tightly coiled. Then, at last, came the moment of release. Instantly the cap was whipped from his head and flung from the stage; he pulled the scarf from off his shoulders, and looked down at the small black book, shaking his head. Then he glanced conspiratorially at his audience, and winked:

Yet, damme folks! – 'twill make a tedious play! …
So – what d'ye think? – Shall NATURE *have its way?*

Spontaneous applause broke out, and a surge of relief and pleasure poured forth. Now a warm smile was lighting up Pinkerman's whole body. He relaxed and looked around at his devoted audience, who were smiling back at him. Their friend had come back to them! Cries of assent greeted each line as Tom's Prologue marched confidently on:

Shall we let Truth *and* Honesty *prevail,*
And offer you a round unvarnish'd tale?
Show men and women as in life they be:
Creatures of passion, candid, wayward, free?
Here, thro' this earthly maze without a plan
They'll steer a course toward what good they can,
Thanks to a loving Tender Courtesan!
You'll view a human world: our only art
Is truthfully to touch the feeling heart.

Pinkerman awarded that line its full weight of emotion, lowering his head slightly and striking his breast in sympathy with the thought. Now at last he could be plain and direct, as if speaking to people he trusted. He had them! ... In the fourth row of the audience, Will glanced sideways at his friend and knew he must be glowing inside. Widow Trotter squeezed his arm, hardly able to breathe. Pinkerman had been shameless, admittedly, but here amongst these people his histrionics had worked their magic. Will and Mrs Trotter knew that the proud young author beside them could now relax and listen as his Prologue reached its conclusion:

Whisper it, friends! – and keep our secret, pray! –
(Reformers have informers in their pay!) –
Poetic Justice *is an old deception,*
An ancient falsehood, a mere lazy fiction.
Our canting preachers propagate the cheat,
And shun the fire, yet enjoy its heat.
Such men attack the sins that they're inclin'd to,
And damn the very vices they've a mind to.

Thus REFORMATION *doth discharge its rage*
And claims the virtue of a spotless page,
Sees crimes in others roundly sent to Hell
While they indulge and think themselves quite well.
OUR *stage presents a true Democracy,*
Whose greatest enemy's – – – HYPOCRISY!

Pinkerman ended the prologue with a confident flourish, and spontaneous cheers rang out all around. He made a low, extravagant bow, then scratched his groin outrageously; and finally he brought his hands together in an attitude of prayer, his eyes raised to the heavens. At each gesture the roars of the audience grew louder, and Tom watched in alarm as one tipsy individual in the front row leapt to his feet and attempted a jig while waving his cap in the air.

'Long live the Fair!' someone shouted from the back.

'Aye! Damn the Reformers!' cried another, to howls of approval.

People were standing to applaud, and to his left a pair of young sparks were attempting to mount their bench but ended up collapsed on the floor.

'The Saints to the Devil!' someone cried, with accidental wit.

'Hands off the Brook Field,' shouted another, more strategically.

Other shouts followed, some more coherent than others. The fervour was increasing by the second. Tom drew his eyes away and risked a glance to his right, where the 'boxes' were applauding more politely. The cry of 'Author!' rang out, and Tom saw it was Lady Norreys, who was beaming under her mask, her gloved hands cupped to her face.

Eyes had begun to turn toward him, and he saw Pinkerman pointing in his direction with outstretched arms. Will patted him on the back, and he could feel a pair of hands from behind pulling him up to his feet. His legs were trembling, and part of him – most of him, in truth – just wanted to run away. He felt poised on a precipice. A warm gust of enthusiasm was buoying him up, and yet he knew that a single step could plunge him down. It was a dangerous moment.

He turned round, and instantly felt on stage himself. He had known nothing like this before, and his mind was agitated. Individual sounds were no longer distinguishable, and it was difficult to see objects distinctly. It took a conscious effort, but he scanned the rows along the back of the booth with deliberate care – and a chill struck him.

One or two faces were conspicuously not smiling, but were glowering with disapproval. At once he thought of Mrs Trotter in the Theatre Royal, and almost choked. There were only a handful of faces, young, sullen, quiet – disengaged rather than aggressive. They were biding their time.

While all this was happening, Pinkerman had slipped quietly behind the curtain, a smile of satisfaction lighting up his features. The job was done – the first job of the evening, at least. The opening scene of *The Tender Courtesan* was being readied. A street in Seville ...

The performance began well. The good will generated by Tom's Prologue had put the audience in a receptive mood, and most of them were happy to leave behind the London of Queen Anne for a world in which unbridled Catholic passions confronted rigid codes of honour, and they were looking forward to the action. They fully expected a kidnapping, a violation, a challenge, and hopefully a duel, with daggers and poisons doing the business – a burning at the stake perhaps (this was Spain, after all)? A gloomy prison would surely be forthcoming, and even a thunderstorm if they were lucky. And over it all they wanted to sense the tyranny of a corrupt State and an oppressive Church, with wicked Papist plots, tortures and confessions. A gruesome death was frankly a necessity, involving a mutilated female corpse if possible. A pair of scheming courtiers and a ruthless Duke would be good – a murderous Cardinal even better. It wasn't much to ask, and they were hopeful. Everyone was well settled on their benches now, and looked and listened eagerly. Around the 'tender Courtesan' they were already picturing a web of intrigue and betrayal ... Surely a terrible crime was waiting to be uncovered? ...

These were impossible demands, and after a quarter of an hour a few adjustments were having to be made. There was still no corpse, and the actors were doing quite a bit of talking. An intricate situation was being explored, and the audience found themselves having to listen to the words.

But if action was lacking, feelings were bubbling up very nicely. Don Leone was being exceptionally cold-hearted, and confronted by his tyrannical father the love-lorn Ernesto was achieving despair with ease – indeed the look in Gilbert's eyes, Tom thought, took it closer to anguish. And as he described his love for Agnes, there was more than defiance evident – it was definitely *outrage*. At one memorable moment Ernesto made to strike Don Leone across the face, and a surprised Pinkerman was forced to shrink back with a look of alarm. By this time his fatherly coldness was coming under strain, and a degree of annoyance was taking over. Within minutes this had become indignation, which in turn gave young Ernesto a renewed boldness. As the exchanges continued, Tom began to wonder if somebody should leap onto the stage and separate the two of them. The audience were gripped. This was a terrific duel of words – and one that was as violent and dangerous as any physical encounter.

For Tom, the scene had an extra dimension of drama as he remembered the disaffected group at the rear of the tent and waited for some disturbance to break out. But nothing was happening – yet. Somehow the emotional heat from the stage was filling the booth and leaving no space for interruption. Perhaps they were becoming gripped themselves?

As scene followed scene the tense atmosphere continued, and passions were mounting with each confrontation. Agnes the novitiate nun was playing her part in this. A wide-eyed Will was delighted to see Lizzy Wright exploiting to the full her capacity to defy constriction – here was a young lady who would not remain a novice for long. This forwardness irritated Peggy Evans, who responded by giving the Abbess of St Clare a degree of exasperation that raised her pompous character to new heights and found an element of suppressed violence there. At one point Will wondered if Peggy was going to fling the holy water in Lizzy's face.

With all this nervous energy being generated and so many niggling provocations increasing the heat, the scene between the two women in Ernesto's life was bound to be memorable – and it proved so. From the very opening of the play Tamara the courtesan had conveyed a surprising degree of allure and assurance. Sally gave her a Cleopatra-like charm, and each physical detail added to the fascination. At one moment, thanks to a delicate sinking of her eyelids and a slight turn of her wrist, Ernesto had been in danger of forgetting the plot entirely. The beautiful fan played between the lovers' faces as if it alone were separating them, forming a trembling barrier as it worked to cool their mutual blushes. Tom was impressed. He glanced at Will and saw a beatific smile.

Lizzy Wright, as Agnes, arrived on the scene in the nick of time, and the skirmishing began in earnest. The words were commonplace enough, but between them the actors discovered a seam of mutual jealousy that made entire sense. At the climactic moment Agnes reached out and seized the fan. Tamara clung onto it tenaciously, eyes blazing. But Lizzy would not give way.

Rarely can a novitiate nun in the white heat of her purity have spoken with such passion:

> Forego your Circean arts! – release Ernesto!
> You have the pow'r to hold him – but, Tamara,
> You have a nobler pow'r – *to let him go.*
> Use it, I pray! *Let young love have its time!'*
> Release him! …

Now it was Agnes who was serpentine. Indeed, Lizzy delivered the final words with a hiss that sent a shiver through the audience. On the phrase about *young love* her grip tightened even more, and her knuckles whitened as she held onto the annoying wrist while the fan bit into Sally's flesh. There was an awkward pause as the two women half-wrestled. To Tom's left, Widow Trotter caught sight of an alarmed Pinkerman gesticulating from the wings.

'Yes – *let him go!'* shouted an enthusiast from the audience fully caught up in the drama of the scene.

'Let *her* go!!' shouted a wit in response.

There was some laughter at this, and for the first time Tom heard an ominous murmur from the back of the booth. But the ribaldry seemed to die down, and cries of 'quiet!' rang out. Tom risked a quick glance over his shoulder and was reassured to see the stout frame of Amos Jackson with a concentrated look in his eyes. Any mischief-maker would have to think twice with him facing them.

The pace of the plot was now quickening, and even the scene with the apothecary had an electric quality. Convinced that much more could be made of his part, Bob Stanley employed his full range of facial and vocal expressions to convey his doubts over the 'poison trick.' The struggle with his conscience had such deep-felt intensity that it suggested the actor was auditioning for Hamlet – and perhaps he was. Several times he looked into the wings to see if Pinkerman was watching.

'Their luck is holding, Tom!' whispered Will, conscious that the nervous energy of the performance was running a risk.

Things hardly calmed themselves during the sub-plot, which thrilled the audience with its exceptionally lively duel. Swords clashed loudly, and patrons in the front row edged back on their seats. Will was delighted to see that Joe Byrne's death was everything the young actor could have wished. Catching the fever of the evening, he twitched and grimaced to fine effect; and long after slumping to the floor he managed to convey the grudging unwillingness with which the human soul left its bodily prison. The watching audience gasped and shuddered in sympathy, and as the body of Don Felipe was finally borne away, a round of spontaneous applause released some of the pent-up emotion.

Over in the boxes, the drama was being well received, although Lord Melksham and his daughter were beginning to conclude that what they were witnessing was opera without the music. Alongside them, Mrs Manley and Lady Norreys smiled behind their masks, amused by the wild theatrical energies on display and appreciative of how a satiric impulse could work its way in at the most solemn of moments.

The Tender Courtesan was reaching its climax, and at this point the audience were so gripped by the drama that the resolution of the love-plot appeared plausible, even natural. All was set for the big scene between Tamara and Don Leone – the false seduction, when Tamara would trap Ernesto's father and extract the crucial vow from him.

And trap him she did – comprehensively. Sally Twiss employed the full range of honeyed arts: she was Circe, Calypso, and Alcina combined – and an unsettling hint of Medea found its way in too. In response, Pinkerman began to sweat profusely, managing the transition from cold-hearted to hot-blooded with remarkable ease. An element of erotic improvisation between them heightened the effect – so much so, that Gilbert's indignation at his entrance was palpable. Ernesto's eyes blazed at his father, and he spat out his words with utter conviction. Tamara shrunk back in surprise and clung to the now passionate Don Leone for protection. When the time came to take the poison, Gilbert lifted the phial defiantly and flung his head back, almost choking as he did so.

The audience were hardly breathing. By now the actors were so caught up in the drama that no spectacular effects were needed. Within the booth, all eyes were fixed, and every heart throbbed as one.

The closing scenes of the play swept on at a high pitch of excitement; and the final moments, in which Agnes embraced the now-resurrected Ernesto, drew tears from benches and boxes alike. At the back of the stage, behind the young lovers, stood Tamara, who was to perform a silent pageant of renunciation and depart like a tragic ghost. But instead she was holding her ground defiantly and appeared transfixed in pent-up fury. It was intended the curtains would finally close on a chaste kiss, with Ernesto and Agnes holding hands; but the curtain-man was hesitating. He watched open-mouthed, like others in the room, while Gilbert and Lizzy clung together in a passionate embrace which had a restless quality that was quite alien to the cathartic ending Pinkerman had envisaged. Embarrassing seconds passed before a loud cry of 'Close the bloody curtain!' rang out from the wings and prompted the poor man to draw the cords and bring *The Tender Courtesan* to an end.

There was a moment of stunned silence before the storm broke. Eager applause and cries of delight filled the tent, mingled with whoops of derision and howls of protest from the group at the back, who had found their voice and were now making their feelings known. Shouts of 'filth!' and 'vile trash!' could be heard above the clapping; and one strident gentleman was declaiming scripture in a string of apocalyptic polysyllables – 'abominable unbelievers!' 'whoremongers!' 'sorcerers!' and 'idolaters!' The words rang out above the clapping; and it was possible to catch the chilling phrase 'fire and brimstone!' before it was swallowed up in the counter-cheers from the benches.

Tom wasn't applauding, but was staring blankly at the closed curtain, struggling to come to terms with the jumble of heart-stopping passion and actorly self-indulgence he had just witnessed. On his left, Widow Trotter's handkerchief dropped to the floor while she clapped heartily, and on his other side Will was applauding in a more measured way:

'I think we can hail that as a triumph!' he said. 'Though a very wild one, don't you think?'

'It was a travesty, Will! A mish-mash of sincerity and crude sensation – I don't know what to believe. Some of it was very powerful … I can only think I was to blame.'

'*Blame?*' said a mystified Mrs Trotter, who had overheard him. 'Yours was the biggest triumph of all. And what a reception you were given!'

'Yes, I was cheered like a hero – but I could have been hanged from a tree just as easily! It was what I'd feared, Mrs T. My prologue stirred everyone up – and all the players seemed to be caught up in their own feelings.'

'But it's the theatre, Mr Bristowe! And how the play gripped us! This was something new – like watching a novel come to life! Something we could believe in. Every thought and passion brought to the surface. We saw into their hearts!'

'You surprise me Mrs T,' said Tom. 'I never thought you would enter into it like this.'

'And why not?' she asked, a little taken aback. 'Don't mistake me – I know this is a theatre-booth. Once I'm back at the Bay-

Tree I shall be my old self, I assure you! – I'll be keeping the accounts and counting the spoons. But it's good to escape for a while.'

She gave Tom an indulgent smile. Sometimes poets didn't understand …

'What's that noise?' said Will suddenly. 'It's coming from behind the curtain.'

They stopped and tried to listen … Yes, it was clear there was some onstage commotion going on. The applause was continuing and the audience were demanding the actors take their bow. But the curtain was remaining closed. What was happening?

A moment later they found out. One eager young man leapt onto the stage and pulled the curtain himself.

The clapping in the booth stopped at once as a chaotic scene revealed itself. It was clear that the drama was far from over. To the left of the stage Pinkerman was slumped in a chair, being fanned by one of the stage-hands; Joe Byrne was clutching his head; and alongside him Lizzy Wright was frozen in a wide-eyed stare into nothing. Everyone else was gazing helplessly at the floor. In front of them was a far from pageant-like Tamara, on her knees, screaming out instructions. But no-one was moving, except for one distorted figure. Cradled in Sally's arms was Gilbert Angell, writhing in agony and clutching his stomach. Beneath his mouth a little pool of green bile was beginning to form.

Chapter Thirty-Five

'CANTHARIDES?'

'Undoubtedly. A substantial dose. Everything points to it: the stinking sweat, the bile, the terrible cramps, the fearful trembling ...'

'But will he survive?'

The physician shook his head:

'He is close to death, Mr Pinkerman. Nothing can retrieve him. The others – and you yourself – are affected but slightly, thank God. But from what you tell me, you have all experienced the excitement of the glands, the heating in the brain. This is the body's response to the stimulating force of the *fly* – its outrageous abrasion of the animal spirits. All indicate the *Spanish Fly*, without a doubt.'

'But can nothing be done for him?'

'Nothing. There is no recourse to a purge – the Cantharides is itself a purgative – and a dramatic one. No, I fear Mr Angell is done for. I wish I could give you hope, but I cannot ...'

'But Dr Radcliffe ...'

'He'll be dead within twenty-four hours, Sir.'

The physician was categorical, and John Radcliffe was never wrong on such matters. Pinkerman and the other players were stunned, and the frightful moaning of Gilbert Angell beyond the door seemed only to confirm the prognosis.

'Can you not stay with him, Doctor?' whispered Lizzy Wright.

The physician's bag closed with a decisive click:

'There is nothing I can do – and I must be at the palace ... Prince George is taken bad again ...'

A smile came to his lips.

'... An odd thing, but I think a little dose of the fly might assist His Royal Highness – a caustic would not come amiss. His circulation is so weak, and the vessels need to be stimulated. I may indeed recommend a blister ... But in any case, he will not see October out, you can be sure of that ... Good day!'

The eminent physician had favoured them only briefly, and a few moments later the man was gone, leaving the group stunned and mystified. They were huddled in Pinkerman's office at the booth, lost for words and puzzled by the drama that had overtaken them. And now Gilbert was dying a few yards away, slumped on an improvised couch with Sally Twiss and Peggy Evans attempting to comfort him as the opiate took effect.

Everyone in the company was exhausted. It had been an astonishing two hours. The febrile activity of *The Tender Courtesan* had left them whirling, and then had come the horror of the unexpected afterpiece. No-one had quite known what to do, and pulses continued to race. It had taken a good twenty minutes for the droll-booth to empty. Many of the spectators were wrought to a high pitch of excitement and unwilling to leave a performance that was far from finished. The knot of mischief-makers, however, had slipped away instantly in the knowledge that retribution had been meted out to the Devil's own. Some of the polite occupants of the boxes hadn't wished to linger either; but the Pophams and their guests hesitated for a time as they contemplated the awkward challenge that lay ahead: what to say to Lady Melksham.

Tom had insisted that his friends should make their way home. He would stay on at the booth to offer what help he could and see if anything might be learned. The triumph of his Prologue was entirely forgotten, and his mind was full of gloomy thoughts about Gilbert and his fate. Such a talented young man, bursting with life and determined on telling the Truth! Well, now he would never have the chance … Tom winced as he recalled their conversation a few hours earlier, and what it had promised. '*So much* promise, Gilbert!' he whispered to himself … And what now? What could they do? He tried to pull his mind back to practical things.

The arrogance of the great Dr Radcliffe had disgusted him, but the man's diagnosis was convincing: Cantharides. Yes, that would explain the contagious madness of the performance. Somebody had administered the drug to the company, but how? And why was Gilbert so seriously affected? The phial of 'poison' was the likely answer. One thing he was certain of: this was another turn in the vicious game someone was playing with the company – a deadly twist of their plot. The theatrical potion had become real poison – the libertine consumed by his desires. The message was clear.

Amidst the ruin of all his plans Pinkerman was determined to hold on. He was still sweating and wild-eyed, but his brain was working rapidly, and he was concerned to observe the forms. He took Tom aside to thank him again for his contribution.

'In spite of what has overtaken us, Mr Bristowe, I don't want your Prologue to be forgotten. Most efforts in that line are trivial – random bolts at best – but yours hit the mark! I only hope I did it justice – there was no elephant needed this time! Your words deserve to be in print. They've become our rallying-cry.'

'Print? Oh no, I wouldn't want … I really have no ambitions for its printing …'

He broke off. Huge disappointment had suddenly shown itself in Pinkerman's face. The man was already close to tears.

A hand reached out:

'But we need it, Mr Bristowe! – we need such things to be said … I fear I've already taken the liberty of sending it to the papers. I fondly hoped it would help our play, d'ye see? But now of course … The *Courtesan* was to carry a message to the world – and when the cheers rang out for your Prologue – well – I thought we might succeed.'

Tom saw clearly and replied warmly:

'In that case, I am happy to stand with you. You have many friends, Mr Pinkerman, as you saw tonight. All is not over. Indeed, with each outrage the theatre's enemies leave themselves more exposed … But how did it happen – *the fly*? Several of you have been affected I think?'

'It can be but one thing, Mr Bristowe – the beer.'

'Beer?'

'We keep a supply of small beer – a couple of flagons of the stuff – behind the stage. 'Tis thirsty work performing, and whistles need to be wetted! Not much is taken usually – though, alas, our Mr Angell does find it helps his confidence. I think he partook more than the others. The drink was set out after this morning's rehearsal – anyone could have meddled with it.'

'So, you think the phial of poison wasn't to blame?'

'That I can't say – the thing disappeared – dropped in the excitement. But 'tis the beer, surely? – Peggy Evans doesn't partake – she has her own little flask of something a mite stronger – and she seems to have escaped … No – our Peggy is her usual brisk self! And she has been finding our antics infuriating …'

He wiped his brow, and Tom noticed he was still breathing heavily.

'… I was close to fainting during that last scene – and Joe Byrne said he thought his head would explode. Sally is still overwrought – and Lizzy too! … but poor, poor Gilbert … he could hardly control his limbs. In our quarrel scene he struck out at me – did you see it? I don't know how the poor boy kept going to the end. His collapse was terrible – so sudden and complete … as if the final curtain told him all was over.'

He stopped. The words had shaped themselves into an epitaph. Pinkerman choked up, and the two of them stood for a moment in silence.

Tom tried to find a glimmer of light:

'I only pray Dr Radcliffe is wrong. The brute was so very pleased with himself – he even rejoiced at the certainty of the symptoms. I'm sure he doesn't want to give us false hope, but …'

He hesitated. There was another question he needed to ask.

'… Something puzzles me, Mr Pinkerman … I was expecting to see Elias Cobb. He was determined on being here, but there's no sign of him.'

'He was certainly here in the booth, Mr Bristowe – no question – and Toby Mudge too – standing at the back. They were keeping an eye on the grumblers. But they weren't there at the final curtain – neither of them – and I've not seen hide nor hair of 'em since.'

Both of them fell silent. Pinkerman's face, usually so animated, was fixed in a helpless stare as if his mind was searching for something to hold onto. So much needed to be done, but the short breathing showed a man close to exhaustion.

Tom's thoughts were also churning rapidly. What had taken Elias and Toby away? And were either of them aware of what had happened? Perhaps not. Full of questions, he looked at Pinkerman and saw a man whose resources were almost spent. There was no cause to trouble him further. What the poor man really needed was some calm and a little time to take stock of events.

But it was not to be. There was a sudden commotion on the other side of the door, and a second later it opened to reveal a frantic Sally Twiss. Her gown was hanging away from her shoulders as if she had been interrupted while dressing, and she was clutching a small bag that was still open. One of her feet was half out of its shoe. She was every inch the pursued heroine of romance.

'They've come for me, Tom! ...'

It was a frightened whisper, and the streaked make-up on her cheek added to the alarming effect.

'... Men of the watch are on their way ... what shall I do? ... Mr Mudge says they'll be here at any moment!'

Toby himself was behind her:

'I ran over here, Mr Pinkerman. Mr Cobb has done his best – but they're determined to present their warrant. We've been holding them at bay! The three of them turned up during the performance, and they'd have burst into the booth had we not stopped them. They were for dragging Miss Twiss away there and then. It took all of Mr Cobb's polite ways – he told them they would certainly start a riot and lives would be in danger. But in the end, it was the promise of a pint of good ale that persuaded them. They agreed to wait till the booth had emptied. Mr Cobb has been delaying them as far as he can – saying they should make the arrest in due form and bring a magistrate. One's now been sent for. He's sure to be here soon.'

'What shall I do, Tom?' repeated Sally. 'If I run away ... or should I stay and face them ... ?

Her fevered mind was racing. Words couldn't keep up.

'... I need to think ... If they question me this moment I don't know what I'll say ... I don't trust myself.'

Pinkerman was also looking at Tom. He was feeling helpless. Whatever they did, they had to decide quickly.

'You need some respite, Sally,' said Tom at once. 'But you mustn't be seen to run away. Can I suggest the two of us disappear into the Fair for a while ... Mr Pinkerman can explain what has been happening – I warrant the men will have no inkling of the disaster – unless word has reached them?'

He looked at the young watchman, who shook his head:

'None at all, Mr Bristowe. I've just learned of it myself. It's a terrible thing. The Watch should have been sent for directly!'

'But all was so confused,' said Pinkerman. 'No-one has been thinking clearly.'

Mudge turned to Tom:

'Can we not work this disaster to our advantage? A case of deliberate poisoning?'

Tom saw the force of this:

'Yes – and the magistrate can be invited to begin the questioning. That will give us a little time.'

'I'll be glad of it,' said Sally quietly. 'I've no heart for running away – not again. You can help me decide what I should do. What has happened to poor Gilbert changes the picture, does it not?'

Tom nodded, glad to see that Mudge seemed easy with the idea:

'Then Sally and I can return to the booth ... But please, make sure Elias is here – he's our safeguard. We can't have Sally carried off without someone friendly to her interest. Is that a sensible course, Toby?'

'Eminently, Mr Bristowe ... Mr Pinkerman, can you begin gathering people together – the ones who are still here? We'll then be ready for the Magistrate.'

Pinkerman was relieved to be active again. He needed to be doing. It would be easy to think of himself as a victim swept along by the current of fate; but William Pinkerman had never been one to allow such a notion. On the contrary, he shared with Christopher Rich the entrepreneur's urge to grasp Occasion as it passed and turn it to advantage. That was more his style. At this moment he could see nothing remotely positive in what had befallen them; but if there was to be a way out, they wouldn't find it by standing still. They must press on.

By the time Elias Cobb arrived with the Magistrate and watchmen, Tom and Sally had stepped out into the night. The May Fair had reached its final wild hour when respectable folk were making the best of their way home – or were lingering around the stalls aware of a nocturnal excitement beginning to tug at them. In the shadowy places behind the booths dark shapes moved quietly, making no sound above a giggle or a rustle of clothes. But along the main concourse the fair-goers' faces were coming alive in the light of dozens of blazing torches which spat and crackled in what was now a fresh breeze. By this time only a handful of hawkers were evident, their cries overborne by raucous shouts and drunken hallooings. The economy of the Fair was working to its close, but some lively business was still being done. Snatchers and filchers were more elusive than ever, and coins slid easily from hand to hand. This was the time for roasted nuts and hot punch. Beyond the booths, the spits had ceased to turn, but the pigs' carcases and scraps of pork crackling were left in the bins for the local ragamuffins to dine.

The two figures who slipped away from Pinkerman's booth could have been mistaken for eloping lovers. A cloak had been found for Sally, and its hood concealed her face. Alongside her, Tom's restless eyes gave him a furtive look as his mind searched out the possibilities. They needed somewhere safe and quiet where Sally could unburden herself.

Over to their left Tom's attention was caught by the waxworks, and he remembered Francis the apprentice. In the confusion of the evening the young artist had slipped his mind. The booth might serve their turn, and his feet led them to it, where they found Mr Price preparing to close the place. He was happy to offer the late visitors a place to sit quietly.

Tom was glad to learn that Francis had indeed attended their play.

'He left here not five minutes ago, Mr Bristowe. There's something he wants to show you. He much enjoyed *The Tender Courtesan*, but in all the chaos he thought it best to slip away. He said your performance had a surprise ending! The lad will be here tomorrow morning if you'd care to call.'

Tom thanked him, and after a few polite exchanges the proprietor left the two of them alone.

At once Sally's whole body seemed to sink in her chair. It struck him that in various ways the girl had been on stage all day. Perhaps she would feel ready to speak her own lines at last?

But still nothing was said. She turned to look at him, and there was a curiosity, even a trace of amusement, in her eyes. But it was Tom who spoke.

'Your Tamara was magnificent! ...' he said.

The remark shot out of him and sounded unbelievably callow – the words of a neophyte admirer. The idea jolted him. Perhaps that's what he was?

'... It became *your* role, did it not? You must have felt that? ... Will told me you had doubts – that you felt much closer to Agnes.'

'Ah, *Will!* ... A young man of nice critical judgment! ...'

The hesitant smile now confirmed itself.

'... Yes, Tom, your friend explained it all to me on Monday. He was very perceptive – and very kind ... Though, when I gave Tamara's character some thought I could see that Ernesto was not for her – such a shallow, calculating youngster! Too willing to impress, and then cheat, his intolerable father. No, I don't believe our simple Agnes got the better of the bargain at all. With such a selfish rover for a husband her life is bound to be a painful one ... No, Tom, Tamara needed to move on. But of course she didn't wish to hurt the young chap. She allowed him to think her a besotted lady rather than a determined woman with a career still ahead of her ... Renunciation indeed!'

During this speech Tom's mind was re-drawing his picture of Tamara – and of Sally too, another determined woman who might well feel trapped between the attentions of Lord Tunbridge and Gilbert Angell – both of them eager to instruct and mould her – yet neither, perhaps, a man for a girl to dream of!

There was silence. Sally could see from Tom's furrowed brow that some mental wrestling was going on. She decided to come to his rescue:

'I'm sorry, Tom. Time presses, and we should be talking of more practical matters. What do you think I should do? I'll truly value your opinion – please speak freely.'

It was an open question, and Tom swallowed hard. He was suddenly wary of giving her advice and needed to be sure of his ground:

'I know you and Gilbert have already been questioned by a Justice – by Mr Hector?'

'Yes, at the theatre when we returned from Holborn, all innocent and trusting. It was an odd occasion. The magistrate's questioning was remarkably brief. He stuck to simple facts ... but I'm afraid in my answers I was less than exact.'

'You mean you omitted to mention certain things?'

'I mean, I lied.'

The words were sharp and pointed.

Tom couldn't help being shocked by the directness and gave her a serious look:

'In what particular? – was it to do with what happened in the property-store? We have kept your secret ... I take it you didn't reveal the truth about what happened in there?'

He was trying to be considerate.

'I didn't reveal any truth at all, Tom ... I denied I had been in the store-room. I must say Gilbert carried himself very well – he let nothing slip.'

'But how did you explain your flight?'

'I turned that to advantage. I said that during the play's interval the Baron had sought me out and accused me of embarrassing him – that we'd had a fierce quarrel – and he had threatened me with violence. So much that I was fearful for my safety. That was when I told Mr Hector of the attempted rape.'

'The assault at your lodgings?'

'Yes – there I spoke the absolute truth – as I did to you and Will.'

Tom was becoming confused. Was Sally telling the truth about her lies – or lying about her truths?

'So, how is it that the story has gone around about you and the Baron in the store-room?'

Momentary alarm showed in her eyes:

'Merely gossip! I know there has been chattering among the actors – they can be such a silly bunch. Petty jealousies, nothing more.'

'But this was more than gossip, Sally. It was a public pronouncement – at a Reformers' meeting on Tuesday night. You were not named, but it was openly declared that the Baron was stabbed during an assignation with an *actress* ... It was said with full confidence – as a thing known.'

'Well it cannot be *known!* – it's a fiction.'

'But it happens to be true ... *Partly* true, at least.'

Tom was becoming exasperated by the slipperiness of all this. He despaired of ever getting a clear picture from her.

There was now anger in her eyes:

'Then one of you four must have revealed it! You gave your word to me – and I trusted you!'

This talk of *trust* was extraordinary, and Tom was about to give her the full force of his indignation ... But something stopped him. He recalled what Will had said about the accusation at the Reformers' meeting – that when Arthur Bedford spoke of the discovery of the Baron's body there had been absolute certainty – and *physical particulars* of the scene ... Tom's next words were thoughtful ones:

'It did not come from any of us, I assure you.'

'Do you swear it?'

'I swear to you! ... but the gentleman was categorical in what he said.'

'Who was this *gentleman?*'

'That I cannot say – not yet.'

Tom hesitated. A thought had germinated: did the Reverend Bedford have his own informant? *Is that why he was so certain?* Tom caught a flicker of doubt in Sally's eyes – as if the implication had alarmed her. It gave him pause. Might a second person have been involved?

He wondered how hard he should press – these were delicate matters. But there was one thing he knew he must confront her with – a question that would soon be raised by someone else:

'You ask me to advise you, Sally – and you know there's only one answer ... I think you should tell the whole truth.'

She rounded on him:

'Ah, the *whole truth* – how sweetly the words fall from your lips! But how can you say that – when you think I killed him? Yes, I've known all along you have suspected me, and now you want me to deliver myself up and confess. Is that it?'

'No, no!'

Tom shook his head violently as if desperate to drive away his doubts.

'You have heard the truth from me already, Tom – in Holborn. Every detail of the scene! Must I re-live it all again for you?'

She reached out a hand to him, but then drew it back. Tom pressed on:

'But could you not tell the Magistrate exactly what you told Will and me?'

'Do you not see, Tom? How can I possibly tell him – when *you* can't make yourself believe me?'

'I do believe you! But ...'

A fatal hesitation stopped him.

'There you are! You cannot bring yourself to do so. And yet you want me to lay myself bare to the Justice? What justice am I like to find, do you think?'

Their conversation was slipping into suspicion and recrimination, and he was not having the better of the exchanges. His own hypocrisy was being laid bare. He expected her to reveal all, but was himself being guarded and secretive.

Ashamed of himself, Tom thought quickly. Sally had sought his help, and he was failing her. Even worse, he had lapsed into an unspoken accusation. Widow Trotter was right: he must trust Sally with what they had learned. He owed it to her to make the bigger picture clearer: who her accusers might be, and what their agenda.

'Listen, Sally! I owe you an apology. I've not been entirely open with you – none of us has! We have very little time ... You need to know what position your accusers are likely to be taking ...'

As briefly and clearly as he could, Tom began telling her what they had learned of the two factions in the Society for the Reformation of Manners, and how the Baron's killing was being exploited. He set out the battle-lines and found himself referring to the 'Reformers' and the 'Zealots'.

'So far, Sally, the Reformers have had the better of it: the Solicitor-General has been looking to place all the blame on the company – a rotten system that cries out for reform.'

'I see the picture … Well, you've solved one mystery: why Mr Hector seemed not to want the truth from me. He already had his explanation and was determined to hold onto it. Is that why he didn't browbeat me?'

'Yes. We think he has been instructed to protect Tunbridge's reputation – the Queen's champion! The Baron must not be allowed to tarnish the reforms! No doubt Mr Hector was mightily relieved that the story you told was manageable. I suspect the arrest of Christopher Rich had been in their minds from the beginning. From what we hear, they are still building a case against him – by foul means, not fair.'

Sally shook her head:

'What games these men are playing! They have no respect for the truth.'

'Yes, and the game is a fierce one. How they question you will reveal their hand – you'll see which cause this magistrate serves. He may be under instructions from the Solicitor-General as Mr Hector was – but it's more likely this new step comes from the Zealots. They are determined to hunt down the Baron and expose him.'

'So, they *wish* me to accuse him? …'

It was an awkward question. Tom kept thoughtfully silent.

'… In that case – do I give them what they want? I assure you I could paint them a sordid picture.'

Tom could see in her eyes how tempting that might be:

'We are back to the big question, Sally – the truth about you and Lord Tunbridge … I hesitate to say more – and it's for you to decide … forgive me … but at our last interview Gilbert intimated that what you had suffered in the storeroom was more than a humiliating assault. Gilbert was determined that the nature of the Baron's violence should be known. He told me it had been … a violent rape … Forgive me, Sally! …'

Those last hesitant words suddenly broke down her defences. After all the control she had been showing – all that self-discipline – this was too much.

She began shaking, and the sobs came surging out:

'Yes – yes – yes – he *raped* me! … Are you satisfied now? Are you *all* satisfied? … But I didn't kill him! – I swear to you – on my soul. I didn't kill him!'

'I believe you, Sally.'

Chapter Thirty-Six

DECKED IN HER exotic robes, the Indian Queen looked down on the coffee-room and met the eyes of Widow Trotter. The doyenne of the Bay-Tree was in need of reassurance, and somehow, above the wigs and through the ripples of pipe-smoke, Mrs Bracegirdle was providing it. The actress's smile was confident, her brow inquisitive and ready to welcome whatever was approaching. Don't despair, the figure was saying – be prepared for it. This royal lady wore her feathers and pearls flamboyantly with as much grace as the awkward artist had allowed her. It was not an elegant representation: the line of the shoulders was quite wrong, the arm twisted down unconvincingly, and the 'pearls' were so huge they must be made of wood ... and yet ... enshrined beneath her gay parasol, she was declaring that theatre was a great adventure not confined to the boards of a stage – that it promised a thrilling journey to anyone with an imagination – anyone prepared to look for the gold dust amongst the sawdust.

Mary Trotter was doing just that, searching for some hope to cling onto after an evening of shock and dismay. Yet it had all begun so well. Tom's Prologue had caught the mood of defiance, and *The Tender Courtesan* had dizzied everyone with a whirligig of emotions, only to fling them back from its world of romance to the distressingly real. When that final grim tableau appeared, the audience knew the stage had been violated – that it could offer no respite from the pain and death the curtain usually held at bay.

At the end of the performance, what should have been a joyous celebration had become huddles of commiseration and conjecture, and parties had dispersed uneasily. The words 'first night' were on no-one's lips, since for this production the first would surely be the last. Nothing was said to Pinkerman, but it was being assumed that for the remainder of the Fair, *The Devil on Two Sticks* would fill the void and the Dutch dancing dogs be given more exercise than usual.

Tom Bristowe's return to the Bay-Tree darkened the mood still further, and as he walked up to the bar, Mrs Trotter saw the ill tidings in his look. The Indian Queen with her encouraging smile became once more just a framed picture. Over in the corner of the room Will had been lingering in the hope that his friend might bring some positive news, and he too guessed the omens must be bad.

But there was a lot to discuss, and decisions needed to be made. And so, disregarding the curiosity buzzing all around her, the Field-General of the Bay-Tree guided her two young men through the kitchen door, placed an order for hot chocolate and cinnamon toast, and settled them at her parlour table. After an extraordinary opening day of the Fair, alone in each other's company they could finally pool their stock of news.

From the first, Tom's account of the scene he had just left turned dismay into horror. Hearing Dr Radcliffe's diagnosis, they found themselves contemplating nothing less than a second murder. What had sent *The Tender Courtesan* veering off into a Bacchic frenzy was evidently not the primal spirit of theatre but the Spanish Fly, and Gilbert Angell had been the chosen victim.

'I can't think it a coincidence,' said Tom. 'Gilbert told me he was determined to bring matters to a crisis. During *The Devil on Two Sticks* tomorrow he was going to denounce the Baron – shame him publicly! It was to be his *moment*, he said.'

'You mean he planned to announce it from the stage?'

'Yes, Mrs T. There was a wildness in his eyes when he told me, so perhaps the Fly was already having an effect. But something else had disturbed him ...'

Tom told them about the obscene drawing found in the actors' shed, and how this had fired Gilbert's anger.

Will gave a low whistle:

'So, you think the poisoning was intended to silence him?'

'I do – but of course it was a terrible risk and put the whole company in danger. That's why I'm wondering if the phial was also tainted – with a lethal dose. It would then look as if Gilbert had been the victim of a larger accident.'

'That's a chilling idea,' said Widow Trotter. 'You have to wonder about the mind behind this ... We can't say we haven't been expecting something of the sort – there have been premonitions enough ... the Reverend Bedford?'

She paused, wondering if this was the moment to tell them of Mr Denniston's revelations – but she held off.

'Well, it's in character,' said Will. 'There's a calculating imagination here: the Cantharides and the obscene drawing were both aimed at the company. And someone has been observing them closely.'

'The drawing was a caricature, but yes, it caught them – and named them ... Gilbert's was an especially exaggerated image. It infuriated him!'

'Could anyone have overheard Gilbert while he was showing it to you?'

'Quite possibly, Mrs T. He was talking recklessly, and there were men within earshot. A lot of hammering was going on.'

Will had begun to frown. His own thoughts were turning to Sally and her place in this sordid drama. Surely Gilbert hadn't planned to expose her in front of the booth audience?

'Did Sally know of Gilbert's threat?' he asked. 'Remember how she swore us to secrecy, Tom! And she insisted to me that the Baron had not been her lover.'

'Yes, and she reminded me of that just now.'

'Just now? You've been talking with her?'

Tom felt an uncomfortable tightening of the stomach:

'Yes, I left her at the booth not half an hour ago. We had some heart-felt exchanges before … It's not easy to tell you this, Will, but we knew the threat of arrest was hanging over her – and … well …'

'My God, they've arrested her?'

Tom nodded:

'Yes, Toby Mudge called to say a Magistrate was on his way. Sally was naturally fearful, and so I slipped away with her for a few minutes and tried to reassure her. She needed to quieten her thoughts.'

'I should have been there!'

'Yes, Will – I wish to God you had been! – But all this came on us so quickly. The two of us walked over to Price's waxworks and were able to talk in private …'

'So, they've come for her!'

Will was clearly shocked and rose from his chair as if the call to arms had sounded. But he could only stand there helplessly, his eyes scanning the room. The whiff of a prison cell was in his nostrils.

At once Widow Trotter was on her feet in sympathy. She reached over for the decanter of madeira on the sideboard:

'I think we should hear what Tom has to say. The picture may not be as dark as we imagine.'

She motioned to Will, and he sat down again while she

filled the glasses and set them on the table. He tried to settle himself as Tom began the account of his interview with Sally. What followed was a deeply uncomfortable few minutes. They all knew her arrest would bring matters to a head. It gave another painful twist to the drama of the evening.

Tom offered a careful summary of what he had learned from her and from his earlier encounter with Gilbert. It seemed the Baron's relations with the two young actors had been closer than they thought – that he had felt able to suggest they act as his informers.

At this, Will and Mrs Trotter let out an exclamation. And an even louder one came when they heard of Gilbert's discovery that Lord Tunbridge already had an informer in the company – and that he could identify the man …

Widow Trotter's ears tingled, and again her thoughts turned to Arthur Bedford – not yet, she told herself …

'Dangerous knowledge, Tom!' said Will. 'Especially when you declare it loudly in a public place – *reckless* is the word!'

'Yes. I suppose it was the Spanish Fly. But Gilbert was being deliberately provoking – and he told me more about Sally. He was in an incendiary mood …'

Tom broke off and picked up his glass with a sigh.

'… Oh dear! I wish there was something bright and hopeful I could tell you – but everything I learned seems to darken the picture …'

He ran a hand through his hair and his head sank to his chest. The words came out as factually as he could make them:

'… At her first questioning by Mr Hector, Sally had said nothing about the Baron's assault in the property-store – in fact she swore to him she had never been in there. But when I asked Gilbert, he revealed that in truth Sally had been subjected to a full and brutal *rape*. I put this to her, and she acknowledged it to be true.'

'Tom! ...'

Will's eyes were blazing.

'... How could you! A rape? The poor girl must have felt it like an accusation – and a shaming one at that! You *put it to her?* – We speak like that in Westminster Hall!'

'I'm sure you handled it more delicately?' said Widow Trotter. 'These matters are not to be spoken lightly – and given Sally's position ... How did she take it?'

Tom's eyes were closed. He was finding it hard to speak.

Will persisted:

'You say she *acknowledged* it? – I can't believe she spoke calmly. Was this *reassuring* her? You are usually so thoughtful about these things, Tom. I hardly credit what I'm hearing.'

'I *was* thoughtful, Will – *I was!* But time was pressing, and I didn't prepare the ground as I should have done. But once I asked the question the truth poured out of her – and I think she felt something of relief. And I know it *was* the truth! ...'

Tom's eyes were now wide open and glittering with moistness.

'... *Sally did not kill Lord Tunbridge!* There was no acting there – her sobs were genuine, and I believed her totally.'

Mrs Trotter and Will looked at each other. Neither shook their head, but both knew they were watching a confused young man who longed for certainty.

'And is that how you left it? With Sally drying her eyes and trying to recompose herself?'

'No, Will, no! Please don't accuse me! I've made it sound heartless – but it truly wasn't. Had you been there you would have seen how the air cleared ... She cried, I admit – but I'm sure it was with relief. And in the end – when she thought of poor Gilbert and what he'd been urging on her – she told me she would tell the complete truth to the Magistrate.'

'Really? And what is the *complete* truth?'

'Very much what she told us at Holborn – but that it had been a *violent* encounter – and that she had fled the store-room when the Baron appeared to have some kind of seizure.'

Widow Trotter was looking doubtful:

'How much better if she had told the truth from the beginning! This change of tune will not do her any favours. They will want to know why she had lied about being in the store-room.'

'But while we walked back to the booth, I suggested she could exploit that. She could say that at the first interview she had told Mr Hector only what she thought he wished to hear – that she had been given to understand that Lord Tunbridge must not be implicated in anything criminal.'

Mrs Trotter was now beaming at him:

'This would set the two factions at loggerheads – very neat!'

'Sally is an intelligent young woman,' said Will.

'And she can be very persuasive,' added Tom.

Here were a few crumbs of comfort; and, as if to solemnise the moment, they set to work on the cinnamon toast which had been languishing untouched in front of them.

Widow Trotter replenished their glasses and readied them for the things she had learned around Adèle Ménage's tea-table that afternoon.

Her story lifted their spirits a little. They saw that in Mr Denniston's friend, *Secretary to His Grace the Duke*, they had nothing less than their own informer. Amidst all the bad news this was a stroke of good fortune; and while they listened to the revelations about Arthur Bedford's activities, they sensed the wind turning in their favour.

'The man is a master conspirator!' concluded Tom in wonderment.

Will nodded:

'Yes, we smiled at his emperor's profile, did we not? – But

it's clear he has imperial *ambitions* too – he's even lording it over the Duke!'

'And he has London and Canterbury on his side ...'

Widow Trotter looked mystified.

'... The Bishop and the Archbishop, Mrs T! Uncle Jack says the two prelates are taking a strong line against the playhouse and are for closing it down. For them it's a way of hitting back at the Court.'

'I think this counts as a grand conspiracy, don't you?' said Will. 'And it seems our Mr Bedford is directing matters.'

'And so far, much has gone to plan. All they need is for the Queen to act. Revoking the Patent requires only the stroke of a pen, and it will surely tempt her. She must be angry at the way her reforms are being frustrated. The Reverend Bedford and his allies must think they are only minutes from success.'

'After all, they are promising her a virtuous nation – a people closer to God!'

A look of concern showed on Widow Trotter's face:

'In that case, is Sally about to hand them the victory? This will be yet another playhouse scandal.'

Will nodded reluctantly:

'Much depends on how it's exploited. Another sordid revelation could sink the theatre entirely, and it's hardly possible to blacken Lord Tunbridge without damaging the Theatre Royal – its very name is becoming an embarrassment. The Reformers will trumpet this as a famous victory – just think how they'll celebrate!'

'But perhaps that gives us some hope?' said Tom. 'After all, if the theatre is closed, which of the parties do you think is going to claim the triumph? Who are the people who will be lording it over this god-fearing realm?'

'It will be the Whigs, will it not?'

'Exactly, Mrs T! – The low-church people. That's why the

Queen, at heart, favours reform over abolition. She wants a virtuous stage rather than no stage at all.'

'And of course, it was her Uncle Charles's company ...'

She stopped in her tracks. They had begun to notice how restless her eyes had become, as if she were looking for something to hold onto.

'... But this is all high politics, gentlemen. As high as they go! I'm sure these lofty matters are very important – but we have to bring our minds back to practical things. *What are we going to do?* ...'

There was mounting frustration in her voice. She sat back in her chair and raised her arms to her two young friends.

'... In particular, what are we going to do *tomorrow?* There is so much we've discovered these past few days. We know how these plotters are working – we know about Merlin and the Red Cross Knight and how Arthur Bedford is organising them – we know their aims and understand their motives – we know what outrages they are prepared to commit. Everything is in place ... And yet events are always outrunning us!

'And tomorrow will surely threaten yet more? *The Devil on Two Sticks* will be a mighty provocation to *the righteous*. Just think of it! – a satire that dares to bring a devil on the stage! What spells will he have? What revelations? Accusations? Surely our plotters cannot let this piece succeed? If *The Tender Courtesan* raised hackles, just think how the *Devil* will fire their anger.'

Tom was warming to her enthusiasm:

'You're right, Mrs T. We must put something in train. We have to see tomorrow as the catastrophe – the decisive scene when the plot will reach its crisis, for good or ill ...'

His face broke into a half-smile.

'... I can picture the look of satisfaction on Arthur Bedford's face at this moment. Do you think he's planning some ingenious climax to his scheme?'

'Yes, Tom … and what he doesn't know – mustn't know – is that we three have laid a scheme of our own!'

Will swallowed:

'Have we?'

His mouth was open. He looked at Tom for reassurance – his friend was still smiling.

'Ah, Will! I suspect our Field-General here is challenging us to come up with a plan for the morrow. Am I right, Mrs T? We must think of Marlborough on the eve of Blenheim!'

Will tried to do just that, but the picture wouldn't hold.

'We can't afford to be spectators anymore, gentlemen,' said Widow Trotter. 'We have to play a part ourselves! Tomorrow's performance will be at 8 – a night-time affair. There will be uncertain light in the darkness. This will be dangerous, but it will give us opportunities too. Let us put our heads together …'

Chapter Thirty-Seven

BY THE TIME the parlour door opened to reveal Elias Cobb's inquiring face, Widow Trotter and her friends had begun to assemble a plan of sorts. It was only when the constable had settled down and made himself easy with a glass of his favourite claret that it grew into something that might count as a *scheme*.

None of them expected Elias's news to be cheering, and it wasn't. He told how Sally had been led away from Pinkerman's booth by two of the officers to be questioned elsewhere, and his demand to accompany her had been bluntly refused. This Magistrate, Mr Grimston (a name that didn't bode well), made it clear that his instructions were firm on the matter; and as for Gilbert's death, he regarded it as a consequence of the May Fair's poisonous character and hardly something to demand a thorough investigation. Elias suspected the man thought a measure of Justice had already been done.

'Of course, it didn't help that Mr Grimston and his cohort had been chased out of the Fair this very morning! He was sporting a black eye and sore back to prove it ...'

Sensing the general disappointment, Elias reached into his waistcoat pocket and pulled out a sealed note.

'... Perhaps this will deliver something more encouraging,

Mr Lundy? I picked it up from the coffee-room just now. It is directed to you at the Bay-Tree.'

Immediately Will's face lit up:

'Ah! Then I know what it must be. I gave the Reverend Tysoe this address – I suggested a meeting. If this is his reply, then it comes to hand perfectly.'

'Mr Tysoe?' said Tom in wonderment.

'Open it!' said Mrs Trotter.

Will did so, and an amused smile began to light up his face:

'I have to say the gentleman writes very much in character. He is eager to continue *our discourse* – and is flattered to believe that I will continue to *manifest* that interest in the work of the Society that he *perceived* in me on Sunday … ah! And he hopes … I'm not sure about this …'

'About what?'

'He *fondly* hopes that I may shortly become *an ornament to the Society for the Reformation of Manners, as I shall surely be to the legal profession*. What do you say to that?'

'I feel you are mocking him a little, Mr Lundy?' said Elias. Is this a meeting you have been seeking?'

'Yes indeed – and his reply has been immediate. It exhibits an immoderate eagerness on his part, verging on enthusiasm. He wishes to meet me at the Garter Coffee House in Jermyn Street, at eleven tomorrow.'

'But this is perfect!' said Tom brightly. 'Just as you hoped. Are you sure you are ready to carry it through? …'

Tom looked at Mrs Trotter:

'… It seems Will's encounter with Mr Tysoe can now be a confirmed part of our scheme?'

'Yes – I can see it fitting our plans very neatly.'

Elias Cobb began to feel he had come late to the party:

'What *scheme* may this be, Mrs Trotter? You all sound

remarkably like conspirators. Am I right in thinking you intend to be off on campaign again?'

'Not just we three, Elias! – Our scheme for tomorrow is a *five-fold* one – and this is not the most daring element of it ...'

The word "daring" made the constable's nostrils twitch – and they were about to twitch even more.

'... No – I think that part is reserved for you ... Yes, my old friend, you have a role to play! And we have already decided what your contribution is to be ...'

Elias Cobb knew that look of hers and what it portended. He had little choice but to listen to instructions.

'... We are convinced it is all to happen tomorrow – so there is no time to lose. We cannot wait on events any longer but have to bring them to their crisis ... Let me recharge your glasses, gentlemen, and then we can set out our plans for the constable. We trust you'll approve, Elias!'

While Widow Trotter played the hostess, he took a deep breath and without thinking delved into his coat pocket for his favourite pipe. A sharp glance reminded him that the parlour was her domain and that only enticing aromas from the kitchen were permitted ... And so, he sat back in a posture of attention. He was familiar with what he thought of as her managerial manner.

'Over recent days we've uncovered so much, have we not, Elias?'

'Yours is a first-rate team, Constable Trotter – none better!'

'Well, today has supplied more of the picture. You need to know how we stand at present, and what we are faced with ...'

After the briefest of preambles – and with the help of Tom and Will – she regaled Elias with an account of the day's discoveries. It was a tale of spying, blackmail, and poisoning, and for all his sturdiness, the constable felt a little shaken by it. It certainly seemed there was an organised plot in train:

'What stratagems, eh!'

Tom nodded:

'Yes, Mr Cobb. *Treasons, stratagems and spoils!* This reaches as far as the Queen herself and threatens to have high political consequences.'

'I have to say the story you give is distinctly credible. This Mr Bedford is a Machiavellian plotter. He has found so much power in only a few weeks!'

'Yes, he's in favour among the great – and he seems to have unlimited resources to call on.'

'And he has something of a playful imagination,' added Will. 'It's a strange thing to say, but it's as if the man is amusing himself – toying with people and inventing scenes.'

'So, you are convinced these people have a plan?'

'Do you not think so, Elias?'

'I do, Molly. And from what you say, tonight Pinkerman's booth is to become his theatre again.'

'A frightening thought, and we've had dark hints of it. We must be ready to meet their plan with one of our own.'

Elias acknowledged all three of them:

'I agree … Now what is this scheme of yours? You must set it out for me. I'm all agog.'

'There are five of us, Elias – and each has a job to do …'

'Five?'

'Yes … the fifth is Lord Melksham. The plot reaches high, and so we need to reach high ourselves.'

Tom picked up the explanation:

'Uncle Jack has promised to call on the Queen's Solicitor-General tomorrow.'

'Sir James Montagu?'

'Yes, Mr Cobb. The two of them are only slenderly acquainted – but my uncle's business has dealings with the Solicitor-General's office, and it would be quite natural for him to call.'

Suddenly the constable glimpsed how Court power worked:

'Well, I have to say, as the pinnacle of your scheme this has much to be said for it! Has His Lordship received his *brief?*'

He glanced at the lawyerly Will, who was following the exchanges with fascination.

'Yes, Mr Cobb – Tom and I talked with him after the play tonight. Lord Melksham was deeply shocked at events and wondered if there was anything practical he could do. We suggested he might warn Montagu of our suspicions – that the theatre company is the victim of a carefully-laid plot – one that is part of a larger fanatic conspiracy that threatens the social order ... the Maypole business being part of it.'

Elias whistled:

'But should Lord Melksham reveal everything? Wouldn't that ...'

'No no! Mr Cobb – it might be dangerous at this stage. No, rather than offer our full evidence, we thought he should raise the *suspicion* with Montagu – nothing more. He should urge him to confront Mr Hector about the matter immediately and ask him *if he has wind of such a plot?* ... The magistrate couldn't then simply dismiss the idea. It would raise doubts – and feed his own suspicions too.'

'Ah! A cunning move. You mean to use Montagu to put pressure on Mr Hector, then?'

'More than that,' said Mrs Trotter. 'As you'll see!'

Elias was intrigued:

'Excellent, Molly! Your scheme is taking shape ... Tysoe – Montagu – what is the third part of it?'

'That's Charles Denniston and his good friend Mr Pomery – our very own informer, or so we think him. Tomorrow morning I shall call at Mr Denniston's Fancy Shop in Katherine Street for another talk. After our tea-table conversation he promised to see if his friend had learned anything further about Arthur Bedford.'

'By your account, they have every reason to fear Bedford – and to want him stopped.'

It was Tom who replied:

'It brings us very close to him, Mr Cobb, and to the workings of that malicious mind. We hope Bedford will betray himself in some way – who knows?'

Mrs Trotter added:

'And I want Mr Pomery to understand the violence of the conspiracy, and what we are facing. As secretary he still has the Duke's ear, and Arthur Bedford must fear him for what he might know. He could be a useful ally.'

'Well, you've tracked Bedford onto his home ground, and that's important – a man's trail is always busiest there, and harder to conceal. I have high hopes of this Mr Pomery!'

Elias was warming to the task and eager to hear more:

'And the fourth part? I suspect Mr Bristowe here won't sit twiddling his thumbs?'

'Nor shall he, Elias! Yes, Tom has a task to perform – a double one in fact …

The first will take him back to Mr Price's waxworks.'

'I know the chance is slim, Mr Cobb – but something may come of the apprentice Francis. I set him to observe during *The Tender Courtesan*. Who knows what a sharp-eyed young fellow with a sketch-book will have noticed?'

The constable beamed:

'There'll soon be nothing more to teach you, Mr Bristowe! This is an ingenious idea. One observant individual can be worth a dozen clumsy officers.'

'And we discovered he likes to sketch around the playhouse.'

'Better and better! Speaking for myself, if I wanted a witness, I would always choose a spectator – someone not involved in the action. An observer often gives a truer picture – they tend to see the details in a scene.'

'Well, nothing may come of it – but Mr Price told me Francis has something he wishes to show me. So I have hopes.'

'And your other task, Mr Bristowe?'

'A walk over to Pall Mall to pay a call on the Pophams. Lavinia has been forbidden to attend tomorrow night's performance, but I need to talk with her about *The Devil on Two Sticks*. Pinkerman has been keeping it a strict secret. I'm sure it will help if we know something of what to expect.'

Widow Trotter lifted her glass and gave them all a look of deep satisfaction. It was not quite on the scale of Christopher Wren contemplating St Paul's, but had something of that character:

'So you see, Elias. We have a grand five-fold *scheme* for tomorrow morning. We each have a mission: Will is to meet with the Reverend Tysoe; Lord Melksham with the Solicitor-General; myself with Mr Denniston; Tom with Francis and Lavinia ...'

There was a pregnant silence until Elias felt obliged to speak:

'And now *my* fate is to be decided, eh? You spoke of it as a challenge. Well, I'm always ready to don my armour in your service, my Lady. I only hope it's not something both violent *and* illegal?'

'It is neither, Elias – you can rest easy. It merely involves some nicely-managed negotiation.'

'Negotiation? I'm no politician, Molly – but shall do my best for you. After all, it won't rank with establishing peace in Europe, will it?'

'Hardly that – just an exchange of common sense, and finding a common interest – and of course holding a large cudgel behind your back.'

'Ah yes – in all negotiations it's best to keep something in reserve. May I ask who will be facing me in the lists?'

'Our Magistrate, Mr Hector of course.'

'What! …'

The constable's jovial chivalry melted away. He contemplated the three unsmiling faces and saw this was no game.

'… That intolerable man? Well, he certainly has all the *political* arts …'

Elias growled out the word.

'… . But will he do anything other than show me the door before I've even sat down? I think he regards me and my kind with contempt.'

'This is where the *cudgel* comes in, Elias …'

Widow Trotter was speaking in a quiet but determined voice.

'… There are things that Mr Hector doesn't know but needs to. Particularly the truth about the Reverend Arthur Bedford. To judge from the Reformers' meeting that Will attended, the two men are at daggers drawn, so you can exploit this – thanks to what *you know* … thanks to *your investigations* …'

Elias noted the pronoun.

'… You might be able to convince Mr Hector that on the matter of Arthur Bedford you are holding scandal at bay – that you have uncovered a potentially serious crime – one that involves the zealots in the Society for the Reformation of Manners and threatens to embarrass Her Majesty and compromise her reforming plans for the theatre. That is no small threat.'

'Ahh!'

The constable endowed the little word with considerable expressiveness.

'At the same time, you might be able to *help* Mr Hector understand how outrageously the Reverend Arthur Bedford has overstepped the mark – and how beneficial it would be for all parties if he and his plots were sent packing back to Bristol … Bristol is a fair city, but it needs to account for its own …'

By this time, Tom and Will were all attention. It was like observing a watchmaker at work.

'... And so, you will have a cudgel in one hand, and a jewelled casket in the other.'

'Ah yes – a threat and a gift!'

'Exactly ...'

Constable Cobb almost flushed at the thought. This was not the kind of engagement he was practised in, and he could see its difficulties starkly. But there was an element of heroic venturing that appealed to him.

'... This will be the culmination of our scheme, Elias, do you see? ... While Lord Melksham is urging Sir James Montagu to consult Mr Hector as a matter of urgency – you, Elias, will be reversing the play by urging Mr Hector to report immediately to Sir James. Each man will then confirm the other's suspicions. With events moving so swiftly, I suspect Mr Hector will not wish to be left in no-man's-land.'

Will was lost in admiration – the legal entanglements in Westminster Hall were as nothing to this:

'If only our politicians could be as far-sighted, Mrs T!'

'This really does constitute a scheme,' said Tom. 'Indeed, it almost counts as a *master-plan*.'

'We may not be able to carry it out in full, of course. But I think there is a clarity of design about it ... But we shall also be at the mercy of events, gentlemen. Something unforeseen may throw us off the track. However, I'm confident we at least have a scheme.'

There were smiles of assent all round, and four glasses were raised to the big adventure on the morrow.

Tom set down his glass and leaned forward:

'I've been thinking, Mrs T ... Can we precipitate events further? You mentioned the crisis – well, I have an idea that might work for us – though it is hazardous and involves a *deception* ...'

The word did not have the negative effect Tom was anticipating.

'Say on, Tom!' said Will encouragingly. 'We are faced with so much deception from our enemies that it would be good to meet them on equal terms.'

'My thought is … might we be able to draw Mr Bedford into a trap? Thus far he has succeeded in keeping himself out of the picture – he's Mr Cobb's 'spectator' *par excellence!* The man seems to be a silent observer, a role he clearly prefers. But could we perhaps draw him out of the shadows?'

Widow Trotter's curiosity was caught:

'How might we do that, Tom?'

'I'm thinking of an urgent note from the Red Cross Knight …'

'Aha! From our mystery spy in the theatre! – Might this flush Bedford out, do you think?'

'I'm not sure – the aim would be to bring him to Pinkerman's booth …'

Will gave a low whistle. This was certainly taking a chance – a very slim one.

'… and I'm wondering if this could somehow be managed through Mr Pomery?'

'I see, Tom … you mean a request from Bedford's informer to meet with him – urgently.'

'Exactly – mentioning *The Devil on Two Sticks* and saying that there has to be a last-minute change of plan.'

'A note from his informer! But would Bedford not be suspicious? The handwriting?'

'Yes, that's a difficulty.'

They thought for a moment, then Will spoke:

'It's a narrow chance, but those anonymous notes – are they not likely to have been written by our informer at the playhouse?'

'Do you mean one like this? …'

Elias delved deep into one of his pockets and extracted a crumpled piece of paper.

'... This is one of the notes Mr Rich received a while ago – I was given it when I fancied I was collecting evidence. It's not much to look at.'

Indeed it was a sad scrap that made its threats in a crabbed, inelegant hand – thankfully not capitals.

'I think this will do, Elias,' said Mrs Trotter. 'I really believe this is a chance we might take. How is your penmanship, Will?'

'Not as untidy as this – but the thing appears to be in the man's natural hand, such as it is. I could certainly have a go. It might work – *if* he is the Red Cross Knight.'

'Good – then let us gather the materials, and you can set about it. Meanwhile, we ought to consider what we'll do if by some miracle the trick succeeds ...'

And so, the unlikely plan was hatched, and the final element of their grand scheme put in place for the morning. After the repeated shocks and frustrations of the past fortnight the Bay-Tree militia were longing for action, and Friday would certainly provide it. Each of them had their respective tasks – difficult interviews of investigation and persuasion, of urging, coaxing and cajoling. The four had agreed to gather at the Bay-Tree at four o'clock on the morrow in the hope that each would have something to tell. And if Tom dined in Pall Mall he might be able to report on what his uncle had achieved with Sir James Montagu.

Twenty minutes later the truant Mrs Trotter made her way back into the coffee-room and was reassured to observe life going quietly on. It was late, and the heartbeat of the place had slowed to the ticking of the tall oak clock. A few customers were sitting quietly and chatting in low tones, and even the rustle of newspapers had ceased. It was at moments like this that she understood how important the chocolate house was to her. It seemed a living character whose moods shifted with the hours of the day. With so much enmity, fear and violence elsewhere, it was good to know that this was her space, and that it offered something of value to others too. It might have settled into a quiet tempo just now, but in a few hours' time it would burst into noise and life – a place of hot news, mysterious rumours, lively scandals, and some tenacious verbal tussles.

No, the Bay-Tree was no retreat. It was a place for thoughts to be lifted and minds to be re-charged.

Friday

7 May 1708

Chapter Thirty-Eight

THE GARTER COFFEE House in Jermyn Street gave an immediate impression of seriousness. It was not, Will thought, the kind of place where people dropped by or popped their heads cheerily round the door. This particular door, in fact, was considerably heavier than the Bay-Tree's, and it opened reluctantly with a warning tinkle. Sober faces looked up as if they had been interrupted. Will immediately registered the broad oak timbers of the floor. The roof beams were solid too, held up by a pair of supporting pillars that lent the place a sturdy and reliable character. It was quite extensive and shunned snugness: the fire looked particularly well behaved. The bar, rather than projecting in a hospitable way, was set into the far wall, and tables were partitioned off discreetly around the side. The Garter was undoubtedly a place for more private conversations.

To judge from the smell there was serious coffee here, with none of the Bay-Tree's more capricious possibilities. At the centre of the room a reading-table for newspapers had several chairs set around it; the walls carried announcements and notices of meetings; and alongside the bar a set of shelves displayed orderly ranks of volumes that looked like reports and books of reference. In character the Garter was altogether tidy, quiet, and plain. It offered everything needful.

Will hesitated. He was a little early, and this was not the kind of place where you joined a chattering group and took your chance with wit. He doubted the place had seen banter for a decade. But now that he was inside, there was nothing for it but to stride up to the bar. No hostess was there to greet him with smiling eyes and silk lappets swaying, but a very different figure. Conscious of the awkwardness, Will placed his penny before a respectable gentleman in a silk neckerchief who smiled politely and spoke quietly:

'Tuppence, Sir.'

Will was taken aback. The place had broken rank. Will supposed this was one way of discouraging the crowds; and no doubt its select clientele was happy with its lack of charm. In any case, it struck him that affability was not something the place would sanction.

Will placed a second penny against the first, and at once an unoccupied recess was politely indicated:

'Mr Tysoe is in a meeting, Sir, but will no doubt be here promptly.'

More curious still. Was this a kind of club? If so, it was a strange one, given that it seemed to cultivate the uncongenial. This *garter* was clearly not a feminine accoutrement but had reference to a token of masculine distinction.

Fortunately Will did not need to sit in silent puzzlement for long. Exactly at eleven o'clock a door in the corner of the room opened, and the Reverend Ebenezer Tysoe appeared with two sober-suited men, who nodded and promptly took their leave.

The look on Mr Tysoe's face indicated that the meeting had not gone well. He waved one arm at the coffee-boy who had been standing to attention by the fire, and reached over to Will with the other. They shook hands as he sat down. The man was tense and troubled:

'I meet continual frustrations, William! I declare that a

"Board of Governors" is the most sluggish of bodies – forever *considering, inquiring,* and *consulting!* It can never be brought to a decision. I am being blocked at every turn ...'

He looked into Will's face and met an open, relaxed expression and a pair of trusting eyes that gleamed at him from under full, light brown hair. Each feature registered and gave him pause. At once he became easier:

'... Ah, well – I'm so pleased we can continue our talk, William. I trust that your father and your aunts are all well? Such estimable people!'

'Indeed, Sir – they are the worthiest of models ... But I'm sorry to hear that barriers are being placed in your way. I take it this concerns your work for the Charity Schools?'

'Yes – it is a continued battle with our nation's establishment. There is so much suspicion about ends and questioning of motives. I can make little progress ... I suspect their own motives are not of the purest!'

Will enjoyed the incongruity, and the naivety tempted him:

'Yes, Mr Tysoe, Charity must surely be allowed to flow freely? – After all, it is an aspect of Divine Grace, is it not? Its fount is in Heaven ... but forgive me – I'm presuming too much ...'

'Not at all, William! Not at all! You say very true – and you put it beautifully. Charity *overflows,* and from them that have much it trickles to those that have nothing. If only I could get these committee-men to understand as much! *Charity,* I tell them, is where Divine Grace meets human love. If we are to fight the Devil and his works, it must be through that.'

Will was astonished, and wondered if he had underestimated Mr Tysoe. Perhaps the man might respond to the human touch? – But he would have to be exceedingly careful and try to hold the conversation to the topic of the Reformation Society. He decided a note of confessional honesty might be effective:

'I must thank you again, Sir, for allowing me to attend your meeting on Tuesday. I have been thinking – thinking long and hard – about the matters discussed, and must confess I find some of them *deeply* troubling.'

Will stressed the word in a way that touched on something fundamental and heart-felt. Mr Tysoe felt the force of it and was drawn forwards in his seat:

'I did not wish the meeting to distress you, William. There were elements of the occasion that troubled me also. I fear that the divisions within the Society were all too manifest, and at times there was an absence of common purpose. We are all about the Lord's work, are we not? To witness such antagonisms was hateful.'

'What I hated, Mr Tysoe, was the current of violence that showed itself. I must say I found the Reverend Bedford's celebration of martyrdom very troubling and – can I say – not a little proud. I accept that *an eye for an eye* is a well-worn doctrine, but the new dispensation of Our Lord was surely to counteract the language of hatred and violence? I must be entirely open with you, Mr Tysoe – I believe the *Jealous God* is very much in contradiction to the God of *Love* ... but I am not practised in such theological niceties ...'

The look on the Reverend Tysoe's face was eloquent. This was no moment to stop.

'... On the matter of the maypole, Sir ... I was there in the Strand when it happened – not many yards away – and the scene was frightening in its violence. The man with the axe may have been a martyr; but there were hundreds of women and children thronging the place, and if the pole had come down, I dread to think what would have resulted. *Murder* cannot surely be God's work, Mr Tysoe? – not that of my Jesus, at least – who suffers little children ...'

Will broke off, allowing the *aposiopesis* its full effect.

Suddenly he felt a hand resting on his.

'Indeed he does, William! You must not blame yourself for being sensitive to such things. All religions have their soldiers and their healers – and you are a *healer!*'

Will sensed a slight healing pressure on his palm.

'The Society is a noble cause, Mr Tysoe. And I wish to do good – for my life to be an example to others – but I fall sadly short. I know what is right, but the *will* does not always master the *deed*.'

'There your heart is speaking, William. And that is *good*.'

Will felt it was now all or nothing:

'But during this past month, Sir … I have begun to attend *plays* – at the theatre. *Three* times. And I feel myself strangely drawn to the place. It is something new and dangerous. I know I have risked my very soul, have I not?'

The Reverend Tysoe felt the stain, and shuddered:

'Indeed, you have touched pitch, William … let us pray you have not been defiled!'

Will expected his hand to be released in distaste – but no. The Reverend Tysoe gripped the sinner more tightly, as if lifting him from the pit, and while he continued to speak Will felt the rhythmic pressure of each emphatic word:

'That theatre is the very *Citadel* of Evil, William! A *pest-house!* It is the place where Satan mocks humanity and plays his deadly games. You must *not* venture there again! Did not my sermon *imprint* it on your soul? Were my words not strong enough to pull you back from *that Hell?* I shall pray for you, William … but you must seek God's forgiveness yourself. The very air of the playhouse is *infectious* – such *unspeakable* crimes … For God's sake, William – and for the sake of your *soul* … Do not venture there! It is a place of *death*. A terrible *judgment* will come!'

Will's hand was beginning to ache.

'I hear it has already come, Sir – to the company at least … One of the actors, as I understand … dead – or dying. There has been another murder, over at the Fair.'

He felt Tysoe's hand stiffen like death.

'What is this? An actor – murdered at the Fair?'

'Yes, Mr Tysoe. It is the latest outrage – and it happened yesterday, in Pinkerman's booth.'

'Pinkerman's …'

Mr Tysoe broke off. He had gone white.

'… An actor, you say?'

'Yes, poor Mr Angell – the one who had that accident with the thunderbox.'

'*Gilbert?* …'

'I heard it at a chocolate house not an hour ago. The poor fellow was poisoned during a performance. It is not easy to say this, Sir, but accounts say the Society had a hand in it – some agent of theirs – a confederate of the axe-man perhaps …'

The Reverend Tysoe looked lost and was gazing silently into the distance.

'… I'm sorry to have startled you.'

'You say *dying*, William. What do you mean? Is the boy not dead?'

'No, but like to die within hours … It was poison. The actor was to take poison in the play, and somebody substituted the real thing. It seems Mr Angell had received a threatening letter cursing him in biblical terms …'

Will saw that the Reverend Tysoe's face was almost mask-like.

'… Could this have been one of the Reverend Bedford's soldiers in Christ, Sir? …'

He stopped, fearing this was a step too far – and suddenly his hand was released. But nothing was said.

Will spoke softly:

'... You are clearly troubled, Sir. Forgive me. I did not know this would touch your own heart so. It is a sad business altogether. Where will this end?'

'Where indeed? ... Oh William – I know not what to think. To meet wrong with wrong – evil with evil – cannot be right. The transgressor will be punished fearfully – but *by the Lord*, eternally. It is not for us to anticipate God's Justice ... I told Mr Angell he was in danger – I warned him!'

'Mr Tysoe ... was this a general warning? Or are you saying you knew of a plot at Pinkerman's booth?'

'The Fair is a damnable thing, William.'

'Yes, but ...'

'The poor, poor boy – I warned him!'

'Did you have wind of something, Mr Tysoe? I trust you were not party to any plan of violence? If so ...'

'No, no! And I made my views clear! But there are those in the Society who wish to drive matters to the utmost – to *push back* against Satan. The Fair is the Devil's own sanctuary ... and yet ...'

Will was becoming anxious. The reverend gentleman was falling apart.

'So, there is a plot against the Fair – against Pinkerman's company?'

'I have no particulars, William – but the thing has been discussed. Arthur Bedford has drawn up a plan ... But I have had no say in it. Indeed, my views are such as to keep me at a distance. Mr Bedford has his own lieutenants ... But where is Gilbert? – I should go to him!'

'Those lieutenants ...'

Will paused on the brink.

'... Might they be Merlin and the Red Cross Knight?'

'William! ... but how ... ?'

'I overheard their names when Mr Bedford talked with you after the meeting. I caught nothing further – except I think I heard him speak of *The Devil on Two Sticks* – am I right? The piece is to be presented at the Fair tonight ... Is there to be another killing?'

Will could hardly have put the matter more starkly.

'I cannot say. I have stepped back from the business.'

'Are these two men agents of the Society?'

'Not as such ... Red Cross is a theatre-man, and I think Merlin is working at the Fair. Please, William – you must not press me! All I know is they are Bedford's people. And he in turn works for the Duke – as I'm sure you know. He has other funds to call on ... But, William, why ... ?'

'Forgive me – *dear* Mr Tysoe. I do not want to give you pain – but too much hangs on this! I am convinced you are not a man of deceit and violence. I cannot bear to think of you as such! ... This has to be cleared between us ...'

Will reached out and held Tysoe's arm. The move was forceful rather than tender, and it gave his words the emphasis he needed:

'... I beg you, Sir, tell me – is there to be a further killing? ... or has another already taken place? Is Gilbert Angell the only victim? ... I am thinking of Lord Tunbridge. If the Reformation Society gives its sanction to *murder*, then I want nothing to do with it. I must shun it – and I must shun its people too!'

Will withdrew his hand. The pulsing rhetoric was shameless, but he was allowing himself to be carried along by its rhythms. He sensed it was the preacher's own language and he would be attuned to it.

The silence was filled by Tysoe's quiet voice:

'Some violence is being planned tonight – that is all I know, William, believe me. Arthur Bedford is most secretive.'

'He walketh about in darkness, Mr Tysoe. He is not a man of light.'

'And you ask about Lord Tunbridge ...'

He broke off, and hesitated.

'... I swear to you, I knew of no plot to kill the Baron. That is the truth.'

'You did not have wind of anything?'

'No ... though the man did stir up powerful feelings, as you saw at our meeting ... But I understood it was a crime of passion – an actress, was it not?'

'That is the Reverend Bedford's accusation – and a convenient one.'

'But William, why are you questioning me like this? I am not accustomed to such a catechism.'

'Because you are a good man. And because I know in your heart you share my fears – that the Society for the Reformation of Manners is changing its character: it is becoming a tribunal that overrides courts of law and social order – an *Inquisition* in all but name. Surely, Sir, this is not something either of us wants? I say this as one who trusts in the laws of this kingdom and the principles of Justice they embody ...'

Will leaned forward and pressed his hand into the clergyman's arm.

'... Arthur Bedford is not a man of our stamp, Mr Tysoe. He is dangerous – a man of violence and hate – not a man of love.'

'What is it you ask of me?'

'All I ask is that, when the time comes – as it shortly will – when Bedford is called to account, you will make your honest views known. I ask nothing more.'

A beatific expression suffused the Reverend Tysoe's face:

'You are a remarkable young man, William. You have the skill of transforming browbeating into a kindly art ... Some day I hope to admire your eloquence in Westminster Hall.'

Chapter Thirty-Nine

CHARLES DENNISTON PLACED the enamelled tweezer-case carefully inside the glass cabinet and laid down his duster:

'This is fortuitous, Mrs Trotter! Mr Pomery and I have just been talking of you. We were wondering whether to send a note round – John thinks he may have a morsel of news to interest you.'

'And I come with a note for him, Mr Denniston!'

'Excellent! Then we have a bargain, do we not? I'm very glad to see you again. I have told John about our conversation yesterday and your concern for the state in which we find ourselves ...'

With a slight turn he laid his hand on the counter alongside an arrangement of silk handkerchiefs.

'... Things do not become any easier – only this morning that hateful Mr Bedford has shown more of himself. But I must leave John to tell you about it. He is in the back room and I know would like to talk.'

Business called; but Widow Trotter remained still and allowed her glance to wander over the display-cases of the toy-shop, taking in the exquisite objects that beckoned all around. The human eye for once was a match for the imagination. Just for a moment she forgot time altogether and felt a familiar surge of delight – the same breathless curiosity that had welled up in her as a child when her chin had reached only as high as the counter and the exquisite snuff-boxes and perfume-jars almost touched her nose.

'You have some beautiful things here, Mr Denniston – this is a treasure-trove!'

'I think of it as the earth's abundance in miniature, Mrs Trotter, drawn here by the four winds. India pays its tribute of ivory and tortoiseshell; Arabia offers its perfumes, Cathay its silks and fine porcelain – and the world's oceans cast up their shells, their amber and mother of pearl.'

'You are quite the poet!'

'Yes, it does awaken a kind of poetical enthusiasm, does it not? ... and yet I am repeatedly told all this fancy stuff is mere luxury – ornament with little use. And of course I have to agree ... But it stirs the soul strangely, does it not? My shop hoards the glittering spoils of *Trade* – the moving power of the world!'

'The world's new religion, do you mean?'

'Well, its magic excites the passions supremely, Mrs Trotter. And are not wars also fought in its name?'

The pair stood there for a few pensive seconds, both sensing that this speculative path led either to philosophy or to satire.

They smiled at each other, and Mrs Trotter made her way through a curtain into the back room of the shop.

John Pomery rose from the desk at which he'd been seated and made her a slight bow, indicating a nearby chair. He was a small, lightly-built gentleman with a thoughtful face that sprang to life as he removed his spectacles:

'Mrs Trotter – I'm heartily glad to see you.'

Lemon cordial was offered and accepted, and within a few minutes the pair of them were comfortably in conversation. It took little time for the name of Arthur Bedford to arise.

'It has all happened so quickly, Mrs Trotter. At one moment I was His Grace's trusted secretary – and the next made to feel a common drudge at the beck and call of Mr Bedford. The man is so much greater than a Chaplain! He arrived in the household like a new Bishop in his diocese, ready to rule.'

'Yes, I've caught sight of him, Mr Pomery. He does have a remarkably imperial countenance.'

'You and your friends have seen something of his power, I know. You have felt the reach of his ambitions ...'

Widow Trotter acknowledged this with her eyes. She was aware that certain things would remain unspoken between them; and there was a delicacy about Mr Pomery that seemed to acknowledge the same.

'... I confess to feeling cast down by it all. Arthur Bedford is vindictive to the extreme. Charles has told you how I found a letter of his and challenged him with it. There was considerable awkwardness. I was given to see how Pride finds embarrassment intolerable. He turned on me and became my accuser.'

'Bedford is a dangerous adversary, Mr Pomery. But what that letter revealed is more than embarrassing. It shows him to be a spymaster – it is direct evidence of his plotting against the Theatre Royal. This is what concerns us. There has been violence – and death –'

'Lord Tunbridge, I know.'

'Yes, but much more. My young lodger, Tom Bristowe, was attacked in Pinkerman's booth, and a threatening note left on his body ... and there was a killing at the booth only yesterday – a young actor ... Mr Angell.'

'Gilbert Angell? No! Heaven preserve us!'

'He had received a threatening note calling down divine vengeance. We believe these threats were made by someone spying on the company – by Mr Bedford's informer in fact.'

Mr Pomery was clearly shaken:

'Do you mean this *Red Cross Knight?*'

'Yes, the gentleman mentioned in that letter you saw.'

'This is terrible news. And you think Arthur Bedford organised the violence?'

'We do – and we have other evidence also.'

'I thought his work against the theatre was mischief only.'

'It has been far more than that.'

'So, when I showed him that letter … he was not only angry – he must have been alarmed.'

'Certainly. The one often prompts the other.'

'He thinks I know his secret …'

Mr Pomery looked up at the wall as if trying to picture the document afresh.

'… *Red Cross* – I took it to be a patriotic reference. The letter seemed to indicate something was expected of this man in connection with the May Fair – that some plan had been laid with him.'

'This is just what we fear, Mr Pomery. Can you tell us anything more?'

'Mr Bedford's letter was expressed in a cryptic manner. But I take it His Grace the Duke was having doubts about the plan. I recall a jotting he had made on it: "Is he sure?"'

'*Is he sure?*'

'That's all – it was nothing to the purpose.'

Widow Trotter thought for a moment:

'But … Could it not mean they were entirely confident of their plan, but had doubts about this Red Cross … Is he *sure?* – Is the man to be relied upon?'

He nodded:

'Yes, that's possible – but I cannot believe His Grace would countenance murder. You cannot think he is behind this?'

'No, no – but is the Duke not determined to have the Fair abolished? Does he not hanker after the land? We think Arthur Bedford is using His Grace's authority for his own purposes – that the Duke and his chaplain have very different motives.'

'That is further cause for Mr Bedford to be afraid – if he is deceiving His Grace in some way.'

'The man is supremely confident, Mr Pomery – and that is his weakness. He thinks to forward his own aims under the guise of the Duke's. You forget he is a violent preacher and believes he owes allegiance to an even greater Lord.'

'That is what I cannot forget, Mrs Trotter. The man is a fanatic! – I know it too well. Indeed, only yesterday I discovered that he is whispering around the household that I am a Papist – to raise His Grace's suspicions against me. I don't think he'll rest until I'm shown the door.'

Widow Trotter set down her glass of cordial, allowed herself to settle more deeply into the chair, and offered him a confiding look:

'That is why we need your help, Mr Pomery ... The man has to be stopped! Mr Denniston tells me you have some news which might be of use to us?'

'Possibly – but perhaps it delivers more of a question than an answer ... Amongst the correspondence taken for posting last night were a pair of sealed letters with the direction in our chaplain's hand: one was addressed to Bishop Compton and the other to none other than Archbishop Tenison.'

Widow Trotter didn't hesitate:

'London and Canterbury!'

Mr Pomery looked amused:

'Yes indeed. Does it not show more than a little ambition? Perhaps a Bishopric is in his thoughts? – He would look very fine in lawn sleeves and a mitre. How does Milton express it? ... "Nor was godhead from his thought!"'

She returned his smile. This seemed excessive – but John Pomery clearly had the measure of their adversary.

'It is a striking picture, Mr Pomery. But I wonder if there is a motive nearer at hand – one that bears directly on our business?'

'What would that be?'

'Perhaps as well as reporting to the Duke, our Mr Bedford has an interest with these prelates? – I understand both are declared enemies of the stage – vehemently so. He can serve the Duke's purposes and also theirs.'

'... And so he strikes two birds with one stone! You are very shrewd, Mrs Trotter.'

'*Three* birds in his case – Mr Bedford's plotting is on a grand scale, don't you think?'

'Yes, a lofty structure ... And you think that I can help you topple it?'

She looked him directly in the eyes and gave a silent nod. He took it as a compliment to his understanding:

'... I see ... What do you wish me to do? Is this some underhand dealing?'

'Of a kind, yes. Though the deception is already in place. You are the innocent means.'

'Innocent? So you wish me to be the vehicle for your deception – not its instigator?'

Mrs Trotter saw that the Duke had an alert and conscientious secretary. She reached over for her bag and extracted the letter. It was a nondescript sheet of paper with the simple direction 'Rev. Mr Bedford.' She handed it to Mr Pomery and watched anxiously as his eyes scanned its contents.

'Ingenious!' he muttered to himself and looked over it a second time. Then his eyes met hers:

'I take it this is not the genuine work of our knightly informer?'

She found it hard to gauge his tone – it could be accusatory or admiring.

'It is not. But we hope it may convince. We took one of the threatening notes as our model.'

He looked down at the sheet again. Widow Trotter watched him intently. Suddenly he stirred himself and spoke:

'Of course, it will have to be somewhat crudely sealed – I doubt our spy carries an armorial seal ring ...'

Widow Trotter breathed with deep relief:

'Do you think this will bring him, Mr Pomery? Would our Mr Bedford even deign to set foot in the Fair? He has been so calm and aloof – setting others to do the business for him.'

'I doubt he has ever been *near* the Fair ... But you express this in such urgent terms – and if the crowning achievement of his plot is at stake, who knows what he might venture? This is where his ambition could trap him ... I take it you want my help in getting this to him?'

'Yes, it needs to be in his hands early this evening. The performance is at eight. We know this is a desperate throw.'

'Well, we have a very discreet messenger-boy. I can tell him the thing was mixed in with my papers by mistake and needs to be carried personally to Mr Bedford without delay ...'

He placed the paper on his desk.

'... Leave it to me.'

'Thank you, Mr Pomery – thank you! You've more than fulfilled our hopes.'

'I wouldn't hope too confidently, Mrs Trotter. It is a doubtful venture. But Charles and I long to see Arthur Bedford encounter Nemesis – an awesome lady even more imperious than himself! Let us see what Pinkerman's booth can do!'

Widow Trotter left Denniston's toy-shop in buoyant sprits, with Mr Pomery's words echoing in her mind. As she walked up Bow Street, she drew herself to her full height and strode with more confidence.

Yes, Nemesis, she thought. Not a woman to tangle with!

Chapter Forty

'Francis is expecting you, Mr Bristowe. He's through that flap over there, putting Mr Cibber to rights!'

Just for a moment an amusing picture formed in Tom's mind, but it was as nothing to the strange sight that greeted him as he stepped outside to the back of the tent. Mr Price's apprentice was seated by a small table with Colley Cibber's head lovingly cradled in his arms. The actor's eyebrows were raised, as well they might be, and his lively eye and eloquent mouth showed him caught at a moment of uncertainty – responsive to the careful way Francis was smoothing his cheek with a silken cloth, though slightly disconcerted by the knife gripped between the young man's teeth as he hung over him.

'Ah! An artist at work!' said Tom spontaneously as he stopped to take in the sight. 'I'm glad to see you're able to repair the damage.'

Francis remained seated and carefully removed the knife from his mouth.

'You must be Mr Bristowe, then?' he said, eyeing Tom with slightly pinched brows.

'Yes indeed. I'm sorry I missed you at the play last night – all was frantic and confused.'

'Is Mr Angell dead, Sir? He looked in a parlous state – as if he'd seen the face of Death himself.'

'I fear he had, Francis. It seems Gilbert Angell is not long for this world.'

'Was it the potion? I think they'd all drunk of it. It was the maddest show – I expected to see Harlequin leap onto the stage!'

There was a raw enjoyment lighting up the young man's features, and he looked like a lively painting himself with the hair sketched in wild brushstrokes. Tom wondered if he should say something about the Spanish Fly, but he held back. There was already enough excitement bubbling up, and they had serious matters to discuss.

A few moments later Colley Cibber had regained a little of his dignity and been set down on the table-top with his questioning look directed toward the tent. Tom noticed what must be Francis's sketching-book lying next to it and was immediately curious:

'I gave you an odd commission, did I not? But Mr Price tells me you enjoyed fulfilling it.'

'Very happy to, Mr Bristowe! It was an open one and I could please myself. I've done a few little sketches. You can choose any for working up into a picture – or I could make a group. Mr Price said you wanted me to observe the audience, and there were a few characters among them too. The play wasn't to my taste, so I was glad to be distracted …'

Tom thanked him and glanced over at the closed book. But the apprentice wasn't for opening it just yet.

'… The best thing by far was your *prologue* – Pinkerman hit the oily preacher well, didn't he! I have a sketch of him. You gave him some good words to say – I was one of the cheerers.'

The remark was delivered casually, but it heartened Tom more than any coffee-house judgment.

'Not everyone agreed with you, I think.'

'No, the dissenters were huddled together at the back. Someone had brought them in. But the play knocked them on the head – they were so caught up in it. I don't think they expected such a fearsome spectacle. Some of the actors almost fought each other, didn't they!'

Young Francis had clearly relished the rough and tumble of the evening. But Tom was eager to know if he'd captured anything that might be useful:

'What interests me, Francis, is any figure who looked suspicious or gave signs of malice. I'm wondering if there was any drama in the audience also.

'It's odd you should say that. I did notice something … but let me show you what I did.'

He took the sketching-book from the table and held it toward his chest, turning some of the pages; then he held it out for Tom:

'Here's the *Reverend* Prologue.'

Tom looked. It was a rapid sketch of Pinkerman executed in a few bold lines, but the character of the preacher was undoubtedly there: the face was turned a little to one side to exhibit a satisfied smile, and the body was slightly bent in a gesture of humility, with the left hand clasped sincerely to the chest. This man carried religion in his look.

'You caught him, Francis. It's our hypocrite to the life!'

The apprentice grinned with pleasure:

'The next one's different.'

And so it was. Tom turned the page and at once saw the familiar Pinkerman sharing a confiding look with his audience: his eyes sparkled in a quick dab of the pencil, and the right hand was held out, drawn lightly as if in natural motion. Where the previous figure was posed, this was dynamic, inviting.

Tom looked up:

'I would love Mrs Trotter to see this. I'm sure she would be glad to have a finished drawing for the Bay-Tree. Could you oblige me? Just between us, you understand …'

Francis was quick in his response:

'I could do it for half a crown – a full crown framed?'

'You have a bargain, Mr Flinn. Keep this to yourself, though.'

This apprentice was clearly a talent, and Tom began turning the pages of the sketching-book, marvelling at the trick of his pencil. He had obviously been observing the audience keenly. A beau was pictured with a *mouchoir* held to his nose which seemed to be twitching fastidiously; an ample citizen and his even more ample lady were viewed from behind, squatting like two large sacks of flour … and then came Sally Twiss as Tamara:

'Definitely the courtesan!' noted Tom, smiling to himself at the license the young man had taken. He had caught Sally in one of her beguiling moves, but had boldly enhanced it: the lace shawl hung invitingly from her shoulder – low enough to reveal most of the left breast – and she held the precious fan so that it was lightly touching her lower lip, which curled to meet it.

'I thought you'd like that one, Mr Bristowe!' said Francis boldly.

'The fan, eh?'

'Yes, she was using it as a weapon, was she not? Flashing it around like a swordsman his rapier! No wonder Lizzy Wright wanted to snatch it from her. That was a rare struggle!'

'You were obviously taken with her, Mr Flinn.'

'Not me Sir, I'm only an observer. But I know someone who was … If you'll turn the page …'

Tom was curious.

'… This gentleman couldn't take his eyes from her.'

Tom turned the page and caught his breath at the familiar face. Somehow Francis had conveyed an image of Lust itself. It was a three-quarter view, and the drawing was rather more finished than the others, as if the artist had been fascinated by the face and determined to hold it fast.

'My goodness – that's a striking portrait!'

Francis didn't reply, but watched Tom intently while he studied it:

'Do you recognise him, Sir?'

'I do indeed ...'

It was unmistakably Amos Jackson, the senior stage-hand. No surprise to find him watching the play – keeping an eye out for trouble among the audience. What was remarkable was the set of the face and the look in the eye. It was a kind of caricature, and yet ... Tom wondered why Amos had been singled out in this way.

'Some artistic license there, Francis?'

'No – *truth*, Mr Bristowe. The man's besotted!'

Tom could give credit to the apprentice's skill in drawing but was unwilling to trust to more:

'You say so, but can there be so much in a single look?'

'I've seen him watching her before – in the playhouse – and in the barn ... and I have a surer reason too – but was told not to speak of it.'

'Told by whom?'

'By him.'

Tom was beginning to feel uncomfortable, as if he had stumbled on something in his path that shouldn't be there. He thought quickly. How far should he pursue this, and where might it lead? He hesitated:

'But ...'

'The eye can tell, Sir – not much can hide from it. Believe me, Mr Jackson is her *admirer*.'

The word was spoken with a knowing emphasis that would do credit to any actor. Tom knew this was more than a youthful impression. Artistic intelligence should never be discounted. But it had to be tested:

'This is important, Francis. I don't want you to break a confidence, but you must tell me what you know. A great deal may depend on it. You say Mr Jackson is Sally Twiss's admirer – you don't mean in any formal way?'

'Depends what you mean by *form*, Sir. I've seen them talking behind the scenes in the theatre. And ... there was the drawing.'

'A drawing?'

'It was between me and Mr Jackson – another commission. I shouldn't speak of it – it was nothing really – but a bit unseemly.'

'Francis – you must tell me.'

The young man avoided Tom's gaze and looked up at the sky as if he wanted his words to be lost in the air:

'He asked me to draw the company rehearsing for the *Courtesan* – show them as a group ...'

Tom knew what was coming and prepared himself.

'... but I had to use some imagination. He asked me to depict them in *caricatura* – without their clothes.'

'I understand, Francis. I've seen the picture.'

The apprentice was astonished:

'What? ... But I took it to be a *private* thing – something he wanted for himself.'

'Quite the opposite, Francis. This *unseemly* picture of yours was displayed in the shed where the players dress, and it carried a threatening message. Gilbert Angell was especially upset by it.'

'Ah yes, I was asked to expand his *tackle* ...'

The young man's hand struck his forehead.

'... By all that's damn'd! What have I done? This was meant to be a secret. Don't tell Mr Price – I beg you, Sir!'

'No, I shall not, Francis – let it remain between us. But on that warranty you must tell me everything you can. You're a sharp observer. You say you saw Sally and Amos talking together. What occasion was this?'

'When I was looking to take Mrs Bradshaw's likeness on her benefit night. I thought she might let me sketch her as Harriet ...'

'In *The Man of Mode?* ... You mean you were in the theatre that night?'

Francis looked puzzled:

'Yes – in and out. I like a benefit. There's usually such a crush, it's easier to slip in behind the scenes without being noticed.

'How do you do that?'

'From Vinegar Yard. I usually wait till the interval, or come in at curtain-time. There's a small door where people sneak in if they don't want to mingle. It's often left unlocked during performances. You're near the costume rooms and dressing-rooms. It's a risk, but if I'm stopped, I say I'm carrying a message for one of the players – I have a note with me just in case.'

'You're a player yourself! Is that when you do your drawings?'

'Not usually – but I *observe*. The place is such a warren. The actors are going to and from their dressing-rooms. Mr Bridge the under-prompter once caught me sketching and I had to show him my book. But since then he's tipped me the wink and lets me alone – I've given him one or two sketches.'

Tom began to marvel at the way this apprentice was setting himself up in business:

'You run a great risk, Francis.'

'I have to be careful. But it's become easier now. My face is familiar, and they hardly notice me – people think I must be somebody's servant. Mr Jackson heard about me and made his proposition at the Fair – said I could wander into the barn during the rehearsal ... but he didn't know I'd already been observing *him!* He sneaked in there himself to feast his eyes. I saw Tamara glance at him more than once.'

'Are you certain of this?'

'Oh yes.'

'Now, Francis. Listen to me. At *The Man of Mode* – during the interval – you were doing your observing?'

'Yes, I'm always doing it. I wanted to catch Mrs Bradshaw in costume, so I went up to her dressing-room – but she had some admirers fluttering round her.'

'What did you see during that time? The smallest thing might be important.'

The young man liked anyone who had an eye for detail, and Tom's curiosity wasn't lost on him:

'This is to do with the killing, isn't it! – Lord Tunbridge being stabbed with Hamlet's bodkin?'

'Is that what you call it?'

'That's when I last saw it – a fine thing ...'

He curved his fingers expressively.

'... In that case, Mr Bristowe, you'll want to know that I saw the Baron that evening during the interval – it can't have been long before the deed was done. He was talking with Mr Jackson. I was very surprised – after all, a Lord and a scene-shifter!'

'But Amos is rather more than that, isn't he?'

'Assistant stage-manager he calls himself – but he has big ambitions ... I said they were *talking*, but it was more angry than that. The two men were at daggers drawn, you might say ...'

The grin froze on his face. Tom couldn't believe what he was hearing.

'... I was too far off to hear anything, but there must have been some dispute going on.'

'Was this before or after you saw Amos Jackson with Sally Twiss?'

'A while after. I saw those two just before the performance began – I'd looked in early to try my luck. The two of them were lurking at the back door when I slipped out. I don't think they even saw me. Both taken up with each other – but uneasy, as if *words* had been exchanged. That was what I noticed – it was only a glimpse, mind you. I came back later for the interval, and it was then I saw Mr Jackson with the Baron.'

There was a lot here for Tom to digest. A pair of dumb-shows, visually precise but wordless. What could be made of them? Francis Flinn had such sharp eyes, but his ears had picked up nothing. Tom thought back to young Bullock's drunken recollections of the evening – his were sounds only. If only the sights and sounds could be fitted together!

'You have the eyes of a hawk, my lad. I hardly dare ask it, but is there anything else you remember from that evening – anything at all?'

'I did see Gilbert Angell in his valet's costume – his arm was in a sling and yet he scratched his neck with the hand – some deception there, I thought. These actors!'

'Was that your only glimpse of him?'

'Yes, he disappeared into the green room. Now that's a place I would love to see. What doesn't go on in there! ...'

He paused.

'... Now I come to think on it – I do recall Mr Grant the prompter stamping his foot and complaining about the setting of the Mall scene – it seems Mr Jackson had been neglecting his duties!'

'Well, Francis, I think we know why! I'm extremely grateful to you. You don't know how helpful you've been.'

'I think I do, Mr Bristowe. Your face has been a revelation – a story in itself ... Might I attempt your portrait – if you've time to give me a sitting?'

Chapter Forty-One

ELIAS COBB HAD never been one to shrink from a physical challenge or from any test of his resolution. He could even show patience when the occasion demanded. But as he stood waiting on the top step in front of Benjamin Hector's townhouse in Duke Street, he felt his confidence draining away.

Confronting a man like Hector on his own terms was not going to be easy. He recalled the offensive way the magistrate had dismissed him from the theatre, and he expected a hostile reception now. Over the years he had observed politicians in action and never ceased to marvel at their ability to be ruthlessly polite. But in this case Mr Hector had dispensed with the niceties. It had been made plain to Elias that he was getting in the way and the investigation of Lord Tunbridge's murder was beyond his competence.

Today he had sent in his name, as form demanded, and fully expected the briefest message to be returned: 'Mr Hector is not at home.' And so it came as a surprise when the servant ushered him inside and asked him to wait in the library.

But any thought of being welcomed was forgotten the moment the magistrate swept in through the door. This was not the cool and controlled figure he was expecting: the gentleman's body was taut, and a flush was rising on his face. He didn't indicate a seat to his visitor but halted a few feet in front of him, rested one hand on an adjacent table, and glared:

'What has been going on, Cobb? Are you behind it?'

The magistrate hadn't bothered to don his wig, and Elias noticed an untidy wisp of hair hanging over his temple. This was annoyance that had spilled over into anger. Elias tried to convey calm:

'You'll have to explain, Mr Hector. I fear I don't see your drift.'

'You don't *see my drift*, eh? Well let me tell you what my *drift* is, Constable! It is Sally Twiss – that pert little actress. She has been taken in for questioning – with no formal warrant! Do you know about this? I assume that's why you're here? Whether to explain or gloat, I cannot tell ... I demand an explanation!'

'It was not on my authority, Mr Hector.'

'Your *authority*? What authority do you have in this affair? You were told plainly the Tunbridge business was none of yours – that it was in the Solicitor-General's hands. And yet you've been sniffing around like a fairground dog. I'm told you were in Pinkerman's booth when the whore was taken up?'

'Yes I was, but had nothing to do with it. I've had little dealing with Mr Grimston – it was evidently on his authority.'

'*Authority* again! Mr Grimston has no warrant – not even the Society for the Reformation of Manners, though that is what he claims. He is at the beck and call of a faction. I understand that *Miss Twiss* (what a sly name!) has been telling tales of a rape and is now accusing Lord Tunbridge in the wildest terms ... and yet when I questioned her previously she had nothing to say about it. The thing is clearly a fabrication – a story she has concocted to blacken the Baron's name.'

Elias began to think a degree of naivety might be useful:

'You speak of a *faction*, Mr Hector. Is this a political business?'

Mr Hector looked at him suspiciously:

'What do you know of politics, Cobb?'

'I know the case touches on important matters, Sir – a member of Her Majesty's House of Lords murdered in such a hole-and-corner way. The circumstances are sordid at best.'

The magistrate's mouth opened involuntarily – such assurance! He scrutinised Constable Cobb with fresh eyes. What did the man know?

'What is *sordid,* Cobb, is the Drury Lane company – the place is crying out for reform – it is a running sore! *Theatre Royal* is a title of honour it no longer deserves. This rape business is a mere distraction.'

'I know little of the political side, Mr Hector. But through my connections with the theatre I pick up pieces here and there. I hear talk and have informants of my own, as you would expect. I get to know of things ...'

Elias was beginning to enjoy being an enigma and was determined to play calm reasonableness for all it was worth:

'... You speak to me as an enemy, Sir – a traitor even. But this is something I do not wish to be.'

Mr Hector was clearly taken aback – by the constable's tone as much as by the sentiment:

'You're a mischief-maker, Cobb! – You have a reputation. It is known you are a friend of the theatre – that you refuse to co-operate with the Society for the Reformation of Manners – that you have turned your back on the Association of Constables and in various ways obstruct their work. As for politics – we know you have associates of your own and do some murky business that way when required.'

Elias didn't like *required,* but thought it best to ignore the implication:

'You speak of my reputation, Sir. That is a precarious thing, is it not? And none of us would wish it to be in the hands of our enemies – neither I, nor you, Mr Hector.'

He looked the magistrate squarely in the eyes.

This was verging on impertinence; but Mr Hector was becoming interested in the drift of the constable's thought. It was curiosity as much as anything which prompted him to continue:

'Sir James Montagu will be incensed when he hears of the arrest. His office is being circumvented, and I owe him an explanation. And Her Majesty will not be happy – you have no idea how far this reaches! You must tell me everything you know of the affair – or I shall make sure you feel the lash for it.'

'You are not likely to advance things by making threats, Sir. I'll happily tell you what I know, and then my advice will be there for the taking. Freely offered ...'

Mr Hector was not used to such frankness. With each accusation Elias Cobb remained calm and direct. The magistrate was beginning to feel like a gale buffeting an oak-tree.

'... The first thing you have to accept, Mr Hector, is that Sally Twiss does not make her accusation lightly. She is no *whore* as you term her, but a young actress whose patron became a violent predator.'

'But this is the old story, Cobb, and you know it. An actress hooking a lord! What did the girl expect?'

'She didn't expect a violent rape, you can be sure of that.'

'But her accusation makes no sense. It seems the girl denies the killing and insists the Baron had some kind of seizure – but that doesn't explain the knife in the back!'

'Exactly, Mr Hector. Why would she invent such a scene? As you say, she altogether denies the killing.'

'With what evidence? Why should she be believed?'

'Why should she not? You will lose nothing by believing her now. If you are still anxious to preserve the Baron's reputation, then I fear that battle is lost. You need to re-group your forces – and move on.'

Mr Hector drew a hand through his hair and looked at the carpet:

'But where?'

Elias took a deep breath and made his play:

'You are aware of the Reverend Arthur Bedford, the Duke of Bedford's chaplain ...'

'Of course I am ...'

The magistrate immediately checked himself.

'... Why do you mention his name? What has he to do with this?'

'You know that Mr Bedford is in great favour with the Duke, and in a few short weeks has made himself powerful within the Reformers' Society – that he commands a lot of support ...'

'I must stop you there. I don't know where this is leading, Cobb – or how you come to be speaking of it.'

'Let us say, I have connections. I know about the division in the Society – how extremely bitter it is. I know, for example, that you are no friend to Mr Bedford and deplore his root-and-branch fervour. I know he is advocating the entire abolition of the theatre – and that such a thing is against Her Majesty's desires. I also know that Lord Tunbridge was entrusted by the Queen with bringing reform – and that Bedford is intent on destroying his reputation and ensuring Her Majesty's scheme is frustrated. I know ...'

'Hold! What are you saying? How dare you take all this on yourself?'

'I take it on, Mr Hector, because I trust to your better instincts. I am willing to conjecture that you would not be displeased if the Reverend Arthur Bedford were to be dispatched back to Bristol and encouraged to stop meddling in affairs of State – for that's what they are, surely?'

The magistrate was lost for words. What he had been hearing was virtually his own agenda. It was uncomfortable, and yet oddly encouraging. He could see that Constable Cobb had been doing more effective work than his own officers. At the same moment it occurred to him that they would both be better sitting down.

Soon the two men were seated side by side with cups of coffee before them, and the constable was setting out some of the evidence that had been gathered about the Reverend Bedford's activities. A constable's report to a magistrate was not usually delivered in such a convivial manner, but Mr Hector was by now eager to hear everything he could, greedily devouring the story of Bedford's machinations. For his part, Elias had begun to think that when he finally emerged into Duke Street he would scratch his head and wonder if he'd been sojourning in a wood near Athens.

But there were cards still to be carefully played, and Elias spoke with caution, holding back a few details while assuring Mr Hector that there was a firm basis for their suspicions. The matter of the maypole was decisive, and when Mr Hector learned about Bedford's direct involvement, he knew they had a chance of success.

Finally, Elias turned to the events of the evening to come and described their fear that Pinkerman's booth would be the site of a further outrage. By this time the magistrate was eager to assert himself and take hold of events that had hitherto been passing him by. Elias could almost smell the eagerness with which the man was ready to take any credit available. He recognised the magisterial gleam in the eye (he had seen it often enough), but on this occasion he was happy to take a step back and let Mr Hector blink in the sunshine.

In the course of the conversation their attention had shifted from Sally Twiss to Arthur Bedford, but Elias was now anxious to bring the talk back to her. He was concerned that Sally should not be declared guilty by default and become an incidental victim of a wider political justice. If Baron Tunbridge was to be exposed (and it was now clear he would be) then Mr Hector must be made to see how this could be turned against Arthur Bedford, and that Sally's evidence might be instrumental. Far from being a distraction, the 'fall' of Baron Tunbridge could bring the fall of Arthur Bedford too.

Elias had been giving the matter thought, and he led Mr Hector carefully through the labyrinth. The clew was complicity. Bedford was employing informers in the theatre and may have entangled Lord Tunbridge in this spying – the Red Cross Knight – whoever he was – would seem to have been working for both of them. This suggested an earlier collusion between them which had turned to enmity and suspicion. Had Bedford and Tunbridge begun as collaborators in mischief? Elias wondered if the Reverend Bedford might have encouraged the reforming Baron to steer into dangerous waters, only to pull back and leave him exposed. This would be characteristic of the Arthur Bedford he thought he knew.

It was only conjecture, but Hector could see it, and indeed he was now warming to an investigation that so far had given him nothing but grief. With the Solicitor-General constantly peering over his shoulder he had assumed that doing as little as possible was the approved policy. And so, when Elias suggested he might like to station a couple of men at Pinkerman's booth that evening, the magistrate leapt at the idea. Not only that, but he knew who they should be:

'I hope you will now think of yourself as working for me, Mr Cobb. And so, if you and the heroic Mr Mudge will regard yourselves as my deputies in this business – you have my authority ...'

The word rang sweetly in Elias's ears, and he had to suppress a triumphant smile.

'... I may even call at the booth myself.'

Elias caught his breath:

'We shall report to you, Mr Hector, so I assure you that won't be necessary. You can safely leave the matter in our hands ...'

It had struck Elias that *The Devil on Two Sticks* wasn't something to tickle the fancy of a magistrate, and this eager new broom ought to be kept well away. The constable was beginning to relish his role of wise advisor.

'... Forgive me, Mr Hector, but can I suggest that you pay a visit to the Solicitor-General yourself, without delay? This is important. With your new information to hand, it will be possible to reassure Sir James that you have made real progress and have uncovered an alarming *conspiracy* – one designed to disturb public peace and encourage the fanatics. You can advise him that Sally Twiss may prove to be your ally – and that Mr Pinkerman's company have themselves been victims of the plot.

This was extremely daring, and the frown on the magisterial brow told Elias he had taken a step too far:

'Don't forget, Constable – it is Lord Tunbridge who is the chief victim in all of this. And we are no nearer to finding his killer. Sally Twiss will have to answer for herself ... If she is to be exonerated, then she must be co-operative – and innocent too, if possible.'

It was a nice feint, and Elias wondered if he should acknowledge it with a smile.

Ten minutes later, it was a confident Elias Cobb who walked back down Duke Street, whistling quietly to himself. He was picturing the four o'clock gathering in Molly's parlour when he would announce his successful joust with the redoubtable Mr Hector. The other three might be returning empty-handed, but he at least had risen to the challenge and would have something valuable to report. At that moment he felt every inch the constable – and had he been built on different lines, it would certainly have put a spring in his step.

Chapter Forty-Two

WIDOW TROTTER AND her friends had no way of knowing how their scheme of investigation was taking shape; but each was confident their own news would change the picture. Alliances had been forged that would surely aid their cause. Will had formed a bond of amity with the Reverend Tysoe; Mrs Trotter had enlisted the practical help of John Pomery; and Elias Cobb was now an official investigator with the authority of Mr Hector and the Solicitor-General behind him. They were in danger of transforming themselves into a fully-fledged counter-plot.

As for Tom, he looked back on his meeting with Francis Flinn with genuine pleasure, but also with a sense of shock at what he'd learned. The more he thought about Amos Jackson, the more remarkable it seemed that the man was Sally's admirer – and not just that perhaps? He was the one responsible for the obscene drawing, and had even been quarrelling with Lord Tunbridge moments before the killing … Was he, then, the informer in the theatre – the Red Cross Knight? It was too much to keep to himself. He felt like running back to Covent Garden at once, and even thought he could take twenty-six miles in his stride. But this Pall Mall visit was important: he needed to learn what his uncle had achieved; and he knew from long experience that visiting the Pophams was always likely to produce something unexpected – usually in the form of Lavinia.

No sooner had Arthur the footman opened the door to him than his cousin ran into the hall and beckoned him into the drawing-room. There was mischief in her eye:

'We must talk, Tom! My stepmother is not happy. Something has ruffled her sails and she's been looking at me suspiciously all morning. She seems to think I intend slipping off to the Fair again. If we're going to talk freely, then we have to talk now ...'

As so often with Lavinia, Tom felt he had some catching-up to do. He was able to manage a few words while being whisked towards the sofa:

'I'm not surprised she's wary. After last night's adventure I thought you'd be locked in your room.'

'Shhh! There's the thing! – your uncle and I made a solemn pact not to enter into minor particulars about the performance ...'

Tom smiled. He could picture father and daughter in collusion like naughty children.

'... but I suspect one of our lady maskers has sent a note round. I detect the work of an informer, Tom! I only hope they haven't revealed anything more dangerous – I've been the victim of hints and silence rather than open accusation, so I think our secret holds.'

'You can count on my discretion, Lavinia. I take it you're referring to *The Devil on Two Sticks?*'

'My mind is on nothing else! To think that in a few hours' time words that I've written will be spoken before an audience. It stirs the soul! ... It certainly beats embroidery.'

'That was never your skill, was it?'

'No, Tom ... I usually stuck the needle in the right place, but I could never master the thread. It always seemed to have a mind of its own.'

'Heaven forbid it should, Lavinia! …' said Tom a little satirically – it seemed to suit the mood.

'… But what about *Arachne's* thread? You must not claim authorship yourself. You've woven this together, have you not – the three of you?'

'A couple of the scenes are ours, Tom. Julia Norreys and I made suggestions, and Mrs Manley wielded the pen. It truly is collective work.'

'Well, you must tell me what you've done with it. I've read the novel, but I suspect you treat Monsieur Le Sage with some licence? I know there's a miniature devil on the loose.'

'It's your favourite subject, Tom – hypocrisy! The thing really is so *apposite* (I love that word!). However, Mr Pinkerman thought that the satire could be polished up a little with a pair of extra scenes – to reflect some matters of moment …'

Tom could hear an alarum ringing in his head – or was it coming from distant Newgate?

'… It's to be performed as a series of revealed scenes. Little Asmodeus lays bare all the shames of the city. He lifts the roof off its hidden vices.'

'Literally so, if I remember rightly.'

'Yes indeed – and there is such fun with the machinery. The audience are able to see what they're not meant to see. It really is perfect hypocrisy, Tom.'

He hardly dared ask the question:

'And – my dear satirical cousin – what scenes has Arachne provided?'

Lavinia's face remained a picture of happy anticipation:

'You'll be very struck by them, Tom – I know you will. The first shows an old nobleman seducing a young actress … and the second one is a clergyman moralising – while a courtesan seduces *him* …'

'What!'

Lavinia was smiling innocently:

'I thought you would like that. Two pictures of our times!'

Not just of the times, thought Tom, but of this moment, and this place.

'You'll be telling me next that Sally Twiss was going to play both parts – as herself in the first, and as Tamara in the second.'

'That's ingenious, Tom – but no. The aristocratic seducer, however, you're sure to recognise – and the hypocrite preacher is a commonplace, is he not?'

It was said with a roguish look. Tom could understand why Pinkerman had been secretive about the play:

'And I thought my prologue was incendiary …'

Lavinia's playfulness was endearing; but given the violence that threatened that evening, he couldn't keep the seriousness from his voice:

'… I don't know what to say, Lavinia. You are handling a dangerous weapon. Do the three of you know what you're doing?'

'Don't be so solemn, Tom! I thought you would *approve*. It's not just men who have the right to be satirical.'

'No no, of course not, but …'

He hesitated. In his imagination he was picturing Mrs Manley and Lady Norreys in a scene of highway robbery – but they were the ones behind the masks, holding the pistols.

'… I shouldn't have spoken like that, Lavinia – You must forgive me! You are a formidable trio. Everything I know of Arachne tells me your scenes will be wonderful – and I promise to bring you a full report on the triumph.'

Tom spoke the words jauntily enough, but his throat dried as he did so. He prayed *The Devil on Two Sticks* didn't release a force they couldn't control.

'Well, I shan't tell you anything more about it, Tom – or you'll be satirical at our expense.'

'Understood. I shall keep your secret *religiously*.'

'No, Tom. Don't do that ... I'd rather you kept it *faithfully*.'

At that moment Tom longed to tell her how much he admired her wit, but something told him silence was the better choice. He heard sounds in the hall and swung round:

'I think we are to be interrupted anyway ... Pax, coz?'

'Pax!' said Lavinia warmly.

Tom's uncle had arrived home fresh from his interview with the Solicitor-General, and after some negotiation Lavinia agreed to leave the two gentlemen to their talk before dinner was called.

Lord Melksham at once poured out two glasses of sherry and became thoughtful:

'You know, Tom, every time I find myself entangled with *government*, I marvel at the subtlety of the political arts. The guile is like no other!'

'Not like the serpent's, uncle?'

'No, not exactly – there's surprisingly little temptation involved. Instead you find you have to come to an *understanding* – politicians use the word like no-one else: with them it means *having the same aims*. If you can reach that point, and get there quickly – then you're made! ... No, Tom, deception is finally less effective than reality, which can be marvellously remedial if administered at the proper time. There's nothing to match the satisfying moment when a politician's smile becomes grateful – when he thinks you can do him some good!'

Tom grinned at his uncle, who was beaming rather like a successful politician himself:

'Looking at you, uncle, I believe you must have concluded a treaty.'

'Ha, yes Tom. But see what you think – it was certainly an informative meeting, and it ended in dramatic fashion. Sir James Montagu is an accomplished player, and in the end it was a pleasure to be matched with him.'

'Did you reach your *understanding*? I'm longing to know.'

'Of sorts, yes. With these discussions it is important to appreciate what obligations the other fellow is under – what forces are pressing on him. And in Sir James's case ...'

A glance from his uncle was enough.

'The Queen?'

'Precisely, Tom – I see you recall yesterday's conversation!'

'Where do things stand with the Playhouse? Is Her Majesty still hesitating about the Patent?'

'More than ever, it seems. She is becoming increasingly suspicious of the Whigs and how they may exploit matters. And so she hangs back, waiting on events. Well, our poor Solicitor-General has been in a quandary. All is prepared, but Christopher Rich's release has thrown things into confusion.'

'So, no charge has been preferred?'

'None – they could hold him no longer. The thing was badly handled from the start, though it has served their purposes. There was no offence to charge him with – just a vague threat spoken in a tavern. Ludicrous!'

'But it has done damage to Rich's reputation?'

'Yes, and the company's – which, as I say, suits them very well ... and now Sally Twiss has been arrested and questioned – and has made the most serious accusation against Lord Tunbridge.'

'Yes, I was there just before she was taken away – she told me she intended to reveal all to the Magistrate.'

'Well, she has certainly done that – as I was about to discover ...'

Tom gave him a questioning look.

'... But first things first ... I began by asking Sir James about his Tunbridge investigation and expected a few lawyer-like sentences to the effect that "enquiries were proceeding, and they anticipated soon to be able ..." *et cetera*. But instead, I was given a lively performance from a stage hero torn by conflicting passions! This is not something one expects from a Solicitor-General – though I suppose the circumstances were exceptional.'

'I shall try to imagine the scene,' said Tom helpfully.

'Then I shall help you ... My timing was perfect. Only ten minutes earlier, Sir James had received the news of Sally's arrest at the hands of Mr Grimston and his officers, and had learned that she is now claiming the Baron raped her during the play's interval – in that same little store-room where he was killed ... Imagine! What could be more open? *Motive* and *occasion* together – nothing plainer. Murder proved! ... And yet a moment later our hero learns that the actress denies the charge vehemently and will accuse the Baron in the strongest terms – that she threatens to reveal the full extent of his turpitude in open court – perhaps with other unwelcome revelations in addition? Nothing more awkward and embarrassing – especially to Her Majesty ... A dilemma!'

'This is worthy of Corneille, uncle!'

'Well, Sir James put on a good show – and I was Solicitude itself, helping him think through the dangerous consequences of bringing Sally to trial. I recalled what you told me, Tom, and I drew his attention to those other people for whom Lord Tunbridge was a deep-dyed villain – a set of men who would relish every drop of scandal – and the more stinking the better ...'

'The Society for the Reformation of Manners.'

'The same – at least the fanatics within it. The picture unsettled him. And so I began adding some other details: evidence of the Society's malicious intentions – the dirty tricks played on the theatre company which have put lives in danger – indeed have brought a new death ... and then the public outrage of the maypole ... I told him of the strong suspicion that these were all connected, and that Arthur Bedford was the plotter-in-chief ...'

'Masterly, uncle!'

'Well, the name *Arthur Bedford* worked like a charm – I saw him shudder slightly as if a fairy's wand had touched his shoulder. It was extraordinary. And from that moment I saw that our cause isn't lost, Tom.'

'But what about Sally? Is he going to press a charge of murder on her?'

'It's too early to say. I could see him brighten at the thought that Sally might be persuaded to maintain her silence if some way could be found to avoid a public trial.'

'This is not edifying, is it? They would demand that Sally let Tunbridge's memory rest in peace. Is that not asking too much of her?'

'Perhaps it is a choice she might be offered? ... But we mustn't jump ahead, Tom. These matters are still uncertain, and I haven't come to our next theatrical moment. I can picture Mrs Trotter's face when she hears of it! ...'

It was a thought that prompted Lord Melksham to reach for his sherry.

'... By this time, Sir James and I were thinking as one –'

'Coming to an *understanding*?'

'– Exactly – I was helping him consider what his next step should be ... and so I urged him to inquire – without delay – if *Mr Hector* had got wind of this conspiracy – and I advised him to seek the magistrate's advice about these new revelations. I went so far as to praise Mr Hector warmly as a man with a sharp nose for investigation who might be able to confirm our suspicions.'

'You are shameless, uncle!'

'Am I not? This counsel was well received, and I was just taking my leave of the Solicitor-General's office with his thanks ringing in my ears, when ... Benjamin Hector himself was announced!'

'You couldn't have scripted this better, could you?'

'Well, I was brought back in, and was audience to a neat little scene in which the sharp-nosed magistrate gave Sir James a convincing report of his investigations – HIS investigations! – into what he suspected was a dangerous conspiracy to force Her Majesty's hand over the Tunbridge affair and encourage dissenting elements among the reformers. Sir James took this as confirmation of everything I had just told him; and for my part I added a quiet remark about *fragile order* and the *dangers of disaffection* ... And so, each of the pieces slid elegantly into place. By this time the Solicitor-General was grateful to both of us, and was convinced that he himself was now master of the whole business – and that everything was pointing to Arthur Bedford ... *but* ...'

Lord Melksham spoke the word carefully.

'... but, he said, where are we to look for *evidence?* ...'

Tom was now smiling too. If the previous scene was Corneille, then this was more like Congreve.

'... At this point, Mr Hector reassured Sir James that he *had a team in hand* who were shortly to report back to him on the affair, and he fully expected to have news very soon. "Good, good!" said Sir James – "you have matters under control, I see!" ... You can imagine how I was enjoying this, Tom.'

'Political manoeuvring as a fine art! Both our puppets performed exceedingly well, uncle, did they not?'

'Superlatively – I couldn't have asked for more ... And that was how it ended – with the word *evidence* ringing in our ears.'

'Well, that is the challenge for tonight,' said Tom. 'Finding sure evidence. If Bedford is intending to make *The Devil on Two Sticks* the consummation of their evil designs, then we have to try and turn it to our purposes – shape it to our own ends ... It has to become the climax of our play, not theirs.'

Chapter Forty-Three

'YOU MUST TAKE the Chair, Mrs Trotter,' said Elias graciously as the four of them gathered in the Bay-Tree's parlour at precisely four of the clock. Given this was her own domain, she hadn't considered any other possibility; but the hostess gave her old friend a courteous nod and invited them all to sit down.

'Thank you, Mr Cobb!' she returned with corresponding politeness.

If this was going to be a formal committee, then it would be a congenial one: a pot of tea and four blue china cups had been set out in front of them, and in the middle of the table were generous slices of baked custard neatly arranged on a dish. It would help stave off hunger until the savoury smells of the Fair began tickling their throats.

She turned to Tom and Will:

'Our esteemed constable now has *authority* in this affair, gentlemen – as we shall hear in a moment. And he promises us some important intelligence!'

A glint in her eye suggested that he was not the only one with hot news.

The two young friends exchanged glances and grinned. They were eager to make report themselves, and for the previous ten minutes had been playing cat-and-mouse with each other.

Will led the way with an account of his meeting with the Reverend Tysoe, and how the revelation of Gilbert's poisoning had come as a terrible shock:

'The poor man was so distracted by thoughts of his dying friend that other things seemed incidental, and it wasn't hard to draw information from him. But I tried to do it considerately – and I think I was even a comfort to him.'

'That's good to hear,' said Tom. 'Perhaps the milk of human kindness isn't entirely soured in him.'

'It's strange, but Tysoe the preacher seems a different animal. Some people aren't improved by a dose of the Holy Spirit!'

'What were you able to gather?' said Widow Trotter.

'No large surprises – but absolute confirmation of what we have suspected. There *is* an organised plot against the theatre, and the Reverend Arthur Bedford is driving it. Mr Tysoe was categorical, but said he had been shut out, which is no surprise given the two men are at loggerheads. But the most important thing is … there is violence planned for tonight.'

'At the booth? For certain?'

'Yes. *The Devil on Two Sticks* is in their sights. He couldn't say more than that.'

A sudden chill descended, and Elias jutted out his chin:

'Well, we shall have to be ready for them.'

'Should Pinkerman cancel the performance, then?' said Mrs Trotter hesitantly. She looked at the others, and they looked at each other. It was an awkward moment. No-one wanted to be the first to speak.

'It's our chance to gather the evidence we need,' said Tom.

'We would have acted merely on presumption – now we can act with knowledge,' said Will.

'Mr Pinkerman must be told, of course,' said Elias. 'And I know what his response will be …'

Widow Trotter nodded:

'Well then, our own plot will be able to *proceed*.'

The words were spoken boldly.

'Does that mean our letter to Arthur Bedford has … ?' Will paused, unsure how to phrase it.

'Yes, Mr Lundy. At Mr Denniston's I was able to have a candid talk with John Pomery – a thoughtful and brave gentleman. He is dispatching your note by a trusted messenger-boy. He was confident it would reach Bedford in time.'

'Excellent!'

'He thought it was ingenious and is willing us to succeed.'

'Of course, he knows about the Red Cross Knight from that earlier letter,' said Tom.

'And Mr Tysoe has wind of it too,' added Will. 'He told me *Red Cross* is Bedford's man in the theatre – and that *Merlin* is working at the Fair. Our two Spenserian informers!'

'Confirmed again!' said Elias with satisfaction.

'Things are taking shape,' said Mrs Trotter. 'If only we knew who these men were – what a difference it would make!'

Will had similar thoughts:

'If only Bedford would take our bait – there is a chance he may lead us to one of them tonight.'

At this moment they became aware that Tom was bursting to speak. He had swallowed a mouthful of tea and set his cup down, and was looking restless in his chair.

'I think I can help,' he said. 'I've a tale to tell that will surprise you all. I learned such remarkable things at the waxworks! …'

With that bold announcement the scene was set. Tom cleared his throat.

'… Mr Price's apprentice is a gifted young man – and a fine draughtsman …'

The others listened with attention while Tom told the story of his conversation with Francis Flinn.

He began with a double revelation: that the obscene drawing

displayed in the actors' shed had been the work of Francis's hand – and had been commissioned by none other than Amos Jackson.

'*Jackson?*' said Elias in astonishment. 'Does that mean he is our Red Cross Knight?'

'It certainly points to him,' said Tom. He is the *man in the theatre*, is he not? A man who could cause a lot of trouble behind the scenes.'

'Not only *behind* the scenes!' said Will, picturing in his mind the burning cloud and falling cannonballs.

'Astonishing!' said Widow Trotter. 'Isn't he the man Pinkerman is employing to keep order in the booth tonight?'

The arrow struck home, and they winced inwardly.

'Pinkey should hear about this at once,' said Elias, flexing his fingers – Amos Jackson was a big fellow, and they would have to be careful.

'Yes, Jackson is very likely our man,' said Tom. 'But there are complications … Francis revealed something even more astonishing about Amos, which you need to know …'

The others sat in rapt silence, imaginations whirling.

'… He is very taken – *besotted* was Francis's word – with Sally Twiss …'

He glanced apprehensively at Will.

'… The young apprentice is the keenest reader of faces, and he is utterly certain of it.'

'*Faces?* – What does he mean? Faces can lie as much as tongues.'

'Yes Will, but he has seen the two of them in conversation – at the playhouse.'

'But Jackson is a stage-hand! – that may mean nothing.'

'What does mean something, Will, is that he saw them together before the performance of *The Man of Mode* – talking intimately … He thought they had been arguing.'

It was as if a thunder-clap had rattled the building. It took a moment for the idea to settle.

'You mean to say your lad was in the theatre that night, behind the scenes?'

'Yes, it's a haunt of his. He seems to come and go as he pleases. He slipped in again during the interval, hoping to draw Mrs Bradshaw; but she was surrounded by her adorers, and so he wandered around *observing* ... It was then he remembers seeing Amos Jackson and Lord Tunbridge having a disagreement.'

There was an intake of breath.

'Lord Bless us!' said Mrs Trotter.

'That must surely seal it?' said Will. 'Amos Jackson is the informer!'

'A maker of mischief, we can be sure – and a quarrelsome one,' added the constable. 'And that man is now behind the scenes in Pinkerman's booth.'

Widow Trotter was looking serious:

'You see what this means, Elias? If our letter-trick succeeds, we have summoned Mr Bedford to the booth to consult with Amos Jackson.'

'A very awkward meeting!'

'Or a neat trick, if it can be properly managed. But it won't be easy.'

'You'll need to discuss this with Pinkerman, Mr Cobb,' said Tom.

'That – and other things too,' said the constable, 'now that I have some authority in the business, thanks to Mr Hector.'

'You survived your interview with him?'

'It was a lively ride, Mr Bristowe, I can tell you! We had a few fences to get over – but once they were past ...'

Elias beamed proudly while the others settled back to hear about his conversation with the magistrate. Will, who had encountered Mr Hector at the reformers' meeting, was curious to learn how the unlikely pair had come to terms.

The constable didn't underplay the drama. He told them how Mr Hector had given vent to his frustrations about Sally's arrest; but once Elias had revealed the plot against the theatre and Arthur Bedford's role in it, the magistrate had seen that the killing of Lord Tunbridge was a part of something bigger and more violent.

'I invoked a threat to civil order and allowed our magistrate to think we are fighting in his cause – that the zealous Arthur Bedford and his forces might be about to face defeat, and a decisive one!'

'Meet his *Blenheim*, you might say?' said Mrs Trotter appropriately.

'Exactly, Molly – and that is something Mr Hector would dearly love to see. He now regards Bedford as a stirrer who threatens the public peace ...'

He looked at Tom and Will.

'... and so he has appointed me his deputy in the business. We now have licence to take our activities a little further, gentlemen. We can act *with authority*.'

The constable reached out for a slice of the baked custard.

'And what about Sally?' asked Will. 'I hope she wasn't forgotten?'

Elias took a moment to answer, hand poised over the dish:

'Now there, Mr Lundy, I think I had conspicuous success. Mr Hector had begun by calling her a common whore – but I settled him down and helped him see that Sally's accusation against the Baron could be a sign of her innocence. I threw suspicion back onto Arthur Bedford – that he had used the Baron for his own purposes. After all, if the two men shared the same informer, it implies they had begun as allies – before Tunbridge began to have theatrical ambitions of his own.'

'Yes, I can see it, Elias,' said Mrs Trotter. 'Arthur Bedford may have used the Baron to help establish himself. Both of them were set on undermining the playhouse.'

'One to destroy it, but the other to refashion it with himself in charge!'

It was an intriguing thought, although the evidence was still insecure. This linking of Bedford and Tunbridge gave them a vivid picture – of a bitter falling out that was still gnawing at Arthur Bedford's soul.

'Well, Elias, I never knew you could be such a sharp negotiator!'

Tom was happy to concur:

'He certainly has the political arts, Mrs T! But you must take a little of the credit yourself. Your idea of setting Mr Hector and the Solicitor-General to confirm each other's suspicions was ingenious – and the stratagem worked to perfection.'

'Does that mean Lord Melksham carried it off with Sir James?'

'He certainly did – he told me the whole story. Mr Cobb had obviously fired Mr Hector up, because he hurried over to the Solicitor-General's office to report on *his* investigations! He arrived just as my uncle was leaving.'

'Ha!' said Elias with surprising good humour. '*His* investigations! Yes, I had offered our findings to Mr Hector on a silver plate, dressed with the finest sauce – and by the end of our meeting he was claiming the whole platter as his. But I'm sure we are happy to let him take the honours – so long as it recruits him for our cause.'

'Wonderful!' said Will. 'And so, are both men with us?'

'Hector and Montagu are both shocked by Arthur Bedford's plotting and determined on teaching him a lesson ... But we desperately need *evidence*. My uncle took his leave with that word ringing in his ears. The suspicions are in place and the story accepted – but nothing can be done on hearsay – not in such an important matter.'

'No,' said Will, 'this is no session-house business. It's something closer to *treason*.'

The thought startled them all. None of them had considered that.

'And we are being expected to find that evidence,' said Tom. 'According to my uncle, Mr Hector reassured Sir James that he had a team in hand who were shortly to report back to him – and he expected to have news very soon!'

Widow Trotter gave the others an encouraging look:

'*A team in hand?* Well then, if that is our commission, gentlemen, it is up to us to fulfil it ... But right now, we must settle a few practical matters for this evening and make disposition of our forces. Tom can tell us something more of *The Devil on Two Sticks* and what we are to expect ...'

And so, the Bay-Tree militia went into close conference.

That evening's performance in Pinkerman's booth seemed certain to be the climax of their adventures. And what a play was in prospect! A miniature demon would be released from captivity and allowed the freedom of the stage, with licence to reveal uncomfortable truths about Human Nature ... and then, at the end, the Seven Deadly Sins themselves would be on display. It was set to be a devilish evening altogether.

Chapter Forty-Four

THE OUTER REACHES of the May Fair were dangerous ground. Beyond the busy areas marked out for organised entertainment, these scrubby fields with their thorn bushes and rickety outbuildings offered a different kind of holiday. Around here things were trackless and desultory – the place barely qualified as a landscape. It was part pastoral, part lawless wilderness, and like many a site of indulgence it had hints of concealed delight. The terrain was seductive. There were not many trees, but the ones that survived were skirted with undergrowth, and bits of straggly hedge remained from the old farm. Here and there, patches of warm turf were shrouded in brambles that gave cover for all kinds of improvised couplings – some of them freely negotiated, others carelessly indulged or violently taken. At play on the edge of things, human creatures joyously fornicated, lightsomely wooed and yielded, or just fucked. According to choice or circumstance.

It was along the margin of this hinterland that a colourful procession wound its way, a little like a bright-skinned adder searching out a warm path for itself; and in the process the scene was transformed into allegory. There were seven variously-attired figures, led by pipe and drum, who danced and gesticulated to the music. The group from Pinkerman's booth had been tripping it through the Fair to advertise the evening's performance; but they were becoming tired now and their cavortings little more than shuffles. The actors were glad to escape the press and take breath. The troop moved on slowly, accompanied by a few ragamuffins who trailed behind, mimicking them with grotesque gestures, like gargoyles warding off the damned. The Seven Deadly Sins were on the march.

In the van was *Pride* – female of course – decked in a whole shop's worth of gaudy jewellery, who was holding a glittering hand-mirror to her face; she had eyes only for herself and gazed adoringly at her thickly-painted complexion of carnation and rose – Art's mockery of Nature. Then came *Covetousness* in a patched-up dirty gabardine, his long-sleeved arms folded round a casket of gold which he clutched to his chest; he looked about him warily as if every human face posed a threat. Treading close behind was *Envy*, who eyed his avaricious neighbour intently while gnawing on a large meatless bone; a serpent made of green leather was curled round his shoulders and seemed to be tightening its grip on his neck. Fourth in line, and by now swinging his wooden sword rather more gently, was *Wrath*; his face was heavily bloodied beneath the antique helmet and his eyes glared out a challenge with every glance. Trailing in his wake was a slighter figure in a linen shift and drooping nightcap who trudged along unwillingly, a spent candle held loosely in his hand: *Sloth* was bleary-eyed and yawned as he looked longingly around him for a place to rest. The penultimate character in the procession was a familiar sight at the Fair, a red-faced man whose large tankard was raised to all and sundry: *Gluttony*'s head was garlanded like Silenus, and beneath a necklace of garlic his other hand stroked his huge pig's bladder of a belly. Finally, bringing up the rear of the pageant and seemingly driving all the others, was *Lust*; his was a body that radiated confidence from an oversized codpiece which bulged through his clothing and lolled out in the shape of a giant tongue.

It was *Sloth* who first realised something was wrong when a stone hit him on the side of the head. His nightcap shuddered to comic effect, and a cry of pain came from his fully-awakened face as he leapt in the air with the shock. Sensing the disturbance, *Wrath* swung round, only to meet a second stone which clattered full on his helmet. His sword was of little use here and he shielded his face with his hands. Within moments all the distinctive figures were under fire, and order was lost as they began scampering in every direction. In a scene worthy of Hieronymus Bosch, the Sins were routed, and jeering insults pursued them through the field. It was here that other less symbolic representations of Lust and Wrath, interrupted in their play, popped their heads round trees and bushes, and shouted curses. Nowhere seemed to offer them shelter.

Not surprisingly, in this place *Pride* was the most in danger, and for once – perhaps uniquely – it was *Lust* that preserved the woman's virtue: Joe Byrne grabbed Lizzy Wright by the arms and shielded her from the hail, encouraging her to run full pelt back to the fair-ground. As the girl raced away, Joe turned on one of the attackers, only to feel a slim blade slice into him.

It was a bedraggled troop that eventually limped back into Pinkerman's booth. A surgeon was promptly sent for and Joe's wounded arm carefully bound up. It was some small compensation that his heroics were the talk of the moment. Also receiving gratulations was Envy, who – albeit not on a par with Samson – had done some useful damage with his cow's bone.

It was tempting to view the incident as a burlesque comedy; but for the players it had been a frightening ordeal. Nevertheless, when Pinkerman suggested that the evening's concluding pageant should be cancelled, there was a defiant 'no' from all concerned – except for Wrath, who declared he was not going to be humiliated a second time.

When word of the assault arrived, Tom and Will, along with Constable Cobb, were sitting with Pinkerman in his office at the booth. The four of them had been discussing the news about Arthur Bedford and Amos Jackson, and Pinkerman had come to terms with the identification of the Red Cross Knight. The revelations made sense to him, and he saw how the trail of violence, disruption and rumour over the past month had been a plot to unsettle the company and make it vulnerable to the reformers. It had fed into pamphlets that presented an image of the theatre on its knees – an institution not worth saving. The idea was no surprise to Pinkerman; but now that he could place Jackson at the centre, the picture was more defined and more uncomfortable. He saw at once that the man had to be confronted as soon as possible. They could not risk letting *The Devil on Two Sticks* go ahead with Amos Jackson free: he must be arrested and questioned. There were little over a couple of hours to go before the performance, so they had to act quickly.

But no sooner was the determination made than the Deadly Sins had crowded back into the booth, nursing their wounds, and this new problem needed to be resolved. In hope of trying to sort matters out, Pinkerman had hurried off to the players' shed with a shout of 'Guard the fort, gentlemen!' It was becoming clear that if there were any deities directing the company's affairs, they must be watching the confusion with delight.

Pinkerman showed his face again ten minutes later, and he had the look of a man trying to hold off despair:

'Well, my friends,' he said to Tom and Will, 'what are we to do? If the pageant is to go ahead – and the common voice is that it shall – then I need to find a pair of replacements. I've procured a new *Lust* in place of the heroic Mr Byrne; but *Sloth* is very dizzy and sore, and *Wrath* has marched off in shame!'

Coming from the company's chief comedian, the words had a comical ring to them, but Tom and Will understood the urgency. The two of them were looking at each other.

'What do you say, Will?' said Tom.

There was a pregnant pause.

His friend yawned and stretched out his arms:

'Oh ... I don't know ... Must we? Can't we just sit and watch like everybody else? It's simply too much trouble.'

Tom's eyes brightened angrily:

'You lazy good-for-nothing! Can't you see the company is in crisis? Here is our friend calling on us to help, and all you can think of is lolling on a bench. I've a good mind to thrash you!'

Tom shook his fist and stamped his foot loudly, while Will blinked and tried to lift his head.

'Gentlemen!' shouted an astonished Pinkerman, making to interpose himself between them. 'This will never do!'

But just as the words left his lips, he detected the sly smiles as each showed appreciation for the other's performance. What a pair!

'Ha ha! Thank you, my friends! You have given me my answer. You are both perfect for the parts! Indeed, I think our new *Wrath* has more mettle in him than the old one, and I have high hopes of *Sloth* – if he can avoid bestirring himself.'

Elias Cobb, who had been watching the scene in baffled amusement, clapped his hands politely:

'Very fine, gentlemen! But can we turn our thoughts back to Amos Jackson? Time is short. I have to question him urgently – and it must be done here, in case we wring something important out of him. He mustn't be allowed to slip away. Mudge and Turley are patrolling the concourse. I think I may need reinforcements.'

'Right now, Jackson is in the tent setting up the scene,' said

Pinkerman, shuddering slightly as the implication of those words struck him. Tom understood at once:

'You will have to examine the carpentry, Mr Pinkerman. If some kind of accident is being planned ...'

'I trust to God there isn't! But yes, of course – we shall put everything to the test before the audience arrives. The stage machinery is finely balanced – literally so. The spectacle!'

'Will anyone be *flying*?' asked Tom uneasily.

'That you can be sure of! But – Jove be praised – there is to be no thunder and lightning. The skies over Seville are uncommonly calm tonight.'

'Seville?' said Tom. 'Is it not Madrid?'

Pinkerman smiled:

'There – as elsewhere – we desert our original. The truth is, we shall be using some of the set of *The Courtesan* – so it has a kind of decorum.'

With so much else on his mind, Elias was feeling the lack of urgency, and he leaned forward:

'Remember, gentlemen, we may soon be favoured with a visit from the Reverend Arthur Bedford ... Someone will have to keep watch!'

'I must leave that to you three,' said Pinkerman. 'What arrangement did your letter propose? You will be the one to recognise his face, Mr Lundy.'

Will began to explain that no precise time had been determined, but 'before the performance at eight' was the phrase used.

'In that case,' said Elias, 'you young gentlemen must station yourselves on the concourse and keep your eyes busy.'

Pinkerman intervened:

'But first, our friends here must learn what they have to do in the pageant. There is little to speak – but you will need to talk with the other Sins – they will instruct you ...'

The complications were mounting on every side. Everyone had important things to do, and little time in which to do them. They really needed to be elsewhere. The mood in Pinkerman's office had grown tense and apprehensive. All of them longed for action. It was like waiting for a storm.

It came sooner than expected, with a sharp knock on the door. The slit deal shook menacingly, and before any reply could be given, it swung open to reveal the figure of Amos Jackson, who stepped purposefully into the room. The man was evidently not happy, and there was a scowl in full occupation of his features.

He had expected to find Pinkerman alone and was taken aback by the four pairs of eyes that were suddenly trained on him – looks that signalled alarm. At once, with a single quick movement, Elias reached across and shut the door behind Jackson, setting his back against it. There was nothing surreptitious about this – it was the closing of a trap. If their man had come into the room feeling annoyed, then he was now on his guard. He looked round, his indignation beginning to mount, and there was an awkward silence.

It was Tom who thought quickest. The closing of the door had been a bad move: the last thing they needed was a cornered animal, especially one as powerfully built as Jackson who in his time had been something of a wrestler and could surely dash down their flimsy door with a single hand.

'Come in, Amos,' he said. 'You've interrupted a private meeting, as you can see! Forgive our embarrassment – but at this point you could well join us. We're discussing something urgent, and you're the man to help.'

'Yes, sit yourself down, Amos,' said Pinkerman. 'Mr Bristowe is right – you've come at the opportune moment.'

Jackson continued to look suspicious. The polite tone was mollifying, but he had called on an urgent matter himself and was not to be diverted:

'Why so hugger-mugger? – Is it about this ridiculous pageant business? …'

Pinkerman looked at Elias, seeking help. But there was no pause: the man was determined to have his say:

'… We have the scene set. The flats are in place, and the machinery looks like it will work, if we're lucky. But if you're to have your pageant, then where in God's name are they to walk? There's no room as I can see, with all those characters parading about – unless they come in one at a time and mind where they step …'

'Hold, Amos!' said Pinkerman in as friendly a spirit as he could manage. 'We'll find a way. *First things first!*'

It was easily said – but where should they begin? This confrontation had come upon them before they were prepared.

Will Lundy took up the challenge – sometimes a witness had to be coaxed into the snare. His voice was confiding:

'We have a pressing problem, Mr Jackson. There has been a threat – a dire threat – made to the play tonight; but what form it will take we do not know. It may be a fiction, but after yesterday's events everyone has to be on his guard.'

'Have you seen anything suspicious, Amos?' said Pinkerman.

'Anyone interesting themselves in the set, or loitering around the place?' added Tom.

They were all joining in now, and Elias was beginning to feel little more than a spectator. Somewhat sheepishly he moved back to his chair.

Amos Jackson trod warily and gave as well-meaning an answer as he could – although he sensed an unspoken accusation hovering over him.

The talk about stage matters proceeded, but the four of them knew the evasions would have to end. Finally, Constable Cobb was ready to change the mood:

'To be direct with you Mr Jackson, we have strong suspicion of the *reformers* – the Society for the Reformation of Manners

– at least the hot-heads of their number. You know well enough how the theatre has been under attack – what accidents have been occurring. Pamphlets pour scorn on the company and relish the thought of its extinction!'

'No, Mr Cobb, *accident* is not the word,' interposed Pinkerman. 'There has been *intent* behind all this. The poisoning of Mr Angell last night has been a terrible shock. For these men, human life is dispensable … I confess, Amos, we fear something of that magnitude tonight!'

Jackson knew he was being pushed nearer the edge, although there was no accusation as yet. He could see they were putting on some kind of act, and he allowed concern to show in his voice:

'Yes, bad things have been happening. And bad people have been interfering in the company's affairs – that I do know!'

It was an unexpectedly sharp remark.

'Oh?'

Pinkerman checked himself. Tom and Will looked at each other. Elias kept his eyes firmly on their suspect:

'And who are these *bad people*, Mr Jackson?'

Again, there was a moment's silence. They were beginning to wonder if Jackson had the whip hand of them.

'One in special I'm thinking of – though he's now gone to trouble another place.'

There was the trace of a smile playing around Jackson's mouth as he spoke – a hint of satisfaction perhaps?

'Do you mean Baron Tunbridge, Amos? …'

Tom spoke quietly, out of a natural curiosity.

'… We know the players were unhappy with his ambitions for the playhouse. Does this mean you agreed with them?'

'The gentleman was a tyrant, Mr Bristowe – and I've heard Mr Pinkerman say as much, more than once.'

'You speak as if you had some dealings with the Baron yourself?'

It was the crucial question.

'The actors felt his shadow over the theatre – though speaking for myself I don't spit out the word *reform* like it was poison. I knew about His Lordship's scheme, and I can't say as it troubled me overmuch. I'm just a scene-builder, after all. What words are spoken on the boards is nothing to me.'

There was an element of defiance in this, but just enough of common sense too. But he had side-stepped the question.

Elias was becoming impatient:

'Did you ever talk with Lord Tunbridge – discuss matters with him?'

Jackson looked at them all. A sarcastic reply about his lowly status would have been an easy response; but this was a direct challenge and it had to be met boldly:

'Why ask me questions when you know the answer? ...'

Clearly, Jackson now understood that he was being interrogated. But the idea didn't seem to throw him out.

'... Yes, I did have *dealings* with him, as you put it – though the word flatters me. In truth, I had things *dealt to me*. His Lordship had great power in the company, and I wasn't the only one to encounter it. Mr Rich, for one, felt the lash on his back.'

'Were you in some kind of arrangement with the Baron?'

Jackson's reply was remarkably prompt:

'Yes, Mr Cobb ... I was his eyes and ears in the company.'

'His spy, do you mean?' said Pinkerman at once.

'The Baron was a sharer in the theatre, and he needed to know what was going on – what the managers wouldn't tell him. He found it useful to have someone like me who could bustle about the place and tell him what people were thinking.'

'So, you informed on company business?'

'Hardly that, Mr Pinkerman. I'm no dealer in *business*. But I heard what was talked about – knew the temper of the place.'

Will Lundy had experienced this kind of cock-sure witness before:

'You paint a very innocent picture, Mr Jackson. I'm sure you were helpful to him … When did your orders change?'

The word *orders* seemed to wrong-foot him. He shuffled slightly:

'Well … The affairs of the playhouse began to concern His Lordship more and more. He was becoming interested in the scandal.'

'So, when did your own *activities* begin? …'

At those words Jackson felt the net tighten. He waited a moment too long, and Will was able to continue:

'… When did you see there was no way back for you, Amos? – that Baron Tunbridge had you in his power and could begin making demands?'

Will was leading the witness, certainly, but was offering him an escape route too. The others watched intently. Jackson glanced toward the door, but was wise enough to remain in his seat and gather himself:

'I said the Baron was a tyrant, and I meant it … I discovered he had secret plans for himself – that he was relishing the scandal – not deploring it … He wanted more. So, yes, I became involved in reckless things …'

'*Dangerous* things!' said Pinkerman sharply – 'you put lives in peril! It was you, was it not, who created the chaos at *Macbeth*? It could have been no-one else. The thunder-trunk – the rosin … You could have killed me! …'

Jackson, who to this point had been alert of eye, lowered his head slightly. There was no point in denying the charge.

'… Amos, Amos!' said Pinkerman, suddenly sounding like a disappointed father. 'How could you do such a thing?'

Jackson was hesitant, disconcerted by the pace of the questioning. This was no time to lift the pressure. Tom spoke:

'Baron Tunbridge had an ally in this, Amos, did he not? At least, at the beginning? … When did the Reverend Arthur Bedford come on the scene?'

Jackson looked up in alarm. For the first time he understood how much these people knew. He had thought he could deny and prevaricate, and wriggle free of their accusations; but he began to see they knew the road ahead better than he did and were watching his every step.

It was Constable Cobb who put the question:

'You are the Red Cross Knight, are you not?'

This was a hammer-blow. Jackson leapt to his feet.

'Hah! That ludicrous name! …'

At that, Elias strode quickly to the door and once again set his back against it. His hands were flexing. He was in position. At any moment he expected the man to make a dash for it.

But Amos Jackson was in no mood for throwing himself into gaol. There was enough of the wily soldier in him and a determination to take matters back into his own hands. He knew his questioners were uneasy and above all curious about what he could tell them. He had learned the scope of their suspicions. They had cast their dice – so, what now? Now it was his turn.

It was Tom who sensed this. He saw they must be patient and not provoke him into violence or flight. Neither would do them any good:

'I'm sure you have a story to tell, Mr Jackson. Please sit down. We ourselves have done too much talking. It's time we heard from you. I suspect there is still much we don't know – and need to know. You need to have your say.'

Pinkerman was also on his feet – but with less subtle intent was reaching for the bottle of brandy on his makeshift desk.

'Hand over the glasses, Mr Lundy,' he said.

This intervention allowed Elias to move back to his chair without embarrassment. A practised ear might have heard the handcuffs jingle in his pocket. The shift of mood served to unsettle Jackson, who suddenly felt he was meant to be celebrating something. He tried to hold his thoughts to the business in hand; but as he looked at the four men, he was reminded of a theatre audience settling down for a performance. He was annoyed at how his resentment and frustration were abating.

But he did not decline the brandy.

'Yes, you see before you *the Red Cross Knight* – what a grand title for a foot-soldier! ...'

He spread his thick arms as if acknowledging applause.

'... You're permitted to smile, gentlemen! I'm part of a game that's been playing out around the theatre and the Fair – though I've been little more than a pawn, if truth be told ... Yes, I was Lord Tunbridge's informer at the beginning – innocent enough – and he made it worth my while. But he began to want more of me, not just to report scandal, but to stir it up – to watch and listen, and retail troublesome gossip. Mr Rich and Mr Grant supplied more than enough between them! And actors' tongues are never at rest – it needed little to get the pot bubbling.

'But the Baron saw that a stage-hand could do more for him – and more was expected of me. The terms improved. Promises were made. I found he had ambitions for the theatre – for a reformed company. The title of *Chief scene-man of the Theatre Royal* was dangled before me! No longer a stage-hand to be ordered around by the prompter, but the man in charge of setting everything up – the carpentry too. After all, with my experience in the booth ...'

Jackson paused, as if looking for some acknowledgment.

'... So, any practical *embarrassments*, so to speak, would be sure to work in my favour. Heads would roll.'

This self-assurance was too much for Elias, for whom euphemism always had a sickly taste:

'You speak of *embarrassments*, Mr Jackson. Do these include broken windows and menacing letters? We know your fondness for obscene drawings, and for threatening death and hell fire. Do your polite *embarrassments* encompass terror and violence?'

'Ah, that's a different story, Constable.'

'Is it? ... Or is it one continued story of malevolence and spite?'

Jackson shied at this and turned toward Tom:

'You mentioned the Reverend Bedford, Mr Bristowe. I have to say things began to change when he made his entrance on the stage.'

'That's an unfortunate image, Amos,' said Pinkerman. 'Unless you intend it as satirical?'

'Perhaps I do. The Reverend Arthur Bedford is entirely taken up with the theatre. It's his *Sodom*. He's unable to turn his back on it! He's determined to destroy all stages – the Playhouse and the Fair – but the very idea breathes life into him ...'

This wasn't news to any of them, but hearing it declared so plainly was a surprise.

'... At first he was Tunbridge's ally. They both had the Society behind them, and one purpose in view ... but then the Reverend got to hear of the Baron's true design, and he was outraged. Tunbridge was to set himself up as the new patent-holder – ingratiating himself with Her Majesty, no less, and ready to do her bidding. In place of abolition, it was to be a plan of rescue – to put the theatre securely under the Queen's patronage.'

'But doesn't Arthur Bedford have ambitions of his own?'

'Put the two men side by side, Mr Bristowe. Their paths may be different, but the goal is the same – their own advancement. If Tunbridge had the Throne protecting him, the Reverend is looking to his Ducal namesake and the princes of the Church. They both disgust me! And with Lord Tunbridge now in his theatre-box in the sky, the Reverend feels more secure than ever.'

Will was suddenly alarmed: if Amos Jackson and Arthur Bedford were so at odds, then his forged letter had surely been torn to shreds.

'Are your relations with Bedford now broken, then?' he asked tentatively.

'Oh no, Mr Lundy, I daren't be anything other than his humble servant still. He has some need of me – though he has his own *factotum* – a creature with none of my compunctions, I have to say ...'

The thought of Amos Jackson having any compunction at all was hard to conceive, but they all saw where this was leading.

'... *Merlin* has no uneasiness of mind. I have nothing to do with him. Bedford likes to keep him as his little fire-dragon – a creature with no sense of danger. And a dangerous man himself! When Mr Bedford gave me my *alias*, he said we were his *two adventurers*. But Merlin doesn't play by any rules.'

'Who is he, Amos?' said Pinkerman quite casually.

'That I don't know. Mr Bedford has enjoyed keeping us apart – so neither knows what the other does. But I have a good idea of Merlin's activities. He's been kept well away from the theatre, but he's certainly busy around the Fair. Your sore head is his doing, Mr Bristowe, I'm sure of that ...'

Tom swallowed hard.

'... And the maypole business too – I suspect he had a share in it. Merlin has his friends who hang around the Dog and Duck and are always itching for a fight. If there's to be trouble tonight, it will be down to them.'

Elias was becoming impatient with the man's story. He wondered how much of fiction there was in it:

'But have you no idea who this Merlin is? That I can't believe!'

'You *must* believe me,' said Jackson. It was spoken not as a plea but as a statement of fact.

'Are you not being deliberately mysterious?' said Will. 'Is Merlin not a convenient scapegoat for you? You can confess to all the slight things and push the capital crimes onto him.'

At this, Jackson looked indignant:

'You're right to be suspicious. I don't claim innocence. But let me tell you this …'

He leant forward, one arm on his knee, the hand held open toward them – it was a gesture of no-nonsense dealing.

'… I confess I had a share in Mr Angell's death – if that's what it proves to be. I admit to it. But it was not designed.'

Elias had heard enough:

'Not *designed?* You mean to say, poisoning the players with Spanish Fly was some kind of accident? A harmless joke?'

'That was not me, Constable,' said Jackson resentfully. 'What I confess to is Mr Angell's *potion*. The young man annoyed me with his pretensions and his delicate ways. I thought I would give him a surprise.'

Now his four questioners were hardly taking breath. It was Pinkerman who asked the question:

'What *surprise* Amos?'

'The strong emetic, Mr Pinkerman – I doctored his love potion. The sickly lovesick youth was meant to spew up all over the stage, and he did so too – to fine effect! But I was not to know about the other drug – the Cantharides. That was none of my doing. The poor boy was hit twice. No wonder the effect was dramatic …'

Tom's mind was working quickly. So, there was no Spanish Fly in Gilbert's phial! He had not received a huge dose of it, as they believed. He had been sedated with a strong opiate in the thought it would ease his death – but … if the emetic had worked so dramatically, then …

'I trust for your sake you speak truth!' declared Pinkerman, cheered by the same thought.

Tom was buoyed up with hope, but knew that Jackson had to be pushed further. The man was too much at his ease. Surely something would unsettle him?

'Tell me, Amos – Did you know that Mr Angell had discovered your identity and was going to unmask you at the play tonight? That he planned to step forward and denounce Lord Tunbridge from the stage. Did you know this?'

The widening of Jackson's eyes was answer enough.

'No, I did not.'

But Tom wasn't finished:

'Did you know he was going to declare the Baron a violent *ravisher* before the whole audience?'

Tom's voice began to crack. This was dangerous ground; but he was determined to press Jackson into a reaction – the man was too composed.

'No, I did not … I would like to have heard it!'

'Oh? … Is that a charge you would endorse? Did you know him for a ravisher, a violator of innocence?'

'I … I can't say …'

For the first time there was hesitation. Amos Jackson was disquieted.

Elias saw it and immediately drove the idea home:

'Young Sally Twiss … Did you know she had become the Baron's victim? …'

There was an uneasy pause.

'… The girl was taken into custody last night, Mr Jackson – on suspicion of murder. You are aware of this?'

'Yes of course – it's the talk of the company.'

'Is it also the *talk* that she has denied the charge – and is ready to speak in open court about Lord Tunbridge's violation of her? To expose him as a ravisher and an evil conspirator?'

'She is brave, Mr Cobb.'

'What do you mean?'

'I mean what I say … Everybody was in thrall to the man. He had a hold on so many – more than you know. Sally resisted him.'

'Are you *sure* of that, Amos?' said Tom slowly. The insinuation was clear.

Jackson looked at him angrily. It was partly anger at the imputation, but also at the way he was being led by the nose:

'I wish to speak no more of it! Tunbridge was a vicious bully.'

Pinkerman had been following the conversation with concern:

'So, Amos, between Arthur Bedford and the Baron, you have been harnessed to two evil taskmasters, have you not? Men who have used you for their own ends. But you seem not to have resisted them. You were *in thrall*? Is that your plea?'

'I make no *plea*, Mr Pinkerman. I am not on a charge. Nor do I beg.'

'Perhaps you should, Amos?'

Jackson was becoming restive, and they began to sense he might be ready to run for it. During the past moments they had been aware of sounds on the other side of the door, which were unsettling the mood. Elias recognised the voices and slipped out to investigate.

During this time, Will had been listening closely to the ebb and flow of the conversation. If there had been any doubt of Jackson's attachment to Sally, his slight reddening at her name dispelled it:

'Yes, you remain in thrall to Arthur Bedford, do you not, Amos? Always ready to do his bidding … But I can see this galls you bitterly. I sincerely think you may be looking for a way to escape his clutches, if you can.'

Jackson was immediately wary:

'Now you're riddling, Mr Lundy. I've told you the truth – and I've said more than enough. You must impute nothing further to me. I'm not here to make bargains.'

'Nor we to offer any ... But surely – would you not like to see the Reverend Arthur Bedford sent packing? Seen for what he is? ...'

There was a momentary relaxation in Jackson's features, as if he had glimpsed a pleasing thought. Will noticed it and was emboldened:

'... You have the chance to be your own man, Mr Jackson. You're a strong fellow – and not just in body. You need to stand up and be yourself again.'

This was rhetorical. It occurred to Jackson that far from being his own man he was about to be recruited a third time. He took breath. But before he could give a reply, the door opened and an eager Elias Cobb reappeared.

The scene swung wildly, almost like a farce.

'News, gentlemen!' he declared. 'Toby Mudge is here with Bob Turley ... It seems we are to expect a visit from Mr Hector – and he intends to bring Sally Twiss with him!'

This was baffling, and questions crowded in. Will was astonished:

'Sally, coming here? Has she been released?'

'No no – she's in custody still. But our Mr Hector has seized the prisoner for himself and is determined to bring things to their crisis.'

'Or cause one!' said a horrified Pinkerman. 'Coming here? The last thing I need is a magistrate descending on the booth tonight. This could be the end! I thought he was going to keep away, Elias?'

'Turley tells me he's not on *Society* business. He's anxious about keeping the peace.'

'Peace!'

The one word summed it all up. Pinkerman had nothing to add. He slumped back into his chair and downed his brandy in a single gulp.

'But there's more, gentlemen … I hesitate to tell you it.'

'Elias! …'

Pinkerman was by now red-faced and not a little desperate. Constable Cobb felt the solemnity of the moment, and his words could not have been heavier:

'It seems Sally Twiss has just confessed to the murder, gentlemen … It was she who stabbed Baron Tunbridge.'

'No! No!'

The sudden cry came from Jackson. It startled everyone. He was on his feet and looked ready to punch the very air in protest.

'Mr Jackson – calm yourself.'

'No! That cannot be. That isn't true!'

Will's thoughts were silently shouting the same. He looked at Tom in despair.

'This confession is not what we expected,' continued Elias. 'Nor what we hoped for. But it gives us our answer.'

'But that is not how it was …'

Jackson spoke the words quietly – and they were the more dramatic for it.

'What can you mean Mr Jackson?'

'I mean … that Sally is innocent … I killed Tunbridge.'

It was said without emotion, almost casually.

'Is that the truth? Think carefully now.'

'Oh yes. I killed him.'

Elias could do no more than play his officious part:

'Mr Jackson – Do you wish to wait for the Magistrate and give him your statement? Or will you tell us now exactly what happened? I assure you, it will not be to your detriment – indeed it might help you speak more freely. In my experience a Magistrate's stricter questioning can be inhibiting – and it sometimes helps to say too much rather than too little.

Amos Jackson gave him a silent nod and sat down again.

Chapter Forty-Five

'I WILL TAKE no guilt on myself!'

Amos Jackson's tone was defiant. If they were expecting to hear an abject confession, then they were mistaken. There was a surprising assurance about him, and as he spoke he looked them in the eye, unabashed:

'I know a great deal, gentlemen – and I've thought a great deal too. And I've come to a determination.'

This was enigmatic.

'And what is that, *may we ask?*'

Elias couldn't keep the ironic note from his voice, and Amos registered it:

'Leave your mockery, Constable. Do you want my help, or do you not? My *determination* – a word you smile at – is to give you what assistance I can.'

'You confess to murder, Mr Jackson – and then expect a tea-table chat?'

'No, not murder, if you will but listen! … You have invited me to speak freely, and your invitation was polite enough …'

Will was feeling uncomfortable at the drift of the exchanges, but before he could speak Amos pre-empted him.

'… Mr Lundy's words a moment ago interested me. *To stand up and be myself …*'

He turned to Will.

'... How easy that sounds, Mr Lundy – *be yourself!* – but with actors all around you, how bloody difficult! ...'

He gave Pinkerman a knowing glance.

'... The playhouse is a place to escape to. Folk come there to be something other than they are. And for three years I've been in their service – happily so! We mechanicals decorate and disguise and mimic and deceive – turn a few pieces of timber into a palace – half a dozen painted flats into a forest – all harmless enough! But everyone knows it's a mockery. The audience shiver with fright when the thunder-trunk is swinging and the rosin flashes, and they cry at the onion tears. It's a wonderful pretence – but it's a world I've been glad of ...'

His expression suddenly darkened.

'... My old life, gentlemen, was very different. As a member of Her Majesty's infantry I faced real cannonballs. I have seen heads fly from shoulders – I have seen a bullet cut down a man as I talked with him ... There was no pretending at *Blenheim!* ...'

Amos may not have been acting, but the drama was immediate. The four of them kept an uneasy silence.

'... But I've since been given my own part, have I not? The Red Cross Knight, who plays his naughty tricks like a marionette in a children's puppet show. How Mr Bedford smiled at the idea ... Yes, Lord Tunbridge and Arthur Bedford! – as you truly say, Mr Lundy, what masters this servant has had!'

'We're ready to listen,' said Tom. 'You must tell your tale at your own pace. If we ask you questions it will only be to clarify. As Constable Cobb says, you are not before a Magistrate.'

Amos Jackson appeared easier at this. They had begun to notice a nervous shuddering of his left knee, as if his body were impatient to be gone. But his face was set and his eyes fixed:

'So, I'm privileged to have my own audience – and one that knows much of the plot already. You know about the drawing,

I take it? The treacherous Francis must have been gossiping. He's a talented lad with a good hand at caricature: the players all stripped of their trappings – bodies without their disguises – a witty satire altogether! And our angelic Gilbert as few have ever seen him, taking his bow. What a well-endowed creature!'

Pinkerman was trying to control his annoyance:

'Your hostility to Mr Angell is clear, Amos. What gave rise to it?'

'Ah, Mr Pinkerman – it was the *eighth* deadly sin gave rise to it. Envy may gnaw at his dry bone, but *Jealousy* has plenty more to feed on – not least himself ... the pains of love! What think you of your philosophical scene-shifter?'

He reached for his brandy.

'I think you have had plenty of time for thinking – too much perhaps?'

'True, Mr Bristowe. I live among the scenes and have a lot of time for watching and waiting. And I suspect you know who it is I watch ...'

He paused almost politely, waiting for the name to be spoken, an eyebrow raised in invitation. But all four kept their counsel. Will was becoming irked by Amos's confidence – the man had just confessed to a killing yet seemed remarkably untroubled, and he was now toying with Sally as if she were his very own secret.

'... I'm unwilling to speak of her, gentlemen – but speak I must ... Sally Twiss is the one true thing in the company. She has genuine innocence, and I cannot bear to see it corrupted. I've had plenty of time to watch that old lecher Tunbridge slavering over her, patting her hand, whispering in her ear, gazing into her eyes. And Gilbert Angell too with his delicate charms cuddling her like his baby sister – and of course Cibber forever sniffing around, eyes a-twinkling, always ready to lead her off for a little *tête-a-tête* ...'

'Did you wish for their licence, Amos?'

It was a pointed question, and he looked surprised at the interruption:

'I'm only human, Mr Lundy. Yes, I was often close to her – almost touching her. But as a scene-shifter I have no *licence* – I am invisible ...'

He glanced at Pinkerman.

'... We slip in and out between the acts like ghosts. But it's we who are the real thing – the truth that must be kept out of sight. We make their magic world seem real.'

Tom found himself uneasy:

'But surely, Amos, on the stage it is the players who make things real – make us believe – not your machines? The magic is what happens when we forget the clouds are made of wood.'

'Sally is *always* Sally!' said Amos with sudden warmth. 'Tamara was *Sally* ... I'm no dreamer ... and Sally knows I see only her – not like the others. I take her for what she is – not for the disguises she wears.'

'You say Sally *knows* ...'

Will paused, hesitant about saying more – but no-one came to help him, and so he went stumbling on:

'... did you ... did you declare yourself to her?'

Amos watched him with interest, aware that something was fuelling Will's questions. He replied quietly:

'I did not need to, Mr Lundy ... She it was who declared herself to me ...'

There was an electric silence. Embarrassed glances were exchanged. The lumbering stage-hand was slipping from view and the eloquent veteran of Blenheim was showing himself. It was unsettling.

'... We had to be cautious. For a hopeful young actress to be consorting with a scene-shifter? No, gentlemen, it wouldn't do. Theatrical vice has its decorums. And so, the game was played out. The blessed Gilbert Angell was forever fussing round her, and the bold Baron Tunbridge had taken to instructing her. What a pair! The brother and the grandfather, each claiming his particular *intimacies*. But how far from lovers!'

A hint of disdain crossed Amos's face. Will choked slightly as the picture formed. He knew there was another scene about to appear, which would come without their prompting. But Elias intervened briskly:

'Time is short, Mr Jackson. You must tell us what happened during Mrs Bradshaw's benefit – that is what concerns us.'

Amos felt the pressure and scowled as the events of eight days earlier began to reawaken:

'You have to know, gentlemen, that Sally had become Lord Tunbridge's project – he had bestowed many attentions on her by way of gifts and advice, and his generosity grew in both, until he felt he had an undoubted property in her. He looked for a return. The man had come to expect little attentions from her – moments of warmth, physical endearments. They amounted to nothing more than fingerings and slobberings ... but they made Sally increasingly uncomfortable ...

'That evening before the play began, she and I snatched some words by the door that leads out to Vinegar Yard, and she told me what had happened a few days before – how the Baron had made a direct attempt on her and would have raped her had she not fought him off so boldly ... I could see her fear, and I swore by Heaven I would have it out with him that very night. The man had to know he had crossed a line – that Sally was no shilling whore to be taken by contract!

'It was a wild thought, and Sally begged me to say nothing. She promised she would confront him when the time was ripe. And so, I stepped back. It was not for me to force the issue against her wishes – unlike that wretched Mr Angell ... But I had not reckoned on Tunbridge ...'

There was a sound outside the door and Amos looked toward it, conscious he might be interrupted at any moment. The thought encouraged him to move on quickly. His voice was tense and short-breathed:

'... When the play's interval came, I noticed the Baron stalk off the stage towards the dressing-rooms. Sally had been *inattentive* and had deliberately turned her back on him – and I saw his annoyance. He had the flushed look of a man itching for satisfaction – lust or anger, it hardly mattered. His eyes blazed like a lioness, and they caught mine as I watched him – perhaps he saw my contempt! It drew him to me – he would have *a word,* he said. I knew what it would be and followed him like a lamb, back to the rear door – his favourite spot for slipping in and out of the place.

'And it was there the Baron's accusations began. There had been a violent falling-out between him and Arthur Bedford, and now my own position was impossible. I was an enemy – a lackey of Bedford's! He said the *interloper* was using me to undermine everything he had worked for – that I was a traitor and had told tales! ... They were the accusations of a man who could see his carefully-laid plans slipping from his grasp ... I was longing to accuse him in turn, but I remembered Sally and kept silent. His words became threats, and he swore he would *never* make me chief Scene-Man. On the contrary, he knew enough of my activities to see me turned out of the place. "You should leave now," he said, "before a charge can be brought – best slip away tonight and not be seen again!"

'That was the moment my resolve broke, and I turned on him. I told him his charges were false, and that I knew enough of his activities to do him real harm. If he called me a traitor, then I would prove one indeed ...

'That was immensely foolish, and I regretted it at once ... "Who are you to threaten me?" he said. "I can break you!" I was torn between arguing the matter out and giving him a beating –

and the thought paralysed me. A second later, gentlemen, he had thrust me out of the door – and bolted it! …'

The four of them looked at the burly Amos in wonderment. It was an unlikely scene, but they could see he was reliving the embarrassment of it.

'… I stood kicking my heels for a minute or two, cursing the playhouse and every soul in it, before I was able to get in again. I was lost what to do … But Fate took a hand, and a moment later I caught a glimpse of Tunbridge further down the passageway – he was slipping into the property-store where they keep the armour, and he held a lighted candle in his hand. It was some kind of assignation …

'But before I could do anything, the Prompter hauled me back to the stage – he was angry! There was a problem with the setting of the scene – and it was at least five minutes before I could sneak away again. I needn't tell you where my feet took me … I assure you my brain had no say in the matter!

'I found myself outside the store-room with my ear to the door, and heard a half-muffled cry. There was no thought about it – I just burst in, and there he was – at least the rear of him! I could see his buttocks rising and falling. He was breathing heavily and thrusting away, with his sword clattering and his silks flapping – like an automaton that needed oiling – so intent on the business that he didn't turn round … over his shoulder I saw Sally with her face crumpled – she was trying to scream but no sound was coming …

'And then it happened. My eyes caught the poniard on the shelf next me, and without a second's thought I had plunged the thing between his shoulder-blades …'

Amos flung his head back and closed his eyes as if wishing to shut out the world and reclaim himself.

'… There you have it, gentlemen – the stupid, sad tale. How easy it appears in the telling!'

'But it hardly ends there, Amos, does it?' said Pinkerman after a few moments.

Amos opened his eyes and sighed:

'You mustn't ask me about motive – about what I was thinking – it's nothing to the purpose … But you may ask about Sally – the heroic Sally! She was remarkably composed and pushed him to the floor as he sank down. He was lifeless from that moment. We looked at each other in horror. Everything was suddenly quiet.'

He stopped speaking, as if expecting the curtain to fall.

Elias was frowning. There were certainly more questions to ask:

'What did Sally say to you, Mr Jackson? It must have been a double shock to her.'

He was straining to keep the tone polite and business-like.

'Indeed it was, Mr Cobb. To speak true, my action must have been the more shocking – a deadly climax. But Sally was practical and in her senses – far more than I was. There was no accusation from her: she knew the deed could not be recalled. She said she would slip away at once – that very instant – and say nothing. And I was to wait a short while, then leave myself. We agreed to keep silent about what had happened and to stay apart for several weeks – until the Fair was over.'

'And that was how you left it?'

'We had to. The interval bell was about to ring. But as she turned away, she pressed her hand into mine and whispered in my ear – they were the words I wanted to hear. She simply said, "I'm free …"'

It was a sentimental moment, and the words fell oddly from Amos Jackson's lips. He seemed to feel their awkwardness and shifted in his chair.

'… So – I killed him, gentlemen … But I refuse to call it murder. The man deserved his fate. I am willing to declare that to anyone.'

Will scrutinised Amos through narrowed eyes. He was longing to open up a further line of questioning, but at this moment it was impossible. Nevertheless, he couldn't hold back entirely:

'Mr Jackson … why do you think Sally has confessed to the killing? Do you imagine it is to save you?'

It was phrased uncomfortably and caught something of Will's own uneasy feelings.

'A fair question, Mr Lundy – but a surmise. All I can say is, you have heard the truth: Sally was the Baron's victim, not his killer. *She is innocent* – you must believe me … I've told you all.'

This had been no simple confession, and its conclusiveness left them a little stunned.

While this was being said, Constable Cobb put his mind to the immediate practicalities. He was facing a man who had just confessed to a killing; he had the handcuffs ready in his pocket, and an arrest was called for … but Arthur Bedford himself might soon be arriving at the booth – no doubt muffled and treading carefully – expecting to meet his Red Cross Knight … How could such a meeting be managed, and, if possible, overheard? Surely a few words would be enough for them. It was an unexpected complication, but a priceless opportunity, and Elias noted the look on Will's face that suggested his mind was on the same track. It seemed they needed to trust Amos further.

It was Will who spoke. With a glance in turn at Elias, he broached the matter of Arthur Bedford:

'Mr Jackson … you have a chance to do yourself some good …'

Chapter Forty-Six

On this second evening of the Fair, the crowds seemed if anything tighter and the voices closer. There was not a breath of wind, and lowering clouds were piled overhead bringing an early darkness. Torches were already being lit along the main concourse, and down the alleyways candles were set in windows. The air was heavy. Spectators could taste the nitre as the fire-eater breathed his flames above their heads. The atmosphere was strangely autumnal, and the smell of roasted nuts and baked gingerbread hung everywhere. Air didn't move but simply became thicker, as if a giant lid were pressing down on the scene and allowing the contents to simmer quietly. There was noise enough, and a busy murmur was building all around, but with no dispersing breeze every sound became muted and more intimate.

Laughter and applause could be heard coming from Miller's booth where Jockey the enchanted Scotchman, his hair magically erecting itself, was encountering a fearsome trio of witches; and on the other side of the concourse an exhausted Sophie and her troupe of rope-dancers were completing their final performance of the day. Along with the sprightly dogs, they had kept Pinkerman's small pavilion busy throughout the afternoon, aching calves and sore feet notwithstanding.

As the dark began to descend on the stalls scattered across the Brook Field, innumerable little scenes were playing out. Clandestine meetings, petty quarrels, confession and accusation, joking and trickery took their turns. Improper behaviour had no meaning here: children smoked, men giggled, women fell over with drink; springtime love blossomed in the gloom; and behind the sheds, things of varying value were being lost, surrendered, and consummated. Little was planned, and everywhere people were taking risks, hoping for the best, chancing their arm, putting it down to experience, counting the cost …

Amid all this randomness, however, an ambitious plot was taking shape in defiance of the Fair's notorious capacity to disorganise. Its participants were doing their best to direct events to their conclusion; but, like everyone else caught up in the carnival, they would have to adapt and improvise.

Outside Pinkerman's booth, an apprehensive Amos Jackson stood half in shadow. His eyes scanned the concourse for the familiar figure who might loom out of the dark at any moment. Time was passing, and he had just slipped into the booth to check that the scenes for *The Devil on Two Sticks* were in readiness. The machinery seemed to be working smoothly: the rotating cogs were aligned and the wires firmly in place … But what was disquieting him more was another scene: his possible encounter with the Reverend Arthur Bedford. The content of the forged note had been explained to him, and he was surprised how convincingly Will had caught the situation. But mimicking his handwriting was another matter: Amos doubted Bedford would be taken in. Would he venture into the Fair? It all seemed unlikely …

But then he thought of the man's curiosity, his overmastering fascination with the stage, and perhaps a need to ensure the consummation of his plans. There was a possibility he might come ... but Amos's self-doubt was growing. Would he succeed in extracting something incriminating? These were false pretences, and Bedford would certainly discover them. How long could he keep the trick going? The scene-shifter wasn't accustomed to performing.

He was also aware that while his own eyes were searching the crowd, another pair of eyes were trained on him. Somewhere Tom Bristowe was watching, ready to act as witness to whatever might occur. It had been agreed that Tom's unfamiliar face would be an advantage in eavesdropping – only this time there would be no convenient chink in the furniture. Tom would have to do the best he could and trust to the crush of the Fair.

Tom in his turn was weighing the difficulties and finding little cause for hope, when he became aware of a tall, slightly stooping figure cutting across the flow of the crowd and moving towards Amos. Amos had his back turned, and as the figure closed in, the shape appeared to loom over him. The head was covered by a hat with its brim turned down almost to the shoulders, and this grotesque effect was confirmed when the man turned. The face appeared muffled, but then Tom realised it must be a beard – a dark, theatrical-looking beard ... It was a chilling sight, but he couldn't help smiling. Here was a stage villain, if ever he saw one! If this was Arthur Bedford – as it surely must be – then the man had arrived in costume.

But Tom's smile died the moment Amos looked round. An expression of alarm flickered over the scene-shifter's face, only to be replaced by a no-nonsense set of the jaw as he prepared for the confrontation. Tom inched his way closer to the pair as they began their dialogue. He couldn't help admiring the determined way Amos had taken up their challenge. They had laid this trap with the Red Cross Knight as their bait, and now they expected the man himself to confront the chief conspirator. There was no script, just trusting to the moment. Tom's heart was beating hard at the precariousness of it all, and he wondered how composed Amos could possibly be. Coolness under fire, he thought – perhaps Blenheim had given him that?

The pair began to walk slowly with the flow of the crowd, with Tom slightly behind, alongside a couple of children happily munching baked apples. Fortunately, the Reverend Bedford had a voice well adapted to the pulpit, and so Tom began to pick up their talk. Amos had agreed to speak emphatically so as to lift the volume as much as possible. But at this moment it was hardly necessary: Arthur Bedford had become angry:

'What! I don't believe you! When do you say you heard this?'

'Not two hours ago – it's the talk of the booth. Gilbert Angell is *dead* – he went into convulsions and lingered through the night – and he expired this very afternoon. He never regained his true senses.'

'But how could this be? It was not to be a deadly dose – we agreed! – just sufficient to put them into a frantic fever.'

'I knew nothing of this. You keep Merlin's activities to yourself. Had you only told me! You know I'm the one who plays games with the company – and how well I've played too!'

'That's nothing to the purpose. We are not playing *games* anymore!'

'But see what has happened? You don't tell me who this Merlin is, so I can't keep an eye on him. Why don't you trust me? The pair of us would be stronger together.'

'How dare you presume …'

'You still think me Tunbridge's man! Let me remind you – *the Baron is no more*. Now I am in *your* service …'

Tom was astonished at the tone. Amos was infantry no longer. He was the artillery – all guns blazing.

'... Mr Bedford! ...'

'Quiet! Do you want the whole fairground to hear? Can we not find somewhere private? You must tell me more. Your note promised something ...'

'In this place there's no privacy without danger – we can slip into the dark in a few seconds, but others may be busy there ... I do have more to report ... let us take our chance. Quickly – down here – follow me!'

Suddenly Amos was guiding this newcomer to the Fair along the side of a skittle-alley where a boisterous game of nine-pins was in progress. The Reverend Bedford was beginning to look alarmed. The Devil was especially busy here – he could see it in the distorted faces, hear it in the abandoned laughter, the mindless cries of triumph, the blasphemous curses of disappointment; he could smell the energy of the sweating bodies – gin-fuelled, no doubt. The Evil was hammering on his senses – a foretaste of Hell! He had put himself in Amos Jackson's hands and was being led into the dark ...

Tom seized the opportunity and wove his way through the skittle-alley and out to the rear on the other side. It was surprisingly dark, and a collection of empty barrels and overflowing bins gave cover. Here was the smelly backside of the Fair. A few yards away he heard Arthur Bedford cough as the stink of urine and faeces crept up his nose – this wasn't the privacy the reverend gentleman had intended. Tom could hear scratchings and scuttlings among the bins and was distinctly uncomfortable himself. He crouched down and tried to listen as Amos and Bedford resumed their talk. With the shouts from the alley to contend with, low tones were out of the question. He unmistakeably heard Bedford speak the name of Pinkerman, then more words ... They were talking about that night's performance.

'... little accident with the machinery? What have you been doing, Jackson? This has not been agreed!'

'I thought I was to use my own invention in such ways?'

'No! You must not act alone. *Macbeth* was a different matter. Another plan has been laid – you are going to throw the whole scheme out. You hinder others!'

'*Hinder?* So you have given Merlin his head! Am I to be dispensed with?'

'Things have reached their final stage and we must be careful. You have no idea of our *negotiations*. The business must be handled judiciously. I cannot expect you to understand.'

'You forget I am responsible for the staging here. If your Merlin is to cause trouble, then I must know of it.'

'That is impossible. No-one is to know. This is in Merlin's hands – and his two recruits ...'

'What! Are there *three* of them? What scheme is this?'

'I cannot say because I have not asked – you know I must keep aloof from this ... But be assured, your allowance will continue. The Society will not be ungenerous, and we cannot have you feeling aggrieved. The Red Cross Knight remains useful to us.'

'But the killing of Gilbert Angell ... will that not lie heavy on your conscience?'

There was a moment of silence. Tom braced himself and held his breath.

'I am sorry to hear of it ... but it is not for us to question Providence. The young man's death was not my doing.'

'It was done at your behest, was it not? The Spanish Fly? If the thing was mishandled, the idea was yours – the intention to harm.'

'How dare you accuse me! Our Lord will use whatever means He chooses. *We* may begin, but *God* will end. He will turn Evil unto Good. The murder of Baron Tunbridge is proof enough of that – dead at the hand of a debauched young actress. How God allows human sin to work His ways!'

Tom could hear the voice of the preacher beginning to soar above the noise of the skittle-alley. There was something uncomfortably impressive about it – the cry of a benighted soul?

Amos persisted:

'Did the *Lord* draw back, then, at the maypole? Did He frustrate your designs and spare the innocent ones?'

'Innocents? No, no – *Philistines!* Their fate is only postponed. Our martyr met a Samson-like end! John Bowling will live in eternity – have no fear! His name is among the blessed.'

'But will God bless the enterprise tonight?'

'We must pray that He does. It is in His hands. He shall refine and purify! This is the place of Evil, and Satan is working all around us … *Ye serpents! Ye generation of Vipers! How can ye escape the damnation of Hell?*'

Arthur Bedford's words rang out, only to be answered by a suppressed scream and a peal of laughter. At that moment, like demons summoned by a spell, a drunken Jack and Jill tumbled into their darkness, looking for some privacy themselves. Urgently in need of relief, the woman squatted on her haunches while her friend began pissing against the rear wall. The man peered into the gloom.

'Beloved Jesus!' he cried suddenly. 'We've interrupted something, Poll! There's a couple of mollies already in occupation!'

'Tell 'em to lug their arses elsewhere!' came the reply. 'These premises is for 'onest folks!'

The scene had changed, and Amos had to think quickly before Bedford could step forward and pronounce *anathema* on the pair of them. He grabbed his arm and proposed a judicious retreat while the man's weapon was occupied. But Bedford remained frozen to the spot.

Tom got to his feet in response to the commotion, and the man saw the movement:

'A third, by God! They have an ogler!'

The woman gave a loud cackling laugh:

'He'll be awaitin' 'is turn, I expect!'

Suddenly, behind them one of the bins banged loudly – somebody was beating it with a heavy stick and the sound was like thunder. The man cried out again:

'Shut yer legs, Poll! 'Tis a whole gang of cock-bawds – there's *four* of 'em now!'

And four of them there certainly were. The couple knew they were outnumbered, and with a 'Let's be off!' they high-tailed it back to the booths.

The fourth figure stepped forward, and in the darkness Tom could make out the face of Tobias Mudge. The watchman was holding his staff and shaking his head:

'Forgive me, Sirs, but I think we should move back to the concourse. These haunts aren't for the likes of you.'

'Toby! ... I take it you're not here by chance?'

'No, Mr Bristowe. While you were watching them, I've been watching you! ... and listening a bit too. I've heard enough for the purpose.'

Arthur Bedford sprang to imperious life and attempted to command the situation:

'And what *purpose* is that, officer? ... What has been going on? ... My friend and I have been discussing private matters, and this young man must have followed us. I think he was looking to rob us! Do you know him? ...'

There was no immediate reply, and in the silence that followed, the intricate truth began to take shape in Bedford's mind.

'... Is this some trap you have set? I demand to see a constable!'

'And a constable you shall see, Mr Bedford … I take it you *are* the Reverend Arthur Bedford, Chaplain to His Grace the Duke – beneath your fairground disguise?'

'Yes, this is the Fair. Why should not a man go *incognito*? A man who wishes to observe and not be seen? There are many worse counterfeits here – the whole place is a masquerade! … What has been going on, Jackson? Why am I being questioned like this? I think we should leave. Our business is completed.'

There was nobody to snigger at the double-entendre, and the phrase hung in the still air. Amos Jackson was silent and remained so while the four of them walked back towards the concourse.

A quarter of an hour later they were all settled in Pinkerman's office, which was making do as a temporary watch-house while the man himself was off supervising in the booth. A solemn-faced Elias Cobb, conscious of his new authority, was fulfilling the role of examining magistrate until the real thing arrived – the much-anticipated Benjamin Hector had not yet materialised. The exchanges were becoming heated as Arthur Bedford began to understand the extent of the subterfuge.

'I shall say nothing to incriminate myself!' he declared. 'This has been a shabby proceeding with no legal justification. It is mere fairground talk! I have nothing more to say to any of you. I demand to be released!'

'That won't be possible, Sir,' said a polite Constable Cobb. 'Your *talk* has been noted. Both Mr Bristowe here, and Mr Mudge, have heard enough to give us concern – and I know Mr Hector has an interest in this – a very great interest. We expect him at any moment.'

'Benjamin Hector? Coming here?'

The Reverend Bedford looked alarmed and glanced around the room.

'We shall be reporting to him, Mr Bedford. There are some serious matters that need to be clarified – some recent events considered. It seems you have given us a lot to think about.'

Bedford was torn between indignant protest and cautious silence. He still hadn't removed the beard, which as it flickered in the candlelight gave him the appearance of a pantomime villain. There was suddenly something absurd about the man. He was looking daggers at Amos, who had been keeping silent, keenly aware that he also would be of commanding interest to the Magistrate. He had already told his story and knew that his fate – life or death – was in play.

They did not have long to wait before Mr Hector arrived. His appearance in the doorway caused a shiver of expectation as five faces turned toward him. Constable Cobb gave a cursory salute with his hand and rose to his feet, ready to make his report. Amos looked Mr Hector straight in the eye, trying to gauge what mood he was in; while Bedford was something of a contradiction – his body had stiffened defiantly, but his face wore an expression of foreboding. And he had suddenly realised his beard was still in place.

The Magistrate's entrance caused a stir; but it was another arrival that provided the surprise. Hector was followed into the room by Toby's fellow-watchman, Bob Turley, who led in a determined-looking Sally Twiss. Amos called out her name, but then fell silent. Arthur Bedford took advantage of the distraction to begin removing his beard – a trickier task than he had anticipated. As he struggled with the thing, Mr Hector eyed him with a degree of amusement:

'Well, I never ... could this be Mr Bedford? I did not think to see you at May Fair, Sir – and certainly not in character. What role do you play this evening?'

Bedford had expected embarrassment, but not this outright mockery. He was struggling to find the appropriate words:

'I deserve your ridicule, Mr Hector. But this foolish disguise had a purpose. I thought to conceal my God-given features in such a vile place – to pass for a heathen so I might go about unremarked and observe the enormities of the Fair.'

'And did you find them?' said Elias, impertinently.

'It is a vile Sodom, Constable! I have witnessed nothing but licence and unspeakable debauchery. The Fair is Hell on Earth – a place of the damned! … I rejoice to see you here, Mr Hector – you are a beacon of light in this terrible darkness! … and I see you have a prime sinner in tow!'

Mr Hector looked at Sally and raised an eyebrow:

'Yes, Mr Bedford. Miss Twiss is in custody, and I have been questioning her closely, I assure you. I am determined that all *crimes* will be punished. Sins are beyond my remit … Crimes – committed and planned – are my concern …'

Bedford winced slightly at the words.

'… As you say, Mr Bedford, the sins of the Fair are *legion* – and I abhor them as much as you … But I have come here on a case of murder.'

'I am being detained against my will,' said Bedford. 'These men seek to accuse me, to bend your ears against me with vile suggestions. You must not listen to them!'

'I shall listen to anyone who wishes to speak, Mr Bedford, and weigh matters accordingly. You must calm yourself. This will be a formal investigation. It will not be a wild game of accusation. I would ask you to be patient.'

But Arthur Bedford wasn't finished:

'In the name of our Society, I beg you! I am betrayed into the hands of sinners, Mr Hector. You must not give credence to these vile eavesdroppers.'

'But I have heard nothing yet. Do you anticipate some degrading charges? If so, then I am bound to hear them.'

'I trust to you as a Christian! *The wicked shall not be unpunished: but the seed of the righteous shall be delivered.*'

The more Arthur Bedford quoted scripture, the more compromised his position appeared. After all, the man had come to the Fair in disguise and been discovered in the dark, behind a skittle-alley, discussing a violent plot with one of his gang. It was an adventure beyond the reach of most Anglican clergy.

Benjamin Hector seated himself in Pinkerman's elbow-chair and took charge, reminding everyone that he was not acting merely as a magistrate but as the representative of the Solicitor-General, and through him of Her Majesty the Queen. This was an unconventional setting for such an inquisition, he said, but with all the parties brought together he was determined to seize the opportunity.

And so, he began the proceedings, in the language of a public meeting rather than – what it was – a huddled gathering in a shed.

'The killing of Lord Tunbridge is a State matter, gentlemen – of exceptional gravity, given the Baron's rank and connections. It is also a delicate one. His sordid end in the playhouse adds to the difficulties of the case. An embarrassment to Her Majesty must be avoided at any cost ... A public trial would open Pandora's Box and release mischiefs of all kinds ...'

Eyes widened and breathing stopped. What was the man saying? No *public trial?*

'... The playhouse has become a place of anarchy and disaffection. It is common knowledge that Her Majesty has sought to rein in its excesses. The reformation of the company was a cause Baron Tunbridge espoused and was determined to bring about. His killing has not only removed the prop on which reform was to be built, but it has tainted the whole enterprise.

It seems the plague of the theatre touches all who come within its sphere, and Lord Tunbridge succumbed to the infection. I have just had to listen to a shocking account of his unbridled lusts! The Theatre Royal, gentlemen, is a tarnished name, and these recent weeks have been a continuing story of outrage and scandal.

'Amid this collapse of the company's reputation, the *Society for the Reformation of Manners* stands as a beacon. Her Majesty therefore has it in mind to accede to the tide of opinion the Society represents – that mere *reform* is not enough! ...'

Tom looked at Elias in despair. The Society was going to win. There was gloom all round. The one person smiling was Arthur Bedford. The Magistrate's oratory rolled on, and an uncomfortable picture began to form.

'... Besides that, Her Majesty has had representations from the highest eminences of the Church, and from His Grace the Duke of Bedford, and especially from the Society for the Reformation of Manners, urging her to terminate the theatre's Patent. She has been unwilling to take that step, but recent events have cast a shadow over the place that cannot easily be lifted. They declare the theatre to be a poisoned well, a sink of iniquity, an ungoverned anarchy ...'

This was the kind of rhetorical language that could roll on indefinitely. Tom and Elias were growing restless. Amos Jackson was staring anxiously at Sally, who was seated on a stool in the corner. The magistrate turned his head:

'... I see you smiling, Mr Bedford ...'

He paused. The tone was cold, ironic. At once the half-smile froze on the clergyman's lips.

'... I hope you do not think you are a mere spectator at this meeting? You will be flattered to know that your associations – your *doings* – have been under scrutiny – and to judge from your presence at the Fair in that ludicrous disguise, you remain active.'

'But Mr Hector! ...'

'I beg you to be quiet, Sir. You shall have your say very soon. We have little time and there is much ground to cover ...'

He gave a judicial cough.

'... First, I need to invite Constable Cobb to deliver his report. Mr Cobb has been acting as my deputy today, and I suspect he may have something that is material to the business in hand ...'

He looked at Tom, then at Amos.

'... Do I take it, Constable, that you and your team have had a fruitful evening?'

It was the turning-point.

The feeling in the room at once changed. Elias did indeed have things to report, the first of which was the identity of the heavily-built stage-hand who had so far been sitting silently with hands on knees, waiting for his moment.

'Mr Hector – let me introduce to you ... *The Red Cross Knight*.'

The Magistrate let out a spontaneous 'Ah!' and looked Amos up and down. 'I begin to see the picture. At our last interview, Mr Cobb, you offered an alarming series of suspicions, and you sketched in nothing less than a conspiracy against the Theatre Royal company, with Mr Bedford here at its head ...'

'But this is outrageous! A vicious libel!'

A red-faced Arthur Bedford had leapt to his feet.

'Mr Bedford – Control yourself! No charge has been brought against you, and no allegation will be accepted without evidence – it is this we are seeking ...'

Hector softened his voice and sought to restore calm.

'... Mr Cobb – you and your team have been gathering such evidence, have you not?'

'We have, Mr Hector. You sought proof for what I alleged, and we are here to present you with it.'

And so, with the assistance of Amos Jackson and the two eavesdroppers, the Reverend Bedford's *associations* and *doings* were laid bare, one by one. It was remorseless. Bedford's unguarded talk with Amos was precisely reported, and the full sinister tale unfolded, item by item, from the dangerous 'accidents' at the performance of *Macbeth* to the more trivial threatening letters, the stonings, and the obscene sketch of the players; it was agreed that the attack on Tom and the provoking of Hannibal the Elephant could both have been deadly.

'It was fortunate indeed that no lives were lost.'

Bedford met the Magistrate's frown with an expression of wide-eyed indignation:

'Neither action was sanctioned by me! You have no evidence – only hearsay!'

Amos hesitated before intervening. He faced the Magistrate:

'I have more to say on this, Sir. The plot is still active, and Mr Bedford has another agent – one more dangerous by far than me – who has been busy. We both heard him admit to this. The man goes by the name of *Merlin* …'

'You choose romantic names for your gang, Mr Bedford! … This *Merlin* – do you know his identity?'

There was no reply.

'Mr Bedford is obstinately silent about it,' said Elias. 'And Mr Jackson is right: this Merlin remains at large, perhaps with two associates … We suspect there may be danger tonight – something yet to be resolved …'

Bedford still said nothing. The Magistrate's exasperation began to show.

'The more of this I hear, Mr Bedford, the more uncooperative I find you. It paints a scene of deliberate havoc – and an entire disregard for human life … I expect you will claim that the poisoning of the company yesterday was none of your doing either?'

The Magistrate looked solemnly at the now perspiring clergyman, and waited for a response.

'I regret Mr Angell's death – indeed I do. It was not meant to happen …'

'His *death?* …'

The Magistrate looked round at the others.

'… I assure you, Mr Bedford, that – no thanks to you! – Mr Angell is very much alive – or he was some twenty minutes ago. Miss Twiss and I left him in good spirits, though with an aching stomach and a wildness in his eyes. Indeed, he had a great deal to say, and his evidence confirms all I have been hearing about your activities.'

'Alive? But …'

Bedford shot an accusing look at Amos, who was himself looking questioningly at Sally. Will could see the two of them were longing to have their own scene together.

The Magistrate continued:

'And there was somebody else at Mr Angell's bedside when we arrived – a personage I would never have expected to see in a thousand years …'

This drew Bedford's attention.

'… However low a stage-player may sink, he is sure to have his *devotees,* and this one is a name that will be familiar to you – Mr Ebenezer Tysoe …'

This was music to Tom's ears. Bedford, however, noticeably slumped in his chair.

'… Yes, another Reverend gentleman!' said Hector ruefully. 'I have to admit, Mr Bedford, our clergy are excessively vigilant in theatrical matters. Both of you show a remarkable adherence to the world of the players …'

Elias was now relishing every delicious word – it was clear that far from being idle, the Magistrate had been pursuing an investigation of his own.

'… What I succeeded in extracting from Mr Tysoe – a highly embarrassed Mr Tysoe, I must say – was his concern over another matter … I refer to the attempted destruction of the Maypole in the Strand. This is the gravest episode in these annals – it is hardly possible to exaggerate the scale of the outrage. If it had not been for the heroics of Mr Mudge here …'

Toby blinked and looked down.

'… we would surely be mourning the deaths of women and children. But God be thanked, the attempt was foiled … I can tell you now, gentlemen, Her Majesty was horrified when the report reached her. In her mind, this occurrence casts a shadow on our reforming cause – taints it with fanaticism, with a contempt for public order …'

Mr Hector's voice took on the dark tones of a hanging judge passing sentence at the Old Bailey.

'… I am given to understand that this violent course of action was discussed – and sanctioned – by the inner circle of the Society, and that you, Mr Bedford, spoke in its favour?'

By this time, Arthur Bedford had come to think of himself differently. Where was Justice here? The sins of the Heathen were being ignored – even exonerated – while he was being humbled and derided. A great weight was pressing down on him, yet he felt an inner lightness. He looked around the room and could see their scorn. It was visible on every face. Something welled up inside him. Was he not being scourged for his principles? Was he not *despised and rejected of men?*

If they expected him to plead in his own defence, then he would not give them that satisfaction. On the contrary, he would return their contempt – not with anger and accusation, but with a quiet determination, a secure confidence in the righteousness of his cause.

And so, with all the evidence taken and the charge-sheet complete, the Reverend Arthur Bedford drew himself up again and spoke calmly and with deliberation. In summary, he told them he would not attempt to wriggle free of these *entanglements,* but would cling to the holy cause he fought for – and which *they* (he looked particularly at Mr Hector) had betrayed:

'It seems, gentlemen, that I have no man's blood on my hands – and that the worst I have done has been to discomfit the Enemy and help undo the work of the Devil. I shall continue to hold fast to that which is good. And in this, I know there are many who will support me … I am not without *connections*. If you pursue me vindictively you may find yourselves routed in your turn …

'But there is one person in this room who must answer before God for a crime beyond my reach. You declared at the outset, Mr Hector, that you had come to investigate a killing – that you were in pursuit of a murderer … Well – *there she is!*'

Everyone's attention turned to Sally Twiss, who throughout the scene had been sitting calmly while from every direction masculine voices had spoken of threats, danger, violence – the language of anger and dispute. She had received glances from Amos Jackson but had tried not to return them – and she looked away from him now.

The Magistrate continued:

'Yes, Mr Bedford. I have had a long interview with Miss Twiss, who has been most forthcoming. I shall not run through the details of the scene she described to me, but it was one of horror. I now see that Lord Tunbridge was indeed the abandoned libertine that you and others have painted. The Queen had put her trust in him and was looking to him to be a beacon to a reformed stage – and now the plan lies in ruins. The embarrassment to Her Majesty is painful, and I have today been informed by the Solicitor-General that she wishes at all costs to avoid a formal trial in which the depravity of a member of the House of Peers will be on public display – feeding the frenzy of all the hacks and scribblers of the metropolis. No. She desires that the curtain be drawn.'

There was a stunned silence. Tom looked at Elias with an unspoken question: was Justice covering her eyes? Both of them were conscious of Amos, who was stirring his limbs and readying himself to speak:

'Sir – I don't know what Miss Twiss has told you …'

Elias interrupted him:

'I'm sure, Amos, that Mr Hector does not wish to revisit the scene of the Baron's death at this moment. If Miss Twiss has given a full confession …'

'It was no *confession*, Mr Cobb …'

Sally intervened sharply. She looked confident, and her voice was firm.

'… I've told Mr Hector what happened – of the violence His Lordship used against me on many occasions. I don't want to visit the hateful scenes again … But I've made it plain: if a public trial comes on, then I'll lay out the full story – every minute circumstance. I have no choice. I shall plead guilty to manslaughter and accept the court's verdict – but the picture I will paint for the jury will be a memorable one, I assure you!'

She turned to the Magistrate and tilted her head as if inviting him to speak. He was only too eager to do so:

'The jury – yes indeed! Miss Twiss has made it clear that the abuse she suffered at the Baron's hands was not to be borne, and that on this final occasion she dared to defend herself from a violent rape. There were no witnesses … but we may well imagine the scene in the costume-room. It was the interval of the play, and the Baron's purpose in luring her there is plain enough … the whole scene is abhorrent. The actress must bear her part for her foolishness, but there can be no mitigation for the Baron's actions.'

Tom and Elias exchanged anxious glances. They were aware that Amos Jackson seated beside them was restless and preparing to speak, and they were desperate to hold him back. Whatever the truth of the scene in the store-room, Sally's account had convinced Mr Hector, and he seemed minded to let the curtain descend. Were Amos to declare himself right now …

'Mr Hector …'

Amos began speaking; but he hesitated slightly, wanting to find the right words. As the Magistrate turned in his direction, Sally gave Amos a direct look whose meaning was not to be missed. The actress was at her most compelling: her eloquent eyes and expressive mouth together spoke clearly to him: 'trust me, Amos,' they said. 'Keep silent and trust me.'

'Yes, Mr Jackson?' said Hector encouragingly.

'Sir … I just want to say that Lord Tunbridge spoke contemptuously of Miss Twiss on several occasions. I do not think he had any respect for her. He was known in the company for a confirmed rake – a man who was once the *confrere* of Etherege and Rochester.'

'A forceful point, Mr Jackson. We have thankfully entered a politer century, and the excesses of the last age are no longer acceptable. The court debauchee is out of fashion.'

On that point everyone could be agreed. A complaisant note was struck; and as if to imprint the thought in their minds, at that moment the door opened and Pinkerman's head peeped in:

'I don't wish to interrupt your deliberations, Mr Hector – but may I please reclaim my office? Our first patrons are beginning to arrive, and we are becoming busy.'

The Magistrate stood up:

'Of course, Pinkerman. We must make way for *The Devil on Two Sticks*, must we not? I shall leave you to your *infernal* work. This is no place for me … On another occasion I might have interested myself. But other matters take precedence.'

Pinkerman had stepped into the room, unable to conceal his relief. Others were rising to their feet.

'If you can restrain yourself a few moments more, Mr Pinkerman, I need to draw things to a close …'

Mr Hector was attempting to maintain some of his magisterial dignity.

'... This has been a valuable meeting, Mr Cobb – and you and your team have done a remarkable job. I shall be able to deliver a full report to Sir James Montagu in the morning ... and I think my recommendations will find favour with him – and with Her Majesty ...'

Elias drew himself up to his full height and nodded silently. Compliments like that needed to echo for a while.

'... If I may have the services of your watchman Turley, I shall return with Miss Twiss. For form's sake she needs to be held in custody – Sir James may wish to question her further tomorrow ... As for you, Mr Bedford ...'

The look on the Magistrate's face noticeably darkened.

'... you will be placed in custody too. My deputy Mr Cobb will make the necessary arrangements. I leave him with you, Constable. You will be kept informed – expect to hear more tomorrow.'

The Reverend Bedford opened his mouth to protest, but judiciously closed it again, recalling his resolution to embrace his humiliation amongst the heathen. This was a time of trial, and he would bear it with fortitude.

A few moments later, Sally had been led out, leaving a tongue-tied Amos wondering what was happening. He felt he had been watching a swiftly-moving scene and was trying to follow the twists of the plot.

Elias reached out and patted him on the arm:

'Courage, man! Sometimes it is good to say little. You must do nothing rash ... Tom here will have to ready himself for the pageant soon, but until then I surrender you to his charge – If I am Mr Hector's deputy, then Mr Bristowe is mine! ...'

The sparkle in the constable's eyes told Amos this was not an oppressive sentence – the scene-shifter's thoughts were whirling, and it would be good to talk matters over.

Elias turned to Arthur Bedford:

'... You are strangely silent, Sir. I hope you will not attempt to abscond from the Fair? I have to remain in the booth for this evening's performance, and I insist you accompany me – either with the handcuffs or without them. I leave that to you ...'

The Reverend Bedford could not disguise his contempt and remained obstinately dumb.

'... I think you may even enjoy *The Devil on Two Sticks* – the protagonist is a figure you know well.'

Pinkerman at this point was rummaging in the drawer of his desk. He paused and looked up:

'Yes, I think Mr Bedford will find our little play illuminating – and the pageant too. It should give you food for thought, Sir.'

Still silence. A strange faraway look had come into Bedford's eyes, as if he felt himself already in some other, higher place.

'May I wish you luck for the performance tonight, gentlemen,' said Elias in the doorway, gripping the handcuffs with one hand and beckoning Mr Bedford with the other.'

'... And now for the *Devil* ...'

Chapter Forty-Seven

WIDOW TROTTER FELT like a Field-General who had devised a battle-plan of genius but instead of leading her forces into the fray was made to languish back at camp waiting for news. Eager to hear how her troops had performed, she was making what haste she could towards the Brook Field. The Bay-Tree had needed her, and at that time of a Friday evening a hackney was not to be had, so she found herself walking briskly down Long Acre and out west to Piccadilly. All the way she had been running difficulties through her mind: how much their commission depended on chance, and how much could go wrong. *Evidence, evidence, evidence* – the word seemed to echo with every stride. Had they managed to lure Arthur Bedford to the Fair? Had they learnt anything about tonight's dangers? Was Amos Jackson indeed the Red Cross Knight? And what about Merlin? Was Gilbert now dead? And what was happening to Sally? Ordinarily the Bay-Tree was a busy news-exchange, but not on this occasion. She was eager for a reunion with Tom and Will, and looked to receive a packet of hot intelligence.

At last she found herself turning into the lower end of the Brook Field, past the Dog and Duck. The place was humming, and a huddle of men round the door were offering noisy greetings to anyone who passed. She fell in behind a couple of characters who were leaving the hostelry evidently refreshed but not in celebratory mood. They were talking and seemed more intent on each other than on the life of the Fair. Both were coatless, with dark breeches and heavy boots; one wore a sleeveless jerkin and the other had a wallet hooked round his belt. As they worked their way up the main concourse the pair's concentration struck her as odd – out of tune with the mood around them.

Her train of thought had put her in a suspicious mood, and the thought grew stronger as they neared Pinkerman's booth and the men at last began to show an interest in their surroundings. Widow Trotter's steps slowed. The two of them had paused to read the banner that was strung across the booth's entrance. Appropriately it was propped up on tall sticks and tilted over at a crazy angle. The cloth pictured the show's unconventional master of ceremonies: a cloven-footed figure in a jester's cap who leaned on a pair of crutches and winked knowingly at his audience. She pretended to dig into the purse attached to her wrist while watching the men's faces closely: what she saw were not looks of amusement or curiosity, but something close to contempt.

But then the pair moved on and Mrs Trotter breathed out deeply. Her imagination was getting the better of her, though her unsettled mood was genuine. The closeness of the air was becoming oppressive, not helped by the acrid smoke from the torches along the concourse. And at that moment, to confirm her feeling of unease, she detected a low rumbling. It was far away, as if distant field-guns were being discharged on the other side of the city. If this wasn't early May she would have taken it for thunder.

'Mrs T! …'

The cry came from behind her, and she looked round to see a beaming Will Lundy approaching, a half-eaten pear in his hand. There was excitement in his eyes.

'... Well met, Mrs T! There's so much news for you – and more to come when Tom finishes his meeting.'

'A meeting? Where is he?'

'In Pinkerman's office – with Amos Jackson, and – you really should be sitting down to hear this! ... . The Reverend Arthur Bedford.'

'Did he come? How wonderful!'

'Not only that, but he fell into our trap – I've heard that the gentleman was most indiscreet.'

'So, you weren't there?'

'Oh no, my face was too familiar. I had to stay out of the way – after all, we had our tethered goat ready. It seems Amos played his part to perfection and Bedford let slip a great deal. Tom was trailing them – and Toby Mudge too ... There is *evidence*, Mrs T! Lots of it ... Mr Cobb has *arrested Bedford!* They are all having a lively time together right now, thrashing things out. I long to hear the upshot of it. They'll surely finish soon.'

Widow Trotter was struggling to take all this in:

'That means ... Amos Jackson ...'

'Is Bedford's agent – oh yes – and was Tunbridge's too. There was a terrible falling-out ... and – the biggest news of all – both Sally *and* Amos have confessed to killing Tunbridge!'

Silence. For once Mary Trotter was lost for words. At this dramatic moment Will took a bite out of his pear and began chewing, stopping the flow of his revelations and allowing her a few seconds to recover:

'You're right, Mr Lundy. I need to sit down. This is too much to take in! You must rehearse it to me in order.'

They soon found a quieter spot at the northern end of the booth where they could hear each other speak, and Mrs Trotter was given the fuller picture. There was a great deal to cheer her, especially the news that young Mr Angell might have survived his poisoning. But it was the double confession that raised the most startling questions.

'Amos must be besotted indeed,' she said. 'Or could Sally be wanting to protect him? ... Perhaps they killed him together?'

'Amos Jackson's story rang true, Mrs T ...'

He frowned.

'... And if so, then all along Sally has been shielding him. She has never mentioned him to us.'

'That's no surprise, Mr Lundy. We shall never know for certain what happened in that store-room. I suspect Lord Tunbridge's account might have told things very differently.'

It was an uncomfortable thought, and Widow Trotter wasn't proud of it.

'We'll get to hear more when their interview is done,' said Will. 'Sally and Amos are in there together – perhaps they'll decide on a story between them!'

Will and Mrs Trotter didn't have long to wait. By now they had both ceased to expect the expected, and so when they saw Tom and Amos approaching side by side and talking genially, they simply hailed them and waited for their news. There was a lot of shaking of heads and raising of eyebrows as they recalled the scene in Pinkerman's office.

'*No trial?*' said Mrs Trotter in wonder. 'Is that really so? Will they not take Sally to court?'

'This is no ordinary case,' said Will. 'The Queen's interest makes it exceptional. From what you say, Tom, the Solicitor-General is embarrassed by the whole affair. He himself may be acting on royal instructions.'

'And the theatre? ... What is to happen there?'

She raised the topic apprehensively.

'Yes indeed,' added Will. 'If Lord Tunbridge is to be silently forgotten, then what about his ambitions for the playhouse?'

'The fate of the company is still uncertain – there's no news as yet. Mr Hector is to report to Montagu in the morning …'

Tom paused and looked at Amos:

'… and with the various dirty tricks now uncovered, the plot against the theatre is proved – Amos here has seen to that. His evidence has been decisive. And it seems our Mr Tysoe has given Hector a full account of the attack on the maypole. The Society for the Reformation of Manners is well and truly implicated.'

Will was astonished:

'*Tysoe* and *Hector* together?'

'Yes – Mr Hector heard about Gilbert's recovery and so he took Sally to call on him … and who should be leaning over the bedside but your clergyman friend!'

'That must have been a heart-wringing scene,' said Widow Trotter '– but no little embarrassment to Mr Tysoe.'

'True,' said Tom. 'And it confirmed his aversion to Arthur Bedford. He was happy to point the finger – after all, the man had very nearly killed Gilbert. I can't see that the Reverend Mr Bedford has any escape now – although at the end of our interview he was defiant and proclaiming the power of his *connections*.'

'Hah!'

Widow Trotter's single syllable captured their thoughts exactly.

'And what about tonight?' asked Will. 'Is trouble still expected? …'

He glanced at Amos Jackson.

'… How safe are we going to be?'

Amos looked uneasy. He had so far kept silent, but knew he was being expected to speak:

'I've told my story, Mr Lundy, and have confessed my part in the plot … but things are out of my hands. *Merlin* is Bedford's prime agent, and what I told you about him holds true.'

'Yes, Bedford confirmed it,' said Tom. 'Merlin is his agent at the Fair – but he has refused to identify the man.'

Widow Trotter looked grave:

'That's troubling. What do you say, Tom? Do you think this Merlin intends to play a part tonight?'

'I do. Bedford's look just now was very chilling – you recall his face in the theatre-box, Mrs T? For all his humiliation, he hasn't lost any of that terrifying certainty. The man still *believes*.'

Will then realised there was something else she needed to know:

'You speak of *playing a part*, Mrs T ... Well, Tom and I have a final revelation for you. As you know, tonight's satirical droll is to conclude with a pageant of the Seven Deadly Sins ...'

She looked suspiciously at the two of them. One was stretching his arms, the other raising a fist.

'... You see before you *Sloth* – and *Wrath!*'

Her reply was a far from droll one:

'That's not good, gentlemen – just when we need you both to be alert and cool-headed.'

Over recent years, Pinkerman's booth had witnessed some remarkable theatrical occasions, and the man whose very name evoked the spirit of May Fair was anticipating another memorable evening. This year was seeing a double experiment. Neither of his presentations was quite the typical fare of the droll-booth – he left that to Miller with his lumbering sea-gods and comic Scotsmen! *The Tender Courtesan* was a drama of human passion and sentiment, and now with *The Devil on Two Sticks* the booth was about to witness a satirical fantasy.

Pinkerman was apprehensive. The thing would have been a challenge at the best of times; but given yesterday's events and the threat hovering over the company, he would be relieved if the performance passed without incident. The theme was dangerous enough, and having a devil loose in the booth had to be something of a risk. He thought of the concluding pageant of the Seven Deadly Sins and wondered if it would have been better to settle on the Four Cardinal Virtues instead ... *Prudence* might have guided him from the outset, and *Temperance* have held the reins; but perhaps *Fortitude* would be there to see them through the evening – and of course *Justice* was always an ideal – if only they could find their way to her!

As Pinkerman peered round the curtain he could see it was a packed house, and he could hear an expectant hum filling the place. The audience had been in their seats for a while, and no-one was now being admitted. People were standing along the back. He was glad to see Elias Cobb in position and was sure he could glimpse a pair of handcuffs ... certainly the constable's neighbour was staring coldly ahead as if wishing he were elsewhere. And over on the aisle at the far side was the estimable Mrs Trotter – wisest and most genial of ladies! He could count a good number of solid citizens, and also some young bloods and a few members of the smart set – perhaps the promise of satire had drawn them in? Finally, his eyes flicked across to the 'boxes' along the left and he smiled to himself. Yes, there they were! – all three of them – dressed in black, their masks moulded into fantastical features. He could see they were attracting attention and adding to the excitement in the room.

From her seat toward the back of the tent, Widow Trotter noticed the curtain twitch and a twinkling eye peep out. No doubt who that was! She silently wished Pinkerman well and tried to let the evening's good news lift her spirits. But her trepidation couldn't be overcome. Although she had heard much to cheer her, the threat of the mysterious 'Merlin' remained, and Amos Jackson's concern had said everything. She was forced to admit that the scene-shifter seemed honest enough; but he had nearly killed Pinkerman and Gilbert, and as for Tunbridge's death – well, the man would certainly be handy with a weapon. He had been working behind the scene at the machines – they had been promised some mechanical ingenuity – and that in itself was unsettling ... And what about those masked ladies over there? Were they fair-goers in masquerade, or pagan priestesses? Mrs Trotter knew Pinkerman well enough to think the latter the more likely.

Sounds of activity were coming from behind the curtain, and she decided it would be a relief when the performance could begin. The seconds ticked by, and she had a last anxious look behind her ...

Her breath caught, as if someone were clasping her throat ... She couldn't be mistaken ... There, at the back of the tent, were the two men from the Dog and Duck. They were not talking, but simply standing side by side, their eyes fixed on the stage. She glanced over to Amos, but he was gazing expectantly at the shivering curtain. And at that instant a drum rolled, a pipe began playing a jaunty melody – and the curtain opened.

The scene was an interior. But this was no ordinary room. The painted backcloth pictured a collection of strange vessels and bottles in vivid colours, all ranged along shelves, and standing in front was a table holding a pile of papers, some heavy volumes, and an odd assortment of instruments – a long-necked flask and glass vials more suited to an alchemist's study; there were spheres and compasses and quadrants too. On the floor stood a large earthenware jar, and an elaborate lamp hung from the ceiling.

At once, a casement window swung open of its own accord and a human figure leapt through it – an agile youth who marked his arrival with a somersault, to wild applause from the audience. He announced himself as 'Don Stulto!' – a student fresh from a nocturnal escapade with a young wife of Seville; he was being pursued by her angry husband and his gang, and had clambered across the roofs of the city to this far-flung garret only to find himself in an astrologer's lair.

The audience were expectant. Suddenly the silence was broken by a loud sobbing, and as the seconds passed the realisation dawned that it was coming from inside the jar, as if the vessel itself were sighing! But how could this be? The neck was far too narrow. A murmur rose in the booth – and then there was silence again as a pathetic human voice was heard:

'Rescue me, Señor, I beg! I have been three years enclosed in this jar. In this house lives a magician who by the power of his art has kept me so long shut up in this close prison!'

'Then you must be a spirit?' said a confused Don Stulto.

'I am a *daemon!*' the voice declared. 'And if you free me I can do you many services! I have power to marry old grey beards to young girls – masters to their maids – virgins of low fortune to lovers that have none ... It is I, Sir, who have introduced into the world Luxury, Debauchery, Games of Hazard – all the chemistry of human desire. I am the only inventor of carousings, dances, music, plays, and every foppish fashion! The theatre is *my world* ... I am that famous *Asmodeo Jingo* – surnamed *The Devil Upon Two Sticks* – and I will help you in your amours. Nothing will be beyond your reach – your every desire will be satisfied!'

'But have you no trick to make me pay for the broken pot?'

'On the contrary, you will be pleased with my acquaintance – I will teach you whatever you desire to know, and discover to you all the faults of mankind.'

'The faults of mankind? ...'

The young man looked suddenly interested.

'... That is true knowledge – that is what I long to know!'

And with that, he seized one of the bottles and struck the jar with full force. There was a sudden crash of sound, and the vessel's sides fell away to reveal a small figure less than three feet high. He had the legs of a goat and his arms rested on two crutches. The creature was long of face, with a sharp chin, a yellow and black complexion, and eyes that shone out like coals.

'What think you of my beauty, Sir?' Asmodeus asked.

'I confess you are somewhat ugly – but if you fulfil your promises to me ...'

'Come then!' said the demon. 'Take hold of my cloak, and fear nothing – whatever the danger appears!'

And with that, the demon turned. The backcloth dropped away to reveal a panorama of tiled roofs, and the pair of them lifted into the air and swung out into the night.

The audience cheered warmly and settled down for what was sure to be an entertainment to remember. The stage began to transform. The student and Asmodeus reappeared, and the little devil pranced about the set, his twin crutches flinging him to left and right at great speed.

'Behold my diabolical powers!' he cried. 'For you, Don Stulto, I will lift off the roofs of all the houses and expose to view whatever is hidden under them! The good citizens of Seville, snug in their respectable virtues, will be shown for what they are ... I will disclose to you the very springs of their actions – their most secret thoughts!'

The student beamed with delight:

'Yes, my little devil – you must show me all! The wit of man is never at rest and I have great curiosity to see the truth of human nature!'

'And so you shall! Under my piercing light all varnish disappears ... Let us begin with the place that is closest to my heart! ...'

There was a flash, and the set began moving. The cogs turned, and there swung into view a remarkably familiar scene.

Asmodeus scurried to the other side of the stage and waved a crutch in the air.

'... This is a *theatre!*' he declared. 'I may call it *my very own house!* ...'

There was more cheering from the audience as the Theatre Royal came fully into view; and by a remarkable trick, the front of it was lifted away to reveal a scene in progress.

'... My playhouse is the constant site of love-adventures. We are now *behind the scenes* – tell me what you see!'

'I see a smug old gentleman with a cane in his hand – a wrinkled countenance, but an amorous briskish eye! ...'

And there he was – Lord Tunbridge – as near as could be. It was a remarkable likeness. And the scene being played out was clear enough. A young actress was in his clutches, and the commentary continued as the old gentleman began pawing her, a leering look on his face.

'... I see an old lecher!'

'Yes – a Machiavel in the games of Love. A *Lord* by day – a *rake* by Night! A gentleman who would reform everyone – but himself! A man who condemns the players, but acts the seducer in his private theatricals! The *green room* is his stage – the *property-store* his field of battle! ...'

The audience roared its approval; and as if drawn by the warmth of their response, Tiny François (for it was he!) leapt down from the stage into the centre aisle of the tent. A demon in form, he moved like a ballet-dancer, and his gruesome face turned and nodded as he caught every eye in the room.

'... Rest your eyes on that scene, my friends,' he declared. 'For the Theatre is the truest picture of human life. It tells us that those who make the greatest figure in the world are not what they seem – no more than the little fellow who takes off his armour in the dressing-room is the hero who had strutted about the stage! ...'

He himself began to strut along the aisle like a general on parade.

'... It is all a well-managed *imposture!* It is the rosin makes the lightning, and the box and balls the thunder! Othello and Desdemona will share a bottle behind the scenes! Greeks and Trojans will happily carouse together! In sum, my friends, the playhouse is much less a cheat than is the world, where those disguises remain forever in place.'

So that was the message – in life, human actors are permanently in character! Widow Trotter could understand why Tom's prologue had so delighted the company.

The little devil scampered back up to the stage and continued to direct the performance. More scenes followed, each one a tableau of hypocrisy and self-delusion. The machines worked smoothly, and as the cogs turned, another representation came into view. Occasionally one scene was set beside another to point up the cheat. To the right, an old miser counted his gold, while on the left his children cast lots for his possessions; to the right, a tired old whore removed her hair, eyebrows and teeth, while in the compartment to the left her client, now returned home, laid down his sword and removed his false eye, his false whiskers, and his wooden leg – before both of them retired to their beds and snuffed out their candles.

At that scene, an unexpected silence fell on the room. People suddenly felt the power of satire to marry comedy and tragedy. It was a moment of magic ... But the picture was banished by a final flourish of drums and yet more leaping by the demon. The play's climax had arrived.

The final tableau revealed itself. It presented a wooden pulpit from which a preacher was delivering a sermon. It was Arthur Bedford to the life! – but it must have been a mask. The figure's gestures were imperious and he looked scornfully down on the array of sinners in the booth before him, an expression of fixed distaste on his face, his every gesture one of accusation. The eyes blazed angrily.

As little Asmodeus delivered his commentary, the audience felt the chill of the scene as if they themselves were being accused. The preacher's finger pointed at each of them. There was an uncomfortable apprehension in the room.

And then it happened. The front of the pulpit lifted away into the air – and there the preacher stood exposed in all his male glory. Widow Trotter wasn't the only member of the audience who gasped at the sight. Slowly the pulpit began to turn like a carousel, and as the back became the front, the preacher's steps brought him into the embrace of a siren-like beauty. Before the curtain began to close, the last words of Asmodeus rang through the booth:

'*Our canting preachers propagate the cheat,*
And shun the fire, yet enjoy its heat.
Such men attack the sins that they're inclin'd to,
And damn the very vices they've a mind to.

Thus REFORMATION *doth discharge its rage*
And claims the virtue of a spotless page,
Sees crimes in others roundly sent to Hell
While they indulge and think themselves quite well.
OUR *stage presents a true Democracy,*
Whose greatest enemy's – – – HYPOCRISY!'

The words of Tom's prologue! Delighted applause rang through the tent. Widow Trotter was thunderstruck, and her eyes met Elias's. The constable sensed the danger of the moment and his face was a mixture of joy and alarm. But the tall figure by his side – handcuffs no longer in sight – remained motionless. Far from protesting at the scene, the Reverend Arthur Bedford kept a cool, statuesque silence.

People's hands finally tired and the applause came to an end – but there was a strange echo to the sound. A deep rumbling could be heard out there in the Brook Field. A superstitious person might have taken it as Heaven's anger at the devilish doings on stage – but Widow Trotter knew a storm was approaching. The thought made her shiver. In a few moments' time the Seven Deadly Sins would be making their appearance, and there was a chance the pageant would be accompanied by unlooked-for sound effects.

But something else was making her uneasy. The moment the final applause broke out she had turned to scan the back row for the men from the Dog and Duck. Perhaps it was disapproval, or was there some more malicious intent? Whatever the explanation, she had seen the two of them silently slipping out of the booth.

Chapter Forty-Eight

WIDOW TROTTER HAD little time to think before there was fresh activity. The piper began playing a merry tune to the accompaniment of some clattering behind the curtain, and young Don Stulto's face peeped round it. With raised eyebrows he looked out at the audience:

'Where is my little devil gone? … That trickster *Señor Jingo* has flown! Does he hide himself amongst you? …'

He stepped out to the edge of the stage and began pacing up and down, shaking his head and tut-tutting to himself.

'… Was I not vouchsafed a sight of all the *faults* of mankind? – And a pretty foolish collection they were, don't you agree? – a gallery of cheats and scoundrels, with enough smooth-faced rogues for a canting congregation! … But the Devil is, I feel dissatisfied – I have a desire for *more* – do you not feel it too, my friends? …'

He paused, and was answered by an approving murmur around the room.

'… We have enjoyed a feast of hypocrites. We have seen Vice disguised as Virtue, and Sin clothed in Holiness; we have watched villains deceiving others, and fools deceiving themselves. All this folly and vice is black enough, I grant … and yet … I yearn for the *very thing* … What do you say? Do you not long to view *the Sins themselves?* …'

It was clear that the audience were more than happy. The benches swayed as everyone settled themselves for what was to come.

'... Follies and crimes, my friends, are but skin-deep – there is always a hand ready to draw the curtain – a trick to cheat the eyes ... but Sin is ingrained. The villain may flee from justice – but his *Sin* will find him out!'

He turned and raised an arm to the curtain and beckoned it to open once more. Now it was he who had become the master of ceremonies.

Something stirred within Widow Trotter. She waited for the scene to appear, feeling distinctly uncomfortable. At that moment there was a heavy rumbling outside the tent – the storm was nearer now ... but something else was echoing in her head:

'Their sins will find them out!'

Her mind went back to that overheard conversation in the New Exchange, and to the phrase that had been spoken with a malicious laugh, as if it was the culmination of their plot. And what more appropriate moment than this? *The Devil on Two Sticks* had been a satirical game, but the pageant of the Seven Deadly Sins would be something more: a darker and more dangerous tableau. She knew Pinkerman had been concerned about it, and perhaps the attack on the Sins during their parade was an omen? She began to think about what she could do.

The curtain opened to a burst of applause, and the first of the figures – *Pride* – entered onto a stage that was now draped in diaphanous cloths – red, blue, green, amber, silver and black, which wove together and swayed like a dancer's veils. The colours shifted and superimposed themselves. It was a remarkable effect and gave her form a moving backdrop of colours, as if the imagination were bringing human pride itself into the tent.

'I am PRIDE!' she began, holding the golden mirror in front of her face and gazing into it while she took little minuet-steps across the stage ... 'I am the vanity of the world, and I see only myself – my beauty, my grace – and my divine power – for am I not a *heavenly image*? Do not men follow only me? Do not even infidels bow the knee to worship PRIDE?'

She held out a long string of pearls and waved them to the music of the pipe.

Mrs Trotter came to a determination. The two men had not re-appeared. While the audience around her were allowing their fancies to play, her imagination was taking her outside the canvas walls of the booth to the Fair-ground beyond. Might some gang be preparing an attack? She looked over at Elias, who remained shackled to his statuesque prisoner – so she couldn't call on him ...

On the stage, Pride gave her blessing to the audience and stepped aside, watching indignantly while the second Vice made his entrance, to very different effect. The shabbily-dressed figure sidled on, his face turning to and fro, hands embracing a locked casket. 'I am COVETOUSNESS!' he whispered as he eyed the audience suspiciously ...

Widow Trotter resolved herself – there was nothing for it but to make her suspicions known. She slipped out of her seat, and a few steps brought her to the back of the room. The audience was intent on the stage and the grating voice that was coming from it: 'It is ever wise counsel,' said the miserly form, "Shut doors behind you! – fast bind, fast find!"' ...

She expected to find the two watchmen, Mudge and Turley, stationed at the booth's entrance, but there was no sign of either. The noisy activity of the Fair was continuing, but it was now overlaid by some riotous sounds coming from the direction of the fields. It appeared that fighting was going on. She inquired of the ticket-man seated by himself at his small table.

'There's a bit of a riot, ma'am, over in the fields there – started just now. Toby and Bob are off helpin.'

Suddenly, as her eyes followed his pointing finger, a brilliant double flash lit up the night sky. Then blackness again. She took a breath, and sure enough, a few seconds later came the crack of thunder like a massive rock splitting in two. She stepped outside the entrance and felt large drops of rain strike her forehead. Her brows contracted. At that moment she realised she had herself become the embodiment of *Suspicion*: surely this riot must be a staged distraction? At this vital moment the booth was left undefended … and yet all appeared well. The voice of common sense told her to return to the pageant, but she knew she would have to make certain …

Meanwhile, inside the booth, a green-faced *Envy* was hissing out his last words, while alternating fabrics of green and silver wove themselves into a pattern behind him in mimicry of the snake that writhed about his neck. This was about to be Tom and Will's moment – a scene Widow Trotter couldn't possibly miss. She stepped into the tent again and watched from the back as *Wrath* made his entrance to a swirl of red and black that shook like battle standards.

'I am WRATH!! …'

Tom's tones were powerful enough, but they were enhanced by a sudden crash of thunder, louder than before. Even Pinkerman couldn't have arranged it better – it was as if Jupiter himself were declaiming from the stage.

Tom wasn't tall, but his helmet – a shiny bronze-coloured creation with a flamboyant plume (the very one that King Hal had sported at Agincourt) enhanced his heroic persona. As Widow Trotter watched him, a lump came to her throat – it was a mixture of pride and fear: admiring pride and anxious fear.

'… I am the twin of *Cruelty* and *Revenge!*' declared the figure, lifting his sword high into the air. She could see Tom's eyes blazing … 'In the heat of war I spare nobody. I make life itself a battle – marriage an angry duel – and politics a warfare upon earth! …'

She could sense a shudder run through the tent. Thanks to the imminent storm, Heaven and Earth seemed in collusion, and Tom had become an elemental master of ceremonies. He stood in the centre of the stage, legs apart, and commanded the room. There was real conviction in his anger, she thought, helped by the heavy rouge on his face – and then she saw that he was looking directly at Arthur Bedford.

'... I am *Murder* under another name! – I rouse the passions and goad them to destroy! I am the enemy of *Peace* and *Love*. No rest is mine – and I allow no rest to others! ...'

At that moment there was a spattering of nervous laughter in the booth. Over to the right a pale hand had appeared holding a burnt-out candle, followed by a long arm, and finally a bleary-eyed face with a night-cap hanging down from it. A layer of white lead gave the skin a ghost-like aspect.

'Who is it disturbs my rest? ... What is this commotion?'

Tom made his retreat, and Will stepped forth, a loose nightgown hanging from his lofty frame like washing on a line. Every move was an effort. He gave *Sloth* a sinuous quality, as if there were no muscle in his body, only tired sinews.

'I am SLOTH! ... I destroy by doing *nothing!* – I weaken every resolution and sap the vigour of men. I am the lazy bosom-friend of Evil, and sleep while evil deeds are done ... I am content to let things take their course ... so, let me lie! ...

A warm murmur came from the audience, as if this *Sloth* was somebody they could understand. But for Widow Trotter the words gave her a new determination. She knew she had to trust her instincts and be bold. And so, she turned her back on the room and left the tent to see if another scene might be beginning.

The rain was coming down hard now, and people were huddling for shelter inside the stalls, beneath awnings and in doorways. As she made her way along the side of the tent she told herself it was a foolish adventure. Her clothes were wet and clinging, and nothing at all seemed to be stirring there. But something drove her on ... She stepped round one of the ropes that secured the canvas roof. This field-side of the booth was dark and empty, offering no shelter at all, and it was hard to make anything out ... But the angry sky changed all in an instant. A flash of brilliance illuminated everything ...

Widow Trotter froze, her chest thudding at what she had just seen. There, without a doubt, was a figure who was not sheltering from the storm but crouching against the canvas of the tent. The man held one of the ropes in his hands and she was sure there had been the glint of a knife ...

Meanwhile, inside the droll-booth the carnival figure of *Gluttony* was lifting everyone's mood. Here on display was an image of grotesque excess, the embodiment of self-indulgence. He was holding a large chop in one hand and waving around a huge tankard of ale in the other – and farting clownishly.

'I am GLUTTONY! – I reck nothing of duty and order! – I feed myself without restraint – in spite of all – and I grow bigger, bigger ...'

By some trick his waistband began to expand as he spoke, and he swung his belly around with glee, his flushed face grinning and winking.

'... You are my friends, one and all! Let us carouse – and may the world go hang! We shall *gluttonize* together – Let others starve! ...'

He bit into the juicy chop. The warmth of the response from the well-fed audience encouraged him, and he continued to parade with brimming confidence, drinking healths at every turn. There was laughter and good cheer in the tent ...

On the other side of the canvas things were very different. In the darkness Widow Trotter took a step forward, but then stopped in her tracks. Her eyes were adjusting themselves a little. The man was certainly one of the pair who had left the booth earlier, and there was no doubting what he intended to do. But it would be foolish to challenge him physically. She must retrace her steps and raise the alarm.

At that moment she heard a shuffling noise behind her. She swung round, hoping to see some assistance.

'Hey! What the devil …'

It was the man in the jerkin. The rain was trickling down his stubbly face and onto a clenched fist that was holding a blade towards her. He was some six feet away.

'… Damn me, Joe! We've got comp'ny! …'

And then his voice became soft and menacing:

'… This is no place for a lady …'

'Hold things there!' shouted the other figure. 'There's a drunken sot fartin' round the stage. We're nearly ready …'

Indeed, Gluttony had been indulging himself, and it was a well-satisfied figure who eventually joined the other Vices now huddling around the pulpit, which still commanded the centre-stage. They were coming to resemble a gang of disreputables thrown out of an alehouse. But among them Tom and Will were trying to remain alert, scanning the booth for anything untoward.

The dancing scarves now changed to red and amber and began twisting together like tongues of fire. It was a fitting invitation to the final Vice, who strode confidently onto the stage with a giant codpiece swinging out from his hose. His face was concealed by a beaked Venetian mask, and a black hat covered his forehead. There was a swagger about the man as he stationed himself at the very front of the stage.

'I am LUST!' he shouted, in tones that made the audience shiver – this figure was evidently no subtle seducer but a blatant arouser of passion. His doublet was flame-coloured, and his hand held a blazing torch. Tom was uneasy – this was an unexpected addition ... Yes, it was the heat of Desire and it crackled menacingly, but it also signalled danger ...

As the rain poured down outside the tent, Widow Trotter looked at the man's knife, then up to his eyes. A flash of lightning showed them creasing into a smile.

'DO IT! ...'

The cry came from the other man, who was crouched behind her.

'... Cut away, Barney! – Do it! Leave her! This is it! ...'

At that moment, something distinctly wrathful seized Mrs Trotter. She reached for her purse and opened it, and as the man's knife lunged towards her she dug into it, and instantly a cloud of pepper covered the man's face. His eyes closed tightly and he cried out in pain, clutching his head. Widow Trotter pushed him to the floor and leapt like a deer over the guy-rope, running back in the direction of the booth's entrance.

Within the tent the seventh Deadly Sin had declared himself to the audience:

'I worship the things of the Flesh! I eat up the body and torment it with desire ... Can you feel its heat? Do you see these *flames?*'

Lust laughed at the audience and tossed his head back wildly ...

And suddenly Tom saw it – a livid scar, which curved under the man's ear. It was the figure he and Will had seen at the Dog and Duck – the one attending the reformers' meeting. Of course, Tom thought, this very afternoon Joe Byrne had been stabbed, and this man had taken his place ...

And at that instant it was clear that *Lust* had deserted his script and was delivering white-hot words of his own. They issued from the masked face like the cry of an avenging demon:

'For, behold, the LORD will come with fire, and his chariots like a whirlwind. He shall render his anger with fury, and with flames of fire!'

Tom turned to Will –

'Merlin! – This is *Merlin!'*

No more words were needed. The man had turned and was lifting his flaming torch towards the tangle of coloured scarves that waved behind him. Tom leapt forward and seized his arm, trying to jerk the torch away. But the man was fearsomely strong, and the flames were thrust towards Tom's face.

The sound of cheering came from the tent as *Wrath* grappled with *Lust*. They were a well-matched pair, and a vivid illustration of mankind's struggle with sin. Several voices cried out for *Wrath,* but one was cheering *Lust.*

And a moment later *Sloth* had joined the action. He jumped forwards with an energetic stride that belied his character and began grappling with the man's other arm.

'*Sloth* has awakened!' and 'Hurrah for *Sloth!'* were the cries, as the audience began to warm to the action, hardly noticing that the canvas ceiling of the booth was beginning to sag downwards above their heads. This was a brilliant climax to the evening – the Deadly Sins had never appeared in so animated a guise!

But *Lust* was exceptionally strong and was now managing to hold the torch to the side curtain. Flames were beginning to lick the fabric. The other Vices were drawn into the action, and cries of delight rang out as *Gluttony* ran forwards to the lit curtain and put the liquid contents of his tankard to excellent use. At the same time *Envy* was entangling *Lust* around the legs, and even a wary *Covetousness* was there to bring his casket down hard on *Lust*'s head – a blow that was at once seconded by *Pride*'s looking-glass. All in all, it was a wild *Psychomachia,* and the audience thrilled to it.

To add to the confusion, Widow Trotter was now in the room shouting to Elias about the threat to the tent, and the Constable had jumped to his feet. It took a moment for him to unlock the handcuffs before he ran through the entrance, commandeering a pair of well-built spectators to follow him.

But it was too late for the canvas roof, part of which began collapsing on the audience's heads. Those seated at the back of the room were now on hands and knees, or were struggling to hold the canvas above them. The stage-end was as yet unaffected, but escape through the booth's entrance was impossible. Curses rang out, and muffled cries of 'Hell's blood!' and 'What the Devil?' could be heard from every direction.

Amidst the growing panic there was one figure who remained impassive. Arthur Bedford, now released from his shackles, rose calmly to his feet and stood alone amid the faithless congregation. Around him, the worshippers of Dagon were in disarray, and their voices of mocking laughter were re-tuned to terror. He knew this was the god-given moment when the blasphemers were to be answered and the whole Satanic crew brought to judgment.

By the side of the stage was a large stand of candles, and Bedford walked with deliberation towards it, knowing exactly what he had to do. God's call had led him to this moment – and he was ready.

But his view was suddenly darkened by three female figures swathed in black, who stood blocking his way. He looked into their masked faces and saw grotesque distortions of the human countenance, shaped respectively into an accusing glare, a grimace of pain, and a howl of grief. It was a devilish Trinity, and it made his blood run cold.

Bedford froze, transfixed by the faces which held him in a single stare as three pairs of arms lifted and turned in a slow dance. They were like some dark force, aeons-old, placing a curse on him – emanations of the universe itself. He could see only them, and in spite of the cries and shouts behind him, it was their chanting that held him spellbound.

'We are the FATES! ...'

The voices spoke in unison.

'... We hold your *Destiny* in our hands ...'

And there, rising and falling before his eyes, was a thick black thread which twisted between them like a writhing snake.

'... We weave the thread of life. Even the Gods fear us, for we have a Knowledge that is greater than any power, divine or human. No-one escapes the path of his Fate! ...'

Bedford was staring, and breathing in short anxious bursts. Somehow he couldn't turn his eyes away.

The three figures chanted, each in turn:

'I *spin* the thread!'

'I *measure* the thread!'

'I *cut* the thread! ...'

Then the dark shape in the middle spoke his name:

'*Arthur Bedford!* ... Your time is *not yet!* ... Your work remains to do ... Self-murder is the blackest Sin – a sin against your Fate. *You must await your hour!* ...'

Bedford's chin was shaking, and the normally commanding features drooped as the words struck home. He swallowed drily. No words of his own could come.

The hesitation was crucial, and before the Reverend Arthur Bedford was able to collect himself, he found his arm firmly grasped, and after a metallic click he heard a very different voice:

'Now then, Mr Bedford – you must do nothing foolish ...'

It was Mudge the watchman, back from the field.

'... Thank you, ladies, I think this gentleman will be cooperative ...'

The three fatal sisters turned to each other and began removing their constricting masks, which had become more than a little oppressive during the evening's performance. Their appearance as the pageant's conclusion may have been prevented, but they were highly satisfied at the improvisation, which seemed to have achieved a genuine *coup de théâtre* – albeit to an audience of one.

'Well, sisters!' said Delarivier Manley. 'The Fates have had their say! We weave more powerfully than we know!'

'And we wove well,' said Lady Norreys. 'It's a rewarding role is it not?'

'It's one I could grow accustomed to!' said the third figure.

'You speak for us all, Lavinia. I think Arachne must be smiling her approval!'

Chapter Forty-Nine

'But what have the *Fates* decided, do you think? ...'

Lady Norreys was partly speaking to herself, and her question went unanswered. She was surveying the stage, where an unconscious *Lust* was lying on the floor surrounded by six Deadly Sins in shocked disarray. Next to her, Mrs Manley had turned to see men from the audience propping up the collapsed canvas roof with poles so as to allow escape from the back of the booth. The third of the Fates was looking with concern at her cousin Tom, who was holding his regal helmet under his arm and rubbing his neck.

The black thread of destiny hung limp from their hands. Was their weaving done?

The booth had gone eerily quiet. Moments earlier, a familiar voice from the stage had been offering reassuring phrases (though no-one seemed to be listening): 'no cause for alarm' – 'sincere apologies' – 'request your patience' – 'unforeseen events' ...' Pinkerman had sounded more like Christopher Rich than his usual buoyant self. Spoken above a surge of bodies, his words seemed like a comic commentary, as if people facing the end of the world were expected to form an orderly queue.

Fair-ground experiences could often be dramatic, but it was agreed that this performance had pushed theatre to its limits.

It had turned in an instant from a satiric entertainment to an unforgettable sermon whose message had been all too clear: Sin is a terrible thing. No ranting preacher could have brought the prospect of hell-fire closer, and as the audience emerged into the night they breathed deeply. The freshening drops of what was now a light rain seemed a benediction. What had they just escaped?

With the emptying of the booth, a degree of calm was restored. Thoughts began to turn to the nature of those 'unforeseen events' and their outcome. Gradually a huge relief settled over the company. The catastrophe had finally come, and somehow they had survived it – but only just. Elias's whispered words to Widow Trotter as he led Arthur Bedford away were sober ones:

'We have escaped with the skin of our teeth, Molly.'

A heavily-shackled Merlin followed shortly after. Once returned to consciousness, the man had become a bundle of fury and frustration, and it took three of them to drag him from the scene, to the accompaniment of a stream of indiscriminate obscenities and snatches of scripture. As for his two henchmen, the Fair had exacted its own rough justice thanks to a group of soldiers who were happy to take matters into their own hands.

In the booth, it wasn't long before Pinkerman's exuberance returned. After the frantic events of the past hour he decided that rather than drift away, his friends might want to talk matters over with a glass in their hand. And so, he invited the Bay-Tree militia and their associates into his office away from the half-collapsed tent, found seats for everyone, and opened a couple of bottles. He was already turning his mind to the morrow and was confident that after setting his team to work through the night the booth would once more be open for business. He announced that he had put an enthusiastic Amos in charge, who had assured him 'the thing would be done.'

'And do not fear! – we shall bring back *The Tender Courtesan!*' he declared. 'Mr Angell is anxious to reassume the role of Ernesto, and I have every expectation that Sally will be free for Tamara. It seems our play bids to become the sensation of the Fair! Reports of yesterday's performance have taken wing, and the ardour of its emotions is much praised. At Will's Coffee House it has been declared *une pièce sentimentale* – which I am assured is a term of the highest commendation in Paris.'

There was some shaking of heads at this bubbling confidence, and in more than one of them was the thought that Cantharides might become compulsory fuel for its performance. Ardour indeed!

But there was no avoiding the darker thoughts that were crowding in – Pinkerman's best port, though excellent, was no magic potion. Tom and Will had resumed their own clothes and were adjusting to reality, but the experience of inhabiting a Deadly Sin was not something either could forget. The look in *Lust*'s blazing eyes had been more frightening than his torch, and the burn on Tom's neck would stay with him for a while as a reminder.

'I have had my fill of Sin, Mr Pinkerman!' said a rueful Will. 'That pageant was too damnably real for my liking.'

'I *was* Wrath!' said Tom. 'When I looked into Arthur Bedford's eyes it seemed to take hold of me.'

Mrs Trotter smiled at her *protégés*:

'Well, you were both mightily convincing. I suspect you've converted a few terrified souls to the path of Virtue!'

The Fates concurred. Now relieved of their masks and black garments, the three of them were slightly less forbidding; nevertheless, something of the power of that darker world hung over them, and the looks on their faces spoke of unease at the role they had played:

'We came to act a part, Mr Pinkerman,' said Mrs Manley. 'But we became the thing itself. We decided Mr Bedford's fate, did we not?'

'... and the fate of a hundred innocents,' added Widow Trotter. 'Nothing was going to stop that man except divine intervention – little did he suspect it would be from the pagan world!'

'There was terror in his eyes,' said Lavinia. 'What will happen to him now, do you think?'

'I doubt our drama has converted him to tolerance and moderation,' said Will. 'But whatever the man's *connections*, he cannot go scot-free. His plots lie open, and too many find him an embarrassment. But a breach of law will be hard to establish – much depends on what Merlin is prepared to reveal.'

'Do we know anything about this "Merlin?"' asked Mrs Trotter.

Pinkerman shrugged his shoulders:

'Very little. Jake Sawyer is his name – that's the one he gave me. I was too trusting and took him on without a recommendation. He was a hard worker and threw himself into things – and he gave no sign of malice. He had worked for the Bedford estate ...'

'Ah, of course ... that's *his* "connection!"' said Will.

'And it's not one that will help our Mr Bedford, is it?' said Tom. 'All this reflects badly on the Duke. *Embarrassment* is hardly the word for it.'

'Very true – the chaplain has overreached himself and presumed too much with his patron. I doubt His Lordship will be forgiving.'

Widow Trotter smiled at the thought:

'I long to tell Mr Denniston and Mr Pomery our news. Bedford's arrest is sure to help them. Without Mr Pomery's aid we should never have lured him into the trap.'

'His part was invaluable,' said Will. 'And as for me – I only hope I'll not be indicted on a charge of forgery ...' He checked himself. 'Thank God the letter wasn't a legal document!'

For an uncomfortable instant an image of the death penalty came into their minds.

'But ...'

Widow Trotter paused and raised her glass to her lips as if to bless the thought.

'... I do believe we've *come through* – have we not, my friends?'

They were hesitant words, but Lady Norreys gave a murmur of agreement. She had been entrusted with the skein of heavy black thread which lay across her lap, and with both hands she slowly lifted it in the air for all to see:

'Look what an involved thread it is! But from what I've learned of your adventures, Mrs Trotter, you have found your way through the labyrinth! ... I only hope the crisis is now over. This will be a blow to the reformers, will it not?'

'We must make sure it *is*,' said Pinkerman, leaning forward as if willing the outcome. 'Their conspiracy has been unmasked!'

This was a little histrionic. It expressed something of the relief they all felt, but they knew the story was not quite done. The future of the company remained in question. Will looked at Tom inquiringly:

'Mr Hector's meeting with the Solicitor-General will be crucial ... When shall we hear about that?'

'I'm hoping Uncle Jack will bring news to the Bay-Tree tomorrow. But Constable Cobb may have word sooner ... and he'll have tidings of his own, no doubt.'

There was a palpable sense of hope in the room; but Will's spirits were being held in check, and he continued warily:

'It's Sally's fate that concerns me. She's been somewhat forgotten in all of this. Her destiny hangs in the scales – and everything I know of Justice tells me it's very uncertain.'

Tom turned to him:

'You've always had faith in her, Will – and I have always doubted her ... But I wonder if Sally is the one who has seen things most clearly? Lord Tunbridge thought he could mould her, and Gilbert seems never to have had the full measure of her – and now Mr Hector is afraid of what she can do – what she might *publish*.'

'Yes, Sally's courage is not in question. If she is put on trial, then her threats will be real. She has more power than ever now.'

Throughout these exchanges, Pinkerman's face had been registering a mixture of hope and fear, and his eyebrows had undergone a troubled journey of their own:

'I just pray the threat is enough, Mr Lundy! I thought she was very brave in silencing Amos.'

'She knew she had the better chances,' said Will. 'Had Amos confessed, the Law would have made him a convenient sacrifice.'

'That was a remarkable moment,' said Tom. 'She was firmly resolved – determined that her story should be the true one.'

'The *Truth!* …'

Will took breath, letting the word hang before them like a puff of smoke about to dissolve into nothing.

'… I doubt we shall ever be certain of that. The Law tries to find the truth, and Justice always thinks it has done so … But finally, all they can do is tell stories.'

'Perhaps that's the way to survive?' said Widow Trotter. 'Tell the most convincing story.'

Pinkerman sighed loudly:

'But it's not always in our hands, is it? I just hope the Queen's plans for the theatre may be set aside – at least for the time being. These have been desperate weeks!'

'I expect summer can't come soon enough for you?' said Mrs Trotter.

'We need time to recover before next season – if there is to be one. At this moment our friend Rich is busier than ever with his plans – the playhouse is full of workmen hammering and sawing. He's a man who shuns all thought of defeat!'

Delarivier Manley's eyes began to sparkle:

'Who knows, Mr Pinkerman? ... I think I may be tempted to write another comedy for you – something just a little *scandalous*. I always think Truth tastes better when spiced with Fiction.'

'Very liberally in your case, Dela,' said Lady Norreys. 'Word has it your *Atalantis* will serve up quite a *ragoût!*'

'Ah! For that, you must wait and see – Right now it's a profound secret. I've certainly had a deal of fun with it. All the best plots are *dash'd and brew'd with lies*, are they not?'

'Sometimes Truth is contraband and has to be smuggled in – I know of a certain gentleman who will credit nothing unless it be *whispered*.'

There was laughter. Lavinia looked at her two witty friends and smiled. It had been a frightening evening, but there was something healing about wit – it seemed to open the mind to fresh adventures, other possibilities. Hesitantly she spoke:

'*Wit* can be an excellent disguise, can it not?'

'How true, Lavinia ... but it can go out of fashion quickly – and we women have to wear it with particular care!'

The easy banter continued a while longer, and what had begun as an anxious committee of inquiry turned into a convivial conversation. Their spirits would not be held down in spite of the circumstances. By the time the party broke up, good humour had reasserted itself and everyone had the feeling that, whatever the next day brought, life would most certainly go on.

Saturday

8 May 1708

Chapter Fifty

THE FOLLOWING EVENING, in the upstairs room of the Bay-Tree the mood continued to be genial. The 'Good Fellowship Room' was dedicated to pleasure, and on alternate Wednesdays it was routinely the venue for the Mutton-Chop dining club. But tonight there were no Tory gentlemen indulging themselves in drunken songs and scurrilous verses. Their large punch-bowl, however, was being put to its accustomed use. After recent events, a Puritanical abstinence was ruled entirely out of order.

The more exotic specialities of the house, including Mr Bagnall's *Hippocrene* and the popular *Aromatick,* also made their way upstairs, along with a series of wooden platters offering choice morsels of food conjured from Mrs Dawes's imagination. The small pieces of toast spread over with cream cheese and bits of artichoke were proving popular, as were the thin slices of cold beef rolled around a paste of mushrooms. The elvers set in a vinegary jelly were meeting more resistance.

Mrs Trotter wanted the gathering to be a party of pleasure – if the news was to be bad, then celebration could turn into consolation.

There was a need for congratulation too, and she seized the opportunity to stand apart and talk quietly with Tom and Will. It was hard to conceive, but somehow the three of them had succeeded in preserving Pinkerman's booth from destruction. Everything had happened so quickly. They were shaken by the violence of the night before, but knew they had to re-live it together.

'Well, gentlemen, was that not a fiendish plot?'

Tom frowned:

'It was devilish, Mrs T. We seemed to sink back into a darker world, and Will and I were trapped in it. The thing was so very real.'

'It wasn't play-acting,' said Will – more of a dangerous ritual. Like the old Moralities must have been.'

'He would have consigned us all to the flames of Hell, Mrs T ... We had the smell of it in our nostrils.'

'And that Merlin was a vicious fighter. He was ready to kill himself along with the rest of us. He and *Wrath* had a manful struggle!'

Tom smiled at his friend:

'*Sloth* was no slug-a-bed either!'

'The two of you fought like heroes – the place was only seconds from destruction.'

'We've heard you were very nimble yourself, Mrs T.'

'I needed to be, Tom – but I regret to say that it wasn't without cost – severe cost ...'

There was sudden concern in their eyes.

'... all that pepper – it cost me half a day's takings.'

'You were well supplied with ordnance!' said Will.

Then Widow Trotter shook her head:

'But Arthur Bedford ... how could any man of religion do such a thing? To take that judgment on himself – and be the executioner too.'

'It's a kind of blasphemy,' said Will. 'But the plot has surely run its course now that he's in custody?'

'Thank God, yes,' said Tom. 'But what can the Law do with him?'

'We may soon hear, once Elias or your uncle arrives.'

'The *Society* will have some explaining to do as well. Their enthusiasm is increasingly dangerous.'

'And the Queen won't like it,' said Widow Trotter. 'These people have shot their bolt. Perhaps we'll be hearing a little less from them in future.'

'I'm not so sure,' said Tom. 'You'll never keep men like Bedford and Tysoe quiet – not when there's a pulpit waiting.'

'A Hell-fire sermon is one thing,' said Will. 'Burning people to death another … The Reverend Mr Tysoe is an enigma. He seems to live so boldly in words, but is fearful of deeds. I can still feel his hand pressing into mine when he thought of what I might *do*.'

'Well, he has evidently spoken out against Bedford,' said Mrs Trotter. 'His words are crucial evidence. And we should never have managed that without your *angling*, Will. I wonder if the two of you are going to remain friends?'

'Now that Gilbert is restored to life, I suspect Mr Tysoe's attention will be directed elsewhere!'

Widow Trotter turned round. There was movement at the other side of the room. The door had opened, and some familiar faces entered.

'Ah! It's Mr Denniston and Mr Pomery – and Adèle too. Good! They will need to know what has happened – forgive me, gentlemen …'

And with those words their bright-eyed hostess skipped off – her Friends in the Garden would be eager for the latest news.

Will watched her go:

'What a lady, Tom! Throughout this adventure it's been she who has held us all together.'

'And given us directions – it's just impossible to say "no" to her. Would she not make a fearsome conspirator herself?'

'I really think Mr Bedford was overmatched from the start.

He stood no chance – the moment he showed her his profile in the Duke's box, his fate was sealed!'

'I think you're right,' said Tom. '*Macbeth* seems so long ago. But that's when it all began.'

'Well, we must trust the Deadly Sins have brought an end to it!'

There was the sound of a clearing of the throat, and they turned to find the author of *The Shoe-Buckle* standing by them. He was clutching an empty glass:

'I could not but hear, gentlemen – the *Deadly Sins!* – am I to credit the frightful news? I hear your Prologue proved to be highly *incendiary*, Mr Bristowe! Did I not counsel you to use discretion?'

He looked down at his glass. Tom suppressed a smile:

'You did indeed, Mr Bagnall, and I should have heeded your advice. We must always guard our words closely and keep them well-ordered. Otherwise, what *ideas* might they excite?'

'I do allow *freer beauties* ... and distance and proportion can reconcile us even to the monstrous ... You must not stand too close!'

'That advice holds for so much, Sir – as I know to my cost.' Tom's hand went to his neck. 'But sometimes we need to grapple!'

A *Thought* struck Laurence Bagnall, and his face became radiant:

'Is that not the wonder of poetry, Mr Bristowe? Nothing in the world should be beyond its grasp. There is nothing that words cannot illuminate or communicate – if we work them hard enough. But we must keep them under control. Our words are our responsibility!'

Will looked at the two poets:

'You are a pair of very wise gentlemen – but I need to refill my glass! I am happy to set aside philosophical responsibility for a while ...'

The hum of conversation was rising in the room. Over by the sideboard, Gavin Leslie and David Macrae were questioning Pinkerman about *The Devil on Two Sticks* and planning their own visit. Nearby, the Bullocks, father and son, were debating the use of comic action on the stage, and how far Nature should be respected – a regular dispute between them that usually ended with some breach of decorum.

Mrs Trotter, having refilled her glass, found her way to Mr Denniston and his friends. She was about to reveal her precious nugget of news when Mrs Ménage plucked her by the elbow and anticipated her:

'Such news, Marie! – Mr Pomery here has received it *from the Duke himself* not an hour since – it is your *Mr Bedford* ...'

Widow Trotter felt deflated but managed to compose her features to a look of interest.

'... He is departing the stage!'

'He is being packed off back to Bristol, Mrs Trotter!' said John Pomery, seizing the reins of the conversation. 'It is the best possible news. I have been asked to arrange for his things to be sent after him ... His Grace seems to be smiling on me again. Does this mean our plot was successful? Charles and I have been on tenterhooks of suspense all day!'

'But this has happened so quickly!' she said. 'Has Mr Bedford fled the scene?'

'His Grace said little, but implied that an immediate departure suited all parties ... and *Hey Presto!* The reverend gentleman is perhaps aboard the Bristol coach this very moment. You must tell us how our letter played out, Mrs Trotter – if these were its consequences ...'

The way was clear, and with renewed relish she gave them the full story of the trapping of Arthur Bedford and the events in Pinkerman's booth. When she reached the violent climax, Mr Denniston shuddered and a look of horror seized him:

'*Nemesis*, Mrs Trotter! What do you say, John? It is a terrifying scene altogether. How very close it came to tragedy!'

'Let us hope a *catharsis* will follow. After such warring passions we long for a spell of calm. There has been altogether too much commotion!'

Mrs Trotter tended to agree, and for a short while the three of them were able to contemplate a life of unruffled routine and quiet reflection – until the door opened and things became ruffled again.

'It's Mr Cobb!'

Every eye turned. The constable strode into the room with an announcement:

'We have come direct from Mr Hector's!'

He left the door open, and behind him a smiling Sally Twiss was ushered in. It was a commanding entrance. She took in the whole audience and gave a slight nod of acknowledgment. At once, all conversation ceased. A radiant Pinkerman threw out his arms to welcome her:

'We have our Tamara!'

The Good Fellowship room was hushed as Constable Cobb was spurred on to tell his tale. He needed little encouragement, and it was soon clear that events had been running at a hot pace during the course of the day. When the sparks of scandal are flying and a wildfire threatens, powerful people can move quickly, and such had been the case. In the end, Arthur Bedford had not so much been given his marching orders as been smuggled away like a case of illicit liquor.

A defiant Jake Sawyer – less influential in his 'connections' – had evidently damn'd and blasted furiously and been whisked off to Newgate where 'Merlin' would keep his two henchmen company and be able to prophesy to his heart's content.

In contrast, the Reverend Bedford's sentence had unfolded with a polite, not to say elegant, inevitability. Anticipating the displeasure of the Queen and wishing to avoid troubling Her Majesty with further sordid revelations, the Solicitor-General had persuaded His Grace the Duke that the nagging doubts he was beginning to have about Arthur Bedford's activities were more than justified, and that a quiet life free of his chaplain's urgings and harryings would be attractive, and consequently that the man's immediate departure for his home city of Bristol would be a welcome solution to an extremely awkward problem ...

In other words, the man was allowed to escape, and all parties could sigh with relief.

If the confirmation of Arthur Bedford's departure from the scene brought a mixed response, Sally's arrival made a happy pendant to it. Pinkerman took her aside and would immediately have entangled her in practical matters had not Widow Trotter and her confederates gathered round to demand her story. She was glad to oblige.

It seemed that Sally's boldness had served her well, and Mr Hector's report to Sir James Montagu that morning had been decisive. In his account, the plotting of Tunbridge and Bedford appeared a single conspiracy, and the Solicitor-General decided that the men's bitter quarrel only confirmed how entangled each was in the other's machinations, with their employment of spies and the outrage of the maypole. The result was that Sally was sympathetically heard. In the end, her resistance to the Baron seemed heroic, and it took little debate for them to agree that Her Majesty's peace of mind would be best served by Sally walking free ...

And there she now was, smiling confidently and speaking with a natural grace – so alive to the promptings of others, so warmly responsive and sure of her story ...

During her account, Will's face began to be shadowed by thought. Sally's confidence was deeply attractive – he loved the way her shoulders worked expressively with her eyes, both attuned in a kind of relaxed assurance – and the turn of the neck and lift of the chin as a smile broke. They were tricks he had noticed before, and which she had used as Tamara. That role, he now saw, was no longer out of her reach. Quite the contrary … How much had Tunbridge taught her? – And how readily had she absorbed those nuances of seduction? Did she end up playing along with the Baron – playing *with* him? Who was the toy? he began to wonder, only to check himself for the unworthy thought. But he couldn't stop. How many performances had she given? How many versions of herself were there? … and why (so niggling a thought this!) – why had she fled to Holborn with Gilbert? Somehow he had avoided the question – they all had. It didn't quite make sense: if things had happened in the store-room as she had said, then why fly off like a guilty thing? They had assumed that Gilbert's anxiety had prompted the flight – or that she had left the Baron alive in that room and had fled to avoid his pursuit. The more Will turned the images of the scene around in his mind, the less clear they became – each time, a slightly different picture formed. And now they were left with two incompatible stories – Amos's truth and Sally's fiction. Was it that simple? Was it Sally who had suggested the flight to Gilbert? Will's mind was cast back to their encounter in his dressing-room. The boy's uneasiness about Sally – did that really fit what they were now accepting as the truth? Was Truth not supposed to be single – *Una*? Could it ever be double? Was Gilbert Angell someone who had offered himself as her knight – not the adventuresome Red Cross Knight in his case but a simple Calidore perhaps? Were he and Amos there to act scenes with her and for her? And was Amos in the end the chosen one – the man who would do the deed? … Will was beginning to perspire a little … might it be that Amos had been prompted – perhaps told of the assignation in the property-store? Was he ready and waiting …? Will stepped back slightly – he was beginning to feel uncomfortable. But his mind wouldn't pull back. It insisted on pressing on with these questions – one after another. Where were they leading? … Was he becoming jealous, and was this jealousy feeding his suspicions? He looked at Sally again closely, and saw she was furrowing her brow slightly before banishing a passing hesitation and allowing a natural smile to light up her face again …

'Are you all right, Will?'

Tom was looking at him, sensing something wasn't right.

'No, all isn't right Tom.'

They watched for a moment together.

'You mustn't doubt now, Will …'

'… How did you know?'

'It's that look on your face. I remember the first time you went to the Playhouse – you were bemused by the performance – wondering how a thing could be true *and* a show. Well, there she is, our Sally – our *actress* – and what a fine, natural one she is. The theatre is her world, remember. She has to belong to everyone, but make each one think themselves special – that the performance is for them alone.'

'But I wonder about her story – her account of things from the very beginning.'

'Yes, Will, there is always something to doubt. We have encountered questions at every turn – I know it as well as you. I've spoken of it, remember! And not always to your liking … But doubt is corrosive. There comes a time when we have to set it aside, or it will never leave us – like jealousy.'

'Yes, you're right, friend Tom …'

He sighed almost plaintively.

'… But it doesn't make the pain less. We have come so far in this business – I know I mustn't doubt now … and yet …'

'You are reading her minutely, Will – and of course you

want to know what *really* happened, so you can close the book and put it back on the shelf.'

'But ...'

'But with an actress, you're going to see her become many different things, each one of them true – or so we hope ... I'm sorry, Will, it's a simple point but needs to be said, and you need to hear it ... I don't want you to be hurt. It is easy to believe your trust has been betrayed and to make it a personal thing.'

'Perhaps I'm doing just that – but remember, I'm also a lawyer ...'

'Yes, and you lawyers always find the *truth*, don't you? – in each case you expose the falsehood! Always weigh everything carefully! Persuasion and performance have no part in it!'

Tom grinned at him with a touch of wickedness. Will looked resigned:

'Alas, that's check mate, I think ... I throw my King over! As soon as the argument moves on to lawyers, I feel the ground shaking.'

Both of them were now beginning to laugh, and in a short time the two friends were mingling around the punch-bowl with the others. The mood in the room was cheerful; but for every expression of relief there was an unspoken disquiet, the thought that at any moment tidings about the theatre's future would arrive to dash their hopes.

And so, when a determined rap at the door was heard, all eyes turned; and when it was Lord Melksham's face that appeared, an apprehensive silence fell. One or two heads nodded in acknowledgment, and his features were anxiously read to see if they boded well or ill.

Tom strode forward to give his own greeting, but he knew that his uncle's message was for the whole room. There was an urgency in his manner which was unsettling.

'I have been with the Solicitor-General,' Lord Melksham announced, 'and I know all of you will wish to hear what resulted ...'

He paused while a glass of punch was held out to him. He took it (a hopeful sign), raised it to Widow Trotter, sipped from it, and looked around:

'... You will have heard from Constable Cobb the news of the Reverend Arthur Bedford's undignified retreat today. All I can say is – a happy riddance to him – and to everything he stands for! Such people give their cause an ill name and turn virtues into vices ...'

There was a warm murmur of assent around the room.

'... And I see to my delight that Miss Twiss is here among us ...'

He raised his glass again and received an enchanting smile in return.

'... so, I shall not repeat a story that will doubtless have been told you already. This outcome is something further to rejoice in – indeed I hope to see Sally Twiss grace the stage of the Theatre Royal for years to come ...'

There was a sudden lightness of heart in everyone. Was this, then, a reprieve?

'... I only wish I could come to you with entire certainty about the future of the company and tell you that all things will go on as before. I doubt they should! Contracts, organisation, book-keeping – all have been erratic. And the chaos of recent weeks – though engineered by evil forces – has revealed an institution that is not in robust health. Indeed, I understand that Mr Rich's future is far from secure ...'

Lord Melksham took another sip of punch.

'... However, it appears that Her Majesty is minded to allow the theatre's patent to continue for the foreseeable future ...'

Polite restraint was momentarily lost in a flurry of spontaneous relief – hands were clasped and glasses lifted.

'... Sir James intimated that the Queen wished to see the *theatrical commotion* (those were her very words!) die down. It was thought that the closure of the Drury Lane playhouse would be inadvisable at this time, given that the scandal has largely been stirred up by disaffected elements among the reformers. Such an extreme action would give comfort to them and encourage those forces that formerly made the State oppressive of the people.'

'Cromwell and his generals!' whispered Will.

'And so, Mr Pinkerman, I congratulate you and your fellow actors on your delivery – at least in this life – from damnation and Hell fire! Long may you fight your eternal struggle with creaking scenes, weak lines, uncooperative machinery, hissing and cat-calls. May the soul of theatre always transcend the body of the stage, and the magic of the playhouse be undimmed!'

These were rousing sentiments and deserved a much bigger audience. Laurence Bagnall, a connoisseur of fine speech, applauded with special warmth and would have immediately entangled His Lordship in a disquisition on the ancient rhetorical arts, had not Widow Trotter steered her honoured guest away. A moment later the two of them were joined by Tom and Will.

'But what about the May Fair, uncle?'

Tom's urgent question drew a slight frown:

'Ah, the Fair! ... I fear the fate of the Fair remains an uncertain one. It continues to give huge offence at the palace. Smithfield and Southwark are distant enough to be endured, but the Brook Field is a near neighbour of Her Majesty. She is said to shiver in her bed at the thought of the Fair invading St James's!'

'I suppose the Queen can terminate it with the stroke of a pen, and there would be no appeal against any proclamation?'

'You are right, Mr Lundy. And I think that moment is close.'

'Another *proclamation?* ...'

The word had stirred Widow Trotter's memory:

'... Do you recall that black-letter broadside, Mr Bristowe?

It was a satiric prohibition against the May Fair, and poor Mr Pinkerman was greatly perturbed by it. Perhaps the thing will be dusted off and printed again – in elegant modern type this time?'

'You may be speaking truer than you know, Mrs Trotter,' said Lord Melksham. 'Her Majesty's proclamation *Against Vice, Profaneness and Immorality* has certainly not been gathering dust, has it? It is forever being reprinted, and I keep hearing it delivered from the pulpit. We are not yet living in a virtuous world!'

'Nor shall we ever, uncle,' said Tom, 'and that gives me hope. There will always be a need for satire, and always food to nourish it. Satire never has to invent – the materials are all around us!'

'And there is quite enough material in this very room!' said Widow Trotter with a sly look. 'But let us not darken our thoughts just now, gentlemen. This has to be a moment for celebration. The punch awaits! … But I would warn you against the jellied eels – there are some experiments best not repeated.

THE END

Historical Note

The Devil's Cathedral

This second Chocolate House Mystery embeds its fictional plot in a specific time and place – in this case, the world of the Drury Lane Theatre and the May Fair during a fortnight in April-May 1708. And once again it proves to be a moment of crisis for the new nation. In *Chocolate House Treason* the context was the party-political conflict of that year; this time the crisis is one of cultural freedom clashing with social regulation.

Londoners in 1708 witnessed an unprecedented crackdown on vice and immorality. Figures given in Alan Hunt's *Governing Morals: A Social History of Moral Regulation* (1999) show many more prosecutions for vice in that year than for any other year between 1694-1737. For 1708 Hunt records in the capital a total of 3,298 prosecutions – for lewd and disorderly conduct, keeping a disorderly house, sabbath-breaking (1,187 of these), and profane swearing (625).

These prosecutions were driven by the Society for the Reformation of Manners, a national movement founded in 1691 in reaction to the libertine excesses of the Restoration. In London its power was considerable, and it issued annual blacklists of offenders. The Society's initiatives against immorality were encouraged by Royal proclamation and the capital's Justices. Blank specimen warrants were being issued for the easy use of magistrates, along with guidance for anonymous informers, of whom there were many; and the Association of Constables was exerting pressure on those who policed the metropolis. But not all constables were willing to enforce these social restrictions, and some magistrates were becoming increasingly suspicious of the radical dissenting elements within the Society.

The power of the Society for the Reformation of Manners was now at its height, and with the support of the Archbishop of Canterbury and the Bishop of London, it waged a determined campaign of sermons and pamphlets against both the Theatre Royal and the May Fair, frequently linked in condemnation. Driving this was Queen Anne's proclamation *for the Preventing & Punishing Vice, Profaneness and Immorality*, which was reissued and ordered to be read regularly from pulpits. Pressure was building for a national reformation that would involve the closure of the theatre and the abolition of the fair.

Two of the leading voices in this movement for moral reform were the Reverend Thomas Bray and the Reverend Arthur Bedford, both of whom feature in *The Devil's Cathedral*. I have based my fictional Reverend Ebenezer Tysoe on Bray (who also did tireless work for the Charity Schools movement). Tysoe's sermon in chapter 17 is largely extracted from Bray's *For God, or for Satan: Being a sermon preached at St Mary le Bow, before the Societies for Reformation of Manners, December 27, 1708*. The Reverend Arthur Bedford, however, appears in the book as himself, though it must be noted that his adventures are imagined – as is his striking profile – and there is no reason to think Bedford was ever involved in violence or illegal activity. But the opinions and words are certainly his own, taken from *Serious Reflections on the Scandalous Abuse and Effects of the Stage* (Bristol, 1705) and *The Evil and Danger of Stage-Plays:*

Shewing their Natural Tendency to Destroy Religion, and Introduce a General Corruption of Manners (Bristol, 1706). I learned a lot about Arthur Bedford from Jonathan Barry's article, 'Hell upon Earth or the Language of the Playhouse', in *Languages of Witchcraft: Narrative, Ideology and Meaning in Early Modern Culture*, ed. Stuart Clark (2001). In giving a picture of the anti-theatre rhetoric of the time, I've drawn from other texts, most importantly the Reverend John Disney's *Essay upon the Execution of the Laws Against Immorality and Prophaneness* (1708), and Josiah Woodward's *Some Thoughts Concerning the Stage in a Letter to a Lady* (1704).

Throughout the novel, the extreme language is entirely that of the preachers and controversialists of 1708 – no invention was needed.

The May Fair, which in 1708 occupied the fields which would become London's smartest district, was notorious for its outraging of public decency and good order, especially after the killing of a constable there in 1702. Being sited so close to St James's, the May Fair was regarded with urgent disapproval by the authorities, and the 1708 Fair was strictly policed – though not with much effect, it would seem. The attacks on the fair came to a head with the anonymous pamphlet, *Reasons for Suppressing the Yearly Fair in Brook-Field, Westminster; Commonly Call'd May-Fair* (London, 1709). This had the desired effect, and the fair was terminated and the animals sold off in April 1709.

It is possible to gain a good sense of the lively character of the May Fair and its activities. Besides drawing material from the attacks on the Fair, I have benefited from other accounts, especially Thomas Frost's *The Old Showmen, and the Old London Fairs* (1874) and Sybil Rosenfeld's study, *The Theatre of the London Fairs in the 18th Century* (1960). Ned Ward's *London Spy* (1698-1700) and Hogarth's wonderful engravings of *Southwark Fair* (1733) and *Strolling Actresses Dressing in a*

Barn (1738) helped supply other details. Ned Ward gives a vivid account of a 'Raffling Shop' in his *Hudibras Redivivus* (1708).

The Theatre Royal closed its doors for the duration of the Fair, and actors were able to moonlight at the fairground booths where they could earn more money and enjoy performing to a diverse and appreciative audience who couldn't afford to frequent the theatre. William Pinkerman (variously Pinkethman, Pinkeman, Pinkeyman), the chief comedian of the Theatre Royal, was the leading entrepreneur of the May Fair, and his booth always attracted the crowds. Pinkerman was a resourceful marketer of his shows. Ned Ward's 'Epilogue Spoken by Mr Pinkeman, upon the Back of an Elephant' (1704) exemplifies the expense and imagination that Pinkerman invested in it, shipping the animal from Guinea along with its handlers. It seems the actual performance of the epilogue within the booth that year was abandoned for health and safety reasons, but the elephant remained a popular draw. In order to award the creature some dignity, I have taken the liberty of naming him 'Hannibal.' Pinkerman's eight dancing dogs, brought over from Holland in 1707, were declared to be 'the wonder of the world.'

Fortunately, there has survived a printed record of the main event in Pinkerman's booth at the 1708 Fair. *The Devil upon two Sticks: or, the Town Until'd: With the Comical Humours of Don Stulto, and Siegnior Jingo: As it is Acted in Pinkeman's Booth in May-Fair* (London: J.R., 1708). I have made full use of this authentic document to bring alive what experiencing the performance must have been like. The additional scenes written by Arachne's Web are of course fictional. The other main production at the booth, *The Tender Courtesan,* is also entirely my invention. Part of me is tempted to produce it, but nothing of the piece exists beyond these pages. I have also invented the pageant of the Seven Deadly Sins, which is performed as an afterpiece to *The Devil on Two Sticks*. This is the kind of raucous interactive event that delighted the fair audiences and is intended to provide a suitable climax to the evening's entertainment. Tom Bristowe's *Prologue to The Tender Courtesan* is sadly fictional – though its finest couplet (rhyming 'inclined to' with 'a mind to') has been appropriated from Thomas Brown's Epilogue to *The Stage-Beaux Toss'd in a Blanket* (1704).

In evoking the world of the Theatre Royal in 1708, I've drawn from various primary and secondary sources, including Colley Cibber's entertaining autobiography, *Apology for the Life of Colley Cibber, Written by Himself*. Joanne Lafler's *The Celebrated Mrs. Oldfield: The Life and Art of an Augustan Actress* (1989) has been particularly helpful.

The action of the novel, from 24 April to 8 May 1708 follows the programme of the Theatre Royal, Drury Lane, as given in the standard reference work, *The London Stage 1660-1800. A Calendar of Plays, Entertainments & Afterpieces Together with Casts, Box Receipts and Contemporary Comment, Part 2: 1700-1729*, ed. Emmett L Avery (1960). This invaluable source documents each production. The performances of *Macbeth*, *Volpone*, and *The Man of Mode* took place on those dates with those actors.

That said, I have expanded the company to include Sally Twiss and Gilbert Angell. The other actors in *The Tender Courtesan* are also fictional, as is the company 'patron', Lord Tunbridge – though after finishing the novel I serendipitously discovered that an actual Lord Tunbridge existed at this time. A favourite of William of Orange, he had been forced to marry the woman he had seduced, had links with the Theatre Royal (his great uncle was Thomas Killigrew, former manager of the company), and he died, aged 59 – *in 1708* . . .

The Chocolate House Mysteries no. 1:

Widow Trotter has big plans for her recently inherited coffee house, not suspecting that within days her little kingdom will be caught up in a national drama involving scandal, conspiracy, and murder.

The new 'Great Britain' is in crisis. The Queen is mired in a sexual scandal, spies are everywhere, and political disputes are bringing violence and division. The treasonous satirist "Bufo" is public enemy number one, and the Ministry is determined to silence him. Drawn into a web of intrigue that reaches from the brothels of Drury Lane to the Court of St James's, Mary Trotter and her young friends Tom and Will race against time to unravel the political plots, solve two murders, and prevent another.

Praise for Chocolate House Treason:

"A stunning debut novel."
— *Sandra Callard*

"Deftly plotted, historically accurate, richly descriptive, and wittily written – this is a charming and compelling mystery. I loved it . . . A fabulous debut!"
— *Cynthia Wall*

"Fairer certainly brings the period to vivid life, so much so that as a reader you feel as if you're living the action as much as the characters . . . The action is fast-paced and incredibly believable."
— *Jonathan White,* Highlights Magazine

"This is an extremely entertaining and civilised read, richly characterised, stylishly written, and cleverly plotted. A well-paced and suspenseful murder mystery is set with originality and wit in a confidently evoked early eighteenth-century London and excitingly investigated by a most unusual and engaging trio of amateur sleuths."
— *Alistair Stead*